PRODIGAL JOURNEY

To Steve,

and for all those who find themselves a long way from home.

THY KINGDOM COME

Volume One

PRODIGAL JOURNEY

LINDA PAULSON ADAMS

CORNERSTONE

Published by:
Cornerstone Publishing & Distribution, Inc.
5427 SOUTH 560 EAST
SALT LAKE CITY, UT 84107

First Printing:
June 2000

Printed in the United States of America
04 03 02 01 00   10 9 8 7 6 5 4 3 2 1

ISBN 1-929281-05-6

Cover design by Adam R. Hopkins
Cover photograph © 1999 Chris Craymer/Stone. Used by permission.

Contents

PART ONE

PART TWO

PART THREE

Acknowledgements

My first thanks go to my parents.

Thanks to Mom, for her patience with me as a small child, when I would beg her for help with writing ideas, then get my own ideas anyway which had nothing to do with hers. Those spelling sentences helped develop the writer within.

Thanks to Dad (yes, you, Dad), for forcing me to take typing in high school. He said it would come in handy someday, even though I didn't want anything to do with secretarial work. Now I only wish I could type as fast as I can think.

Thanks to Eric Knight, my first editor, for his initial confidence in this book. His enthusiasm created greater confidence in me and helped me realize it was a project worth pursuing.

Scott Parkin was instrumental in my writing group to point out spots needing serious work in the first draft of this manuscript, and this is a much better story today because of his insight.

Profuse gratitude goes to Steve, my husband, for thinking this was a terrific and worthwhile project all along, and encouraging me to keep going in spite of setbacks, often being much more excited about it than I was. (I love you, honey.) Thanks for keeping me going when I felt like I'd gotten myself in over my head and wanted to stuff this whole thing through a paper shredder. (I couldn't have done this without you. Honest.)

Last of all, thanks to Richard Hopkins, my editor and publisher, for taking on this project, being a pleasure to work with, and for finally making my dream come true of seeing my novel in print.

About the Author

Linda Paulson Adams lives in Jackson County, Missouri. (Honest. We didn't make that up.) She has been married for eleven years, has four young children, three cats, and one dog (not counting a few foster animals that come and go while looking for permanent homes).

She was born in Baltimore, Maryland, attended high school in Hollister, California, and graduated from Brigham Young University in Provo, Utah in 1990 with an Associate's Degree in English.

She has been writing stories since she was old enough to print in pencil, and squeezes in time to work on her craft often late at night or when she really should be doing something else much more mundane, such as sorting socks. She has published poetry and short fiction. This is her first novel.

She also volunteers for the Humane Society and Keeshond Rescue, a community service she embraces out of her love for animals. She fantasizes about someday having Real Furniture and a tidy home, collects unique salt and pepper shakers and nail polish colors, and has always been a connoisseur (and consumer) of fine chocolate.

Preface

Shortly after moving to Missouri over seven years ago, I became fascinated with both the history and the prophesied future of Jackson County. I was especially interested in the prophecies made by Joseph Smith, as recorded in the Doctrine and Covenants of The Church of Jesus Christ of Latter-day Saints, that this would be the place where the Latter-day Saints one day establish Zion, the New Jerusalem.

The first chapter to this novel was penned soon after the birth of my third child in 1993. It is not "Chapter One;" in fact, it is a chapter very near the end of the book. I don't want everyone turning to it first so I won't say which one it is. But after writing that chapter, I had to find out more about Alyssa. Who was she? Where was she going? Where had she been? As I wrote, discovering the answers to my own questions, I realized she was intertwined with a fictional world revolving around the prophesied establishment of Zion, the New Jerusalem, in Jackson County. Before this, I had only written short stories and poetry (yes, the poetry in this volume is mine, though attributed to fictional characters). As I wrote bits and pieces between changing diapers, feeding babies, and watching my children grow before my eyes, Alyssa's story also grew until it became longer than one book, then long enough for an entire series.

While doing the research for this novel, I learned there are not only prophecies about these future events but a great deal of folklore. Much of this folklore is attributed to Joseph Smith, though no one can prove he was the actual source. One such legend is the popular notion that this area will be "swept clean" of all its inhabitants before the Saints return to build Zion. Most likely (if the statement was made at all), the "sweeping clean" has already taken place, during the desolation left by the Civil War. However, the concept made for a fascinating idea on which to build a fictional series.

Of course, this series is not based on fascinating ideas alone. In fact, the characters in this novel are far more important than the events that surround them. Like signs of the times in every era, the events that fulfill prophecy are often incidental to the lives of those who live them. In the same way, the events prophesied for the future of the New Jerusalem are woven into the lives of the characters in this book. By looking carefully, one can find where I have pulled this or that idea or event from scripture and sometimes, from Mormon folklore.

The story itself depicts a world fully ripened in iniquity, far ahead of our own real world. I have tried to describe this world as delicately as possible, but in order to depict the extent of the wickedness that will likely precede the Second Coming, and to remain true and faithful to the characters and their story, certain things had to be shown, said, or made clear. Some of these things could offend the tender feelings of some readers. I can only say that I have made the content of this work a matter of much prayer and study in the hope that my depictions would be appropriate but never offensive.

This novel, and the series, is merely the product of my overactive imagination, not an attempt to predict the future. I have received no more revelation on the subject of the Last Days or the Second Coming than anybody else. It begins with a fictional Foreword that is actually part of the novel. It is not a true Foreword in the usual sense and is certainly not meant to be a doctrinal statement.

I have enjoyed researching this topic and it's been fun speculating on all the possible ways events could play themselves out. This is simply one way, one extremely fictional and imaginary way, things could happen.

Linda Paulson Adams

Foreword

There is a world coexisting with our own but on a different plane—separated by a "phase variance," if you will—that is invisible to the human eye. The existence of this alternate world is manifest in the unexplained, all that is considered paranormal or supernatural. It includes phenomena from ghosts to angelic visitations, and is sometimes manifest in those events we call miracles. These phenomena arise when our two worlds intersect in such a way as to allow interaction between the two planes.

The beings who inhabit this world are at war.

One side in the conflict are those banished to this earth from the eternal realms beyond for evil deeds, beings of great intelligence who chose a dark path. These are forbidden forever from taking on corporeal form. They covet physical experience, for in a body is power—more power than they can ever possess. They know this. Denied for eternity from feeling physical pleasure or pain, they possess a seething, jealous hatred for humanity and seek its destruction.

On the opposing side are beings of light who often defend us against these powers of evil. They also possess great intelligence and fight to protect humanity from the destruction the evil ones crave.

This war is a fight for our souls. We spring from the same God, the same source of life as they. The beings of light consider us their brothers and sisters, and our success becomes theirs also, for they are motivated by the purest form of love.

Though our natural eyes cannot see them, both light and dark entities can shift in and out of our realm; their unimaginably subtle form makes this possible. The physical nature of our bodies, our incredibly massive and rigid atomic structure, prevents us from contact with their world.

Most of the time.

Prologue

There was a time in American History we would all prefer to forget. The year 2023 brought tragedy in its wake. In that year the popular but radical televangelist, Reverend Alluvius Blankenship, decided the President of the United States was the long-prophesied Anti-Christ, the man who would give the world a few years of peace, then bring in the Tribulation prophesied in the Bible. That was his interpretation anyway.

He secretly purchased three nuclear warheads and, as we understand it now, carefully planned for a time when the President would make a political visit to "that den of iniquity," Southern California. Destroying the "wickedness of Hollywood" was a bonus to him. He swore he dropped the bombs on Los Angeles, San Diego and midway inbetween to stop the Anti-Christ and prevent the Tribulation. He even claimed he received a message direct from God. But the bomb that hit San Clemente destroyed the San Onofre nuclear power plant, irradiating most of California when it blew. Nuclear waste and fallout spilled into the Pacific, and drifted far enough north to contaminate the entire West Coast all the way to Puget Sound.

In spite of all the destruction and mourning he caused, there was no Tribulation, a benefit he claimed credit for to the day of his death. But there was no Rapture either, no Second Coming and none of the other signs his followers anticipated. Instead, the Californians who survived moved inland and started to rebuild their lives.

The whole incident frightened us terribly, revealing our easily forgotten but latent capability to do harm. Reverend Blankenship was arrested, tried for crimes against humanity and convicted, though he always denied he had done anything wrong.

His close followers disbanded and were never heard from again, but the impact of their actions didn't disappear with them. The Blankenship incident was the single-most destructive blow to Christianity in history. It completely crushed the Evangelical sects, and caused intense hardship for every other Christian faith, declining memberships, failing donations. Social pressure and public ridicule only helped continue these trends.

When the ash finally settled, there was a time when the sun became bright again and there was a semblance of peace. It was during this time that Alyssa Stark came into the world.

She was five years old when President James Antonine Garrison, then newly elected, drafted the New Constitution and burned the original in Capitol Mall. It was a great celebration. I watched it on the holo. I remember feeling sick to my stomach, without knowing why.

But the people, the majority of them anyway, loved him. He promised change, and he gave it to them, every change they wanted. Many things once outlawed were legalized and taxed—gambling in all forms, narcotic drug sales, prostitution. Commerce was freed from regulation. The FCC and FDA, the FTC and the laws preventing monopolies, were all discarded as chaff. Anything could be bought if one had enough cash or credit, and the government profited.

This was a great relief to many, allowing the newly honest employment of thousands. Prisoners were set free if the activities for which they had been charged were no longer criminal . . . as long as they could cover the price of an appeal and waiver of sentence.

The President's motto was "A true democracy founded on freedom in its purest sense, not on the 'prohibitions' our ancestors called freedom." In every speech he reiterated his theme, saying that we should be free to follow our dreams, whatever they might be, that moral restrictions were limitations of our truest freedom.

How I tired of hearing that speech as the years went on.

Under the new law, things went on nearly as before. At first. Life continued on its way, and few noticed the bureaucratic changes, not right away, at least. Many were still reeling from the shock of the Los Angeles disaster and the effects of relocation, trying to rebuild their lives and livelihoods. Highways were repaired, taxes collected, the Senate and Congress elected as usual.

The Electoral College was eliminated, of course. Technology allowed every citizen to vote online, through the Internet. Each vote was registered on the Federal Electoral website and counted on their central computers. Supposedly.

Term limits became a thing of the past, even for the Presidency. "Jag," as his supporters called him (for his initials), said that if the people loved him and wished him to continue in office, who was he to refuse them? Oh, how they cheered when he was sworn in for his third term, and later, his fourth. He called himself the President of the People.

A New Bill of Rights was passed, a distorted, condensed version of the original. From what I know, there used to be an amendment on freedom of religion, but that was omitted. A few individuals were upset by this, but they learned that silence was preferable to making objections. It was easy to ignore their fate, especially with the Blankenship trial fresh in the public memory. Too many people were still angry, especially at anyone who believed in Christ.

What happened to those poor souls remains a mystery more shrouded than that old Roswell story, and one that has been far less researched. I certainly don't know what happened. I can only say that they disappeared, and the reports of dissent didn't last long.

Membership in all Christian faiths continued to dwindle. Laws were enacted to prevent active proselytizing for these religions. No member of an organized faith could discuss their beliefs unless they were specifically asked for information. I've always been grateful that I did ask, although it was not until several years later. In doing so I discovered answers I had always searched for; answers that have brought me peace, in spite of the many hardships that followed after our family's baptism into The Church of Jesus Christ of Latter-day Saints.

In the meantime, America prospered. All was well. The President's popularity was never better in the polls. Or so the news reports said.

The Atlantic Subduction Trench formed the year Alyssa turned nine. She told us excitedly how she felt the shaking beneath her feet as she shoveled the driveway, only to learn later that the Atlantic seaboard from Maine to Florida had crumpled under the North American continental plate. The ocean floor just off the East Coast dropped to a depth of as much as six miles in some places . . . instantly and without warning. They felt it as far away as Denver.

In less than an hour, the resulting tsunami destroyed everything in its wake, sweeping the East Coast of all civilization from Boston to Atlanta and as far inland as RoanokeThe kilometer-wide fissure that opened along the Appalachians still seeps and bubbles at unpredictable times. The water receded, but rebuilding was not a popular option. From the Appalachian Fault to the former Eastern seaboard, the land trembles so frequently and so violently that only the most stubborn of Easterners remain.

No one on either coast felt safe anymore. As a result, our Great Midwest urbanized at an alarming rate. Construction boomed, with skyscrapers and highways going up faster than ever before. Zoning codes were minimal, purchasable. There was no time for lengthy arguments in city council meetings over what should be built where. It became an architectural menagerie.

The President, away from D. C. when the tsunami hit, erected a Palace in the middle of the new metropolis. It became renowned as the Ninth Wonder of the World, though I never went to see it. It was great and spacious, and many grand parties were held there. Anyone who could afford the price of the tickets could attend. There were plenty of ways to earn the tickets if one wanted them badly enough, especially if one were young and pretty or had other useful talents.

The new capital became known as Central City. It was larger than the former state of Maryland. It bordered Des Moines on the north, Omaha and Wichita on the west, and Springfield on the south, and soon contained the largest population of any city on earth, by many millions. Thankfully it never did spread quite close enough to urbanize our own beautiful Eastern Iowa, but we worried sometimes.

It was a great hub, with twenty-eight airports and over three hundred mass transit systems. By satellite at night the continent appeared to have a great eye in its center, unblinking, unwinking, but ever in motion, with strands of light radiating from it, marking the highways like arteries and veins.

This is the era in which Alyssa's coming of age began.

Beverly Richardson,
Richardson Family History

PART ONE

Chapter 1

Secrets

It is long afterward, sometimes,
Before we find meaning.
It distills in our
Souls
As
Sand
Sifting through
The hourglass of our lives
Falling softly down, grain by grain.

Hourglass,
by Paulo Vernon,
21st Century poet

"**W**ait for me!"

"It's a race, lame brain, I'm not waiting!" Peter cried.

Laughing, he ran faster. He didn't look back to see if Alyssa was gaining on him. Nimbly he jumped the rocks and small burrows that were common to the little meadow. While their families stayed at the campsite and picnicked, they went off exploring. When they were together, exploring always turned into racing, sooner or later.

"Peter, wait!" she repeated, her voice angry now.

He laughed again. "You're just trying to trick me," he yelled over his shoulder without looking back. "I won't fall for that again!" He ran faster.

Alyssa's voice got farther away as he ran. "Peter, wait! You have to! Come back!"

When he finally reached the top of the hill he stopped, breathing hard. He put his hands on his knees and dropped his head down. At last he turned and looked up. She wasn't behind him, and he had to straighten up to look for her. There she was, no more than a few meters from where the race began, sitting in an odd position on the ground.

"Why didn't you tell me you were hurt?" he yelled over the distance, tired and angry with himself now. She didn't answer, and he couldn't see her face.

Quickly he ran back, muttering under his breath.

"What happened?" he called as he got closer.

"I fell in some kind of hole," she said. "The grass was long and I didn't see it coming."

Peter reached her, panting with the exertion. "How bad is it?"

"I heard it snap." Her voice broke. "It hurts bad." Her lower lip trembled and she tried to blink back tears, but a few spilled out anyway.

"Oh great," Peter muttered. "Look, I can go get my dad. He could drive his Jeep out here. If you broke it, we'd better not move you." He paused, trying to collect his thoughts. "Or maybe it's just a sprain. It could've been a stick you heard snap. Did you try putting weight on it?"

Alyssa nodded and a small whimper escaped. She hung her head and then her body shook with sobs.

"Hey there, don't cry," he said. "We'll have you fixed up soon. It'll be all right." He stood, shifting his weight from foot to foot, scratching his elbow nervously. She still looked down at the ground, visibly shaking, but not making a sound.

Finally she sniffed and said, "I ripped my T-shirt too."

"So?" He sat down near her, pulling his knees up and wrapping his arms around them. "I think we've got bigger worries than that. Huh?" He tried a small laugh.

She looked up. "You don't understand. This was brand new. I ripped it on this stupid dead branch when I fell." She shoved the branch away angrily, wiping her tears with her hand and sniffling.

"It's just a shirt." He shrugged. "Come on, do you think you can lean on me or something? I can help you up. If it's just sprained you could make it back. I might be skinny but I'm strong." He stood up and held out his hand.

"She'll probably never let me wear a T-shirt again. I finally got her to let me have one. Now I'll be lucky if I ever get to play outside again."

"Maybe she'll be glad it's not worse. It's my fault anyway, I mean, I started the race."

"I'd have won easy if I hadn't fallen and you know it."

"No way. I've been training. I'm tired of getting beat. You're littler than me."

She smiled. But then a shadow came over her face. "Peter, you have to promise not to tell," she whispered.

"Well, gee, it's obvious you're hurt," he said. "We need to get you some help."

"No, dummy. I mean you can't tell anybody that you saw me . . . you know . . . cry." Her face flushed red as she said it and she looked away.

"What's the big deal? You're hurt pretty bad."

"Alyssa Stark never cries," she said, straightening herself up as much as possible. She winced. "Never."

"You just did. Gotcha," he said.

She was not amused.

"Hey, I'm sorry. Why not? I still cry sometimes, if I have to. And Julia cries all the time."

"Alyssa Stark does not cry," she repeated in a stiff voice.

Peter was silent, thinking. He sat back down with a thud, and looked at her hazel-gray eyes. She stared straight ahead, glanced at him, then looked away. There was fear in her eyes, and anger, and an overwhelming sadness. He had never noticed it before.

After a long moment he said, "I haven't ever seen you cry. Huh?" *Not even when her mother scolds her in front of me.* Maybe that's why they got along so well. She was tough, unlike other whiny ten-year-old girls.

"Promise," she said fiercely, "you won't ever tell."

"I promise," Peter said. "I mean it. You can trust me." He looked into her eyes again. "It'll be our secret." He smiled.

"Okay. Our secret."

"Now," he said. "Enough of this. I didn't get a First Aid merit badge for nothing. Let me see that leg. Maybe I can tell if it's broken or not."

"Oh no you don't! Don't you dare touch me!"

"I know what I'm doing, honest." He reached for her leg.

"That's okay, I'll wait for your dad, thank you." Her eyes were wide as she tried ineffectively to push him away.

"I have to at least find out if you're bleeding before I leave."

"All right. See?" She turned her leg over with her hands. "I'm not bleeding. I just can't walk. Go get your dad, please!"

"Okay, okay! I'm going!"

****

The ride back to the campground in the Jeep was quiet. Alyssa sat with her legs stretched out in the back seat. Peter sat in front with his dad, Phil Richardson. They didn't talk.

When they arrived Alyssa's mother was already in hysterics. "Whatever did you think you were doing, child? How could you be so stupid?" she yelled, opening the door of the Jeep before it came to a complete stop. "I can't believe you could be so *stupid!*"

"Now, Joan, it was an accident," Phil said from the driver's seat.

She gave him a nasty look. "I doubt that," she said. "This is all your fault, isn't it, Peter? You're always encouraging her! I should have known better than to let my daughter run off exploring with you. From now on Alyssa, you are not to go wandering around places you have no business being. And you will not play outside for three months. Not even the backyard. Is that *completely* clear?"

Alyssa said nothing, only nodded.

"The truth. How did this happen? What idiotic trick were you trying to pull this time?" She stopped and lit a cigarette, taking a drag on it and replacing her lighter in the pocket of her slacks at the same time.

"It was just a race, Mother," she replied softly.

"A race? You were racing? The country around here is not the place for track and field, young lady, and you know better. You know better. Just look at you!"

"Yes, Mother," she said.

Phil's voice low and threatening, "Now Joan, that's enough. Any more of that in front of me, and I promise you'll regret it. She's hurt enough, can't you see that?"

Joan looked at him coldly with her steel-gray eyes and slammed the car door shut. She walked around to the driver's window, which was down. In a harsh, barely controlled whisper, she said, "Don't you dare tell me how to discipline my children." She blew smoke out her nostrils.

"I wasn't referring to your *discipline*." He spat the last word out like an oath.

"If you had any discipline yourself you wouldn't have had so many little brats, and they wouldn't be running wild, encouraging *my* child to endanger herself this way! I'll take care of this the way I see fit."

Phil glared at her. After a long pause he said, "I'll drive her to the hospital. I expect you'll meet us there?"

"You will not," Joan said. "She is my daughter and I'm taking her."

"I'm afraid her leg is too bad to risk moving her again," Phil said, holding her stare.

Beverly, his wife, came up behind Joan and cautiously put her hand on her shoulder. Joan flinched and pushed her hand away. "Joan," Beverly said gently.

"What?" she answered, voice still tense. But her gaze dropped to the ground, away from Phil's, and her shoulders slumped slightly.

"Joan, I'll ride with you to the hospital. I think you're much too upset to drive. Come on. I'll take you to the car." She spoke quietly.

"Too upset . . ."

Joan's voice lost its edge and she turned away from the Jeep, walking back toward the picnic table as if in a trance. Beverly walked next to her, placing an arm around her shoulder as they went.

"I don't know how she does it," Phil muttered under his breath.

Peter had been staring down at his fingers during the whole episode, but he looked up to see Joan walk away.

"You okay, Alyssa?" he asked, turning around to face her.

She nodded and looked out the side window. "Fine," she said.

"Peter, I want you to ride back home in the van with Isaac," Phil said.

"But Dad . . ."

"You go home with Isaac," he said again. "Your mom has to go with Joan to keep her calm. Ike can drive you kids back home just fine."

"He only has his permit," Peter said.

"He's been driving tractors since he was your age. He knows what he's doing, and if he gets stopped you can say it was an emergency. We can afford the ticket if we have to. It'll be all right. I've watched him, he's very safe when he wants to be."

"Look, Dad, I'm not all that worried about his driving, I just . . ."

"I know," Phil said, looking at his son. "But I think it's in everyone's best interests if you're not at the hospital. That's final."

"It wasn't my fault."

Phil pressed his lips together. "I know, son. But that's not the issue right now."

"It wasn't his fault," Alyssa echoed from the back.

"I believe you kids," he said, then sighed. "I do. But some people just don't . . ." He broke off his sentence. After a pause, he said, "Go on, Peter. Go tell your brother he gets to drive home."

Reluctantly Peter got out of the car. "See you around, Alyssa," he said. "Hope your leg's all right."

She smiled her twisted little smile. "I'll be fine. See you."

He shut the car door and walked off to find Isaac.

****

It was a year before he saw her again, in spite of his mom's best efforts to appease Joan's injured feelings and imagined slights. Peter was glad when their holiday and summertime visits got back to normal, the way they used to be, getting together often, the two of them playing wonderful practical jokes on her big sister Lauren.

But he missed her that year. It was boring without her.

Chapter 2

Celebration

Four years after Alyssa broke her leg at Camp Keomah was the last time America celebrated the Fourth of July. Outmoded ideas like patriotism and respect for our heritage having faded, Independence Day meant little more to the masses than watermelon, fireworks, and incinerating marshmallows over a fire. Parades and flagwaving were the debris of a former day, an unenlighted day of subservience to paralyzing and dangerous religions, a day of closed minds. Or so they said. But they were wrong. Their minds were much more closed than mine, I always thought.

The President and his supporters worked to make the day a holiday in his honor instead. They worked in the dark, like tunneling moles eroding precious foundations to enlarge their own burrows, never emerging for light or fresh air. He created the New Freedom, the New Democracy. It made sense to claim this day for himself too, the last vestige of glory and honor remaining for the old ways. As though he did more than play on everyone's unstable emotions to gain his power in the first place.

A nation in fear, having suffered through so much tragedy and loss, looked up to him with near reverence for support and redemption. Carefully planned propaganda ensured all that. A simple matter, really. Most wanted to trust him. They didn't even try to see through it. They swallowed it whole without thinking.

You see, I remember. I was old enough. I went to school before they started teaching the Revised History. I knew how our forefathers fought for their freedoms. I felt something was amiss with all this. It bothered me, like a fly buzzing in the back of my mind, but there were too many other things going on in my life. As if I could've changed anything anyway.

But Peter and Alyssa were unaware of these things back then. They were so young and uninterested in the growing political turmoil as it unfolded.

Beverly Richardson,
Richardson Family History

It was hot, humid. The smell of charcoal freshly ignited hung in the air, and the landscape around the farm was lush and green. The sky was a deep, unobstructed, cerulean blue. The acrid charcoal mingled with scents of summer wildflower, honeysuckle and the usual farm smells—fresh corn, new-cut hay, the heavy scent of farm animals sweating in their various pens and stalls.

In past years, the two families had taken several days together for the Independence Day holiday. They camped or took long sightseeing trips. Traditionally, it was the most time they spent together the entire year.

This year was different. Alyssa's family lived in upper Des Moines, a two-hour drive west of the Richardson farm. Joan was unusually busy this summer, with increased museum responsibilities she said, and could not afford more than one day away from work. So this time they met at the farm, and only for the day.

Perhaps it was for the better.

If the tension ran higher today between the two mothers than usual, if the seams of their friendship were beginning to fray and shred in opposite directions, Alyssa tried not to notice.

She and Peter were busy.

Lauren sat under the ancient live oak tree in the large, deep-set front yard, facing the road. She was reading a book, scowling, sitting carefully on a small blanket to keep from getting dirty.

As she read, Alyssa planted a trail of evenly spaced peanut butter globs along the gravel drive and across the lawn. Her heart thumped with excitement and a vague sense of danger. When she was two meters away from the tree she stood directly in back of Lauren, hidden by its large bole. She looked behind her to see Peter following the pathway of peanut butter leading a very large, very ugly, blue and red-headed gray turkey. The turkey's limited concentration was focused on snatching each mouthful, then hunting around for the next bite.

Laughter erupted from behind the house as the other three Richardson children tumbled around in a rambunctious game of hide and go tackle. She and Peter had left the game to spy on Lauren.

Her timing had to be perfect.

Alyssa squatted low to the ground with the large plastic jar of peanut butter. If she moved too soon, Lauren might notice. Slowly, silently, she crept toward the bole of the tree. The turkey was finding his way closer, louder now with his gobbling. She wished he would shut up. It worried her some, but she knew her sister became completely absorbed when she read, especially when it was one of those sleazy romance novels. The noises probably wouldn't register until it was too late.

Very carefully, Alyssa scooted the jar of peanut butter around the oak's trunk until it was right beside Lauren, then crept away. She saw Peter's light blond hair sticking out from behind a tree on the opposite side of the gravel drive. He waved to her to join him. Increasing her speed as she fled, she reached him panting and out of breath. Peter turned sixteen in the spring and was now a head taller than her.

"He's almost there," he said, motioning her to look. Afraid to even breathe, they stood transfixed, watching the old turkey work his way along the sticky path. Lauren hated all animals. Ugly ones were somewhat worse, but in truth she was as repulsed by a kitten as she was by a vulture. Or a live turkey.

Lauren sat unmoving and stiff, not leaning against the tree. She scowled as she read. She had darker hair and eyes than Alyssa, but her face was the exact tight, pinched face of her mother; a perfect replica. Alyssa was always glad her features resembled those of her father more, even if her hair had to be light and her eyes gray like her mother's. But they were not quite the same color; Joan's eyes were the cold gray of hardened steel. Alyssa's were more the gray of a rain cloud, or a lake on a stormy day, flecked with odd bits of color.

"You should have heard her this morning," Alyssa said. "Mom made her come. She insisted she didn't need to come to 'another idiotic gathering with those puerile people.'" She snickered. "She actually used 'puerile' in a sentence, can you believe it? Mom was about ready to let her stay home until she said that. Lauren's been perfectly awful since she turned sixteen. Thinks she's so *mature*." She made a gagging noise.

The turkey was now practically beside Lauren.

"He won't hurt her, will he?" Alyssa asked, tossing her short tousled ponytail. She spoke more out of curiosity than concern for her sister's well-being.

"Nah. He's got a nasty temper, but he's harmless." Peter grinned. "As long as he's not provoked."

They looked at each other mischievously.

"Hey, look," Peter said.

Their eyes grew wide as they watched the turkey put his whole head inside the jar of peanut butter, feeding noisily as it clucked and gobbled with delight.

"I never thought he'd get that close," Peter whispered in awe.

"She doesn't notice anything when she reads," Alyssa replied.

Finally Lauren noticed, and provoked.

"Get that thing out of here!" she shrieked. Startled, the turkey backed away from its jar. "Get out! Shoo!"

Lauren kicked at it and batted it on the head with the book as if to frighten it, to make it run away and disappear. But its feathers ruffled and puffed out. Suddenly, the mottled gray and black turkey looked twice its size. Red-rimmed yellow eyes stared her down as the warning clucks grew louder.

Lauren screamed and ran. The turkey gave chase.

Peter and Alyssa let out peals of laughter as they watched the melee. The other three Richardson children, one older and two younger than Peter, came from their game in back of the house, drawn by the screeching of both tormented girl and vicious beast. When they saw it they laughed, the younger ones cheering for the turkey.

Lauren ran, screaming hysterically. In her fright she headed first toward the street. The turkey followed close behind, squawking. Then she doubled back and bolted for the front door, hair streaming behind her. Once inside, she turned toward her pursuer. The screen let out a long sigh as it leisurely made its way closed. Realizing the bird would follow her inside, she screamed again and slammed the heavy wooden door shut. It cut her scream short when it closed, muffling the sound.

Still ruffled from the excitement, the turkey preened a few of his wing feathers and strutted off the long front porch. From there, he headed back to the tree in search of the coveted jar of peanut butter.

As their laughter died down, Alyssa put one hand on her fledgling hip and asked, "Aren't you getting too old for this?" She raised her left eyebrow.

"Not when the fun's this good," Peter smiled. He looked at her. "But I think we'd better get out of here for a while."

"Good idea."

He grabbed her hand and ran with her into the cornfields to their left from where they faced the house. They followed a path perpendicular to the driveway and away from the scene of the crime, running through endless scratchy rows of corn until they were both breathless. Peter kept a firm grip on her hand all the way. She didn't take notice until they stopped to rest in one of the many tractor paths that crisscrossed the field. He gave her hand a gentle squeeze, and seemed reluctant to let go.

"Hey!" she said, pulling on her hand. "What do you think you're doing?" She looked at him indignantly.

"Holding your hand," he said and dropped it. "We'd better sit down," he said, looking around. "I'm tired, and I'm as tall as the corn anymore."

He flopped down on the grass in the pathway between the stalks. Alyssa sat down more gently. She was aware of something unusual and warm inside, something strangely different than the warmth she felt from exercise.

"You might be taller now but I can still beat you in a race," she said, raising one eyebrow. She sat facing him, her legs crossed.

"Only if I let you," he laughed. His hair was the color of golden sunshine, and it sparkled. She had never noticed that sparkle before.

"You lie," she replied. She felt uncomfortable thinking about his hair, and shifted her legs again.

He shook his head and pursed his lips trying to be comical.

She grabbed a handful of grass and threw it at him. He grinned and batted it away. Then he ran his hand through his soft hair, something she had seen him do a thousand times, only now, this time, it had a certain charm to it. She looked away, studying the cornstalk next to her.

"Well," he said, looking down at the ground and then up at her. Their eyes met. His gaze held hers a long moment. "They're like looking into a kaleidoscope," he whispered. "Green if the light hits them one way, blue if it reflects another . . . then these other colors flicker in there, winking in and out, like . . ." "Excuse me?" she said, clearing her throat.

"Did I say that out loud?" he said, his eyes widening. He blushed very red. "Uh, never mind, nothing."

"Nothing?"

"Yeah, nothing. You have weird eyes. So?" He looked away.

"Weird eyes," she said with a smirk.

"Well," he said, and coughed, "Uh . . . I got a new phone, wanna see it?" He reached into the back pocket of his jeans.

"You and your toys." She grinned.

"Oh, right," Peter said, pulling out the device. "It's not a toy. Mom needs it to call me in when I'm out in the field." He flipped it open, revealing the video screen and keypad.

"Boy, that's tiny." She laughed. "How do you see anybody's face on that thing? Where's the speaker?"

"Here, see? See, I can get the news and stuff on it, too. It's got pretty good video. Top of the line . . . No way, look at that, the Colts are actually winning! I can't believe it."

"Yeah, but why do you need expensive stuff like that? You could just get a basic unit."

"What, and have only black and white?"

"Good grief. Black and white. Now there's ancient history!"

They sat facing each other, offset to each other's left. She nudged him with her knee. "Lemme see it." He handed it to her, and she inspected it. "So the sound comes out here."

"Yeah."

"And here's the laser eye for your digital interface back in the house?"

"Yeah, isn't that cool? I can upload all your phone calls and store 'em forever."

"Why would you want to do that? No privacy, I swear, there's no privacy anymore. You can't say anything anywhere without somebody recording it. Good grief. Probably a satellite up there taping us as we sit here in this field."

"Could be. So?"

"Yeah, I guess you're right. Doesn't help to get all paranoid, does it?" She handed it back to him. "Well, that's pretty neat. It's better than Dad's pager, even."

"Oh, it's a pager too. And e-mail, and its got web access, but the screen's too small. The text comes up too tiny to read, and if you change the point size then it takes about ten years to read anything. It's a pain." He closed it and put it back in his pocket.

"Yeah, I guess it would be."

They were silent, listening to the breeze rustle through the corn, drinking in the scent of the growing stalks, green and firm.

"So, what do you think's happening back there?" Alyssa asked, nodding her head in the direction of the house.

"Hope somebody got Harvey back in his pen," Peter said.

"Not safe to go back yet?"

"Not yet."

"I wonder what my mother will do this time," Alyssa said.

"Let's just hope nobody saw you with the peanut butter. Huh?" he said.

"It'll be obvious it was us," she said, shaking her head. She twisted the end of her shirttail in sudden worry. "Obvious."

Some things were just too tempting to resist even when she knew the consequences of upsetting her mother's favorite daughter. But she had been upsetting Lauren ever since she was born, according to Joan.

"Hey, you know," Peter said, sounding uncomfortable, "Joan seems weirder every time we see her. Is it just me, or is she really?"

Alyssa laughed. "It's not you. She's weirder. She keeps collecting more and more archeological junk. Has to replace what keeps *breaking*."

She twisted her mouth in a wry smile. "Nice thing is, she's at the museum so much now we don't have to put up with her. Even Dad seems happier when she's not around, for all he fusses about their not spending time together. He's started puttering around with his model trains again. And cooking gourmet food, too." She waved her arm with a flourish and wrinkled her nose in disgust. "Most of it doesn't taste very good, but he puts so much time into it I'd feel guilty if I didn't eat it. And then Mom's never home for dinner anymore either." She smiled a wan smile. "It's been nice."

Peter looked at her tousled hair and smiled. The smile faded from his face and he knitted his brows together, then took a deep breath.

"Alyssa," he said softly, gently.

His tone of voice caught her full attention. She looked deep into his eyes, noticing their crystal blue as if she was seeing them for the first time, and tried to decide whether they were more like the sky or the sea, which she had never seen. Perhaps a star superimposed over the color of the ocean. It frightened her even to think that way.

She raised one eyebrow. "What?" she asked.

"Do you think our parents will stay friends forever?"

"I never thought about it much."

"Have you noticed how they're getting along lately?"

"I try not to pay attention if I don't have to."

Peter swallowed hard. He seemed reluctant to speak. "You should. They've been fighting a lot," he said, and his eyes dropped. "I've overheard some of their video conversations."

"What about this time?" Alyssa asked.

"I'm not certain," he said. His eyes shifted. "But it sounds serious."

"How serious?"

"It could be ending." He fidgeted nervously, pulling at spikes of grass with his fingertips.

"Hey, it's probably nothing to worry about. I doubt Mom's going to try too hard to lose her only friend. I mean, they've known each other since high school or something. Our age."

Alyssa twisted her shirttail around her index finger, dropped it, then unfastened and refastened the bottom button of her blouse. She felt an odd sense of dread. Could it be true? Peter rarely lied, if ever, but she knew he didn't always tell her everything, sometimes for her own safety. Some things she was better off not knowing.

Although Joan had been gone more frequently, when she was at home, she was more tense and hostile. That much was true. But Alyssa knew better than to pay attention, much less try to find out why.

"Your mom is so stable," she said, looking down again, her fingers still buttoning and unbuttoning, "I always thought she was so cool the way she does things. She can get along with anybody. Mom is calmer for weeks after they see each other. I don't know why, but when she's not around Beverly . . ."

She didn't finish her sentence. She stopped playing with the button. Then, in a small voice, she added, "That year after I broke my leg was the worst ever." She had never admitted it, not even to Peter.

He nodded with a look of understanding.

She sat and thought for a few minutes in silence. It was a comfortable silence, even though the subject was not. Neither had ever felt the need to fill every moment with trivial conversation. Alyssa enjoyed the silent times, the quiet thinking times, just as much or more than talking. The girls at school chattered like jays. Alyssa had sought without success to understand them. She preferred Peter's rare but more comfortable company to any of them.

Peter stared into the cornfield and sighed.

She said, "I've wondered if these trips would go on forever. I always hoped so. Mom is so much more settled afterwards, and it's so nice here." She fidgeted with a blade of grass, looked up at the clear deep sky. "But what could she want now? If they . . ." She would not finish the sentence. She didn't dare to think of it.

Peter turned to watch her.

"Everything ends, you know," Alyssa said. "Mother always says nothing lasts forever. I never wanted to believe she was right. Not about friendship, anyway." She slapped her hand against her leg. "Why does she always have to screw everything up? It's her fault, isn't it?"

Peter drew in a breath, hesitating.

"Isn't it?"

"Yes and no."

"You are so annoying, Peter."

He smiled. "Tell me something I don't know."

"Why don't you just tell me? You know, don't you? You rat. What's it about this time?"

"Alyssa, I can't say." His voice was strained.

"Why?"

Stray thoughts of how his hand had felt in hers, running through the field, vanished as she felt frustration rise. She had to know.

"I've promised not to talk about it." He stressed each word.

"So? Promised who?"

"Your mother."

"When? Where?"

Peter's expression was pained. "On the phone. Six months ago."

"I don't believe you. I've seen you twice since then." She stared at him, angry, folding her arms against her chest. "How could you not tell me something this important?"

He rubbed one hand along the grass at his side, back and forth, fidgeting, then scratched his head above his ear. "It didn't seem like it would be a big deal then," he said. "You know your mom, she keeps pushing issues. She's blowing this whole thing way out of proportion."

"What whole thing? You're driving me crazy! I'd rather go back up to the house than sit here with you!"

She half stood up.

"No, don't go," he pleaded, catching her hand with his as she tried to stand. "Please," he said, pulling gently on her hand, as if to see whether she would pull away from him.

She didn't. Instead she settled herself back down to a sitting position.

"I can keep secrets," Alyssa said.

He held on to her hand, squeezing it tightly. "I know," he said.

They looked into each other's eyes, Alyssa's confused, Peter's pleading with her not to ask.

"It was just Mom," she said. "It was a dumb promise."

"It's not just that it's a dumb promise," Peter said.

He stroked her hand, relaxing to a gentler grip. She looked down at their connected hands, then up at his face. She made no protest.

"If I tell you and your mom finds out, then I know for a fact," he paused, taking a deep breath, "I know I would never see you again. And I don't want that to happen."

"She won't find out," Alyssa said, tossing her wheat blond ponytail.

Peter continued stroking her hand softly. She gave his hand a soft squeeze. It was warm. The touch was delightful. Her world reeled with a wash of confused emotion.

"Thing is," Peter said quietly, looking down at their hands, "I've been wishing I could see you more often, not never again." He gave a small laugh, a half-smile. "Trying to come up with excuses. Something your mom just might buy if I was lucky. But I can't come up with anything believable except the truth, that I want to be with you." He paused. "And I'm positive she would dread anything happening between us."

"True," Alyssa said.

As his words registered, her throat went dry. She had never thought about anything happening, not before now, his hand in hers, new emotions flooding through her in waves of turmoil.

She had a sudden awareness that something was happening, this very moment, changing their perceptions of each other, perhaps even of life itself, something she didn't fully understand.

She realized that her mother's opinion of Peter wasn't high, especially since the accident. Joan still blamed him. Joan never forgave anyone anything. Anything romantic happening between them was certain to be forbidden, absolutely.

In the back of her mind she was surprised her mother hadn't threatened her about this before, warning her away by fear and intimidation. After all she and Peter were close. Joan would have sensed this. Perhaps she didn't wish to bring new ideas into Alyssa's mind, ideas she might not have come up with on her own.

"Alyssa, I don't want to lose you," Peter said. He ran his other hand through that thin blond hair. It fell back in his face. "Not now."

Alyssa stared at him. She felt terrified and thrilled at the same time. She couldn't speak.

"Alyssa, you're my best friend. You've been my best friend for . . . forever. I can't help how I've been feeling. If I could never see you again, I . . . I don't know what I'd do with myself." He looked at her, pleading with his eyes that she would understand. "I don't know how smart it is to tell you, or if you even care, but I don't know how I'd go on without you. You mean too much to me. I've been holding back for a long time, trying to push it away, you know, telling myself it doesn't make sense, but I can't anymore. Not if I might lose you."

We're holding hands, she thought. Trying to ignore what she was feeling thrill inside her as she heard his words, she said, "So you won't tell me after all?" Her voice didn't come out with the force she had hoped.

Peter sighed. "One track, aren't you?" He looked into her eyes, reaching into her soul. "I've told you, the truth could separate us forever."

"If I know Mother," she said, "It will anyway, whether you tell me or not."

"Truth?"

"Truth. Swear it." Alyssa looked quite stern. She was well practiced with that look.

He sighed. "To be honest, I was going to download the call and put it on my phone here so I could play it for you. I mean, not that you won't believe me, but I thought it might be better for you to see for yourself. But anyway, Mom deleted it all. Or locked it up so I couldn't find it or something. Anyway, I couldn't get it for you. Sorry." Peter smiled apologetically. Then he raised his right hand, still holding hers with his left. "Your mother has forbidden us as a family to discuss the subject of religion with her impressionable young children." He said it in a near-perfect imitation of her mother's prim, lilting and too-precise voice, blinking his eyes rapidly as he finished the sentence to complete the impression.

Alyssa would have laughed—Peter could copy her mother to the last detail—except that the content of what he had just said stunned all joy out of her.

"Religion? That's ridiculous. I don't believe in God. Why would she even bother with a thing like that?"

"I saw her myself. She gave us quite the lecture. Had us all come in front of the screen so she could see everybody. She pointed that bony finger of hers and said, 'Especially you, Peter.' I'm surprised Mom didn't just hang up. Wish I could've found it for you, it was incredible. She insisted that none of us influence your tender, open minds by clouding them with archaic religious ideas. She fears you would be permanently psychologically disturbed by false beliefs that distort the truth of established, proven, scientific fact."

Alyssa made a rude noise with her mouth. "What does religion have to do with anything?" She sighed.

She watched a ladybug crawl up a blade of grass, nudged it so it would crawl up her finger, pulling slightly against Peter's hand as she leaned to reach for it. "I fail to see the meaning in it. Seems like a bunch of hocus-pocus gibberish to me. Can you imagine honestly believing in heaven? Some happy place we all go when we die. Or hell? Some big red goblin in tights waiting to poke all the wicked sinners with a pitchfork. Crazy stuff."

The ladybug flew away. She watched it go. Peter's eyes smiled at her, but he said nothing. "So there," she said. "Do I sound psychologically disturbed to you?"

He grinned, squeezing her hand. "No more than usual."

She feigned a kick toward him and smiled, then grew serious again. "But that doesn't explain why Mom would suddenly go off on a kick about it. Unless . . . Oh." Her eyes widened. She paused, collecting her thoughts, comprehension forming. "Oh," she repeated. "Your mom . . .

you . . ." She stumbled, not knowing quite what to say. "I guess I just insulted you. Sorry." She looked down at the ground, away from their intertwined hands, away from Peter's lucid eyes.

"It's all right. No offense," Peter said. He sighed. "I might as well say it. We're joining a church, a . . . Christian church, Alyssa."

"Really?" She looked at him incredulously. "You've got to be kidding."

"Tomorrow, in fact, it'll be official," he said. "I never felt anything like this before. It's so different," he said, and paused. "There is a God, Alyssa. Whether you believe in Him or not, and I feel like we've finally found Him. He's real, not the invention of some philosophers. I can feel it. It's more real than anything I've ever known."

Alyssa paused briefly and looked away, unsure how to react.

"Well . . . whatever," she said. "Still. Why would Mother care so much what you guys do? So you don't discuss it. Big deal."

"Your mother's barely put up with Mom's religious feelings before. Mom has always believed there must be something more, but she hasn't done anything formal about it, like this. Joan has always tried to tell Mom she's misled, and I think for a while there, Mom sort of believed her. I guess you never paid any attention. But Joan can't handle Mom believing in it this much."

"What about you?" Alyssa said, raising an eyebrow.

"Well, I really do believe it. I can feel it like a glow inside me that it's the right thing to do. I feel close to God for the first time in my life."

"Hmm," she said.

"And Mom, well, she knows what she knows. Mom says she's actually heard real answers to her prayers. She says that's never happened to her before. And, well, you know Mom; she sticks to her word. She can't just pretend it's not real. And you know what Joan says about reality and truth."

"Science is the only certain truth," she said, in a parody of her mother's voice. She looked up. There was real pain, real concern in his eyes; she recognized it. "Mother hates to be wrong, you know. More than anything."

It was her turn to stroke his hand for comfort. She wasn't sure her mother *was* wrong, but how could she be sure? The things Peter had told her were too strange for her to imagine believing in them herself. But it seemed the right thing to say, if it would help him feel better.

"It's tearing them apart, Alyssa. Mom is trying so hard to keep it from getting in the way. She tries not to bring it up, she insists it won't change anything between them, but Joan won't leave it alone . . ." His voice trailed off.

In a moment he continued. "The last time you came, they argued all day about it. Mom cried that night. I started worrying you might never come back, and if that happened I might never see you again, and then I realized how I felt about you. I don't want to have to lose you over this, Alyssa. I don't want that to happen ever."

"I don't want it to happen, either, Peter," she said.

The thought that she could lose Peter, her only real friend, frightened her terribly. And she could lose him over an argument not her own, an argument over something as silly as differing beliefs. Over things no one could even be certain were true or untrue.

She felt pain and joy at once. Joy at her new understanding of their feelings for each other, mutual, thrilling emotions; and pain from the fear of the unknown, never knowing when or if the argument would or could be resolved. Her mother was certainly vehement in her opinions. If it did strike too deeply . . .

"We'll never know when it's the last time, will we?" she whispered. "We won't know until it's too late." She pounded her free hand into the ground.

She wondered that with her mother's multiple inconsistencies, she had never allowed that thought in her mind before. She had taken their outings to the Richardson farm, going places together with Peter, totally for granted, never thinking of the possibility there could come a time when it would not be a part of her life. The only part she looked forward to. The one thing that made living bearable.

A stray piece of remembered conversation entered her mind. "You know, Peter," she whispered, "I think we almost didn't come today. I overheard Dad saying something like, 'Now Joan, you're just being petty.' I didn't hear what she said back. I didn't know what he was talking about. Maybe she was trying to get out of coming. And then Lauren said that thing about 'puerile people,' and Mother got all huffy and insisted that we were *all* going."

Peter leaned over to her. He let go of her hand and placed his hand gently on her thin shoulder. His face was very close. Alyssa could smell the salty-sweet aroma of his hair blowing in the breeze. "If even this could be the last time," he said softly, earnestly, "and we won't know it until it's too late, I don't want you to leave without saying goodbye."

They looked into each other's eyes for a long moment. Alyssa's heart beat faster.

"Have you ever been kissed?" Peter whispered, barely audible.

She mouthed the word "no," shaking her head.

They stared at each other, Alyssa gathering in every detail of his familiar, but somehow new, features. She swallowed a lump in her throat.

"You?" she whispered.

Peter shook his head. "No." It was barely a voice at all.

The wind stopped blowing. The insects held still for them, the birds also; even the corn seemed to be waiting, listening, silent in anticipation, as though all nature held its breath.

The sun shone down on them as he gently pressed his lips to hers.

The kiss was warm and sweet and soft. It was a new sensation. She never imagined a kiss would feel like this, the gentle feeling of softness against her lips, the emotions that flooded her when they touched, the scent of his face and hair so close, so intimate. Peter reached up, to hold her chin in his hand.

It felt like eternity.

Their lips parted. He held her face in his hands, looking deep into her eyes. She reached up and touched his soft, slightly wavy hair.

"This is how we'll say good-bye," she whispered.

"Every time we're alone together," he whispered back.

"It'll be our secret."

"Our secret."

The breeze picked up again as they looked in each other's eyes. It rustled the corn and their hair, ignoring them now as it passed through them.

"When I'm old enough," Peter said, scooting around and taking her in his arms, "I'll come and get you, and carry you away with me, and we won't have to worry about anything separating us ever again."

His arms felt like the most natural place for her to be. She was surprised they had never thought of holding each other like this before.

"When I'm old enough," she said, "You know I'm leaving home and never looking back." She paused, then whispered, "Will you be there to take me away?"

She looked up at him, and took one of his hands in hers, interlacing her fingers with his, smiling at the strange wonder of the magical sensations she felt.

He nodded. "You better believe it," he said. After a pause, he added, "I have my license now, and next summer Dad'll probably let me drive to Des Moines by myself. We can arrange secret meetings."

"Like an old cloak and dagger movie," she smiled. "High adventure!

Spies, secret hideouts and passwords." Her face flushed with the thoughts of danger and excitement. She sighed. "Talk about getting in trouble."

"Yeah," Peter said. "Tell me about it. Even I probably wouldn't get away with it too easily. But I could."

"Uh-huh," Alyssa said, her sarcasm evident.

"I could," he repeated, and held her tight.

In the trees the robins and jays sang and scolded each other noisily, the crickets began their early evening hum, the scent of grilled steak and chicken filled the humid July air, and fireworks exploded in her heart for the first time.

Chapter 3

Verdict

Well, it didn't go well today. I wish so much they had stayed for tomorrow, but Joan couldn't be convinced. I know we're all ready for our baptisms, though. I feel the truth of this Gospel down to the marrow of my bones. Even Andrew understands it, though it seems he's still so young.

It's hard to believe he'll be eleven next week. Seems like yesterday I gave birth to him in the kitchen. Silly me, trying so hard to get all the peach jam put up before he came. He was two weeks early, and I figured it for false labor until it was too late. He came so fast. The paramedics didn't even get here until after I delivered. They found me and the baby lying on the kitchen floor, surrounded by sheets and towels. I can still see Isaac and Peter, little wide-eyed boys trying to help me, and baby Julia crying in the living room. The house smelled of burnt jam for days . . .

I guess childbirth has been on my mind lately.

As for the others, Julia hasn't gotten too difficult since turning thirteen, though I expect her to. She's still moody and picky, but besides whining more she's been manageable. At sixteen Peter is the same as always. Isaac is excited about being nineteen. He's already talking about serving a mission as soon as he's able to go.

No matter what Joan says about four being too many, I'm proud of each of them, and of the faith they're developing. They're so amazing. It's hard to imagine what all the upcoming changes will bring to our family though . . . as much as I'm anticipating all the blessings, I do wonder what else will change, and how.

Joan was so upset today. It didn't help matters that Peter and Alyssa pulled off another of their practical jokes on Lauren. I doubt I was hard enough on him afterwards. I'm amazed Joan didn't make them leave immediately, after that incident.

Maybe she was thinking of Chuck. It was good for him to talk to Phil while they were grilling together. Most of it bored Phil to tears, he said—Chuck's exotic foreign recipes for marinades. Thank goodness he didn't let Chuck try any of them. I like my food plain old American, thank you very much.

Joan made him wear a tie again, poor man. To a Fourth of July barbecue. But that's like her. Chuck was so hot today he was dripping with sweat. He told Phil how Joan never lets him wear anything comfortable. I think the truth is she never lets him own anything comfortable. Chuck said she goes through his drawers and throws out his favorite clothes as soon as they show any signs of wear, which isn't much, in her book. No wonder he's always scratching, with all that starch.

Well, at least the food was good, the salads came off, and there was plenty to go around. We have to be nearly self-sufficient, with crop sales so undependable. It's nice not to worry about having enough.

Peter did seem a little funny tonight after they left, but I haven't had a chance to talk to him about it yet . . .

Beverly Richardson,
personal journal entry

Peter and Alyssa strolled casually up to the house. He was careful to keep a good distance from her as they walked across the large back lawn. Alyssa glanced over at him just a little, but said nothing. They had agreed to act like nothing out of the ordinary had happened between them.

Lauren was nowhere in sight.

The family was making final preparations to eat. Beverly set a macaroni and vegetable salad on the table, then wiped a trickle of sweat off her brow and into her short, dark, curly hair. She looked up and saw him.

"Peter! Where have you been?" she called. "You know you have to put your things away after you play with them."

Peter reflexively looked over to the turkey pen. The turkey was back in it, strutting around as though nothing had happened. Then he saw the open jar of desiccated peanut butter on the table.

Beverly stood straight, arms folded across her chest, a stern look on her face.

"Sorry, Mom, I'll get it," he said, flushing.

He knew he had just admitted guilt by looking for the turkey. He didn't meet her eyes as he grabbed the jar and headed for the kitchen.

"Don't you dare put that in the cupboard, young man!" she said. He looked back and saw her turn to Joan, adding, "I'll deal with him."

Joan sat primly at one corner of the table and nodded. She was very stiff, but whether it was her usual stiffness or a bridled, barely contained rage was difficult to tell. She was dressed in a pastel silk blouse and slacks, accented by a string of hand-knotted pearls. Her pale blond hair was pulled back in her usual severe hairstyle.

Her too formal clothing was in sharp contrast to his mother's. Beverly had on a bright blue T-shirt and floral Bermuda shorts, and her feet, as usual, were bare.

In the kitchen, Beverly said, "Peter, I am very disappointed in you. You know he can't eat that much peanut butter without getting sick. Poor creature's been hacking it up all afternoon. You're in charge of cleaning his pen for the next week."

Peter breathed a sigh of relief. "Is that all?"

"We'll just save this," she said, taking the jar out of his hands, "for when he needs a special treat. Can't exactly use the rest of it now, can we? Or should we use it only on *your* sandwiches?"

Peter looked at her quizzically.

She continued, "You know full well it was wrong to scare Lauren like that. You know how much she hates animals and being here. You don't need to make it worse. For Heaven's sake, things are tense enough without this wrench thrown in. What were you thinking?"

Peter shrugged and looked at the floor.

"So. You're also grounded from all privileges for one week. Your phone, please?"

"But Mom . . ." he started.

"No buts," she said firmly, holding out her hand.

Peter closed his mouth. He knew it would be a full week, no more, no less, no variations. Her pronouncements were fixed and firmly enforced. He reached into his back pocket and handed it to her.

"But you won't be able to reach me if I'm out working," he said.

"I'll let you know if I think you need it. You can have it back next week."

As they walked back to the door, she murmured in his ear, "I am fully aware it took two to engineer that little trick. But for *her* sake I won't mention that fact to Joan. And you are to pretend I just made your life very miserable."

"You did," he answered in a low voice.

"You can't change the consequences of your actions."

"I know, I know."

She gave him a quick hug and pushed through the door, picking up another bowl of salad as she went. Peter paused in front of the sink, then turned on the faucet to wash up. He looked at his hand where he had held Alyssa's, and decided he couldn't bear to wash it. Gently, he pressed his palm to his cheek, then turned off the water and went back out into the streaming sunlight.

****

As Chuck sat down at the large picnic table, Peter saw him unbutton the top button of his shirt and begin to loosen his tie. Then, at a glare from his wife, he buttoned it up again. Peter smiled at Alyssa, but she didn't seem amused.

The children swarmed to the large table and began noisily passing food around, eating almost directly out of the serving bowls, most manners forgotten.

"Hey, that was my piece of chicken," Julia said. "I called it!"

"No, you didn't," Andrew said.

"Kids," Phil said, exhausted.

"That's mine!" Julia said.

"No, it isn't. Here, have the Jell-O instead."

"I hate green Jell-O!" she squealed. "Come on, give it back!"

Andrew grinned evilly and sucked the meat off the chicken bone with a loud slurp.

"M-o-o-o-m!" Julia whined.

"Can't you control *any* of your children?" Joan asked, irritation showing in her voice.

The argument immediately quieted down and the meal took on a more somber mood.

Alyssa had sat down as far away from her mother as she could get and still be at the same table. Peter let Andrew sit next to her, and took a seat opposite her and to one side. There was an empty place where Lauren should have been.

"Joan," Beverly said after a while, "This cake is simply too gorgeous too eat."

"No it isn't," Andrew said.

"You really shouldn't have gone to the trouble," she said.

Peter watched as Phil sliced a good-sized chunk out of it and served it to Andrew, then cut a piece for himself. It was shaped like a waving American flag, frosted with whipped cream, with fresh raspberries and blueberries delicately placed to form the Stars and Stripes. The white interior had four layers of filling, each a different fruit flavor and color.

"Well of course I didn't bake it myself," Joan said. "I had it done."

Chuck muttered, "Don't know what use the flag is anymore. President's probably going to plop his own face there in the blue part one of these days, instead of all those stars . . . How come there's still fifty of 'em anyway? Anybody but me think that's stupid?" He jumped suddenly, as though Joan had nudged him under the table, none too gently. "Oh, you know it's true, Joan, even if you did vote for him. As if New York and Jersey were states anymore . . . Or Rhode Island, or Connecticut, for that matter." He bit into the corn on the cob he was holding and was silent.

There was an uncomfortable pause, which Beverly broke. "You know, Joan, it's really too much. The *cake* should be in the museum!"

Joan laughed unexpectedly. Beverly had a knack for striking Joan's sense of humor, which was odd enough that she wouldn't laugh or even smile at an ordinary joke.

Phil looked around the table. His eyes fell on the empty place. "Where's Lauren?" he asked. Beverly nudged him with her elbow.

"Sulking," Julia said, loudly enough to be heard across the table.

"Oh," Phil said quietly, and looked down.

"You children all know she's much too mature for that kind of sick humor," Joan said.

Andrew said, "She didn't look too mature an hour ago!"

"Andrew, hush!" Beverly snapped back. He took a large bite of his cake.

"So Chuck," Phil said, speaking too loud, "When are you taking that vacation you were talking about?"

"Oh," he answered, relief showing on his face, "Four weeks. We decided last week we'd go to Hawaii. Just the two of us." He looked at Joan. "We've both needed a vacation for a long time now. Why don't you tell everyone the details, honey."

Joan, successfully distracted from the subject of Lauren, began to tell all about which islands they would visit, which places she had already seen, and the various amenities of the hotels they were trying to decide on. Her lilting voice dominated the remainder of the dinner conversation. It seemed to Peter she must enjoy hearing herself speak.

". . . you don't want to go to Oahu, because everyone goes to Oahu. It's too civilized, like visiting Central with a few palm trees and beaches thrown in. Not real vacationing at all. Why, last time I was in Hawaii, on that dig, you remember, the Polynesian cultural profile project? Well, that was several years back, true, but anyway, we found this remote little spot with a little bay and one tiny hotel. What was it called, Chuck?"

"I don't know, I wasn't there," he said sourly.

"Oh, well, I *told* you about it, didn't I? Never mind. Anyway there's this one little tiny cove spot that tourists hardly ever visit because it's so hard to get to. We had to fly in by helicopter. I remember that. Why, I thought Jack and Darlene were simply *insane*, you know, for trying, but I've never had a more thrilling air ride in my life. The beaches were absolutely breathtaking. What a view that was. Oh, and it turned out there were some simply *marvelous* artifacts, not too far beneath the surface either! Jack had such a nose for those things. No one on the staff ever questioned his hunches, did you know that, not after the amazing Queztocoatl find back when I was just out of college. It's a shame he had to retire, that asthma that would never clear up, you know. Strange thing, that. It kept getting worse, and you can't very well *dig* if you're allergic to dust!"

She laughed at her own observation, an out-of-place sound, her voice almost a cackle. "Well, that's near the village where I think we ought to make our reservations, although Chuck disagrees, but that's only because he hasn't seen it, you see. But then on the island of Hawaii itself there may still be a few remote places, certain spots *have* been protected . . ."

Her voice went on and on without any sign of tiring.

"You have to stay alone with *her*," Peter whispered across the table to Alyssa, motioning discreetly toward the house, "for two whole weeks?" He made a sour face.

Alyssa made a similar face and nodded. She picked up her corn on the cob and bit into it.

"I don't envy you," he said.

"I don't either," she said, swallowing.

****

As Alyssa got into their car late that night, after brilliant fireworks were reduced to fading ashes, after Julia had gone upstairs to bed and Andrew had fallen asleep on the lawn, she heard Joan say to Beverly, "You haven't changed your mind, have you?"

Through the car window she saw Beverly shake her head then frown. "I think you know by now how strongly I feel about this, Joan," she said. "Are you sure you can't stay for tomorrow?"

"What, and watch? You have got to be joking. You couldn't pay me enough."

"It would mean so much to me."

"It would mean much to *me* if you would come to your senses. You can't possibly be going through with this. You just can't, dear. Can't you see how twisted and convoluted it is? It's simple *brainwashing*. That is all. There is absolutely no logic, Beverly, no logic in this decision whatever."

"I know what I know. There's no other way to explain it than what I've already said. Please stay. Maybe then you'll understand."

"I couldn't possibly manage to witness such a disgraceful scene."

"Joan, please. I have to do this. I wish you would try to understand."

"Well." She couldn't see her mother's face in the dark, but could imagine the polite but terse smile her mother often used. "I guess that's it then."

"See you on Labor Day?" Beverly asked, hope in her tone of voice.

"We'll see." Joan climbed in the car. "Let's go, Chuck," she said. He already had the car running.

"What was that all about, Mother? Aren't we coming for Labor Day? Did they want us to stay over tonight?" Alyssa asked.

"You should know by now when things are none of your business. Have you not yet learned when to keep your mouth and eyes shut?"

Joan didn't turn to address her daughter. She stared straight ahead. Alyssa knew then it was not just the incident with Lauren that bothered her mother. Her mind was suddenly full of questions, questions she knew she couldn't ask. Even if she could it was unlikely an answer would be provided.

The rest of the two-hour ride home was silent.

Lauren scooted as far away from Alyssa as possible in the back seat and sat stiffly, like her mother, arms crossed tightly in front of her chest.

As they drove off, Peter stood a little behind his mother, trying to look aloof. They hadn't had any more time alone the rest of the evening. Alyssa could do no more than wave a casual good-bye as she climbed in the car.

They had shared only the one kiss, but she remembered the warmth of his lips on hers. She thought about his soft tender words, the warmth of the sun on his hair, the green smell of the cornfields in the breeze.

"*We'll see*," her mom had said to Beverly. In the same tone she used on Alyssa when she meant that she would never, never get what she wanted.

Maybe this *was* the last time. A lump slipped from her throat to the bottom of her heart.

A light blinked past her window as the car sped silently along the highway. She would not cry. She was in control. Without visibly flinching a muscle, she fought the painful aching in her chest, her constricting throat, the stinging in her eyes, as she stared out the car window. She concentrated intently, willing the feelings away.

Still she felt his lips pressing against hers in her mind, his fingers in her hair, her hand in his . . . and her soul betrayed her. But she would not give in to tears. She was strong.

She remembered the joy she felt only hours before, the new feelings that sprang to life today . . . only to die. She leaned her head against the car window and shut her eyes, feigning rest. The memories of the afternoon were sweet. The present, this silent car ride, was bitter. The future she dared not think about.

She opened her eyes briefly, and shut them again. She couldn't watch. Deep down, she felt she might never travel along this road again.

Chapter 4

Sentencing

I had this lovely Waterford china plate that I found in a quaint little antique store in a forgotten part of Central. I'd been shopping all day long and my feet were so tired. I walked in and was browsing around, and there was this wonderful potpourri going somewhere. I remember the whole place smelled first like old wood, because it was so old it was an antique itself, you see, and then cinnamon. Such a lovely cinnamon smell. This plate was mounted up above the back shelf, pretty as a picture. I remember they wanted $675 for it and I managed to talk the owner into letting me have it for only $503. It was such a rush, bargaining the price. How I loved that plate. The pattern had the most delicate white bas-relief figures all around the edge, and such an exquisite shade of blue.

Funny, I don't quite recollect what happened to it. I'm positive I never would have sold it, but I haven't seen it anywhere in the house for several years.

Joan Stark,
from an interview about
her private collection

The next night was Thursday. During another strange and unpronounceable meal from her father, complete with exotic garnishes, Alyssa's mother came home early. She stormed through the front door in a fully developed rage and slammed it shut with a vengeance, rattling the whole house.

It was a small single-level ranch-style house. Although her parents both earned higher than average incomes, the one point Chuck stood firm on was that they did not need a larger, flashier house. It was big enough for the four of them, if just barely, and he liked it. Joan compensated by cluttering it with expensive and frequently ugly—sometimes gruesome—artifacts, and furnishing it with bulky antique furniture. It emphasized the cramped feeling.

Her collection of ashtrays, rarely emptied, littered every dresser, shelf and counter. She had at least one anywhere it might be needed.

A few of the artifacts fell off the wall with the rattle from the door.

"It's done!" She bellowed, startling the three others at the dinner table. Chuck put his fork down. "She went through with it. She did it anyway. After everything I told her!"

She picked up the nearest object, a Mayan head ornament, and hurled it at the wall. It impacted with a dull thud.

Lauren slipped quickly down the hall to her room. Alyssa would normally have followed suit, but today she felt fastened permanently to her seat even though logic dictated that she move. She had to know.

"Trouble at work, dear?" Chuck asked calmly.

An antique china plate hurtled into the kitchen. It crashed into tiny pieces on the table and scattered piercing shards of blue china into his food . . . and Alyssa's hand and forearm. Small red drops of blood welled up from several places on her skin.

Silently she conceded to logic and became unfixed from her chair. Slipping down the short hallway into the bathroom, she locked the door behind her as her father idly picked pieces of china out of his food.

Alyssa turned on the cold water and carefully pulled the glittering slivers out of her hand one at a time, using tweezers. She winced at one between her thumb and forefinger that went particularly deep as she strained to listen over the running water.

"I will never forgive her for this!" she heard her mother shriek. "Never!"

More thuds. It was lucky for Chuck he was a large man. Her aim was usually none too good, and what did manage to graze him didn't do him much harm. He never threw anything back. She generally did not aim directly at him anyway, unless he was the object of her rage. Tonight he was not.

Alyssa continued to run the water over her hand and arm. Most of what her mother said was unintelligible gibberish, punctuated by hysterical weeping sobs. She watched casually as blood mingled with water and ran in a pinkish swirl down the drain.

She'll tell me I shouldn't have had my elbow on the table in the first place, she thought.

A loud banging on the bathroom door startled her.

"Yes?" she answered, trying to maintain calm in her voice.

"Open the door." Joan's voice was forceful.

Fear swept through her like an Arctic wind. "I'm occupied, Mother," she said, keeping her voice polite.

"I said open the door!" Louder, more pounding.

"Joan . . ." she heard her father say feebly.

Bracing herself, she unlocked the door and swung it open.

"Yes, Mother?" she said, careful to keep her wounded hand behind the door. Seeing the physical evidence of her wrath only made Joan more uncontrollable, like a shark smelling blood in the water.

Alyssa blinked slowly, maintaining a completely undisturbed expression. Her mother's eyes were red and mascara trails wound down her cheeks. Her silk dress was badly rumpled.

She pointed a skeletal finger at her daughter. "You. You will never see your friends again! You are forbidden to make any kind of contact with anyone in the Richardson family. Anyone! Do you understand? Never!" She lowered the pitch of her voice. "And if you do you may not live to regret it."

Her tone was ice and it froze Alyssa like a statue. Joan stopped to take a long drag on her cigarette, suckling it as a baby would its bottle while she closed her eyes.

"Yes, Mother," she said.

She decided to take a risk, even though the throbbing in her hand warned forcefully against it. She felt compelled to know more, to see if she could find out her mother's reason for doing this to her, for ruining everything she had ever found good in her life.

She took the mental equivalent of a deep breath and said, "Everything seemed all right yesterday. May I please ask what happened?"

It was a mistake. Joan slapped her face, hard. The force knocked her head against the door frame and upset her balance. Her legs were strong though, so she quickly regained her balance without falling.

"I'm very sorry, Mother," she said, quelling her anger, creating the artificial tone of respect in her voice that she hoped was believable. Her temples pounded from the blow.

Her mother turned down toward the end of the hallway, trailing smoke. How her mother managed never to drop her cigarettes remained a mystery to Alyssa. She could never figure it out, and often thought curiously about it at times like this. It helped to distract her mind.

Joan hesitated and turned back. Alyssa's hand covered part of her face, but the red welt showed through her fingers.

"You may not leave the house tomorrow," she said.

Alyssa always stayed home when the bruises were obvious. She nodded and held her mother's eyes with hers. She refused to let the pain show.

Joan's face twitched uncomfortably. "Beverly Richardson has done an absolutely unforgivable thing. She ruined everything there ever was between us. It's all her fault. Do you hear me? She's insane! This time she has gone too far. Too far!"

With these words she lunged toward her daughter, blind with the need to strike out at something. Alyssa flinched before she could force herself not to, then mentally cursed herself. It was a sign of weakness. But Joan stopped before she reached her. Tears ran freshly across her face.

"You will *never* ask me about this again."

Alyssa stared at her mother, expressionless, as she turned back down the hallway.

"Did you hear that, Lauren?" Joan yelled, pounding on her oldest daughter's door. "No more Richardson's!"

"Good!" Lauren's voice practically sang through the door. "Good riddance!"

Joan slammed into the door with both fists, hard. Weeping, she slid down to the ground in a heap. Alyssa crossed to her own room. Her father stood in the entrance to the hall.

"Alyssa," he said. "I . . ."

"Forget about it," she mumbled, and locked her door.

Sometimes she hated him as much as she hated her mother . . . for just standing there, watching. Sometimes she even felt sorry for him, but not for long.

It was his fault she had been born in the first place. When she was very small and supposed to be asleep, on a night when company was over, she had crept into the hallway and overheard Joan talking about it. It had been a bad day. Alyssa hadn't behaved, and Joan was in a fine mood for complaining.

"*You know I never wanted to have that child,*" she had said. The memory still stung.

"*Now Joan, you shouldn't say things like that,*" she heard a woman's voice say.

"*Why not? It's the truth. What's wrong with the truth? Truth is truth, isn't it? Might as well not skip around it, you know. It was all Chuck's idea. He just had to try for a son. Just had to. Didn't you dear. We were both so disappointed when the genetic testing came back.*"

"*Well, I wasn't—*" her father's voice had said. She wasn't sure what he planned to say.

"*We thought about it, you know. It wasn't too late at that point. We thought hard about it,*" Joan said next. Alyssa knew now what she meant, though at the time she had been too young to understand.

"You did, I didn't," Chuck had replied.

"Little creature has been a pain from the beginning. Thank goodness you gave up on the idea of having a boy after that, dear. Would I ever submit to that torture again? Certainly not! A bad idea from the start. Did I ever tell you what a horrible pregnancy that was?" Those were her exact words, Alyssa remembered.

"Yes, well, Danielle, I think it's time we were getting along, don't you?" a tired male voice said, after which she had crept back into her room quietly before anyone saw her.

She sat down on her bed and fumbled with the handful of plastic bandages and the tube of antibiotic ointment she had grabbed from the bathroom counter. Her thoughts were far from her father now.

It was final. Peter was gone. He would no longer be part of her life.

She considered the reality of it. If there was a God, at least he had allowed them to say goodbye. But she wondered if it really was a kindness. Maybe it would have been easier if Peter had never kissed her, if he had never told her how he felt, if she had never felt that queer feeling in her chest when he held her hand.

Then that same God had torn them apart. Or had her mother torn them away from God? Of course, if there was no God, the whole thing was pointless, and the Richardson's were just plain stupid.

In a flash of comprehension, she understood why her mother was upset. She thought they had all lost their grip on reality. Perhaps they had. Why not let it pass? Aren't people allowed to think what they want to? This new church of the Richardson's surely wouldn't harm her or change her. Peter said they'd been thinking about this decision for six months. Six months he had kept silent, not pushing any sort of beliefs at her, not saying anything at all.

But she couldn't tell her mother she knew that. Not without risking serious injury for knowing much more than she was supposed to.

It was too confusing. There were too many gaps in what she knew. It prevented her from coming to any kind of conclusion. The true facts were beyond her understanding. And now there was no one who could explain them.

Of course, Peter could.

Forbidden to make any kind of contact . . . Her mother's words stung her.

She shuddered to think of the consequences if they did arrange a secret meeting. She might be able to hide from her parents, but Lauren was nosy. Lauren would find out if her mother didn't, and would make sure that her mother knew.

She placed a bandage on her forearm, and opened another one methodically.

She wasn't stupid. Love, true or not, would never be as important as survival. Neither would vague perceptions of religion. She had already sacrificed ballet lessons, the softball team, various possessions and friendships to the whims of her mother. Yes, Peter was lost. Definitely. She could accept that.

She would miss him, of course.

Alyssa placed the last bandage around her ring finger and inspected her hand. The smaller scratches didn't need attention. She rubbed a little ointment into them anyway, watching the shiny stuff leave its greasy mark on her skin.

A tear leaked out of her left eye before she was aware of it. Then another.

She listened to the noises in the hall. Her mother was wailing in dissonant cadences up and down the scale. Her father's calm but earnest voice filtered through occasionally as he tried to comfort the woman he inconveniently but desperately loved. He would also lose a friend, Phil, with this turn of events. That didn't matter to Alyssa.

As she listened she also realized that when Joan noticed which items she had broken and remembered their replacement value, a whole new cycle of rage and crying would begin. It was always so. It would be a long, loud night.

She considered the two tears making their way down her cheek. No one would hear her or think of her tonight. Perhaps this once she could.

She curled up around her pillow and wept, bitterly, deeply, silently, as silently as possible, which for her was little louder than the breathing of sleep. She hadn't cried once in four years, not since the day she broke her leg racing Peter.

Peter. She felt his kiss on her lips again and the tears came in earnest.

She knew suddenly that she was lonely, lonelier than she had ever been. For years she had looked forward to the regular holidays they shared together. She didn't realize how much until now, when she thought of no Labor Day, no Thanksgiving, no Winter Holiday with Peter.

There was nothing left to look forward to. The days when she knew she was happy were always the days with Peter. Those days she felt free, at ease. The Richardson's accepted her for who she was, what she was, didn't try to change her or curse her because she wasn't what they expected or wanted her to be.

There was also the frightening, and far more immediate, prospect that there was no one left who could keep Joan calm.

She wept deep into the night. Finally the emptiness so consumed her that there were no tears left; still she found no relief from her anguish.

At that most bitter moment in the darkness, a warmth suddenly surrounded her. It felt similar to Peter's arms around her, only it made her feel somehow brighter inside. It was as though someone was there with her, giving her strength and comfort. As if someone wept with her, grieved for her. She breathed deeply and soon felt as calm and peaceful as a butterfly floating above a spring meadow.

As easily as the sorrow came, it was gone. She fell into a deep, silent sleep, finally untroubled by fear.

Chapter 5

Secondary Education

ARTICLE V, SECTION XIV, 13. *The legal age of adulthood shall be age seventeen years for allowing participation in previously-labeled adult activities: the consumption of alcohol, cigarettes, any other recreational narcotics, engaging in sexual relations, the admittance into establishments of business which provide, allow, or assist said activities; or the earliest age at which an individual is deemed capable to consent with mature knowledge of the natural possible consequences of their actions. Inasmuch as the actual age of maturity is individual, exceptions shall be allowed on an individual basis. 14. As some citizens are capable of determining said consequences younger than seventeen, the following shall be set forth: A permit for citizens under the age of seventeen years who pass minimum requirements establishing sufficient maturity may be obtained and renewed annually. Permits must be signed by the parent or legal guardian of the citizen. No such permit shall be required for any individual over the age of seventeen years, and no permit may be issued to an individual under the age of thitrteen years. Maturity may be determined by psychological evaluation or the judgment of the Court. Specific fees and regulations for said permits shall be established by Congress. 15. Instructional courses on the above mentioned activities, and possible hazards and benefits of participating in such, may be provided for those citizens wishing to undertake them, and are strongly recommended. Such courses may not be mandatory, as so doing would be an express violation of ART. II, SEC. I, 1 (Personal Individual Freedoms).*

The New Constitution

S ummer vacation was a new nightmare. Until now, it had always been her favorite time of year. She looked forward to going to the Richardson's so much; she didn't even realize how much until it was no longer there to anticipate. It hurt, if she allowed herself to think about it, which was a luxury she didn't frequently indulge.

Emotions were useless to her now, without Peter to share them. She squashed them like insignificant insects.

The trip to Hawaii came and went, and she and Lauren survived one another without incident. Both Joan and Chuck seemed happier afterwards, for a time.

Alyssa secretly thanked whatever powers there might be that Joan had to work increasingly longer hours at the museum. She received another promotion, and often came home too exhausted to criticize Alyssa for the things she didn't get done around the house, her clumsiness or her lack of manners.

But her rage was as unpredictable and inflammatory as ever, more so with the loss of Beverly's stabilizing influence. The smallest detail could set her off, such as Alyssa forgetting to take out the kitchen garbage, or leaving the toothpaste out on the bathroom counter. Alyssa knew the signs well, and was good at staying out of sight when necessary.

In August Joan went on a month-long dig somewhere in Brazil. Alyssa allowed herself to feel a small amount of pleasure at this. But there was still Lauren to deal with during the day.

Lauren had been given a car last winter, on her sixteenth birthday. It was a luxury sports model, bright blue. As soon as Joan left for Brazil she began to use it to bring boys home. Not always the same boy, and not always boys Alyssa thought were at all attractive.

Alyssa found herself, for the first time, wishing desperately for a larger house. With only the three bedrooms, living room, kitchen and small suburban yard there were literally no places to go to escape this new form of torture.

The first time, however, the boy brought his own car, and opened the door without knocking. Alyssa was watching television and nearly jumped out of her chair.

"You're not Lauren," he said, and headed down the hallway in the direction Alyssa pointed.

She stared after him, eyes wide in bewilderment. Soon she had to turn the television up louder to drown out the noises coming from the bedroom. It was disgusting.

After he left, Lauren found Alyssa in the kitchen and grabbed her from behind with one arm around her waist. Hot breath hissed onto Alyssa's neck as Lauren's other arm came up around her throat and tightened. Alyssa swallowed hard.

"What'd I do?" she choked out. "Let go!"

"If you breathe a word about this to anybody," Lauren said, "I'll kill you."

If there was one point Joan had made clear, it was that her daughters would never, never become promiscuous. They had both heard her lecture on that subject, minus any useful details, many times. It was the only education on reproduction she ever offered them.

"We both know what'll happen if she finds out. Don't we?" Lauren was not quite of legal age to engage in such activities without a permit signed by their parents. Joan would, of course, never sign such a thing. So Lauren would be in legal, as well as familial, hot water if she were found out.

Lauren squeezed tighter. Alyssa hadn't protested the restraint. She gagged and made a motion with her hands. She didn't doubt her sister could carry out the threat if she wanted to. Lauren loosened her grip.

"All you had to do was ask," Alyssa said, her voice shaky. "You don't have to do that. Let go of me!" She licked her lips, which were suddenly dry. "I'm good at keeping secrets."

Lauren released her. "Glad we understand each other."

Alyssa rushed to the bathroom, shaking, and leaned on the counter to catch her breath.

•••••••

So it happened that Alyssa usually went outside or took a walk when the boys came over. She was certain sex was disgusting, and had no curiosity about it whatever.

Lauren seemed to sense this. Often after a boy left, she would seek out her sister and describe their activities to her, in explicit detail, relishing every moment. Sometimes she recited the entire account through Alyssa's closed bedroom door. She had never been talkative. Now she wouldn't stop talking.

Alyssa made no response to these discourses, and asked no questions. If Lauren caught her out in the kitchen or the living room, Alyssa refused to either acknowledge her presence or leave the room until Lauren finally gave up and went away in a huff. It was the perfect silent treatment. If Alyssa hid in her room, or stayed away entirely, it would be a sign that she was annoyed by the monologues. So she simply kept to what she was doing, going about her business, painstakingly ignoring her sister.

By the end of the summer there was not much about the subject of sex that remained a secret to Alyssa, except for actual experience. And, thanks to Lauren, she was thoroughly uninterested in that. In fact, she was certain she never wanted that particular experience. The loss of control over her body's functions, the physical intimacy with another human being and other things Lauren described as pleasurable were utterly revolting to her.

On rare occasions when she felt the odd physical urges arising in her own body, she fought them back as easily as she fought back tears, pain, anger.

She wouldn't give in to these feelings, she decided. She wouldn't become like Lauren. She would maintain control. Control of her actions, her emotions, control of anything in her life that she could claim to be hers. That included relatively few things outside herself, but she could master everything within her. She was strong. Nothing would ever control her. She was determined.

****

Alyssa began her sophomore year at Rodham High, turning fifteen in September. To her surprise, on returning to school she discovered that Lauren had suddenly become very popular. They had both been fairly unknown before. The obvious reason for her popularity caused Alyssa some unwanted attention. Now she was *Lauren's* sister.

Thankfully Rodham was a large high school, so she rarely saw her sister during the day. That was a great relief after enduring such close quarters with her during vacation.

But she wished she could crawl away unseen every time someone asked her if they were related. Especially the boys, the ones with the same look in their eyes that Lauren had developed over the summer, a burning look that made Alyssa feel deeply uncomfortable. It was not at all the way Peter had looked at her.

The good thing was that it was Lauren's senior year. She applied to a nearby art school that was slightly too far away to commute daily, and was accepted for the following year. Alyssa would be free of her then.

"I'm leaving, I'm leaving," Lauren chanted when their parents were not home. Alyssa could now look forward to something. Lauren would soon be out of her life.

****

Alyssa spent her time at home in her room, studying her schoolwork. She enjoyed the calm rationality of algebra, geometry, physics, mathematics, the hard sciences generally. These were fresh and emotionless concepts, specific, precise. Problems could always be solved, using proven methods. It was refreshing to her to work out even the hardest formulas. She enjoyed the mental exercise, the feeling of control and comprehension as she grasped each new concept.

She impressed her science teachers with her calm, quiet dedication to her studies. They wondered at her soberness. Most students didn't genuinely want to learn, doing only enough work to earn passing grades. And few of those who cared actually understood the concepts as well as she did.

Her algebra teacher asked her once about her irregular absences. They were more frequent this year because Joan's anger became less restrained as the months without Beverly passed. But Alyssa was strong and stubborn. She could stay in her room indefinitely, as long as she had her books to read and study, avoiding her mother until Joan forgot about whatever it was that made her angry. Her mother wrote the excuses herself. But her algebra teacher wasn't that easily convinced.

"I don't believe you're sick that much, Alyssa," Mr. Henderson said.

She shrugged. "I get a lot of colds," she said, looking off at the chalkboard.

Algebra was her last class of the day. She stood at her desk packing her backpack, and looked at her watch. If she missed the bus she would have to walk. She didn't want to walk. It was raining.

"Come on. You never even sniffle in class. You're not sick, and you love school. I can see that."

"So?" she said, looking at him absently.

"Well, so I know you're not cutting class."

"What about it? I said I was sick." She hefted her backpack onto her shoulders.

"Look. I'm just going to ask. Is your father hurting you?"

"My dad? No way! He couldn't hurt anything if he tried. He couldn't put powder on a flea."

"Well, I've seen him, and not to offend you, but he is pretty big. And he seemed, well, preoccupied to me. Are you sure he's not messing around with you?"

"Of course I'm sure. I never heard a more stupid thing in my life. I mean, no offense to you, but he doesn't have it in him."

"You can tell me. It's all right." He looked at her closely. "There's counseling for this sort of thing."

"Mr. Henderson, my dad would never hurt me. It's my mother who would . . . if anyone." She shifted her backpack, uncomfortable about saying that much.

"Your mother? Mrs. Stark? But she seemed so *nice* at conference," he said. "She was so affable and interested in your classes. And she's so small—skinny, like you are. How . . ." He looked confused.

She shrugged. "Hey, if you don't want to know, don't ask," she said.

"That's not what I meant, I meant, I just don't see how—"

"Well you don't know her very well, do you?"

"But she's such a *pillar* of the community. I've gone to hear her speak. I would never have guessed . . . I often wondered what it must be like for you, I mean, she's hardly unknown in her field, you're practically the child of a celebrity where archaeology's concerned . . . You see, it's a hobby of mine."

Alyssa scoffed at him.

"Look, are you certain you're not just protecting your father?" he said, finally.

She sighed. "He is so harmless it's pathetic. Look, let's just forget we had this conversation, okay? It'll be worse for me if you try to do anything about it. If you go around messing up her precious career because of this little talk, then I'm completely sunk. I mean it. And it's not that bad. It really isn't. Honest. She's just, you know, more . . . strict than some parents are." She shrugged her shoulders.

"Are you sure there isn't anything I can do?" he asked.

"I can take care of myself," she said. "Honest. I'm fine. And I need to go."

"Well . . ."

"Look, I have to go *now* or I'll miss the bus," she said, hurrying out. Her footsteps echoed on the tile floor as she left.

****

Alyssa didn't excel in humanities, however, spending only enough time on those areas to earn the passing marks she needed. History confused her. It changed every year.

Early in the school year she had raised her hand. "I'm sure I learned in second grade that Washington and Jefferson were heroes," she said. "Wasn't one of them a President?"

"You learned lies," the teacher said. "They were unenlightened men who plunged this country into centuries of stagnation with their moralism. They plundered the native peoples nearly to extinction while setting up a government which indoctrinated and restricted the rights of its citizens. It was a government with no vision of how large and powerful this country could become. Their ancient system soon became powerless to serve its citizens properly. It may have worked for them, back then, and it was a brave attempt at a new form of government, but that's all. Our new system was desperately needed and is much better than their old ways."

"But what about that monument. I saw a picture of it once, this big mountain with four faces carved into it. Wasn't Washington one of those faces?"

The teacher gave her a stern look. "They were nearly worshipped once, that's true, but it was in the past and a grave error. Personally? I was glad when that thing was destroyed."

She didn't ask about it again. It would only mean more difficult questions on a longer test. She was always glad to return to her scientific studies where the answers didn't change and her questions were welcome.

****

A group of girls tried to befriend Alyssa that year, almost as one would take on a project. There were three of them, Valerie, Mikalah, and Holly. They came up to her giggling about something and asked her to have lunch with them.

She complied. There was no specific reason not to, though she preferred spending her break in the school library studying.

"Are you Lauren Stark's sister?" Mikalah asked. "I mean, like, wow. She is so cool."

"Uh, yes, I am," she said warily.

"I mean, all the guys just *go* for her. You know?"

"I've noticed," Alyssa said with a sour twist of her lips.

"Wow," Mikalah said, smiling. "I mean, she must be *so good.*"

"Look, I'd rather not talk about her, okay?"

"Come on, Mickey, leave off," Holly said.

In the middle of lunch, Valerie said, "So, who do you like?"

"Oh, nobody, I guess."

"Oh, come on, there has to be somebody," Holly said. "Everybody has a crush on somebody."

"Well, I don't," Alyssa said. She wasn't sure Peter counted, not now. Even if he did, she didn't feel like telling these silly girls about him.

"Come on, you're just hiding it," Valerie said. Valerie wore heavy makeup and dyed her hair blond. Her brown roots were evident. "What about Jim Decker? Jim's so cute."

"Who's he?" Alyssa asked without interest.

"He's right over there, with Bart and Mart, the twins," Mikalah said. "I like the twins."

"You can't like both of them," Holly said. "*I* like Bart."

"Yes I can," Mikalah said. "They're identical anyway. Besides I heard they do *everything* together." She giggled.

"So do you think he's cute?" Valerie said.

"Oh, I don't know," said Alyssa.

"How can you not think Jim Decker is cute?" Valerie said. "He's divine."

"I think there's more to it than just being 'cute,'" Alyssa said.

"Well that's the most important part," Mikalah said. She had bright blue eyes and dark hair, with freckles dotting her pale skin. She often wore red. "After all, if a guy's not cute to start with, well, *yuck*. I mean, sure, he might be a good kisser and all, but who'd want to find out? And the ugly ones, usually they don't have enough experience to be good anyway, so you've wasted your time. I found that out."

Alyssa ate her sandwich.

"So you don't like anybody?" Holly said. Holly had long brown hair and dark skin. She wore a wide silver metal belt around her tiny waist.

"I already said that."

"You have to like somebody," Holly insisted.

"Why?" Alyssa asked.

"Well, you just *do*. Oh. Maybe, um . . . Are you, you know . . . Are you a lesbian?" Mikalah asked.

Alyssa made a face. "No way. Gross."

"Hey, there's nothing wrong with it," Holly said. "Nothing to be ashamed of. Maurine Jenkins is that way, did you know that?"

"It's not gross," Valerie said, defensively. "It's just different. That's what my mom says."

"Well, I guess *she'd* know," Mikalah said, and giggled.

"Sorry," Alyssa said. "I didn't mean any offense."

"It's okay," Valerie said.

"So. If you don't think Jim's cute, who do you think is cute? Just, you know, objectively," Holly asked.

Alyssa sighed. She wondered if it was time for class yet, and looked at her watch. *Too much time left*, she thought. "It's just not something I think about a lot. I have a lot of other stuff to worry about."

"Like what?"

"Well, my schoolwork for one thing. And I have to take care of the house and stuff."

"Everybody does that," Valerie said.

Holly said, "You have to have a social life. I mean, don't you even think about it? You've got to at least think about it. What do you think about in Henderson's class?"

"I think about algebra," she said.

"Oh, brother," one of them said. She wasn't sure which. She'd been studying her napkin. They all sounded the same to her.

"Well, you could go out if you wanted to though, couldn't you? Shoot, you're so pretty. It'd be a waste, not to go out, with your body."

It was Valerie.

"I guess," Alyssa said. "Actually I don't know if my mom would let me."

"What, she doesn't want you to go out?"

"I don't think so. I haven't asked."

"Why not?"

"Well, with my mom you have to be careful. She's pretty picky."

"Oh, one of those," Holly said. "My mom begs me to go out so she can have the house to herself, with her Roberto. Now there's one ugly dude. Barf."

The girls giggled, then all were silent for a moment. Finally Valerie said, "You know who I like?"

"Who?" The other two girls huddled closer to her.

Valerie blushed slightly and confessed. "Derik Brown."

"Derik Brown!" Mikalah said. "Does he like you?"

"I think so," she said, smiling. "He passed me a note in second hour."

"What'd it say?" Holly asked, her silver belt jingling.

"Um, if you don't mind," Alyssa said, standing up, "I do have to get going."

"You do?" Valerie said, looking at her briefly, then returning to the tale about the note.

Alyssa nodded, though the girls were no longer paying attention to her, and headed for the library.

****

She found little in common with them, but for some reason they sought her out, and on several occasions managed to convince her to come and eat with them, although their constant chattering about boys didn't interest her. She couldn't bear to think about any of the boys in school in the same way she did Peter. She kept those feelings locked up tight. Better to ignore them, pretend they weren't there, than allow the pain to overwhelm her if she gave them any thought.

After the Winter Holiday break, it came out that Jim Decker Himself had a crush on her.

Did she like him back?

She was completely uninterested.

When they utterly failed to arrange for her to go on a date with him, they came to find her for lunch less often. They were friendly when they saw her, but Alyssa was glad to have her time back, and didn't seek their companionship.

Chapter 6

In the Name of Self-Defense

Public displays of mutual affection are expressions of normal, youthful behavior, and shall not be suppressed so long as the activity does not interfere with a student's time in class or schoolwork.

Rodham High School
Student Handbook

There came a day in March, before spring had fully come, when Alyssa was followed around school all day by a boy with greasy long black hair, dark hollow eyes, and skin that was too pale, as though he had lived in a cave his entire life.

"Hey, I know who you are," he said. "If you're anything like your sister I can't wait to try you out. I think I'm in love."

Alyssa couldn't recall seeing this one with Lauren before. He asked vulgar questions about her personal behavior, and told her repeatedly what he wanted from her. With questionable thanks to Lauren's summer education, Alyssa knew exactly what activities he had in mind, and felt sick to her stomach.

She was good at ignoring things until they went away, but this one would not. He followed her to all her classes, waited around the door until class got out, sat down by her at lunch and described activities that completely ruined her appetite.

She had no safety in numbers today. It came to her that one advantage the gossipy chattering groups of girls had was that they protected each other from unwanted advances. Even that brainless Mikalah might have been of some help. Alyssa scanned the cafeteria; it was raining outside and crowded indoors, but she could see none of her would-be friends. She couldn't eat, and finally got up to throw her lunch away. Of course he followed her.

She was good at the silent treatment; it worked well on Lauren, but this greasy boy was like a loathsome shadow she couldn't shake. On the way out of the cafeteria she said, "Get lost," but that didn't help at all.

"You've noticed me," he said, clutching his hand to his chest. "I'm in heaven!"

She ran for the bus as soon as she was free of class, but he was waiting for her outside the front door. She was afraid he would follow her onto the bus, but he didn't.

Instead, he called after her, "You can run, Angel, but I'll be here tomorrow waiting for you. I'm in love."

This would have to stop.

****

When she got home she knocked on Lauren's door. It opened. She didn't say "Come in," or anything else sisters say to each other. She only looked at Alyssa and said, "Yeah?"

Alyssa's face was free of expression as usual. She spoke quietly.

"I know I made you a promise. But I refuse to live with creeps coming on to me because they hear I'm your sister and think I'm just like you. Either you spread the word to your friends to leave me alone, or I'll tell Mother everything. I mean it. Then you'll be free to do whatever you want to me. I don't even care. I refuse to live this way."

Lauren laughed nonchalantly. "She'd never believe you. *I'm* the perfect one, remember." Her brown eyes were dark and hard to read, but there was a note of sadness in her voice. "Besides, I'm legal now."

Alyssa waited patiently.

Lauren scratched her head. "If you'd loosen up a little, it wouldn't be a problem. You'd like it a lot if you just tried it once. I can hook you up with someone really good. Nice and romantic."

Alyssa's blank expression didn't change.

"What? Should I tell them you're still a virgin?" Lauren asked, smirking.

"I'd rather you didn't announce that fact."

There was a pause.

Lauren sighed. "So who was it today?"

"Blaine Draper, Dryden, something like that," she replied. "You know, the one everybody calls Diaper-Head."

"Ugh." Lauren shuddered. "Even I wouldn't . . ." She looked around, tapped her foot twice. "Okay. If you don't want to have any fun, that's your choice. I'll spread the word to leave you alone."

"Thank you."

Lauren shut her door. Alyssa could only hope it would help.

****

The next day Blaine was waiting for her by the door of her first class. She walked right past as though she didn't see him, but he reached out and grabbed her by the waist when she was in the threshold, where she couldn't escape. Pulling her out of the doorway, he pressed her against the wall.

"Angel," he whispered. "I missed you. I dreamed about you all night. Want to hear? I had some real sweet dreams." He licked his lips.

"No," she insisted. "And my name's not Angel. Let me go."

She pushed him back, but he pressed harder against her. She was glad she had books to push with. Her mind raced as her eyes darted around, looking for anyone she recognized as a friend. There were always couples in hallways like this. She knew one more was unlikely to be noticed.

She hated attracting attention to herself; screaming was so undignified. He couldn't pursue the matter too far here, not in public. The school drew a line between what was considered public affection and intimate behavior, the latter requiring one of the privacy rooms, none of which were nearby.

But she hated being restrained. He was stronger than he appeared, and taller than her. It was likely that passers-by wouldn't even see her behind him, he was so close.

He pulled her tighter, backing her into a little corner made between the wall and a row of lockers.

"I'm sure once I kiss you, Angel, you'll forget why you're fighting it. You're being a tease. I've got to have you. Deep down you're a kinky lioness waiting to be released."

"No! I am not!" she said, rare anger showing in her voice.

She was now deeply frightened. All thoughts of remaining calm and emotionless were gone. She started to struggle.

"Don't touch me. Let me go. Now!"

"See? Angel, you *are* a lioness. And *I'm* going to be the first to release you." He leaned in to kiss her.

"I said no!"

In a simple act of self-defense, she turned her head away, and jerked her knee upward. But her books slid out of her hands, and the movement failed. The only result was that he pulled her even closer.

With her head turned, he couldn't reach her mouth. Instead, he kissed her neck, viciously. It hurt. It was also wet, warm, and slimy.

She winced and let out a small cry of pain.

"Knew you'd like it," he mumbled through hot breath. "Mmmm.

You're so delicious, my Angel. I can't wait to find out how the rest of you tastes."

He continued the painful attack on her throat. She struggled to push him away, but he pinned her hands expertly and pressed his body up against hers, the books no longer protecting her.

She let out a scream. It couldn't be helped, even if it was undignified. At this point, she no longer cared.

"Leave her alone," a deep, gruff voice said from behind her attacker.

Surprised, Blaine stopped and looked around, then loosened his grip. Alyssa struggled free and took several steps away from the wall. A large senior stood there, someone Alyssa recognized. She had seen him with Lauren several times. She thought his name was Garret, something with a "G," anyway, but it escaped her. She noticed a small crowd had gathered, but didn't know any of the other faces.

"Why should I?" Blaine retorted. "She's mine. You can't have her."

"I am not your property!" Alyssa spat out, the adrenaline causing her to shake with anger.

"Doesn't look to me like she wants you. I said leave her alone." He folded his muscular arms in front of his chest. She remembered hearing Lauren say he played defense on the football team. "And it's not me that wants her. Lauren says you leave her sister alone or else. She sent me to check up on you, Diaper-Head. *I'm* the *'or else.'*" He stared Blaine down.

Eventually the smaller boy swallowed. His eyes darting from Alyssa to the intruder, he said, "If you change your mind, Angel, I'll be waiting."

The football player took two steps toward him as he backed away. "You can't stop me from dreaming about you," he said, then turned and fled.

"Thank you," Alyssa said to her rescuer, and began picking up her books.

"No problem," he said. "Anything for Lauren."

He bent down and helped gather her papers.

"Thanks," she said again.

He handed the papers to her. She looked up at him. He wasn't bad looking, and his face was friendly.

"Sorry I didn't get here sooner," he said. "Lauren just told me about it this morning."

"I'm glad you came when you did." She paused and shifted her books. "Well. Thanks, uh, Garret?"

"Garth. Name's Garth. Sure. Anytime." He turned and walked away.

She heard footsteps running behind her and turned around. Holly and Valerie were coming toward her.

"Alyssa!" they said together.

"You all right?" Valerie asked.

She nodded. "I think so."

"What happened to you?" asked Holly.

"That Blaine Diaper guy, he, uh . . ." she couldn't finish. The words wouldn't come out of her mouth.

"I heard it was him," Valerie said, looking at Holly wide-eyed. "Megan said there was a crowd and when she saw it was you he got to, she came to find us."

"How long has he been following you?" Holly said.

"Just since yesterday," Alyssa said.

"Oh, man, I was sick yesterday," Holly said. "You should've *called* me. We'd have stuck by you like glue today. He's so creepy. I mean, there's ugly, and then there's *creepy*."

"I didn't think to. Guess I'll know better from now on." She managed a wan smile. She couldn't bear the thought of something like that happening again. "Boys usually ignore me, I didn't know what to do."

"You going to be all right?" Valerie asked.

"I think so. I mean, he didn't actually hurt me, it was just extremely gross." She shivered.

"You sure?" Holly asked, flipping her hair behind her back.

"Yeah."

"Hey, I gotta get to class," Valerie said, still out of breath. "I have too many tardies first hour anyway. We're real sorry, Alyssa. See you around, huh?" She ran off.

"Me too," Alyssa said. "I better get in there." The hall had cleared out surprisingly fast.

"All right," Holly said. "I'm real sorry I wasn't here." She put her hand out, touched Alyssa lightly on the arm. "Let me know if there's anything I can do. Call or something."

"Thanks."

The story of what happened spread around the school and went through various changes, as gossip will do. One or two girls came up to her that day who had never spoken to her before and said, "I'm so sorry." But nobody, not even Holly, thought to tell her about the mark on her neck.

Alyssa was not vain and didn't like mirrors much. She didn't preen in front of them like other girls her age. Of course, she knew what a hickey was, and had an idea how it was done, but not even Lauren had mentioned what it felt like to get one. She had no idea Blaine left visible evidence of his attack.

She was so distraught her hand shook every time she held a pencil. She couldn't concentrate, even in algebra. All she could think about was getting home where she was relatively safe. Odd. Home had never felt safe before.

In her preoccupation she forgot that her mother was coming home early that day to pack for a flight. She was the keynote speaker at an important archaeological conference and would be gone for three days.

So as Alyssa came through the front door expecting relief—a few quiet hours of study before the misery of sitting through one of her father's odd dinners, then hiding out in her room the rest of the night—it happened that her mother was carrying her garment bag into the living room.

Of course Joan saw it immediately. It was a large and bright purple mark on the right side of her fifteen-year old daughter's neck. To a mother like her it could mean only one thing.

She dropped her bag. Alyssa stood in the doorway, belatedly remembering her mother was going to be home. Ordinarily she wouldn't forget such a vital detail. She knew instantly that her mother was angry just from seeing her in the doorway, but didn't know why. Was she overdue for some kind of imagined discipline? It was so hard to tell what Joan was going to forget and what she wasn't. She braced herself.

"Hello, Mother," she said carefully.

"You little *slut*," was all that hissed from Joan's mouth.

"Pardon?"

Confusion rattled around in her brain. Joan had never used that particular word to insult her before. Had her mother found some lingerie item of Lauren's lying around and assumed it was hers? She adjusted her backpack on her shoulders. Perhaps Lauren had left something out on purpose, maybe planted it in her room even. She wouldn't be surprised. She would have to tread with extreme caution.

"How did you get that?" Joan said in a low voice, pointing.

The hair on the back of Alyssa's neck bristled. She was more dangerous when she talked softly than when she yelled. She was like a cobra winding up for its deadly strike.

"Get what? I don't know what you mean, Mother?"

She carefully set her backpack down on the floor, trying to behave normally while making sense of the accusation.

"These are so common you don't even notice them anymore? Is that it?"

She stepped closer. Alyssa was exhausted from her emotionally grueling day. She was unprepared for a confrontation. She had tried to come up with correct answers but had found none. Joan came closer. Alyssa felt as trapped as she had that morning.

Joan reached out and lifted Alyssa's hair from her neck. Alyssa looked at her with confusion.

"It *is* exactly what I thought it was," Joan said. "Do you mean to tell me you don't know what this is or how it got there?" She prodded Alyssa's neck with her fingernails.

Dimly Alyssa realized what must have happened. "Is there something on my neck?"

Joan slapped her across her face, mocking her words. "'Is there something on my neck?' I'll say there is! Why, you little whore! Next I suppose you'll try to tell me you're still a virgin!"

"But I am!"

It was the wrong answer. She was slapped again. "Don't you lie to me," Joan said. "You don't come home with those if you are!"

"It's never happened before! There was this boy at school, he's been following me around and today he attacked me in the hall before school and he cornered me and I couldn't get away from him." Her words came out in one desperate breath. She gasped. "It felt horrible! It hurt! I didn't want him to touch me! It was awful but he was stronger than me. I'm lucky I wasn't raped!"

She realized she was too close to tears, losing her stable defenses right in front of her mother and took a deep, calming breath. Her cheek stung.

"*Liar!*" Joan whispered. "You did this on purpose because you knew I'd be home! You knew how important this presentation is to me and you just had to ruin it!" She paused, ideas forming. "No wonder you stay in your room all the time! Having sex orgies in there, are you? How many have you done at once, five at a time? More?"

Stunned, Alyssa silently mouthed the word "no," shaking.

"Not in *my* house you won't, young lady!"

"No, Mother, please, didn't you hear me?"

"And now that you're caught you make up asinine stories like this! Pretending you didn't even like it! I don't believe that for a second."

She punctuated her sentence with another blow, this time with her fist. It was the first time she had ever used a fist on Alyssa. She was wearing a sharp jeweled ring that cut into her cheek. The sting was intense.

"It's the truth, Mother, I swear it," Alyssa choked out, forgetting not to raise her hand to her jaw, forgetting to ignore the pain, not to let it show.

"Even if it was true, he wouldn't have been after you if you hadn't been asking for it, you little tramp. What have I told you? Haven't you heard a word I've said? Serves you right!"

"No! Please, listen to me," Alyssa pleaded.

"Shut up!" Joan yelled.

Lauren opened the front door just then, home from school. She took in the scene in the living room and said, "Just came home for a snack," then headed for the kitchen.

"Wait a minute," Joan said. She held up Alyssa's hair, pulling sharply on it. "Lauren dear, you were at school today. Do you know anything about this? Alyssa seems to think it was quite the public incident."

Lauren turned around to look. "My goodness, what *is* that?" she said. "Is that some kind of rash? Are you sick?"

Alyssa looked at her in complete disbelief.

Joan said, "It's a hickey, Lauren. Don't tell me you're seventeen years old and haven't heard of a hickey."

"Oh!" Lauren said. Her voice was syrupy sweet. "So *that's* what they look like. No, Mother, I have no idea how she got that." She pulled a granola bar out of the cupboard and headed for the front door. "I'll be back late. Sorry, I haven't heard anything," she said, and left.

"So you are a liar," Joan said, as the sound of Lauren's car faded down the street.

The absolute betrayal sent Alyssa's mind reeling. She should have expected it, but she wasn't herself today. Backing away, she bumped into the chair next to the television.

"No," Alyssa mumbled as she shook her head.

There was no way out. They were alone, and there were no rules here but Joan's. She thought of running, opening the front door and seeing how far she could get on foot. She realized it wouldn't be far. Even assuming she could outrun her mother, which was likely, she had no money and nowhere to go if she left. While it was true she dreamed of leaving home, she meant to plan it out better than this when she did. She needed to pack things, take along food, cash, clothes, not run out the front door empty-handed. She dismissed the thought. It would also appear an admission of guilt, and she refused to do *that*. It would only further seal her fate. She would have to see this out and defend her innocence.

She blurted out, "Lauren knows about it, she sent a friend of hers on the football team to stop this guy!"

"*Lauren*," Joan said, "would never lie to me. She has never lied to me in her entire life. But you, you've been lying ever since you learned how to talk. She doesn't even *know* any of those filthy football players. She's an *artist*. And even if she did, why would she care to help you, after all the nasty tricks you've pulled on her your entire life? Get the facts straight if you're going to tell a believable lie. You are nothing but shameful, child, shameful, for even trying to bring her into this! She had nothing at all to do with it. You heard her yourself."

Alyssa was flabbergasted. She had no defense but the truth, and her mother refused to hear that. All she could do was stand there with her mouth hanging open stupidly.

"So. I bet you don't even know his name, do you. And close your mouth. You look like a dumb guppy."

"It was Blaine. Blaine Dry... It sounds like diaper. They call him Diaper-Head. Dryson? Dryden? I can't remember."

Her mind was so confused that she didn't realize until too late that this was also a very wrong answer.

"That's proof! You're a full-blown filthy whore! You don't even know his name!"

Her mother began to swear in earnest, using explicitly crude language that in a small part of the back of her mind Alyssa was surprised her mother even knew, words Lauren used around her all the time in her attempts to annoy.

As Joan yelled, she pushed Alyssa, knocking her against the television entertainment center. It was an antique, manufactured long before the built-in large screen wall models became stylish, and the corners were pointed. Two figurines fell off the shelf onto the floor. One was clay, and it shattered.

"Now look what you've done!" Joan shrieked. "My Aztec! You clumsy fool, stand up and take your punishment!"

She grabbed her daughter's shoulders with both hands and squeezed, shaking her as she dug in with her perfectly manicured fingernails. "Stand up, I tell you! You worthless piece of whoring *trash*!"

She shoved Alyssa backwards. A stab of pain tore through her head as it connected with another sharp corner of the entertainment center. Her head was spinning.

"I am not!" Alyssa yelled, and cursed back at her.

She was angry now. It boiled up in her blood as she fought to control it. The day had been too long, the events too draining, for her to keep up her placid front. She thought about trying to hit Joan back, but was too afraid. She had no chance of overpowering her, not now, with her head pounding so badly.

She fell over, losing her balance.

"Don't you *dare* swear at me, you ungrateful wretch. Get up!" Joan shouted, kicking her in the ribs with her pointed shoe.

Alyssa winced.

"I said get up!"

Joan kicked again, finding new words to insult her with. And again. And again. She wouldn't stop.

"Fifteen years I've put up with you," she screamed. "And this is how you repay me! It's not bad enough that you're clumsy. It's not bad enough that you can't get along in this family. You have to go sleeping around just to spite me! And then you tell blatant lies about it! No punishment could possibly be severe enough for you!" She kicked still harder.

Twice Alyssa kicked back, holding her head in her arms. It was fruitless, and only served to increase Joan's rage. At last Alyssa lay motionless on the carpet, curled up to defend herself against the blows.

Her body seared with agony. But she wouldn't cry. Her mother's curses barely registered in her brain as she concentrated on not breaking down, not showing Joan how intense the pain was.

She knew she was innocent. She *knew*. Wrapping that thought around the pain, she concentrated on it, feeling it in every fiber of her consciousness, with every blow, a righteous indignation nursed by the agonizing sensation of unfairness and misery that made up her entire existence.

Then she fell into a warm, comforting blackness.

Chapter 7

Negotiations

Negotiating is a fine art, requiring much of give and take by all parties involved. Where there is obviously more "take" by one party than "give," in both political and personal contracts, a sense of fairness is often lost.

The New Diplomacy Handbook,
Dilworth Hunter, c. 2017 AD

Her father's voice woke her. "Alyssa, please, wake up." He shook her, panic evident in his tone. Slowly consciousness returned. And pain.

"Alyssa, who did this to you?" he said.

"Oh, right. Who do you think, Dad?" she mumbled, memory returning. She didn't know if Joan had ended her assault before or after she lost consciousness. Everything hurt. She moaned.

"She couldn't have done this. She'd never do this. She's never . . ." Her father's voice trailed off. "I told her she was never to . . ." After a pause, he continued. "I just came in. She left a note on the door saying she left for the airport an hour ago. I can't believe she left you like this."

Alyssa opened her eyes. The room was blurry and spinning. She tried to raise up on one elbow. Every movement hurt.

Chuck pounded a fist into the floor with a curse. "What did she think she was doing? Why? *Why?*" His voice broke.

Alyssa blinked. Idly she wondered if he would have stopped her if he had been home.

"Because of this, I guess," she said, and raised her head to show him her neck.

Chuck sounded surprised. "How did that happen?"

"I told Mother the truth," she said, "but she didn't believe me. There was this guy following me around at school harassing me. He caught me in the hall this morning and did this before somebody could stop him." Was it only this morning? It seemed years ago. "I couldn't get away from him—he was too strong. I didn't even know he left a mark. I didn't know. Mother saw it when I came home, and she freaked."

Chuck sighed. "I'm so sorry." He paused. "Even if it did get there the usual way, that's the way things are, part of growing up anymore. I don't know why she can't accept that."

Alyssa tried to focus her eyes on him. "She called me a slut."

"Oh. Yes, I suppose she would have."

He was silent a moment, staring at the floor. His brown hair was rumpled and needed a cut badly. He ran a hand through it with a sigh, and continued.

"Her mother was like that. Joan always hated her for it. She's so picky about this sort of thing because of that."

Briefly Alyssa's mind followed this new tangent. *Grandma?* She had been dead for years. It was odd to think of an old woman that way.

Chuck said, "So you know, it doesn't matter to me. What you do or don't do is your own business. You're practically a grown woman now. You'll make good decisions about all of this kind of stuff, I know you will, you've always been responsible. But in the future, make sure nothing ever shows, you know what I mean?"

Alyssa groaned. "Even you don't believe me."

"No, I do," he said. "You're smart enough to cover it up if you'd known about it. I know why you stay in your room so much . . ." His voice trailed off, and he was silent a few moments. "Just be careful, you know, in the future. You know, you might actually want one of those someday." He made a feeble attempt to laugh.

"I seriously doubt that," she said. "It hurt."

He got up from his sitting position on the floor next to her. "Here, let me help you up. Can you walk?"

"I think so." She struggled to get up, holding on to his arms.

"Do you need a doctor?" His tone of voice told her he sincerely hoped that she did not.

"I think I'll be fine."

He helped her walk to her room. "Are you sure? Because I could drive you, to, to, a hospital somewhere."

"I should be all right. I just need something for the pain. It hurts to move."

Chuck winced. "I think I have a prescription left over from when my back went out."

She had a black eye, blood in her hair, bruises on her arms and jaw.

"It's never been this bad before, has it?" He was very pale. She thought he looked frightened.

She shook her head. "No."

"It really hasn't? You promise? Tell me, sweetie, please. Has this happened before? Ever?"

"No, she just lost it this time. I didn't even remember she was going to be here, and then I didn't know there was a mark there, I was just going to go to my room until dinner. I didn't even know it was *there*. I didn't *know*. And then I broke one of her statues, that ugly little clay thing, and she just, she just . . . exploded." she stopped and took a deep excruciating breath.

Chuck began to cry. "Oh, sweetie . . ." he said, and put his arms around her. She leaned on his broad shoulder, but it hurt too much to return the gesture.

"I'll be all right, Dad, I'm always all right," she said with an effort. His sobbing bothered her.

"You know, I think we really, we need to take you to the hospital," he said, after a moment, between sobs. "We need to. We have to find out how bad this is. Come on, let's get you out to the car."

****

Her time at the hospital was a blur. It was a long ride there, and she tried to sleep on the way, to rest, to find some relief. But it hurt so much to breathe.

The faces and voices all ran together in her mind, especially after they gave her an injection of some kind of painkiller. She felt a little like she was floating, though she knew she was being prodded, examined, looked over. She answered routine questions, but as soon as a question was asked she forgot it again. A few comments filtered through her numbed mind.

"No, wasn't him . . . this one's definitely a woman's shoe. See the mark there?"

"They have insurance?"

"Yeah. No problem there . . . notified . . ."

". . . need to call the authorities then . . ."

". . . already paid fines in full up front, plus extra . . . locking up the record . . ."

"Good news, sweetheart. That spot there on your head won't need stitches . . ."

". . . cracked ribs . . . scan shows at least three here . . ."

". . . nothing else broken . . ."

". . . get some rest, everything will be just fine . . . back to normal in a few weeks."

Later she remembered one nurse leaning over her, with a kind face.

"What happened to you, you poor thing?" she asked.

Alyssa turned her head carefully. "I came home with this," she said, "but it wasn't my fault."

The woman squeezed her hand, and she felt all buoyant and warm again. Again their words were a blur.

". . . my daughter . . . came home with a baby . . . wouldn't do that . . ."

"Some people . . ."

". . .world coming to these days . . . just wish . . ."

Out of the haze came a loud voice. "Ready to go home, Alyssa?"

She opened her eyes. It was a doctor's face, smiling kindly.

"You take these," he said, handing her a prescription bottle, "every four hours as long as you need them, all right? And if you have to you can take two at a time, but be careful, they're pretty potent."

Once back in her own room, medication taken and her father gone, Alyssa fell on her bed. They had gotten her into an uncomfortable disposable gown at the hospital and later helped her back into her clothes. It was too painful to repeat the procedure.

Her sleep was fitful and disturbed. She dreamed nightmares, her puzzled brain frantically trying to sort out the fractured pieces of the day. She woke more than once with a startle reflex, a sharp intake of breath that scorched through her lungs. Breathing was agony. The medicine didn't help much with that.

****

She couldn't return to school for a week. Then she was instructed to say that she had been in a car accident. Joan could no longer meet Alyssa's eyes, turning away to light a cigarette when she saw her, but she didn't want anyone asking questions, that she made clear. Alyssa had been frustrated by her before, but she truly feared her now.

The spot on Alyssa's jaw remained a sickly green. Her ribs hurt too much for her to walk quickly for several weeks. Breathing remained painful for much longer.

Her algebra teacher gave her a stern look when she stepped into the classroom.

"Was this really an accident?" he asked her privately after class.

She nodded her head. "Oh, yeah. You should've seen the car. Totaled. I get to go to a chiropractic specialist and everything." She wasn't, but that's what everyone said after car accidents.

"You're certain."

"You think I don't know what an accident is? Come on."

"You could have a court case with this," he said. "I know an attorney who does cases like this. You could win."

"Nope," she said. "The car hit a tree. Can't sue a tree."

"You're sure this didn't have anything at all to do with that boy?"

"What boy?"

"Blaine. Come on. We all heard the story, Alyssa. I know what happened. Day after that, you miss school for a week and come back banged up. Are you trying to tell me the two things aren't connected?"

"Oh, that? No way! My folks went and got me my permit when I turned thirteen. They don't care about that stuff at all. I can do anything I want." It was a flat-out lie. She didn't have a permit, didn't want one and wouldn't dare ask, but she hoped it would satisfy Henderson's curiosity. "In fact, my dad was taking me out to dinner for a consolation prize. Sun got in his eyes and he missed a turn. Ran right off the road."

The teacher let out a frustrated breath through his nostrils as she left.

Holly also asked her about it, with the same results.

"You said you didn't know if your mom would let you go out, I remember that. That was the first day you had lunch with us."

"Look, my mom was out of town that day." A half-truth. She didn't like lying, but she had an intuition about when and where it might be necessary. "My dad was taking me out to dinner 'cause he felt sorry for me. But we had an accident." *Keep the stories straight,* she thought to herself.

Holly gave her a look.

"I'm all right. Doc says I'll be back in shape in a few weeks. Did I tell you I'm seeing a chiropractor?"

"All right, if you say so," Holly said. "Have it your way."

"I'm *fine*," Alyssa said.

"I said, okay," Holly said. "I believe you already, okay?"

She left it at that.

****

Over the following months Alyssa noticed her parents arguing more loudly, more often, more intensely. She ignored it. It was pointless to make sense of them. She stayed in her room and studied.

Every time Joan passed her closed door she had a new kind of insult to spit at her. "Tramp," she would say, or some other synonym. The meaning was clear. Alyssa ignored that too. She knew the truth. That was what mattered. But she was determined more than ever that what her mother believed about her would never come true.

****

Soon it was May, with only a few weeks left in the school year. Holly stopped her between classes. "I can't figure you out," she said.

"What do you mean?" Alyssa asked.

"Well, it's like this, see. I've been wondering about you and Jim."

"Oh, not that again. You're going to tell me he still likes me or something? Brother."

"No, that's not it. It's like this, see? The most marvelous guy in school chases after you and you blow him off. If he asked me out I'd go in a heartbeat. And then that thing with Blaine, well, nobody would go for him, but you come back to school all messed up. And no matter what you say, I mean I'm not blind. My dad used to work my mom over pretty good when he was living with us, and she'd always say she walked into a wall. Hey, nobody walks into that many walls. But look, that's not my point. I'll let you stick to your little story if you want. Here's the thing. I was wondering if you were *afraid* to go out with Jim or something, but maybe you did like him after all. See, that I could understand. We can help you, I mean, if you want. We all know how to sneak out."

"I just don't think Jim is that great," she said, feeling uncomfortably transparent. She thought her accident story worked fine, so she decided to ignore that part of Holly's comments, for the moment, and focus on the question at hand. "Look. He had you girls all asking me for him. You bent over backwards, but he didn't. He's never said a word to me himself. Not even hello. I mean, I never even noticed him *looking* at me." Not the way Peter looked at her, anyway. Not even the way Lauren's boyfriends sized her sister up. "What am I supposed to think?"

"Well, he's *shy*," Holly said.

"The guy I'm interested in isn't afraid to tell me how he feels," Alyssa said.

"There is a guy?" Holly said, smiling. Her face brightened. She tossed her long, dark hair back over her shoulder, like a fashion model. "I knew it! I just knew it. Tell me about him. Is he cute? Is he in school here?"

Alyssa hesitated. She didn't intend it to come out sounding like there was. How did that happen? She only meant to give a simple explanation.

"Um . . ." She looked toward the bulletin board on the other side of the hallway, unsure what to say next or how she could back out. "Well, there was, once, but my mother won't let us see each other anymore."

The words were out before she could call them back.

"How tragic! How romantic! I never would have guessed. What was wrong with him, what didn't she like? You want to sneak out behind her back?"

Alyssa paled. "No way! Not with my mother I don't."

"Oh? So it wasn't a car accident, was it?"

"What happened between us didn't have anything to do with sneaking behind her back." She tightened up, beginning to feel cornered. Her side still hurt sometimes, and she didn't feel like talking about it. "I've never done that."

"Well, you should try sometime," Holly said. "It's not as hard as you think. She'll never know."

"My sister would find out and tell her."

"Oh, Lauren? Yeah, she seems the weasel type. But we could help you out, you know. There are ways."

"He lives too far away anyway. It wouldn't work."

"Long distance, too? Wow. Totally romantic. Wait till Valerie hears about this!"

"Oh, please, Holly, I wish you wouldn't." She reached out on impulse to touch Holly's arm, her eyes wide as the color drained from her face. Blaine's memory was far too fresh. If Joan heard about her and Peter somehow . . . The thought absolutely terrified her. "I mean, it's not something Lauren even knows about, I mean, well, she knows him, but she didn't know there was anything between us. Oh crap. I should've kept my big mouth shut."

The bell rang. Alyssa became visibly agitated. "Shoot, I'm late for Henderson's class, he's gonna kill me." She adjusted her backpack on her shoulders and nervously shifted back and forth, torn between continuing the conversation and leaving.

"I'll go with you," Holly said. Together they moved down the hallway to the staircase and up.

"It's like this, see," she began, moving quickly down the hallway as she twisted the end of a backpack strap between her fingers. She spoke very fast, looking down at the tile floor speeding by under her feet. She felt exposed and resented having to say anything so personal and private to this girl. But she had to explain or endure the risk of the rumor getting back to her sister. She couldn't bear that.

"My mother didn't know there was anything between us, or Lauren either, but see, me and this guy, our moms have been friends forever. And this summer they had this huge argument, and now they won't see each other anymore and so I'm not allowed to see him again *either*, but it's not at all because there was something between us. Only me and him knew that. In fact we barely figured out our feelings at the same time they had this big fight, so it never got to be anything at all, really . . . so it's better for me if I move on. Does that make sense?"

"Maybe," Holly said. "I'm trying to follow you."

"So anyway it would be very, very bad for me if Lauren found out and told my mother, see, since Mom didn't like him much anyway, and she didn't know about the romantic part. If you talk, sooner or later it'll get back to Lauren and I'm sure to get busted over it."

She was shaking. They reached the door of the classroom and Alyssa lowered her voice to a whisper. "So please, please don't tell anybody, I'm begging you. I never should've said anything in the first place. If any stories get around, Mother will have my head on a platter. Literally."

"So I was right? That bruise on your face and stuff. There was no accident." Holly wrinkled her brow.

Silently, Alyssa nodded her head, then felt a horrible thing—tears bubbling up, getting close to the surface. That was simply not allowed. She looked Holly straight in the eyes and fought for control, forcing the emotions back down into the cool, quiet place where no one could see them.

"You know, there's crisis centers for that kind of thing, Alyssa. My friend Jennifer, she . . ."

"It's not like that," she said. "She's never been like that before. It won't happen again."

"You don't know that."

Holly's eyes were compassionate. It became more difficult for Alyssa to keep her composure, and she turned away.

"Look, just keep it quiet, please. About everything. As long as you don't tell anybody else about this guy or the truth about the accident, everything will work out fine," Alyssa said. "I know how to manage her."

"Are you sure?" Holly asked.

"Sure I'm sure," she said.

"Well, you can trust me. Honest. I'll be quiet if that's what you want."

"Can I?" Alyssa asked, pleading with her eyes, her face still pale.

"Honest." Holly smiled. "If it's like that, I won't tell. Promise. Secret's safe with me. I know how it goes."

"Oh, thank you," Alyssa said. "Thank you." She put her hand on the door. "I better get in there," she said.

"See you around," Holly said.

Alyssa went in and took her seat in the front row. Mr. Henderson pretended not to notice. She had never been late before. She breathed a sigh of relief when he ignored her and continued with the lecture, and hoped desperately that Holly would keep her promise.

She did. Alyssa never heard anything circulating around school about it, and Holly never brought it up again. But after that day, when they saw each other in the hall or ate lunch together with Valerie and Mikalah, they shared a knowing smile. Holly's was compassionate and caring, Alyssa's simply grateful.

As things worked out, Holly started going steady with Jim Decker before the school year was up, which made the smile between them even bigger.

****

That summer a letter arrived from Peter. Alyssa got the mail that day, fortunately.

Usually there were only bills and junk mail, but here was this little envelope, hand-addressed to her. By sheer luck she was alone in the house. She took it to her room and locked her door anyway. Her hands shook as she opened it. An emotional flood saturated her. She hadn't allowed thoughts of Peter to stay in her mind since the day . . . the day after . . . Her chest felt like it would burst with warmth, remembering. She felt her face grow warm and red.

The letter was short. It was in Peter's small, neat handwriting, and read:

Dear Alyssa,

I know your mom won't allow any contact between us. I'm so sorry. I think about you all the time. I keep trying to email you, but it always bounces. Has she changed your address? I hoped I'd be able to write you once in a while, at least. This is killing me. I worry about you so.

I hope you're okay. I wanted you to know that whatever happens in the future, I do know that what we chose was right. We've been so *happy since, except for missing you. Things are so much better for all of us. I only wish your mom could have accepted it.*

I know I'm taking a big risk even mailing this to your house. I hope you don't get in trouble. But I have to know if there's any chance we could see each other this summer like we talked about last year. I have permission to come, anytime. My feelings for you haven't changed in the least. I miss you terribly.

If I don't hear from you in two weeks, I'll assume your answer is no. But please, please write me even if we can't meet. Or call me. Or something. Please!

Love,
Peter

Her pulse beat rapidly in her throat as she read it. Lauren was gone, and her parents were both at work. She checked her watch. She had the afternoon to herself. She read the letter again and again, trying to memorize it. But she was better at memorizing algebraic equations and geometric proofs, and the words kept escaping her.

She felt an ache in the center of her soul. *"My feelings for you haven't changed in the least. I miss you terribly . . ."*

There was only one thing she could do.

She went into the bathroom and struck a match then held it up to the letter. Watching the flame catch hold of the bottom corner and begin its work, she held it carefully over the toilet. Her mother could never find this. She wasn't sure if Joan ever poked around her things, though she suspected as much. The evidence had to be destroyed. It was blessing enough that she'd gotten the mail and been able to read it. If someone else had seen that letter first—she was horrified at the possible consequences. Her heart beat fast as she watched the flames start.

Then she saw the date on the letter and nearly jumped. It was July the Fourth. It had been one year exactly. She thought she would melt.

Peter's signature blackened in the flame. How had the holiday passed without her noticing? Oh, yes. They called it President's Day this year or something, and neither of her parents had bothered to take the day off. She recalled there were a few fireworks set off in the neighborhood this week, but they hadn't reminded her. The significance of the date had slipped by her completely.

Holly's words suddenly bubbled up from her memory. *We could help you out, you know. There are ways . . .*

Quickly she blew on the flame, trying to put it out. It wasn't enough. She smashed the letter flat between her palms, letting out a little exclamation of pain as she felt the heat. But it was short-lived. She crumbled the ashes that clung to the paper into the water and flushed them.

Then she looked at the scorched letter. The writing was still readable, with only a few words on the bottom missing. Her hands trembled. What was she thinking? She reached for another match, then put it back in the matchbox. She felt she must be losing her mind. She couldn't possibly do what she was thinking. Could she? It was far too risky. She vacillated desperately between burning the rest of the letter—forgetting it ever arrived—and calling Holly.

Finally she burned the envelope but folded the letter carefully, after shaking off the rest of the crisp browned edges. She flushed the ashes down the toilet and went to the phone, dialing Holly's number.

The girl was surprised to see her on the screen. "Oh, hi there!" she said. "What's up?"

"Can I talk to you?" Alyssa said. She wondered if her face showed the agitation she felt. She tried so hard to be rational, to be in control, but right now it was too difficult.

"Well, sure, what's on your mind? I got nothing to do today. I was supposed to go to the mall with Mom, but she had to go in to work."

"I was wondering if you could help me. You remember when we had that talk outside of math class last year?"

Holly's eyes widened slightly. "Oh yeah, of course I remember that."

"Look, don't say anything else, I can't talk here. How far is it to your house? Would it be all right if I came over?"

"Oh, well, I think so."

"Shoot. I didn't mean to invite myself. That's impolite. Mother's always telling me to be polite. I'm sorry. If you're busy, well, it's not that important. It can wait."

"Nah, I'm not busy. Come on over."

"Is it far?"

"You know where Second Street is? Is that close to your house?"

"Yeah."

"It's right off Second." She finished giving directions.

"I'll be right over. But I'll have to be back by four, before anyone figures out I left."

After she rang off she deleted the record of the phone call and the record that a call had been made, then checked to make sure the computer system hadn't cached it anywhere. It took a few minutes; maybe it was a little paranoid, but she felt she could never be too sure. She knew her way around the system inside and out. Her competence at math and formulas paid off there. Tricks like this were pretty simple, but she never knew what else her mother might have programmed in. Sure, she could delete the record of a phone call; but if she dared to call Peter himself it could set off a whole alarm system for all she knew. Joan was funny about things like that. She knew better than to call or e-mail him from the home system.

She walked the whole way, briskly, burning off nervous energy as she went. She guessed it was only two or three kilometers, from the time it took.

Holly's house was a lot like her own, small, except it was bright and cheery on the inside, light colors on the walls, sparsely furnished in a modern style. It was odd to see her outside of school. She hardly realized that visiting friends was something most girls did, and frequently. She felt strange about it.

"So, what's happened?" Holly said. "Is it good or bad?"

She told her about the letter and after some coaxing, showed it to her.

"Wow," Holly said, after reading it. "He sounds so sweet. And he can spell, too. Shoot, what did they *do*?"

"I'm not supposed to know, but he told me they joined a church. A Christian church."

"Hm. My dad . . . well, I don't get to see him that much—which isn't a bad thing—but he always said religious people are fruitcakes."

"Yeah, well, my mother thinks so too. She said I could never contact him again."

"That's so severe. I mean she must've freaked."

"Oh, you could say that." She paused. "So, is there anything I can do? I mean, he can't just send letters to my house like this. It's dumb luck I was the one who found this. I've got to make him stop."

"Make him stop? You've got to be kidding! This is like, a real love letter!"

Alyssa blushed. "Oh, come on, I've known him my whole entire life. He's more like a brother . . . Well, until last summer he was anyway," she said, considering. "But look, I'm fried if he does this again. I wondered if I could maybe use your e-mail or something. If I do it from home, I'm afraid Mother will find it."

"Oh, I'm really sorry, but I can't." She sounded sincere.

"Oh . . ."

Holly laughed. "We don't have a computer at home. My mom's funny, she doesn't believe in them. Well, that's not it exactly. She works with them all day. I think she doesn't want to come home and fool with it. They'd make her work around the clock if we had one. She says I get all the training I need at school, so we don't need one here."

"That's weird."

"Maybe." She shrugged.

"You don't even have email on your phone, or TV?"

Holly hesitated. "Well, we do, but it's the one thing I'm absolutely not allowed to touch. She's afraid I'll get hooked up with, you know, the weirdoes out there who prey on teenage girls." She smiled.

"Oh." She wouldn't ask Holly to break a rule for her sake. "Well, I can't call him either. It's long-distance. Should I write a regular letter?"

"You could call from here. It's all right."

"No." She twisted the bottom of her shirt into a knot. "I just couldn't."

"Sure you can. What's the number? I'll dial."

"No, I can't, I mean I just *can't*. I don't know what would happen to me if I saw his face again."

Holly laughed, a light happy sound. "Girl, you *do* have it bad. What are you worried about? I bet we can work out a way to get you together! This summer . . . next week even! You could be in his arms again, like that." She snapped her fingers.

"No, Holly, that's not what I want."

The idea was too crazy. Things had changed since last summer. The beating over Blaine was still fresh in her memory. Then there was the thought of having to break it off with him again. That thought was too much for her to handle. The risks were too great.

She unknotted her shirttail and twisted it again. "I just can't."

"Don't you want to? You're nuttier than I thought. What'd you come all the way over here for? You said you wanted help, didn't you? I'm helping!" She was smiling, teasing her.

"I know, I know. Maybe I'm just not ready to see him again, then miss him for another year. I don't know if I can risk it."

"Pretty big risk?"

Alyssa nodded. "I'm not sure it's worth it . . . for just one visit."

"I see." Holly pursed her lips, thinking. "Well, I think it's worth it."

"I don't know about that."

"Maybe you have cold feet. I mean, this guy sounds like he's in love."

"Yeah, well." She coughed trying to choke down the emotions she felt rising in her throat. "Tell you what. If I do call him, I'll let you know, okay? I get an allowance once in a while, when Dad remembers about it. I could pay for the call. But I just don't think I'm ready. I don't know if I could handle it. Not yet."

"Okay. Are you going to let me help you write back, at least?"

"All right." She smiled.

They went to Holly's room where she got out some stationery and a pen. Alyssa wrote several drafts, as Holly encouraged her. She felt flushed and flustered the entire time she was there, like a part of her, a very private part, was being cracked wide open. It was very uncomfortable. But she smiled a lot, and she had to admit it was fun being with Holly.

She ended up mailing these words:

Dear Peter,

I miss you too. But things are much worse here than they used to be. Please, you mustn't write to me again. It'll be very bad for me if you try to write or get in touch in any way. I'm not sure how Mother booby-trapped the email, but I don't dare send anything that way, or she's sure to find out.

I've been forbidden to see you or contact you ever again. Even doing this much is dangerous for me. I can't do anything more than send you this one letter. You know how Mother can get. But I promise I will keep all our secrets in my heart.

We have to go on without each other. It's the only way, at least until I can leave home. I'll always treasure our time together, the only truly happy memories I have. Thank you for everything.

Don't worry about me. I'm getting along all right. In a couple more years I'll be free. Maybe then, if you're still around, I can call you.

Yours,
Alyssa

"Girl, that is absolutely heartbreaking," Holly said, reading it over.

"Well, maybe," Alyssa said.

"Aren't you even going to cry? Shoot, I read that and I want to cry. It's so sad."

"No, no, I'm all right. Really. And hey, thanks for your help. You've been great."

She dropped the letter in a public mailbox on her way home, hoping it would be enough to prevent Peter from writing again and bringing with it another, surely worse, beating.

****

Two Saturdays later, the members of the Stark family were all constrained to eat an early dinner together. In the middle of it, Joan made an exultant announcement.

She took Chuck's hand in hers and exclaimed, "We're moving!" His hand looked limp.

"I have bought us all a dream house," Joan continued. "My speaker's fees have added up, and we've been saving, and your father *finally* agrees we must have a bigger home."

She smiled broadly, but the smile didn't fit her face well. It was unusual on her, garish.

Joan patted Chuck's hand. "It's about time we *look* like we earn those middle-six figures!"

He looked glum and pale. The cordon bleu, one of his better dishes, was off-flavor tonight as well.

Joan had finally won. She was in high spirits. She seemed almost giddy as she popped the cork on a bottle of champagne and poured a glass for Chuck and herself.

"To the new house," she toasted.

Chuck raised his glass briefly and downed it in one gulp. Alyssa raised her eyebrow. He never drank anything that fast. She felt sorrier for him than she ever had.

Chapter 8

Gifts

Oh, what a glorious year, when we purchased the Braithewaite house. It was a breathtaking home, with every amenity I ever dreamed of having. I was so pleased with my dear Chuck for agreeing, at long last, that it was a necessity. After all, we could afford it. I was making plenty of money, and Chuck's engineering department wasn't doing too shabbily either, for once.

A brand-new house. It felt like a fresh start on something. I was so anxious to furnish it properly, the way it begged to be decorated. I spent quite some time shopping then.

The realtor told us it was outfitted with the most advanced of filter systems, but I enjoyed so much the newness of it that I couldn't bring myself to smoke inside the house. Me!

I kept my cigarettes out on the deck in back, waiting for me on that little wrought-iron table by my favorite outdoor chair. I found a wrought-iron ashtray to match, an Early Colonial. It was a handsome thing, diamond-shaped, with tiny roses worked into the ornamentation.

The view was lovely from there, facing West, and in summertime I could catch the sunset when I arrived home from work. I had to go all day without smoking at the museum, or else walk so far away from the building it wasn't worth the effort. So it was refreshing to come home and relax out there with my feet up on that little footstool. Some days my feet would hurt so much, much more than when I was younger. But the specialist could never find anything wrong with them, you know.

Have I written yet about that footstool? Now that was a real treasure . . .

Joan Stark,
Memoirs

Moving irritated Alyssa. It required her to be out of her room more often while she packed things, bumping into her parents and Lauren far more frequently than she liked. Joan at least seemed pleased with the whole process.

"It doesn't matter to me," Lauren said to Alyssa. "I'm already packed. Two months, and my semester starts."

Alyssa just stared until she turned away.

They all went to see the house when it was completed, while it was vacant. It was odd, all four of them riding in the car together. They hadn't done that since . . . since Peter. Over a year ago. Quickly, Alyssa slammed the gate shut on that memory.

It was a prestigious, elaborate house, freshly built. It had what realtors call excellent amenities: huge plate glass windows, vaulted ceilings, most of the basic functions automated or voice-operated thanks to the household computer system. A true dream house.

Alyssa's closet was nearly as large as her old bedroom. She also had her own private bathroom and shower. She could see the advantages of that right away.

She couldn't count the number of times Joan had caught her for discipline by lying in wait in the hall until she came out to serve some basic biological need. It was one way Joan managed to inflict punishment. Sometimes it was for an old infraction of house rules, something Joan suddenly remembered that had happened weeks before. Sometimes, though, she forgot why she was standing outside Alyssa's door and wandered off. She was unpredictable, patternless.

This behavior confused Alyssa's analytical mind. She often guessed wrong, assuming Joan must be gone when, in fact, she had remained silent out there, waiting, like a predator stalking its prey. Alyssa didn't like making that mistake. It made her paranoid about leaving her room, and left her wishing that she knew how to install a peephole in her door.

If she was to remain a virtual prisoner in her room anyway, the prison might as well be well equipped.

It was an upstairs bedroom. There was a built-in bookshelf along one wall and a built-in student desk for studying next to that. The walls were clean and bright and white, and two large windows along the same wall as the desk let in plenty of sunshine. All she lacked was a refrigerator and stove, she smirked. This could be all right after all.

The kitchen was immense, with vaulted ceilings and skylights, a cooking island in the center, every modern kitchen luxury imaginable.

A large box sat on the island.

"Open it," Joan said excitedly to her husband. "It's for you!"

Alyssa and Lauren looked at each other. It was not like Joan to buy things for other people. She rarely thought to, or remembered to do it when it was expected. Even at Winter Holiday, they both knew it was

Chuck who purchased their presents.

Chuck opened the box and peered inside.

"It's that cookware set you've been wanting for months," Joan said.

Chuck lifted a large heavy pan from the box. It was a beautiful enameled forest green on the outside, white on the inside, with brass trim and polished black handles.

"These are the ones," he said, forcing a smile. "Thank you, honey." He put the pan back in the box.

"Aren't you going to take them out? It's the complete set," she said. "Complete. Every single piece."

"There'll be time for that later," he said. He smiled again, but without cheer. "It's very thoughtful. Thank you."

They continued the tour. There was a parlor, an entertainment room, a study, several guest rooms, a large open basement that Joan presented to Chuck as his.

"This will be your space for your trains," she said. "You won't have to hide out in that cold garage anymore when you putter with them."

The garage here could hold four cars, plus storage. Alyssa wondered if her own car would ever be garaged there, and doubted it.

"Alyssa will be going to a new high school, of course," Joan went on as their footsteps echoed through the empty house. "Wellesley Memorial. It's smaller, dear, but equally as accredited as Rodham. Your credits will all transfer over."

It was a sunny day, and the large windows let in generous amounts of light. Alyssa hardly heard her mother's monologue as she showcased the features of the house, using her best museum tour voice. She wondered instead how long it would be before she was set to work cleaning all the multiple panes of windows. She imagined how she might reach the high ones, picturing herself on a tall ladder wiping them down, trying not to leave a single streak.

"And Lauren, I have a wonderful surprise!" Joan's voice faded back into her consciousness as they walked back through the living room. "The best one of all. This house is only a twenty minute drive from campus. You won't be needing that apartment after all! You'll stay right here, with us." She smiled as sweetly as she knew how. It was clear she felt she was doing Lauren an immense favor.

"Thank you, Mother," Lauren said blankly.

Her eyes were far away. There would be no more discussion, that much was obvious. Lauren would attend college from home.

Transferring was out of the question. It was the best art school in the nation.

"And if you do change your mind and decide to major in archaeology after all, there's a wonderful school only fifteen minutes south of here."

Somehow Lauren managed a wan smile.

"Coincidence, dear, coincidence," Joan smiled, and patted her eldest daughter on the shoulder.

"I'll have to get out of my lease," she said blankly. "It might be hard."

"I took care of that for you already, sweetheart," said Joan. "The day we accepted the counteroffer."

"How thoughtful of you." Lauren turned away from the kitchen. "Which way was the bathroom?" she said, her tone casual.

Alyssa twisted her mouth into a sour expression. She burned the conversation into her memory. No matter what Joan said, the location of the house could hardly be coincidence. She, on the other hand, would not be trapped so easily.

Soon after the date of their tour, they moved in. Joan was thrilled at the prospect of having something worthwhile to decorate. Her artifacts were no longer cluttered haphazardly throughout the house.

And she didn't throw them. Not as often, anyway. In fact, to Alyssa's surprise, Joan picked on her very little after the move.

But she spent more time at home, fussing over the exact placement of objects, bringing more antiques and artifacts to furnish the elaborate house, a house that finally suited her. She had an Early Colonial room, an Aztec room, an Egyptian room, a Graeco-Roman room.

Chuck spent most of his time after work setting up elaborate train tracks. There was room in the basement for any configuration he could dream up. He built tiny shelves along the walls to house each individual car. Saturdays he spent shopping, collecting more and more pieces, browsing through antique stores for rare finds.

Once in a while he showed one to Alyssa. She would smile vaguely and say, "That's real nice, Dad. Is that the one you've been looking for?"

He took her with him once, but her feet were tired at the end of the day, and she ended up with a blister on her left heel. After that, she made excuses not to go again. She couldn't catch his enthusiasm. It was dreadfully boring to her.

He cooked less time-consuming meals in the new house so he would have more time in the evenings to work on his train projects. It was a relief to have standard American food again, meatloaf, macaroni and cheese from a box, fried chicken from a nearby deli. The cookware hung

GIFTS

professionally above the cooking island, gleaming, sparkling, new . . . but unused.

He also began to drink beer.

Lauren kept odd hours with her college schedule. Classes began shortly after the move, and sometimes she didn't come home at night. She could do as she pleased and Joan never questioned it. Lauren always explained that she was out with sorority activities, or in the studios working on projects. She had to work whenever her muse struck her.

But she couldn't leave home.

At the end of August, Joan called Alyssa out to the deck one evening, where she was wont to spend time alone after work sitting in a high-backed wrought-iron deck chair with her feet up. Alyssa never went out there unless called.

She felt strange standing next to her mother's chair and shifted her feet, worried that perhaps she had committed some inexplicable wrong. The breeze had an early fall chill, but it blew the cigarette smoke away from her, so Alyssa was glad for it. She was also glad she no longer had to smell the myriad of ashtrays that were strewn around the old house. For some reason Joan had taken to smoking outdoors, and had placed most of her ashtray collection in a glass cabinet in the parlor.

"My dear," Joan began, "I've gone down to the school and gotten your classes. I think perhaps you'll like them this year. I've enrolled you in beginning paleontology and ancient Greek history. This school doesn't require so much math as your last school did, so you shouldn't have to work nearly so hard doing all those endless formulas." She took a long drag on her cigarette.

Alyssa cleared her throat. "I don't believe I'll be going into archaeology, Mother."

"You won't?"

"I believe we've had this conversation before."

"Oh. So we have. Yes, that's right. Well, I supposed, since Lauren has developed an artistic talent that cannot be ignored—you've seen her work, haven't you, dear?"

"Oh yes. Plenty of it." She twisted her mouth into a sour grin. She stood just back of her mother's chair so Joan couldn't see her face.

"Yes. Well, I supposed that since she has chosen an artistic career for herself . . ." She sighed and stopped.

I'll say, Alyssa thought. *She calls it an art form anyway.* Lauren's "work" was hardly what her mother supposed it to be.

" . . . that perhaps you might be interested in becoming the next archaeologist in the family."

"Actually, I was planning on becoming a mathematician. Maybe a physicist."

"Gracious. What does the world need more of those for? You'll never find a satisfying job that way. Are you certain?"

"I *enjoy* doing those 'endless formulas,' Mother. Just like Dad."

"Now Alyssa. Just because your father is an engineer doesn't mean he *likes* it."

Alyssa rolled her eyes. She knew differently. If there was one thing she could talk to her dad about, it was math. Formulas, theories, the revolutionary giants—Copernicus, Einstein, Brooks.

"I am ten times the scientist your father is," Joan continued. "But don't let on, dear, it would crush him." She put out her cigarette and turned in her chair to face her daughter. "I didn't figure you would ever amount to much of anything anyway," she said with a sigh. She had dark circles under her eyes and her cheeks looked hollow in the fading light. "I suppose you can go ahead and take your silly math courses then."

"Yes, Mother."

"I'll call the school tomorrow and adjust your schedule, once again." She sounded irritated.

"Thank you, Mother."

"You may go now." She turned back around to face the sunset and lit a new cigarette.

Alyssa silently went back in the house and climbed the staircase to her room. She felt a vague sense of anger, but squashed it. She didn't have much longer until graduation—two years. All she had to do was hang on until she had the diploma in her hand. Then her escape would be real, tangible. It was almost close enough to taste.

****

The following Saturday Joan brought home dozens of packages. This in itself was not unusual. What was unusual was that she brought them up to Alyssa's room.

"I have your new school clothes," she said brightly, knocking on the door.

It was such a strange thing for her to say that Alyssa figured it must not be a trick and opened her door out of perverse curiosity. Chuck always took her shopping for those things. He gave her his card and a reasonable limit, then waited outside the store entrances at the mall while she tried things on.

"Yes, Mother?" she said, a puzzled look on her face.

"Yes, dear, your school clothes."

She was loaded down with garments on hangers in plastic bags. Paper bags were strewn in the hallway, all bearing the names of the most lavish department stores.

Joan smiled. It was almost a Cheshire grin, it was so wide. "I had the most marvelous idea. Now, well, I don't know if it will work, but I assumed we could at least give it a go, you see. I was looking for a new suit to wear to my conference next week, and I happened to pass by the Junior department, on my way to the women's suits, and it struck me. This may be a way to help you out with, you know, your little problem." She cleared her throat.

"My little problem?"

"Yes. You know. Your *reputation*." She whispered the last word as though it were a dread disease.

"Oh."

Perhaps she should have left the door shut. Mother was in an odd mood, and Alyssa couldn't tell which way it might turn.

"Here, would you hold these?" Joan said, thrusting a pile of slippery, plastic-wrapped clothing into her arms.

She brushed past Alyssa through the doorway with more clothes and shopping bags and dumped them on the bed. Alyssa bristled. This was not good at all. She didn't like her mother being in her room. She felt invaded, and wished she would leave. But she couldn't ask her to. Not without the very real risk of lighting a fuse.

"Good. Now, if you'd like to look at some of these things . . ." Joan paused and looked around the large room, taking it in. "You know I do hate what you've done in here. Are you sure you won't let me decorate it right for you? An ancient Welsh theme, perhaps?"

"I like it fine, Mother."

It was sparse, the furnishings modern and bright. She had it painted a pale pink, with a coordinating wallpaper in a tiny floral print on the long wall. Her father had allowed her to choose the furniture and matching bedding and window treatments herself.

"Teenagers," Joan sighed. She almost sounded motherly. "Well. I suppose it'll have to do. Just keep your door shut when we have people over, it's so mundane I'd rather no one saw it."

"Yes, Mother." *What people?* Alyssa wondered. Joan hadn't

entertained since . . . she couldn't remember when.

"Yes. Now, back to the issue at hand. I talked to all the store clerks, they were so very helpful. They helped me select all the latest fashions and colors for you, in the most modest styles available. Some of the things on the rack! Oh! I couldn't believe it. It's been such a terribly long time since I shopped in the Junior department, do you realize that, dear? Do girls actually wear those things with the holes in the sides? And there were these rubbery jumpsuits with holes cut out everywhere. Simply *appalling.*"

"I suppose some of the girls do," Alyssa said, wondering where her mother was headed with this. She dropped a load on the bed as well. "But Mother, what if these things don't fit? Do you even know my size?"

"I have a wonderful tailor, dear, he does lovely work. Lovely. I know about what size you are, dear, I am your *mother.* But if it doesn't fit exactly right he can make it most flattering. Don't worry about that a bit. These are the latest styles. You should fit right in, in this new school, and be able to get a new start. Don't you think?"

"A new start?"

Alyssa was flabbergasted at the pile of clothing on the bed. She lifted the price tag on one of the blouses and raised her eyebrow. Joan began removing the items from the plastic bags and carrying them, one by one, to Alyssa's closet.

"I've set up an appointment with him to come next week."

"Who?"

"The *tailor.* I mentioned him already, didn't I? Your listening skills, child, still need some honing."

"Wouldn't it be easier to take back what doesn't fit and get it in a different size?"

"Why are you so set that they won't fit, silly girl?"

Alyssa felt a sense of defeat. Some of the things on the bed were pretty, true, but most of it looked like clothing Joan herself would wear. She wondered if they actually did come from the Junior department and not the Old Crone department Joan shopped in. From the look of things, there would be no inoffensive way of returning them and choosing her clothes for herself. Not this year.

"You see, dear, if you have all these lovely things to wear, and they're all so very modest, see? You keep this blouse buttoned all the way up to the top, that's the way it's supposed to be worn, the woman assured me, and perhaps you'll be able to leave that nasty reputation behind you. It's a new school. You can start out fresh. Nobody knows you here, and if you go carefully, no one has to know about . . . well, about, you know, your *shadowy* past. You can turn over a new leaf here. If you try. I do believe it could work."

Alyssa looked at the clothes. She picked up one blouse that caught her eye and held it up to herself.

"Yes, isn't that one especially nice? You see, it might not be too late. If you turn yourself around now, that is. To be on the safe side I'd say you shouldn't be seen with any boys this year at all, in school or out. And especially not going on any dates. None of that for you until you've reached seventeen at least. I suppose I can't *legally* stop you after that. But no more of that sort of thing for you. Not if you plan on changing your . . . *ways* . . . for good. Which I fully expect you to do."

Alyssa definitely did not like the turn of this conversation. It was like being forced to admit guilt where there was none. But she couldn't be ungrateful, either. No small sum of money had been spent on the clothes lying heaped on the bedspread. And it appeared Joan was giving her a second chance to prove herself, of sorts. That was something Alyssa wasn't sure had ever happened before.

"Well, thank you, Mother, this was . . . thoughtful of you," she said, after a pause. "I'll take all of that into consideration."

"Why certainly you will. I sincerely hope I shall not be disappointed this time." She turned to go.

Alyssa nearly collapsed with relief when Joan left, shutting the door behind her.

"I suppose I will be out of one shadow, won't I?" she whispered to herself. "Without Lauren, it *will* be a fresh start."

She continued to put the clothes away in the closet. Maybe she could get her father to take her out shopping anyway.

****

Peter was seventeen that September. He approached Beverly at breakfast on a day late in the month.

"Mom," he said, "I've been worried about Alyssa. Her letter was so cryptic."

"I know," Beverly said. "I worry too." She took a sip from her water glass as they sat together at the kitchen table.

"I'm going to see her," he said.

"Peter, I'm not sure that's a good idea."

"Right now! How could things get any worse? If we can prove anything's happened to her, I can bring her back here!" His face was flushed with excitement, even through his deep tan. "Would you and Dad be willing to take her in? If she wanted to come?"

"Peter, that's not wise." She paused. "A year apart is a long time at your age. And I think you should take a good long look at yourself. Aren't you still getting over Heather?"

"Mom, that's not fair. This isn't about Heather. Heather was nobody."

Beverly looked carefully at her son and sighed. "You certainly didn't act like she was nobody, before she dumped you," she said.

"Mom."

"If you're going to go, Saturday is not the smartest day to do it. Everyone could be home. She could be in for some fierce discipline if you so much as show up. That letter was a warning, Peter, to stay away. Don't push it further. You'll only make things worse for her."

"Exactly what I mean! She must be in trouble. She needs our help."

"Why don't you think about it for a while longer. If you still feel like it, go next week. This isn't the kind of thing to do on an impulse."

"I *have* been thinking about it. And I have to go today. It's her birthday, Mom. She's sixteen. Today!"

She paused. "May I remind you that you are not a medieval knight rescuing the fair maiden from the dragon's teeth. Please be realistic. It's possible you could be charged with any number of crimes by the police."

"Sixteen is legal for a lot of things, depending."

Beverly sighed. "Only if she's bothered to get a permit, and you and I both know what that means."

"I know."

"It wouldn't be good at all."

"I *know*."

They sat looking at each other a long time in silence.

"I just have to know how she is. I have to try," he said finally.

After a long pause, she said, "If she comes with you, we'll try and find someone who can foster her. I won't stop you if you're sure it's the right thing to do." She leaned over closer to her son. "But if this little escapade doesn't have a happy ending, Peter, you are going to have to promise me you'll stop carrying this torch. I know how much she meant to you, but you have to accept your losses, no matter how much it hurts." Her voice was firm.

"I know that. She said the same thing. But I have to know. I have to know if I've lost her or not. There's no one else like her. Nobody I've gone out with even comes close."

"You're still very young," she told him. "You've hardly dated. There are millions of wonderful people in the world you haven't even met. Though you don't believe that right now."

"I know," he said. He grabbed his car keys and jacket. "Thanks, Mom. I'll be back tonight." He gave her a quick kiss on the cheek.

She stared after him as the wan fall sunlight filtered through the window, and sighed.

****

Peter arrived at Alyssa's old house at noon. There were tricycles and toys in the driveway, candy wrappers and paper cups strewn on the lawn. The noise of children playing filled the backyard. A bicycle lay collapsed next to the front door.

He checked the address in his pocket. Yes, he had remembered it right. It had been a long time since his family had visited, that was true, but it looked like the house he remembered. Still, Joan would never have tolerated the yard in this condition.

He rang the doorbell. A brown-haired woman in her mid-thirties answered it. She wiped her hands on an apron and pushed her hair out of her face. "May I help you?" she asked.

He was almost speechless. "Uh, um, I was looking for the Stark family? They lived here?"

"Oh!" She smiled. "Yes. We bought the house from them about a month and a half ago. Nice couple." A pause. "Though I'm not so sure about their daughter."

"Their daughter?"

"Yes, Mrs. Stark said she was one of the reasons they were moving, and we heard some very bad things about her from the neighbors after we moved in."

"What sorts of things?"

"Well, I'm not one to talk, really . . . but it seems she was a, a porn star, can you imagine? They tell me there were all sorts of goings-on here whenever the parents weren't home."

"Goings-on?" Peter swallowed.

"Yes. Boys coming and going constantly, that sort of thing. Well, it's just talk, I suppose. But all in all, I'm glad she won't be nearby to influence my children."

"Which daughter was this, do you know?"

"Oh, I think it must have been the youngest. Mrs. Stark said her oldest was an innocent, a real delight. Yes, I'm sure it was the younger girl. Terrible, don't you think? To start so young."

Peter was flustered, but struggled not to show it. "Do you know where they went? It's important that I find them."

"Oh, you know them?" Her expression changed slightly. She seemed ready to apologize, but cleared her throat and said, "Well, no, of course not. That's never part of the real estate transaction, you know."

A small girl about three years old appeared behind the woman, sucking her thumb, and pulled at the leg of her mother's pants. "Just a minute, Beth," she said, looking down. To Peter she said, "I'm sorry, we never talked to them about where they were moving. I'm afraid I can't help you." She smiled again, motioning to her small daughter. "I have to go, I'm in the middle of a project. Good luck to you."

"Thanks," Peter said as she shut the door.

He felt in a trance. In the car he pounded his fist on the steering wheel. *A month and a half! Why didn't I come as soon as I got that letter? Why?*

He spent the afternoon in libraries, postal centers, any computer terminal or information booth he could access, searching. All the terminals required palm print identification before he could log in. Every way he tried to access it, the information was blocked.

"The information you have requested is restricted," the computer would say. Or "Unlisted." Or "Access denied." There was no loophole he could find that would get the computer to ignore his identity.

Alyssa would probably know how to do this, he thought. She had always been better at programming, not to mention simple hacking for the sake of pulling a practical joke. Her knowledge would have come in handy now . . . some of it, anyway. He tried to keep the thought from filling his mind.

He asked the information center employee to look it up for him, thinking perhaps Joan had blocked out only his family from access to their information, rather than creating a general-public unlisted restriction.

"I'm sorry, we're not allowed to do that," she said. "If the computer won't give it to you there is usually a reason. The palm ID is there for security purposes, for the protection of our citizens."

"Can't you even tell me if it's a general access restriction or specific just to me?"

"I'm sorry, we're not allowed to give out that information."

"Look, I just need her address, that's all I want!"

"I'm sorry. People still have trouble with stalkers these days and other undesirable sorts." She gave him a suspicious look. "It's my job to ensure their personal freedoms are not infringed. If you're not from a collection agency . . ." here she paused and raised an eyebrow at him expectantly. Peter shook his head and she continued. "Then there's nothing I can do for you."

"I see," Peter said, and left.

After three more hours of getting nowhere he gave up. At a different information office he tried pretending he was a bill collector, but the palm ID gave him away again and he could produce no license. This resulted in an even more suspicious look from the employee. The entire afternoon he pushed away the nasty things the woman had said about Alyssa, his Alyssa . . . it just couldn't be true.

When he had exhausted every logical avenue he could imagine, he tried just driving around, to see if somehow he could feel out where she was. He tried to imagine which direction to go, to sense her presence by connecting with her on some deep psychic level, but it took not more than twenty minutes to realize he was being stupid, foolish, and wasting precious gas besides. He "felt" absolutely nothing, nothing but a rising anger. He turned the car around in a fierce arc, nearly running it into a ditch, and headed home.

****

He arrived well after dinner. Beverly was doing needlework in the living room, waiting. She looked up expectantly and saw the look on her son's face.

"What is it?"

"They moved," he said. "A month and a half ago."

"I'm sorry, Peter," she said, getting up to embrace him in a comforting hug. He was taller than she, and he leaned over her holding her tightly.

"I couldn't find her," he said. His voice began to crack. "I don't know where she's gone. None of the computers would give me the new address. She could be anywhere. Nobody would help me. I even went to a real estate office, but they just laughed at me."

His body shook with a sob that Beverly felt in her soul.

"And the woman living in their house . . . she said the most awful things . . . I'll never find her now."

"Oh, Peter," she said. "I am sorry."

She held him close as he broke down in her arms. In a way, she knew his catharsis was healthy. For him, Alyssa was lost.

****

That Saturday, Alyssa's father awakened his gourmet flair and baked her a birthday cake. He didn't ask her what she wanted or what her favorite flavor was. He simply consulted his cookbooks and decided that an orange torte would be just the thing. It turned out beautiful, icing artistically drizzled over the top.

It was just the two of them for dinner that night. Lauren hadn't been home all day, and Joan was spending the afternoon and evening with museum investors, entertaining.

He grilled chicken for her outdoors, on the built-in automated grill that came with the house, and made twice-baked potatoes and fresh sautéed green beans, all of which she liked very much.

After dinner he presented her with the cake, complete with sixteen glowing candles.

"Thanks, Dad," she said. "You know you didn't have to go to all this trouble."

"I wanted to," he said. "It was fun. Been a little time since I've gotten my cookbooks out. Happy Birthday, honey! We could sing, I guess, but I'd feel a little silly, don't you think?"

"Yes, I think so. This is fine. Thanks."

She blew out the candles and accepted the slice of cake with grace, gingerly biting into the odd delicacy. There were currants in it too. She hated orange flavor, but she disliked currants even more.

"Wonderful," she said politely as her father beamed.

She ate the whole slice, wishing she could at least pick out the currants. But it wouldn't be considerate, so she kept at it.

"I got you something," her father said when they finished eating. He got up from the table and produced a box about the size of a large notebook. "Open it," he said.

She removed the paper, recognized it immediately and gasped.

"Dad!" She smiled broadly. He had done something right. "I can't believe it!"

She unzipped a fine brown leather case. Inside was her very own personal computer. She recognized that it was the top of the line model and said as much, wondering aloud.

Chuck grinned. "I got a promotion too, you know. It has all the latest software and hardware installed, access to all the net servers, everything."

It wasn't just a computer. It was also a television, videophone, stereo, everything in one compact package.

"It's wireless, and the mouse is built in, there. It prints, if you slide the paper in here, see? But I can get you a standard-size printer and larger speakers for your room if you want. Extra battery power, more memory. Whatever you want. I can take you shopping next week for accessories and software and stuff. If you like it."

She held it carefully in her hands, inspecting all its accessories. "Thanks, Dad. It's perfect." Her face glowed. She laughed, a short delighted sound. "It's really perfect!"

"I also got you this." He held out another box, much smaller.

She opened it. Inside was a full carat marquise-cut diamond dangling on a long fine gold chain. It sparkled in the light of the crystal chandelier.

"I thought you deserved something beautiful too," he said. "You're growing up quite pretty."

She blushed at the compliment. She didn't think about her looks much. She kept her blond hair long, straight down the middle of her back, with just a few bangs. It was the color of ripening wheat. She wore it that way mostly to avoid having to spend time on it. She used only a little makeup. Joan would never approve of more and she didn't like spending the time to put it on in the first place. But she had become rather striking in appearance, regardless. That she could not hide from the mirror.

"Thanks, Dad," she said. "It's beautiful."

"You might want to, uh, not tell your mother about that one."

"Oh?"

"She might think I already spent too much on the computer, you know?"

"I get it." She smiled. "She'll start in on you, huh?"

"Maybe. I don't know, maybe not. For now, just wear it to school and stuff. I told her about the computer though, and she thought that was a good idea."

She smiled. "I can keep a secret, Dad."

She put the necklace on before going upstairs to her room to play with her computer, and start transferring her files over from the main home system. She was pleased to have one of her own, though she never would have dared to ask. It would be very useful. This was the one thing her room lacked. She had never had her own television or phone to herself before.

He had remembered her birthday. That felt very nice.

****

After Winter Holiday, in January, a quiet girl named Debra casually joined her one day in the cafeteria.

"Is it okay if I sit here?" she asked.

"Uh . . . sure. Have a seat," Alyssa responded, although she was a little startled.

She usually ate alone. She had made no effort to make friends at the new school. She enjoyed her anonymity after that awful year in Lauren's shadow.

Debra was African-American, and her hair was cut very short. Her face was round even though she was thin. She wore round wire glasses that accentuated this feature, but they didn't hide her large, deep brown eyes or long lashes. Alyssa had seen her before but hadn't paid any attention. She noticed so few other people.

"I'm Debra Gray. Are you new?" Debra asked.

"Yeah, sort of," Alyssa said, taking a bite of her sandwich.

"We've lived here forever. Are you a junior?"

Alyssa nodded.

"Me too." She unpacked her lunch and began to eat.

"So where do you live?" Debra asked.

"Braithewaite Street."

"Oh. Up there," Debra said, looking glum.

"Something wrong with that?"

"No, nothing. You must be rich, huh?"

"Oh, I don't know, I never thought about it."

"You never thought about it?"

"Not like that," Alyssa said. "I never thought of it as 'rich.' We moved from a small house, so it's been a little weird I guess."

"Really?"

"Yeah, my mom's been bugging my dad to move for years. Power struggle, you know."

Debra looked confused.

"Don't your parents fight over things?" Alyssa asked.

"Yeah. But I wouldn't call it a power struggle."

"It always is. Watch closely next time. You'll see how it works." She smiled.

Debra smiled back. She had beautiful teeth. "We'll see. I don't think it's like that with them though."

"Suit yourself."

After their first meeting, she started to look for Debra at every lunch time. Alyssa found she liked her, largely because she was quiet and didn't ask too many questions. She also liked the fact that Debra *didn't* talk solely about boys. It was refreshing, a nice change after all the pestering about it from the girls last year. Holly had been nice, true, but she always thought of them as shallow.

At first they talked about trivial things: the weather, if classes had gone well that day, what those classes involved. But gradually their conversations deepened. Alyssa was always wary of revealing information that felt too personal, but Debra's easy manner relaxed her.

"Man," Debra said angrily one day, in the middle of the term. "I just can't make it in Mrs. Simon's class."

"Why not?" Alyssa took a bite of mashed potato. "Simon's easy."

"I'm afraid I might not even pass," Debra said with a sigh. She barely picked at her lunch. Despite her slender physique, she usually ate like she was famished. "I don't know what I need advanced algebra for anyway." She sighed. "I'm going to teach English. What's algebra got to do with that?"

"You could change your mind later," Alyssa said. "I mean, you can't make much money teaching."

Debra looked at her, puzzled. "I don't intend to work for a lot of money."

Alyssa waved her fork, chewing another bite. When she swallowed, she said, "Come on. Everybody works for money. That's why you work. Even my sister works for money."

She said, "What does she do?"

"Oh. Uh, come to think of it . . ." She considered a moment, raised an eyebrow. *Legal* didn't mean moral or socially acceptable in Des Moines, and Alyssa felt a certain degree of embarrassment about Lauren's career, the one she had carefully hidden from Joan. But it hadn't taken her sister long to turn her newfound high school hobby into a high paying profession. "One of those . . . entertainment sort of careers."

"Oh." She paused. "So she's an actress?"

"Hm, not exactly . . ." Alyssa took a drink of water, thinking for a long moment. Or was she? Lauren had mentioned film to her once, but Alyssa wasn't sure the type of movies Lauren was in really involved "acting."

She hesitated. "Let's just say she's an artist. She goes to New Rockford, started this summer."

"Wow. That must be expensive."

"She's on scholarship."

"That's hard too. New Rockford's pretty selective. I have a cousin who's really good, but she didn't even get in, much less get a scholarship."

"Let's just say my sister earned it." Alyssa cleared her throat and mumbled, "One way or another." Then she said, "But you were talking about Simon's class." She had a gut feeling that Lauren's warped sense of ethics weren't the sort of thing her new friend would understand.

"Yeah. I just can't get it, and I don't even know why I should have to."

"Hey, they make me take history. I don't know why anybody needs that when they change it every year. I read this quote once. It said, 'History is a bunch of lies everybody agrees with.'" She laughed. "I like that. I can never get it straight, but I try."

"Do you think you could help me out, maybe?"

"With your math? I think so."

"Really?"

"Well, it's easy for me. I don't know if I could explain it so it's easy to learn or not, but I could give it a shot."

"Are you sure?"

"Sure." Alyssa smiled.

Debra smiled back with obvious relief. "That would be so great. I have to get a scholarship if I'm going to get to college at all, and I can't make it without algebra. I've got my job down at the library, but it isn't enough, even if I save my whole check until graduation."

"Yeah, I'll probably need a full scholarship, myself. Maybe you could help me out with the history, huh?"

"Your parents aren't going to cover it?" Her eyes opened wide.

Alyssa shook her head. "I don't know, but I'm not going to depend on it. Mother wanted a baby archaeologist, and didn't get one with either of us, so I doubt she'll want to pay for me to do what I want to do."

"She sounds weird."

"Well, you could say that . . . and you'd be right." Alyssa smiled.

"Hm." After a pause, Debra said, "So if we do this, would it be better for me to come to your house or the other way around?"

Alyssa took a drink to help her swallow the bite in her mouth, then added, "Might be better if I come over, first. I'll have to talk to my folks about it. They're not used to company. Maybe we can trade off after a while."

"Sounds like a plan." Debra grinned. "Is this weekend good to start?"

"I'm not doing anything." She finished up her dessert, an apple cobbler that was not too bad for cafeteria fare. She hated to admit it, but she had eaten quite well before her father quit cooking, and now she missed it. But the cobbler was decent. And it was either this or fix her own lunch, which she disliked even more.

"Saturday afternoon will work for me," Debra said.

"I'll be there, then. About two?"

"Okay. Hey, thanks, Alyssa." She picked up her tray. "This means a lot to me. See you around."

"See you."

Alyssa stayed in the cafeteria sipping at her water glass for a while after Debra left. She wasn't sure what to expect from this arrangement. She hoped she could teach the concepts her brain easily absorbed, but she didn't know if she could explain them to someone else. She knew she liked Deb, quite a bit, and wanted to help. She just hoped her parents wouldn't mind if she had company sometimes.

Chapter 9

Breach of Trust

I was very surprised when I heard they sold the old house. Chuck was the only child of his mother, and he had lived in that house, with her, ever since any of us could remember. When he married Joan, she moved in with the two of them.

His mother passed away about three years later. She was only sixty-some, I suppose, but her health was never good, not in the years I knew her. She was always coming down with some disease or another. Chuck wouldn't hear of a nursing home, afraid she'd never know where she was. He couldn't stand the thought of her being more disoriented than she was already. Joan kept trying to convince him to send her off, but he stood his ground. His mother came first. She died in the hospital though, of pneumonia. If she had died in the house, Joan told me back then, she wouldn't have lived there afterwards, no matter how fond he was of the old place.

So of course, I wonder what happened that he would let her sell it . . . I'm sure that's how it was, he would never have done it on his own.

Beverly Richardson,
personal journal entry

"**L**ook at this!" Joan said, later that week. "Have you seen this report card?"

"Since when have you paid attention to my report cards?" Alyssa asked. "I didn't think you cared."

She was in the living room on her way to the kitchen. Having run out of snacks and feeling hungry, she had come out for something to eat. It would have been nice to have a portable refrigerator in her room, but she was uncertain how to approach it.

"Are you being rude to me?"

"No, Mother, no," Alyssa stammered.

Shoot, she thought. *Bad timing.* She could have waited to eat, had she guessed her mother's mood. She shifted her weight from foot to foot while she tried to think of an easy excuse to disappear, but Joan had her eyes trained on her daughter, clutching the printout of Alyssa's grades in her bony hand. No, she would have to play this one out, see where it went.

"Joan," Chuck said.

He was watching television tonight on the huge built-in wall screen, instead of playing with his model trains in the basement as he did most evenings.

"Well, have you seen it? She has a C minus in History! Can you imagine? A C *minus*!" She went over to him and thrust the paper into his lap.

"I got A's in all the math and science classes, though," Alyssa said.

"But a C minus! That's a hair's breadth away from a *D*!" She turned back to Alyssa. "What do you think you're doing? Don't you study? Haven't you been paying attention in class?"

"It's confusing, Mother, I have to re-learn new things every year. Whatever was a right answer last year, this year it's different. I can't even get current events straight. This term we studied the Blankenship case, and the facts are all different than they were last time I learned about it. I got most of the answers wrong on the final."

"Don't give me excuses! No daughter of mine is going to disgrace me by failing *history*, of all things!"

"She did get A's in math," Chuck said. He read the printout. "Right here. Biology, A. Physics, A. Trig, A."

"It's not an excuse, it's the—" Alyssa started, and was interrupted.

"Are you skipping class? I'm going to have to talk to your teachers, the principal."

"Mother, I never—"

"Don't talk back to me! This is unacceptable. You'll be grounded for this, grounded for a month at the very least."

"Grounded from what? How? I don't *do* anything," Alyssa said. "I don't ever *go* anywhere."

Joan slapped her hard across the cheek. "Don't talk back to me! Didn't you hear me?" The room was huge, with a cathedral ceiling, and her voice reverberated through the house.

Chuck stood up. "Joan!" he said.

"What?" She turned to him angrily.

Alyssa rubbed her cheek. "Geesh," she said.

She always got C's in History, American Civics, all those classes. This had never come up until now. Whatever brought this on she would never know. Then she thought of Debra, and how she had promised to tutor her on the weekend. Which was tomorrow. She couldn't be grounded. She had just made a friend, and Deb needed her. Being grounded *could* mean something.

"You promised," Chuck said.

"So what?" Joan said.

"You *promised*," he said again.

"So? What are you going to do about it?" she said.

Chuck opened his mouth as if to say something, then shut it.

"That's exactly what I thought," Joan said.

"But you promised, Joan." He seemed stunned, like a fly struck by an unseen swatter.

"Well. I'm almost late for my meeting with the curators," she said, checking her watch.

"It's Friday," Chuck said. "There's a new movie on."

"I told you about this meeting last week," she said.

Alyssa carefully moved on into the kitchen. The subject of the argument had inexplicably moved away from her, as sometimes happened. She had to come up with some way to continue with the tutoring tomorrow, in spite of the unexpected punishment. Otherwise she would have to explain her absence to Deb, and that could be embarrassing.

She was still hungry. She rubbed at the sting on her cheek while she looked in the cupboards and refrigerator.

"I *did* tell you," her mother said to her dad. "This is important. It's been a horrible week with them fussing about that Bangkok exhibit. They won't be satisfied with anything until it's one hundred percent. There's nothing I can do about it, *they* called the meeting and *I* have to be there. You know that as well as I do. I can't miss this meeting and I won't."

Chuck said something unintelligible, and Joan went out the door. Alyssa heard it slam.

Chuck stood transfixed. "She promised," he said blankly.

"Dad, I have a friend who wants to tutor me in history," Alyssa said. She came back through the living room with a glass of milk and a napkin with two doughnuts in it. "Do you think that might help? I was supposed to go over to her house Saturday. What should I tell her?"

"Huh?" he said, looking over at her.

"I'm supposed to go to a friend's house tomorrow for tutoring in history. Can I still go, or am I grounded?"

"Tutoring. That might be just the thing. Yeah, I guess you could go, I don't think that's quite the same," he said. "It'd be like school. You wouldn't be grounded from school, now would you? Sure, honey, go ahead, I think she might not mind that . . ." His voice trailed off.

She finally caught something he had said a moment before. "Promised what, anyway?" she asked, trying to sound casual. He looked weird to her, standing there like a mannequin. Something about it was disturbing.

After a moment more he managed to focus on her. He raised his eyebrows.

"Has she hit you since we moved?" he said, his voice faint.

"Huh?"

"What I said. Has she hit you since we've been here, in this house?" He was suddenly reanimated, as though he had been in a trance and just come out of it.

Alyssa shrugged. "Well, sure, a couple times," she said. "So? Not nearly as much as she used to, though, after . . . well, you know, that one time," she finished, her voice trailing off. "Helps to have my own bathroom."

"Damn," he muttered. "*Damn*." He sat down on the couch with a thump.

As she stood there watching him she began to comprehend. She set her snack down on the end table and went over to him.

"Dad," she said. "What exactly did she promise?"

He looked up at her, his eyes blank again, looking shrunken, deflated, like a balloon when the air is beginning to come out.

"She said, if we bought the house, she'd never hit you again. She swore it."

"Did she tell you that? Oh, Dad, why did you buy that story? She probably made it up to win you over. You know how badly she wanted all this." She waved her arm to indicate the house.

"No," he said, shaking his head. "It was my idea."

She sat down on the couch next to him. It was a designer couch made of ivory jacquard, very soft. It felt like she melted into it whenever she sat down. She shifted, trying to lift herself up.

"Why did you do that, Dad?" she asked.

"I did it for you, honey," he said softly, his eyes changing again. "I wanted you to be safe, to make sure that would never happen again, you know, what happened last year. What she did to you."

"You did?" She felt something strange and flushed warm when he told her. "You did that for me?"

She didn't know what to think. She had assumed he finally caved in. She let out her breath slowly and was quiet.

After a minute she said, "Did you really think it would work? Honest?"

"I hoped," he said. "I really hoped." He put his head in his hands. "I don't know why I thought it would. But then I thought she was doing so well. So much better this year. I just . . . wish there was a *way* . . ." his voice trailed off again.

"Well, you know," Alyssa said, "Now that I know, I can rat on her." She grinned, looking at him, and patted his arm. "Hey, maybe she forgot she promised. You think? It's possible." She laughed, but the joke was empty.

"I'm sorry, honey," he said, looking back up. His eyes were soft and brown and warm.

"For what?"

"I did think it would help," he said.

"I know. I think that was really . . . really . . ." She wasn't sure. She knew it meant something, but she didn't know what the right word was. "Really nice of you. I know it must've been hard for you, you loved that old house."

"No," he said. "It wasn't so hard. I thought I was protecting you."

"You did," she said. "She's not nearly so bad. She loves this house. It's all right."

She picked up her glass and napkin, then put them back down.

"Looks like you're short a beer or two, Dad," she said. Heading back into the kitchen, she got one for him and popped the seal on the can. She handed it to him.

"Here. You'll feel better in a while."

"Oh. Yeah, I suppose you're right," he said, and sat there staring at the huge television screen. "Thanks, honey." He raised his lips to the can.

She took her snack and went up to her room.

Chapter 10

Confidences

The Blankenship mindset still persists, though I assure you, Sir, we are doing our best to flush out the perpetrators and correct them of their faulty reasoning. There are many more than we originally thought. Perhaps an increase in our budget would assist us in finding them for you.

Victor Caldwell,
private memo to the President

She went to Debra's the next day. It wasn't far, so she rode her old bicycle. She knew at first sight that she liked it. It was an old house, comfortable and noisy. There were a lot of children running around the yard playing.

Three of them, she found out, were Debra's siblings. The rest were their assorted friends. Their family had two large, friendly dogs which came up to inspect Alyssa on her arrival. Debra's father was balding and round. What was left of his hair was short, tightly curled and mottled with gray in a way that made him look distinguished. He was outside in the crisp early spring afternoon, wheeling landscaping rock in a large wheelbarrow.

"Hello," he said, panting a little from the exertion as he set down his load in the middle of the lawn, "You must be Alyssa. I'm Harold Gray, Deb's father. How're you doing?" He held out a broad hand.

"Fine, thank you, Mr. Gray," she said, shaking the offered hand. It was a much firmer squeeze than she was used to.

"Dr. Gray, actually," he said, "but please, call me Hal."

"You're a doctor?" she said, wrinkling her brow. She knew by observation that Deb's family wasn't affluent, and wondered at the apparent incongruity.

He laughed. He was not much taller than she was, and wore glasses nearly identical to Deb's. "Ph.D. in Humanities. I teach at Weaver College."

"Oh," she said. Weaver was a local junior college. That made more sense.

"Why don't you come inside? Deb's expecting you. Flint, get *down,* boy!" The last was directed at a large gray dog jumping toward Alyssa's face to lick her. The dog obeyed but continued to nip at her heels and sniff her bicycle.

"Thanks," she said. "He's all right. We don't have any pets, but I like dogs."

"Well, he's old enough to know better," Hal said.

He took Alyssa to the door as Debra came out. Flint chased the other dog into the house when the front door opened, knocking Debra to one side.

"Hi!" she said with a smile. "I was wondering if you were here yet. Are you ready?"

"I think so," Alyssa said, feeling a little overwhelmed.

Her own house was eerily quiet much of the time. This much activity swirling around her made her feel unsteady. Hal called the dogs back out as a group of small boys came careening around from the side of the house, in the middle of a game that appeared to be tag.

The living room was tidy, but cluttered. There were stacks of school papers heaped on top of a small piano. The furniture was well kept and attractive, and the décor used soft muted colors.

The front door slammed behind them, startling Alyssa.

Deb laughed. "I take it your house is quieter," she said with a smile.

"A little."

"The kids are so excited to get outside again after being cooped up all winter. You know how that is," she said. "They get spring fever. Come on, we'll go to my room where it's a little quieter."

She led the way through the hall. A little girl sat at the end with a pair of scissors and construction paper.

"Rochelle!" Deb said. "You're not supposed to have scissors in the hall! Look at that mess! You clean that up, right now."

"You're not Mom," the girl said. She had the same large soft brown eyes as Debra. Her long hair was woven into tiny braids that bounced when she looked up. Several multicolored beads were worked into the ends of each plait.

"You know where that belongs," Deb said. "Now do it."

Rochelle made an elaborate sigh and scooped up her things, leaving a trail of paper scraps behind as she went. Deb went past where she had been sitting and through the last doorway. "This is my room," she said.

"Was that your sister?" Alyssa asked as she entered.

The walls were painted a soft blue. Faded patchwork quilts covered two beds, one against either wall. A basket of folded laundry was nestled on one of the beds with an assortment of stuffed animals. A student desk occupied one corner.

"Yeah, I have to share a room with her too, the little squeak," Deb said.

"How old is she?"

"Four." Deb sighed. "She can be real sweet sometimes, but other days, watch out. Then she's just a pain all the way around."

"How many brothers and sisters do you have?" Alyssa asked.

"Three brothers. She's my only sister. I'm the oldest," she said.

"Whew." Alyssa sat on the bed. No wonder there was so much noise here.

"Manning is next after me, then Gordon, then Abel. Rochelle's the baby," Deb said.

"Oh," Alyssa said, a bit overwhelmed by the sheer volume of children.

They got down to work. It frustrated Alyssa at first that Deb didn't understand some of the basic concepts of algebra. It was all so elementary to her. As they went along, she figured out that Deb *could* understand it. It was just that Mrs. Simon's method of teaching wasn't working for her. Alyssa thought up other ways to phrase things. It was exciting to see comprehension form behind Deb's eyes. Debra got excited too.

When they reached a stopping place, Alyssa mentioned that she had been grounded for getting a C minus in history, but that her father let her come over anyway. Deb wanted to go over that with her, to make things fair. They spent the next half of the afternoon working on that subject.

"It's like this," Deb said. "I hate it, a lot, but you have to give them exactly the answers they want to hear on the test. I mean, what would happen to me if I went and put down that Christianity itself didn't have anything to do with the LA tragedy, it was just one man's insane interpretation of his religion?"

"They'd lock you up in the loony bin," Alyssa said. "Besides which, you'd fail the test."

"Yeah. See?" Deb said.

"Well, you *would* be nuts. You've got to have a pretty good imagination to come up with that in the first place, and then have a lot of gall to put it down as a real test answer. That guy was a fruitcake. I don't know why we even have to study a whole unit on him. It's more boring than the unit on the Cold War."

"Yeah, well." She paused. "I agree he was a fruitcake. But a lot of innocent people have suffered needlessly for years because of what he did. And he was only one man. But you have to give them what they want to hear. Follow exactly what Kramer says and spit it back out the same way. Don't interpret. He doesn't like that. I always get in trouble when I try. I had him last year for Nineteenth Century and barely managed a C, because I mouthed off too much."

"You?" Alyssa said, incredulous. "You're so quiet."

"Usually, but some things irk me. Then I can't keep my mouth shut when I should."

"I know what you mean," Alyssa said, smiling.

....

The night after she visited Debra's house, Joan was absent. Alyssa wandered out of her room and decided to keep company with her father in the basement. He looked very surprised to see her, but smiled broadly.

"Come to see what I'm doing down here in the dungeon?" he asked.

"Yeah, I guess so," she said, laying her hand on a plywood table that was about waist level. It was a meter long, with an elaborate miniature landscape built on it. There were six like it in the open basement room. On this one there was a mountain at each end, bridges, and a convoluted train track running all over the scene. It was covered with artificial grass and tiny artificial trees and shrubs. On further study she noticed that he'd made one of the mountains into a volcano, and went over to inspect it.

"I call that one Mount Joan," he laughed. "Don't tell your mother. Watch." He pressed a button and the volcano rumbled and spouted smoke and ash into the air. Alyssa jumped back with a start.

"Like it?" he asked.

She laughed. "That's pretty good, Dad."

"I put a microchip in it so it erupts unpredictably at random intervals."

"Really. Mt. Joan, huh?"

"Yep."

"Why?"

He laughed. "Well, this way, I never know if the train's going to be in danger when it comes around, see? Higher risk factor. Actually, I never put any of my collectors' pieces on that track. I only use those over here, on this table."

He pushed a button. The room filled with the whish and whistle of miniature trains spinning their wheels along tiny metal tracks, the whir of several engines coming into motion at once.

"I was fixing some of the interfaces tonight, but I think I've got it wired correctly now. You're just in time."

He showed her the rest of the tables. He had one landscape for each type of land formation: a desert, a rainforest, the American Old West (that was the one with Mt. Joan), and a polar express. He was delighted to explain his plans to interconnect each section so that someday his make believe world would be united into one great masterpiece.

"Want to help?" he asked. "I could use a steady hand sometimes."

"Sure," Alyssa said.

She followed the directions he gave for setting the glue and applying the tiny artificial trees to the artificial turf. He had two more tables that were just masses of wire and miniature wood framing. She helped him mold the mountains and landscaping on these out of a special compound he used. They worked mostly in silence, Chuck giving her careful instruction when necessary.

"Go easy on that stuff, it's expensive," he said once, and then added, "But you do have to use enough to get the effect you want. You know, you're pretty good at this."

"Thanks," she said. It was interesting putting it all together. He worked from a blueprint he had designed himself, each table a segment of the master plan that he would push together and link up when completed.

When he got tired he sat down in a large leather recliner and turned on the basement television, letting the trains run smoothly around the tracks.

"I'm beat," he said, putting his feet up. Then he put them back down again with a thud. "Shoot," he said. "My beer's empty."

He shook the can, and tossed it into a trashcan by his chair, then started to get up.

"Oh, I'll get it, Dad," she said.

"You will?" he asked.

"Sure."

"Thanks, sweetheart."

He put his feet back up, and started flipping channels with the remote. Upstairs, she realized she didn't know how many he went through, so she grabbed a six-pack and brought it down to him.

"Here you go," she said, her feet landing heavily on the stairs. "How much?"

"Wow, you think I'll get through all that before it gets warm?" he asked with a smile.

"Is warm bad?" she said.

"Oh, it depends," he said. "Sometimes."

"I'll take whatever you don't need back to the fridge if you want. I'm going to bed, anyway."

"You are?" he said, looking a little disappointed.

"I'm tired," she said with a shrug.

"Yes, well, I suppose it's past your bedtime." He opened one of the cans she gave him.

"So do you want me to take it back up?" she said.

"Take what?" he asked, staring at the television screen.

"Any of the beer. I brought too much."

"Oh. No, sweetie, this'll be fine," he said, looking over at her and smiling. "You run along to bed. Your mother home yet?"

"I didn't check."

He nodded and took a drink, then said goodnight.

"Night," she said.

"Sweetie?"

"Huh?"

"Why'd you come down here?"

"I don't know," Alyssa said.

It was the truth. She had felt strange ever since his confession about buying the house for her sake. She didn't quite know why she had left her room and found her way down there. She shrugged.

"Well, you're welcome, anytime. I liked the company," he said.

"Sure, Dad," she said, and went upstairs.

****

Alyssa began to visit Deb regularly for tutoring. At first she went just on Saturdays, then after school once or twice a week as well. Both of them saw their grades improve as a result.

In spite of all the boisterousness and energy surrounding them while they tried to work, or maybe because of it, being at Debra's house filled something inside her, an empty spot that had been void since she lost Peter. Had she sat down and thought about it, forcing it to the front of her mind, she might have realized how similar the Gray's and the Richardson's were. They were both easygoing families, rambunctious, affable, surrounded on all sides by small children and pets, their homes generating that internal musical hum that comes from a network of people working together, serving each other with a common cause.

But she didn't think about it. She only knew she liked going, and that while she was there she felt relaxed and carefree. There was an unspoken feeling that she couldn't possibly come to any harm. In many ways her visits were rejuvenating, like breathing the fresh green air of spring after being indoors all winter.

Alyssa also began spending many nights with her father, building his elaborate tracks. It was painstaking, precise when it came to laying the track. Everything had to be exact to make the trains run to his specifications. She enjoyed the precision. It was very logical and mathematical, and it satisfied her. He praised her for her patience when he watched her redo lines and curves of track she had put in carefully, pulling it all up and beginning again if it wasn't perfect.

There were nights she stayed and watched television with him too, after he flopped into his recliner, exhausted. More than one weekend evening she fell asleep in a little wing chair next to his, waking with a start to find the time had elapsed into the wee hours of the morning with Chuck snoring loudly in his recliner. She would quietly tiptoe up the stairs and find her way in the dark to her own room.

And sometimes, on the nights when she stayed, when he was far into his beer for the night, when he looked at her with that vacant look in his eyes, sometimes, on those nights, she would confide in him her dreams and hopes for the future. Things she hoped that in the morning he wouldn't remember, things she could easily deny, if he asked.

But she felt good just to share them with somebody.

Chapter 11

Freedom

Today begins a new era for each of you. You have your whole life before you. Remember what you've learned in your four years here, and remember us with fondness.

Romeo Jackson, Keynote Speaker,
Wellesley Memorial Commencement Exercises

At length, her coveted graduation day arrived. As soon as she got home from the midmorning ceremonies, Alyssa finished packing her things to leave. She packed her computer in her suitcase along with her favorite clothes. One large suitcase would be sufficient. There were only a few personal effects she wanted to take, nothing that would remind her of this place. She didn't care if she ever returned.

She wore the diamond from her father, concealed under her blouse. Joan still didn't know about it. She had worn it under her clothes always.

She and Deb had signed a lease together on an apartment near the Central University campus, in the heart of Central City. Their friendship had grown during their senior year. Alyssa had applied to Central U mostly because that's where Debra ended up getting a scholarship. It was a good enough school, though not the best, but sufficiently far from home for her to escape.

It was supposed to be a decent apartment, from the advertisement they saw, but neither of them had seen it in person. Deb wouldn't be down until the end of summer, but Alyssa was unwilling to wait one more day. In the last year she had done computer work, programming and web page design for small businesses, while Deb did the editing and proofreading. They both made good money. She had saved enough that she could afford to leave early and pay the full rent during the summer months. She would live alone until Deb arrived in late August.

She left her door open as she packed. Joan had come to the commencement exercises with Chuck. Now she passed by her daughter's uncharacteristically open door.

"What do you think you're doing?" she asked.

"I'm leaving. What's it look like?"

"Leaving where, child? Why, you're attending the National Institute of Archaeology, which is only a fifteen minute drive away. There's no need for you to pack a suitcase. I turned in your papers last fall, and they accepted you, thanks to that girl helping you with your history grades. I may have had a little pull getting you in, but that doesn't matter, see? It's not what you know but who you know. That's the way society works. Haven't I told you all this before? I'm sure I have. In fact I'm certain I recall going over this with you. I've selected your freshman classes, and I believe you'll thoroughly enjoy Dr. Holgren's insight. He only teaches the special honors courses, but I think you'll be able to handle it just fine, the way you've brought up your grades so nicely. It took some doing to get you in *his* class, of that I can assure you."

"You can't stop me," Alyssa said. "I'm seventeen now." She zippered the case shut and hefted it off the bed to the floor.

"Well, must you leave *today*? This is quite sudden, isn't it? I certainly expected you to put more thought into your future than this. NIA is a fine school. High credentials. It's not my alma mater, but there isn't a better school in existence today."

"I've dreamed about this day since I was eleven years old, Mother. I'm not staying in this house one minute longer than I have to."

She put the last of her toiletry items in her backpack and zipped that too. Joan blinked.

"I told you. I've been accepted at Central U. I've taken care of my classes myself. I am never going to follow in your footsteps, even if I liked archaeology and history, which I don't. I've made that perfectly clear. I can't believe you've conveniently *forgotten* that every time I've said it."

She stopped, gaining control of the anger she felt rising inside; then, feeling a rush of adrenaline, she pressed on. "Maybe you think you can mold Lauren, but it won't work on me. And it doesn't work on her either, did you know that? She just makes you think it does. She snows you blind. You and your lifelong search for truth. The truth is staring you in the face every day, right here, but you refuse to look at it. You don't know the first thing about either one of us, especially not her. And you'll never know me, I can promise you that. I don't know why you'd bother to keep me here in the first place. I assumed you'd be glad to be rid of me."

She shouldered the backpack as Joan stood aghast.

"How dare you! Why would you say such things?"

"We both know you never wanted me. That's no secret."

Joan's eyes bulged. She blinked again, swallowing hard. She seemed to be holding her breath.

"How would you know . . .?" Her voice came out a shocked whisper.

"I'm not stupid, Mother. It's only obvious."

Joan continued to stare wide-eyed. After a long moment, she continued, "But your *father*. Your father needs you here. You can't go, it'll ruin him. It'll absolutely ruin him. He depends on you. He needs you. He'll be lost without you here to help him. Can't you see that?"

"He's just fine. I'm leaving. Nothing you can possibly do will keep me here another minute." Her tone grew increasingly ascerbic.

"I'll be most happy to buy you your own car so you can drive to class," Joan said, trying out a smile.

"Mother, that is about the most shallow thing you have ever said to me." Bitterness was evident in her voice. "Give it up."

Joan stared at her. Though she was not interested, she knew exactly what her mother saw. Alyssa had become strikingly pretty, more attractive than Joan had ever been. She resembled Chuck more than her mother. She could present quite a charismatic figure if she chose, and today she chose.

Joan's nose twitched and the fingers on her right hand rubbed together, missing a cigarette. Alyssa stared straight back at her mother, arms folded, waiting for her response, her eyebrows arched.

After a long icy pause, Joan said, "Perhaps I should've had the abortion after all."

She turned and continued down the hallway, her linen slacks marking her steps with a soft swish as she went. It was the last thing Alyssa heard her say before she left the house.

****

Lauren had begged her for weeks not to go. "Please don't leave me alone here," she said, in tears. Crying always bothered Alyssa. It was a sign of weakness, irrationality. "You can't do this to me."

"Why not? You've got plenty of money from your . . . film career. You're an adult. Nobody's forcing you to stay here. You could move out any time you want."

It was true. It hadn't taken long for Lauren to find that she had discovered a highly profitable, legal, and—so far, for her—enjoyable profession, if not one that was very reputable. And she excelled at it, apparently. The art degree she was slowly working on was a cover-up, but a good one. She explained her large savings account to her mother as coming from the sale of her "art." It wasn't a total lie.

"Why don't you? What's keeping you?" Alyssa pressed her.

"You'd never understand," Lauren said, and was quiet. She turned away. "I don't think she'll let me go unless I get married, and I couldn't bring myself to that . . . even then I wonder. Every time I bring it up . . ." She shrugged.

"Well, I'm going," Alyssa said. "I'm not that stupid and spineless."

"But you can't go, you just can't," Lauren repeated. "Don't leave me alone with her."

"Watch me!"

****

Her father sat on the ivory jacquard sofa in the living room when she carried her suitcase in. His presence surprised her. He rarely existed above the basement level anymore, and always carried a can of beer with him, or had one close enough that he could reach for it. His once muscular physique had been replaced by a flabby belly that hung out over the waistband of his slacks. Today, the traditional can was absent. She looked around the room, searching for it.

"What are you doing up here, Dad?" she asked, setting down her suitcase.

Chuck stood up. "I came up to say goodbye to my little girl." He had a faint smile on his face.

She noticed that he looked much older than he had just a few years ago. His brown hair had nearly all lightened to gray, and more wrinkles showed on his face than she had ever noticed before. Perhaps it was the bright sunlight in the room. They used a strong light to work under, at night on the trains, but otherwise the basement was dim. Still she should have noticed. It was odd noticing all at once that her father was old.

The world landscapes were finished, and Chuck had started a new project: period pieces of the history of rail transportation, built to scale as accurately as he could make them using historical data.

"I thought my leaving was a surprise," she said.

She picked her suitcase back up, and put it down again. He knew about her classes and her plans to room with Deb, but she hadn't mentioned the exact time she planned to leave, not even when he was passed out on his easy chair in the basement.

"I know more than you think, honey." He laughed a humorless laugh.

"I was pretty sure you'd want to go today. I'm not that oblivious. Look, I just wanted to know how you plan to lug that thing to the transit station." He pointed to her suitcase.

"Taxi," she said.

"Would you let me drive you instead?"

Alyssa twisted her mouth into a pucker. "I don't know about that. How about you let me drive the car, and then you take it home from the station."

She searched the room with her eyes for the missing beer can.

"I'm dry," he said. "Don't worry, I can drive. I made sure of that. Not a drop since five o'clock last night. Wasn't easy."

She sighed. "Okay, then. I guess so."

****

At the station, waiting for the transit train that would take her to the heart of Central City, Chuck said, "I have a surprise for you. You'll like it."

They sat together on one of the smooth metal benches in front of the platform. Alyssa raised an eyebrow.

"I don't know how much you've saved, but I have a little account that Joan . . . that your mother doesn't know about. I set it up quite a few years ago. It's yours, to help put you through college." He pulled a folded envelope out of his shirt pocket and handed it to her. "I can send you this much every month. If you need more, just ask. Once you set up an account there we can do this electronically, but I thought it'd be fun to see the real green money for a change."

She opened the envelope and gasped. Inside was a large sum of cash, more than sufficient for tuition and any other expenses she might incur living away from home.

"Are you sure about this?" she said.

"I can afford it, don't worry. I've saved it just for you. It's all yours."

"No, I mean, are you sure Mom doesn't know? She'll bite your head off for this."

Chuck laughed. "Yeah. I'm sure. She would have spent it already if she'd found it."

"Good point." She smiled.

There was a pause while she stowed the envelope in her purse. The transit train pulled in front of them with a metallic whoosh of brakes and steam, bringing with it an acrid smell. A group of passengers disembarked, raising the decibel level noticeably. In a few more moments the car, freshly empty, stood waiting.

Alyssa looked up from her purse and said, "Looks like it's time for me to go. Thanks, Dad. For everything."

"Let me know when you get that account set up."

She smiled. "I'll be in touch."

He smiled back. Then, awkwardly, he asked, "Can I hug you?"

"Yeah."

For all the time she'd spent in the basement with him, watching his silly toy trains speed along on their tiny electric tracks, with all the talking they had done, she wasn't certain he had ever reached out and touched her. The embrace was unnatural and clumsy, the physical contact felt cloying and strained, but something deep inside her relished it, drinking in the familiar smell of her father up close and intimate. Something else, however, begged for it to be over quickly. It made her want to run, to be free of him and everything his presence stood for.

He whispered softly, "I love you, Alyssa. I've always loved you. I just want you to know that before you go."

"I know, Dad," she managed to whisper.

His words intensified the feeling she had. They made her feel more than a little embarrassed and slightly queasy. She swallowed hard, realizing she was about to shed tears if she wasn't more careful. She was angry with herself for allowing silly sentimental emotion to get in the way of this moment, the moment she had waited for, hungered for as long as she could remember. Escape was in her grasp. The last thing she needed to feel was a desperate, foolish need to cry. She fought the feeling back with all her energy.

He released her, and it was all she could do to avoid running into the train car to find her seat. She forced a smile as she waved a final goodbye.

****

Never in her entire life had Alyssa imagined anything as immense as Central City. She had visited the northern part a few times in her early childhood, on shopping trips, but this was nothing like the fuzzy images her memory provided. Nothing here was familiar, except the names of a few national chain stores emblazoned across an occasional building or billboard.

Before she had been on the transit train an hour, she was already deep into the city. The skyscrapers were endless, networked together like some great half-finished jigsaw puzzle that wound its way high above her making it difficult to catch a glimpse of the sky. She wondered who lived and worked behind all the endless windows, how they could stand being so squeezed together. Then she realized that she was about to become one of them herself.

Some of the buildings were built right on top of older structures, the new springing out of the ruins of the old. The City had grown so fast out of such great necessity that building crews hadn't always taken time to clear the debris. After a time that debris simply became part of the landscape. The inhabitants forgot it should have been cleared away, or didn't care to spend the time or resources to get rid of it. So they built right around it.

The highways above and below the train were in shadow, buildings eclipsing the light that shone from above, smog and pollution making the air hazy. Down below at street level she could make out neon signs advertising places of business. The atmosphere was dreary and gray.

It would be another two hours of this same city landscape before she reached the Central U campus and the apartment building that would become her new home. She sighed and wondered if she would ever see anything green again. There were occasional breaks in the skyscrapers, places where the train ran smoothly on its rails above the houses and residential plots below. Here and there she caught a glimpse of something green and growing, but it was such a fleeting vision, she couldn't be certain what she saw.

She was pleased to see that her destination was sufficiently far away, and it looked like a place where it would be easy to get lost. She felt a great sense of liberation at that thought. Here in this labyrinth of cityscape, perhaps, she could make a new life for herself. One only she would be responsible for, where no one would try to control her or tell her what to do, how to feel, how to act. Finally, she was free to become and do whatever she wanted.

It frightened her just a little to realize that she wasn't yet sure what that would be.

PART TWO

Chapter 12

Housekeeping

I can't believe it. They let her go off on her own and she hardly knows how to read a recipe. I've started to wonder what else she's never been taught. But I can only teach so much at a time; and some things, the most important things, I don't know if I'm even capable—not to mention allowed—to teach her.

It's so hard. I hate that the law disallows anything you could possibly call proselytizing for any religion, especially Christian faiths . . . At least we can still preach openly in foreign countries, for the time being. The President is lobbying hard to get all religious feelings defined as mental illness. (I pray it never goes through.) As for now, I can't say anything about it to her at all.

Debra Gray,
personal journal entry

The apartment was small, located in a low-rent college district, but the living area was large enough to be comfortable. It was on the third level of a five-story brick building, not far from the university campus. The front door opened to the outside, with a cement walkway and cast-iron railing. At the end, a metal stairway led to ground level.

The entrance opened into a living room with an old orange and brown plaid sofa in the center, torn at one end. There were two end tables, and a small desk opposite the sofa. A television set occupied the wall on the left side, facing the sofa. The tiny kitchen was at the back and had a window over the sink. The only eating space was a bar separating the two areas, with four tall barstools for seating.

There were three doors lined up along the right-hand wall of the living area. The two bedrooms were on either side, with a bath in the middle. After looking at them both, Alyssa chose the bedroom toward the rear of the apartment. The view from this room looked out on the central courtyard. The small apartment complex was made up of four red brick buildings in a square pattern. From the third floor, it was a decent view, and it had a lawn, something green to look at.

The apartment smelled dank from layers of occupants, old carpet, and too little fresh paint or air. The first thing Alyssa bought were deodorizers to mask the unpleasantness.

****

A few days after her arrival Alyssa awoke from a dream, a shred of suppressed memory floating in her mind. Peter's lips on hers . . . the softness of his touch on her hand, her mouth . . . the warmth of the summer sun shining on them, that last fateful day together.

She remembered one thing in particular, her own words saying, *Will you be there to take me away?* and Peter's voice, *I'll come and get you, and carry you away with me, and we won't have to worry about anything separating us ever again* . . .

She was free! Her mother was no longer there looking over her shoulder, watching every move, booby-trapping the e-mail and phone lines to ensure she never contacted the Richardsons. She felt a giddy sense of happiness rush through her soul. At last she could see Peter!

If he's waited, she thought.

The giddy feeling gave way to apprehension. Logic told her the answer would be no. It wasn't reasonable to expect that he'd be sitting by the phone, counting the days until she was free to leave home. She had practically told him to forget her, and after that letter she hadn't heard from him again. Of course, they had moved after she sent it. He might have been unable to contact her after that.

Anything could have happened in the last two years, anything. But maybe . . . maybe he could still be waiting, holding on. Maybe he was waiting for her to call him, waiting for this very day.

She was torn between excited anticipation and the more rational, logical thought that he would have moved on. She could no longer bear not knowing.

She went to the phone to dial the number, the main phone, from the wall in the living room. Her mother could have bugged her personal computer for all she knew. One of these days soon, she would have to take it apart and install new components, to eliminate that risk, however minor it might be.

As she started to dial, she realized the number wasn't going to come easily to memory. Finally, she had to dial information and look them up. When she got the number, she breathed a sigh of relief. It looked familiar. Memory told her it hadn't changed, it was the right number. It felt right.

Her palms began to sweat. This was silly, irrational, unlike her. She wiped her hands on her pants.

What do I look like? she thought, panicking.

It wasn't a subject she gave much attention, but this time it sent her running to the bathroom to check her reflection. She brushed her hair and put on some makeup—the right way, for once. Debra had taught her how, but she rarely bothered. Once she was satisfied she looked her best, she went back to the screen, took a deep breath, and punched in the number.

Mrs. Richardson answered the phone.

"Hi . . . Mrs. Richardson, it's me, Alyssa Stark. Remember me?"

The woman seemed taken back a step, then smiled. "Hello, Alyssa! How are you? It's been so long! You look . . . marvelous."

"I'm doing pretty well, now. I start school at Central University this summer."

"Central? I see." She wrinkled her brow, slightly.

"Yeah, it's far enough away from home, but still not too far from . . ." Alyssa smiled, wishing she hadn't brought the subject up.

Mrs. Richardson nodded. "Of course. Yes, it certainly is that. How is Joan?"

"She's okay. I guess. Happy with her career, at least."

"That's good." Mrs. Richardson didn't pursue it further.

"I was calling . . . I was wondering . . . Is Peter home? May I talk to him? A few years back we talked about maybe getting in touch after I finished high school, once I was away from home. Mother forbade any contact with you, but I'm free of that now."

"Peter . . . yes, well . . . Actually, Alyssa, he's not here."

"I can call back another time. When will he be home?"

"No, you see, he's not living at home now. He's . . . gone to China to do . . . some humanitarian service work." She seemed to be choosing her words carefully.

"China?" That didn't seem like him. She wrinkled her brow. "Service . . . like the Peace Corps?"

"Yes, something like that." Mrs. Richardson smiled.

China, half a world away, but still . . . as close as the click of a button.

"Would it be all right if I called him there, or e-mailed or something?"

Mrs. Richardson frowned. "I'm afraid not. It's a very remote area he's in, still quite undeveloped. They don't have much technology there. In fact, we don't get to hear from him that often ourselves. We usually have to wait for him to get in touch with us."

"Oh." That wasn't so good. Not an easy solution, anyway. "How long will he be there?"

"A couple of years. He made a long-term commitment to the work."

"Oh." Alyssa's turn to pause. "Well . . . When he gets back, maybe?" she said, hope still in her voice. "Or can you tell him hello for me?"

"I think . . ." Bev bit her lip and looked off to her left.

Alyssa followed her gaze. A girl about Alyssa's age had just walked into the Richardson's living room. She had dark blond hair, brown eyes, and a willowy build.

"Mom, where'd you put that . . ." she said, and stopped. "Oh, I didn't know you were on the phone."

Mom? Alyssa thought. "Hi, you must be Julia," she said.

But the image of Peter's younger sister didn't fit this person. She remembered Julia having dark hair and blue eyes, like her mother.

"No, I'm Topaz. And you're . . .?"

"I'm Alyssa, Alyssa Stark. An old friend of Peter's."

The girl's eyes narrowed ever so slightly.

"A childhood friend," Mrs. Richardson said.

"Oh," Topaz said, and brightened. She looked Alyssa up and down. "I see."

"I think I'm missing something here," Alyssa said.

Mrs. Richardson cleared her throat. "Topaz is Peter's fiancée," she said. "They plan to be married after he returns from China."

Suddenly everything clicked together. Mrs. Richardson's apparent hesitation, her careful choice of words, now made perfect sense. Peter hadn't waited, and she had unknowingly placed the woman in an uncomfortable position.

"Oh! I see," she said. "Well." She forced a smile. "Congratulations, of course."

There was a pause, and Alyssa continued. "I take it Peter never mentioned me, then?"

"No, I don't think so," Topaz said, shaking her head.

"And you didn't go with him to China?"

The girl giggled. "Are you kidding?" Mrs. Richardson gave her a look. "I mean," she said, straightening, "Of course not. I have no interest in mucking around in Third World dirt like he does. It's just not for me. We have everything planned for when he gets back."

"Well, that's . . . wonderful for you," Alyssa said. A thought came to her. "You're not worried he'll find someone else while he's there? That's very . . . trusting."

A wide smile. "No chance of that," Topaz said. "Not if I know Peter. And I do, quite well."

"I suppose you would," Alyssa said. "Well, I wish you both luck. I was just calling to say hello, maybe chat a bit about old times."

"Sure," Topaz said. "No problem."

Mrs. Richardson said, "We're glad to know you're okay, Alyssa. It's good to see you."

"Thanks," she said, suddenly struggling for control of her emotions. "And tell Peter . . . tell him I'm very happy for him. It looks like he's found a wonderful . . . wife."

Topaz smiled even more broadly. "Thank you," she said.

"Tell me, Alyssa, what are you studying at CU?" Mrs. Richardson asked.

After a brief but difficult interchange that allowed some catching up and filling in on both sides, Alyssa rung off. She felt strained, glad the call had ended, and sat down heavily on the faded couch.

She had not prepared herself for the crush of disappointment she now felt. She knew—she had known before calling—how irrational was her hope, how whimsical her childhood dreams. But she didn't realize until now how much they had meant to her.

China? A fiancée?

Obviously he hadn't looked for her, or waited for her at all. He hadn't even mentioned her, his first kiss, to his fiancée. She knew she had been the first. She just . . . hadn't given thought to who he might kiss *next*. For her, it had been the first and only. She knew she was unusual in that way, and sighed.

Humanitarian service. That puzzled her. Topaz made it sound agricultural. Well, that might be like Peter; he had always been fascinated by plants. Slowly, it dawned on her that she really didn't know whether it would be like him, or not. She only knew the boy. Not the man he had grown into during the few years they were apart.

With horror, she realized she might cry. She felt her throat tighten, her chest begin to ache, and blinked rapidly to hold the welling tears back in. She fought it, pushing it down, because it was *silly*, silly to imagine . . . it was only an off chance anyway that he might have remembered . . .

When she wrote, she had told him to move on. Apparently he had done exactly that.

He forgot me, she thought. *He hasn't even mentioned me.* Somehow she could handle the thought of him being gone, away, even engaged to be married to someone else, someone who seemed quite nice; but the thought that he had *forgotten* her swept her away.

The weight of it threatened to crush her heart, and she could no longer hold back the tears. Finally, she let them come, but quietly, ever so quietly. She was glad to be alone, glad no one could see, ashamed of her need to cry over such a silly, irrational thing. Wasn't she stronger than this?

She only allowed herself the luxury of tears until she could pull herself together and stifle the unbearable emotion. She locked it up in a dark corner of her heart, hoping it would stay there forever.

Classes would begin in two days. She had plenty to keep her mind and her time occupied until then, fixing up the apartment, shopping, orienting herself to the campus. She wouldn't think about this. She would do as Peter had done. She would move on.

She took a deep breath and rose to her feet, then stood still in the middle of the living area until she felt strong again.

****

When autumn came, Debra arrived along with a bundle of suitcases, boxes, and other assorted baggage.

"Wow," she said, coming through the door. "This is so nice."

Alyssa greeted her. "Are you kidding?" she said, smiling. "The furniture stinks. I didn't want to buy any, though. This is just what was here."

Deb said. "I expected it to be smaller than this. This is great! How have you been?" She dropped her things and gave Alyssa a hug.

Alyssa was glad to see her. She called every week to talk, but it was never enough. She was lonely without her, especially since calling the Richardson's house.

"I've been good," Alyssa said. "Need any help with your stuff?"

"I think I've got it," Deb said. "Jon helped me."

"Hello," a male voice said.

Jon, Deb's boyfriend, stepped through the doorway. He was a little taller than Deb, with a slight but strong build. His smooth chocolate skin was a shade or two darker than Debra's, but his eyes were a slightly lighter brown. He wore stylish glasses and kept his hair cropped very short, accentuating his naturally good looks. He had a touch of shyness about him that was endearing.

"Oh, hello," Alyssa said. "How've you been?"

"Just fine," Jon answered. "Thanks." He set down more bags with a loud grunt.

Jon and Debra had been dating since spring. He was nice, and Deb was happy around him. They had an easygoing relationship that seemed more a casual friendship than an outwardly romantic one. He treated Alyssa all right, and didn't mind if she hung around when they were together.

"Taken good care of Deb for me?" she asked.

"I try," he said with a smile. He went out and pulled a large cardboard box back in through the front door.

"You big goof," Deb said. "As if I need taking care of."

"Are you going to Central U?" Alyssa asked. "I thought Deb said—"

"No," Jon said. "I just drove her down. Then I'm off to New Hopkins."

"Oh, that's right," Alyssa said. "Pre-med. I didn't know they had an undergraduate program."

"Yeah, they do," Jon said. "I'm in the dual-degree longitudinal track. The one you can't get in unless you're very good." He grinned.

"He was so excited," Deb said. "You should have seen him. He jumped so high when he read the acceptance letter, he nearly knocked a hole in the ceiling." She laughed. "Partial scholarship, too."

"That's great. You staying a while?" Alyssa asked.

"No," Jon said. "I've gotta be there tomorrow. I'll help Deb settle in, then I'm off. It's an hour's drive from here."

Alyssa nodded. "I haven't done anything to your room," she said to Deb. "It's the one on the right, to the front."

"Have you had a good summer?" Deb asked, picking up a suitcase and heading for the door Alyssa indicated. Jon followed with more luggage.

"Yeah. It's been nice and quiet around here."

"Good neighbors?"

"I haven't bothered to meet many of them," she said.

"Well, that would be just like you," Deb said, with a smile.

Alyssa smiled back. "Yeah, you do know me," she said.

When everything was mostly unpacked, Deb and Jon went out for dinner. They invited Alyssa, but she declined. She figured they would need time alone together, and neither of them pushed her to come along once she refused. When Deb came back with a smile on her face but exhausted from the day's traveling, Jon didn't come up with her.

The following morning, Deb went to inspect the fridge and let out a yelp. Alyssa came out of her room, where she'd been studying. Inside the refrigerator were leftover fast-food containers, a carton of milk, and a few unidentifiable objects, but it was mostly empty. Deb checked the cupboards, which were also virtually empty.

"Good grief, Alyssa, didn't your mother ever teach you to cook?"

"Huh?"

"Don't you know how to cook?" Deb repeated. "You don't even have any flour, or sugar, or spices, except salt and pepper!"

"So?"

"What have you been eating?"

"I go out a lot," she said. "There's a pretty good café around the block."

"What else?"

"Oh, macaroni and cheese, frozen dinners, you know," she said with a shrug. "Cereal, that sort of thing."

"Nobody taught you how to cook, girl?" She put her hands on her hips in disbelief.

"Well, no."

"I thought you said your dad was some kind of chef or something."

"Yeah, for a while, but I never watched him," she said.

"Good grief. I can't believe they expected you to get by on your own, all alone out here, without even knowing how to cook."

"Dad sends plenty of money. I don't have to."

"But it's not healthy," Deb complained. "It's amazing you haven't gained weight."

"I only eat when I'm hungry," Alyssa said.

"Then you're probably malnourished. Come on. Where's the closest grocery from here? I'm going have to teach you how to cook."

"Deb, you don't have to do that."

"Oh yes I do. It'll drive me nuts to watch you eat like that, and I'm certainly not going to do all the cooking myself."

"I'll wash the dishes, honey," Alyssa said in a syrupy voice, and laughed out loud.

Deb laughed too. "No way. We're going to share this. Get your purse."

"We'll have to take the tram to the store," Alyssa said, going to the couch for her purse. "It's too far to walk."

"How far is it to campus?" Deb said. "Jon took me around last night after dinner for a tour, but I didn't pay attention to how far it was from here when we were in the car. Is it a long walk?"

"It's close. About ten minutes, walking," she answered.

"Not bad," Deb said.

When they returned from the store Alyssa got her first cooking lesson.

"It's not that hard," Deb told her. "See, it's just a lot of math and chemistry." She smiled, showing Alyssa a recipe in the cookbook. "Things you're good at. Simple stuff. You read the recipe, you measure the ingredients just like it says, you create a chemical reaction, and—voilà—you end up with dinner."

"Okay," Alyssa said, unsure of herself. She had spent as little time in the kitchen as possible. That way she didn't have to worry about cleaning it.

"Lucky for you I brought pots and pans, and dishes. Really girl, I don't know how you survived here all summer."

"Like I said, the café," Alyssa responded. "I didn't bring much with me when I left. Just a suitcase, actually. You brought half a house."

"Good thing I did," Deb said, grinning.

"I bought whatever I needed when I needed it," she said. "Sheets, towels, pictures for the walls, silverware and stuff. It's been fun."

"Ah, what would it be like?" Deb mused, shaking her head.

"Hey, I can buy you anything you need, too," Alyssa added. "My dad's been generous."

"Oh no," she said. "I didn't mean that for real. It's just that . . . the whole concept is so weird to me. I've never been able to buy anything I wanted, brand-new. We watch every penny in our house." She looked down at Alyssa's efforts. "Okay. Next, you get that knife there and cut up this meat into little pieces."

"Ew," Alyssa said. "No way. I think I'll be a vegetarian from now on."

"Oh, fine, I'll do it," Deb said. "You get used to it after a while." She began to cut the beef. "You boil the water for the noodles. You do know how to boil water?" she asked with a smirk.

"Hey, I can make macaroni and cheese," Alyssa retorted. "I figured that out."

She got out the one large saucepan she owned and filled it with water, putting it on the stove to boil, then adding salt.

"Good," Deb said. She may have been joking, but she looked relieved.

"You didn't think I knew that much, did you?"

"I hoped you did."

They continued the lesson, and ended up with a fine stroganoff dish and a side of green beans.

"Oh, come on, who needs vegetables?" Alyssa asked. "Nobody's looking over your shoulder to make sure you eat them here."

"They're healthy," Deb said. "Good for you."

"You sound just like my dad," Alyssa said, but she ate them anyway. "Hey, this stuff is good. Guess I'll keep you after all." She smiled.

It was nice to have company. She had gotten used to being alone and enjoyed it very much. So much that she wasn't sure how she would react to Deb's coming. Of course she missed her. But until the moment she arrived, Alyssa didn't know how she would react. She had never lived with anyone outside of her family, and that wasn't exactly a pleasant experience.

Even though Deb had only been around one day, it was as though a burden had been lifted off her shoulders. It was nice to have someone to talk to again. Deb was a good, comfortable friend. After her call to the Richardson's, it was wonderful to have company. The loneliness she had felt eased instantly with her presence.

Deb smiled back. "Of course you'll keep me, silly," she said. "Did you think you could get rid of me?"

They both laughed. It was an unexpected relief to Alyssa to have Deb there, in person. It was like taking a deep, cleansing breath of country air and drinking it in.

When Saturday night came, Deb said, "Tomorrow I won't be here much. I'm going to see Jon at school. I'll take the tram. Is that all right with you?"

"Of course," Alyssa said. "Hey, we're all grown up now, remember? Go, have fun."

"I'll probably be gone all day," Deb said, looking a trifle worried.

"Sure. I won't worry about you," Alyssa said.

Sunday morning Deb got up early and dressed in her nicer clothes. She tamed her short curly hair as best she could and put on low heels with a bright African print dress.

"Wow," Alyssa said. "You look nice. You never dressed up that much for Jon before, did you?"

"Thanks," Deb said, blushing. "I figured, well, if I see him only once a week now, I might as well look good, huh?"

"I guess so," Alyssa said. "Have fun."

"I will. Thanks for understanding."

"No problem."

"Have you dated anyone this summer?" Deb asked.

"Nope. Too busy studying."

She didn't tell Debra about the come-ons she had received from the guys in her apartment complex. It was too embarrassing. One of them,

Ray, was fairly adamant in his advances. He rang her doorbell one day in early August.

"Look, Alyssa," he said, "I'm not looking for a long-term commitment, you don't have to worry about that."

She looked him over. He was, she had to admit, attractive. At least on the outside. But the longer he talked, the less attractive he seemed, and the more she wanted him to go away.

"You're just so hot . . . you're driving me crazy. I've gotta find a way . . . Won't you even consider it—a nice dinner first, a movie maybe? Or the theater. You the type that likes the theater?"

"Ray," she said, "I'm just not interested."

"Why not? Something wrong with me? You don't find me good-looking. Is that it?"

She sighed. "You just don't get it."

"No, that can't be it . . ." he muttered. "But I know you're not seeing anyone else. The guys say you won't go out with any of them, so I know it's not just me. What is it then? Why do you let that incredibly gorgeous body of yours just . . . just go to *waste* like that? Don't you ever wanna, you know, share it a little?"

"I'm not 'going to waste,' thank you," she said, and moved to shut the door.

"Wait!" he said. "I'm just trying to understand. You *are* straight, aren't you? I mean, you're not seeing any women either as far as I know . . . Or is that it? Because I've converted more than one in my time. I could show you, babe."

"Yes, I'm straight," she said, her voice tired. She ran her hand through her hair, a gesture of frustration. "I'm just not interested in dating. Okay?"

"It makes no sense," he said, pleading. "Come on, just once? *Once?* I promise, I'll make it so nice. Candles, romance, the works. Best you ever had, I promise, and that's a promise I know I can deliver." He smiled broadly.

"I said *no*. Now deal with it." She shut the door, sighed heavily and rolled her eyes. How much of this would she have to put up with?

From the other side of the door, as his footsteps moved off, she heard him say, "If you ever change your mind, you know where to find me. 510B."

She wanted to scream.

Since calling the Richardson's, the whole idea of romance and dating had lost its attraction. It seemed a waste of time and money on frivolous things. With men like Ray, the only reason to go on a date was to get into bed. She shuddered at the thought.

What could possibly be so fascinating about *that*? Lauren had never found happiness there, not as far as Alyssa could tell. Pleasure, yes; but love? Never. And as far as she could tell, Lauren had never found self-worth, well being or contentment either.

She preferred to keep her emotions in check, under control. It was easier that way. She had no desire to place herself in situations that could easily get out of hand, to risk losing control over the privacy of her body, or worse yet, her heart. She was determined not to give either away freely.

Losing Peter had hurt . . . it still ached, though she blocked it out. She simply had no desire to endure that pain again.

Chapter 13

Hush

Hush, little baby, don't say a word,
Daddy's gonna buy you a mockingbird.
And if that mockingbird don't sing,
Daddy's gonna buy you a diamond ring.

Traditional children's song

Chuck called and checked on his daughter once or twice a month. He talked to her about his job, his challenges with co-workers, his new train layouts. Some of them he had sold, and for a good price. He didn't mention the rest of the family much, and Alyssa didn't feel like asking about them either.

Frequently they left the connection open while they both worked, she with her books studying, and him painstakingly fitting pieces of track together, talking to each other as they used to while she was at home. He would show her a design and ask her opinion, then say, "Wow. You know, you're a better engineer than I am, sweetie."

Leaving the line open like that didn't bother her at all. In fact, she looked forward to his calls, even if she did let him do most of the calling. She didn't like the risk that when she called, her mother might answer.

But there also came the times he called late, long past midnight. Alyssa was usually up studying, so he didn't often wake her. But she soon learned that if the phone rang from home after midnight, to proceed with caution.

"Hey, little Alison," he said, the first time he called that late. His voice was slurred, and the words ran together so she could hardly make them out. "My little bitsy baby grown and off to school, look at you." He reached toward the screen with a tickling motion of his fingers. "Ho! I made a rhyme! You know I was the one changed all your diapers and fed you and all that when you were a bitsy baby? I was the one sang you lullabies. I can't believe you've gotten so big so fast. It's flown by, and you're gone now, and you're not coming back, are you? I think you told me that."

"You've gone through more than your six-pack, haven't you, Dad," Alyssa said with a frustrated sigh.

She looked back at her schoolwork. She had a mid-term the next day and wanted to cram all the information into her head one last time before morning. The work here was much harder than in high school, and the classes were so large that she hardly knew her professors. She was no longer a special pet to any of them. She noticed that a couple of the professors had favorites, but they weren't so much the smartest students as the prettiest. She didn't care to become one of those. They reminded her of Lauren.

So she had to work harder than she ever did before to get the grades she wanted. She wanted them perfect, and perfection was difficult.

She pulled at a section of her hair that always seemed out of place no matter what she did. This call was unexpected, and she wasn't sure how to deal with it. Usually he passed out asleep when he had too much. It was unusual for him to be alert at this hour.

"How much have you had?" she asked.

"Oh, I dunno, not enough yet." He laughed and looked at the can in his hand, shook it. "My baby, baby Alison, look at you now. All grown up. You gonna look at me, or not? Look up. I miss your face. Oh, that sweet little baby face, my little moon pie. You used to have this curl at the end of your hair when you were a baby. It's gone now. Look at that. Long, and straight as a stick. But so pretty with those eyes of yours. My baby Alison."

He put the empty can down, and popped open a new one. The foam bubbled up and spilled over his fingers.

"My name is Alyssa, Dad."

Her voice was terse. The longer she was away, the easier it became to distance herself from where she had lived. It was like another life now.

"I know, I know. Your mother didn't like 'Alison.' So what? I can call you what I want, can't I? Hey, have you ever had a dream you just can't remember in the morning? I hate that. I had this dream yesterday, what was it about, something to do with some kind of zoo, and the architecture of this building was so odd, and there was a . . . a goat, I think. Something like a goat. But different. It had wings or something. Made no sense. But I know it did while I was dreaming it, I just know it. Hey, now I remember what I called to ask you. You remember how you loved that story about Rose Red and that little gnome with his beard stuck in the log when you were little? What was his name? Was that Rumpelstiltskin, or somebody else? What story was that?"

"I don't remember, Dad."

"No, I have to know," he said, taking another sip. "I won't be able to sleep until I find out. You have to tell me. See, I'm doing a new track, and it's all about fairy tales, and I gotta know his name."

"I don't remember, Dad. I don't think I ever read that story."

"Sure you did. Read it all the time. Snow White and Rose Red and what's-his-name. He had this long beard and they kept cutting pieces of it off. It made him so mad."

"No Dad. I never liked fairy tales. Ask Lauren."

"She isn't home."

"She's the one who liked fairy tales."

"But I have to know what the little gnome's name was," he pleaded, and hiccuped. "It's driving me nuts."

"I have to go now, Dad. I need to study."

"You know what your problem is? You're too serious. You know I can't remember you ever laughing? Or crying either, come to think of it. Not since you were about, oh, six, I think. Maybe five. Didn't you ever feel anything? How'd you do it? Maybe you could show me. I'm feeling way too much these days. I miss you so much, sweetie, it hurts. My little girl." He started to sing, off-key. "Hush little baby, don't you cry, Daddy's gonna buy you a lullaby. And if that lullaby don't sing, Daddy's gonna buy you a mocking . . ." He stopped. "Wait," he said. "That isn't how it goes." He began again. "Hush, little baby . . ."

"Goodnight, Dad," she said, and moved to cut him off.

"Oh, don't go. Please talk to me."

"You're drunk."

"Sure, so what? You used to talk to me all the time when I was drunk. What's the difference now? You think I don't remember what you told me?"

"Call me when you're sober, Dad. Goodnight."

"But the little man . . . Why can't you talk to me like you used to?"

"Look it up," she said, frustration rising in her voice. "I'm going now. Goodbye."

She cut the connection before he could say anything else, then slammed the screen down on the laptop. It frightened her that he might have been conscious enough to remember the things she told him. She thought she had been talking to a stone wall, or at least a wall void of hearing or perception. Her hands shook.

****

Joan called for the first time in December.

"Your father tells me you refuse to come home for Holiday. Why won't you come back for Winter Holiday? Everyone comes home for Winter Holiday. It's a *tradition*. It's unjust of you to sit there in that puny, forsaken little excuse of an apartment and not budge an inch to come home to visit us even once. Your father's desperate to see you, don't you know that? Janet's and Paula's daughters are coming home. Paula is taking everyone to Rio this year. Janet's holding a reunion. Everyone is going to be there. Not one person will be missing. And me, what do I get? An ungrateful little cretin who just *sits* there refusing to come for one little holiday! Some present!"

"Well, Mother, you're helping a lot," Alyssa spat out. "You're such a thrill . . . And since when did you care what your co-workers do over the holidays? You haven't been sociable in years."

"You are so incredibly rude! Did I ever teach you that? Did I? You've never spoken to me this way!"

"I wonder why," Alyssa muttered.

"Perhaps it's the university culture. I will attempt to ignore this horrifying attitude you seem to have developed. Perhaps we can rectify that once you're home. That place must be a terrible influence on you. Aren't you aware that your absence is tearing this family to shreds? You should see your father. He's in a terrible state."

"I have seen him," Alyssa answered, leaning back in her chair, folding her arms in a hostile posture.

It was dark in her room with only her small study lamp by the bed. She knew Joan couldn't see her well that way. She was actually amused, waiting to see how worked up Joan would get in front of the video screen, knowing her mother was powerless to harm her.

"So what about it?" Alyssa asked.

"This is all your fault! If you would just come home he'd get better. It's ruining all of us!"

"There's nothing the matter with him!"

"Must I say it out loud?" Joan said, staring, her voice a harsh whisper.

"Say what?"

Joan looked behind her, then whispered, "You of all people should know he's *drinking* too much. And he refuses to get any *help*."

"As if I could do anything about that!" Alyssa said. She leaned forward again and stared viciously into her mother's steely gray eyes. "You drove him to it!" She pointed her finger, her voice bitter. "Demanding your precious big house, and always knocking his career like it was nothing, treating him like dirt for twenty-some-odd years . . .

and getting away with it. It's no wonder he drinks. He needs something to drown you out. You should be glad that's all he does!"

Joan took a step away from the screen, her eyes wide.

Alyssa continued. "He started it when we moved to that house, not when I left for school. My leaving had nothing to do with it. Not one bit. If you weren't such a tyrannical control freak, you'd realize you were the problem, not me! You don't want me home. You just want to get your way! Well, you won't. Not with me. Not anymore."

In a cold whisper Joan replied, "You are a despicable piece of flesh even to suggest such things. You will come back here for the holiday. Then you'll see, your father will return to normal."

"I don't like your idea of *normal*," Alyssa said. "Dad understands why I won't come home. And he'd be fine if you weren't on his case all the time. Quit nagging him."

"He isn't dealing well with this situation. You must help him. He can't stand your being gone."

"Seems to me it's you who can't stand it. He's your problem, not mine. He never bothered you about your cigarettes. You know he hates cigarette smoke? He ever tell you that to your face? Did he ever tell you he's afraid they're going to kill you one of these days? Do you even know how much he wants you to quit? I bet you don't, because he's too chicken to stand up to you and tell you. He's afraid of you. Your own husband's afraid of you. Did you know that?"

Joan ignored her and held up a slip of paper. "This argument is superfluous. I've already purchased your airline ticket. Nonrefundable. You'll be on flight 3406 out of Central Airport West, 1:50 PM—"

"You can eat that ticket. I'm not getting on any plane just to put up with more of this crap."

"Don't you dare swear at me, young lady."

"I'll swear all I want." She demonstrated. Then, after Joan turned from red to white to blue in shock without getting a word in, Alyssa terminated the call.

She grinned wickedly. "You old witch. It's about time I got to tell you off." It was highly satisfying. She took a perverse delight in knowing that Joan couldn't hurt her now no matter what she said. All she had to do was hang up.

She was glad Debra was gone at the moment. She had never heard Deb swear, so she was careful to watch her language when she was around, though it really didn't take much effort. But Alyssa was sure Deb would have been shocked even without the bad language. Some things about her family Alyssa just didn't talk about. Deb's family was vastly different. There were things, like this, that she wouldn't understand.

The phone rang again. The call was from her home number. She ignored it.

****

Deb, of course, went home for the two-week holiday break. Jon came to pick her up and take her back. Most of the time, Deb went to see him on Sundays, but sometimes he came instead and took her out for most of the day. They always dressed up, and Jon usually wore a tie and sometimes brought her roses when he came. Alyssa thought it was cute.

At home, Deb used to meet him frequently in sweats or a T-shirt. She didn't worry much about her clothes then. Watching her friend now made Alyssa smile.

But there was something else about Jon's visits. Alyssa felt a twinge of envy that Debra had someone there for her. She kept that hidden, however. The absence of male companionship in Alyssa's life wasn't from lack of opportunity, if she could call Ray and the other guys who repeatedly called and asked her out, "opportunities."

Debra never questioned her persistent refusal to date these men. When Alyssa would slam the phone down and repeat some scrap of the conversation, saying "Can you *believe* that?" Debra would laugh right along with her.

She had told Deb about the phone call to the Richardson's when she finally got up the nerve to talk about it, in November.

"I called Peter this summer," she said. "Right after I got here."

Debra smiled. "Brave girl! How did it go?"

Alyssa shrugged. "He's getting married," she said. She didn't include the foreign service work. It was too strange, in her mind, to explain. Best to leave it out.

"I'm so sorry," Deb said, her face falling. "I was sure he meant more to you than you let on. Are you okay? Really?"

"Oh sure, I'm fine. I mean, it wasn't realistic to expect him to pine away for me, you know."

"Oh, I know . . . still . . . Was he happy to see you? Did you talk for a while? Catch up?"

"Actually, he wasn't there when I called. I talked to his fiancée."

"Oh." Deb wrinkled her nose. "Joy."

"Yeah," Alyssa said. "But I'm all right."

Debra gave her a big hug.

She kept reminding herself she was fine without him, alone, without any love interest. She wished it would *feel* that way as she pushed the emotions back down, forcing them away again.

The two weeks was a long time without Deb, longer than she thought it would be. The summer had gone fast in comparison. That was before the apartment carried the echo of Deb's voice and footsteps, and all the fond memories they had made, popping popcorn, watching movies, staying up late at night talking.

She was lonely now, and struggled to keep herself occupied.

Maybe, she thought, it wouldn't be so bad to go home and visit. *No,* she thought, strengthening her resolve. She nursed her contempt for the idea by reopening memories, old wounds in her mind, reminding herself why she never wanted to return.

****

Over one year later, in January of her sophomore year Alyssa, then nineteen, still hadn't returned home. Not once, not even for a short visit. With no young men in her life, there was little to distract her from her studies as she pursued a credit load that would speed her through her degree program in just over three years.

She had the unreasonable fear that if she went home, she would never find a way to escape again. The feeling reminded her of dreams she once had where she tried to get out of a maze but couldn't find the exit, from which she would awaken drenched in a cold sweat.

Her father talked of coming out to visit her, but he had not. Vacation time was difficult to get, he said, and Joan had too many things she assigned him to do. It was more an unfulfilled dream than anything else. Alyssa wasn't even sure she wanted him to come; it would be strange introducing him into her environment.

Deb continued seeing Jon, talking frequently about her hopes, frustrations and feelings about him. She wondered if they would eventually marry, if he was too shy to ask. Alyssa told her not to get that serious yet. She was too young and he had too much school left. Sometimes she wondered how much of her friendship with Debra was spent on parenting each other, and laughed to herself about it.

Joan called her unexpectedly early one Thursday evening that month. The sky was gray and dreary. It had refused to snow or rain or allow the sun to shine for two weeks.

"Hello, Mother," she said without enthusiasm. She had been

expecting Chuck; he was due to call. She might not have answered had she known it was Joan and not him. She noticed mascara running down her mother's cheeks, and added, "What's wrong this time?"

Joan had been calling more frequently, complaining about her absence taking its toll on her father's health and well being. Alyssa wondered about that. She didn't believe her mother cared about anyone's well being but her own. To Alyssa, this was just a vain attempt to control her from a distance, and it wasn't going to work.

A few months ago Joan telephoned to say that Chuck had lost his job and if they lost the house as a result, it would be Alyssa's fault. If she had been home, this never would have happened. Alyssa had hung up before Joan could work herself into a full-blown tantrum. But first she reminded her that Chuck was an adult and capable of making his own decisions. She told her mother again it couldn't possibly be her fault. Besides, it was an empty accusation. Chuck made plenty of money on the side from selling his train sets. And if things got really tight, all they had to do was sell off a few of Joan's precious artifacts.

Saying it aloud, however, didn't stop the nagging worry that maybe, just maybe, it was partly her fault . . . or all her fault.

No, she thought. Their problems simply could not be her fault. Logic told her it wasn't possible. She shook off the dreadful feeling as best as she could, but it persisted. When her mother confronted her now, it was hard to avoid that feeling, and she was quicker to anger because of it.

"It's your father," Joan said this time, her voice shaking.

"What did he do this time? Get another job and get fired on purpose just to spite you?"

"Alyssa, be serious for one second if you can possibly manage it. Listen. Your father is *dead*. He died of a heart attack this afternoon. I came home early from the museum tonight, and went downstairs to see if he was going to start anything for dinner . . ." Joan looked away from the screen momentarily toward the stairway. "He was sitting there in his rotten old chair, staring into space with a moronic grin on his face, holding a wretched can of beer." Her voice raised in pitch during the whole speech, and cracked when she said "beer."

"No," Alyssa said, shaking her head. "No. He's too young. You're making this up. This is a sick joke, Mother. Cut it out. I'm not coming home. It won't work."

Lauren appeared behind Joan, a wraithlike incarnation of her mother now, only her darker hair marking the difference between them. Alyssa had forgotten how striking the resemblance was between the two. She noticed only that, in contrast, Joan had developed deep lines around her lips from pursing them into a frown too often. She looked far older than her actual age.

Lauren's color was also bad; she was much paler than Alyssa remembered. She hadn't spoken to her sister since leaving home, and was startled to see her now. Chuck mentioned last summer that Lauren had moved out, got her own art studio and apartment. He told her it was about time, but Joan was beside herself with the house so empty. He had laughed, a hollow chuckle, and said, "I guess I don't count," then turned back to placing artificial shrubbery on his newest creation.

"It's true," Lauren said, shaking Alyssa's thoughts back to the present. "I'll fax you an autopsy report when it comes, if you want. His liver probably would've gotten him, if his heart hadn't given out first."

"Lauren, you could be less graphic," Joan said, her voice sharp.

"Sorry, Mother," Lauren said. "But it's a fact."

Alyssa was stunned. She stared blankly away from the screen. "Thanks for telling me,"

"You must come home for the funeral," Joan said.

"You have to," Lauren echoed.

"When is it?"

"Saturday," Joan said.

"I have a mid-term I can't miss. Sorry."

"A mid-term in January? On a Saturday?"

"Yeah." Mentally she cursed herself. She was a better liar than that. "We have tests on Saturday a lot," she added with a noncommittal shrug. Maybe that would help.

"Alyssa, we're talking about your father here! They'll have to let you out of it! I'll fax the dean with an explanation. They're certain to understand a . . . a *passing* in the family."

"Right. My father," Alyssa said. "The man solely responsible for bringing me into this world. Like I said, thanks for telling me."

She hung up before her mother could rebut that statement and embark on the sermon about how dreadful her entire pregnancy, labor and delivery had been.

She sat down on her bed as the shock of it sank in. She wanted to go. She wished she could go. The last few months he'd given her extra money, and he hadn't called drunk once since he lost his job. But the thought of going was too much. It was too final. He couldn't be dead, just like that. She knew Joan would think up some reason to make her stay. She would definitely come up with something.

Anger welled up inside her. Why did she have to be afraid to go home? Why couldn't she feel safe going to her own father's funeral? It was obvious Joan still wanted to control her life. That was why she always begged her to come home. In fact, if it weren't for Lauren affirming the story, she would have thought it was some sick joke Joan had invented to bring her back.

Then another thought came, one that terrified her. The money. Joan would find out about his secret account now that his estate was in her hands. Her college career would be over. She didn't have nearly enough credits to graduate yet.

If she did go to the funeral would it ease the hard feelings between them enough that Joan would continue to dole out her college fund? No. The likelihood was she wouldn't even have the money to return to the CU campus. She might even be prevented from leaving the house. She had no desire to go back there, to that prison, even for this. Joan would purchase a one-way ticket. She'd have to pay for her own return. It was near the end of the month, and she had used up her allowance already. She had no idea that it would be her last.

She generally spent the money frivolously, on apartment furnishings and useless gadgets that caught her fancy. She bought computer software and accessories she rarely used. Often, she bought clothes and other things for Debra she knew her friend couldn't afford, and sometimes helped her pay for her books. She even let Deb use her long distance account to call her family and talk as long as she wanted. At first Deb had objected, but when she realized how much Alyssa wanted to do that for her, and that she could afford it, she relented.

Deep down, Alyssa enjoyed having money, very much. She took it for granted. It had always come easily. Her father was generous with what he had. Now she might have to work for it. Many students did, even while carrying a heavy schedule. She wracked her brain for a plan, one that would allow her the time to hold down a job and still keep up her arduous schedule.

It had been hard earning money in high school, before she had the college fund to rely on. Now her studying took up all her free time. She had no social life. Others thought her strange. She never went to parties or bars like the other students in her apartment complex. Central U had a national reputation for being a "party school." She was the exception to the rule.

Even Debra must have thought she was strange, though she never said so. Deb didn't go to those places, either. She had her own circle of friends. They were nice, and they weren't into partying and drinking. But Alyssa didn't connect with them either. Most of the time she stayed out of sight when they came over. Sometimes she chatted, but she found them about as strange as they must have thought her to be.

She decided not to think about missing her father.

Debra came home about two hours later to find Alyssa still sitting on her bed staring at nothing, an empty feeling somewhere inside that must have shown on her face.

"What happened?" Deb asked, "What's wrong?" The sound of concern was in her voice.

"My dad died this afternoon," Alyssa said with a shrug, as though it were casual news.

"Oh no." Debra sat beside her and placed a hand on her shoulder. Alyssa made no response. "You must feel awful."

Alyssa snorted. "That would hardly be the word. He's . . . he was the biggest, I don't know what, I ever knew. He let my mother walk all over him and never said boo about it his whole life. He died of a heart attack. His cholesterol was always high, you know." She paused a long time before she continued. "It was bound to happen sooner or later. His health hasn't been good lately." Her voice sounded more like a newscaster than someone telling a personal story that ought to carry deep emotion.

Debra took a breath. She seemed unsure of what to say. Alyssa's eyes weren't puffy or red. Her cheeks weren't wet. Her voice was steady, devoid of feeling.

"Haven't you cried? I'd be devastated if my dad was suddenly taken like that."

Alyssa didn't answer. She thought, *Sure, if I had a dad like yours I might miss him too.* It wasn't her biggest problem at the moment. She had to find a decent way to earn money, so she could finish her degree. A college degree was everything. Employers wouldn't give her a second look if she didn't have a degree. Honest, decent employers, anyway, with respectable business pursuits.

Deb continued, "When I was a kid, I had a favorite dog, Betsy. She was the best dog I ever had, I mean, way more obedient and loving than Fritz or Flint." She laughed a little. Alyssa had been knocked over by those two big dogs almost every time she came over. "Anyway, she got hit by a car and I couldn't cry about it for days and days. I kept pretending she was still around, calling her. But she never came. I was pretty little, maybe four or five. My dad finally sat me down and talked to me about it. After that I finally was able to cry. So, you see, I know sometimes it's hard to get started, but I know I always feel better once I let it out, you know . . ." She paused, wrinkling her brow in concern. "Come to think of it, I've never seen you cry, Alyssa. In all the time I've known you." She looked at her with a puzzled expression on her face.

"I don't cry," she said. She spoke firmly, so Deb wouldn't pursue it further. "The worst thing is I haven't saved any of the money he sent me. I don't know where tuition will come from next semester."

"I won't call my family on your phone bill anymore," Deb said. "I could take back some things . . ."

Alyssa waved her hand. "No. It's all right. Don't worry about that. I'd have just spent it on something else."

"Won't your mom send it?" Deb asked, even more puzzled.

Alyssa looked at her. "Hardly. She never even liked me."

"Well, I know you feel like that, Alyssa, but I doubt it's true. She's got to care about your college success. She's got to."

"No way. She always acted like I was a burden. Then when it came time to go she didn't want me to leave. It was so queer." She picked at a tiny hole in her bedspread. "Kept trying to get me to be an archaeologist, like her, like it was the most prestigious thing in the world. She hates my major. She thinks computer engineering is dumb, that the market's saturated already, but it's not. Then she calls me all the time telling me I better come home because Dad's getting worse. Well, that's not my fault. It's not my fault if he misses me. He understands me. He knows."

"You could've gone home for the holidays. That might've helped," Deb said.

"No, you don't understand," Alyssa said. "She just wanted to get me back to keep me there. She'd say it was to help Dad. Well, that's not my job. She was just mad because she had to look after him when I left. And of course there was nobody left to do the housework and stuff. Oh, yes, then she *had* to hire a housekeeper. It was *such* a hardship . . . Then when Lauren finally moved out she really blew a gasket. Started in on me again full bore, like it was all my fault things didn't go her way."

"You spent a lot of time with your father in the basement. I remember you telling me how you two worked on all his train layouts and stuff. I don't see . . . How did he need looking after?"

"Well, nobody else in the family hardly ever talked to him."

"Oh," Deb said, but it was clear from her tone she didn't understand.

"My family's not like yours," Alyssa said.

"I know that," Deb said. "I just didn't realize it was so . . . lonely."

Alyssa shrugged and stood up, moving toward the bedroom window to look out on the central courtyard, though there was nothing much to see at the moment.

"I can't even go to the funeral. If I do, I'll never get back here. Somehow she wouldn't let me escape. I just know it. I can't afford both the ticket and school. Even if she bought me a ticket home, I'm sure it would be one-way. I'd have to come up with the money to get back here, and I don't have it."

"You're being unreasonable," Deb said. "Did she actually say that? I'm sure you could get there and back."

"You don't understand," Alyssa said. "You don't know my mother. This is how she works. She manipulates absolutely everything, and when she can't, she freaks."

"So you're not going to the funeral?"

Alyssa shook her head. "I'd be stuck. I swore when I left I was never going back. I meant it."

"Not even for that? I mean, it would just be a weekend trip. This is your last chance. You'll never get to see him again."

Her words brought a flash of memory Alyssa found unwelcome just then—the last time she *had* seen her father . . . at the train station, the cloying hug, his unique scent, her desperation to get away.

"*I love you,*" he had said. She didn't remember saying it back. Not then, not ever. She pushed the thought away.

"I'm not interested in looking at a dead corpse in a pretty wooden box. What is there to that?"

"Closure," Deb said and paused. "That's why they have funerals, girl." She put a hand on her hip and looked Alyssa in the eye. "So this is why you never come with me and Jon when we go home for breaks. You made some weird promise to yourself never to visit them again? Don't you ever get homesick? Not even a tiny bit?"

"Look. Try to understand. See, Mother wanted to have Lauren, sort of, but one was enough. My dad was the only one who even wanted to have another kid, and even then, he wanted a son. So finally he talked her into it and they had me. But I was supposed to be a boy. And I wasn't . . . She wanted to get an abortion, but he convinced her not to. So I was a disappointment to both of them. They ruined my life before I was even born. I mean, he made things decent for me and stuff, but I always had this feeling that somehow I wasn't quite what he wanted. Look, I know I never told you this before, but you have to understand. It's like prison, not the kind of thing you go back to once you get out, not by choice anyway. No way am I going there again, especially if he's *not* there. He was the only one who ever cared."

"Oh, Alyssa," Deb said, sitting down on the bed. "I had no idea."

"Don't feel sorry for me. It's just the way it was, but I don't like talking about it. And right now I need to figure out how to come up with some money." She got up, patted Deb on the shoulder. She looked lost and confused. " . . . in a way I can live with and still be able to keep up my studies."

Alyssa switched on her computer. Deb stayed and watched for several minutes.

Finally she said, "I don't know if you need me to stay or go."

"Whatever. I'm all right." Alyssa didn't look over. Her fingers clicked on the keyboard. "I'm going to check with the people we worked with before, in high school. Their website's been looking shabby lately. Maybe they could hire us again. I've been designing graphics for that one class. I've gotten a lot better."

Debra sighed. "Okay . . . I guess I'll go get dinner. Come and get me if you need me."

"Sure," Alyssa said.

Later, Alyssa could hear Deb finishing up the dinner dishes. She watched through her door as Deb wiped her hands on a kitchen towel, then leaned against the counter and sighed. She looked away as Deb came back into her room.

"I really think you should go," Deb said.

Alyssa fussed at her computer screen, clicking keys vigorously. The screen shifted images every few seconds.

"What?" she said, pretending not to have heard.

"I honestly think you need to go."

"Why?"

"You'll regret it later, I promise you."

Alyssa grunted. "I doubt that."

"Look, I know you two were close."

"I wouldn't call it that."

"Well, shoot, he's the closest thing you had in your family. You need to be there. I'll do whatever I can to help you get back here, if that's what you're worried about." She rubbed her hand through the back of her dark curly hair. "I'll talk to my folks, and I'm sure they'd be happy to help pay for your ticket. We can pool our resources."

Finally Alyssa turned around. "You guys can't afford that."

"I'll find a way."

"You would do that for me?"

"Yes, I would."

Alyssa sighed. "You shouldn't have to. I'll figure it out somehow."

"So you'll go?"

"I really don't want to."

Deb looked at her.

Alyssa pushed her foot down and slid her chair away from her desk. "Fine. You and your closure. Why do I have to room with somebody minoring in psychology?" She rolled her eyes.

Deb smiled. "Okay. Call and tell them you'll be there."

"No. I'm not going that far," Alyssa said. "I might go, but I'm not telling them. Not if I can help it."

" Fine. Whatever. Just go, please?"

"All right."

****

She called around until she found the right funeral home, stubbornly refusing to give her family any notice of her arrival, even to ask where it was being held. She left early Saturday morning by commuter plane to Des Moines. It was a short flight, less than an hour, and she was filled with dread the entire trip. As she rode in the taxi, she pored over her itinerary. Had she scheduled enough time to get to and from the airport and the funeral home and still make her return flight? She wasn't about to stay overnight.

She had bought the ticket herself, on credit. Her father had given her his card number long ago, and it worked. It hadn't been cancelled yet. *What a blessing*, she thought. Deb didn't need to do any pooling of resources after all. But Alyssa had been touched by her offer. It was a noble gesture.

She felt absolutely black inside as she walked through the door and whispered that she was there for the funeral of Charles Alison Stark. The attendant nodded and escorted her in the right direction. She wondered how much they were paid to look mournful all day long.

It was bitter cold outside, and she kept her long black dress coat and knit hat on. When she warmed up a little she peeled off her black leather gloves, loosening one finger at a time. She was early. There was no one else in the room, just the little brass urn with her father's ashes inside. But that . . . the ashes . . . didn't count. Inwardly she was glad it wasn't a coffin. She wouldn't have to participate in a viewing, wouldn't have to look at his dead body.

She shuddered. The urn was sitting on a heavy oval table. There were flowers all around it, mostly yellow gladiolas, and some blue flowers with long, very narrow petals. One arrangement was of a dozen white roses. There was soft music in a minor key playing from some sound system; she thought it was a familiar classical piece, but hadn't studied enough music to know its name. She didn't like being the only one in the room, with that thing—the urn. She began to feel nervous, jumpy, and got up to find the attendant.

"Excuse me," she said. "Is there somewhere else I could wait until everyone arrives? I . . . I don't much like being first." She didn't relish the thought of being there when Joan walked in, either.

"I understand," he said, and led her to a sort of waiting room, with two overstuffed sofas and several chairs, none of which looked comfortable. She chose a chair.

"Thank you," she said. "I thought it was at eleven o'clock?"

"Twelve," he said. "It was moved back an hour."

She nodded. "I see."

It would be tight getting back to the airport in time.

"The family was instructed to arrive at eleven-thirty, to be seated in the front row for some quality time with one another before the rest of the attendees arrive. Would you be . . .?" He looked at her quizzically.

She shook her head. It was bad enough to be here. She certainly didn't want to *sit* with them. That would be going too far.

She slunk into a back row seat a few minutes after noon, purposely late. The room was full. She recognized her mother in the front, the back of her head, her hair pulled into the severe chignon she usually wore. Her hair was a different shade of blond than she remembered. It looked unnatural. She must be dyeing it, to cover the gray. Alyssa tapped her foot nervously while the eulogy was delivered, then noticed that she was annoying a large woman in black rayon sitting next to her and stopped.

The whole time she was in a state of near panic. She wondered if she could get out before her family caught sight of her and delayed her just long enough to miss her flight; wondered why Deb had made her come like this, why she had listened to Deb and why this was important at all. She had the persistent feeling that none of this was happening, that it was some sort of bad dream, vivid but eerie. Surely she would wake up soon, Chuck would call next week, his usual self, they'd chat about her classes, her studies and his work while he pieced his little segments of track into intricate designs.

When it was almost over, she slipped out unseen. At the doorway she stopped, noticing a small table with an open book on it and a pen. She hesitated, then turned to look at the cover. It was a guestbook. She had a sudden urge, and wondered whether to fight it or not.

Nervously, she picked up the pen and signed her name, then hurried out, breathing hard.

****

Monday evening Joan called. "I see you didn't care enough to come."

"I was there," she said. "I just didn't care enough to say hello."

She was surprised at the depth of hostility her tone revealed, and wondered why she had even bothered to answer the phone. Maybe a part of her still hoped it would be her father.

"You are so rude. Where were you? If you were there, didn't they seat you? You were supposed to be up front with the family. You said you were staying for your mid-term. Or was that yet another lie?"

"Why should I be polite?" Alyssa said unwilling to hide her bitterness. "I was there. I signed the guestbook. Check it."

"I shall do that," Joan said. "But that doesn't excuse your behavior. You have a duty to honor your father's passing properly. Protocol dictates that if you were there, you should have taken your place with the family."

"Look, you should be glad I came at all. Don't talk to me about duty. You didn't even say goodbye to me before I left home. Isn't that a duty? The last thing you said to me before I left was . . . do you remember? Do you even remember? You said 'I should've had the abortion.' What protocol is that? For both our sakes, let's just pretend you did. Problem solved. No more worries about Dad, either. Seems to me he found the easy way out."

"I never said such a horrible thing to you!"

"Hasn't anyone ever told you your memory is selective? You did so."

"My memory is perfectly accurate. I am certain I never said such a thing. You are a most ungrateful human being. Didn't your father mean anything to you? You know he would have wanted you seated in front with us." She began to cry.

"Listen to you. What a bunch of garbage! You say yourself there is no afterlife. If he's not around to care whether I was there or not, why should you? The only reason you wanted me to come home is so you could have someone to take it out on. You're just mad because I didn't do what you wanted, so here you are calling up all righteous and indignant that I wasn't there, but—a-ha!—I was, and now you're mad you missed the chance to catch me."

Joan pursed her wrinkled lips. "You wretched little—"

"Oh, cut it out," Alyssa interrupted. "I'm tired of hearing it. Give me one good reason why I shouldn't hang up."

"I suppose it never occurred to you I might miss you."

Alyssa snorted. "You mean, you miss beating me. Taking it out on Lauren now? Don't like that, eh?"

"How dare you!"

"You don't fool me. Not for a minute."

"Whatever makes you think I would want someone as unpleasant as you are living in my house? I had no intention of *catching* you, as you say, much less—"

"Like I said, give me one good reason," Alyssa repeated, lifting her hand to close the connection.

Joan stopped mid-sentence, and her expression changed. "Actually, I do have one. This would have been much simpler in person. I need your signature on a statement, and it's exasperating to do this the hard way when you were right here on Saturday. I can't believe you didn't even stay long enough to tell us you came." She sighed.

"So, what do I need to sign?"

Her voice became stiff. "I am required by law to inform you that your father left you an inheritance, and deliver it to you. I need your signature and thumbprint showing you received the money."

Alyssa hoped the exhilaration she felt wasn't too visible. "He what?" An inheritance? This was totally unexpected. It changed everything.

"He left you some money. It's willed directly to you and I am legally required to make certain you receive it. I don't even know where he got it." Joan was visibly disturbed. She cleared her throat. "His attorney seems to know all about it, however. For some reason they must have thought it necessary to have a sworn statement from you. Personally I think that's rather extreme, but it's in the will."

Alyssa gave her a twisted smile, then quickly erased it from her face. It must be the rest of her college fund.

Thanks, Dad, you're smarter than I ever gave you credit for. To her mother, she said, hoping her voice was expressionless, "I'll give you the number to my account here and you can transfer the money over. Fax me the statement. I'll sign it and put my thumbprint on it." She typed the number, hoping her voice had been expressionless and bland.

Joan punched some keys at her end of the connection. "I can't fax the statement," Joan said. "It must be the original document, signed the old-fashioned way. This is why it would've all been much simpler in person on Saturday. I'll have to mail it to you. You must sign it in the presence of an attorney and have it notarized within ten business days."

"Well, you could've told me that in the first place, and I might've hung around."

"As if you gave me the chance."

"As if you couldn't have called and told me."

"As if you would've answered the phone."

The computer beeped. At the bottom of Alyssa's screen a message came up. "Transaction complete," it read, stating the amount of the deposit. Any amount was more than she hoped for, but it was still not quite enough to complete her education. She would have to figure the math later. Still, it would get her much farther than she had originally thought. Maybe through the end of this year, or if she was careful, longer than that.

"This eats you up, doesn't it, Mother?" she said.

"What?" Joan said acidly.

"Having to give me this money."

"I admit I would never do it voluntarily. It's a waste of good funds."

"Did you know Dad was using it to put me through college? He's been sending me an allowance every month. You might as well know. See? I knew all along he didn't want me to come home. Who's the liar now?" Her laugh was a mean sound. "You and your never-ending search for truth. Well, now that you have the truth do you like it?"

Joan took a deep breath through her nose, her lips pursed, discomfort apparent in every feature of her face. "He did so want you to come home. You could have visited. He missed you dearly."

"He could've come here."

"Your ingratitude is pathetic. Nothing you have ever done amounts to anywhere near this large a sum."

"So, what happens to you if I don't sign and return the dumb paper?"

"I'll sue you for it," Joan said. "And don't think for a moment I won't."

She terminated the connection before Alyssa could cut her off first. Alyssa shivered and shook herself, relieved the conversation was over.

Immediately she called the bank and changed her account number. One could never be too paranoid when Joan was involved.

Chapter 14

Elation

We have found that certain forms of this drug bring out latent capabilities in the human brain with a fair degree of reliability. Such phenomena as telepathy, telekinesis, and some form of communication with a previously unknown intelligent lifeform are consistently reported. From our latest findings, it appears the psychic phenomena can be explained entirely on the basis of such communication. Test subjects can give directions to these unseen beings in some manner. That they are not imaginary is partially evidenced by the direct relationship between the directions given and the observed psychic phenomena.

Further, we have discovered—purely by accident as reported in our earlier memo—that certain quantum sub-phase readings coincide with the appearance of these "hallucinations." That is, certain fluctuations take place at the exact moment the subjects claim to be in contact with these unseen beings. We are now in the process of testing for and detecting the specific fluctuations that characterize these hallucinatory episodes using a Quantum Sub-phase Detection Device (QSDD).

In order to continue with our research however, we require Presidential approval for further testing on human subjects. As more volunteers are currently in short supply we feel it necessary to implement a slightly more aggressive procedure to acquire subjects fitting our demographic requirements, as described in the attached material.

We are aware of the potential for controversy over this, should it become public, but His Presidency can see the potential benefits of continued judicious pursuit of this matter, especially if the tests prove successful.

We look forward to your reply.

Federal Department of Research,
Confidential Memo to the President

A lyssa wouldn't admit that her father's death affected her in any way, on any level. But a crushing, heavy weight threatened every corner of her mind, every turn of her thoughts. Even with the emotional control she had taught herself, she didn't know how to make this go away. It ached, tore at her heart. She didn't understand it. She had convinced herself she didn't love her father, only felt sorry for him when she felt anything at all.

She pushed the feeling away. It made no sense. There shouldn't be any pain associated with his death. Sure, she would miss his phone calls. But she still had his money, she could continue her education, and life would go on in its usual way.

Still, gone was the only part of her home that was ever home to her. Chuck was the only part of her family she halfway wished to claim, even with his imperfections. Yet she refused to acknowledge that this intense pain meant she did truly love him, in a deeply buried way. In her mind she could hear the comforting sound of his trains swishing along their tracks, and mentally replayed his odd middle-of-the-night phone calls, their quiet conversations when he needed to hear her voice. She had felt a deep sense of security in knowing he was there, piecing together his odd train contraptions. When she imagined the train sets silent, the basement still, she shoved the thought away with great force.

She refused to grieve.

Classes were attended regularly. She completed her assignments, studied and took her tests as she always had. But something was missing. It was just a routine, without the excitement for learning she normally had. It felt a little like she was the one who had died, leaving just a hollow shell.

Aside from the pain's vise-like grip on her heart, she had no other feelings at all, about anything. It was more difficult to sleep at night, however. She either lay awake in bed for hours, or filled the time studying. Anything to keep her mind from wandering back to her father's basement, with its silent trains.

A few weeks after the funeral, Deb went home for a long weekend.

"Are you going to be okay?" she asked. "I'll be gone for three days."

Since the funeral, Deb hadn't left her for more than a few hours. Jon came up to visit on Sundays, and they disappeared for a little while, but most of the day the three of them hung around together.

"Call me if you need to talk, or anything. Call collect. It's all right. I'm here for you, even if I'm at home. You know that, don't you?"

"I'm fine," Alyssa replied. "I told you, there's nothing wrong with me.

Go on, get out of here. Go have fun. Tell Rochelle she's still a little brat, even if she thinks she's growing up. Tell her I think her missing teeth make her look like a jack o' lantern."

Deb smiled. "Still, I'm worried about you. You haven't been yourself. Are you sure you're not depressed . . . ? You still won't talk about it."

"Nothing to talk about. I'm all right. Go on, Jon's waiting for you."

But that night her loneliness grew intense. As she sat alone in her room, it seemed a great weight on her soul. And the internal pain, as usual, refused to be relieved. She needed to escape it somehow.

She could hear the laughter and the usual boisterous noises coming from the adjoining walls, happy conversations and games going on in the courtyard below. It was Friday, the beginning of a long weekend, and the weather was unusually warm for February. It was one of those rare winter days that gives the feeling spring is just around the corner. It had been a long, cold winter, and people were taking advantage of the weather, carrying on outside after months of being cooped up indoors.

She felt hollow. With Debra gone, there was no one to laugh with her, if she'd wanted to laugh. She had made few other acquaintances, by choice, telling herself that many friends and a social life were unnecessary, time-consuming. She saw her fellow students waste time partying or pursuing entertainment when they should have been studying, and it always resulted in lower grades. It seemed pointless. She had goals and objectives, and that didn't leave time for gaiety.

She looked out her bedroom window down into the courtyard, and saw two couples, one walking hand in hand, the other closer together in an embrace. She thought of Peter, and missed him. Was he home, married by now? She didn't want to embarrass herself by calling again to find out. He had forgotten, and so must she.

If Peter was lost to her, was she right to refuse dates as she did? It kept her in control, true. She reminded herself of that. But it also kept her from . . . from finding the happiness the couples below, in the courtyard, seemed to enjoy.

At the moment, she was restless. She wondered why she felt so terribly dark inside. She couldn't shake the feeling, and wondered if maybe it was the lack of such entertainment in her life. Was it necessary to keep such a tight rein on her feelings? Her control prevented pain. But maybe . . . maybe it also prevented the experience of joy.

As her thoughts wandered in these unsatisfying circles, the doorbell rang. She looked through the peephole to see who it was. It was Manuel, from 130A, who had asked her out once before. He was slightly more decent than some of her other would-be suitors. She opened the door.

"Hey, Alyssa."

"Hi, Manuel. What's up?"

"Well, that roommate of yours is gone for the weekend, isn't she?"

"What's it to you?" She felt slightly on edge at the question.

"Eh, she's . . ." He seemed to skip over whatever point he originally had in mind. "See, there's a bunch of us, we're walking downtown tonight, doing some shopping, having a good time, you know. We wondered, maybe you'd like to come along."

"And what has Debra got to do with that?"

"Well, I kinda figured maybe she wouldn't let you go, or something. Maybe she wouldn't like it."

"What does she look like, my mother? I follow my own rules," Alyssa said. "Why?"

"Oh, well, she just doesn't seem the type for it, that's all."

"But I do?" She wondered if she should be amused.

"Well, she's kind of attached, you know? That guy. Her boyfriend."

"Oh," she said. "So is this kind of, a date sort of thing."

"It could be." He grinned. "Doesn't have to be. Just a party, a good time, you know? You don't have to stick with me, or anything like that, unless you want to. Just come along. Have some fun, eh? It's Friday."

All her restlessness gathered inside her. She heard herself say, "What the heck. Sure, I'll go." She did feel an itch to get out, to do something . . . something different for a change. Let go a little. But just a little.

"All right!" His face lit up with excitement.

"I've gotta put my shoes on, get my coat. You going right away?"

"We'll wait for you. We'll be hanging at the bottom of the stairs. I'll go tell everybody," he said, and left, smiling wide, with a skip in his step.

Walking alone in Central City at night could be dangerous, in spite of computerized surveillance in public areas. She would be in a group, but still, there might be danger. Murder, theft, and outright rape were illegal, of course, even if many of the things that tended to cause them were not. One of the first things Alyssa had purchased on arriving at college was a small pocketknife, a switchblade that was short, sharp and ready to defend her in an instant. She took a weaponry class that first summer and learned how to use it, should she ever have to.

She carried it on the rare occasions when she went out alone. Her off-campus travels were usually limited to the café, the grocery store, the movie theater and sometimes the mall, and she almost always had Debra with her then. She had never used the blade, but she put it in her pocket anyway, before leaving. She fingered it in her pocket as she went down the apartment stairs, careful not to press the button, slightly apprehensive about what she would find ahead of her.

It was a convivial group as it turned out, and they welcomed her energetically. She knew most of their names, or at least their faces, from passing on the stairs or crossing paths in the common laundry room.

They walked briskly among the looming skyscrapers that twinkled their cold lights high into the clouds of smog. The streets were acrid with the stench of garbage, fuel and the smoke of many factories. She didn't know where they were going, but as the conversation around her continued, she got a clearer idea of where the group was headed.

"Hey, you remember Joe last week?" Ciara said. "What a riot!"

They all laughed. Joe had been taken away by Security after appearing in the courtyard stark naked with a loaded gun.

"What was he on?" Brent asked.

"Acid," Ciara said. "He was dead sure aliens were coming to get him!"

"Lucky he didn't hurt anybody," Alyssa said.

"Ah, Joe's harmless," Manuel said.

"What you getting tonight?" Gilly asked.

"Oh, the usual," Ciara said. "Good old crystal meth and some of that heavenly Thrill Ride."

"I'm gonna get some Thrill Ride for you, babe," Brent said to Donna. They were holding hands. "For both of us."

Donna laughed. Alyssa didn't like the sound of it.

"I'm going for something different," Gilly said. "I haven't tried Joy Song yet."

"Oh, that's good stuff," Nick said. "You'll love it."

It seemed the rest of the group agreed.

"And don't forget the tequila," someone else said. "Who's getting the tequila?"

"Are we all pitching in on the joints again or is everybody getting their own?" Manuel asked this.

There was some discussion, almost an argument, over the issue. It took a few minutes to settle it.

So, she thought, *this is the kind of "shopping" Manuel had in mind.* She had assumed something very different.

When the New Constitution was put in place, the word 'drugstore' took on a whole new meaning. This had to be the type of place they were headed. Under the law, a 'pharmacy' was strictly for medicine. A 'drugstore' was a place where recreational drugs and alcohol were sold.

By law they were required to be separate from pharmacies. Gone was the old-fashioned way of drug lords, cartels, shady deals in dark alleys and exorbitant prices for a single "hit."

They made movies, mostly comedies, about that era. Spoofs, making fun of how silly it was when narcotics were illegal. Marijuana was now a lucrative cash crop in southern Texas. Heroin and cocaine were sold hand in hand with cigarettes and liquor. The medicinal benefits of marijuana were advertised on national TV, and companies competed for recognition as the highest quality brand. There was nothing furtive about it now, and anyone over seventeen could buy.

"Gilly, you remember that time you got tanked on speed?" said Dave, another of the guys. "Awesome, you were so awesome."

Gilly laughed, another unpleasant sound to Alyssa. "So, you think I should get speed instead?" She smiled, teasing him.

"I'd like to see you on Joy Song, I think," Dave said.

"It's a shame Marie dropped out," someone else said. "She was great."

"What happened to Marie?" Alyssa asked.

"Oh, she couldn't get off crack cocaine," Manuel said. "Ran out of money to buy off professors for grades too. She had to go home."

Brent said, "She was careless. You gotta know when to say 'when.'"

Donna said, "That reminds me. Brent, while we're there, don't let me forget to get my heroin refills for my IV kit back at home."

"Little bit keeps you going, hey darling?" he said.

The general public looked down on excess and overuse. Rehab and detox centers were never short of patients, but occasional, social drug use was routine, even expected.

"Dave, you did remember to double-check the reservation tonight, didn't you?" Ciara asked.

"Would I forget? As in-demand as the Tiki Room is?" he said. "We're cool. Thanks for pitching in your share early this time, everybody. Helped a lot."

"Was I supposed to pitch in some money?" Alyssa asked Manuel, walking beside her.

"No way, not this time," he said, smiling. "Your first time in the Tiki Room's on me."

As the conversation turned to the "Tiki Room," Alyssa grew more and more alarmed. She had never heard of the place, though they were obviously all familiar with it. It was located deep in the local red-light district, apparently a hot spot for group parties . . . the kind she had only vaguely heard of, and was horrified to think of joining. Being near people on drugs was one thing, but the kind of casual group sex they were talking about was not, *definitely* not, something she wanted to watch, not to mention participate in.

Manuel must have picked up on her growing discomfort. He whispered to her, "Hey, like I said, you won't have to join in anything you don't want to. Don't worry. It'll be fun, even if you're just hanging out. Okay? Cool?"

She nodded her head, and said, "Thanks. I'll remember that." She would have to find a way to back out.

The buildings were endless, and her apprehension grew as the talk went on around her, becoming more explicit and vulgar with each block. The air seemed charged with some kind of sexual energy, a delirious anticipation, once the conversation turned to the subject. It became evident this group was anxious to reach their destination for the evening, and Manuel was no exception.

After about twenty minutes, she found herself looking in the window of a brightly lit liquor and drug store while the others went inside.

"Come on," Manuel said. "What're you getting?"

"I haven't decided yet," she said, trying to sound noncommittal.

"I can help you pick," he said. "There's plenty to help you unwind."

She was certain "unwinding" was not what she wanted. She felt uneasy even walking inside, but she was anxious to hide her inexperience. She had never been in such a place before, and always assumed they would be filthy somehow, with cockroaches creeping furtively about the shelves.

Instead, the store was bright and clean, with colorful displays of small bright boxes proclaiming their redeeming benefits and advantages over other brands. The talk was lively. It was like watching children set loose in the proverbial candy store, pockets full of loose change.

Manuel made several suggestions for her, and so did Dave, Nick, and Brent individually. They nudged Manuel and whispered in his ear, something she didn't quite catch, but she got the idea they were negotiating with him for their "turn," once they got her safely to the Tiki Room and properly intoxicated. It made her sick. She pretended to look over the packages in the aphrodisiac aisle they pointed her to with interest, but volunteered few questions of her own.

Ciara, Gilly, and the other two girls filled up small baskets of little boxes, giggling and laughing and talking about the benefits of the different products and brands they were buying. Nick and Brent went to the refrigerator case and chose the alcohol.

Dave came up to her and whispered in her ear, something about his prowess and endowments being of far higher quality than Manuel's, and brushed his hand against her shoulder.

She forced a smile and said, "I'm sure you think so."

"I know so," he said.

"Well," she said. "I suppose you might."

"Hope you're a lot looser once you're loaded," he said, laughing.

"That's for me to know," she said.

She cleared her throat and moved off quickly to another aisle. Soon the group was paying for their purchases at the counter. She made a plan, to stay here in the store until they were long gone, then disappear back home, alone. She felt more than a little stupid for agreeing to come, and had no idea how to back out of her situation gracefully yet retain a degree of dignity. All she knew was that she absolutely could not continue with them past this point.

Manuel was last out the door. "Haven't you found what you want?" he asked. "You're worse than my sister. I thought *she* took forever."

"I'm still deciding whether I want the Joy Song, the Thrill, or something else," she said, holding up a couple of boxes. "Don't worry about me. You go on ahead, and I'll catch up."

"You know the way all right?" he asked.

"Sure," she said. "Who doesn't? I'll be right behind you."

"Don't you want me to wait for you?"

That would certainly ruin her meager plan. "No," she said, trying to sound casual. "I think I'll be a few minutes still. I don't want to forget anything." She made herself smile. "Go on," she said. "I wouldn't miss it. Sounds like a great time."

"All right, then. Make sure you tell them at the door, you're with Dave's party," he said, and went out the door as she sighed her relief.

She was the only customer left.

"So, what's your pleasure?" the druggist asked, after a minute. "You're not like them. I can tell."

She looked at him. He was slightly taller than her, and solidly built, with longish brown hair that curled around the nape of his neck and brown eyes. He was not unattractive, she thought, then realized it wasn't like her to sum up a man like that. Then, it wasn't like her to be in a place like this, either.

"What do you mean?" she said, clearing her throat.

"Anything in particular you're looking for? Seems like you're having a hard time finding exactly the right thing. Can I help you?"

She shook her head. "I don't know."

She did more casual wandering down the aisles, wishing he wouldn't talk to her. She just wanted to bide her time until the group moved far enough ahead. She didn't dare go look out the window for them. Not yet.

"We carry everything, all licensed brands," he said, and cleared his throat. "And a few *unlicensed* ones . . . We keep those in a safe room in the back, but I can show you, if you're looking for one of those."

"Oh. Well, is there anything in particular *you* prefer?" she asked. "What would you recommend?"

"Employees have to be drug-free. Company policy." He grinned.

Alyssa smiled back. She didn't feel a threat, but she kept her hand on the knife in her pocket, fidgeting with it just in case.

"That's a pretty stupid policy, don't you think? You can't recommend anything that way."

He laughed. "Can't have the employees stealing them blind. That wouldn't be wise either, now would it."

"Oh, I guess not." She tried to laugh back.

She felt odd, with him watching her every step. But it wasn't the look of a storeowner watching for theft. It was the look of a man at a woman. Whenever she looked up, there were his warm brown eyes again, meeting hers. Oddly, instead of feeling her defenses shoot up, on guard, all her nerves bristling, she felt soft and strange inside. Warm.

"You're not going to the Tiki Room with them, are you?" he said.

He had a mellow, smooth voice. It seemed to vibrate through her like a pleasant electrical current. She shook off the feeling, with an effort. Maybe the group's energy, their conversation and excitement, had rubbed off on her somehow. She couldn't explain it.

"Excuse me?"

"You're not going with them, are you?"

"Is that any of your business?" she asked. She had been so distracted by the *sound* of his voice that his words took a moment to register.

"This your first time?" He leaned on the counter, his chin on his hands.

"I don't think that's any of your business, either," she said. *Did it show?* She didn't want to appear a novice. That seemed, somehow, embarrassing.

"Sure it is," he said. "Look, I can find you something gentle. Make sure you don't go off with something too harsh on your system. That's part of my job. Plus we offer a 15% discount to first-time users."

"I wouldn't worry about that," she said.

"You didn't like those other guys' recommendations," he said. "If you were going, you'd have taken them up on it. They knew the best stuff."

"Oh, they did?"

"And you didn't. Therefore I conclude you are 'A' not going with them, and 'B' more likely than not a first-timer. I'll bet you're just waiting around until they're gone, then you'll go home, or somewhere else, but not with them."

She felt transparent, and she didn't like it. "Oh, please." She rolled her eyes. "You think you're so smart, do you?"

He chuckled. "Just observant. I call 'em like I see 'em."

"Look, I just don't want to end up doing anything too weird this time," she said, trying to create a cover story. She didn't want him to know he had guessed correctly. "I don't know them very well yet."

As she said it she thought of how an uncontrolled drug-induced display would humiliate her. It was one thing when Joe from the football team wandered outside naked in the snow and thought he was hunting aliens; it would be another if *she* was the one that had security called on her. Then there were the guys, never in short supply, who made it plain what they'd like to do with her if they ever managed to get her alone and willing. She didn't need to give them a chance. Was that why Manuel had invited her along in the first place? He certainly hadn't made it *sound* like an outing for drugs and uninhibited sex. She wrinkled her nose unconsciously. Of course, it may not have been an intentional deception. He may have assumed she knew what he meant by "a party."

The druggist laughed again. "Then what'd you come with them for?"

The question brought her back to the present moment. "I could manage the Tiki Room without any help from this stuff," she said, indicating the products surrounding her.

He laughed outright. "Now I *know* you've never been there. You couldn't. And nobody does."

"What? Are drugs a prerequisite for getting in now?"

He was still smiling. "Not exactly. But trust me. You could never keep up without some sort of enhancement. You'd need to be stoked on a huge dose of ginseng and kava kava root, at the very least."

She sensed that her game was up. Her voice softened, dropping its defensive edge. "I guess I came because I wanted to feel, I don't know, better. I just want it all to, you know, go away for a while."

She turned away. Why was she explaining this to a total stranger? She wasn't even comfortable mentioning it to Deb, her restlessness, the intensity of her loneliness. How could she tell anyone that this awful *something* inside her was so painful she could hardly stand to live with it; that if it didn't ease up, she wasn't sure she wanted to go on living?

"But you're right, I don't think the Tiki Room is the answer," she said softly.

"I, for one, would hope not," he said.

As she stood there fingering the brightly colored boxes, meandering through the aisles, she began to wonder if the answer was *here* after all. Could any of these things make the pain go away? At least for a little while? She started to read the packages more carefully. Debra was away for the weekend. If she took something back to her apartment and locked her doors, no one would ever know if she made a fool of herself.

Her curiosity was piqued. She looked through the aisles, trying to remember what she knew about the few she had heard about.

Just once, she thought. *Maybe just once wouldn't hurt me, and maybe I could feel a little better.*

She looked . . . Heroin, no. Too strong, and she didn't like needles. Beer, wine, vodka: definitely not. Too many memories of her father sitting in his chair. Besides, it would take more than a drunken stupor to ease the pain she felt. Marijuana? Probably not strong enough either.

She found a section of products labeled "mood enhancers" and looked through them with greater interest. *One of these, maybe . . .*

The druggist let her look for a while, without saying more.

"What about this one?" she asked finally, picking up a plain white box with black printing. It looked overly ordinary.

He came out from behind the counter toward her.

"No," he said. "No, you don't want that one." He reached out for the box and she pulled it away from him.

"Why not?" she asked. "What's wrong with it?"

He dropped his hand to his side. "It's experimental."

"Is it addictive? I don't want anything addictive."

"Hard to say. Like I said, it's experimental. *Very* experimental. Look, please, if you've never done anything before, you don't want to start out with something that heavy. Marijuana's a lot better for a first try. Please. It's good stuff. We have seven of the major brands and three gourmet varieties, including one imported from Europe."

He tried to hand her a different package. She ignored it.

"I never said I was a beginner," she said, still determined to maintain her dignity. "Just tell me, what does this one do?"

She peered at the fine print on the box for a list of ingredients. They made no sense to her. She didn't recognize any of the chemical names.

"It's called Elation. It's the trade name for something unpronounceable. It's got LSD, and part of it is that chemical they discovered that triggers the near-death experience in the brain. There's some other stuff thrown in too. It's not here for recreational purposes at all." He paused. "Look, I shouldn't tell you this and I could get myself fired or worse, but some of the drugs in here aren't entirely for fun, okay? Some of them are plants for government research. They're trying to find out if the brain has latent capabilities that can be brought out by these drugs. Personally I think it's a crock. But what it does mean is some of them are terribly dangerous."

"That still doesn't tell me what it does," Alyssa said stubbornly. She held the box tightly. "What's it like?" All she knew was that it wasn't among the ones the others had talked about or bought.

"I don't know," he said. He opened and closed his fists nervously. "Please, put it down. It could kill you."

"How?"

"It's totally unpredictable. Sometimes it simulates death." He looked at her intently. "Sometimes people don't come back."

"Death, huh? Is it painful?" she asked, raising an eyebrow.

He gave an exasperated sigh. "You are way more impossible than I gave you credit for when you walked in here," he said. "How should I know? Probably, yes. Excruciatingly painful. Agony. Will you put that down? Please?"

They stared at each other. Alyssa considered the impact of what he was telling her. But if she was anything, she was stubborn. His nervousness piqued her curiosity even more. What did it matter to him anyway? She examined his expression, looking for meaning. She noticed he had long eyelashes and smooth skin, a well-shaped mouth . . . but with effort, she pushed those thoughts away.

"Why do you care?" she asked. "You've never seen me before."

He dropped his eyes. "Sorry. It's just that you're not like everybody else who comes in here. I can tell. I don't want you to hurt yourself." Looking up again, he said, "Look, please let me get you something else. Marijuana's what I recommend for a first try. Gives a good buzz. Takes the edge off whatever it is that's bothering you."

"If I just wanted to take the edge off, I'd grab a beer, like my . . ." She looked away, angry that she almost spilled herself to a total stranger, and angrier still to realize she was befuddled by the fact that he was actually quite attractive. It interfered with her usual feeling of control.

"Please," he said. "If you'll put that down, I'll buy you the pot myself."

"You still haven't told me exactly what it *does*," she said.

"That's because I don't exactly know," he said. "Something like an acid trip, only worse. It can be very good *or* very bad. All I know is it's not dependable."

She couldn't quite remember what she'd heard about acid trips, except for Joe's experience the group had recounted on the way over.

"So?" she said.

"This is extremely touchy stuff," he said.

"I'll be careful. How much?"

"You can't take more than one at a time or it'll kill you for sure. I do know that much."

"No, I mean, how much does it cost?" She took out her ID card.

"Six hundred. Each."

"Okay, so how many are in here?" she asked, unfazed, reading the box again.

"Tell you what. Would you do me a favor?"

She arched her eyebrow at him, hoping she looked stern.

"Please just buy one at a time. In fact, it's illegal to buy more than four at once."

She sighed. "All right." She handed him her card.

He reached for the box and she let him take it from her. He opened it and took out one of the small plastic wrapped pills. He took her card, handed her the tiny packet, and went up to the register to complete the transaction. He swiped the card, then looked at the screen. A flicker of expression came across his face, then vanished. He cleared his throat.

"I'll need your palm print too," he said.

"Why?"

"Gotta make sure you're seventeen. Controlled substance for minors," he said, grinning.

"Oh, please," she said. "I do not look that young."

"Rules," he said still grinning, and shrugged.

She gave an exasperated sigh and placed her right palm down on the electronic pad. It returned a beep.

"There, see?" she said. "I'm legal. Now you can download my whole bio. Right?"

"Really. Would I do that?" he said, keeping up the banter.

"I don't know," she said. "Do you want to?"

"I'll keep this box right here, just for you," he said, ignoring the question, and put it under the counter. Then he returned her card. He smiled again, but seemed more nervous. "At least then I'll know you're still around. Alive, I mean. I work most nights, but if you come in when I'm not here they might not know what you're talking about. Try to make sure it's me you talk to, would you?"

"You work on commission or something?"

"Uh, something like that."

"Is that box going to be okay under there?" she asked. "Don't go getting yourself in trouble for my sake. You don't even know me."

"Oh yeah. It's fine. You're the only one buying this stuff."

"With your sales pitch, I'm not surprised." She smiled.

"I usually don't have to say anything. It can't guarantee a good high for the price. People like guarantees."

She turned to go. "Any idea how long this lasts?"

"Anywhere from four to eight hours. It can paralyze you while you're on it but you won't know that. You could come out of it pretty stiff and sore but usually the paralysis isn't permanent. At least, that's what I've heard." He fidgeted with the buttons on his keyboard.

"Have you heard anything else?"

"Will it change your mind?"

She considered. "No."

He didn't look up. He seemed young at that moment. She thought he was probably not too many years older than she.

"I've been told it's like traveling to another dimension. It's supposed to feel awesome but it backfires unpredictably. That's from the LSD in it. You won't know what's happening around you once it kicks in. And if you take stimulants to counter that effect, it doesn't work and it can cause permanent brain damage. Don't drink any alcohol with it at *all*. And don't . . ."

"If I cared so much, I wouldn't be buying it," she said dryly. "I'll be back if I need it again sometime."

"Would you come back even if you don't? So I know you're still here?"

"Why is it so important to you?"

"You remind me of my sister," he said in a low voice. Looking away, he added more softly, "She wasn't so lucky."

"She took this?" she asked, motioning with the little packet.

"Nah, not that," he said, looking back toward her.

"Well, I'm sorry."

Why, when none of the men in the apartments or her classes made any impression on her, did his looks and manner appeal to her? It made no sense.

"I'll come back," she said. She wanted to, even if just to talk to him again, hear that mellow voice. It would be worth the trip.

"I hope so," he said, then cleared his throat. "I mean, you're far too beautiful and young to die."

She flushed red in spite of herself. He said it so tenderly, as though he meant it. It gave her a fluttery feeling inside that she was completely unfamiliar with. Well, not completely, perhaps. The thought unnerved her, and it made her angry that she had blushed.

"Yeah. Well. I'm sure you say that to everyone who comes in here," she said, and left before he could say anything else.

He seemed so different from the guys in her apartment complex. Why hadn't she brushed him off like the rest of them? Why had it been so hard? He must have caught her off guard. That was all.

On the way home she wondered if he really needed the palmprint, or if he was just trying to find out who she was. She smiled mischievously. When she first got to school, she had encoded her ID card to validate transactions without the viewer or cashier seeing her name. She was sure that was the flicker that crossed his face. It was almost consternation, she thought. Her ID also had an encoded signal that deleted her account number after the transaction was complete, so it was nearly untraceable.

She usually just bought groceries and household things, so there was no real need for so much privacy. But she didn't want Joan, or her father for that matter, to check on how she spent her money, then fuss at her about it. Mostly she had encoded the card because she could. She was a skillful hacker and enjoyed having fun with her talent.

That was why she made the comment about downloading her bio. She knew he would try. If it wasn't already on his mind, it would be now. Her smile grew broader. She had taken care of that long ago, also. She liked her privacy, so she had encoded her bio on the government mainframe making it virtually untouchable by anyone who didn't have her private series of access codes. Her palmprint had to be registered and on file by law, so she had made sure strangers could only access the most basic information; her birth date, place of birth and sex. No name or account numbers would show up. Any such request would summon a menu demanding an absurd number of passwords protected by algorithms even her math professors couldn't solve.

She never thought it would come in handy, until now. It was just for fun, but she didn't like the idea that anybody could get her palmprint and download all kinds of information about her. She doubted that even the government could break her coding, not that they would have any reason to try. She was just one puny citizen who never did anything to call attention to herself, so it would likely never be looked at anyway.

Wouldn't he be surprised when he still couldn't find anything on her, even with her palmprint. He'd have to be a far better programmer than she was to override the passwords and booby traps she had encoded into her files. That was highly unlikely. She laughed silently to herself.

When she got back to her apartment, she locked her door, then double-checked the lock moments later. In her room, she took the pill out of her pocket and placed it on her desk. She looked at it under the fluorescent study light, and paced her room, rubbing her hands together until they were sweaty.

She ran her hands through her hair. She was beginning to sweat all over even though it was February and she hadn't turned the heat up when she came in. The evening was nice out, but it was still cold.

Well, she didn't *have* to take the thing. She had gotten back home safely. Wasn't that enough? To know she was safe at home, and not demeaning herself in some Tiki Room with total strangers?

She felt a thrill of anticipation, the exhilaration of risk. This little white pill could kill her. She might not come back once she tried it, and there could be other side effects.

The thought should have frightened her away. Instead, it was somehow appealing. Was it curiosity that beckoned her, or something else, something about the way she'd been feeling since her father died? She didn't know, but if she didn't come back from wherever this took her, she didn't really care. There just wasn't anything in her life that was worth putting up with the pain she felt.

Deb would miss her, certainly, but she was strong enough to deal with the loss. She had Jonathan and her family. She would move on. Joan would probably be glad she was gone. Her father couldn't possibly care anymore. He was dead.

And what about Peter? She felt a rush of anger at the thought. He hadn't even cared to wait until she was free. He had gone and attached himself to the next available female as soon as he could. *My feelings for you haven't changed*, he wrote in his letter. Ha! He wasn't there when she called for him. He promised, but he wasn't there.

No. He was no longer a possibility, no longer someone who could be part of her life. She could only guess how she would feel, as someone's wife, if a former . . . *what? what was I to him? A former love?* . . . if a former love showed up and tried to edge her way in, even if only as a friend. She wouldn't like it in the least.

So did it matter? No one cared if she lived or died. It was easy to believe. Once she thought about it long enough, she became convinced. Life would go on without her on its stage, and probably without knowing she had been there at all.

Most likely, she would still be around in the morning, and with luck, none the worse for it. So what could it hurt? If it killed her, she'd be written up as an accidental overdose . . . and her pain would be over. That in itself was a positive benefit. And if not? Well, her doors were locked tight, Debra was away, and no one had to know what she did over the weekend. No one was there to look over her shoulder, tell her what to do. Or not to do.

Then again, she thought, she could just flush it down the toilet. Or save it. Or even take it back. Was it refundable? She had forgotten to ask. It didn't matter. She had wasted more than that at one time before. It was only money.

Maybe the best choice was to save it, but what better time was there than right now? And if she saved it, who knew but what Debra would find it. Then she was sure there would be a fight. No, that would be no good. If she was going to try it at all, tonight was the night to do it.

Her curiosity over its effects was insatiable. She took it out of the tiny clear plastic wrapper, put it down on her desk, and looked at it for a while. She wandered around the apartment, trying to avoid the choice in front of her. The little pill seemed to call to her, like the strange foods from Alice in Wonderland with little labels on them, saying *"eat me."*

Finally, she came to a decision. Grabbing the pill, she gulped it down with a drink of water before she could change her mind again. Then she sat on her bed and waited.

The thought occurred to her that she should try to vomit it back up and give up on the whole idea. A tendril of fear reached toward her as she wondered what she had done. She stood up with the intention of heading for the toilet, but her body began to quiver. Quickly she lay back down on her bed, unable to stand.

It was an indescribable rush, a surge of pure emotion. She had absolutely no control over it. She tried, and felt anger rise at her failure. Then she found she didn't care. It was like dreaming, only more powerful, more vivid, more *real*.

Suddenly she was in the dark, a vivid purple darkness, spinning like an ice skater caught in an endless twirl. A hideous deep violet monster appeared above her and she felt fear. No, the monster *was* fear. It opened its mouth, gaping terrible black rows of teeth before her, and she screamed and screamed again. She was dizzy from the spin when the fear-monster swallowed her up in its giant maw. Then she became the monster, roaring, gnashing her ugly black teeth against the darkness, twisting, shrieking, frightened, terrified of herself and the horrible blackness she had become.

Suddenly she passed some kind of portal and was herself again, swimming in a sea, a blood red sea. The sea was pain. She thrashed in its murky waters and wept convulsively, as she had never done before. How long she wept that way she didn't know. She dodged sharks and spinning knives, odd fish of the kind that live in the bottom of the deepest oceans, emitting eerie light. Finally, she found herself floating in a direction that must have been the sea's surface. She swam toward it.

Again the scene changed. She broke the surface of the sea and leaped out, flying through a yellow-green sky to the sun, a sun of radiant light. On she flew, breaking the atmosphere, coursing through the blackness of space, soaring to the distant white hot globe. Like a moth, uncontrollably, she flew toward it, not caring if it burned her into ashes. She approached at an impossible speed, feeling she had crossed vast distances in mere seconds. A thrill of euphoria consumed her.

When she reached the gaseous sphere, she plunged in headlong, doing a somersault with all the grace of a professional diver, a splash-free, perfect score. And she wasn't burned in the least. Inside the sun was joy! Intense, giddy, ecstatic joy! She didn't know that such intense feelings existed. Swimming inside the gases of the immense star, she didn't want to leave, ever.

Selfishness consumed her. She didn't want anyone else to enter and share this great joy with her. Immediately the joy vanished and she became the star. She felt magnificent, powerful, huge. She had never felt so big and so important. But something else was happening to her. She was hot, too hot. There was pressure, excruciating pressure. She screamed as she exploded into a flaming supernova.

Now she was disjointed, flying particles scattered in space. She gathered herself together, how she didn't know, and felt intense relief.

Then another portal, a new scene, appeared before her eyes. All was light, the purest white she had ever seen, and in the light she felt a love so magnificent she couldn't bear it. Here she wanted to stay even more than she had wanted to stay in the star of joy. It was a longing more intense than any she had ever known before.

Then she looked down at herself. She was muddy, stained and filthy.

Her shoes left awful footprints, blood red, all over the pure white background. She was dirty, impure, filthy and filled with shame. She didn't belong in this place. She couldn't stay here, no matter how much she wanted it. She couldn't handle the shame of her own filth.

Turning, she ran with all her strength, flailing her legs and arms and diving gracelessly back into the dark red sea of pain that loomed before her, filled with the most intense guilt and sorrow she had ever felt.

The scenes before her mind began to increase in intensity. She wept, she laughed hysterically, then howled in seething rage. They carried her mercilessly, as a twisting roller coaster carries its helpless passengers from one thrill to the next. She had no idea emotions could feel like this, could *be* this, could be so wonderful, so terrible, so overwhelming, all at once. She felt like a living kaleidoscope, twisting through space, her mind reaching into new galaxies of sensation.

Her body convulsed on the bed. Her entire frame shook. Her eyes rolled up, open but seeing nothing, darting about wildly as they might during a dream. Her voice made only a quiet whimper of protest.

****

When she awoke the next morning she lay twisted on the floor, her head throbbing. She looked at the clock. It was noon. She straightened herself, and sat up.

Why was she on the floor? She had been asleep, but before she went to sleep . . . Oh. Her brain felt like it was trying to shred itself from the inside out. She stood, shaking as with a fever.

She remembered most of the experience, clearly now. The awesome power of it frightened her. But something inside felt better after the violent rampage of emotions, the screams, the weeping, the fierce rage. She felt calmer. The pain had diminished to a degree she could tolerate. She took a deep breath and released it. The sun shone through her window, and she reached to open the curtain.

Had she screamed and laughed as loudly as she thought she did? It would be mortally embarrassing if the neighbors had heard. A lot of them would have been out all night. Still, after abandoning the group from last night, she hardly needed rumors to start circulating.

No, she realized. It was unlikely anyone had heard. Security would have come to quiet her if not to see that nothing was hurting her.

Good. No one would know. She had made a useful discovery. She could use this newfound drug when she felt her cool interior cracking. When Debra was gone anyway. She wouldn't approve if she found

Alyssa this way. That was certain. But aside from the headache, she felt relaxed, almost giddy. It had been such a rush, not at all dangerous.

There was water left in her glass. She found some painkillers for the headache and took them with the rest of the water. She was still sleepy. She reclosed the curtain and got under the covers.

This time, she didn't wake up until the next morning.

Cursing herself, she jumped out of bed. Her body felt mostly normal again but it was ten AM . . . *Sunday*. There was a physics research paper due Tuesday, and she still had to write the final draft. And an exam in engineering, and a calculus exam Wednesday. There wasn't enough time left to do the work. She had planned to spend Saturday at the library; now that day was gone.

She worked feverishly through what remained of the day, berating herself for her stupidity. But there was still Monday. She could go to the library then. It wouldn't make up for the lost time, but at least she felt better. Her emotions weren't as difficult to keep in check as she worked. She was able to concentrate better. If only she hadn't slept so long afterwards, or had that terrible headache, maybe it would have been completely worth it.

Debra returned the next evening. By that time, Alyssa had finished her papers and was poring intently over her engineering text as though nothing out of the ordinary had happened.

Her research paper came back fine. She didn't score quite as high on the two exams as usual, but she chalked it up to the foreshortened amount of time she had to study.

****

Weeks went by. Her mother hadn't called since the day of the funeral, but Alyssa could feel the emotional pressure building up again. She did extra schoolwork, attempting to keep her mind occupied, but the pressure, the ache in her soul, continued to increase in spite of all she did to ignore it. Finally she could ignore it no longer. She needed some relief. It had to go away. It just had to.

She decided to take a walk into Central City again, this time alone and hoping none of her "friends" from the first time she went would shop for their drug supplies at the same time. She told Debra that she had to get some groceries and would be back shortly. Deb was busy studying. The walk would take about as long as the tram to the grocery store. She remembered seeing a convenience store on the way; she would pick up a few things on her way back to keep up appearances.

Furtively, she tucked a plastic grocery bag from their usual store into her purse for the things she would buy later.

It felt so dishonest. She wasn't in the practice of lying to Deb, and it was difficult for her. But lying was better than telling her the truth. Deb wouldn't understand. Worse yet, she would probably try to stop her if she knew. And Alyssa didn't want to be stopped.

The druggist looked at her with obvious relief. "Oh, good. You're still alive. I was worried about you," he said.

"Thanks," she said. "But I think you're weird for caring."

"Bad for business to lose customers that way," he said, and coughed, covering his mouth with his hand. He was hiding a blush, she could tell. Seeing that made her feel warm inside again, which annoyed her.

She took her ID card out of her pocket. "Actually it worked fairly well," she said, handing it to him.

He sighed melodramatically. "So I have to start worrying again?"

"Afraid so."

"How was it? Was it like I heard? You know . . . so I can tell my other customers, since I don't get to try the stuff myself." He leaned over the counter toward her.

"It's a pretty good rush," she said. "Very, um, emotional. Powerful." She blushed slightly, and looked away.

"No chance I could offer you a simple, delightful little aphrodisiac instead?"

"Hardly," she said, suddenly cold as steel. She wondered what had drawn her to him the first time. *Aphrodisiac!* He was just like the other guys after all.

"They're much less expensive."

She cleared her throat and gave him her most icy stare. "Money," she said, "is not an object."

He avoided her eyes and gave her a pill from under the counter. "So will that be all for you today?" he asked with a blink.

"Well, actually I was wondering if you have anything to keep me from sleeping so long after it wears off?" she asked. "I didn't have enough time to study for my exams afterwards, I was so tired. I'm lucky I got decent grades. Not so good as usual, but I did lose a day of study time."

"You *are* an odd sort," he said with a puzzled smile. "No, there isn't anything like that. A simple stimulant might work. Caffeine might do the trick. You'll probably just have to get used to it."

"Will I?" she asked. "Get used to it?"

"Depends," he said. "This is uncharted territory. I told you that."

"Don't worry about me," she said as she went out the door, one hand in her pocket fingering the tiny plastic package.

"I will worry," he said. "And come back, please," he called after her. "I have to know you're all right."

She wondered while she walked home how often she could afford this release and still manage to get through school. She tried to figure the numbers in her head, weighing the high price of the drug against what she needed for tuition and books.

That night she waited impatiently for Debra to go to sleep. When she finally heard her snoring in the next room, she placed the pill on her desk as before and looked at it. Maybe she could save it for a while this time, in case she needed it more later on. She was torn between fear of the horrors she had seen the first time, horrors she knew would intensify as the night wore on, and the need to release the internal tension she felt, the war she waged every second against her underlying emotional pain. But she had so little . . . so little to live for, and the need won out over her doubts.

She made sure to climb in bed and set her alarm this time, loudest setting. She swallowed the tiny white pill and pulled the covers over her head to wait. If she didn't get to class the next day maybe she could explain to Debra she was sick. Then she gasped.

It began.

Chapter 15

Promises

I have serious doubts she's the best choice for Peter. I try not to let it show. I know it bothers him that I think this way. Topaz was so much nicer, more easygoing, but none of us could blame her for not waiting around that long. Not even Peter. When all the missionaries were called home, six months before his mission should have ended, she was already married to John Bryant. He seemed much more troubled about having to come home early than he did about losing her. But he had to come. The religious atmosphere everywhere in the world was too dangerous for open proselyting, and the Prophet and the Apostles said "the times of the Gentiles were fulfilled." Personally, I was glad to see him back, safe and unharmed.

. . . But he can throw himself into relationships so fast, especially this one. He's barely been home, it seems. I've tried to tell him to take his time, but he never pays attention. Maybe this one will work out after all. It's about all I can hope for. He's so anxious to get on with what he calls "life," settling down, having a family of his own, taking over the farm so Phil can retire . . . I'd hate to have to watch his heart break again. It's hard to be so unsure, and so powerless to help.

Beverly Richardson,
personal journal entry

"Wait for me!"

It was the nightmare again. The voice was like an echo in Peter's mind, barely audible as it pierced him to the center of his soul.

"Peter. Peter, wait for me!"

He stood on top of a grassy knoll. The wind whistled around his body, chilling him. He shivered.

Again she called. Yes, it was a woman's voice. "Wait, please!"

Jackie? he wondered. No, that wasn't her voice. Who then?

He was so cold.

He turned to run down the hill, away from the voice. It was eerie and haunting and somehow familiar. But he couldn't run.

"Don't leave me! Please! Wait for me!" she cried.

The sky above him was dark, full of storm clouds. He turned around to face where the voice might come from.

Suddenly Jackie was by his side. She wrapped her arms around his waist and her fingers were like ice. He gasped at her touch.

"Peter, let's go. I don't like it here. It's creepy," she whined.

"Can't you hear her? She might need help," he answered, shifting, wanting to run toward the voice now.

"Forget about her, let's go!" She pulled his arm, jerking him partway down the hill. Her grip was so frozen it burned.

"Peter, wait for me," the voice pleaded, desperate.

"Get me out of here!" Jackie screamed, working herself up into one of her tantrums. "I don't like this place!" Her voice rose with each syllable.

Somehow he wrenched himself free of her. The wind was so fierce he had to yell to be heard. "No! You go on ahead. I'll catch up later."

"I'm not waiting for you, Peter," Jackie said, and turned with her usual melodramatic flair. She flounced down the hill and disappeared.

The dream always ended there. But this time, he didn't wake up.

"Wait for me!" The voice was much closer now. The wind subsided a little. He stared into the murky darkness at the bottom of the knoll.

Far away he could make out a figure, a young girl, about ten, wearing muddy jeans and a torn T-shirt. She waved at him, her wheat-blond hair pulled back in a ponytail.

"Alyssa?" he whispered. "Is that you?"

She smiled at him, the smile he remembered from so many years ago.

"What's the matter?" he asked.

"Wait for me. I'm coming to you," she said.

The light began to fade away into darkness. The wind became louder. "Why?" he shouted. "When?"

"You're the only one left who loves me, Peter." The wind carried her voice to him, eerie and echoing. "Please, wait for me."

He strained to see her in the fast fading light. "But where are you? I tried to find you!" he cried. "I did! I couldn't find you! Where are you?"

"I will come to you." It was a whisper, an echo; he couldn't be sure of the words, they were so faint in his mind, then she vanished from sight.

"Don't go!"

Suddenly he awoke, his body drenched in sweat. He shivered violently under the covers. It was a warm mid-April night, but he was as chilled as the time he got caught in a sudden blizzard bringing the cattle in from pasture.

Sleep fled from him. He turned on his lamp and checked his fingers for frostbite, then shook his head. It was just a dream. *You don't get frostbite in April, idiot.* He stripped off his wet nightshirt and got a clean dry one from his dresser, and hurried back under the covers, shivering until he began to feel warm again.

The images in the dream burned before his eyes. What could it possibly mean? *Wait for me,* she said. Over and over. *Wait for her? Why?* It made no sense.

How old would Alyssa be now?

About nineteen, he thought. *Closer to twenty? . . . A year and a half younger than me.*

His mind was keenly alert. The intensity of the dream jogged his memory, denying further sleep. There was a day the two of them had played on that hill together. Only it had been high summer then; there was no storm, no wind, not a cloud anywhere.

It was the day she fell and broke her leg at Camp Keomah.

Peter remembered running at top speed to get his father, Joan's hysterical tirade when they got back to the picnic site, and finding out much later that she had broken her leg in two places and was in a cast for months. But he had never seen her cry again. Or wear a T-shirt.

His reminiscing taught him nothing. What was she doing in his dreams? Alyssa had vanished from his life years ago. He gave up on his dream of rescuing her after that miserable day wandering her old neighborhood, unable to find her new address. His mother had been right. He had forgotten and moved on. He had heard nothing more from her or of her since . . . His mind must be playing tricks on him, acting out a long-lost fantasy. That was all.

He had thought he found true love with Topaz, and she was a much more recent memory than Alyssa. But it was never deep, certainly not enough for marriage, although that was something he hadn't known before he left. He had been infatuated with her, in love with the idea of marriage, more than with her. He hadn't been that surprised to get her letter saying she was dating John Bryant, and later, to receive the wedding invitation. In a way, her marriage had been a relief. Once he was in China and realized how little he actually missed her . . . yes, his mind was supposed to be on the Lord's work, but still, his true feelings had given him away. Or rather, the lack of them. It simply hadn't hurt that much to lose her.

But the way he loved Jackie, that was different, very different. He was surer of love than he had ever been with Topaz. Soon she would be his wife, and the very thought thrilled his soul. He loved everything about her. No one else could replace her dazzling influence in his life. She was so beautiful, so vivacious, so perfect.

It's just a crazy dream after all, he thought. *Maybe I never quite let Alyssa go.*

He told no one of the nightmares.

****

He had always thought love at first sight was a fantasy, until he met Jackie. It was during a big Valentine's day church dance. She was new. He asked her to dance and didn't let her go all night. They talked on the phone nearly every day afterwards. There were days he was desperate just to see her on the other end of the line, to hear her melodic voice.

She was the most beautiful creature he had ever seen. She had fiery auburn hair and light freckles powdering her pale porcelain skin, offset by deep brown eyes, large and mysterious. He was dazzled. She was spontaneous, unpredictable, undeniably feminine, and he truly loved her. He was absolutely sure of it.

It was rare to find a beautiful woman who held the same high values he did. Many times he had been disappointed.

"So will I get to see you every Sunday from now on? I don't know why I haven't noticed you at church before," he said, flirting as they danced to a slow romantic tune.

"I have a Sunday shift at work that I can't change," she answered.

"Then you need a new job," he said.

She laughed. He fell in love with that sound in an instant. "I wish," she said. "There's nothing else available. I like my job anyway. It's all right."

"Do you get to go to church at all?" he asked her, concern evident on his face.

"Oh, of course," she said without hesitating. "Don't worry about me, I take care of myself," she said, laughing again.

Six weeks after they met, he asked her to marry him. Never before had anything felt so right. She was both surprised and elated to say yes.

Soon after that, arguments began. Her temper, which he had not seen before his proposal, began to flare up frequently. Peter credited it to the stress of engagement. He loved her. He could learn to live with her temper tantrums. And he let her win, most of the time. Things would smooth out after the stress of the wedding was over. She would get better; this was temporary. Weddings were always stressful. Then it would be like their first magical days together.

****

"He's never going to get you that ring, you know."

Gert looked over at Jackie while they stirred their coffee, on break from work. It was a small, bright, but bleak break room, the only décor on the wall being posters describing sanitation procedures, reminders about the necessity of handwashing and a personal products dispenser. The chairs were metal and small, the table a chipped white veneer stained from long use.

She and Gert shared a shift this rotation where they worked for the Public Health Department, administering vaccines, filing endless paperwork and other menial quasi-medical tasks considered beneath the level of the medics and physicians.

"Yes he will," Jackie responded after a pause, putting down her stirrer. "And I knew you were going to say that."

The two shared so many work hours together they knew each other's reactions by heart. Gert had short, jet-black hair, a deep tan and a short wiry frame. She was five years older than Jackie and had been divorced, twice.

"You barely know him. He could be really weird."

"He's not Mark." Mark was Gert's first husband.

"I know, but I'm telling you, you're rushing it."

Gert took a sip of her coffee, still too hot, and winced.

"Look, I know I feel different when I'm around Peter," Jackie said. "I feel so good. It's like nothing I've ever felt before. I can't explain why he wants to marry me, but it's the best offer I'm ever going to get. I'm jumping at the chance and you can't scare me out of it."

Gert sighed. "You don't have to get married, you know. You don't need a man to live."

"They are useful," Jackie grinned.

"What about your blessed vodka?" Gert said. "Does he know? He doesn't drink at all, does he?"

"No way does he know! Days I see him, not a drop. But it's okay, I'll quit by the time the wedding gets here. I'm already slowing down." She took a long swallow from her coffee cup. "He'll never have to know. He thinks I'm as much of a teetotaler as he is," she said. "I've managed to wrap that boy around my little finger. He's flipped. He thinks I'm *perfect*.

Did I tell you that? He says I'm the most beautiful woman alive. He'll do anything I ask him to." She smirked, making no effort to hide her pride in front of Gert.

"We both know he's not giving you *anything*. *You* of all people." Gert said with a wink.

"Shut up," Jackie said, getting up for a refill. She poured it quickly, carrying a packet of sugar back to the table. "I told you he's too straight. He doesn't even kiss me like he means to take it anywhere." She shrugged her shoulders. "Not yet. But he'll come around."

Gert snickered. "Doubtful. He's probably gay."

"I told you, he's not Mark," Jackie retorted.

"Touché." Gert took another sip. "But, you'll never see that ring."

"We picked it out already. That rock is so huge I'll barely be able to lift my hand," she said. "He just wants to wait till my birthday to give it to me. Isn't that romantic?"

"I've seen his kind before. You'll be lucky to get a skinny gold-plated band on your wedding day. Trust me. Then it'll rust in a couple of years and you'll know you've been gypped."

"That's not true! He is too sweet for that!"

Talking to Gert always unsettled her. Jackie chalked it up to Gert's own bad luck with men, but she succeeded in raising doubts in Jackie's mind, pulling at the loose strands of thought she would rather not pick up and be forced to confront. They knew each other too well.

Disturbed, she went on, "I told you how we picked it out, didn't I? Trying on bigger and bigger diamonds and he didn't even gulp once?"

"I've heard your hokey story. 'Oh Peter, oh please can I have this one?'" she mocked, batting her eyes at a fictional figure in the air, then looking squarely across the table at Jackie. "He'll never be able to afford it."

"He put a huge deposit on it, I saw."

"Was it refundable?"

"I don't know." Her uneasiness grew.

"Come your birthday, he'll have some sissy excuse. That's always the way it happens. But you'll go ahead and marry the bozo anyway, because you feel so *nice*, telling yourself it'll get better someday, and meanwhile you're married to a farmer. You! Well, let me tell you something, girl, 'someday' never happens. And you'll never be a good little farm wife, popping out babies, churning butter and milking cows!" Gert laughed wholeheartedly.

"Peter's not like that!" Jackie stood up, pushing her chair away from her. She picked her cup up off the table and went to the small rust-colored sink to rinse it. "I swear, he would never dream of letting me down. And I won't need to milk any cows, either. He's not that backwards, it's not like I'm marrying into a time warp or something. I swear, you can be so stupid. He's going to let me have my own career. He said so."

"I'll believe it when I see it," Gert said, leaning back in her chair and crossing her legs, cup in hand. She sipped at it, obviously amused. "Some illustrious career you've got, anyway."

Jackie finished rinsing her cup, and turned around to face Gert, pointing her finger. "Tell you what. I bet I can have that ring on my finger by tomorrow. I'm seeing Peter tonight. We're going to dinner and then dancing till late." She twirled in her pale green uniform. "I bet I can coax him into giving it to me now. He should only have one or two payments left. Didn't I just say I can get him to do anything?" She smiled. "That ought to prove it to you."

"A hundred dollars says he won't," Gert said.

"A hundred . . .?" Jackie blinked. She put her cup in its place slowly. "Well. He is crazy about me . . . Tell you what. You're on." She went to the door, break over, smiling. "You'll see that ring tomorrow morning."

Gert stood and went to the sink with her cup. "Like I said. I'll believe it when I see it. *If* I see. I think I just made me an easy hundred bucks."

****

Peter picked Jackie up at her apartment. She looked stunning, as always. Her long auburn hair curled softly, gently flowing over her shoulders. She wore a soft rayon spring-flowered dress cut just above the knee, but full-skirted for dancing.

"Jackie, you look incredible," he said.

"As usual," she said, and winked.

He opened the car door for her as he always did.

"You are too much of an old-fashioned gentleman, Peter," she said, getting in.

"And you love it," he said.

She laughed, the light airy sound that he loved.

On the way to the restaurant, she took his hand in hers and said, "Wasn't it tonight we were going to pick up my ring?"

"I told you it would be your birthday present."

"Oh, Peter," she said. "Why not just surprise me tonight?" Her fingers moved to dance across the back of his neck as she spoke. "I hate telling all my friends about you and not having any ring to prove I'm engaged. Some of them don't even believe you exist. When are you going to meet them?"

"It's only two weeks till your birthday. Be patient." He turned to her briefly and smiled, but his knuckles showed white as they clutched the steering wheel in anticipation of a possible mood swing. He could never predict them, and no matter how he tried, he still hadn't figured out how to avoid them.

"Oh, come on, honey, it's not far out of the way. Why don't we go get it right now? Won't it look nice on me at dinner tonight? Please?"

He glanced over to see her smile and cross her legs, effectively raising her skirt a few inches higher on her thigh.

When he didn't answer right away, she said, "By the way, do you like my new dress?"

He glanced over at her. "The colors go nice with your hair," he said, frowning a little. "But I do think it's a bit short." He reached over and patted her knee gingerly, effectively smoothing the skirt back down, then returned his hand to the steering wheel.

"You're so silly about that kind of thing," Jackie said, and crossed her legs the other direction.

"It's not silly, it's careful. We'll be getting married soon enough, sweetheart," Peter said. "You know that as well as I do."

"So are we going to the jeweler's before dinner or after?" she asked.

"Jackie!" Peter said, frustrated. "Look. You know darn well I don't get paid till the end of the month. I wouldn't be so specific if I didn't have to be, but look. I'm flat broke right now. I have enough to take you out tonight, but nowhere near enough to pick up your ring, not until payday. You know that. There's nothing more I'd love to do right now than put that ring on your finger, but it'll have to wait."

"What about your credit? It's good, isn't it? Everyone else in the world makes payments."

"I'm not going to use credit to pay for something I can pay for in cash in a few days. We've talked about this before. It's just a few more days, Jackie."

"But I really want the ring now!" She began to whine as she spoke. "Please, Peter, turn here."

"I can't!"

"The turn is right here! Come on!" Her voice began its familiar elevation in pitch. "Right here!" She pointed anxiously down the street as they passed the intersection. "It won't take more than a minute, and they'll be closed after dinner!" She was becoming hysterical.

"I wish you would calm down," Peter said. He held the steering wheel stiffly, which caused his driving to be somewhat jerky as he changed lanes. A car honked. "I am not going there tonight."

"I *am* calm!" Jackie said anxiously. She turned around in her seat to look longingly back toward the intersection. "You just don't understand me at all. I really need this!" Her expression became increasingly distressed as she watched the intersection disappear behind them. "If you don't get me that ring right now, Peter, I'm not sure I can believe you really love me."

"You'll have it. This is just going to have to be something you wait for." Her words stung. "I do love you, Jackie, more than anything. Please believe me. I want to, but I can't. Why do you have to keep bringing it up? Huh?"

"I'm tired of waiting for you, Peter!" Her voice was almost a wail. "And I don't feel really truly engaged without a ring!"

The previous night's dream bubbled up suddenly and haunted him. *Wait for me, Peter*, Alyssa's small eerie voice echoed in his mind. The recurrent dreams had begun shortly after he proposed, but he didn't know whose voice had been speaking those words . . . not until last night. Jackie's dream voice also echoed in his mind, sharper, more dissonant, selfish: *I'm not waiting for you . . . Peter.*

With an effort he shook the echoes away and came back to the present moment.

Jackie began to sob. "I do wonder if you really love me, Peter," she said. "You can be so mean."

"Mean? I'm not being mean! I would never do anything to hurt you, honey. I've tried to explain this logically. Why don't you understand? I just can't do it, or I would. Of course I love you!" He took an exasperated breath. Why was she so childish? "But you know," he continued, "sometimes I wonder the same thing about you. I think you love getting your own way more than you love me."

"That's not true!" She continued to cry, fumbling through her purse for a tissue. "That hurts, Peter! I just wanted to have my ring, so I could show everybody at work tomorrow, and I'm so tired of trying to explain, and they don't understand, and they think you're no good for not giving me a ring, and . . ." She stopped to blow her nose.

"You will have it. Your birthday is not that far away. Please cheer up, sweetheart." He made a sharp right turn at the restaurant's driveway, almost passing it and barely missing a pickup truck as it left the lot.

The driver honked.

Jackie took a compact out of her purse and looked over her face. "Now you've ruined everything. My mascara's running everywhere. I look perfectly hideous!"

Peter pulled the car into a parking spot, crooked, and slammed the brake. "We're here. And I did not touch your makeup. Please stop blaming me for everything that goes wrong when it's clearly your fault we're having an argument in the first place."

She cried harder and turned away from him. He thrust a hand through his hair in frustration, then placed his other hand on her shoulder.

"Honey," he said, "I didn't mean that. I'm sorry. Come on, let's go in."

"Maybe after I fix this mess," she sobbed. "If you still want to go in there with me. You must hate me. You act like you hate me sometimes."

"I think you still look beautiful," he told her. "I could never, ever hate you. I love you, Jackie."

"No. You couldn't, could you. You're just too nice," she said, adding an empty laugh.

She wouldn't get out of the car until she had returned her face to its perfectly made-up state. Their conversation lapsed into silence while she fussed over it.

They didn't speak again except to order, and then not to each other.

Near the end of the meal, Jackie said, "You know, when we first met things were different. You used to be so wonderful to me, Peter, and now you don't even consider *my* feelings."

"What do you mean, used to?" Peter said, holding his fork in mid-air.

Maybe it was time to get to the bottom of this. He was tired of circling around in the same argument. So far he had tried to ignore her outbursts in the hope they would resolve on their own. Maybe the dreams were getting to him, maybe his patience was just wearing thin, but he felt the need to speak up for himself. It was time he took a stand.

"I take you everywhere and anywhere you want to go, and I pay for absolutely everything. I bring you flowers, all the time. I even hold your purse—makes me feel like an old man sitting outside the dressing room holding his wife's purse while she tries things on! What more do you want?!" He punctuated each sentence with an emphatic wave of his fork.

"Well, you wouldn't take me to the jeweler's," she said. "And you won't even try to understand how much it means to me. All you can talk about is money, like a little money is more important than my deepest feelings."

Peter dropped his fork on his plate. It rang out with a clatter. Several pairs of eyes looked over at their table.

"Jackie!" he whispered. "I thought we finished that discussion!"

His blue eyes burned with an emotion even he didn't understand. He shouldn't be this violently *angry* at someone he cared so much for. Should he? It was so frustrating—so exasperating—to explain the same thing over and over again, and still get nowhere. It was like spinning wheels in a mud hole. He shook his head to clear it away.

Softer, he thought. *Calm down.* "Why are we fighting over this?" he said. "I love you. I'm terribly sorry I can't do it right now. I know it must be hard on you. Can't you understand why we have to wait?"

A few diners around them chuckled. Peter, his angry eyes only on Jackie, paid them no attention.

"I can understand you want to make my life difficult," she said with a pout.

Peter let out an sigh and picked up his fork again. They continued their meal in silence.

"I'm kind of tired," Jackie sighed when they were in the car again. "I don't feel much like dancing tonight after all."

"Me neither," Peter said. "I'll just take you home so you can get your rest. I know you have to get up early tomorrow anyway."

"That'll be fine," she said.

The thirty minute ride to Jackie's apartment was silent also.

"See you Saturday?" Peter asked when he let her out of the car.

"Sure, honey. Two o'clock as usual." She still seemed sad, but less hostile. She gave him a little kiss on the lips. He returned it accompanied by a short but earnest hug. "I'll let myself in," she said.

He watched her climb the two flights of stairs while he leaned on the open passenger door. She waved when she got to her apartment and flipped the lights on from inside. He waved back, shut the car door, got in on the driver's side and started the engine.

Chapter 16

Deception

"Jackie, you are going to church there, aren't you?"

"Sure, Mom. Gosh, when are you going to get off my case?"

"I'm sorry, honey, it's just that . . . Well, your stepfather and I, sometimes we worry about you, after that incident . . ."

"Do you have to bring that up again? When are you going to forget it? Why won't you leave it alone, huh?"

"Jackie, it's just that we worry."

"I told you, I messed up once, okay? Once! And it was a long time ago. Drop it. Please. I'm doing fine, going to church, all that. I've got lots of friends here. And my roommates are great."

"So. Are you seeing anyone?"

"Oh, Mom, you know me. Nobody serious."

exerpt from phone conversation
recorded by Jackie Halladay

Alyssa was high again.

All was black around her, but she could feel others nearby, people, a vast crowd. The last few times she came on this journey she had noticed others around her. Many of them moaned as if in pain. Tonight they were speaking to her.

"Welcome," one voice said soothingly, but it didn't feel soothing. "We're so glad you've come back to us. We missed you."

"We are your friends," another said.

She didn't want to be friends with that *thing*. It wasn't quite . . . human. Though it bore a human sort of shape, it was vile. She didn't know how she knew that, she just did. She pushed away, trying to escape.

"Come with us," a female figure said. She had long gray hair and dark hollow eyes. "We're glad you're here."

"I don't want to come with you," she said. She didn't like this kind of fear. She preferred the deep violet fear-monster that devoured her. This was cold, sheer terror. "What are you going to do to me?"

"Good, good," said a womanly figure with revolting yellowish hair and

183

terrible teeth. "It is good to be afraid." She laughed a hideous, hollow laugh.

Alyssa turned to run, to find a portal she could pass through. Where was the sun? The sun with that awesome joy inside it? It had been so long since she found that.

It was not the same every time. The last few times, since she noticed she was not alone, had become more terrifying and far less ecstatic.

The gray-haired one laughed also. "Yes, that is good. We need your fear. Come."

She reached out her hand and grabbed Alyssa. It was barbed, as though she used a pronged metal trap rather than a hand. Alyssa began to bleed.

"Ouch!"

"Yesss! Yessss! Pain!" The other one licked up the blood with a delighted squeal. "Give us your pain, child, give it to usss."

Alyssa screamed. "Get out of here! I want the sun! Send me to the sun!"

All the creatures surrounding her recoiled at this. She didn't know why. The grip on her hand was released.

"Leave her!" A booming voice echoed in the darkness. "She is not ready! *Fools*!"

Alyssa crouched in what she hoped was a corner and wished this segment would hurry up and be over. A black figure in even blacker robes came forward.

"She has to *want* the pain, you imbeciles. Obey the rules or suffer the punishment!"

The figure struck the two who had accosted her, bowling them away, screeching. The dissonant noise hurt her ears. The black figure was like ink, watery and shifting, fluid in movement, though human in form like the others.

"So sorry," he said, lifting Alyssa's chin with misty fingers. His touch felt like liquid hydrogen flowing through her body. "They shall have to behave more presentably in the future. We are all so pleased you have come again to visit us. Perhaps someday we can help you make your stay here more . . . permanent. When you are ready."

She closed her eyes to the blank darkness of his face, trembling in absolute horror. It was a face, a human sort of face, with the usual features but terrifying to behold. She didn't want to stay there. She wanted to get out.

"I frighten you," he said, and laughed a laugh that was more horrible than anything she had ever heard, even here in the depths of this realm of torture. "Good."

He left, inky black robes flowing behind him, and she melted into the darkness, devoid of any strength, sobbing. No other scene befell her that night, for which she was grateful. Soon she faded into an exhausted sleep.

****

The remaining two weeks until Jackie's birthday passed with little mention of the ring. Jackie appeared to have accepted the delay. But the silences between the two while they were together became longer and more frequent. When they did talk, they discussed necessary things, the wedding plans, who was to call the caterer, the florist, and which photographer would be available, since Jackie's first choice fell through. Nothing substantial. Nothing that might bring up an argument. They both avoided such topics.

They only saw each other twice a week, due to conflicting schedules and the fact that she lived a good thirty-minute drive away from the Richardson's. It had never seemed enough time together before. Now Peter found it too much.

The day arrived for him to pick up the ring at the jeweler's, the last Saturday in April. He had tried to forget the recurrent dreams of Alyssa, but always since that night she had been in the back of his mind, haunting him.

Had he truly loved her? He was only sixteen then. How much can a sixteen year old boy know of love? Every time he brought her up since, his mother had emphasized what a silly, romantic notion it was to look for her. She couldn't have grown up with any values at all. Not according to the terrible things the neighbors had said.

Had she really become a porn star? Why should I wait for a . . . porn star?

It was unreasonable to think she would have found the Church, and therefore repentance, or to think he could convert her if he did find her. The world she grew up in was vastly different from his. The type of woman she was sure to have become would never match the illusion that remained in his memory. He knew his mother was right, and he had accepted it. Or he thought he had. He stopped talking or asking about her before his mission, before Topaz, but partly it had been because he was tired of hearing the lecture.

Alyssa had been wonderful, spunky and tough as well as fun. He never had to guess at what she was thinking like some kind of mind reader, or try to impress her with presents and flowers, or use tender words that didn't express what he honestly felt. None of the girls he had dated since were even remotely like her, though he had to admit they often had some physical resemblance.

Secretly he cursed himself. It was wrong to think about another woman while picking up his bride's engagement ring. And a woman who only existed in his memory at that. Jackie had anxiously awaited this day, her birthday, the day he had promised to give it to her. He could hardly wait to see the look on her face when she saw it, when he placed it delicately on her finger.

Besides, Alyssa could never be the same now as she was then. He sighed. What fourteen-year old tomboy needs flowers or romance? Even if she had never left, if this ring was for her and not for Jackie, who could know that things would be any different? And every couple fights. He had seen his parents argue and resolve differences hundreds of times. He knew it didn't mean they weren't in love. They were still very happy together, after twenty-five years.

The arguments must be from the stress, he thought again. *At the heart of things, we really are in love.* It was true love; he was certain of it. He knew how he felt when he decided to propose. He had never been so sure of anything in his life. By comparison, proposing to Topaz had been silly and ill-timed. This was completely different.

At the car, he opened the ring box. The one-carat solitaire glittered and flashed in the sun. It was a flawless cut, and a rainbow of color flashed from it in every direction.

A cloud passed in front of the sun and the light disappeared from the diamond. Suddenly it looked like nothing more than a frozen crystal, an ice chip. It felt cold in his hand.

So cold. Frozen. He shuddered involuntarily.

It must be the jitters everyone talks about, he told himself. He closed the box carefully and pocketed it. *My nerves are playing tricks on me. Jackie and I love each other.*

It felt like a piece of lead in his pocket.

****

"Look how beautifully it shines, Peter," Jackie said.

The weather was warm and wonderful. Jackie stood under a lamppost in the park where they walked, holding out her hand to the light. She was in unusually high spirits, and had been ever since he had picked her up at her apartment, before they went to dinner. He had given her the little box over dessert.

Peter admired it with her, holding her left hand tenderly. "Looks like it's shining just for you," he said.

"Oh, you," she said. "Stop it." She smiled and took his hand. "Let's keep walking," she said.

The heady smells of the green and flowering trees filled Peter's head and made him feel . . . something. Happy. Relaxed. Deeply in love. There were no voices echoing tonight.

Soon they came to a place on the walking path where it was darker. The moon wasn't yet up, and the lamplight was far away. The air filled with the humming song of crickets. The gurgling sound of the little brook that ran through the park was their orchestra. They paused, and Jackie leaned against the trunk of a large tree.

"It's beautiful tonight," Peter said. "And so are you."

Jackie smiled and reached up to kiss him. He put his arms around her waist and returned her kiss. Their kisses were always innocent, sweet. But this was different. This time her touch wasn't soft and tender. It burned with a desire both passionate and urgent. She placed her hands around his neck, pressing his lips to hers more forcefully, opening her mouth to his, pulling her body in tightly against him.

He felt the powerful rush of hormones and his mind raced. *Why is she starting this? Now?* he thought. It wasn't gentle, inspiring, as before, but designed to kindle a raging fire. Where did she learn to kiss like this?

He had always been careful to avoid igniting the fire of easy passion. Always cautious not to take things too far, he had never kissed this way before. It involved a level of passion he intended to reserve for marriage. The ease with which she went there now suggested it came out of practice and experience.

He pushed her away, reeling from the shock.

"Jackie," he said, "what do you think you're doing?"

She took no notice of the rejection. There was a look in her eyes he hadn't seen before. He had seen it in others, other places, other couples' eyes. It was the intoxication of desire.

Leaning up to him, she whispered in his ear. "We're *alone*, Peter." Her voice was deep and husky. "No one's going to see anything here. Relax. If you'd rather, you could come home with me tonight." Her voice beckoned, promising immediate fulfillment of long-harbored desires. "You could stay over. My roommates all went home for the weekend."

She kissed his neck, fingering his earlobe. Her other hand moved slowly down his back, lower than he was used to. He twisted between holding onto restraint and responding to his body's passionate urge to give in to her touch, to encourage her forward, to reciprocate. His stomach went into knots.

"We'll be totally alone there, if you're nervous about someone coming down the path," she said again.

Again he pushed her away from him, this time holding her shoulders in his hands, arms fully extended. He was tempted by her words far more than he cared to admit. Her touch drove him crazy with desire. But the timing was all wrong. He wanted his angel before marriage. Only afterward could he hope she would play the part of the harlot, but just for him. At the moment he held the wrong one in his arms and the shock took the breath right out of his lungs.

He gave her a gentle shake. "Jackie, what's gotten into you? Why?"

The trance was broken. A new fire took light in her eyes, the more familiar fire of anger.

"Why not?" she asked. "Don't you even *want* me?" Her voice cracked as she expressed the pain of his rejection. "Don't you *feel* anything? Are you made of stone or something? What is it with you?"

"That's not it. Of course I feel something. Believe me, I do. I do want you . . . very badly. But it's wrong now, Jackie. Not before the wedding. I shouldn't have to explain that to you. You know that as well as I do," Peter said. "Don't you?"

He pleaded with her, his eyes begging her to understand, his heart on fire, his mind appalled, unwilling to accept the reality of her blatant proposition. But he couldn't escape the thought. *This can't be the first time she's tried this with someone.* It made him sick to his stomach. The crickets continued their joyful song and he wished they would stop.

She laughed halfheartedly, not the same laugh he was used to hearing, and tossed her long curly hair back over her shoulders, then reached up and plucked his hands off her shoulders, holding his hands in hers.

"Don't tell me," she said, swinging their hands together as she spoke coyly, "Don't tell me you actually believe all that nonsense they teach us about a little pleasure being so wrong, especially when it's between two people who really love each other? I *love* you, Peter." She swung her arms behind her back, wrapping his hands low behind her waist, and reached up to kiss him again.

He broke off the kiss, wrenching himself free. "Yes, Jackie! I do believe it! And it's not nonsense!"

He turned and headed in the direction of the car.

"Peter, how stupid can you be?" she called, trying to catch up with him. "Nobody will ever know if we do anything! Why can't you . . ."

"*I* would know!" he shouted, turning back to face her. "*You* would know. And *God* would know. That's three too many people right there!"

Turning, he kept moving, aware his argument sounded stupid and that it might not be the right thing to say, but he was too upset to find better words.

Finally she caught up to him and kept pace, not reaching out to him. She was silent.

"What I want to know is," he said after a long pause, not slowing his pace, "Is why have you kept this from me? I was positive we felt the same way about this. I've tried so hard not to even think about doing anything physical with you, to make sure I did nothing to damage your innocence, or mine, before our wedding night. Well, some innocence you've got, after all!"

He looked over at her profile as they walked. The pain and hurt in his eyes must have been obvious. He blinked back tears. One fell down his cheek anyway. He wiped it away with a single angry motion.

"I don't know," she said. She looked at him, reading his expression. "I guess it's that birthday champagne talking. Or does *that* offend you too?"

As he turned his head away he caught a glimpse of her smile a twisted, spiteful smile, out of the corner of his eye, and walked faster. She struggled to keep up without running. His car was in sight now.

"I can *not* believe," she added emphatically, "That *I—me!—I* actually managed to find the *one* man left on earth who might actually be saving himself for his wedding night. You have *got* to be joking."

Peter didn't answer. He got in the car without opening her door. She got in, slamming it shut behind her.

"So now I'm not even a lady anymore, am I? Is that how it is?"

"Stop it!"

He turned the key in the ignition.

When they were out of the parking lot he said, "I don't know what you are right now. I'm taking you home. And I have to tell you right now, I don't know if I'm ever coming back. I'm not at all sure I can handle this."

His hands shook as he gripped the steering wheel. He stared straight ahead, not daring even to look at her. They drove twenty minutes in tense silence.

"Is this the end then?" Jackie said at last, softly, sliding her left hand under her leg. The ring disappeared as she smoothed her blouse with her other hand.

"Maybe," Peter said. "I don't know. I need some time to think." He looked over at her with a sad sigh. "I love you so much, Jackie. I don't want to lose you. I mean I didn't. Especially not like this." He relaxed his hold on the steering wheel. "At least tell me . . . tell me why you were drinking. That's a shock too. That would be a start. I have to know why you're doing this to me. It hurts, Jackie."

"Well, that at least wasn't all my fault," she said, with a sigh, suddenly more humble. "I didn't buy it or anything, see? I didn't go looking for it. My roommates had a birthday party for me and spiked the punch. Then when they told me, I figured a glass or two wouldn't hurt too much, just this once."

"I guess you can see it did," he said.

Jackie looked down, then out the window. "I'm so sorry," she said. It sounded genuine.

"Me too," said Peter. He drummed his left fingers on the steering wheel. "Look, I have to be honest with you. I don't know if I can deal with this and still marry you. Looks to me like you're not the woman I thought you were. At all."

"I know," she said, still looking out the window.

"I have at least a thousand questions. And I don't think I can handle the answers tonight. I'm not ready to listen."

Jackie nodded her head.

They drove on silently.

Peter's thoughts ran in circles around each other. He tried to make sense out of this woman, this lovely being he had thought he knew so well. He was still silent as he parked the car at her apartment.

"See you?" Jackie asked, opening the passenger door.

Peter looked at her sadly. "I don't know."

She didn't try to kiss him goodbye.

****

Jackie walked up the two flights to her door and unlocked it. Closing the door behind her, she felt her way through the kitchen in the dark. A small beam of light filtered through its window. She opened the far right cabinet and pulled a small sack of flour off the shelf.

"Ah," she said, reaching into the back and removing a liter size bottle of vodka. It was about two-thirds full. "Nobody else has found you yet." She smiled dreamily. "Good. You won't ever let me down like that, will you?" She unscrewed the lid.

Taking a glass from a different cupboard with one hand, she held the bottle gently like a baby, as if it were too precious to set on the counter. She leaned against the wall dividing the kitchen from the living room and slid down to the linoleum in a slump.

She began to pour.

****

"You're home early, Peter," Beverly said when he came in the door. "Again."

She was cross-stitching on the couch, needles, charts, and floss colors scattered all about her, magnifying lenses low on her nose. She looked up at her son, her concern evident.

"I know, Mom," he said, as he shut the door. He tossed his keys on the end table and flopped into the soft brown recliner. He ran his hand through his blond hair, his expression pensive. "Everything started out so great for us. But as soon as I proposed and stuff, she changed, like *that*." He snapped his fingers.

Beverly continued stitching. "Are you sure it's the right thing to do? That you haven't rushed into this?"

"I'm sure, Mom, I felt it."

"Past tense?" She looked up.

"I know you don't like her much. But I love her. I love her so much it hurts. I don't know what to do anymore." He didn't dare tell her what Jackie had said and done tonight.

"I like her fine, Peter, it's just that something has never quite settled right with me about her. She seems very nice. I just can't put my finger on it."

I bet I can, Peter thought to himself, but he said, "I need some time to think about it. We had a big fight tonight. I don't know where we're headed anymore."

"I thought it would go well tonight, finally getting her the ring and all."

"Me too." He picked idly at a hole in the chair's upholstery, pulling out a bit of the stuffing.

"You're old enough not to pick at that," Beverly chided.

"Sorry." He stood up, wiping the stuffing off his pants. "I guess it's just nerves."

"Make sure you keep praying, Peter. God will help you."

"I have been." He stared at the ceiling, then out through the wide French kitchen doors far into the night. "I just can't seem to find the answer no matter which way I turn."

"If you're sure it's the right thing, you know I'll support you all the way," she said. "But if it isn't, I'm not going to sit here and let you ruin the most crucial decision of your life. This is important, Peter. You don't want to mess this up. You remember your Uncle Theo and all the trouble he went through with Bonnie before the divorce. And look at how their kids have turned out."

"I know, Mom. I've heard all about Uncle Theo." *A million times,* he added silently. He looked back at her, then turned for his room. "I guess I'll get to bed. Maybe it'll make some sense in the morning."

"Good luck," she said. "For your sake, I hope so."

****

As he lay in bed thinking, he wished for once that she were not so beautiful, so hard to resist. *Why did she do it? Asking me to her apartment like that. Why?* It was so overt, so presumptuous, her intentions so obvious. And then when she saw she'd hurt him she dug in deeper, twisting the knife she had thrust into his heart.

She was so different tonight. Was it the alcohol? Did it alter her true personality or unleash it? How could he ever know? He hadn't smelled anything funny on her breath, or tasted anything on her lips when he kissed her. Maybe there wasn't any. Maybe that was a lie as well. His mind ran in vicious circles, making no sense out of anything.

Sleep evaded him for hours before he finally found it.

****

At two AM, when the bottle was empty, Jackie reached up to fumble the hand-held telephone off the wall. It clattered to the floor. She groaned as she stretched out to find it in the dark, its screen glowing. She dialed a number, audio only.

"Kevin?" she said, in that husky soft voice, the voice that hadn't worked on Peter. "Me again. I need you to come over." She laughed, a deep-throated soft sound. "Mm-hmm, *right* now. Thanks."

Chapter 17

Gambling

If I'd known she was playing Russian roulette with her life, I would never have left her alone. I feel so stupid for not recognizing the signs. I hope I can forgive myself, someday.

Debra Gray,
personal journal entry

Before the end of April, Alyssa was using Elation every weekend. She forced herself to regulate it that much, in spite of the increasingly desperate need she felt for its effects.

She would go out Friday to get it, then save the pill in a hiding place in her desk drawer until Saturday night, waiting in anxious anticipation for Deb to go to sleep. Deb went to bed early Saturday nights, so she could get up early and spend the day with Jon.

Alyssa had learned to act like she was "back to normal" around Debra so she would worry less, and visit Jon at school again. It was easier to hide that way; she could sleep all day Sunday and Deb would never find out.

"Hello again," the druggist said. "It's my Friday night girl."

She greeted him with more affability each time, getting used to his easy, flirtatious manner, and actually looked forward to the opportunity of seeing him again, even if she made the visits as brief as possible.

"Told you I'd be back," she responded. Another week she told him, with a mock whisper, "I don't think this stuff is as dangerous as you say it is. It's so cool. You should try it."

His face was instantly serious. "Oh yes it is," he said, then paused. "It tears me apart watching you play with that dynamite."

"So get a new job," she said, handing over her card. She enjoyed the flirting. It was new territory for her, and she found it exciting.

"Can't," he answered. "It was supposed to be temporary. But I have this irrational compulsion to know what happens to my favorite customers. See?" He swung the register's computer screen around to face her. "I'm always checking the obituaries." He sighed and looked in her eyes. "If you never tell me your name I'll never know if you're in them or not. I'm Rob," he said, looking up at her hopefully.

"I know, it's on your name tag, *Rob*," she said, smiling. "You can't find it, can you," she said, raising her eyebrow with a grin. "Can't find my name with that computer." She was in a good mood. Her high the last weekend had been ecstatic, with none of the dark figures appearing. She had found the sun of joy and it had been eternities before the supernova came. After that she had traveled in a lush green jungle of sheer indescribable happiness. She hoped this one would be the same.

But it was always different. Completely unpredictable. Always elusive, the risk of death thrilled her. Even the nightmare terrors were worth the risk when compared to the chance she might get to that wonderful place again, and feel the absolute joy, the elation from which the drug apparently got its name.

"All I can say is you must be an awfully good hacker if *I* can't crack it," he said, bringing her thoughts back to her surroundings.

"Really?"

"Yeah, really. I'm not half bad at the game myself."

"Well, you never asked for my name, either, you know," she said. "The old-fashioned way."

"So I'm asking," he said, returning the raised brow.

She gave him a catty smile. "Maybe next time. I like being mysterious."

He leaned on the counter, head on his chin. "You are impossible, aren't you?"

"I'll be back," she said, tossing her ponytail behind her.

****

"She comes in every Friday. Like clockwork."

It was strictly an audio transmission. Rob spoke quietly into the air. The hidden receiver picked up his voice.

"See to it that you're there, then," came the other man's voice. It was a deep, gravelly bass. "Get any details you can out of her. We need your report. You did try to talk her out of it?"

"Yeah."

"She knows the risks."

"Yes."

"She suicidal?"

"Probably."

"Keep her talking until we get the information we need. Do whatever you have to. And if she does knock herself off find out where her body ends up."

"Yes, sir."

"Any luck establishing a positive ID?"

"Not yet. She's done something to her personal files. I haven't cracked her encryption codes yet."

"All right. Keep working on it, you're the pro. I'll be in touch. Oh and Rob . . ."

"Hm?"

"Nice work. If this one goes well you're looking at a significant promotion. And I do mean *significant*."

"Thanks." The connection was terminated. He smiled to himself, a smug smile as he tossed the box he was holding loosely in his hand and replaced it under the counter.

"*Alyssa Stark*," he mumbled under his breath. "Daughter of Joan Stark—no small celebrity in her field, that one—and the recently late Charles Stark. Age, nineteen; sophomore at Central U; major, computer technology and engineering, grades excellent . . . until this year's midterm report. Hm, what a shame. Not a bad job of programming, darling. But not good enough." He paused, and picked up the box again, studying it.

"No need for the boss to know that yet, is there?" He smiled to himself, pleased. "Certainly not."

****

Alyssa's hard-earned high scores were now barely passing.

All she cared about was that she pass. The professors that would accept cash bribes she paid. She forgot she had once made a resolution not to do that, a pact she made with Debra to fight against the amoral ethics that went on in some of the classrooms. She had to pass these classes. She struggled between the reality of what she was doing to herself and the illusion that she could continue in the direction she was headed and still graduate.

She told Debra nothing, especially not about her bribes. She felt miserable about hiding from her, but Deb was always so good about everything, so kind, so helpful. She couldn't bear to let her down by telling her the truth.

And Deb *would* make her stop. She knew that. Debra had definite opinions on things like that. She was too good, sometimes. So Alyssa found she preferred to lie than hurt her roommate's feelings. And she became good at it. Convincing. The ease with which excuses slipped from her lips frightened her.

The term would be over in one month. She only had to survive that much longer and she could rest. Sweet rest. She could skip a term if she wanted to, or needed to, and work, maybe. Earn some money to replace her rapidly depleting account.

At the beginning the relief had lasted so long. Now the pain returned so quickly, too quickly. And it was worse each time it returned, agonizingly difficult to handle. She counted the hours, the minutes before her weekly trip to the drug store. She promised herself she would not afford it more often than that, but it called to her, it begged her to come for it. Eventually, she couldn't resist the summons. She became incapable of resistance.

Gone were the times when she let the capsule remain on her desk, anticipating, lovingly regarding it for hours while she distracted her mind with something else until she got up the nerve to take it. Now, as soon as Debra was sound asleep on Saturday night she threw open the desk drawer and tore off the wrapper. She always remembered to have a glass of water ready. And sometimes she didn't even need that.

She swallowed the pill . . . and struggled again in an inky darkness, creatures all about her, grabbing her, tearing her hair, shrieking. She shrieked with them and struck out, white-hot with rage. She lashed out with lightning that flowed from her fingertips, arcing out in violent streaks, destroying the grotesque creatures briefly illuminated by the flashes. She gloried in the gore she had created when they were all destroyed, stomping about the crushed and burned remains, laughing at what she had done, splashing bile and ichor on her boots. Warrior's boots.

The orange glow of fire shone in the distance, the glow of her victory. She was the conquering hero coming home from the kill. She grabbed one of the hoary heads by its hair as a trophy and ran to the source of light.

This was different from the earlier times, when she first started taking the pills. Each time, the images in her mind had become more concrete, less dreamlike, with more people and images joining her. The more she took the drug, the better her mind focused on the strange scenes. It was like slowly focusing the lens of a camera, making sense of the vague images and filling them in, detail by detail. The images she saw now were so vivid she couldn't readily tell the difference between being in this place, acting out the part playing before her eyes, and her own normal waking reality.

More battle! The orange glow of bonfires lit the battle scene, a field of millions, dead and wounded. In the midst of them about thirty soldiers in strange armor fought bitterly. She heard swords clashing together, the grunts and groans of impassioned conflict. She could smell their sweat even above the hot stink of the bloody corpses that surrounded her. The head became a sword in her hands and she raised it above her with a mighty battle cry, racing forward.

As she ran, she saw that the dead were women, children, men, old and young, and while the vision horrified her, yet she ran on through the field, stumbling to meet the battling survivors.

"Who is the victor here?" she cried. "I fight only for the side of victory!"

"There is no victor here," a man whispered from behind a large rock. "They all shall die."

She threw her heavy sword down in anger. "It's stupid to fight without a victor! One side should surrender! There will be no kingdom left!"

"True," the voice answered. "Their kingdom shall be given to another."

"I do not fight for fools!" she cried.

The rush of battle, the adrenaline coursing through every vein, the frustration of stillness when one is keen and anxious to fight. She considered rushing in and slaying them all for their gross stupidity. Three more fell beneath the sword as she watched. In an odd way she enjoyed the grisly scene, feeling the part of the fierce warrior. *But a warrior for what cause?*

It didn't matter in the end.

She sat on the ground heavily, shaking as the aftereffects of anger flowed out of her body. She watched until the last two warriors were left, then with great exertion one finally slew the other, but he also fell to the ground, dead or fainted. As the last man fell, she felt a profound sadness for the dead surrounding her. The face of a beautiful woman lay next to her. A small child lay in her arms. Silent. Both slain in battle. She began to weep. The depth of her sorrow was unbearable. She wanted out of there now, fast, and she cried for escape.

The scene shifted, mercifully. She found herself upon a grassy hillside, sunshine streaming all around her, the carnage of the battlefield gone from her sight. This was happiness. She watched sheep, little spring lambs bounding with glee as lambs do in the warm sunshine, and relaxed as one of the little ones wandered away from the flock. A thunderstorm threatened on the horizon. She tried to run to the lamb when she saw it fall and lame itself on a rock, but she was helpless, paralyzed somehow. Was tonight only to be an exercise in frustration? She needed no lessons in that.

Wolves howled in the distance, and the howling grew nearer. Yet her paralysis continued.

Why can't I move? I can go anywhere I want! It's my dream!

But it was not just a dream, and she was trapped as the lamb bleated for its mother.

Her distress increased as she feared she would see the lamb torn to shreds by the approaching wolves. She had fought fierce battles, inflicting gore and death on ugly minions, but she didn't want to witness this. It was cruel and unfair. She heard eerie laughter behind her. It was the wolves' howling. Their howl was the sound of laughter. They saw the helplessness of their prey and rejoiced in their pending triumph.

The lamb continued to bleat. It lay on the grass, crippled. She twisted in agony, powerless to stop the awful scene.

As she watched, she became aware of the feet of a man next to the injured lamb. He scooped it gently up into his strong arms and cradled it, calling it by name. She couldn't hear the name. She wanted to, but she knew it was the lamb's name.

The wolves halted their approach and retreated. Their baying faded away in the distance. Tears filled her eyes as she realized she wanted to become the lamb, to be cradled in those arms, to feel what the lamb felt.

She watched the man scratch the soft little ears, coo to it, talk to it, murmuring softly in words she couldn't understand, perhaps another language. Selfishly she tried to move, to become the lamb as she had done before with other things, but she couldn't. She couldn't stand it any longer. She wanted this. Surely this would be the height of all ecstasy, and she wished to feel it for herself, more than anything, but she was paralyzed. It wasn't fair.

Then the man looked up at her, his face gentle and kind. He said nothing, but looked directly at her. There was such a profound depth of sadness in his gaze that she felt a sudden, bright, burning shame. It was the shame she had felt before, whenever she found herself in the midst of that blinding white light.

A light grew around the man and his lamb. It bleated and he stroked it, ever so gently, still watching her, saying nothing at all.

"I'm sorry," she whispered, mortified that she had thought to intrude on their moment, their love, the kindness between the two of them. She was chagrined at her selfishness. She couldn't meet that anguished gaze and turned away, at last mercifully released from her stasis. She wandered along the grassy knoll now, stumbling as the thunderstorm approached with its warm spring rain.

She became a raindrop and soaked into the earth, hoping she would disappear.

****

As the weeks dragged by, her thoughts became less connected, losing their typical streamlined logical edge. It was so frustrating. The pain inside was much worse now than when she started taking the sweet little white pills. She hardly remembered why it was there, no longer conscious of what had caused it. She only knew there was but one way to make it leave, even if it was for an ever shorter time.

She refused to accept the idea that the drug was now controlling her. She would never have allowed such a thing only a few short months ago.

She came out of the terrible highs fearful now, harrowed up by the images, wishing she could forget the vivid scenes of graphic violence that coursed before her eyes. Immediately after these trips, she was powerfully afraid to try the drug again. But always her need for relief from the agony in her soul, and the pull the drug had on her, overcame that fear. Always there was the hope that next time it would be good, that she would experience the magnificent feelings of happiness, laughter, the endless light of ecstatic joy. No, she only wished it was endless. It always ended. That was the problem. If only she could find a way to stay there, forever, and never return to the reality of her life.

It was increasingly hard to concentrate on real events as the hallucinations became more intense, more real. Her cash account depleted rapidly, especially with the hefty bribes she had to pay her professors for passing grades as the end of the semester approached.

She was even testy with Debra at times. She apologized after every outburst, explaining it was due to the stress of increasingly difficult class work, which was partially true, but it was getting harder, mostly because she couldn't think clearly anymore.

Debra didn't complain. She nodded her understanding, sometimes giving her a hug. "I know it must be hard for you," she would say. "I wish there was more I could do to help you get through this."

It frustrated Alyssa that Deb was so patient with her, so *nice*. She was desperately afraid Deb would find out, and worse, that she would make her stop. She didn't want to stop. It was the only thing that made the pain bearable; the only sense of identity and purpose left in her life.

****

There came a time when Alyssa gave her wrist to the yellow-haired womanish being willingly, and fell into absolute despair while she madly enjoyed the pain from the strange torture. She awoke after that experience horrified, clutching her forearm, looking for scars.

There were none. But her wrist ached, throbbing, where it had been touched.

After that, fear got the better of her for a time, and the next Friday night she stayed home to watch videos and pop popcorn with Debra.

"It's been a while since we've done this," Deb said, smiling. "I'm so glad. You must be doing a little better."

They told jokes and laughed, and Alyssa hid her nervousness and jitters behind a forced smile.

Saturday night was much harder to get through. She stayed up, in the kitchen, trying a recipe she suddenly decided she wanted to learn. It was hard, not the recipe but the act of cooking. It reminded her so much of her father, his strange gourmet meals. She had to blink many times; her eyes kept blurring over the text of the cookbook.

Well past midnight, she fell asleep sitting in the barstool at the kitchen counter, without finishing the project.

The following week, she sat taking notes in one of the large lecture halls, struggling to concentrate on physics. Suddenly, the willowy gray-haired woman from her drug-induced dreams appeared in the empty seat next to her. Her hair flowed around her head as though she were underwater.

"Hello, my dear child," she said.

Alyssa nearly jumped out of her skin. She dropped her pencil and leaned over to look for it, then looked back up. The creature was still there, laughing at her.

"Did you miss me? I missed you terribly. You didn't come." The voice was filled with petulant disappointment. "I hoped it would be *my* turn."

Alyssa looked down the row to see if anyone else noticed an overly tall, wraithlike woman, with hair containing a life of its own, suddenly appear in the lecture hall. The hair was mesmerizing, floating around her face in wisps. Alyssa blinked and looked away. It was so real. She must be seeing things, hallucinating in broad daylight. And she wasn't on the drugs either. She had skipped last week.

This creature just referred to that too, she thought in fear.

The thing showed her the pencil. "Looking for this?" She handed it to her. Alyssa took it cautiously. She didn't speak to the being, or try to touch it. She knew better.

The apparition continued to talk for several minutes, then disappeared as suddenly as it had come. Alyssa was quite shaken. Rob had never mentioned this particular side effect. But she could hardly blame him for that. He said all the time he didn't know much about it.

After that, daytime hallucinations began to come more frequently. At first they came once or twice a week, but as time progressed, the creatures came to visit her nearly every day.

And she couldn't manage to skip more than the one week. The drug called to her too strongly, too powerfully for her to resist its summons the next Friday. But she didn't mention the side effect to Rob. Something held her back. Perhaps it was pride.

Shapeless dark things jumped out of the walls at her as she walked to classes, spooking her. Shadows she couldn't escape drifted toward her, overwhelming her with fear and panic. They passed through her like an icy wind. Sometimes they darted at her, taunting her, daring her to chase them.

You will be like one of us, they whispered. *Join us. Come be a part of us, forever.*

Sometimes they had the semblance of faces she couldn't quite recognize, like shadows. But sometimes they were the same creatures she saw when she was high. Some had become truly familiar, as individual as human faces.

She continued to wish that the memories of her experiences there —wherever "there" was, she thought of it as a specific place—were not so vivid. She became skittish, eyes darting about in paranoia as she walked to class, and she jumped at sudden noises. She didn't *want* to become one of those things, even if it were possible.

What remained of her logical mind told her it was all a side effect, not real. *Not real. Not possibly real*, she told herself. But that didn't make them more manageable.

****

Debra went home for a four-day visit during the last weekend in April. Knowing she wouldn't be checked on, Alyssa splurged. She felt increasingly like Deb was looking over her shoulder, and it bothered her. She persuaded Rob to let her have three pills, maybe even four at once.

She didn't have enough money left in her account for even one pill, and had no more credit accounts to draw on. Joan had canceled her father's credit card. About a month earlier, she tried to buy groceries with it and was refused. She brought the diamond necklace with her tonight instead, the gift from her father. She hadn't worn it much since he died. Now she pulled it from underneath her shirt, unclasped it, and handed it over the counter.

"Please, Rob," she begged, "I swear I'll only do one at a time."

"Oh, honey," he said sadly, dangling the fine chain between his fingers, "I wish you wouldn't do this."

But he couldn't say no. The necklace was worth four pills, one more than she hoped for. That meant she could stay high all weekend.

****

Sunday afternoon Jackie woke up to the piercing headache and intense nausea of a hangover and a man in her bed who was not Peter. Memory returned to her slowly. As it did, she felt even sicker. She stumbled into the bathroom to take care of the nausea. Afterward, wiping her face with a washcloth, she caught her reflection in the mirror. Disheveled hair, horribly tangled, no make-up, a hickey—right *there*? She cursed.

"Kevin! Kevin!" she yelled into the bedroom. The sound of her own voice pounded in her head. She swore, reminding herself not to shout.

Whisper! she thought.

"What, sugar?" the near-unconscious man mumbled. "You wasted me."

"Haven't I told you before not to leave any marks?" She was furious, throwing a pillow at him as hard as she could.

"Oh, like he's going to find it," he said, waking up. "You wouldn't be calling me anymore if he was likely to see that. What time is it?"

"I don't know." She looked back at the mirror and cursed again.

"I gotta get out of here, sugar, it's past two," Kevin said, jumping up. He was gone in less than a minute.

"Fine, leave," she mumbled. "Just be that way." She turned on a cold shower.

When reality sank in, she began to weep, and crumpled to the floor of the shower, cold water pelting her frame until she was thoroughly chilled. She was still sick to her stomach. Peter was supposed to be here in sweet surrender, not Kevin again. That had been the plan. It was to be the perfect birthday. First the ring, then a magnificent weekend . . .

Why? Oh, yes. She remembered his rejection.

She couldn't stop crying then. It hurt so much. She couldn't understand why he let her down, going on about God and being watched and right and wrong.

We're in love, aren't we? Brother!

She had met monks who were more willing. She hadn't gotten anywhere with him. Nowhere. Not even so far as decent making out in the back seat of his car. One or two good kisses, enough to get started, then . . . nothing. He put a stop to everything and took her straight home . . . alone.

Eventually she kicked the shower off with her foot, but she was powerless to get up. Her roommates had promised her they wouldn't return before five tonight. She didn't need to move just yet.

And to top it off, Peter had broken up with her for good. *Or had he? What did he say, exactly?*

She cried fresh tears when she remembered that part. She had ruined everything. The thought nagged at her, as it had done before, that he *was* too good for her after all. She pushed it away, but knew she had ruined her one shot at a decent guy. Her only shot. He was so nice to her, so much nicer than any other guy she knew. So *worth it*. He treated her so well, like a queen. Like she was on a pedestal. Oh, why? Why was she so stupid? He would never marry her now. Never.

If he knew the truth.

She clung to that thought. Only if he *knew*. A plan began to form in her mind. Arranging all the details in just the right way so he would believe her would be hard work. It would be a gamble, risking which details of her life she could share and which would ruin things even more. Something would have to be said, to explain herself. She remembered that much—he wanted an explanation.

There might still be a chance she could pull it off. She had played the game wrong, made a bad call, that was all.

He must really believe in all of it, just as he said.

The concept was new to her. Well, she would have to adjust her approach, then. And she might have to accept waiting for his passion until the wedding, like he expected. It might be interesting to have someone that pure and innocent, someone she could teach, mold . . . Yes, the thought did attract her, very much, even arouse her.

If there's a wedding at all . . .

Thinking that her plans, her hopes and dreams could all be fatally ruined, and by her own doing, kept her weeping most of the day. But he certainly didn't know everything . . . that was her trump card.

She would have to play it for everything it was worth.

Chapter 18

Shattered

i dream a dream one night
of a priceless spinning vase twirling in the air
i reach to stop its reckless spin
but it sways into a wild elliptic dance,
faster, faster, out of control
i try to catch it as it falls and i miss

i miss

it shatters to a thousand glittering shards
they pierce my skin and poison me
with devastating spite, cold as hate
you should have let me spin, the pieces hiss
didn't you know how valuable you were, is my reply
i sit among the sparkling glass, bleeding as
i try to piece the fragments into one

i find i am exhausted on awaking

Shattered,
by Debra Gray

Saturday afternoon Alyssa came out of her second high. She had waited, sleeping off the effects of the first before taking the second dose. This time she shook violently, still feeling the aftereffects of a violent rage. She didn't want to be back yet. It couldn't be over so soon.

She found the third pill and swallowed it. She relished the sense of danger, the knowledge that each time could be her last. There was nothing but pain to live for anyway. And her money was gone. There would be no way to get more pills. *No more pills.*

She felt anger knowing the mythical "last time" hadn't happened yet. She came back again. So many times she had risked it. Yet death still evaded her fragile grasp.

the only practical solution. There was no other way to silence

204

the horrible pain, the terrible voices that screamed at her now during class, trying to force her to respond. They no longer whispered airily, picking up pencils and blowing puffs around her hair to spook her.

We want you, Alyssa. You belong to us. You're ours, the voices said.

Their faces were clear now, no more shadows, human in form but terrifyingly not so. She knew them. And they knew her. They laughed at her when they saw her fear, feeding on it. They followed her mercilessly, hanging about at the edge of her peripheral vision, cackling, scratching at her arms with hideous barbed fingers. Perhaps she was going insane. They couldn't be *real*.

If only the misery that was her life would end. If she could only find the sweet silence of death, the blissful sleep that would put an end to her misplaced existence, perhaps then she could rest.

There was only one way to be sure.

As the third pill began to take over, she swallowed the fourth in desperate hope.

"Sorry, Rob," she whispered. "I know I promised. One at a time."

She screamed as the overdose penetrated her brain.

****

At home in her family's roomy ranch-style house, Debra worked to finish a term paper due at the end of the break, amid invitations from her younger siblings to come and play.

"Okay, Rochelle, I'm coming," she said, finally leaving her notes. After two hours of playing Monopoly, she excused herself to get back to her work. Jon was at his family's house, but she had a date with him that evening.

"Aw, Deb, you're on holiday," her brother Abel complained, scrunching his face. He was twelve and had been winning.

"I know. But I have to finish this paper or I'm in big trouble."

It was three o'clock Saturday. When she returned to the desk, she took a deep breath to clear her mind and help her remember where she was. Yes. Time to get out the research on child social development, compare Piaget and Erickson with the new articles by Ziffield and Rodgers and . . . Where was that notebook? The blue one she put all that stuff in.

"Mom, have you seen a blue notebook kicking around this weekend?"

"Hm? No, Deb, I haven't. We haven't touched your things."

"I know."

"Have you checked your backpack?"

"Yeah, I'm going through it again now."

"Is it important?"

"I can't finish this paper without it, and it has to be done before I go back."

"Oh. Well, we'll help you look."

After another two hours of thorough but fruitless searching, Debra flopped down on the couch in the family room with a sigh. Her mother sat down next to her. "All right. Let's think. Do you remember packing it with your things?"

"I think so . . . wait . . . No, I can't remember seeing it in there. I assumed it was because I always have it with me."

"Could it be in Jon's car?"

She called Jon. He searched the car thoroughly, but couldn't come up with it either.

"I didn't get anything out on the ride home," she said. "We just talked."

"Okay. Well, maybe it's back in your apartment. When did you last work on it?"

"It was Monday. I think. The days blur together, you know?"

Her mother laughed. "Tell me about it!"

"Where was I? I got the papers copied at the library, took them home, and . . . Oh. That's right. I studied in Alyssa's room Monday. I read the articles in her room. I must've left them there. No, that can't be right. She always has everything exactly in place, so if I left them there she would have moved them to the living room or the counter or something. But I haven't done any work on it since. That's the last place I remember seeing the notebook."

"How is she, by the way?"

Deb shook her head. "Not good. She's gotten so touchy. I have a feeling something's not right, but I can't put my finger on it, except that she still won't talk about losing her father, not at all, and it's been over four months. I'm waiting for her to open up. I've never seen her cry. Maybe she keeps that private. She does spend time alone in her room."

Her mother nodded. "You keep your eye on her?"

"She's trying hard to push me away. But I'm not letting her, not totally. A few weekends ago we watched movies together, and she seemed more herself. Jumpy, maybe, but more like she used to be, before the funeral. She seems kind of . . . almost paranoid, in a way. But I don't know what she's afraid of."

"Well." Her mother rubbed her hands on her legs then stood up.

"There's still the matter of finding your notebook. Can you finish your paper without it?"

"No way."

"I guess you'd better go get it then."

Deb sighed an unhappy sigh. "I don't want to go. It seems like it's been forever since I've been home. I miss you guys."

"It's good to have you here, too." She hugged her daughter tightly.

"Maybe I could stay and use the local library instead," she said. "Or skip the paper and make it up later."

As she made these excuses, a horrible feeling came over her. It was black and dark and frightened her. She pulled away from her mother.

"What is it?" Mrs. Gray asked.

"I don't know." She knitted her brows together, puzzling it out. "I . . . I think I have to go back, now," she said. "I have no idea why. I've just got to get there. Something's wrong. Terribly wrong." She looked panicky.

"Call Jon," her mother said. "He may not be ready to go, you know. His family misses him too."

She called, and in an hour's time she was with Jon in his car, headed back to the apartment.

"This is so awful, Jon," she said. "I have this terrible feeling that something's wrong and I don't know why. Can you go any faster?"

"I can't afford a ticket," he said.

"I know, I know. Just hurry, okay?"

The ride took entirely too long. She was a nervous wreck by the time they arrived.

"Alyssa? Alyssa? Are you home?" she called. "I'm back early, I know, but I left some papers here. Are you home?"

There was no answer, no sign of her, and her bedroom door was shut. Deb sighed, exasperated.

"Do you think she went out for dinner?" Jon asked.

"I have no idea. I hate to open her door, especially if she's not home. She likes her privacy."

"I know."

"But my papers really *could* be in there . . ."

She sighed. The black feeling became worse as she moved closer to the door.

"Alyssa? Are you in there?" she called, knocking loudly. She paused. Silence.

On impulse, she flung the door open. The underlying panic she had felt exploded. Alyssa lay contorted on the floor, halfway under her bed.

Deb shrieked. " Alyssa! What's the matter?"

But Alyssa's wild, wide-open eyes didn't see her. Her skin was grayish blue. Her body shook uncontrollably, convulsively.

"Help!" Debra screamed. "Jon, help me! What's wrong with her?

He looked almost as confused as Debra as he rushed to Alyssa, Looking into her eyes, he grasped her wrist and felt for a pulse.

"Oh, man," Jon said. "Looks like she's having a seizure, Deb. Or she's OD'd on drugs. Shoot, honey, I don't know. I had a class on drug reactions and side effects last term, but I've never seen anything like this up close." After another moment he added, "Her color's very bad, Deb. Pulse is extremely weak. I can barely find it."

Debra flipped Alyssa's computer on and hit the emergency channel.

"What's happening? Is she dying?" she asked anxiously.

"I don't know," Jon said. "She might be." He looked up at her and there was pain in his eyes. "This looks bad, baby."

Deb nodded as she spoke to the emergency crew on the phone, giving the address and situation.

"You didn't know she was using anything?" he continued. "Oh, man. This is bad."

"No," Debra said, her voice rising, becoming agitated. "She's been touchy since her dad died, but I never saw her like this, ever." She began to cry, sitting on the bed.

"Don't blame yourself, baby," Jon said. "It won't do any good."

Alyssa made a sharp gasp and went limp, then stopped breathing.

Debra screamed.

****

She swam in an inky darkness.

Come, come to us, the voices said. *It is time.*

There was a long, dark tunnel leading down. It seemed like it would never end. The tunnel was quiet and still, void of the turbulence present in other places she had wandered during her highs. The voices were silent here, and she was alone. There was a point of light at the end that gradually grew bigger. She moved toward it as though she were floating. She felt strangely free.

It is time, she thought.

****

"You know mouth-to-mouth, don't you?" Jon said. "Help me out here, I'll do the CPR. Prop up her neck. We've got to keep her going until the medics arrive." He moved into position and started working.

"No, Jon, give her a blessing first!" Deb said, her voice high-pitched and anxious.

"I can't, Deb, I'm not supposed to do it all by myself."

"Yes you can! Do it! She needs you! You have to!"

"Debra," he started. "Listen. Number one, it's against the law."

"Are you just going to sit there and watch her die?"

"I'm giving her CPR!"

"Jon, *please!*"

"Deb, if we don't get her heart started she could suffer brain damage. She could end up a vegetable even if she makes it!"

"That's why she needs a *blessing*," Deb said.

Jon relented. Reaching for an object attached to his key ring, he opened a little vial and placed a drop of oil on her head, closed it and laid his hands on her head. He mumbled some preliminary words, then spoke firmly and with great force.

"Alyssa, I command you to live. I say unto you, it is not your time to die, and command you to cease risking your life in this manner. If you follow this counsel from this time forward, you shall be healed and protected from the evil forces which surround you and seek to bring you harm, and you shall again find purpose in your life. You have much to do in building up the Lord's kingdom here on earth, very much. And I say through the power of the Spirit which is in me that when the time has fully come, you will have a sure witness of the truth your soul seeks, if you but open your soul to receive it."

He finished in a whisper, using the nearly forbidden name of Jesus Christ, then without pausing, turned himself around to continue the CPR.

"Now help me out with the mouth-to-mouth, all right?" he said, pumping his folded hands on her chest.

Debra nodded and complied. "Thank you," she said, wiping away tears, and breathed air into Alyssa's lungs.

For a long, long, moment the only sound in the room was the quiet thump, thump, thump of Jon's CPR and the soft sigh of Debra breathing air into Alyssa's lungs in synchronous rhythm with Jon, followed by his barely audible whisper as he ticked off the beats.

There was no change, but the two of them continued their feverish work, not daring to break the rhythm.

"What was that all about?" Deb whispered between breaths.

"I don't know," Jon said. "The words just spilled out of my mouth. That's the way it happens sometimes."

"She'll never join us," Deb said. "What were you thinking? She's not the type."

"I know that," Jon said, irritated. "You're the one who asked me to give her a blessing. Don't knock how it came out. They weren't *my* thoughts, you know."

****

At the end of the tunnel, Alyssa found herself in a place that reminded her of her old pediatrician's waiting room, full of strangers, oddly quiet. Gone was the rage and anguish she felt earlier in the journey. Here was peace. Diffused light came from all directions. She took a chair and sat down, feeling strangely lightweight, as though released from some familiar pressure.

"Alyssa, sweetie, what are you doing here?"

She jumped out of her seat. Her father was in the chair next to her. She hadn't recognized him when she came in.

"Dad?" she said.

"Yes, it's me," Chuck said. "But you're not supposed to be here. I'm afraid you won't be able to stay." He looked at her with longing. "It's good to see you though. I've missed you so much. So much."

"Where are we?" she asked. "I mean, where am I? What are you doing here?"

His face looked soft and friendly; his eyes smiled at her, but she perceived they were full of sorrow. "I'll be waiting right here for you. Don't worry about me. I'm all right. They have trains here that they let me work on."

"Trains?"

He smiled, and nodded. "Yeah. I keep myself pretty busy." His expression changed. "Now you must get back. You're in danger of staying too long. They won't like that at all. Hurry, go back the way you came."

"I don't want to go, Dad, I like it here," she said. "Who are *they*, anyway?"

"You must go. I'm sorry."

Instantly she was watching her body from above. She watched as Jon did something strange to her head. Without knowing why, she flooded with fury. What was Jon doing near her anyway? How did he get there?

She rushed toward him. Whatever he said was not only powerful, it was pulling her back and she didn't like it. She couldn't make out his words.

"No!" she screamed. "Stop! I'm not going back. I won't!"

But her mouth remained silent.

****

An ambulance wailed its approach. It seemed to take forever, then the siren cut abruptly.

"You know we're both in deep trouble if anybody finds out about that blessing," Jon said through his teeth, keeping up his steady rhythm. "She didn't ask for it. She could sue us. I could go to *jail*."

"I know," Deb said, between breaths. "But I won't tell if you don't. It's not like she *could* have asked for it, you know."

"Should we even tell her?" Jon asked.

"Boy, I don't know," Deb said. "I doubt she'd appreciate it. First off, she doesn't even know we're religious. It's safer that way, until she figures it out for herself. I'm surprised she hasn't already, us going off to church together every Sunday. But for as bright as she is, she's not very observant when it comes to people."

"You're probably right," Jon said. "Let's not say anything, not yet."

Moments later a paramedic crew of three entered the room, hustling Jon and Debra out of the way. They inserted an IV into Alyssa's arm, drew blood, and connected her with wires, sensors and tubing to an automatic resuscitation unit for oxygen and CPR. They checked manually for vital signs.

"I'm pre-med, New Hopkins," Jon said. "Second year."

"Good," one of the medics said, a wiry blond woman. "Looks like you kept her going. Good job. We'll take over from here."

She inserted the blood sample into a diagnostic analyzer. A miniature centrifuge spun the glass tube while its computer probe searched the sample for known foreign compounds.

"Either of you know what she OD'd on?" she asked.

"No," they said together.

"I didn't even know she had a problem, and I'm the best friend she's got," Deb said, sniffling.

"Could be one of the new ones," one of the other medics said, a man with a long black ponytail down the middle of his back. He spoke with a Spanish accent.

The analyzer beeped.

"Damn," the woman said, reading the screen. "Elation."

The two men echoed her concern with more colorful epithets. The third man, an older, heavy-set fellow, pulled a syringe out of the medkit and filled it with a serum.

"I don't care what anybody says, some of these drugs ought to be illegal," he said, injecting it into the IV.

Seconds ticked by. Alyssa gasped.

"We have respiration," said the man who injected her.

"Don't get excited yet," the woman said to Deb, waving her to a hush. "This is the trickiest stuff on the market. Backfires all the time. You know how many people this stuff kills on the first try? I'm sick of it. It's caused far too many body bags for my taste, and it's getting worse lately. I don't know why people even bother with it. Too dangerous. Frankly, guys, you're just plain lucky she's still here."

Debra started to cry.

"I'm getting a pulse here. BP 60 over 35 and rising," said the man with the ponytail.

Alyssa began to shake again.

"More stimulant," the man taking vital signs said. He shook his head. "We're losing the pulse, temp's going too high. Have to stabilize her, counteract the paralysis."

The other man injected another dose in the IV.

"Too much of that and we'll lose her for sure," the woman said.

"I know it, Jane!" the man requesting more said. "But if she stays under any longer she'll be a vegetable, if she makes it at all."

****

Alyssa blinked. She gasped for breath and nearly choked on it. Air rushed into her lungs and stung.

"What's her name?" a man's voice asked.

"Alyssa." It was Deb's voice.

"Alyssa, can you hear me?" the man asked. "Can you hear me?"

She blinked again, and moved her head toward the voice. Everything was fuzzy.

"Where are you?" she mumbled.

The voices seemed to come from behind her, around her. Whose voice was that anyway? She was talking to someone, in a room. Who was it? It was someone important, she knew that, and the conversation was unfinished.

"Let me go," she said to the voice. Her speech was slurred. She struggled to be understandable. "I have to go."

The memory was already fuzzy and fading fast. Desperately she clung to it, to no avail. It slipped away as easily as a handful of beach sand would slide through her fingers.

"Alyssa, wake up. Can you hear me?" the voice repeated.

"Who are you? Let me go!" Her voice was desperate. She started to struggle. "Don't touch me!"

"Don't struggle. Please. You've experienced a major overdose. Your condition is critical," a woman's voice said.

She laid her head back down hard on the floor with a thud and stopped struggling.

"I'm still alive?" she moaned.

Her vision cleared slowly. She was in her room, on the floor, surrounded by strangers in medical uniforms. And there was Deb, and Jon with her. She felt vaguely that she should be angry with Jon, seeing him there, but couldn't remember why. She shook her head. Jon never did anything that would anger anybody. He was too docile and mellow to bother a soul. She breathed deeply and let that feeling slip away too. There was no tangible reason to cling to it.

"Your roommate found you. You're very lucky to be alive," the female attendant said. "Jane" it said on her name tag. "You'd be dead by now if it weren't for her."

"Lucky?" she said, and cursed irritably. Her tongue wasn't responding well.

"20 cc's of tetralanine with folate, Jack," Jane said. "Sounds like she needs it."

Joe inserted the medication into the IV after Jack handed him the needle.

"What's that?" Alyssa asked in a suspicious tone. "What are you doing to me?" She didn't like doctors.

"Antidepressant," Jane said. "I'll leave you with a prescription and I want you to take it. It'll keep you from trying to kill yourself again."

****

Debra leaned forward, worried. She asked quietly, "Are you sure that's what she was doing?"

Jane said, "I'm sorry, honey, but yes. Nobody takes that much Elation for any other purpose. It's sold in highly controlled dosages, and it's expensive. I don't know how she came to with the level of the stuff she's got in her bloodstream." She lowered her voice. "It's easily the most dangerous substance on the market. It's got a synthetic chemical in it that triggers the near-death experience. Remember that study a couple of years back? The controversial one, where scientists proved there's no such thing as life after death, proved that the whole near-death phenomenon was just a chemically induced reaction that taps into a different part of the brain? Got 'em the Nobel Prize?"

"Yes," she said with a sigh. "I heard about it."

"Well, that's what she was taking here. The stuff is loaded with those chemicals, plus acid. Supposed to give you powerful hallucinations. Problem is, too often it takes people a little too near death. They *don't* come back."

Deb's expression went blank. She sat down in the chair by the desk. "Is that what she was doing?"

"I need you to make sure she takes this." The woman handed her a prescription bottle. "Even if she doesn't want to. Spike it in her food if you have to, if you care about her. I also want you to keep it for her, since there's enough in there to cause serious brain damage if she takes it all at once. Anybody who takes that much Elation is damned serious about suicide. Even junkies won't touch the stuff."

A tear ran down Deb's cheek. "Okay. I get it."

"I'm sorry," Jane said. "But it's the truth. Might hurt, but it's better that you know. This stuff here should help with the withdrawal too. She'll need your help. It's horribly addictive. Assuming you survive each hit, that is. You've gotta watch her for signs of relapse, switching to other drugs, anything like that."

Debra nodded. She wiped her eyes. "I knew she wasn't doing well since her father died, but I had no idea she was this bad off."

"You think you can take care of her?"

"Sure." She nodded again. "I'll take care of her. I'll watch her like she was my own child."

"You'll have to," Jane said.

****

It was so hard to stay awake. So hard. Alyssa wanted to go back to that place. She had almost made it to . . . she wondered where it was she had been. She knew she was talking to somebody, someone she knew. But she couldn't remember who. It faded away like a dream does in the morning.

The IV man, Jack, said to her, "Alyssa, listen to me. There's only one way to get all this toxic crap out of your bloodstream quickly." He turned up the speed on the IV drip to maximum. "We flush it out."

"No, no, it sleeps off," she mumbled. "Just let me sleep it off." She was so tired.

"No sleeping for you, girl," Jack said. "Can't have you wandering off into unconsciousness for a while yet. First we flush."

"Great," she groaned.

"Jane, where's that RL enzyme solution?" Jack asked, rummaging through the medkit. "Is it A or B, with Elation?"

"B," Jane answered.

"Got it," he said, inserting yet another syringe into the vial and drawing out the liquid. Then he inserted the needle into the IV.

"What's that?" asked Alyssa, perturbed. She didn't like the feeling of being connected to all this wiring and tubing. It was uncomfortable, invasive. She wished they would all go away and let her go back to sleep.

"Helps the flush, honey," Jack said. "Gives your liver and kidneys a nice boost."

"We can stay here and take care of this business until we get another call. All right with you, Martinez?" Jane asked.

Martinez, with the ponytail, nodded. "I'm not off till one," he said, checking his watch.

"I have to get up," Alyssa said. She was still drowsy, but suddenly aware of the rapid effect the IV drip was having on her system.

Jane helped her to her feet. "Do you think you can walk?"

Alyssa nodded.

The next few hours were among the most irritating in her life. They pumped enough fluid into her for a small wading pool. And with her sobriety came the usual shattering headache. She was lucky the rescue team got no other calls. They would have had to leave her IV in with Jon and Debra to take care of her until they were able to return and follow up.

Ambulance companies were privately owned, sharing the emergency channel and dividing the territory into regions for effective emergency care throughout the city. They did a good job. Crews carried all necessary equipment on board for common emergencies, and they only used hospitals when absolutely necessary. Those were run by separate corporations and were in direct competition with each other and the emergency care companies, although in the years since deregulation, they had become more specialized.

They would have had to take her to one had she not resuscitated. And most rescue teams didn't like to do that, for good reason. Hospitals didn't provide much emergency care, except for the rich. For students like Alyssa, without health insurance, it was rescue team policy to avoid hospitals whenever possible, for the patient's sake.

The law allowed hospitals to extract payment in forms other than money when neither cash nor insurance was available. The government argued that this policy allowed hospitals to provide better health care by making up the losses they incurred treating mandatory charity cases. Every citizen had the guaranteed right to health care, or so the "freedom-to-treatment" law said; no patient could legally be turned away. But the law also said hospitals had the right to profit from their business.

Translated into reality, this meant payment could be made in other forms. One permitted by law was "voluntary extraneous organ donation." This might mean a kidney, perhaps. But many hospitals interpreted the "extraneous organ" clause of the law rather loosely, to mean "any organ without which a body can still sustain life." It was generally the hospital's choice, and many were ruthless, circumventing the "voluntary" clause altogether.

Through the whole ordeal Alyssa felt one consistent emotion, anger. She was angry that she had survived, that she had been ripped away from death when it had finally beckoned her to see the secrets it held beyond its gates. She had a definite sense that something *was* there waiting for her, something better than the life she knew. This was something she had never known before.

After the medics left, she sat on her bed and rubbed at the bandage on her arm where the IV had been. It was two o'clock in the morning. Deb sat opposite her in the study chair, watching. Tears ran freely but silently down her cheeks.

Alyssa looked up. Her face was nearly back to its normal color. Her long blond hair was matted and tangled from two days of neglect. She felt uncomfortable in her clothes and in desperate need of a shower. She saw Deb and her tears, and for the first time realized that her actions had affected her friend. At this, her anger flared again, then faded.

Suddenly she felt a deep sense of guilt, the shame she had felt when facing the man with the injured lamb in her . . . whatever it was . . . hallucination might be the right word. Again she wished she could disappear. But this was reality. She couldn't turn into a raindrop and vanish here.

Silence weighed heavily on them. Finally Alyssa said, "I'm sorry, Deb." She looked away and picked at the tape on her arm.

"Why didn't you tell me?" Deb asked, her voice breaking from the tears. "I could've helped you."

"I knew you'd make me stop. I didn't want to stop."

"How long has this been going on?"

"Since February."

She couldn't look up or meet her friend's eyes. She didn't like seeing the pain in them or knowing it was a pain she had caused, intentionally. It felt worse than the agony she had been suffering to know she had hurt someone she cared for so much, more than she had cared for anyone in a long time. She was only now keenly, achingly aware of that fact. She had ignored it until now.

Debra caught a sob in her throat. "How did this happen? I mean, I feel so stupid. Here I am, minoring in psychology, and I don't know *how* I missed it. I should have guessed. I know you haven't been yourself in months. I just didn't know it was this serious."

"The first time was when you went home for a weekend, so you never knew," Alyssa said quietly, still pulling at the medical tape. "After that, well, I was careful. I knew you wouldn't like it if you knew, so I kept it from you."

"Like when you said you weren't feeling well that other weekend and stayed in bed."

She nodded. "Yeah, that was one time. Most of the time, I, uh . . ." she looked away. This was hard. Maybe she didn't need to say anything more.

"You what?"

"I waited till you were asleep Saturday nights and then took it."

"You started sleeping in Sundays about then. That's right!" she said. "Why didn't I notice? I just thought you were tired . . . And then . . . then I was gone the rest of the day."

She couldn't bring her eyes up to look at Deb. She barely nodded.

"But I was here, Alyssa. You could have talked to me. I've always been here for you. Why did you have to lie about this? I only wanted to help you, and you pushed me away."

"You wouldn't understand," she whispered.

"I would. I'd try. All you had to do was talk to me."

"I couldn't. I don't . . . I don't know how."

"I was *here*," Deb repeated with a mournful sob.

Alyssa felt the tightness in her throat, the ache in her chest that meant the beginning of tears. She had hurt Debra when her friend only wanted to help her. The weight threatened to crush her. All the lies she had told to cover up her habit, all the money she had wasted, all the pain she had caused . . . It was too much to bear alone.

For the first time in years she allowed the tears to come. She had done a terrible, awful, selfish thing, and it hurt not only herself but someone else. Someone she cared for more than she realized.

"Oh, Deb," she choked, catching a deep breath. "I'm so sorry." She held her face in her hands. "I never meant for this to hurt you. I just wanted to die."

Debra crossed the tiny room and put her arm around her shoulder, as she had done the day Alyssa's father died. This time, however, Alyssa leaned into her and wept freely, openly. She hadn't wept in front of anyone since she was a child. She was ashamed to. She felt weak, helpless, flayed open. But she could no longer hold it back. Sobs wracked her frame as the emotion of a lifetime threatened to drown her soul.

Debra held her tightly and wept with her.

Chapter 19

Haunted

It appears that once a sufficient conditioning point in the drug therapy is reached, the subjects can see these alien lifeforms even during normal sobriety, so long as regular doses are being administered. We are uncertain as to the cause . . .

It will necessitate further research until we discover the cause for this observation, and whether subjects with (or without) the necessary conditioning might be able to contact them without the use of the drug at all . . . Such a benefit would be of great use to us, considering the risk of its unpleasant side effects.

Victor Caldwell,
private research notes

Sunday came and went and Peter didn't call Jackie as usual.

Monday morning, she called him. "Peter, I'm afraid I've made a terrible mistake," she said. She was sobbing. "Can I come and see you this morning?"

"I have to be in town today. Aren't you supposed to be at work?"

"I'm too upset to work. I got the day off. I really need to see you. Please."

"I can go into town this afternoon, I guess," he said. "If you come here I can see you. But I'm not going to your apartment, I'm sorry."

"Thanks, Peter. I'll be there soon."

Peter, watching from the front window, came outside when he saw her drive up. It was a cloudy but warm day. The wind ruffled gently through his hair.

Jackie's long auburn hair was pulled back in a curly, unkempt ponytail. She wore jeans and a long oversized T-shirt. Peter noticed she didn't have any of her usual makeup on and that her eyes were puffy from crying.

"Where can we go to talk?" she said as she got out of her car.

"Right here will be just fine," he said politely. "We can sit down on the front lawn."

She sat down under the large live oak tree, the same tree Lauren sat under so many years ago, reading on the Fourth of July, when she was taunted by a turkey that had long since gone to Thanksgiving dinner. He remembered that now. So much had changed since then. He didn't know why life had to keep getting more complicated, or why memories of Alyssa kept haunting him.

Peter sat down a few feet away from his fiancée, facing her.

"Well?" he said.

"I need to know what you've decided. Do you need more time? I mean . . ."

"I was kind of waiting for an explanation from you before I made up my mind."

"Peter, I am so afraid of losing you," she said. Tears began to run down her cheeks, but she held her eyes steadily on his. "When I think I might have lost you, I just, I just can't handle it. I don't know what got into me Saturday. I wasn't thinking straight. I don't know what I was doing."

"I don't either," he said. He folded his arms across his chest.

"You know I was baptized four years ago," she said. "It turned my life around."

He nodded.

"I never wanted to have to tell you about the life I had before that, but I guess . . . I guess it's time. I was afraid if I told you, you wouldn't love me anymore. Or that you'd leave me, or hate me for what I used to be. I had a terrible life, Peter. I was so messed up. I didn't want to disappoint you. You keep saying how perfect I am, and really, I am so not perfect it isn't even funny." More tears came, and she had to stop talking to regain her composure.

"How bad was it?" he asked. "You'd better tell me everything now if you want me to even consider getting married." He shifted his position on the lawn.

She was silent a few moments before she began to speak. "I've never told anybody how it really was, who didn't know me back then, anyway. I've tried to erase everything, but it keeps coming back up to haunt me, no matter what I do to escape. I mean that's part of why I moved here, to get away from my reputation, from my old friends." She sniffled, then continued.

"See, I was pretty wild in high school, you know, I went to all the parties. I had a, you know, quite a few boyfriends, and I was always, well, pretty physical with them, uh . . . well, you know what I mean. I drank a lot then, too, Peter. I mean, a lot. I'd wake up with horrible hangovers, throwing up, the whole bit, and not even remember where I'd been. I guess I was running away from my family problems." She sniffed. "I've worked some of those out. Tried to, anyway."

"So you were an alcoholic?"

"I wasn't that bad, no. I only drank on weekends. When I found the Church, Peter, it changed everything. I cleaned up my life, turned everything around, and I've been totally careful ever since then. I promise." She twisted her tissue in her fingers and wiped her eyes.

"So what was last weekend all about?"

"I told you the truth. I didn't think one glass would hurt too much, after all, champagne was always my weak spot. I didn't know what it was going to do to me. It brought out a lot of, of those old feelings, you know, feelings I used to have around my old boyfriends. You know," she said slowly, as though choosing her words carefully.

Peter said, "No, I don't know. What are you trying to say? Just say it, why don't you."

"Oh, Peter, please, don't make me say it. Please."

"Say what?" He pressed her, digging in where he could tell it hurt even as she had done to him, twisting his own knife. Maybe then he could come up with the truth.

"Don't make me."

"Jackie, how many 'boyfriends' are we talking about here?"

"Oh, I don't know, five or six. I guess. I'm not even totally sure. I told you, sometimes I couldn't remember where I'd been after I woke up." She looked away from him and started to cry again, her shoulders shaking. "I'm not sure what I've done. If you don't want to go through with it, now that you know the truth about me, I . . . . I'll understand." She leaned on the tree, shaking with sobs.

"Jackie," Peter started, concerned. He felt a sick feeling in the pit of his stomach. "You're telling me you're not even *sure* how many men you've slept with? Is that what you're saying?" He didn't want to say the words out loud. The thought appalled him so completely, the thought that other men had already touched her, in places he wouldn't allow himself to think of touching until they were married. And more than one other man. Some she might not even *remember*.

He wasn't certain at that moment that he wouldn't throw up. It revolted him. He always thought he had a forgiving heart, that if someone he loved made terrible mistakes, he could forgive them. Even this mistake, especially if it was before their baptism or just once or with one person, well, things like that can happen. He knew that. He wasn't that naïve. It hadn't happened to him; it was true he had carefully saved himself for his future bride. He had thought until this moment that he could understand and forgive someone who hadn't managed the same level of self-control. But thinking about this, of what she had been and done . . . it twisted his gut in a way he had never experienced before. He was silent a long time, thinking about it, feeling sick inside.

"If you don't love me any more I can just go," she whispered at last. "I'm not anywhere near worthy of a man as good and sweet as you are."

This pulled him out of his reverie, and shifted his train of thought. "Hey. Hey, you said yourself it was in the past, right? Before you even knew better? How can I blame you for that? You didn't know it wasn't right. You're not responsible for something you didn't know. Don't you understand that? When you were baptized, it took care of all that, just like you're new again."

He was shaken and shocked by her revelation, but the nausea subsided some. It was still a lot to swallow. He had never suspected as much, but he concentrated on this last idea.

"*Brand* new. Sweetheart. Don't you understand? It was all washed away then."

He imagined her in a white baptismal dress, coming out of the water bright and clean with baby-pink newborn skin, gorgeous and radiant. It was a bright picture, and his mind clung to it desperately.

She took a deep, shaking breath. "I guess so, but . . . I'm just never sure . . . It's so hard to feel like I can forgive myself sometimes."

Don't tell me you actually believe all that nonsense they teach us about a little pleasure being so wrong. Her words rang out from his memory. The uneasy feeling in his stomach returned and flip-flopped.

"It *is* all in the past now, isn't it?" he asked suddenly, biting his lip, the mental image of her new purity shattering before his eyes.

Jackie turned to face him. Her lower lip trembled. "How could you even *ask* me that, after everything I've told you? I just laid my whole awful life in front of you! How *could* you?" She began to cry again. "That hurts, Peter! I've tried so hard! I could never tell this to anyone else. Not my friends, especially never my parents, nobody! My mom caught me once—*one* time, years ago—and I've never been able to live it down. She tells *everybody* about it. Why do you think I don't want your parents to meet them? That's why, that's the real reason. Imagine it!" She paused for control. "The truth is, I haven't told my mother about you. I just know she'd ring up to make sure you 'knew about my *past*.' And every time I call home it's the same thing, re-hashed over and over again . . .

Please, please, don't tell me you're going to do that to me too. I couldn't stand it."

Peter felt horrible for asking. It was wrong of him to rub it in. It must have been heart-wrenching for her just to open up to him about it. He tried to imagine how he would feel if the situation were reversed, making a brave attempt at empathy.

"I'm sorry," he said, reaching out to put a hand on her shoulder. "It's just that it occurred to me that if you slipped with the champagne, it's possible that . . ."

"It's hardly the same thing, Peter!" she wailed.

"I'm sorry! I wouldn't know!"

Then, more gently, he added, "This is a lot for me to take in at once. A lot of what you said Saturday and what you're saying now doesn't jell."

"You know I wasn't myself then," she said, regaining her composure and sniffing. "You know it. I told you that. I already said I was sorry."

"Which side of you do I believe, Jackie?" Now he was crying too, surprised himself that the tears came.

"*This is me*, Peter, this is who I really am, not whatever it was you saw Saturday. Oh, Peter, I'll do anything I can to get you back," she pleaded. "You're the most wonderful thing that's ever happened to me. I can only guess how much it must have hurt. How much this hurts you. I can't stand to think about it. My only hope is that you'll be able to forgive me, someday, and love me in spite of everything I've been."

"I'll try, Jackie. I will try. But it might take a while. And you have to promise me this is the truth," he said. "No more secrets. Please. Don't keep anything else from me. This is about all I can take. I couldn't handle anything else. Not right now." *Not ever*, he added mentally.

"I promise," she said. "I won't surprise you with any more secrets." She smiled, and took his hand in hers. "And honestly, I do want to wait for . . . sex, as much as you do. I'm sorry I said what I did the other night. I love you so much. It will be perfect, it will be. It's just that I've never had anything this . . . pure before in my life. I've never known anyone like you. The other guys, back in high school, see, it was the only thing they wanted from me." She shrugged, and turned her head. "I wanted to be loved so terribly. I was so lonely all the time . . . it was the only way I could feel . . . Oh, Peter, don't you see, I really don't deserve you? You're too good for me." She looked at him with those warm, captivating eyes, and he melted.

"I'm still going to have to work this out, Jackie," he said. "But I want to. I honestly do want to. I've never loved anyone the way I love you. I want to be there to protect you, and help you when you're hurting. I *need* to know how you feel. That's what I'm here for. And that means you need to talk to me, and I need to be able to understand you. Because I don't want to lose you either. You mean more to me than anything." He lifted up her pale porcelain chin with his hand.

"Oh, thank you, Peter," she whispered. Her soft brown eyes looked into his with ultimate tenderness.

He leaned over and kissed her then, and it was warm and sweet and innocent. Her past didn't matter. It was past. His heart swelled with love for her, and forgiveness, and in that moment he was certain she was meant to be his wife.

****

Debra stayed by Alyssa's side all weekend. She left her paper unfinished, untouched, in her backpack.

Once Alyssa got started, she told Deb everything, from the beginning. Everything she had left out of the story because it was too painful for her to inflict it on anyone else. How her mother had hated her since before she was born, had beaten her, insulted her, constantly. How her father stood by and did nothing but watch, except for the deal he made for the big house. How painful it was. The more she talked, the more it hurt. Before the weekend was over she was hoarse.

Deb simply listened. She didn't judge or offer advice, but held her tongue.

And Alyssa learned to cry.

She could comprehend all the basic laws of physics and recite the periodic table backwards. But no professor had taught her anything as essential to life as this. It was the answer she had been searching for. It actually had a purpose. It was the relief the drug never provided, that it *could* never provide. She had always pushed it away, thinking her tears were useless, a sign of weakness in the face of the enemy. They wouldn't change anything. They never changed anything for her mother, with her endless cycles of hysteria.

But there was a purpose. They changed her on the inside, albeit slowly. The drug, on the other hand, had been nothing but a false stimulant of uncontrolled, mindless emotions brought to life in vivid images. It was purposeless. She could see that now.

Somehow during the weekend the burden she carried subsided to a degree that it was almost tolerable, and Monday night she put into words, finally, the thing that had gnawed at her during her entire life.

"I guess I don't have any idea who I am, Deb. I don't have any purpose, any sense of who I am. I came into existence by a fluke of nature twenty years ago. I mean, you could call it a mistake and it wouldn't be far from the truth. I know my dad wanted me, sort of, to begin with anyway, and toward the end there I liked spending time with him so much, even if I did think his trains were silly. I just wanted to be with him. But with him gone I feel like I don't have any reason for existing at all." She paused, catching her breath, forcing the words to come out. "I miss him so *much*. And he's gone forever. I'll never see him again. I never thought it would hurt like this, or happen this soon."

More tears welled up and brimmed over.

Deb said quietly, "*I* want you to live, Alyssa."

Alyssa wept more earnestly then.

"Let it out. Take a deep breath." Deb put her arm around her.

"Thank you, Deb," she said, after a while.

"For what?"

"For still caring, after all I've done to hurt you."

"That's what friends are for," she said. "I'm here for you."

"Have I ever been there for you? I feel like all I've ever done is hurt you, and you're still here."

"Sure you've been there for me. Every day. You're a terrific person, Alyssa. I mean that."

"I've been so selfish." Then, in the next ragged breath, "Oh, I miss my dad," she said, and wept again.

****

"Are you going to be all right?" Deb asked Tuesday morning as she shouldered her backpack.

"Yeah," Alyssa answered. "I'll even make it to class on time." She stood in front of the mirror brushing her hair. "I'm ready to go back. I feel much better."

"Good," Deb said, shouldering her pack, watching her brush out her hair. "I'll go ahead then."

"Deb?"

"Yes?"

"Thank you."

"Hey," Deb smiled. "I'm just glad I got here in time. I was terrified you weren't going to make it."

Alyssa felt more pangs of guilt. She stopped brushing. "It's good to know you care."

Deb nodded. "I do." She left for class.

Alyssa put her hairbrush away and picked up her own backpack. She sighed. There wasn't much for her to do but finish out the term. That meant getting to class herself.

The morning had the feeling of a dawn that comes after a long and dangerous thunderstorm. The quiet rang in her ears. After all the commotion of the last several days the regular morning routine seemed strange and methodical, like going through the motions without much energy left to give them. There was a feeling of sadness that stayed with her; not the anguish of the previous nights, but a feeling of hopelessness and loss as she considered what was left of her future.

She had no money for tuition and little hope for a solid career without a degree. She would be lucky to find any job at all with her dreams of graduation shattered. There was probably less practical reason now for living than before, when all her hopes were ahead of her.

Her pointless spending had ruined the one chance she had to finish her degree. She had wasted all her father's money. The entire sum. It was gone even before she had given up the necklace to Rob. Was that only last Friday? It seemed eons ago. She had no cash, no job, no assets for collateral.

Even so, something felt better. She had Deb, someone who honestly cared about her. She *mattered* to somebody. It was a new feeling for her, to know she really, truly mattered in someone else's life. It had been too easy for her to feel invisible, lost, anonymous, to forget anyone who might care about her. That blindness had nearly ruined her friendship. She wouldn't make that mistake again.

She hadn't had such a good friend since Peter. Although she shared her apartment with Debra, she hadn't thought to share much more than that until now. They studied together, true, and helped each other with classes as they could, but she had never let out the feelings that burdened her before this weekend.

She thought of Peter briefly, and more kindly than she had since she spoke with Mrs. Richardson on the phone.

He had been on the edge of her thoughts over the weekend, her only happy memories of childhood or home. She was thankful he didn't seem real anymore, more like a dream than a memory. Over the weekend, she told Debra some of the pranks the two of them had played on Lauren when they were little, before life became complicated and tore them apart. As she talked she had wondered aloud what would have happened, had Joan not been either so adamant, or so terrifying to defy.

But that cycle of speculation was meaningless. She knew it as soon as she mentioned it. The past couldn't be changed. She had to live in the present, and Peter couldn't be a part of her present. He was gone. He had chosen his life, and it didn't include her.

Yes, the past was past. She had little future left, and she had to find a way to deal with that. Somehow.

She went to class and took careful notes. Part of her mind felt different, she knew. It was much harder to concentrate now. She had a terrible headache that came and went. The medics had explained she would have to live with it for many weeks, until all the effects of the drug cleared her system. They also explained the importance of not trying to deaden the pain with anything strong. She had to live with it or risk addicting herself to some new substance.

It was so hard connecting her thoughts in class. Once she thought she heard an evil cackling behind her and jumped. But it was just a pencil sharpener. The medics had warned her she would probably have flashbacks or hallucinations for a long time. They also told her it might be more difficult to concentrate, maybe for the rest of her life.

It began to sink in what she had done to herself.

In the middle of her favorite class, advanced physics, she suddenly jumped up and walked out of the lecture hall. She felt a new surge of anger, this time at herself. She couldn't stay in class. She couldn't even think. Physics, for the first time in her life, was hard to comprehend. She had lost control of her actions. And doing so had ruined a part of her brain that she would never get back.

Never.

You won't get away from us that easily, a voice laughed in her head. *We know you'll come back to us. They always do.*

It disturbed her, but she tried to ignore it. She walked briskly around campus, wanting to run to burn away her fury, but not wanting to attract attention by bursting into a sprint.

She found herself approaching the huge university gym and went inside. After checking out some equipment, she found a vacant racquetball court and took her anger out on the ball in private. She beat the ball against the wall, hitting it repeatedly. In only a few minutes she began to sweat. She hit harder. Her hair flew wildly as she swung the racquet. She had left her hair down and now it got in her face, tangling between her fingers and mouth when she tried to brush it away.

You'll be back, dearie. We miss you. We will come for you.

Get out, she told the voice, shuddering.

She couldn't believe how out of control she had allowed her life to become. She was talking to voices inside her head. Did she have any shred of sanity left?

When had she lost control?

Slam. Bounce.

Why hadn't she trusted Debra? She slammed the ball harder.

Why had she ruined her brain, her precious ability to think? Didn't she know that's what would happen? Wasn't she smarter than that? She knew what drugs were all about. They taught all that propaganda in high school about how stupid addictions are and how to be careful when choosing and using drugs. Wasn't she paying attention? Did she honestly think it couldn't happen to her?

Whack. Whack.

The ball flew across the court. Her breath came in ragged gasps. She was out of shape to boot. Why did she have to live with pain in the first place?

Whack.

Why did she have to live at all? Why hadn't the stuff killed her? She'd come so close! It wasn't fair.

Whack. Bounce. Whack.

Finally she slammed the blue rubber ball into the wall so hard it burst. It wouldn't bounce any more with a tear in it, so she paddled it into the floor, yelling, cursing it for breaking.

Suddenly she stopped. She was screaming at an inanimate object.

She plopped down hard on the court and began to cry. Drawing her knees up to her chest, she hung her head over them as her shoulders shook.

She wept a long time. When she finished she realized it was late in the afternoon. She had to get home or Debra would worry about her.

It was good to know someone would.

Chapter 20

Rob

He's obviously just flirting with her. I'm not sure exactly what he wants, but it can't be completely altruistic. And she was snowed. Completely. She sees through all the rest of them, why can't she see through him? He's no different than the other guys who chase her, not in my book. If she had a nice boyfriend before, somebody more like Jon maybe. Then she'd know. He made me so mad. But there's nothing I can do. She just got angry when I said something.

Debra Gray,
personal journal entry

Alyssa dreamed that night she was inside her brain, tiny, running through the convoluted masses of cells, finding synapses fried, connections burned to ash. She tried desperately to piece the fallen cords of nerve back together, to rebuild the ruined connections. She thought the dream lasted all night. She couldn't remember any other dream in the morning, and awoke tired, with a headache. The medics said no analgesics.

How stupid. She took a pain reliever to ease the discomfort. She didn't need that constant a reminder of her stupidity. She had to concentrate.

Classes were extremely difficult, no different than the day before. She fidgeted. She couldn't concentrate. The odd voices, the eerie laughter in her head, were constant. She couldn't see the awful creatures anymore, and for that she was grateful, but she could sense their presence. The side effects would cease, the medics said, in time. As long as she stayed off the drug. But the voices still frightened her. The medics told her it might be years before she couldn't hear them any more.

Eventually, as she knew it would, Friday came again. There was one more thing she had to do. Rob would worry about her if she didn't show up.

She explained this to Deb.

"No way are you going back there," Deb said. "You're still having withdrawals."

It was true. The headaches were intense, and the pain killers weren't terribly effective. The night before, she took a sleeping pill to knock out the pain so she could rest peacefully. She felt an intense pull, a need to delve into those bizarre depths in the recesses of her mind, to go on just one more exciting adventure, but she thought she could manage going to see Rob without begging him for more.

She feared the highs now more than ever. With her eyes open, she realized that during most of them she had been frightened, weeping and abusively battered about by those *things*, the nearly-human creatures of her imagination. The times she actually felt what its name promised—elation—were extremely rare. She was desperately afraid to go back to that place in her mind, wherever it was, even as she felt the intense urge to try it once more.

She wanted to live now. That was the biggest difference. Each day that desire became stronger. She wasn't as willing to risk her life as she had been only a week ago. Deb spent a lot of time with her, talking, and it felt good. In fact, Deb hardly let her out of her sight except for class time, and she made her take the antidepressants religiously.

"I'm strong enough not to take the stuff again," she said. "Besides, I don't have any money left to buy it. Don't worry. I can handle going there. Honest."

"I don't think so," Deb said. "This is an extremely bad idea."

"Well, you know where I'm going, don't you? I'm telling you about it, aren't I? You can search me when I get back. Promise."

"That's not it. For all I know you won't *come* back," Deb said, agitated. "This is a *really* bad idea."

"Come with me then," Alyssa said. "Please. Would you? He worries about me. He's my friend too."

"Why would he care? Why do you care whether he's worried or not? Oh, please, don't tell me you're attracted to this creep."

"Of course not. Don't be silly. And he's not a creep. Look, it's just that I promised. Please, come with me."

Deb sighed. "Okay. You win. I guess I'll have to."

When the two of them walked in Rob was visibly surprised. Deb looked around nervously, arms folded across her chest. She didn't hide her distaste for being inside such a place. She had said she wouldn't set foot inside if it weren't to protect Alyssa.

"Well," Rob said. "What's this? Bringing me a new customer?"

"It *means* Alyssa nearly died of an overdose last weekend," Deb said. "Thanks to you. But she's done with it, and she won't be coming back any more." She looked at Alyssa. "Okay, he's seen you. Can we go?"

Rob's face paled. "It's not my fault," he said, coming around the counter toward them. "She begged me for it. How can I say no to those eyes?" He looked sad as he stopped a few feet away from the two of them. "Are you okay?" he whispered. "You didn't go one at a time, did you. You promised me. I trusted you." He reached his hand toward her.

She blushed. "The overdose was all my fault, Deb," she said. "It was my choice. I did it on purpose. Don't blame him, he just works here." She stepped closer to him, "I'm sorry, Rob. I know I promised, but I couldn't handle it. I wanted to tell you myself that I . . ." she stopped suddenly, just short of reaching out for his hand.

She *heard* it calling to her from under the counter. *Come, come, come to me, my love*, it said.

Another voice said, *We miss you. We need your pain. Come back to us. Share with us.*

She took a deep breath, swallowed hard. "I won't be needing it any more." She mustered a smile.

A multitude of voices screeched and wailed as one. She shook her head to clear them. They were stronger in this place for some reason, and she flinched.

He didn't take his eyes away from her face. "Good. I can breathe again," he said, with honest relief. "I did make her promise me, only one at a time," he said to Deb. "How many did she—"

"You promise me you won't let her buy any more of that junk," Deb interrupted. "And then I'm going to wait outside. If I have to hear any more of this conversation, I'm going to puke."

"I promise," Rob said. "And I'll be more than glad to keep that one."

"Deb, wait," Alyssa called. She sighed as she watched Debra walk out the door and lean with her back against the plate-glass window, her arms folded. "She didn't want me to come here," she explained. "She didn't even want to come in."

"It's okay. I understand," he said, then cleared his throat. "Well. She called you Alyssa, huh?"

She looked out the window at Deb with chagrin. She hadn't mentioned their little game to her. "Yeah. Secret's out, I guess." Then she looked at him. "But you won't be looking for me anymore in the obituaries so it doesn't matter, does it?"

"It's a beautiful name. So lovely . . . Alyssa. I like it."

Alyssa smirked. "I never thought of it that way."

"Why not? It's like a melody. It fits you perfectly."

"I was named after my father. His middle name was Alison."

"Oh," Rob said. Then, with a start, he added, "So, wait a minute, does this mean you're going? You won't be back again?"

"I guess so." She turned slightly towards the door.

"Wait. Can I see you again? Please?" he said. "I mean, not in here, not as a customer. I've worried about you so much, you coming in here buying those suicide pills every week." He paused, gazing at her intently. "I feel awful I haven't been able to stop you. I know I haven't helped you any, obviously, and I'll understand if you never want to see me again. I know why *she* doesn't want you to." He pointed to the window, "She's an open book. But it would make me so happy if this isn't goodbye for us, if you would see me again. I'll miss you. I've gotten used to worrying about you. Please."

Alyssa looked at him a long moment. Her heart beat faster hearing his words, but she tried not to show it. "I suppose that would be okay." She hoped she sounded more nonchalant than she felt. Her eyes shifted from Rob to Debra and back again.

"No shop talk," she added, her head pounding suddenly. *Did the analgesic wear off so quickly?* "I don't want to talk about this. It was horrible, all of it. I want to forget it ever happened."

"Hey, I didn't want you to get started in the first place, if you remember," he said. "Look, I just want to see you. No commitments or anything. And no shop talk."

"Okay," she said quietly. "You can call me." She gave him her personal number.

Outside, Debra was unhappy. "What took you so long?"

"He asked me out," Alyssa said. She was careful to say it casually, careful not to smile. She shrugged her left shoulder.

Deb stiffened. "You said no, right? You *did* say no."

Alyssa shook her head.

"What did you do that for? I can't believe it. I think I'm going to be ill."

"Oh, get off it," Alyssa said. "He's nice. He just wants to see me again."

"Yeah, he wants his customer back. He's losing a hefty commission, isn't he?"

"Cut it out! Rob isn't like that. He never wanted me to get started in the first place."

"Well, he didn't stop you either," Deb said.

"He tried. You know how I can be." She gave her a sheepish grin.

"What could you possibly see in him? He's not even attractive."

"Oh, right, and Jon is Mr. Universe himself," she retorted. Then she felt bad. Jon *was* quite good-looking.

"Well, *I* think he's gorgeous," Deb said.

"See? Touché, then," Alyssa said, and Deb was quiet. Alyssa could tell Deb was fuming inside, but said nothing else.

They walked together in the dark of the city streets, factories humming, traffic noise surrounding them. Sirens and horns blared out from all directions. The moon tried to shine through the smog, but without much success. It smelled especially dank in this sector of Central City. Too much moisture and not enough daylight, not enough sanitation.

Alyssa hadn't taken this walk with anyone else since that first night, when Manuel asked her to come along. It was odd to have company, odder still not to feel the tiny plastic package in her pocket. She missed fingering it. She fiddled with the little pocketknife instead, but it didn't help.

She wanted to turn around and run back. Suddenly it was quite urgent. She *must* go back. She felt them, felt the creatures pushing her, impelling her to go back there and see if there was a way she could convince Rob to give her one more hit. Just one more time wouldn't hurt. Maybe there was something she could trade for it.

You could trade your body . . . he's very attracted to you, a voice in her mind said.

No, she rejected the thought. *Never.*

Images of Lauren loomed in her mind. She could never stoop *that* low. She might think of something, though. She had cheated death before and never ran into trouble with the game until she took more than she should at once.

Her heart beat in her throat. She fought it, fought the desperate impulse to run. She had to. She reminded herself of her conviction, her fear, her promise to herself.

Besides, Deb would follow her and scold her like a mother hen if she went back. She had to show her she was strong.

After a long silence Debra said, "I don't have to say I think this is a very bad idea."

"I figured you would."

The words brought her out of the turmoil and gave her something else to think about. She was relieved. It would be easier to fight with Deb about Rob than to admit she still needed the drug.

"You don't have to feel obligated to him, you know."

"I don't," Alyssa said. "Like I told you, he's a friend, in a weird sort of way. He's different. He tried to talk me out of it from the first time I went in there."

Debra exhaled an annoyed sigh. "He is still a druggist, Alyssa. He is *not* your friend. No matter what he says, he doesn't care about you. He's only in the business to make a profit. I mean he's obviously not doing it to improve the world. I swear, without people like him willing to sell that garbage . . ."

"No, it's the other way around. If people want it, it's going to get sold. It's not like he's the owner or anything. He just works there. It's a job. That's all."

"Don't get me started on this. Those things should never have been legalized in the first place. It's wrong."

"The regulations make sure people don't get crummy stuff, and it's kept everything aboveboard. Look at how it's helped the economy. That's on the news all the time. It created a lot of decent jobs. And it's saves a lot of lives, too, since people don't have to worry about going to jail or getting killed shipping the stuff anymore. It raises a lot of money in taxes alone."

"It nearly took *your* life, don't forget that."

"Because I wanted it to!"

"Every time?"

Alyssa didn't answer. She felt scolded again, and more than a little upset. After a long pause, she said, "He really is nice. You know I don't go out with just anybody. I wouldn't have said yes if I didn't want to."

Deb didn't answer immediately. She was walking very fast. Finally she said, "Promise me you'll be careful. This is very risky."

"I will be careful. Don't worry. I'll even tell you everything that happens to the last detail. Besides, it's just one date. Not a major commitment." She made her voice sound casual.

It would be her first real date. Not that she hadn't been asked, but she never even wanted to accept a request before. Putting the other guys off had always been easy. But she felt a definite flutter of excitement about this one. It made her giddy to think he still wanted to see her. He had grown on her, and now that she thought about it she had looked forward to seeing him every weekend and coyly flirting with him almost as much as she had looked forward to getting high.

"All right. I won't try to control your life, you'd just get mad at me anyway."

"You have been rather motherly this week." Quickly she added, "Not the same as my mother, of course. I mean, in a nice way."

Deb made a 'humph' sort of sound and continued walking.

"How did you feel when you first met Jon?" Alyssa asked. "Didn't you know him before I met you? Did you feel anything?"

"Well, it wasn't love at first sight," Deb said. "That's for sure. He was a brat when he was younger. He used to tease me to death. But we became good friends after a while, the year you and I met, and then . . . Well, you know the rest of the story."

"Yes, I remember," Alyssa said, laughing.

Many nights in their senior year, Deb had kept her up late on the phone trying to figure out what to do, once she realized she was in love. It had taken Jon months to clue in.

"Well, that's the best part overall, the friendship."

"I see what you mean," Alyssa said.

It was never too hard to distract Debra by discussing Jon. They spent the rest of the walk home talking about him.

•••••••

"Almost lost her. She OD'd last weekend, and she's got help with her. Company."

"She ever tell you about hallucinations?"

"No. She's a closed book. I can't crack through all her ID encryption coding either. Still don't know who she is or where she's from."

"So is this a dead end in your opinion, Robert?" The man's gruff bass didn't sound pleased. "Should we hand her case over to the boys at the computer lab?"

"No, that won't be necessary." Rob grimaced. Then he smiled, knowing the other man wouldn't see. "I found a way to keep in touch with her anyway. Maybe on a more *personal* level I can get her to talk. We'll have to see."

"No emotional attachments. Rules of the game."

"Since when am I prone to that? You know me. I know the rules."

"Keep counting on that promotion then. I'll throw a bit of an advance into your next check, for incentive. I think you've earned it."

•••••••

Alyssa was nervous the next day. Rob was to meet her at the café for lunch. She changed clothes three times, then realized he was used to seeing her in grubby jeans and wrinkled shirts. She left the third outfit on and started brushing her hair. She sprayed down the one lock of hair on the side of her head that never would stay flat, and became annoyed with it, brushing it over and over again. Finally she just put on a headband.

Maybe he wouldn't be there at all. Then she could forget about it and consider his offer a common courtesy to departing customers.

But he was there. And her heart did a little skip when she saw him.

Somehow she had always thought of him as inseparably connected to the store. She never saw him anywhere else. His presence here, in a place she frequented with Debra, was incongruous. He was out of his uniform too, and looked sharp, stylishly dressed.

Nice clothes, she thought. *Expensive*. "Hi," she said shyly, sitting down.

"Hi." He smiled. "I thought you wouldn't come."

She looked at her watch. "I'm not late."

"I know. But I was afraid you wouldn't be here. That friend of yours . . . I was afraid she'd talk you out of it. I can tell she doesn't like me."

"Oh, Debra's all talk," she said. "I do whatever I want."

"It's nice to see you, you know, somewhere else," Rob said.

"I was thinking the same thing," she said.

They talked quietly in the booth all afternoon.

****

A few days later they met again, this time for dinner.

He made her laugh, with his lighthearted, easy manner. He was terribly flirtatious, and Alyssa found she enjoyed the outrageous attention. She was unused to anything like it. During the meal she caught him watching her more than once with a rapt, lost look in his eyes.

She smiled. "Stop that!" she said.

"Stop what?" he asked, straightening himself in his chair.

"Looking at me like that. You look silly."

"Oh. Well. Sorry. It must be the pasta." He rolled his eyes. "I always get this weird kind of indigestion when I eat here. We'll have to try a different place next time."

"Next time?" She raised her left eyebrow. "Who says there'll be a next time?"

"Why not?" he countered. "Don't I just take your breath away?" He gasped dramatically.

She grinned. "Oh, all right. Why not?"

The next week they saw each other three times. Rob called every day to see if she was free for dinner or a movie a few hours before he wanted to meet. Twice she was not, and said so. She still had to study for her exams and finish final drafts of term papers. Finals were fast approaching and she wasn't ready. She couldn't spare every moment for him, whether she wanted to or not.

While they were together Alyssa found she enjoyed his company, his exaggerated compliments. When he didn't try to hold her hand or make other physical advances, she relaxed and became more comfortable talking to him. She would never say so, but being physically close to anyone still frightened her. Even when Deb hugged her, she was uncomfortable with it.

Rob smiled easily and laughed at her jokes, and she could tell by the lost way he looked at her that he thought she was beautiful. It wasn't an act. He flirted outrageously to hide behind his feelings, but she saw through him and was genuinely flattered. She enjoyed feeling beautiful and being the sole object of his attentions. Something about it felt very good.

"Tell me about your family," Rob said the second week.

It was Monday. They had taken a walk, the weather being nice, and stopped in a small park to sit on a bench.

There was a City ordinance that required parks. Some study years earlier had shown that people needed greenery on some deep psychological and physiological level. The parks were an effort begun a few years later, in hopes of reducing crime, increasing morale and raising taxes.

"So what are you, my self-appointed therapist? Do we have to start with my traumatic childhood?" she teased.

"Course not. I just want to know you better."

"Is that all?"

"Sure, you tell me yours, I'll tell you mine," he said with a wink and a laugh. "So, how traumatic was it?"

She laughed and said, "Well, I grew up hating my mother." She surprised herself. Those were not the words she had intended to say.

"Why?" He looked in her eyes. She could tell he meant it. He honestly wanted to know.

She started to explain, and found she had a bizarre compulsion to spill everything to him, her whole life. She found herself telling him things about her past she hadn't even told Debra, and she had been fairly open with her. It seemed more natural to share them with him.

Deb struggled to comprehend some of the things she told her. He didn't. He understood perfectly.

"So why didn't you just leave?" he asked after she had talked for a long time. "You could've left when you turned seventeen. At least a year sooner. And why didn't you ever hit her back? Didn't you want to?"

She could have balked at his questions, refused to answer. Instead she sat quietly, thinking. "I guess I was too scared. I never did run away. I always knew I could get out once I finished school, and I didn't turn seventeen till my senior year anyway. My birthday's in September."

Rob sighed. "I'm sorry it wasn't different for you."

"Was it different for you?" she asked.

"Not much, really. Feelings are about the same, anyway. I don't even remember much of my childhood. Bits and pieces. I remember moving, a lot." His eyes looked far away.

"Why?"

He shrugged. "Mom's told me about it, some. My real dad was a vicious alcoholic. Your dad sounds like he was at least quiet about it."

"My father wasn't an alcoholic." She bristled.

Rob snorted. "Ha! *You* are in denial. Floating down De-Nile on a homemade raft. You just told me yourself he drank himself to death."

"I did not. He just drank beer."

"Beer's alcohol."

He stared at her until she looked down. That was a twist. She had always prided herself on her ability to stare anyone down. It was a strange feeling.

"Okay," she said, turning away from him. "So you've made your point. What about it?"

"Hey, I'm sorry," he said, reaching out to touch her shoulder. Just briefly. She looked back at him. "But would you feel any better if I said, okay, you're right, he wasn't an alcoholic? Let you keep on pretending? Huh?"

"No," she said, shaking her head.

"All right then."

"So what about your dad?" Alyssa said. "You were talking about him."

"My ma left him when I was little, six or seven maybe. I still have the scars." He pushed up his sleeve to show a large ugly white mark on his upper arm. "See that?"

Alyssa gasped. "How did you get that?"

"Ma told me it took over thirty stitches." He was quiet a moment. "Pa got carried away with a whiskey bottle one night. She told me I was about four. I don't remember it though." He shrugged.

"Didn't she call the police? What about the people who stitched you up? Wouldn't they have known?"

She was horrified. She had felt sorry for herself her entire life; but even Joan would never have done damage like that.

"Maybe," he said. "But Pa had plenty of money. You can buy anything you want with money, if you have enough. Probably paid the doctors to shut up. Far as I know, he never went to prison, or therapy.

"We moved around a lot after she left him. I went to at least three different schools each year. Got kicked out of most of 'em." He smiled. "Like I said, I can't remember most of it, not until I was about twelve or so. Ma's filled me in on some things, like where all the scars came from, but she keeps quiet about a lot of it. And she was no slouch when it came to discipline herself."

"And here I thought my life was bad," Alyssa murmured.

She imagined Rob as a little boy, wondering how he must have felt; wondering what sort of people could do things like that to a small child. It simply dwarfed anything she had to complain about. She felt a sudden, intense compassion for him, unlike anything she had ever experienced for another person.

Rob looked up. "Hey," he said. "Hey." He touched her shoulder lightly again, this time leaving his hand there. "No fair comparing. It all hurts the same. It's okay. I've come to terms with most of it. I'm all right."

From that night on they had plenty to talk about. His sister had died at sixteen of a heroin overdose.

"How can you even do what you do for a living then?" Alyssa asked him when he told her the story of his sister's death. They were in the café where they had met for their first date, having dessert. She was suddenly very angry. "How can you justify doing what you do when drugs killed your own sister?"

"She died a long time ago, before it was regulated. She got some really bad stuff. She was a junkie back when it was a lot more dangerous to be one. Plus she was a lot older than me. Mom was only fourteen when she had her, hadn't even met my Pa yet. I was only about ten when it happened. They didn't put the regulations in the law until years after they legalized it. You knew that, didn't you?"

"That doesn't change the facts. You sell heroin right along with pot and anything else scientists can cook up in their labs. An overdose nearly killed *me*. How can you even live with yourself knowing that?"

Her voice rose, an angry edge in her tone. The thought sickened her.

"No shop talk, remember?" he smiled, taking a bite of his dessert.

Alyssa put her spoon down. They shared similar tastes in food, often ordering the same thing from the menu. Today she was eating the same rich chocolate concoction.

"I remember. I made the rule. But you can't back out of this one that easily." She stared at him until *he* looked away this time.

"Well." He took another bite and swallowed. "It pays well. Nice benefits. I get to meet some very interesting people," he laughed and looked back at her. "You are something else, you know? I never even thought of it that way before. Maybe I do what I do so I can rescue poor beautiful lost souls like you who remind me of her." He gave her a wink.

"How many 'lost souls' have there been?" Alyssa asked, arching her brow.

She didn't like the thought this brought out. She enjoyed thinking of herself as the only woman he had ever paid attention to in his entire life. While she knew, deep down, how illogical and completely unlikely that perception was, she liked preserving the illusion.

Rob lowered his eyes. His flirtatious manner vanished. He looked back up. "Just you, so far."

"Likely story. Like I'm the only girlfriend you've ever had in your life. You expect me to believe that?"

"Oh, so you're my girlfriend now?" he grinned.

"No," she snapped, and looked out the window.

"Do you want to be?" he asked, his tone serious as he looked at her.

"I don't know," she said. "You'll have to explain yourself better than that if you want me to consider it."

"Alyssa, honest, you're different," he said. "Everyone else, they just want a kick, a thrill. Something to put a spark in their weekend. I told you from the start I knew that about you. That's not what you were looking for, or we both know you'd have gone on to the Tiki Room with the rest of them."

"I'm not sure how flattering that is."

"Do I have to flatter you all the time?"

"Well, I'm getting used to it." She smiled.

"I idolized my sister," he said quietly. "She was so beautiful. She had long blond hair, like you. Only her eyes were bright blue. Yours are different, so mysterious. I can't quite figure out what color they are."

She looked at him, then looked down at her dessert.

"So what about you?" Rob asked after a pause. "Everything about you screams you're a control freak. The way you order things on the menu. 'Put the dressing on the side, and get the garnishes right this time. And if the mahi mahi isn't fresh flown in today, I don't want it.' I mean, really! And then it has to be just *so* or you send it back to the kitchen. 'These fries aren't hot enough. There's too much mustard on this burger. I ordered this *without* pickles.'"

"My dad was an amateur chef. I'm picky," she said. "So?"

"Well, there's also the fact that you have to pick out where we're going. You don't like to be surprised. I have to tell you exactly where I'm taking you or you freak out. Then there's the way you fuss at that little piece of hair that tweaks out on the right side and won't lie flat." He gestured at her hair, and she fussed with it automatically, putting her hand down only with an effort. "You said so yourself. The first time I saw you, you talked about being in control. What did somebody like you get out of taking such a powerful drug? You surrendered your precious control to it. Why? How did you manage to justify that?"

"Emotional release. I couldn't do that naturally, but I'm learning." She was on the defensive now.

"Repressed, are you?" His eyes glimmered.

"I've lived my life well without emotions, yes, but that's just the way I am. I wouldn't call it repression."

It struck a nerve that he had noticed so many details about her habits. She didn't realize he had. It wasn't comfortable knowing her behavior revealed so much about her personality. She felt piqued. Especially since he was right on every point.

"You think it's been easy for me?" she said. "You of all people should know it's powerfully addictive. I couldn't help it much after the first time or two. You should know that."

"I bet you couldn't stand not controlling the aftereffects. Unable to control whether you got a headache or not. Did those ever bother you? Sleeping too long? The headaches?"

"And I notice you didn't warn me about those, either, before I walked out with it."

"I did too. I tried," he said. "You were the stubborn one. I wanted you to try something else, remember? Come on. How did you deal with it?"

"No shop talk," she said, shaking her spoon at him.

"I answered *your* question," he said. With a dramatic sigh he added, "I just wondered if it interfered too much with your precious control of everything in your environment . . . So I can understand you better." He paused. With a sigh, he said, "It's not important though. I don't mean to drag up *pain*ful memories."

She conceded defeat. "Oh, fine. As long as we don't talk about this all the time. Yes, it bothered me. It still bothers me. I don't know if I can forgive myself for that, ever. You know I probably won't finish school."

"I know," he said. "I'm sorry too. I'm sorry I had anything at all to do with that. But there's one thing I'm not sorry for."

"What's that?" she asked.

"I'm not sorry I met you." He looked deep into her eyes. "Ever since that first night you came in, I don't know why, but my life hasn't been the same since. You've turned me upside-down and sideways."

"Yeah, well, neither has mine," she said, uncomfortable with his confession. "You try having your life ripped inside-out by that drug."

This brought something else to her mind. Maybe he knew something more. Could he? It was worth a try. "You know, I probably shouldn't mention this. It's too weird."

"Mention what?"

"Well, since the subject is up . . ." she said, and left off, smashing leftover crumbs of her dessert with her fork.

"What?" he asked.

"You ever hear about any truly weird side effects?"

"Weird? Weird how?"

"I don't even believe it myself. But I . . . I just have to tell somebody," she said, speaking faster as she gathered her courage. "I don't know if you'll understand this or not, but I know Deb wouldn't. I've got to know if I was going crazy. So here goes. Some of the . . . the same creatures I saw when I was high . . . they came back to haunt me during the day."

"Creatures?" Rob asked with interest.

"Yes. That's the best word I can think of. During the highs the rush was incredible, but there were these *things* . . . people, sort of . . . Hallucinations, is all they were, I guess, but they were terrifying. The kind of things that crawl out from your worst nightmares. They wanted my pain, my fear. It was like they fed on my sensations somehow. Well, after a while I started seeing them when I was *sober*. They talked to me. I heard voices, saw shadows jumping out of the walls, hallucinations like that. It was freaky. Most of the creatures were gruesome, horrible. So I about flipped when I started seeing those *things* in broad daylight." She shivered. "At least that part is over. I can't see them anymore, thank goodness. I mentioned it privately to the medics and they told me it was normal. Flashbacks, hallucinations, all pretty common side effects reported for Elation. But I noticed you never mentioned any of that."

"You're hearing voices too? What do they say?"

Alyssa shook her head. She felt insulted, as though he was teasing her. The look on his face was too intense. He couldn't be that serious.

"I don't remember well," she said.

"You were sober when it happened?" He smiled. "Come on, you've got to remember. Go ahead, tell me."

If she didn't know better, she'd have thought he wanted to pull out a notebook and pencil to take notes like a psychoanalyst. That would be too much. He *was* teasing her.

"I said, I don't remember." Her voice was terse. She put her spoon down and looked at him sternly.

We'll have you still, a voice echoed, laughing in her mind. *Keep lying. Lying is good. It's your greatest gift. You'll find your way back to us soon enough.*

She hoped her face didn't register the shock she felt hearing something strange once again.

"You really don't want to talk about it?" he said, his mood and look shifting. "I believe you. I wasn't making fun or anything. I didn't mean to sound . . . Maybe another time you can tell me all about it?"

"I doubt it," she said, irritated.

"Really, I would like to know. If it's important to you, I want you to share it with me. I'm glad you brought it up."

"Never mind," she said.

"I'm sorry," he said, and paused. "No more shop talk?"

"Yes," she replied. "That would be good."

"Hey, uh, there's a bunch of new movies premiering tonight. You wanna pick one? We'll be just in time to make one of them if we leave right now," Rob said, checking his watch.

"Sure. I could use a good comedy about now. You're wearing a little thin." She nudged him under the table with her toe.

They left the restaurant and drove to the theater.

****

"Got something," he reported late that night in the dark of his apartment. "Have to work on her more though. She's touchy."

After a silence the other voice said, "What is it?"

"She did hear voices, had hallucinations. Sober, just like you said. But she wouldn't go into any detail. Whatever she saw gave her serious creeps. I couldn't press her any further without raising suspicion."

"Get the details."

"Of course, sir, but give me time. It's not like she's a lab patient. There are limits out here."

****

The future loomed in front of Alyssa with more than a vague sense of foreboding. But at least she wanted to face it now. That was the big difference.

It didn't matter that she needed two sleeping pills to get to sleep now, to prevent the nightmares. The evenings she spent with Rob lifted her sadness. It was different from the kind of friendship she shared with Debra. There was a definite underlying excitement to it.

She studied, but without the fervor she used to have. She just wanted to pass her classes, even though it wouldn't count for much. She didn't have enough cash to pay her professors for any more passing grades. When the term was over she would look for a job. She sent out advertisements, resumes, but so far no offers came back from the Internet companies she had worked for in high school.

Debra stopped complaining about her seeing Rob.

"I guess he's all right," she said after the second week they had been seeing each other. "You do seem happier after you've been with him."

Alyssa smiled. "I told you he was nice."

"And he treats you all right? He's so polite when he comes over. I think it's pretty funny how he tries to kiss up to me." She laughed. "He doesn't have to."

"Yeah, he knows that. But he's sweet. He wants you to like him." Then she added, "We're good friends, is all. For now."

"Hm," Deb said. "Well, that's how me and Jon started. Look. I'm sorry I fussed at you over this. I guess I misjudged him. If you're happy with him, then I'm happy for you, too."

"Thanks. That means a lot to me."

****

The week of finals arrived. She had agreed to see Rob only after her last one was over.

"How did you do?" he asked when they finally met at the café. "I missed you every day this week."

"I did all right, I guess. As if it matters now." She looked melancholy.

His comments were slowly losing their facetious nature and taking on a more meaningful tone.

"You know," he said softly, "Some days you seem as fragile as a delicate blown-glass sculpture. And other days you act as though your very sinews were cabled steel, strong and inflexible."

"How am I supposed to take that?" she said, looking over.

"Just that you're a mystery to me," he said, smiling. "You fascinate me. And I can't figure out which you are, today. Glass or steel."

She found it unusual, somehow, that he hadn't even tried to hold her hand, yet. She had seen him reach for her, out of the corner of her eye, once or twice, but he pulled his hand back each time. She hadn't encouraged him.

"You're a little strange yourself," she said, smiling back.

She was sure other guys would be expecting "more" by this point. She heard people talk. If dating was going well, most couples had slept together by the third or fourth date. But he hadn't pushed. She was glad for that, relieved. She would have to drop him if he became demanding, she was sure.

"And how am I to take that?" he asked.

"Call it a compliment," she said.

He laughed.

Through the window of their booth the city lights winked cheerlessly, the traffic passing by, oblivious to their existence.

"This place stinks," Alyssa said, looking out. "Nothing outside that window cares that my dreams are completely ruined. Nobody cares about anything anymore, except money. All anybody ever wants is more money. Sometimes it makes me sick."

"What's wrong with having money? Doesn't your family have plenty?"

"I never told you that," she said, looking back at him.

"You didn't?" he said, wrinkling his brow.

"I don't think so."

"I guess I figured it out from the way you dress. Some of the things you've put in your apartment aren't cheap either. College students don't do that unless they've got families with money to burn."

"Oh, they don't?" she said.

"Of course not. Nobody has their own money like that by twenty-one. Oh, then there was that little line you gave me once, about 'Money is no object.'" He grinned. "Besides, you think I believe Debra bought the original Nagel in your living room?"

She smiled. "I see what you mean. Well, you're right. Dad sent that, actually, for my last birthday. Before he passed away."

"I can tell a lot about people from watching them," Rob said. "It's kind of a gift I have."

"So I noticed."

"What about asking your mother for money?" Rob asked. "You haven't even talked to her about it, have you? I bet you haven't talked to her since your dad's funeral."

"Would you ask *your* mother?" she responded.

"Good point. But it wouldn't hurt to try."

"Well, you're right. I haven't talked to her since right after the funeral. That's when she handed over my dad's money, my inheritance. But if I called, I'd have to tell her where all that money went. I can't face that. I can't tell her I wasted it. Then she *could* tell me how right she was about me from the beginning, what a useless waste of a human being I am, and I'd start believing she was right. No way. I'm not going to set myself up to listen to that. It's bad enough as it is." There was pain in her eyes as she looked at him. "You wouldn't still have my diamond necklace, would you?"

Rob shook his head. "It wasn't mine to keep. If there was any way I could get it back for you, I would. You have to believe me."

After a pause she said, "I figured as much. Just had to ask." She looked out the window again.

"You look so sad tonight . . . I'd like to help you," he said. "But I don't know how."

"I don't know either." She paused. "You know, I never had a definite plan, anyway. My only goal was to get away from that house. I never thought much about what would happen to me after I left home. I figured I'd finish school though, at least."

"I know how much you love school." He paused, reaching his hand forward. But again he left it on the table. She saw, but didn't take it. "Can I help? How much is tuition?"

"Rob, I'm not going to let you pay for my education," she said. "That's not an option."

"Too much commitment?"

"Definitely." She nodded her head. "I couldn't let you. Besides, you couldn't possibly make that much money. You can't have *that* much to throw away, with your job."

"I wouldn't be throwing it away," he said with a smile. "Besides, I have other resources I can draw on."

"Thanks, but no." She sighed. "My mind isn't the same. I can't make the mental connections, I can't concentrate, I can't even study well anymore. I don't have what it takes now even if I did have the finances to finish my degree. It's okay, Rob. I have to learn to cut my losses."

"Am I one of them?" he asked, wrinkling his brow in worry.

"Huh?"

"Am I one of your losses?"

"Oh. No. I'd say you're probably the only good thing that's come out of this whole mess."

She smiled a faint smile, but there was little happiness behind it tonight. Surely she enjoyed his company; but he was also deeply intertwined with the reasons for her sadness, the losses she felt. She didn't feel very talkative. After several minutes of silence, Rob slowly stretched out his hand to where hers lay across the table and touched her ever so gently.

"Is this okay?" he whispered, gathering her hand into his.

Alyssa looked down at their hands.

"Sure," she said.

She squeezed his hand a little. It was different, touching like this. But she was so sullen this evening, on the close of her untimely last day of college, that her hand was limp; she felt no thrill of excitement in his touch. She might have, had he tried on a different day, later maybe.

"Is my timing off?" he asked. "I don't want to push you, if you're not ready. I can let go . . . That glass sculpture, you know . . . I certainly don't want to break it." He smiled at her, a warm, melting smile.

She felt safe, the way he spoke, and something inside her relaxed. He understood somehow . . . there would be no pressure for physical involvement from him. His words put her at ease, and his touch was gentle and kind. His skin was very soft on hers.

"No, Rob, this is fine, really," she said, attempting a smile and squeezing his hand again. "I'm just down, that's all."

She didn't mind holding his hand. There was some electricity to the feel of his skin on her fingers. She couldn't deny that.

But it also didn't do much to comfort her.

Chapter 21

Waiting

Peter and I haven't fought as much lately, at least. I'm trying hard. I'm talking to him more, even telling him some of the deeper stuff. Not everything. I'm not that stupid. But he really tries his best to understand. He cares so much. I don't deserve that, but he can't possibly know the truth.

I'm more nervous than usual around him, but at least he hasn't noticed. He keeps saying we'll just put that little "episode" behind us. He was going to try to see me every other day, but after that night he said it was best we keep our time together limited until after the wedding. I agreed, though for different reasons I guess . . . I nearly blew everything, and the wedding's only a month away. A June wedding. Just like I've always dreamed.

I'm still trying to recover from the shock that my best lines didn't work on him that night. I wonder if he really does want me that way. He says he does, and I'm trying to believe him, hoping he really will come around after the wedding like he says. I'd die if he didn't. Just die. In the meantime I'm trying to keep things to a minimum, trying to be very careful about it, but a woman has to cope with this kind of frustration somehow. Alcohol alone won't do it for me, never has.

Jackie Halladay,
diary entry

It was a night late in May when Peter dreamed the dream again. But it was a little different this time.

Peter was standing with Jackie in her wedding dress, together on the grassy knoll. Her ring sparkled on her finger, larger than life. They kissed. It was wonderful and enticing, the way she kissed him that night in the park. He quivered with anticipation and reached to caress her as he longed to, when again the voice came so faint, so piercing.

"No! Peter! Wait for me!"

He turned to the voice. Again the wind blew a chill through his bones. Jackie grabbed his hand and pulled him away. Her touch was icy, so cold it burned with frost.

"Wait for me," the voice repeated. It was desperate. "Please."

"Who are you?" he asked the voice.

"I am not waiting for you, Peter," Jackie said and vanished.

"You already know," the voice said plaintively, and it was right.

"Why do I have to wait? Wait for what?"

"*Wait for me.*"

"Why? I have to know why."

He saw nothing but darkness ahead, swirling clouds obstructing his view. There was no one, no image of Alyssa visible this time.

"You'll understand in time. Just wait for me . . ." The voice faded away and he awoke in a cold sweat.

He tensed his muscles in frustration. He was promised to Jackie. They were in love. He promised her he would take care of her, share the rest of his life with her, grow old with her. She was the most wonderful thing in his life. He had to have a better excuse than a silly dream to break that promise.

Fitfully he fell asleep again.

****

Alyssa awoke gasping for air. Was it a nightmare or another haunting flashback? She couldn't remember clearly, but it had something to do with Peter and another woman, a beautiful woman. The woman was taking him away from her. He wanted the woman badly . . . he was burning with desire for her. Alyssa didn't know how she knew that, the images were blurry, but she *knew*. And she hated him for it. She was livid, green with jealousy. She ached to be near him, to hold him close. She called to him, she begged him to wait, but he didn't see her, didn't know her anymore. She wanted him like she wanted nothing else in her entire life. She longed to have him back, to have him sweep her up in his arms and carry her away with him. He belonged to *her*, not to that . . . that woman.

She sat up in bed, breathing hard. *Now that is totally irrational,* she thought.

She remembered calling Mrs. Richardson, remembered clearly meeting Topaz on the phone and being told Peter was marrying her when he returned from China. She already knew that, she had dealt with it. Why would she dream about it now?

She shook off the potent feelings of jealousy, the fierce sense of possession. But there was something odd . . . something not quite right . . . she had a hard time placing it.

The woman in the dream was not Topaz.

Topaz was blond, she was sure she remembered that much. This woman had the look of a movie star, a supermodel, with vivid red-auburn hair. She shook her head, clearing her thoughts. That was more than ridiculous. She didn't remember his fiancée being anything overly spectacular to look at.

Her imagination surely must have run away with her, this time. It was crazy. The nightmare gave her an overall prickly feeling of creepiness. Yet she found she ached for it to return, to sleep and dream it over again, if only to be near him once more. He had felt so close . . . so near she might have reached out and touched him.

She flipped on the lamp by her bed. How could she have a nightmare anyway? The sleeping pills suppressed them so she could rest. Oh yes. She had been so tired when Rob finally left she had forgotten.

After they left the café, they decided to watch TV at her apartment and he had stayed late, both of them staring at the mindless drivel of programming until they couldn't see straight. Debra had gone to bed early, claiming one last final in the morning.

On the couch Rob had put his arm around Alyssa and pulled her close to him. With surprise, she found it was actually comfortable. Before the evening was over she rather relished the closeness. She was glad he had taken her hand in the café. And he didn't try to kiss her or make further advances during the evening, which she also appreciated.

"Must be more side effects," Alyssa said to herself, rubbing her temples. The headaches were at last beginning to fade during the day. She didn't need the pain killers as much as she used to. But maybe she needed a stronger sedative at night.

She didn't like to dream. Her dreams relived the nightmares of her drug-induced images in all their terror. They never included the joy.

She lay back in bed and settled into the covers. Her last thought before dropping off was to wonder why she had dreamed such an odd dream about Peter, tonight of all nights when things were going so well with Rob.

Again she wished for the dream to return. She could almost feel him, close enough to hold in her arms. She wanted him so passionately, him and no one else . . . and wanted *him* to want no one else.

Finally she slept.

****

The next day was Saturday. She met Rob for dinner.

After dinner, they walked to the park. It was not too far from the café. The evening was warm, the air refreshing, as they neared the green lawns. This particular park had a beautiful fountain with brass statuary, and tonight they sat on one of the benches next to it.

He had taken her hand as they walked, and didn't let it go when they sat down. But something about it felt different to her, less comforting than it had been the night before.

"I take it you're feeling a little better tonight?"

"I guess so," Alyssa said. "But Rob, I've been doing some serious thinking today. About us."

The truth was Peter hadn't left her mind all day. Her longing for him, after the dream, barely faded during the daylight hours. He would be home and married by now . . . wouldn't he? She knew he was lost to her, knew how wrong and illogical it would be to run to him and try to steal him away from his wife. Still, she had even entertained that thought, if only momentarily.

Of course she had immediately banished the idea, aware of its utter madness as well as the improbability of succeeding in such a rash, malicious venture. Such things were not in her nature.

Her thoughts had then moved from Peter to Rob . . . analyzing her current feelings for him, trying to explain, even to herself, how she felt. If nothing else the dream had confused and befuddled her, more than any mere dream should have. Many things concerned her about Rob—his job, the circumstances under which they had met, always the underlying temptation (or was it a *hope?*) she felt, but kept hidden, that he might bring her something from the store.

"Serious thinking? That doesn't sound good, hon. Never a hopeful sign."

He looked in her eyes, his expression saying he hoped she was not about to say what generally follows that sentence in a relationship. She held his gaze, swept in by the emotions she saw there.

"Oh, I guess it's nothing."

She bit her lower lip. She hadn't expected to forget what she was going to say. His eyes were a warm chocolate brown, and the way he looked at her was intoxicating. It took her breath away.

"Then it was nothing, Alyssa, nothing at all," he said, and softly leaned in to kiss her.

She closed her eyes and let him. It was a delicate, light kiss. Soft. But the sensation on her lips brought back a vivid memory, one she had long blocked from her mind, the memory of a cornfield, birds singing, crickets . . . her only other time.

She pushed the thought away and put her hand up to touch Rob's cheek, returning his kiss. Then she found herself imagining he *was* Peter, that it was he she kissed, giving her passion to him alone.

Again she was filled with illogical, anxious longing. She forced herself to remember this was Rob. *Rob*. She hadn't expected it to be so difficult. She felt confused and a little dazed.

"Wow," Rob said, when the kiss ended. "I could get used to that."

She blushed, but said nothing.

"Do . . . do you want to walk some more?" he asked, after a pause. "I feel so . . . out in the open. If I'm going to kiss you I'd like to feel like we're alone."

"Sure," she said. "It's a nice night."

She squeezed his hand as they stood up, and in spite of her confusion, she felt a thrill that Rob was planning to kiss her again.

There were more trees at the other end of the park, a paved walking trail designed to give the impression one was in a forest. The underbrush was left untrimmed and allowed to grow wild. The effect was nice. The trees had been transplanted there when the park was built giving it the feeling that they had been there for years. They stopped under a large tree and sat down on the soft grass beneath it.

"This is better, don't you think?"

"Yes," Alyssa said, leaning against the tree. "Much nicer. It actually smells good here. Can't smell that city stink as much."

"Good point," Rob said. "Um, hey, I brought something along tonight, but I'm not sure it's the right thing." He reached into his pocket.

"You did?" *Something from the store?* she wondered. Her hopes . . . and fears, raised at once.

"Yeah, I don't know, considering everything . . . but I thought you might enjoy it. You tell me right away if I'm wrong and I'll put it back."

He pulled out an odd-colored thing that reminded her of a cigarette, but not quite.

"Rob, that's a joint, isn't it? Why did you bring it?"

"It is. I thought . . . actually, I don't know what I was thinking, now that I look at it."

"I don't smoke," she said. "Mother was a chimney."

"I wondered about that," he said. "But I couldn't remember, so I brought some in a pill, too."

She saw that a small capsule was also in his hand. One eyebrow went up. She had forgotten it came that way.

"Please don't be mad at me. I know how withdrawals are so hard, and you're not feeling too upbeat lately . . . I thought it might help, but I'm not so sure," he said, shaking his head. "Now that I think about it maybe it wasn't such a good idea. I'm sorry."

"I'm not mad . . .," she said, her voice trailing off. Was it like Elation, maybe? Only less potent, less dangerous? She had no idea, but she didn't want to start anything new. Still there was that problem with sleep she was having. She felt edgy. The sleeping pills helped, but they weren't quite enough. It might be worth a try if it would help her sleep.

"You're not?"

"Not really . . . Will it help me sleep?" she asked, putting her hand on his. He had moved to put the items back in his pocket, but stopped.

"You're not sleeping well, hon?" he asked with concern.

She shook her head. "Nightmares."

"What kind of nightmares?" He moved a little closer and put his arm around her.

She fidgeted and looked away, then leaned into his embrace. "Those things I saw. The creatures I told you about. I relive all the horrible parts of it in my dreams. Never the good parts. All those creatures and voices . . . all the violence . . . the hallucinations I had during the day too. They scare me so much. I still hear their voices, sometimes. I don't know how to make them go away." She was shaking. "I wonder if I'm going crazy."

"I'm so sorry," he said. "Man, do I feel guilty. I helped you get those nightmares." He looked decidedly uncomfortable. "Maybe if you talk to somebody about it, it would help."

"Somebody like you?" she asked, an involuntary shudder going through her as she thought about sharing the graphic, grisly images with anyone. "Are you sure you can handle it?"

"Try me," Rob replied, and held her tighter. "I promise I'll try. Not much fazes me, you'd be surprised."

She talked. She told him everything, all the details—the gray-haired woman who appeared to her in class the first time, the yellow-haired one who leeched out the pain from her wrist, the fear monster, the blood-red pain, and especially the inky black taskmaster who terrified her most of all.

When she was finished, Rob was quiet.

"It's so strange," he said. "You talk about them so clearly, like they're unique individuals or something."

"It feels like they are. The familiar ones, anyway."

"And you still hear their voices?"

"I haven't for a while. Just when I sleep." It was the first time she realized she rarely heard them in daylight hours anymore.

"Well, that's good," he said. "That's very good."

They were silent. Then he looked down at his hand, still holding the marijuana. The joint was sweaty from his palms. His hands were also shaking, she noticed.

"Hey, you're scared," she said. "I'm sorry. Too much detail?"

"No," he said. "I can handle it. Not much fazes me. Like I said."

"But this does."

"Uh . . . it's not that exactly," he said. "It's all right. Don't worry about me, hon. It's you we need to be concerned about." He paused, then motioned with the object in his hands. "I can't promise this'll help you sleep any better. It just makes you feel different. A buzz. Not quite the same as being drunk."

"I've never gotten drunk," Alyssa said. "Watching my dad was enough for me. Hey," and she cleared her throat, "You promised you weren't going to sell me anything." She hated to say it, but she had to address the issue straight on.

"Are you sure you're not mad? I don't want you mad at me."

"Of course not."

"Well, I'm not selling it to you. It's free, a present. But I'm taking it back. It was dumb to bring it along."

"No," she said.

If it would help her sleep, she wanted it. Uneasiness entered her mind, a strong inclination to refuse and make him put it back in his pocket. She brushed it off. Maybe it *would* help her nightmares go away. That alone was worth trying it. Wasn't it?

"It wasn't dumb. Do you mind if I try one? One of the pills?"

"I only brought one, but I don't think you ought to . . ."

She took it out of his hand. "It won't kill me, right?"

"It's never lethal, no."

The feeling to refuse nagged at her. Again she struggled inside, and rejected it. But the sleeping pills weren't fixing the problem well enough. The nightmares were cutting through her sleep in spite of them. She was up to two tranquilizers at night and ready for three, but afraid. She didn't want to work up to a potentially lethal dose. She felt true friendship now, a reason to live, knowing how much others cared about her and that she cared about them. She was done with risking suicide, and this was never lethal. She did feel better, with Debra's watchful care and Rob's attentions . . . except for the night terrors. She had to find a way to be rid of them.

"I didn't bring any water," he said.

The pill was not too big, and in capsule form. Looking at it, she said, "I won't need any," and swallowed it before she could change her mind again.

"Are you sure you want to do that?" he asked.

"If I wasn't, I wouldn't have taken it," she said, not as sure as she sounded.

He paused. "Would you mind if I lit up?" he asked, indicating the joint still in his hand.

She laughed. "I remember hearing something about a drug-free company policy. You can't have any."

"That doesn't apply to tobacco, alcohol or pot."

"Oh, it doesn't?" she said. "Why not?"

"Nobody's that clean. Not in Central City, anyway. They wouldn't have any employees."

She laughed again. "I guess I don't mind. Go ahead."

He took out a lighter and lit it, inhaling deeply once it caught.

"That smells odd," she said.

"Don't tell me you've never smelled pot before. Come on. How sheltered can one person be?"

"It's not that, it's just that it reminds me of something."

What? she wondered. Oh yes, she had smelled this occasionally walking past the windows of some of the apartments in her complex. But there was something else. It escaped her.

"You really surprise me," he said. "I didn't think you'd go for this."

"When does it start to work?"

"Soon," he said, taking a drag on the joint. "It's quick."

She realized in another moment she was feeling a little heady. It made her want to giggle. That was bothersome. Elation had been very different. And when she'd taken it, she was always alone. Why hadn't she thought of that? Now she might end up embarrassing herself. Maybe she should have taken it home with her. No—that wouldn't have worked either. Debra was home.

"Which is faster?" she asked, trying to keep concern out of her voice. "The pill or the joint?"

"They're about the same," he said. "There's an injectable form too, but I'm not fond of needles."

"Oh, you're not *fond* of needles," she said, and giggled. She couldn't help herself. "Who's *fond* of needles?"

He laughed too. "You'd be surprised at the weirdos out there."

She giggled again. Suddenly everything he said was so funny. It *shouldn't* be funny. It made no sense. She tried fighting it but laughed out loud anyway.

"Weirdos, weirdos," she said. "Such a goofy word. Tell me all about them."

"Maybe," he said. "Later."

When his joint was finished, she said, "Oh, is it gone?"

It seemed so disappointing, so terribly *sad*, that everything he brought along was gone. Suddenly she felt like crying, and hoped she could control that. Not in front of Rob. The drug made her feel small inside her own body, pushed out of the way. It was almost as though she were in a car, and the marijuana had pushed her out of the driver's seat, leaving her helpless except to watch while it drove her wherever it wanted.

"Try not to think about that, sweetheart. There's always more where that came from."

"Oh, okay." She felt light and giddy.

He leaned in and kissed her, pulling her body close against his. "There's more where this came from, too," he said.

"Oh . . ." she said. "How very nice to know." At least that felt nice, quite pleasant, in fact. She closed her eyes, waiting to be kissed again.

He reached up and held her head in his hands, running his fingers through her hair. He kissed her passionately, not softly as at first. Alyssa felt lost in the kiss, brilliant bursts of light exploding inside her. It was extraordinary. She had never allowed anyone this physically close to her, never imagined the thrilling sensations it would bring to her entire body. It was thoroughly breathtaking. Lovely, except for the haunting feeling that it wasn't her but the pill.

"Oh, Rob," she mumbled through the kiss.

He continued, and she reached her arms around to pull him close, leaning heavily against the large trunk of the tree. She breathed deeply, inhaling the scent of his skin, noticing the scent of the lingering smoke in the air. One of his hands moved through her hair, the other he used to stroke tenderly down her back. It was sheer electricity.

Yet something inside her still wasn't right. The feel of the pill's control remained an irritation in the back of her mind.

From her lips, he moved gently to kiss her cheek, brushing her hair away with his mouth. He leaned down to her smooth, pale neck, and kissed her throat delicately, sweetly, as though savoring the feel of her skin on his lips. It sent more electric currents through her body and she quivered, thrilled and annoyed at the same time.

"Oh, sweetheart, you're like . . . an angel," he said, whispering in her ear. "An absolute angel. Oh . . . oh wow."

Angel. Angel, you are a lioness. . . Knew you'd like it, you're so delicious, my Angel . . .

She pulled suddenly away from him, dark memories bursting through the pall of the drug and the intensity of his kisses. *Blaine. That awful Blaine from high school.*

She started to shake and broke contact with him, almost getting up, stumbling, sitting down again. Her head felt so strange. Her neck hurt with the pain of a memory. Rob hadn't kissed her that hard. She knew that. She struggled to gain control of her thoughts, remind herself that Rob was nothing like that creep.

"What's wrong?" he asked, deep concern in his dark brown eyes. "I'm so sorry, I don't want to pressure you . . . If you're not ready there's no rush, I can wait . . ."

"Nothing," she said anxiously, turning back toward him. "It's nothing. Just . . . just don't call me Angel. Ever again. Never. Please."

There was a quiver in her voice that she recognized. She struggled to steady it. She would not cry, not here, not now, and definitely not about that. She remembered the beating and felt a real pain in her ribs, another consequence of Blaine's actions. The fuzzy memories of the hospital, how much it hurt to walk, to breathe for weeks afterward. She moaned unconsciously.

"Don't ever call me that. Please. Never." She didn't realize she was repeating herself, over and over as the memories surged up.

"I'm sorry, honey, I won't . . . I promise."

Her vision went in and out of focus.

"How long is this stuff supposed to last?" she asked.

She didn't enjoy any of the sensations it brought on, and it was terribly difficult to fight against them. She struggled for control, to get back in the 'driver's seat' of her own body. But it took more effort than she was used to, and was much more futile.

"I don't know, depends," he said, leaning against the tree. "Those pills are pretty strong."

"Can I go home now?" she asked, still fighting the urge to cry with all the strength she had left. She sounded like a little child.

"You don't want to be with me anymore?" he asked, sounding a little like a hurt puppy.

"No Rob, I do, I do," she said, scooting back over next to him. "I'm sorry. I just got, uh, scared all of a sudden. Bad memories . . . that's all. It wasn't you. Honest."

"Who was he? I swear, I'll kill him. He ruined you. I knew there must be something . . ."

"It was nobody. Not worth talking about."

"Okay," he said. "If you say so."

He tried clumsily to put his arm around her, and almost poked her in the eye. They both laughed hysterically. She felt completely out of control.

"This is too weird," Alyssa said, still laughing. She fell backward heavily into his lap and reached up to touch his cheek.

"Can I kiss you some more?" he asked, looking down at her, his hand caressing the length of her side. "Oh man, do I want to make love to you, Alyssa." His voice was quiet, but intensely passionate.

He paused suddenly, the look in his eyes saying he hadn't meant to reveal that much aloud. He changed his tone. "But . . . but please, don't worry, it doesn't have to be now, I can wait as long as it takes . . . I mean, right now, oh just let me kiss you." He leaned over her.

Gently she pushed him away, giggling and shaking her head. She couldn't quite take in the impact of his words, his emotion. The evening was already too much to handle. She felt more like teasing him than being serious.

"What kind of girl do you think I am?" She sat up straight, and dread overcame her. Her own voice frightened her. "Oh, Rob, you really, really better stop. We have to stop. Mother will beat me to death if she finds out what we're doing. No way. I'm not allowed . . . Not at all, not *ever*." She felt about ten years old, and wished her voice, at least, would come out normally.

Rob soothed her. "She'll never know, I promise. I'll never tell. Just kiss me." His voice pleaded with her.

"Oh Rob, you're so silly." She giggled again. "Give it a rest."

Out of the blue, a thought startled her. "That's it!"

"What?"

"That's it! Why the smoke smells familiar! It's Mother's cigarettes . . . mostly they smelled like cigarette smoke, but there was this smell too. I thought it was just that new brand she switched to."

"Your mom smoked pot?" Rob laughed.

She shook her head. "They were cigarettes. Not joints. No way would she . . . she's too uptight, Rob. Should see her. Buttons everything to the top button, looks like she can't even *breathe*." She stopped. "This is too weird. My mother and pot. She's too *old*."

"Cigarettes laced with it are pretty common. Didn't you know that?"

She shook her head. "All those years Mother was smoking pot. I feel pretty dumb." She paused. "You think Dad knew?"

"He'd have to be more than stupid not to have known."

"That's too strange, too strange," she said, and was suddenly incredibly sleepy. "Take care of me, Rob."

She brushed her hand against his cheek, and leaned her head on his shoulder. Then she shut her eyes, and was promptly asleep.

****

Some time later Rob shook Alyssa awake.

"Hey," he said. "Wake up, we better get you home. We fell asleep. It'll be morning in a few hours."

"Hm?" she said, smiling with her eyes shut, snuggling her head into his chest.

"Hon, we gotta get you home. I have to work in the morning."

"How come you have nights off anyway?" Her speech was slurred. "I thought you worked nights."

"I rearranged my schedule."

"For me?"

"Just for you, sweetheart. Come on, get up."

By the time Rob had halfway dragged her home, supporting her heavily so she could walk, and returned to his own apartment, it was four-thirty AM.

His phone rang as he walked in the door.

"Robert, where have you been?" his boss's voice insisted before he could even say hello. The screen was blank. "You were supposed to check in with your report three hours ago. Do you think I like waiting up? I had half a mind to send someone out after you."

"Sorry," he said sleepily. "Glad you didn't. Look, I forgot it was Saturday. What are you, my mother? Checking up if I break curfew?"

"This is an extremely important case you're working on. Don't forget that. Your report was due hours ago."

"Yes, sir. I understand."

"Have you gotten any more information out of that girl?"

Rob stiffened, suddenly wide awake, all senses keen. "No," he said, nonchalantly. "But I'm doing my best, sir."

"You have one more week. If you can't get it out of her yourself you'll have to bring her in here for questioning. We just lost subjects thirty-eight and forty-one."

He grimaced. "I told you to turn down the meter on that machine."

A pause. "Your advice was noted and booked, Robert."

"Hmph." *Noted, booked, but unused.* He shuddered.

He didn't like this game anymore. It was leaving a bad taste in his mouth. Forget the nice tidy Swiss account he was building up. It could rot there for all he cared. Some things weren't worth it.

"Understood, sir. One more week."

****

Monday Alyssa met Rob again. She was glum over dinner.

"Debra found out," she told him. "She was livid."

"How?"

"I hadn't showered and she came in to wake me up, since she never heard me come in. Maybe you didn't notice her sleeping on the couch there. She was trying to wait up for me. She smelled the smoke on my clothes."

"What did you tell her?"

"I told her I hadn't smoked any. I said it was from a party we went to."

"And?"

"She didn't believe me. She thought it was you. But I didn't admit it."

"You lied?"

"I suppose you could call it that if you want to. I didn't, you recall, actually *smoke* any."

"You lied to protect me. Wow." He grinned at her. "You know she'll see through that."

"Maybe. But no I didn't do it to protect you, I did it to keep things the way they are. I don't need to lose Deb's friendship right now."

"And you don't need to lose me."

He was smiling himself silly, looking at her with his chin in his hand.

"I didn't say that." She looked out the window.

He reached across the table and took her hand. "Don't tell me you didn't feel anything when I kissed you the other night."

She looked back at him, smiling again. "I wouldn't say that either."

When the tab for dinner was paid and the dishes were cleared away, she said, "Rob, I did do some thinking about what happened Saturday."

"What about it?" He tried to smile as he fussed with his napkin.

"Well, Deb said—"

"Is this about Deb or is it about you and me?"

"It's about *me*. She was so disappointed I'd gone back to drugs for help. I insisted I hadn't, but she kept after me. We had such a fight. I figured it's hardly the same, but . . ."

"It isn't. Marijuana's harmless unless you make a habit of it."

"That's what she's afraid of! What *I'm* afraid of," she amended.

"Oh, honey," he said. "I told you I shouldn't have brought it. I was stupid to give it to you. But you practically begged as soon as you saw it. What could I do? I can't say no to you. I don't know what I was thinking." His eyes pleaded with her.

"Exactly. You can't say no. Honestly, I hated the marijuana, but what if there were something else? All I'll ever have to do is ask, and there it is. It's all too easy." After finally making this mental connection, she had been quite irritable all weekend.

"Alyssa . . . "

"Deb said as long as I keep burying my problems I'm not going to get any better. It doesn't help anything."

"And?"

"You'd better not bring me anything else," she said.

"Is that your choice or hers? You can't let her run your life either. You'll never be happy that way, Miss Control Freak."

"It's mine." She sighed. "I think she's right."

"It's up to you. You didn't like it, really? I thought you did."

She looked at him. "Well. I thought I would. But it's not at all like the Elation. The only benefit was I did sleep well . . . I think." She paused, then swore. She thought she *had* slept soundly. But the sensations of being out of control, before falling asleep . . . that was unbearable. She didn't feel like discussing that at the moment, though. Rob apparently *liked* those same sensations, and wouldn't understand. "I hate it when she's right. She's always right. It's annoying. But listen. I just can't get started on that, or anything else. It won't help anything."

He smiled at her. "Okay. If that's what you want, then I promise. No more. No matter how much you beg. I never want to hurt you."

"Oh, you don't have to promise . . . I'm pretty sure I don't want to go there again."

He laughed. "You don't sound like you even know what you want!"

"I want to feel better. But not with drugs. That's not the answer."

"Do I help you feel better?"

She smiled a faint smile. "I think so."

"And so does Deb?"

"Definitely."

"We'll help you pull through then. I'm very sorry I set you back. I won't do it again."

"I won't ask for any, either," she said.

"I'd just tell you no," he laughed. "But remember, I can still kiss you anytime you need it. That's not a drug."

She grinned, remembering the electricity she felt, hoping it had been more than just the drug.

"Come on," he said, "Want to go for another walk?"

They walked along the city streets this time, looking in shop windows and talking of the things they would buy each other if they had the money. Rob owned a fine car and dressed very well, but he never revealed his income to her. She assumed that issue was private, anyway, but she wondered once or twice, fleetingly, how he appeared to do so well on only a store clerk's income.

They held hands the whole time.

As it got late, they headed back to her apartment. Outside the building, he walked her around to the side, not the front entrance, and leaned up against the red brick wall, pulling her in close to him.

"What's this about?" she asked. "Aren't you taking me in?"

"Do you mind so terribly if I kiss you goodnight first?" he asked.

"Here? Why?"

"Why not?" He smiled and held her, his arms around her waist.

"Why not?" she said, lifting her arms around his neck in anticipation.

As they kissed, it felt far different to her than it had on Saturday. Her mind wandered. This was not the same. *Not the same as what?* She searched for the answer. Again the memory, her adolescent kiss in the cornfield. *Peter.* The complete rightness of it. This kiss was dull, flat, only the touching of lips, a mere physical sensation. It was not a connection of souls like her first kiss had been. There were no fireworks.

The pain of being stripped away from him forever bubbled up from somewhere deep inside. She couldn't bear it. Why did she want him *now*? She had pushed all that aside, long ago, to be left in the past. Let him go. Let him have the life he chose. Leave it alone. It made no sense. She tried again to keep the memories and longing away, but she couldn't this time.

Another memory intruded, one of carelessly handing all her money away to the man kissing her . . . week after week, destroying her future with his assistance. It pricked her conscience deeply.

She pulled away carefully, trying not to show her discomfort.

"Is something wrong?" he whispered, running his fingers through her hair.

She didn't look up, but took a deep breath. "I don't understand it myself." She leaned against his chest, trying to think. "I've been having such a good time with you."

He continued stroking her long blond hair.

After a moment, she whispered, "I remember what I wanted to talk about the other night before you made me forget."

"Don't say it, sweetheart, please don't say it," he whispered back, shaking, holding her tighter.

"Rob . . . It has to be said. I can't help thinking about how we met. Where you work. I try to ignore it, but I keep remembering things. It hurts, Rob. I'm finding it hard to forget."

"I'll find another job," he said. "I was ready to quit anyway. I'll do anything for you, I mean it."

She stepped back a little to look at him. She hated to see the pain in his eyes. "I know you would. But a new job won't change my memories. It wouldn't be fair to you to keep up a charade."

"Maybe fate brought us together. If I know one thing, it's that nothing changes the past. But we can find a happiness together that grows out of pain. We can do it, I know we can. Together." A tear welled up in his eye and spilled out.

"Rob, this addiction I've gone through . . . this is a part of my life that needs to be put solidly in the past. I know now that every time I see you, I'm either going to hope you've brought me some more effective drug relief, or remember how much I've lost since the day we met. I've completely ruined everything I ever had to look forward to," she said, separating herself further from his arms. "It's awful. All I ever wanted for myself was an education, a career. That hope is shattered now. And like it or not, you were a huge part of that process. It's very hard for me to deal with. I don't know that I can."

Her voice cracked as she spoke. She didn't know it was going to, and she fought it. It was one thing to let go in front of Debra as she had. Crying in front of Rob would be a different matter entirely.

"Please don't do this," he said. "Please. I need you in my life. I want so much to be with you." He took her hands in his, and his voice trembled. "I love you, Alyssa, I love you so much."

He looked at her so earnestly, it was difficult for her to hold his gaze.

"That's just it," she said, emotion coloring her voice. "I know how strongly you feel. And it's not fair of me to lead you on. You've been so good to me. But I know . . . I know I'll never be able to love you the way you love me. You're tied to this part of my life that's painful for me even to think about. I don't want to remember it. You can't undo your part in it any more than I can separate you from it. And every time I look at you, I remember. I see you in the store, at the counter, taking my money and sending me home with those pills."

"I know it was horrible," he said, touching her cheek gently. "But think about this. It's scary to fall in love, Alyssa. Everyone gets scared when it happens. It's a perfectly normal stage, and that's all this is right now. Really. We can work through it together. I'm frightened too, but I know it'll be all right. That's why they call it 'falling' in love. It's like free-falling off a cliff . . . thrilling and terrifying at once, but you don't crash when you get to the bottom, Alyssa. You don't. The parachute opens in time and we have a soft landing, in each other's arms. Let's give it some time . . . Did I move too fast for you on Saturday? We don't have to—"

"That's not at all what this is about." Parachutes, cliffs, these were not what she had in mind. He didn't understand.

"We can work it out, together."

"No. I can't work it out, Rob. I know that now. I've been trying but I can't. When you kissed me just now it was missing something. I'm not sure what. It's just that . . . I shouldn't have to be controlled by a drug to enjoy kissing you. That should come naturally, and it's not coming naturally to me. I have a hard time being comfortable with it at all."

"Our first kiss was natural," he said. "By the fountain."

"I know." She looked down. She couldn't tell him. Peter had intruded on her thoughts then too. Why couldn't she push those thoughts away tonight? *Go away.* It was no use. Even at this moment she ached for him. That one pesky, horrible dream, awakening feelings she thought were long dead. Rob was real, she reminded herself. Peter was fantasy, an unobtainable daydream. Her feelings made no sense.

"Who was he?" Rob whispered, startling her out of her thoughts. He *couldn't* know what she had been thinking. "Who hurt you like this, that you can't let yourself go to enjoy being with me, kissing me?"

"Rob, no, you have it all wrong," she said. "I'm missing something, that's all."

"No, I don't have it wrong," he said. "Somebody hurt you. Very badly. Something terrified you Saturday. And now it's the same thing again."

"It's not the same thing," she said firmly, looking up.

"Then what is it?"

"I already told you." She held his eyes steadily. It was difficult. "If we met some other way, some other place, maybe this could work out. It's not you, and it's not somebody else's fault." Her own voice broke finally. "I just can't do this. I'm sorry. Maybe I never should have gone out with you in the first place."

A solitary tear rolled down her cheek and she looked away. *Maybe Debra was right from the beginning.* She dared not say that aloud.

"Don't say that," he said, panicking. "That's not true. I've enjoyed every minute, every second, I've been with you."

"Me too," Alyssa said.

She was silent a long time. He didn't move, and she couldn't force herself to look at him.

Finally she said, "There was someone else, once."

"I can tell. Please, tell me about it."

"We were just kids. I was so young. It was nothing to begin with, it was over almost before it began, but I loved him so much. I haven't felt that way since for anyone. And I find I can't be with you without thinking about him."

"There's nothing like a first love," he said, his voice tender.

"I guess not," she said.

"And you're so worried about that? Honey, it doesn't matter to me if you've been in love before. It's just another part of who you are."

"But when you kiss me I think about him, wishing you *were* him. Pretending. I see his face when I shut my eyes, not yours. It feels so wrong. I shouldn't be doing that. It happened the first time, and it's happening again tonight. I'm trying not to, but I can't help it."

"Alyssa, that's okay. I don't mind. As long as I'm here for you, that's what matters to me. I love you. I can wait for you to sort it all out. Those images will fade in time."

"You're saying you don't mind if I pretend you're someone else when you kiss me, like that's *normal?*" she asked. "And what if they don't fade away? What then?"

"I guess I could have plastic surgery," he said, and laughed. More seriously, he added, "Honey, everybody thinks about their first love once in a while. Everybody wonders how things might have been. What if this, what if that. It's *all right.*"

"Oh?"

"Sure, as long as you're not still seeing him. Or planning on it."

"No, I haven't seen him since I was fourteen," she said. "Last I heard he was getting married, anyway."

"Well, good for me, then." He looked intently at her. "Is he the one who called you 'Angel?' What is it you were afraid of Saturday, won't you tell me? Did your mother . . . what did she have to do with it? She did something to you, didn't she. I'm sure of it."

Alyssa stiffened. Joan had hurt her both times; first emotionally, ripping Peter away from her, then physically, inflicting the beating after Blaine's attack. But Rob didn't need to know everything. "No. Saturday was a different issue entirely."

"Don't you want to talk it out? Wouldn't it be better?"

"No," she said firmly. "I'd rather not bring that up again."

"I'm sorry. I . . . I won't."

His eyes were full of unasked questions. She nodded her head. They could remain unasked.

"Thanks."

"Oh, Alyssa. If only I could save you from all your memories." He ran a finger softly down her cheek. "If only I could set you free. You're everything I ever hoped to find in a woman. I'll do anything for you, absolutely anything I can."

"Uh-huh," she said, arching her eyebrow and catching his hand in hers. "Right."

"I mean it. You're the only woman I've ever fallen for this deeply," he said. "This has never happened to me before. The way I feel about you is utterly indescribable."

"Don't tell me *I'm* your first love," she said. "I won't believe you."

"Not in the typical sense, no; but I know I've never felt this way about anyone in my life. You have to believe me."

"So. We're back to where we started, that this just isn't fair to you. I don't feel the same way."

"And I'll tell you again, I don't care. I'll do whatever it takes to make you happy."

"I need some time to myself to think things over, Rob."

"How much time?"

"I don't know," she said. "Maybe a week, maybe longer. I don't know."

"A whole week?" He faltered. "More?"

"Yes, at least."

"We could just be friends," he said.

She sighed.

"I don't think I can stand not seeing you that long."

"Rob." She looked at him, begging him to understand. "I need time."

"I know," he sighed.

They looked into each other's eyes.

"May I kiss you goodbye?" He whispered.

Alyssa nodded. "Don't worry. When I'm ready, I'll call. I promise."

He kissed her, carefully, tenderly, gently. She awkwardly returned his kiss, feeling none of the thrill she knew she should feel if someone she loved desperately were kissing her, if Peter were there kissing her. She shoved that thought away. It was stupid.

Why can't I just forget about it? I'm just hurting Rob. And possibly myself.

"Goodbye," he said sadly. "But I want you to know I've always loved you. And I always will. I'll be waiting by the phone every second."

She nodded. "Goodbye, Rob."

She watched him walk away into the night.

****

"Screw this filthy job," Rob reported in person two days later. "I quit."

"You can't quit that easily, 47."

"Robert to you." He paced the room, refusing to sit in the heavy black alligator chair in front of the man's enormous white marble kidney-shaped desk.

"You know the rules about emotional . . ."

"Aaah." He waved his hand. "No worries there I assure you. I could've earned an Oscar for my performance. And she *still* dumped me. Look. You lead me along on a string, dangling some huge promotion in front of my nose, and I won't ever see it. Why? Because I can't manipulate people into telling me what you need to know for your lousy research. So I quit. I'm tired of this game."

The large man sighed, exhaling tobacco smoke. It was an inferior quality cigar, and it stank.

"You know the rules. If you can't do your job well, we just can't promote you. We only promote the best."

"You know damn well *I'm* the very best." He flopped down finally in the large alligator chair. "I'm tired of manipulating. And dead tired of being manipulated by scum like you."

"Rob, let's be reasonable human beings here. We're on the verge of discovering a whole new plane of existence . . ."

"You've got a whacked-out dangerous drug on your hands is all you've got. You'll make more with that new hormone-producing crud you synthesized, if you ask me."

"For the last time this is not about profit, it's about a major discovery."

"Not about profit? You lie. It's always about profit."

"Robert! This is about proving that there are other life forms co-existing with us on this planet! Life forms that are aware of us! Observing our actions! Can't you even comprehend what that means?"

"Yeah, I know what it means. It means you're crazier than I thought you were."

"We don't even know if it's an alien presence or an indigenous one. And we almost had hands-on proof, except for your incompetence." The man's deep voice raised in pitch and speed with his excitement.

"Yeah, *almost*."

Rob stood and crossed the room to stare blankly at the heavy teak bookshelf in one corner. Tolstoy, Darwin, Steinbeck, Marx. *The Complete Roswell Report*. Stalin, complete works. *The APA Encyclopedia of Psychosocial Disorders*.

He continued. "That's the key word here, isn't it? Maybe your proof just plain doesn't exist. You thought of that?"

"She is the only lead we have left. You must pursue it further. You have three more days to get the information we need and then you'll have to bring her in."

"It's not reasonable to do that," he said. *These imbeciles wouldn't care if they killed her*, he thought. *Killed her! Like the other leads. All in the name of this stupid, lunatic research.* "She won't come willingly. She doesn't believe me anymore. Or trust me. And I did find out one thing, turns out she's related to a public figure. Anything happens to her and we're in hot water with the media."

"Which public figure? What's the relationship?"

"I can only say you wouldn't want to touch this one, I assure you." He could play that up. Joan Stark was hardly that much of a celebrity, but as it was not a complete untruth, his bluff came off much more believable. "The President would *not* be pleased. You're better off if you don't know. Trust me." He knew, after years of working with this man, what tactics would work with him and what would not.

"Use something on her then, to get the information. Slip it in a drink."

"I told you before, she's not a player!" He turned around to face the man behind the desk. "First off, she doesn't touch alcohol. Second, she'd see through any trick like that before it even took effect. In fact, I already tried, and it didn't work. Look, didn't I tell you I quit? I'm not bringing her in for you!"

"We have other agents who will."

"And the media will be down your throat in milliseconds no matter how much you pay. You aren't as high up in the hierarchy as you'd like to think, and you know it. Find someone else for your guinea pig. And if I'm not mistaken you still don't know who she is."

"But you do, 47."

"*Robert.*"

"And your inventive little device will work just as well on you as it does on our other subjects."

"You wouldn't dare," Rob said, his face turning slightly pale.

"You also won't find work elsewhere if you leave us now."

"You can't blackball me. I have an excellent record."

"Think again."

"It won't change my mind."

He hoped he didn't look as unsettled as he felt.

"It would be difficult to let you leave knowing everything you know about the research alone, much less the methods involved. We'd rather not lose your expertise at this point. You ought to know that by now."

"But I don't *believe* any of it. I think you're all insane. Your scientists have so many half-baked ideas simmering on those Bunsen burners of yours you've forgotten what the real world is all about. Nobody will believe you even if you have hard evidence. You won't be able to make a dime off of this, even with media propaganda. They'll lock you in a padded cell and throw away the key."

"Rob, I like you." The large man puffed on his cigar.

"Huh?" The sudden change of subject caught him off guard.

"And because I like you, I'm not going to kill you. Probably a mistake, but I'll let you slide . . . this time. I believe you know what you have to do. And I don't think you're stupid enough not to do it. You bring her to me. Since you already know her, you're the best agent to do it without raising her suspicions until we have her safely locked inside."

Rob's face paled to ashen white. "*Kill* me? Over a stupid job?"

"We told you when you joined our ranks this was far more than a job. May I see your right hand, please?"

Incredulous, he held his hand out across the solid marble-topped desk. The man pushed a button concealed on his side of the desk, and an electronic buzz sounded, a crackle, a sizzle.

"Ouch!" Rob cried out, heat searing through the palm of his hand. He shook it. "What'd you do that for?"

"I've destroyed your ID device. You no longer work for us, officially."

"Fine with me. That's all I wanted."

"And we'll see to it that you no longer work for anyone else. I also strongly recommend—if you value your life—that you bring us the subject for observation by the deadline. If you can perform that task to my satisfaction, I may be inclined to reinstate your position. With a full bonus, and the promotion."

Rob shook his aching hand. The metal device generated quite a bit of heat when its computer chip fried. He could feel the pain sear up to his elbow. No, his shoulder. He had a sudden headache. It must have been implanted next to a nerve.

If he was lucky he could have it surgically removed. He knew a few people. Maybe he could find a fake one, have it put in, change his identity. If he could find a connection who also altered fingerprints. That would require microsurgery; it would be more difficult to arrange.

****

The large man took a long pull on his cigar as he watched Rob leave, stepping quickly from his office and down the hall. The man chuckled. The boy had been given a decent scare. He wouldn't be back. Not without the girl anyway.

And if he lost her, he wouldn't return alive. That much was certain.

Chapter 22

Unveiled

    Todd (coming into the room): "Sorry to keep you waiting. I uh, I just had to go check on something in the kitchen."

    Jackie, smiling: "I know all about the camera, Todd."

    Todd: "Oh. I--I--y--you want I should turn it off? I'm . . ."

    Jackie (with light laugh): "No, I don't mind at all. I never do. Besides, I'm only free about two more weeks. You may not get to see me after that."

    Todd: "Okay, uh, well, great then. Um, it's nice to finally meet you . . . Wow, you're gorgeous . . . Kevin's told us a lot about you, but he didn't tell us you were such a knockout."

    Jackie, laughing: "You never saw his tapes of me, I take it?"

    Todd: "No, he never shows us those. Keeps that for himself."

    Jackie comes close to Todd, and takes his hand. Her speech is slurred, as though slightly intoxicated.

    Jackie (with a toss of her hair): "Well, that would be like him. And thanks. You're pretty cute yourself. You have great eyes."

    Jackie and Todd look at each other.

    Todd: "Uh, thanks. You think so?"

    Jackie: "Oh, I definitely think so."

    Todd retains Jackie's hand.

    Todd, whispering: "You're sure it's okay Kevin's not here?"

    Jackie: "Oh, I'm sure. I came in anyway, didn't I? See, I need someone right now. That's his loss, wouldn't you say?"

    Jackie runs two fingers along Todd's throat and through his hair.

    Todd nods his head.

    Jackie (tossing her hair again): "And your gain. Besides, maybe I think Kevin's gotten a little dull."

    Jackie raises her eyebrow and traces her index finger down Todd's chest to the second button on his shirt.

    Jackie: "Maybe I'd like to get to know you better instead. Find out what you really like doing. I just love making new discoveries, don't you?"

    Todd: "Oh, yeah. I can't wait to discover—"

    Jackie (interrupting): "Just remember, the only rule I have is no marks. The only rule."

    Todd: "Yeah, Kevin told—"

    Jackie (interrupting again) puts a finger to Todd's lips.

    Jackie: "Shh. That's quite enough about Kevin. I want to know more about Todd."

    Jackie moves to the center of the room, facing the camera lens, dead center. She looks straight at it, then at Todd, and smiles.

    Jackie: "Now be a dear and close the shade, would you?"

transcript of video,
from a private collection

Two Saturdays before the wedding, the Richardson's held a big family barbecue. It was hot and sunny and the mood of the day reminded Peter of many happy times from his childhood.

Isaac, his older brother, and his wife Anna, had come in from town to celebrate with them. Anna was expecting their first baby at the end of the month and looked large and hot and uncomfortable. Isaac beamed with pride.

    "It's unusual to have everyone home at once," Beverly said to Jackie. "I'm sorry none of your roommates could make it. We'd have been happy to have them."

    "You know how it goes," Jackie said. "Maria went home this weekend, Liz and Nadine had to work, and so on."

    Peter said, "Is the chicken done yet, Dad? It smells delicious."

    "Twenty minutes," Phil gave notice from his grill.

    "Andrew!" Beverly called to her younger son, now seventeen. When he appeared in the kitchen doorway, she said, "Can you go get the salads?"

    "Coming," he answered.

    "Did she make fifteen salads again, Peter?" Jackie whispered.

    Peter laughed.

    The twins, Jordan and Kellie, ran up behind them. "Tag!" they said simultaneously, one tagging Peter and the other tagging Jackie. Then they ran off to the lawn.

    "Come on," Peter urged his fiancée, and ran after the babies of the family, pulling her along. The twins were five now. Jordan claimed he was oldest since he was born an hour before his sister. They arrived in the early spring, several months after the breakup between Beverly and Joan.

    "Careful, you'll knock over the tables!" said Beverly.

"Oh, no, not the salad!" said Andrew, in a high-pitched falsetto as he placed three large bowls on the table.

For once Jackie joined in the chase, laughing genuinely as the adults played with the youth and children alike in a boisterous, rule-free game. Isaac, Andrew, and Julia joined in. Anna, of course, chose to sit out.

Peter overheard his dad say to his mother, "When was the last time they all played like that, Bev?"

"I'm not sure if I've ever seen Jackie let loose like that," she answered. "I suppose it's a good sign."

Her response pleased Peter. He wanted so badly for his mother to like her.

He had stepped back from the play momentarily to listen to his parents. As he turned back, Kellie ran up behind Jackie and yelled "Boo!" then tickled her sides. Jackie yelped with surprise. She fell down in the grass and grabbed Kellie's ankles, tickling the back of her knees while she pulled the girl down with her.

"Gotcha back!" she said breathlessly.

Peter beamed. He was so happy seeing her accept this childish attention and respond in kind. Andrew and Jordan bumped into the two girls, and shortly everyone joined in the giant tickle fight, emitting shrieks and squeals of delighted laughter.

The game deteriorated into sheer silliness, Andrew rolling and wrestling with Jordan, the girls all howling and tickling each other. Isaac threw a giant blue plastic ball to Peter, and they played a game of "keep away" over everyone's heads.

After a while Peter tired out, and moved to one side. Not long after, the group broke apart, exhausted as well. Jordan and Kellie ran off in a new direction to play a version of tag combined with hide-and-seek. The older ones got up more slowly, laughing from the physical joy of their romp.

"Oh my!" Jackie said, between giggles and deep breaths, "I don't know the last time I laughed this hard!"

She stood and brushed the grass off her jeans, and looked up smiling at Peter.

But he was no longer smiling.

"What's the matter?" she asked.

Looking around, then behind her, she turned back to face him.

A hush fell on the rest of the group. Julia looked away. Isaac lay on the ground, breathing hard. Peter and Andrew stood together, staring.

Finally she looked down to inspect herself. Her blouse had come partly undone and slipped off her shoulder during the roughhousing. A large, ugly purplish mark could be seen just above and partly covered by her brassiere. It was fairly fresh.

"Oh no. Oh, please, *no*," she said when she saw it. She pulled her shirt quickly back over her shoulder and buttoned it, her face flushing deep red. "No, not now . . ."

"Masterpiece of a hickey there, bro," Andrew said to Peter, with a mock punch to his brother's arm. In a mumble, he added, "Though I must say I'm surprised. You know you're not supposed to be—"

Peter found his voice and interrupted his brother, batting him away with his hand. "I didn't put it there."

It was a terse whisper. He felt sick to his stomach.

"Oh," Andrew said. He put one hand over his eyes and slowly drew it downward, rubbing his face. "I see."

Jackie could hold Peter's stare no longer.

"No," she repeated in a horrified whisper. "Please, not this, *now*." Tears ran down her face. "Oh, not *now,*" she mumbled, and dashed past him into the house, crying.

Beverly got up and followed her as Peter stared into the empty space where Jackie had stood. In the distance he could see the twins laugh as they ran around the trees by the stables, ignorant of events at the house.

"I think I'll check and see how my wife is doing," Isaac said. She was only a few meters away. He got up quickly and went over to her. After a moment's conference, he said, "We're going for a walk. Doctor says it's good exercise for bringing on labor, you know."

"So she says, anyway," Anna added with a forced smile.

They strolled off hand in hand, in the direction of the barn and stables.

Peter finally sat down on the ground with a thump. Andrew sat next to him and put one hand on his brother's shoulder.

"You had no idea she might be . . .?" The question hung in the air, unfinished.

"None," Peter answered. A suppressed sob shook his body. "She said she had no more secrets." His tears came freely, and he leaned his head on his younger brother's shoulder. Andrew pulled him in tightly and held him as his body shook with the pain of his tears. "No more *secrets*."

Slowly the sizzling and popping of the grill ceased as Phil pulled the chicken off the grill and without a word took it into the house.

"Why did I believe her?" Peter cried out. "I feel so stupid!"

"Hey," Andrew said. "It could've happened to anybody." He scratched his head.

Could it? Was he just blind? What signs had he missed so completely? Peter felt as though his heart had been wrenched out of his chest and flung away. He was completely consumed by the empty ache it left inside him. Time passed unnoticed as he leaned on his brother's shoulder, sobbing.

After a moment that seemed infinite, Beverly came back outside. She said quietly, "Will you talk to Jackie?"

Peter didn't turn, but in his peripheral vision he could see his mother, with Jackie standing behind her in the doorway looking down at her feet. The sight burned into his heart and memory. He nodded, and motioned Andrew to go. His brother silently got up and slid into the house.

Jackie came and sat down beside him, wiping away a silent stream of tears. They didn't say anything for what felt like an eternity.

Finally Peter broke the silence. He said, bitterness filling his tone, "Don't you even try to tell me that was some accident with your vacuum cleaner." He refused to look at her.

"Peter, I . . ." she stopped, swallowed hard. "I wasn't going to make up an excuse. It's exactly what you think it is. I'm sorry."

"I don't want to know how it got there. I don't *think* I want to know why, and I *know* I don't want to know who."

She nodded her head. "I promise it'll never happen again," she said.

"Jackie, I would never, ever be able to believe you. Not after . . . after everything else you've lied about. You said, no more secrets. You said, you had solved your problems."

"But Peter, it wouldn't happen again . . . not after we're married and I have you . . ."

"What kind of fool do you take me for?" he said, finally looking her in the eye.

"How's a girl supposed to hang on so long?" she said, anger coloring her voice. "You can't possibly understand. A woman has *needs*, Peter. Once you've experienced it, it's not like you can . . . I mean, even you've got to do *something*, don't you? I look at you and I don't know how you can stand it, even if you've never had—"

"'*Needs?*'" he said. "Have you ever heard of self-control? What about patience? What about *my* need for a wife I can trust? "

"You'll never understand until you've been there," she said, crying again. "I've been so awfully frustrated . . . what was I supposed to do?

You wouldn't . . ."

"You were supposed to wait!" Peter said, his voice rising. "And maybe I don't 'understand' from experience, but I've had friends who've made mistakes, and they manage to live without it afterwards. It's a choice, Jackie. You always have a choice."

"It's not that simple, Peter. You don't know how it *feels*. It's a lot more difficult than you think."

He stood up, angry, and took a few steps away from her. "Jackie. I've been raised to believe that when God gives a commandment, he provides a way to keep it. You could've found that way, if you tried. But you didn't! What makes you think you'll find it after marriage?"

She was silent for a moment. "Why do you always have to bring God into everything?"

"Why do you have to keep Him out? You know what I've said is true."

She stared at him, then turned away.

"Tell me," he said. "Since we've been dating, how often has this happened? I don't believe this is the only time you've been 'frustrated.' In fact I wouldn't believe you if you swore it. And you know what else I can't figure out?"

"What?" she said, equally angry now.

"I don't see how you thought that thing would be completely gone in two weeks. Did you think I wouldn't notice it on our wedding night? Did you? Nevermind you'd be going through the temple when you shouldn't. Good thing, for your sake, you didn't. I suppose you lied your way through your recommend interview. How could you live with yourself after that? What was the plan, Jackie?"

"Shut up!" she said, not looking up. Quieter, she added, "It would be gone by then."

"And if it weren't?"

She sniffed. The pride and hostility left her voice, and she spoke softly. "Well . . . I figured it might be dark, at least the first night, knowing you . . . and I was pretty sure I could encourage you to, well, um, cover it up with your own, maybe . . ."

"And what if that didn't work? What if I'd found it then?"

"Well, we'd have been married already," she said.

"I suppose you think I'd *stay* married after something like that?"

"I don't know," she said, sobbing again. "I don't know. I'm so sorry, Peter, I'm so, so sorry."

"Yeah. Well. I'm sure you are . . . now." He took a long pause. Thoughtfully, he said, "You'd never have told me, would you. If this . . .

if this hadn't happened today."

She shook her head. "No, I wasn't going to, that's true. I knew you wouldn't understand, and it would only hurt you . . ."

Peter swallowed. "I think you'd better go."

She nodded her head. "I know. I understand."

"And don't plan on coming back. Not ever."

She nodded again. "I figured as much."

They stood for a moment in silence. Then from her spot on the lawn, Jackie looked up at him, several feet away.

"Peter, will you ever forgive me?" she asked. Her voice was barely audible. "I've really hurt you . . . I know I have. I'm so sorry. I just . . . you were so wonderful . . . your love meant so much to me . . . and I knew you'd never want me if you knew everything . . . lying was the only way I knew to hold on to you."

"Well," he said, his voice also losing its angry edge, "You can see it didn't work."

"Will you forgive me?" she pleaded.

He looked out over the fields, the orchard, the stables; anywhere but at her. Her question hung in the air for a long moment, wrenching his soul with deeper pain. "I can only promise you I'll try," he said eventually, his voice hoarse. "I will try."

She took a deep, ragged breath, and stood up. "Okay," she said, very quiet. "Thank you . . . I can't ask for more than that."

He still didn't look over at her.

"I'll go now," she said, and headed for the house.

He nodded his head, barely. He couldn't bring himself to say *goodbye.*

After a few minutes he walked across the lawn, toward the orchard, and sat down again. He raised his head when he heard her car engine start, and listened to the sound of the wheels on gravel turning the car around, pulling out, then turning into the road. He listened until he couldn't make out its sound any longer.

She was gone.

Later that day he found the ring she had coveted so much. It was left behind, lying loose on the kitchen counter.

Chapter 23

The Library

We have run into a small predicament, it seems. Agent 47 has not returned as I expected. The homing device I activated in his ID also appears to have malfunctioned.

Victor Caldwell,
private memo

"I quit my job," Rob said.

It was Saturday, almost a week since Alyssa last saw him in person.

"Rob," was all she could say.

She wore her hair wrapped up tightly in a bun, which kept it out of the way while she worked. She and Deb were giving the apartment a thorough cleaning, and she had gone into her room to take the call.

She regarded him sadly. "A new job is not going to do it. I think I made that clear."

He called every day. The more he called the less she wanted to talk to him. And today she was busy.

"You did," he said, "I'm looking for something else anyway. Something decent. For you. But not just for you. I realized my ethics were getting warped. You taught me that."

"You didn't need to do that," Alyssa said.

"Yes, I did. I'm glad I did. I told you, I'll do anything for you, and I mean it."

Alyssa sat down at her desk and faced him close up. "If you thought this would change anything, Rob . . ."

"I miss you too much. I need you. Please say you'll see me again. Just once. Please."

"Rob, I asked for time, and you're not giving me any. You keep calling. Every day I'm more certain I have to move on . . . I need to forget, put it behind me. It's the only way."

"I can help you forget. Please. We can work through this together."

She whispered, "Listen. You know I don't love you the way you love me. I can't promise I ever will. You know that."

"I can live with that."

278

"Give me a good reason why *I* should have to live with it."

Her response took him aback for a moment.

"Because time changes a lot of things. Because I love you. Because you're scared. You're afraid to let anybody love you, Alyssa. Believe me, I know that feeling."

"I'm not forcing you to love me. And it's not true. I'm not scared."

He paused a moment. "Please just let me see you. Give me one more chance. Feelings can change."

"They certainly can. You're not giving me any space, and I don't like it. I told you I'd call and here you've been bugging me all week."

"Alyssa, please. Just meet me at the café. We need to talk."

"We are talking."

"In person. I need to see you again," he said. "This hurts too much."

"No. I meant it. Bye, Rob." She cut off the connection.

It didn't occur to her to be more polite. He was bothersome, but she still got the weirdest warm feeling in her chest when she talked to him, saw his face on the screen. But she tried hard to ignore that, to make it go away. The only logical and right decision was to make a clean break. It was the only way.

She went back to her work and told Deb about the call. Frustrated, she asked, "How do you get rid of them when they're like that?"

Deb shrugged. "I've never had to. I don't know." She smiled, scratching her curly head. She adjusted her glasses. "I'd love it if Jon was that desperate for me, actually."

"Try dumping him and see what happens," Alyssa said, furiously scrubbing imaginary spots in the kitchen sink.

Deb laughed. "Nah. I don't want to risk it."

Alyssa continued scrubbing, then turned on the water to rinse. "I feel so bad. I can't put my finger on it. There's nothing wrong with him. I know I don't feel the same way about him as he does about me. It's just not, I don't know, *there*. Something is definitely missing. It's not fair to keep seeing him if I don't feel it, is it? I mean, he says that doesn't matter, but it matters to me."

Deb was going through the couch. She had the cushions pulled off and strewn all over the floor. She bent over the springs, and reached into the back of it with her hand.

"Were you really in love with Peter?" she asked. "Or anyone else, ever? I mean, do you have anyone to compare this with, what you have with Rob?"

"I'm not sure." She wrinkled her brow. She *had* been comparing. That was half her problem.

"How can you not know?" Deb said, laughing. "You have to know."

"I think I was too young to know if it was love."

"But you thought so at the time, right?"

"It's still hard, even now, to think about him. Still painful."

It made no sense that it would be, after all this time. She closed her eyes a moment, then turned around and looked at Deb. She leaned back against the sink and twisted the wet rag in her hands.

"I was only fourteen, remember. Did I tell you about his starry blue eyes . . . Man, he had gorgeous eyes." She paused. "But we were just friends, until our last day together. It didn't have time to become anything else," she said.

"Your mother stopped it."

"Yes." Pain washed over her and she shuddered. Memories of her mother screaming, the shattered blue china plate, picking the fragments out of her hand . . . it all raced before her eyes. The reasons for the sudden separation had never been entirely clear in her mind, though she knew it had something to do with religion. She decided not to mention that part to Debra.

"His mom and mine had some great big fight and after that I was forbidden . . . we never saw each other again. I did try, once . . . I told you I made that phone call . . . but by then it was too late."

Tears she had denied herself came back suddenly, and she caught her breath.

Deb pulled something moldy out of the couch. "Oh, gross," she said. "Look at that. I think it was an apple in another life. Why don't we do this more often?"

She straightened up. Alyssa had gone silent. Debra walked over to the kitchen to throw the thing away and saw she was crying.

"I'm so sorry," Debra said. "It must have been awful." She washed her hands and then put her arm around Alyssa's shoulder.

"I guess it still hurts more than I thought. I mean, obviously, he forgot about me . . . It's not like I really expected him to . . . I mean, I told him he shouldn't wait . . . but the reality of it . . . I guess it hit me hard, anyway." She wiped her tears away quickly with her sleeve and took a deep breath. "I'm fine now."

"You sure?"

"Yeah. I feel silly. It was all so long ago."

"So? Love isn't silly."

"Feels like it. Nothing makes sense."

"So," Debra said, "being with Rob doesn't compare, is that it? My mom says every time you love, it's different. You can't expect to feel exactly the same this time."

"I suppose. But Rob doesn't make me feel the way I felt then. I don't think he ever could. It was so magical, so romantic . . . then my mother shattered it. But it's vain to dream of what would've happened between us, if she hadn't . . ." Her voice trailed off momentarily. "What's done is done. I can't get that part of my life back. Not ever."

"No, that much is true. You do need to move on, whether you stick with Rob or not."

"I thought I had, that's the strange thing. And I don't see why I should have to settle for less than what I felt back then."

"You're right, you don't. And Rob did give you that joint, too. That was lame. I still haven't forgiven him for that."

"He did not give me a joint." Alyssa started.

"Look, I know you lied to me. I'm just sorry you felt you had to."

"It's not a lie," she said.

"Alyssa," Debra said, chagrin in her voice. "Please."

She was pricked. Softly, she said, "It was a pill. A marijuana pill. He had the joint." She felt horrible inside, and dark.

"And you couldn't just come out and tell me that." Disappointment colored her voice.

"You were so mad. I knew you'd hate him forever, and I didn't want that."

"Look, I knew you were lying, and I was pretty sure he didn't have to force you, either." Deb looked at her. "I know everybody makes mistakes, and I can only imagine how hard it's been for you since the overdose. I don't hate him for it. Or you. I was just . . . very disappointed."

"I'm sorry," Alyssa said. "I really am. About the whole thing. Lying, doing it in the first place, everything."

Deb shrugged. "It's all right. Forgiveness is something I work at. It does help to have you say it, though." She smiled.

"So you must think I'm right to let him go, aren't I?"

"Is that what you think?"

She ran her hands through her hair, twisting the loose strands back into the bun. She remembered Rob, moving his fingers so lightly through it, and felt that achy feeling inside again. His lips *were* soft. She couldn't help remembering that.

She pushed the thoughts away. "Oh, I don't know," she said. "I can't make up my mind. I think I'm sure and then I'm not. I keep wishing he would give up. Why doesn't he just give up?"

"If he loves you, why would he give up? Unrequited love is a terrible thing."

"Must be."

She sighed and turned around, starting to scrub down the countertop and cabinets.

"You remember how I was before Jon and I got together."

Alyssa laughed. "Boy, do I. You were a wreck!"

"You said he thinks you're scared. Are you sure that's not it?"

"I'm sure."

But she did feel some fear. Rob himself didn't frighten her, exactly. Something else about the whole thing did. She couldn't place what, though. She knelt down and scraped at a drip of dried-on pancake batter stuck to the cabinet. "I need to put past mistakes where they belong. I'm afraid I'll keep wanting him to bring me drugs," she said, frowning. "I'll tell you though, after that incident he did swear he'd never do it again, no matter how I begged."

"He did?"

"Yeah. And I'll be honest with you, I didn't exactly want him to make that promise. It was his idea."

She unstuck the spot of batter with her thumbnail and rubbed it clean with the rag.

"You think he can keep that promise?"

"Probably." She sighed.

"You know," Deb said, reflecting, "It seems to me he absolutely adores you. Truly. That's rare these days. Not easy to find."

"Yeah, but if I don't feel the same way . . ."

"I think you're scared," Deb said, bending down and looking her straight in the eye. "That's what I think." She stood up again. "Although I'm not completely on his side or anything—I'd rather you found someone safer, someone who wasn't tied to this mess you've been through—I do think he really, honestly cares for you."

"Oh, so this is just me being scared, is that all?"

"Mm-hm. Mostly," she smiled.

After a pause Alyssa looked away and asked, "How's Jonathan acting?"

"Scared!" Deb laughed, then went back over to work on the couch. "Seriously, I don't know where we stand. He's dating a few other girls he met at New Hopkins. I'm free to do the same, he says, but I'm not interested in anyone else. You know the guys here."

They both laughed.

"I don't mind too much, though." Deb shrugged. "He just wants to be sure, I think, before he commits to more. I'm not worried."

"Sure you're not." Alyssa threw her a look.

"Oh, stop it. We never said it was serious between us."

"That doesn't mean it isn't," Alyssa grinned.

Deb pursed her lips. "It isn't."

****

Alyssa had just enough money left for one month's share of the rent and some groceries.

Monday morning she went out, after their vigorous weekend cleaning the apartment, to look for a job. She started the day with a haircut. It was an impulsive move, and it cost some of her remaining money, but she had thought about it many times. Especially after the busy weekend, having to keep it up or in a ponytail, she felt like her hair was getting in the way.

"Cut it off, all off," she told the stylist. "Give me something easy."

"You sure?" the stylist asked, hesitant, holding up the long golden tail in the mirror. "All of it?"

"I'm sure. I'm tired of brushing this mop out all the time."

The stylist gave her a short, sassy cut above the nape of her neck that she could blow-dry quickly, sweeping it away from her face. It changed her look completely.

Debra was surprised when she saw her. "Why'd you cut your hair?" she asked, walking around her. "It's cute, but you look so different. Wow! You look . . . different!"

Alyssa grinned. "It feels different. Lightweight. I feel free, like I could fly."

It did look good. The stylist said it was more businesslike, and should help her look professional in interviews.

Rob called again that night. "You changed your hair?" he said, after his initial hello. "It was so long and beautiful." He looked pained.

"Do I need your permission?" she asked.

"No, I meant—"

"You won't love me anymore without it?" she teased.

"You won't get rid of me that easily," he said in a teasing tone. "But you look so *different*. I loved your hair."

"I was tired of it," she said. "You want long hair, you grow it."

"No, it just surprised me, that's all."

"So what is it now? As if I didn't already know," she said, putting her hand on her hip.

"Can't you just come talk to me?" he asked.

He looked pale. She adjusted the color on her screen. That wasn't it. He *was* pale.

"I don't know what good it would do."

"Please. I miss you so much. I need to see you again. I have to."

"You're not giving me time."

She was feeling peeved and cranky from a long disappointing day of job-searching with no luck. She wasn't ready to deal with him.

"I don't have much more time," he said.

"You're a pain in the neck, you know that?"

She let her grumpy feelings increase and pour out on him. This had to stop. It hurt too much, and he was pathetic.

"I didn't call yesterday," he said.

"Yes, and thank you. It was a relief."

She didn't know why, but she felt like being mean. She was tired of trying to be nice, and tired of his calling, tired of fighting him away.

"Please, Alyssa," he said. "This is vital. I have to see you. Just once."

"Oh, all right," she said with a sigh. "You've worn me down. I suppose you won't stop this nonsense until I do. I'll meet you at the café tomorrow, noon."

He smiled broadly. "Thank you so much. I'll be there."

****

The next day at the café Rob sat anxiously, shifting his position and looking around every few minutes. It was five after noon.

At ten after he stood up from the booth, paced to the restroom door and back, and sat down again. He punched a drink order into the automatic terminal.

At fifteen after, a plain waitress with dark circles under her eyes brought the drink without a word or a nod.

"No tip for her," he muttered to himself. He checked his watch every twenty seconds, sipping his cola between checks.

At twelve thirty-five he stood up, leaving the money for his drink. He felt hot and sweaty, and the ventilation in the place was poor. He headed for the door to wait outside.

At the exit he almost bumped into her. He didn't recognize her at first, forgetting she had cut her hair.

"Alyssa! I was afraid you wouldn't come!" He couldn't help smiling. The angry words he had meant to dump on her didn't come out. She was just too beautiful.

"So I'm late. So what?" she said.

"Just seeing you again is divine." He sighed, gazing at her. "Can we go somewhere else?" he asked. "Let's take a walk. We have to find a quiet place to talk."

Alyssa raised an eyebrow, a wary look in her eyes. "I prefer it here."

He took her hand in his and pulled her along the sidewalk outside the café. She followed, but he could feel her resistance.

"It's hot in there," he said. He leaned over to her ear and whispered, "We could be watched in there. We need to get somewhere we've never been together."

"Shouldn't be too hard."

"I know a library not far from here," he said, walking rapidly, nearly dragging Alyssa along behind him. "Have you ever been there?"

"Where's your car?" she asked.

"I sold it."

"What? Why?"

"Had to."

"Why?"

"Oh, it had a few bugs," he said, with a quirky smile.

"Couldn't you just fix them?" she said.

"Listen, I'll explain when we get there."

"Where?"

"The library. Come on!"

"Wait a minute!" she said, wrenching her hand free after they had walked about three blocks. She stopped in the middle of the sidewalk. "Why should I come with you at all? Watched by who? Why are you worried about being watched? You call *me* a control freak. Look at yourself! How do I know this isn't some paranoid, psycho scheme to take me away somewhere and nobody but you ever sees me again? Do you think I don't know how many wackos there are in this city?"

Rob stopped, looked at her, cupped her chin in his hand. "Right. Nobody will ever see us again. Funny. Very funny," he said. He laughed and took a deep breath. "No. Just to the library, Alyssa. Come on, we have to hurry." He took her hand again and pulled her along, turning right at the corner.

At the next block they turned left.

Alyssa said, "Okay, so if we're being watched, how do you know we're not being followed? And I thought you just wanted to talk!"

"I do. It's cameras. Not people. I know. We'll talk once we're there. Not out here."

"You're scaring me," she said, and stopped again.

"I'll explain everything. Come on." He pulled. She held her ground this time.

"This is too weird, Rob."

"I'll explain, *in the library*." His face felt flushed. It was warm, humid for June, and flies buzzed around them. One landed on his face and he brushed it away. "Please. Come with me." He pulled on her hand. "I can't talk here."

She went. "I think you've lost your marbles."

"No. Found some." He grinned at her and continued his frenzied pace through the streets, bordered on either side by both towering skyscrapers and stunted squat ancient ones.

The architecture of Central City was bizarre, a product of the haphazard nature of its construction. It had overflowed into the farmland and small towns so rapidly that contractors hadn't bothered to tear down old things first, if they were sturdy enough to build on. In this quarter there were lofty professional towers next to run-down suburban homes now used for small businesses, small town business streets with high-rise apartment complexes looming up behind them.

This montage had a dramatic effect on light and shadow. Streaks of light pierced through where it seemed a shadow should have been. Where they now walked, ominous shade from the taller buildings cast gloom on what had once been the cheery streets of a small community, a casualty of rapid growth.

They approached the library. It was an ancient stone building nestled among modern edifices of polished glass and shining metal. It was in the middle of a square, and had a real lawn, flowers, and ornamental trees in front. Sunlight shone down on it with the brilliance of noon on a cloudless day in early summer. No shadow seemed to enter its domain.

It was a domed building and once had been impressive. Now bricks fell out of its walls and lay in small piles around its foundation, and what was left of those walls were speckled. As they approached, it became evident that the speckles were not from the natural color of the stone but from a proliferation of graffiti.

People milled around the gardens, some picnicking in the shade, some wandering aimlessly around the greenery, some taking their exercise on a lunch break. There were a few gardeners in overalls pruning the trees and planting new flowers in the beds.

They walked quickly up the granite steps to the front entrance together. By this time Alyssa was panting from exertion. Still Rob didn't slow down.

On opening the door, she started to say, "Why—"

He cut her off with a finger to his lips for silence. "Hush," he whispered. "It's a library, remember?"

They walked up two more flights of granite steps inside, crossed a floor to a small door, then up another flight of metal stairs. Their soft rapid steps rang through the deep stairwell. Only then did he slow down. Finally, he pushed open a metal door in the wall to their left and pulled her through.

They were in a small study room, all four walls the same cinder block, whitewashed, no decoration and no windows; the steel door was the only exit. There was a large wood-veneer table, chipped, with rusted legs, and four soft swivel chairs for furniture. A single fluorescent light hung from the high ceiling. There were no books and no shelves.

"We can talk in here," Rob said, shutting the door. There was a digital lock on it, which he activated. It beeped.

"Well, you could've chosen a more romantic meeting place," she said.

"It's soundproof, don't worry," he said, smiling, sitting down in the chair to the left of hers. "Lead-lined walls. And I've checked it out for hidden wiring. It's clean."

"Rob, you're frightening me," she said. She sat down in the chair nearest the door. "None of this makes any sense. Who cares if it's soundproof? Hidden wires? What are you talking about?"

"I don't mean to scare you, but I may scare you more before this is over. Look, if you feel anything for me at all, I need you to listen, because you're probably not going to like anything I have to say." He took a deep breath and looked at her.

"How so?"

"Oh, man." Rob leaned back from the table and stood up. He laughed to himself, flatly, and turned around, his back to her. "I don't even know where to start."

"The beginning's usually a good spot," she offered.

"I don't know if I can even go back that far," he said, and sat down again. He took a deep breath. "I'm the one in trouble. It's me. They're after me. They're looking for me everywhere. They think I know too much. Maybe I do. I don't know." He placed his elbows on the table and buried his head in his hands. "It has nothing to do with you. Well, in a way it does. Well, actually, no, it's got a lot to do with you. I've probably put you at risk just bringing you here. Shoot. I just have to talk to somebody. I only want to talk, Alyssa." He turned his head, resting it in his hands, to look at her pleadingly, sideways. "I didn't mean for this to frighten you. I know I'm acting strange, but it'll all be clear in a few minutes if you'll just let me talk." He looked at her, trying to meet her eyes.

"Well," she said, with a hint of sarcasm and disbelief. "So who's after you?"

"The government. I was such an *idiot.*"

Alyssa cringed. "You know they'll find you."

"I think I can manage them. I still have a few cards to play."

"What have you done, Rob?" she asked.

"Alyssa." He took a deep breath and wondered if any of this would be easier if she were not so breathtaking, if he didn't feel so strongly about this woman in front of him, if his heart didn't nearly leap out of his chest with longing every time he was near her.

He'd have turned her in months ago if it weren't for that, as soon as he'd broken through her encryption codes. Knowing that about himself turned his stomach. He would have turned her in and forgotten about her, banked the bonus and taken the promotion, bought that vintage Ferrari and taken a long-overdue vacation to Bermuda. It nauseated him to realize what he would have done. What he used to be. What could have happened to her.

Now she looked at him expectantly, waiting for him to speak, with her left eyebrow raised just so, the way she did. That incredulous look she gave him whenever he flirted for her attention.

He took another deep breath and pushed his chair away from the table.

"Alyssa, I'm not a druggist. I never was. That was a front. What I *am* is a government agent. I have been since I was seventeen. It's all I ever wanted to do since I was a little brat. I thought it would be so cool, you know, playing all the spy games. Thought I could be some kind of *hero.*"

He stood up. The words were hard to push out of his mouth. Everything he said after this would probably ruin any chance he still had with her; but it was time. She had to know the truth. He couldn't play this way any longer. She was in danger.

"Well, that's not the way it is in real life. See, I was working for the DR—the Department of Research—when we met." He looked away. "My assignment was to make full reports on anybody taking Elation. Use any means possible, standard procedures, blah blah blah. I was making a killing for doing virtually nothing. A cake walk. Best assignment I ever had."

He stood up and walked to the other side of the room. "Then you came along. You were the only one crazy enough to take the stuff who fit their protocol as an ideal subject. The only one." He laughed another empty laugh. "You, of all people. I was supposed to get a cushy promotion when this was over. Would've nearly doubled my salary. But then I . . . I fell in love with you. And that's absolutely against the rules. *All* the rules." Finally he turned and looked at her.

She held his gaze steady, saying nothing. She was pale and her eyes were wide.

"I fell in love the moment I first saw you, Alyssa. Watching you try to get away from that crowd you were with, pretend you weren't a novice. I couldn't help it. It just happened. And it's grown from that time since. I've never loved anyone my whole life, not like this. I love you so much it hurts. And loving you made me realize something."

He came back toward her and leaned against the back of the cushioned chair. "They didn't care about you, or anybody else. All they cared about was their stupid research, finding the proof they need for their studies. They don't even think of people like you as human beings, with lives and feelings, or families. Do you have any idea what they're doing with genetics now? Do you know what they're getting away with?"

"I don't want to know," she said quickly.

"All right, fine. But listen. They were glad you already wanted to die. They hoped you would so they could do your autopsy themselves without attracting attention."

"Why?"

The thought of it made him ill, imagining little pieces of her body scattered about the lab in sterile pans and petri dishes. "I guess they could learn something that way. I don't know what. Look. They didn't care. They didn't care what I did to you as long as they got the information they wanted. The whole thing has been like a light coming on, you see? It started that day you bugged me about my sister. Remember? You got mad that I could be selling drugs when she died from an overdose."

"I remember."

"I was doing all right until then. I was humming along just fine. Life was going pretty great. I knew how I felt about *you*, but I was doing a great job rationalizing what I was doing for them. I thought I could keep up both charades, the one with you and the one with my department head. But then you said all that stuff and it made me think hard about what I was up to, what I was all about. And I realized my job didn't make any sense anymore. I wasn't helping anybody except myself. Some hero. You were right. Dead-on. It didn't make sense for me to be doing what I was doing. It was completely unethical by anybody's standards.

"And now they're breathing down my neck digging for tidbits of information. Lately the boss started to see through me, thinking I might have fallen for you and asking questions. I couldn't take it anymore. So I quit."

"You really did quit?"

"Yeah."

"Rob, they don't let people in your line of work quit. Do they?"

"No." He sighed. "They fried my government ID. I had to have it surgically removed." He showed her the pinkish-red scar on his right palm. "And I have to disappear within the next few days. If not sooner. He wants me to think they're just letting me go. I'm lucky to be alive. But if I don't vanish fast enough, Alyssa, I won't be."

Alyssa studied his face. She let go of the armrests and leaned toward him. "You expect me to believe all this? Is this the truth or is this just some half-baked scheme to get me back in your life?"

"Both." He grinned at her, but there was sadness behind his smile, and fear. "I know I'm way out on a limb here, but I want you to come with me," he said.

He sat down in the chair and scooted it in close to her. Alyssa stared at him, a confused look on her face.

"I'm having microsurgery tonight to get my fingerprints altered. For what it's worth. It might just buy me some more time."

"Fingerprints, Rob." She paused and let out a frustrated sigh. "Even the old retinal scans at the airport would find you out. And you can't change your DNA."

"I know, but it might buy me time. I know a few tricks."

"How do I know you're not just telling me a story?"

"I showed you my hand," he said. "Would I do that to myself just to get you back?"

"I hadn't pegged you for a Van Gogh, no." She sighed. "I guess not."

"So what do you say? Will you come with me?"

"Do you think I'm crazy?"

"I hope so. I hope you're crazy enough to think about it. Please. I know I've deceived you and lied to you, and I won't fault you if you hate me from now on for everything I've done. I know I'm taking that risk telling you all this. But this is the truth. I won't hide anything from you ever again. You can trust me. I promise."

"Don't you think being with you will put me at risk too? Do you think I'm crazy *and* stupid?"

"They can't legally do anything to you without exposing themselves. You're a private citizen. The last thing they want is to be found out. Public opinion on human test subjects is still—"

"The key word here being *legally*."

"I've protected your identity so far. They don't have any idea who you are."

"That's what you think."

"No, that's what I know. See, I broke through your passwords and encoding long before you told me your name. It wasn't easy. You're a pretty good hacker, you know that?"

"You *what?*"

Maybe he should've left that part out. Too late now. "It was my *job* to do that, Alyssa. I was only doing my job. But what I didn't do was report that information to my superiors. I was supposed to. I didn't because even that early on I wanted to protect you. I wanted you all to myself."

"If you found out that easily who I am, why can't they? You've endangered me as well. What were you thinking?"

"They can't because I deleted all your ID files from the government mainframe. Every last one."

She blinked. After a moment she said, "That's impossible."

"No, it isn't. I know how."

"But, how could you dare do that without talking to me first? Maybe I don't want you to do that."

"Believe me, Alyssa, you do. And I'm talking to you now, aren't I? I'm telling you now. I went as far back as I could. Your birth certificate isn't even on record anymore."

"So I'm not even a living person, to them? How am I supposed to find a job? And of course I haven't. At least now I know why. You've ruined everything. Thanks a lot."

"I'm saving your life here, and you're worried about a job."

"Yes, I am!"

"Just think, no more taxes for life." He tried a smile. She didn't return it, but looked at him coldly. "They have no way to find you now. You'll be safe."

"So why don't you delete your own records then?"

"I have. And when I get my new fingerprints I'll have all the tools I need to create a new identity for myself and start over, clean as a whistle."

"If you're *that* good, then why aren't you in charge of the CIA or something?" She folded her arms and raised her eyebrow.

"One of the unwritten rules is not to let on how good you really are. It's all a big game. A gamble. If they knew I was that good they'd be afraid of what I could do to them. I'd have been dead long ago. Or in charge, yeah." He tried a laugh but it fell flat.

"Rob, this is giving me the creeps. I don't know if I believe you."

"I understand."

"How could you get me into this?" She looked straight into his eyes. The expression on her face was so full of pain and hurt that he had to look away.

"You're the one who took the stuff. Not me," he said. He couldn't bear that look.

"You sold it to me. First you ruined my chances at a decent career and now you've ruined my entire life!" She stood up, angry. "What's left of it, that is!"

"I did not ruin your career! Using the drugs did that for you, plain and simple. It was your choice. *Your* choice. Not mine. Remember, I offered to pay for your college, but you didn't go for it. I had the money. I *had* the *money*. I'm trying to make up for what I did to you, don't you see that? I even took a huge risk trying to buy your diamond back, but I couldn't get it. And maybe I should remind you, you didn't want your life then anyway! You threw it away every time you came in that shop. And I told you not to do it!"

He was angry too and turned finally to face her. This was not the response he'd planned for in his hours of thinking about this moment, if it ever came to be a moment. He had rehearsed and rehearsed how it might go, but this reaction was not one he was prepared for. It would have been easier if she had broken down and cried; maybe then she would have allowed him to comfort her. He was unprepared for her anger.

"Was that part of your instructions too? Reverse psychology?"

Rob stiffened, paled. His anger dissipated. "Yes." He paused. "It helps us avoid liability." It was a whisper. "But it was more than that. I really *didn't* want to see you go through this. It was torture for me, watching you."

"Well. So that's how it was." She was silent for several minutes.

He had no comeback, no retort, nothing to say that wouldn't make matters worse. He kept the silence, waiting.

"I notice you didn't try to stop me after that first time. And you were always begging me to come back. Come to think of it, that's exactly what you did with the marijuana, too," she continued. "Yeah. It was the same thing. You kept saying, 'No, no, no, let me put it back in my pocket.' What were you trying to do?"

Rob bit his lip, watching her while she paused again. Her logic frightened him.

Her eyes went wide. "It's obvious, now that I think about it. I remember now, you said . . . You wanted . . . you hoped I'd take it so maybe I'd feel like sleeping with you. That's it, isn't it? Do you think I can't see through that? You're just like the rest of them after all! You jerk! You big jerk!" She wept, hot tears of anger. "And to think it almost *worked*!" She turned toward the wall, away from him, but her sobs were plainly audible.

Horrified by her words, Rob said, "Alyssa, no way. No *way*. That's not it at all. Honey, I wouldn't want anything you weren't ready for. I could tell you weren't ready. Your first time shouldn't be like that. Please, don't cry, don't cry. Please."

"I am not a—" she started in, turning her face to him again.

He cut her off. "Yes you are. I had my suspicions all along. You had to be either a virgin or you were physically hurt. That Saturday I figured out it was both."

"How did you . . . No, don't answer that," she said. Her face flushed red and she turned away.

"It's nothing to be embarrassed about, Alyssa," he said. "In fact I'm impressed, touched, even. And I respect you. I would never dream of touching you if you weren't completely ready for it. Honest. You've got to believe me, hon. I simply wouldn't dare, no matter how much I . . ." He stopped and took a deep breath, then ran his hand through his hair. His forehead was sweating. "Besides, if that's all I wanted from you that night, I could have had it."

"That's not true!" She flashed another quick glance at him.

"It *is* true. You were stoned. You couldn't possibly have resisted me for long. Nevermind that a good part of the time you were asleep."

She turned around, slowly, her eyes burning with hate or anger. She wiped tears from her cheeks with the back of her hand. "You didn't . . . You *didn't* take advantage of me, while I was sleeping?"

He recognized her look for what it was—horror—and recoiled.

"Absolutely not! Alyssa. You have to believe me. The thought never, *never* crossed my mind. I fell asleep right after you did. Honey, I would *not* do that, not to anyone, and never to you, especially not after whatever you've already lived through. Whatever it is you won't talk about. I'm not that kind of a man."

He couldn't tell from the look on her face if she believed him. She still shook, as though sobbing, but her tears had ceased, and she made no noise.

"I'm *not*. Trust me, Alyssa, if I was going to make love to you I'd want you to be wide awake and completely ready and willing," he said. "I'd want you to have the experience of a lifetime . . . something you'd remember forever, something you'd *want* to remember forever. Please, you have to believe me. I am *not* like 'the rest of them.'"

"Okay," she said, narrowing her eyes. She took a deep breath.

"Look, all I wanted that night was to help you feel better. You were so down. I couldn't stand not being able to help. Listen to me, please. I didn't push you, did I? No. I didn't. When you said no more, I stopped. I *stopped*. And no, that's not at all why I brought the pot along. It *was* stupid. Very stupid. For all I know I've put you back on a road neither one of us wants you to be on. I've been kicking myself ever since."

She took a few more deep breaths while he spoke and wiped one last tear from her face.

After a long pause she looked him in the eye and asked, "So why did you bring it, then?"

"I thought . . ." *No more secrets. Tell the whole truth.* He let out a sigh. "I thought maybe I could still get the information they wanted. Maybe I could get it from you with the help of that drug. Still trying to please everyone, I guess, play both sides of the game. But I changed my mind. I'm not giving it to them no matter what the cost. You're worth far more than that to me. Far more than anyone could ever pay. You have to believe me. I could never, never do that to you."

"So how do I know you're not working for them now? How do I know this isn't some elaborate plot to get the information they want? Huh? You expect me to trust you after all this?"

"Because you gave it to me already," he said, his voice barely a whisper. "Before you took the pill that night."

"*What?*" she said. The blood drained from her face.

"They wanted to know all about those creatures you saw. Every last detail. They always do standard drug testing before they release a product on the market. During the routine testing, they discovered people could see these things and talk to them when they were sober, so they started researching the side effect. The boss swore it was proof of other intelligent life on the planet, some such nonsense, and that this drug somehow worked on people so they could see these life forms. I don't know how. It was so totally cockeyed I didn't see how anyone could believe it. I certainly didn't believe it then, and I still don't. They're just some hyped-up LSD flashbacks. Anyone with a brain in their head would know that. I definitely did not think it was worth you dying over it. Or me. Or *anybody*."

He thought about the other subjects; there were forty-one that he knew about. Maybe more. He had never met any of them.

"They think those things are *real*? Not hallucinations?"

Her face went from white to gray.

"The appearances are backed up by quantum sub-phase readings and other coincident activity in the subjects' peripheral visual and auditory nerve pathways. But the quantum sub-phase data alone isn't enough to prove it."

"Of course it isn't. You can't get accurate readings on that level. Heisenberg's uncertainty principle."

Her response startled him at first, then he remembered how often she had mentioned her physics classes. "We have a machine that's overcome Heisenberg's theoretical limits . . . a little, anyway. It measures quantum energy and momentum accurately. When this thing was invented it was a bit startling, but it does work. Still, the data it's come up with isn't quite enough on its own. They know it's detecting *something* with a good deal of accuracy, but they don't know exactly what they're measuring. Could be sub-phases of the quantum particles, maybe perturbations in Lewis Little's elementary waves. Anyway, lab rats don't talk much, and human volunteers are hard to come by, considering the risks. There's always a few weirdoes. But they needed a test group. Subjects who didn't know anything was supposed to happen, who weren't on a bunch of other drugs. Who weren't being paid to say anything. You know, not the weird ones."

"I feel sick," Alyssa said. "I think I'm really going to be sick." She sat down and rubbed her forehead. "So did you tell them?" she asked. "Do they know what I saw?"

"No way. They don't even know that I know."

"Why didn't you tell them?"

"Alyssa, I *love you*. When is that going to sink in? Don't you know what I'm giving up for you?" He paused, slightly irritated. "In fact, they gave me until today to coax it out of you the easy way. If I couldn't then they wanted me to bring you in to the lab. They have this machine there . . ." He shuddered and paused. "It's not something I could ever put you through. I couldn't bear it."

"Today?" She looked up.

"That's one reason we're here. I designed this room myself, a couple years ago. Their scanners can't penetrate it and they don't know about it. We're safe in here."

"Are you sure?"

"Positive."

"Well, Rob, if you told them all the details, wouldn't this all be over with? Why don't we just go there, and tell them? If it'll save us both from harm."

"Oh no. They'd want you to *talk* to them."

"To the government people? I could handle that, to save myself. If—"

"No, no. *Them*. They'd keep stoking you up on Elation, lower doses if you were lucky, for the rest of your life, so you could see the things and talk to them *all* the time. Relay messages back and forth, that sort of thing. I heard they were looking for a spokesperson among the test subjects. Somebody to be a reliable contact. They had the gall to call it a 'dignified ambassadorial position.' I wasn't supposed to know that much while I was working on this end of the case. But I had a couple of sources, and I found out."

"Oh," Alyssa moaned. "But you would be safe if you told them, right?"

Rob swallowed. "Cushy promotion, loads of perks." His voice was completely flat.

"And you haven't done that?" she whispered.

"I *won't* do it. They'd still have you," he said. "Boss told me I'm welcome to have my old job back if I bring you in. If I don't, they'll crawl the city looking for me. That's the deal. I know how terrified you are of those things, real or not. I knew it when you first mentioned it. No way on earth would I deliver you up to that kind of fate. I'd die first. And I mean that." He sat down again.

Alyssa looked dumbfounded. "This is much worse than I imagined."

"I know."

They sat together in silence.

Rob was first to speak. "I don't believe them. It's got to be just a weird side effect everyone who takes the stuff gets. Just like the medics told you. It messes with your brain chemistry. That's got to be all it is. They just want to stoke you up and keep you all high and visionary the rest of your life, all in the name of research. And who knows how long that life would be, considering the risks. It's such a crock. I don't know how I put up with this crap as long as I did."

"Do you know if the other people saw the same exact creatures I did?" Alyssa whispered.

"I have no idea."

"The medics seemed familiar with the symptoms," she said. "It can't be that big a secret."

"They know about it, but the government can't question them."

"Why not?"

"It might be easier, but it raises suspicion. The medics don't know the side effects mean anything. If they suspected, they'd start getting ideas, start poking their noses into things. They'd let loose the whole nasty business to the public. They don't get along well with the DR. Hospitals are subsidized by tax money and they aren't. Medics don't like that at all. They're in direct competition with the hospitals, which means they're in competition with the government, which means they're suspicious of anything the government tries to ask them, especially where the Department of Research is concerned. Government's tried to buy a few of them out before but for some reason it never works. I don't know why, they offered plenty."

"Well then, why don't *we* let it loose? They shouldn't be able to get away with this! It's going to happen to someone else, don't you see? Maybe you can save me, but what about whoever comes along next? They're going to keep trying until they get their . . . ambassador, or whatever they call it. Why don't you take it public?"

"Tell the press?" He blinked at her without comprehension.

"Yeah. I have the number for the medics who rescued me. They've done a couple of follow-up calls. We could talk to them first for support, and then take it to all the major news stations in the City. You'd be a hero, Rob! This is your chance to be what you always dreamed. Don't you see?"

"A hero? I don't think so."

"Are you too chicken to expose something that's as morally and ethically wrong as this? Is that it? You're *scared*? I thought you had more guts."

"It's not a matter of courage at all. Alyssa, you're forgetting who's in control here."

"Oh, right, the government controls every single media station in the country. That's not possible. I hear bad things all the time about the stupid government. If they controlled absolutely everything they wouldn't let anything scandalous get out at all."

He found her ignorance appalling, and had to remind himself that he was privy to many things she and the rest of the American public were not. He could only stare at her, willing her to believe.

"No way," she said.

He didn't change his expression.

"It can't be true. That's impossible," she said.

"Alyssa, if I've learned one thing in the years I've worked for the government it's the fact that it controls a lot more of our lives than anyone thinks possible. More than you're willing to believe. Do you remember hearing about the Arizona polio epidemic three years ago? Government sent a bad batch of live oral vaccine out there. Two hundred children died and thousands more were crippled."

She shook her head. "That's not how I heard it."

"Have you been to Arizona lately?

"Never."

"The people were told the vaccine must have been ineffective against this new strain of polio, that the virus mutated and we were working on a new vaccine to combat it. You want the truth? The vaccine the government shipped out there infected the kids with full-blown polio. That's the truth. They covered it up so neatly that out here, you never even heard anything happened. Arizona's been under quarantine ever since. Can't leave, can't go in. We told them it was to protect the rest of the country from the new strain, and most of the citizens were so freaked out they didn't complain. It's to protect the government's butt, is what it is. They let people leave, the people will talk."

"How do you know that?"

"I was *in* Arizona," Rob said. "I was there. On follow-up assignment. In fact, I wouldn't put it past them to have done it on purpose. The President doesn't like those independent militia groups out that way, and they were getting powerful before the quarantine went into effect. I'm sure he felt threatened. He's not entirely sane, in my opinion. But I never could find concrete proof of a conspiracy. Just good guesses. And I looked hard."

"Oh, you did."

"You bet I did."

"So what else don't I know?" she asked, rolling her eyes.

"I'll bet you thought they really did find a cure for AIDS, don't you?"

"Sure, it was all over the news . . ." she stopped. "You're making this stuff up to scare me into going with you, aren't you?"

"Honest, I wouldn't do that. I can get you all the nit-picky details if you want them. I have some of the files on disks I've stashed away. Thought I could use the data for blackmail someday if I had to." He sighed. "Only now I'm in a different department, so the people I'd have to blackmail aren't the same. Great, huh?"

"Well, there's got to be some way to get this out in the open."

"Only if you want hundreds of innocent people to die along with you. If the medics get wind of it and try to do anything, even as a group, they'd all be wasted. And it would look like a convenient accident. Are you ready for that? You want to be responsible for the lives of the people who saved your life? Do you?"

"But . . ."

"Look. That's the way it is."

She twisted in her seat. "Just the way it is? You have no power to change it, even once?" she asked uncomfortably.

"They'll keep this quiet no matter what it takes. If they ever do get proof of these things' so-called existence and go public with the information, they'll never tell how many people died in the process of obtaining it." He was emphatic. "I've seen these people work, Alyssa. They can make people disappear. No one ever knows what happens to them. Not even their closest family."

"Did you ever make anyone . . . disappear?" she asked, her voice sounding dry.

"No. That's not part of my job. I don't have the right psychological profile for it. So they say. I didn't want any part of it anyway. Bad enough I have to know it happens."

"So there's nothing we can do?"

"We can run away together. Save both of our lives and leave this whole mess behind us."

"Rob, how is that going to help?"

He reached over and took her hand in both of his, stroking it. "We'll be together. I know how they operate, and I know how to get away without being found. Believe me, I had a detailed plan for this made up three years ago. Just in case. After a few years in the service, I realized I might need it someday."

He took a deep breath. "I'll be happy just to be with you. Like this. I don't need anything else if you're by my side. Just seeing you, having you near me, is enough. I know you say you don't feel as strongly as I do. But Alyssa, I know you must feel something. If you didn't, you wouldn't have come here at all. I know I've been annoying since you broke it off. And I know you have a perfect right to hate me for everything I've done, everything I am and stand for. But I don't want to leave you. I don't want to live without you. And I can't stay here anymore. It's the only way I can escape. I was thinking we could go out somewhere in the country, maybe Montana, and raise some sheep together. I can pay cash for a good sized ranch, and it'll never be traced. Ever since I was a kid, I always thought sheep were cool, you know? They're quiet and harmless, and they never hurt anyone. Plus you don't have to kill them to earn a living. You sell their wool, and they get hot in the summer anyway, so it all works out fair . . ."

He could see she wasn't listening. "Alyssa, I need to know if you'll come with me."

She looked at him. "Rob, I don't know."

"Marry me," he said, impulsively. "Come with me to the country. I love you. We'll forget all this ever happened to us. Start a new life. Please. Will you marry me?"

The shock registered in her eyes and she pulled back away from him a little. "Rob, I can't do that."

"You've said yourself there's nothing left for you here. Have you found a job yet?"

"No. I can't now. You know that."

"Then there's nothing keeping you here. But *I* need you. I love you. Even if you can't love me as deeply as I love you, or whatever your deal is, as long as we're together, I'll find a way to make you happy. I promise. I'll do anything for you. I know I can make you happy. Whatever you need, you'll have it. Please. Just promise me you'll think about it. Don't say no right away. Please." His eyes glistened and he felt close to tears.

"Are you certain they don't know who I am?" she asked mournfully. "Do I even have a choice here, Rob? Either I go with you, or wind up dead? Or worse, a, a spokesperson to some kind of . . . alien intelligence?"

"I'm as sure as I can be, under the circumstances. They could be hiding it from me that they know, but I doubt it." He sighed. "I'm pretty good at reading the boss. If I have anything going for me at all it's that I was very good at what I did."

"Good enough to pretend you love me?" she asked. He heard a sob catch in her throat.

"No," he choked. "Not that good. It's real, Alyssa. This is the most real thing I've ever felt. You have to believe me."

"How do I know you won't turn me in if I say no?"

"I could never, ever do that to you. I'd turn myself in to the machine first. I'm willing to do it to save you if I have to. I would do that for you. Please believe me."

She took a long deep breath that exhaled in a sigh.

"Promise me you'll think about it. We could be happy, I know it."

There was a long pause while they looked at each other.

"All right, I promise." She sighed. "But it was hard enough to work out my feelings before this. This is a lot for me to handle at once."

"I know . . . but I have to know by tomorrow," he said, his face revealing the pain and worry he felt. "I don't have much time."

"Tomorrow . . ." Another sigh.

She stood up, leaned over to him and brushed his cheek with a kiss. He pressed a button to unlocked the door. The lock beeped and the door swung open.

"I have to go," she said. "Am I safe if I leave this place alone?"

He checked his watch. "Should be. Go home a different route. Take a bus to the mall or something first. That'll help. You know, it might be a good thing you cut your hair. If they've gotten a visual on you somehow, the new style will help disguise you."

"Rob, I'm scared. I wish I didn't believe you."

"I know. I'm so sorry."

"What about you? Will you be all right?"

"I'll make it fine. Don't worry about me."

"I don't want to think about you *not* making it."

"I'll call you?"

She nodded. "Tomorrow."

****

She wandered back to her apartment in a daze, taking a circuitous route as Rob had suggested.

Chapter 24

Crossroads

> *This decision is so hard. Maybe I should try writing this out like a math theorem and see if that helps.*
>
> *Eeney, meeney, miney, mo, catch a tiger, let him go . . .*
>
> *Two roads diverged in a wood, and I . . .*
>
> *And I what?*
>
> *How's that go again? I never did do well in English, just physics. But even Einstein couldn't help me out on this one. He'd just tell me it was relative.*
>
> *And on top of all the other issues, I have this persistent, nagging feeling that I would put him in danger if I went. And myself. It's an odd feeling. Seems bigger than my own thoughts, and kind of like it comes from a source outside myself . . . A good source, not like those horrible voices certainly, but ominous still. I don't understand it.*
>
> Alyssa Stark,
> note found on her personal computer

All was quiet when she returned to her apartment. She found it peculiarly discomforting. Sitting down on the plaid couch, she waited, but she didn't know for what. Maybe something would come to her.

It was a lot to take in, as she told Rob.

She knew deep down that he loved her; she could feel it. But she wasn't certain if what she felt for him was love. Marriage was a frightening concept. Running away with him, escaping the reach of the government, was more frightening still. She knew she could do it if she wanted to badly enough. She had always been stubborn once she made up her mind. But she simply couldn't enter into such a binding contract without a strong love to hold it together. And it would be a binding contract, whether it was made official by a marriage ceremony or not. She might not be able to contact anyone she knew, except him, for as long as she lived, or at least until the danger was past, if it ever was. She would be committing her entire life into his hands. Into exile. Permanently.

It was asking too much. There was no guarantee he would be able to get away safely alone, much less dragging along an inexperienced accomplice.

But if what she felt was love, she wasn't sure marriage was what she wanted, even under ideal circumstances. The thought of creating a family of her own, the possibility of having children someday, terrified her. Her father had tried his entire life to please his wife without success. Rob wanted to do that for her. He said he loved her, he needed her. But did she need him? Would their marriage turn out the way her parents' had? Would she become her mother to Rob's Chuck?

And he had lied to her, then lied for her, trying to protect her. He deleted her ID files, somehow, without her permission. Was that love?

Her thoughts circled around each other, twisting, trying to make connections. What did love matter anyway? What purpose did it serve? She didn't need it. She had never needed it. No matter what Deb said about it.

If I go, I face my whole life alone with him, and . . . a bunch of smelly sheep . . . If I stay, I could be found and tortured and no one will ever know. If I go, we could make out under the Montana sun all day long . . . If I stay, I could have a normal life. They might never find me. Or need me. And I might get a real job after all.

Yeah, right, and mushrooms grow on the moon.

She literally felt dizzy. When Debra came home from class at dinnertime she was still sitting on the couch, staring blankly at the ceiling.

"What's the matter?" Deb asked.

Her words startled Alyssa. "I didn't hear you come in," she said. She wiped her hands up and down on her jeans, fidgeting.

"How'd it go with Rob?" Deb asked. "What did he want?"

"Rob," Alyssa said softly.

She looked up at her friend, quieting her hands. Deb put her purse on the end table and put down her backpack.

When Deb looked over at her again she said, "He asked me to marry him." It just spilled out.

"I can't believe it! What did you say?"

She shook her head "no."

Several minutes went by in silence.

"Alyssa," Deb said.

She had almost forgotten someone else was in the room, and jumped out of her seat, then caught herself.

"What?"

"You're very pale. Have you eaten anything today?"

"Huh? No, I guess I haven't."

"Are you hungry?"

"No."

"I'll fix you something anyway. You've been sitting on that couch all day, haven't you?"

She vaguely recalled getting up once to use the restroom, but nodded her head. Deb got up and crossed into the tiny kitchen, pulling ingredients out of the cupboards.

"Are you going to think about it at all?" she asked, trying to sound casual.

"I broke up with him before he asked, if you remember." Alyssa forced herself to listen and participate in the conversation, pulling herself up as though coming out of a great deep.

"Breakups don't have to be permanent. You've been moping around like a cloud with nothing to rain on ever since you dumped him. You've hardly even smiled lately, and you were smiling so much."

"Really?" She was barely able to listen.

"He totally adores you. He seems like he'd do anything for you. You have to figure out if you're not just afraid of the whole idea, you know. Marriage isn't all bad."

"Yeah. He'd do anything. I guess so."

"Wouldn't hurt to think about it."

"It's more complex than that," she said.

"Like how?"

"He's going off to be a sheep farmer or something. In Montana."

"He's leaving Central City?"

Alyssa nodded.

"When?"

"Tomorrow."

****

In the end she said no. She didn't let him know how close she had come several times to saying, *Yes, I will run away with you. I will go on this great adventure.* In a way, she found the prospect exciting. It made her heart beat faster when she thought about it. But logic prevailed, and she stuck to it. It was the only decision that felt *right*.

She hated being responsible for hurting him. He called several times that night and the following day, always from a different phone, a payphone or hotel, usually. After the first time she had to unscramble the rest of his calls with a list of passwords he gave her. He suggested several ways to get out of trouble in case they found her, and uploaded potentially necessary files to her computer, all the while begging her to come, then begging her to reconsider after she said no again.

She wished she could be certain she didn't love him; that would have made it easier. But she was sure of one thing, that she would use him if she went, use his feelings to twist him into becoming whatever she wanted him to be. He might not care if she did. But she would care. She didn't want to be like that. She wouldn't become her mother. She would spare him the misery of a life like her father's. The longer she thought about it, the more she convinced herself that this is exactly what *would* happen to them. Her parents were the perfect example of what the two of them would become. It would never work. They were both better off alone.

The last call was the hardest.

"You won't reconsider one last time? I have to go, now. How fast can you pack your things? I can be there in thirty minutes."

"I'm sorry, Rob. I just can't." She ignored the leap in her heart that said, *Go for it, you fool, he loves you. Last chance.*

"But I can't ever come back for you. And I can't tell you where I'm going. It would put you at risk. I wish you would come. Are you sure you don't have your bags waiting, torturing me until the last moment?" He tried to smile.

"No, Rob, I can't. It's better for both of us this way."

"Couldn't you come as a friend? A business partner? Just so I can still see you, talk to you sometimes? Just talk?"

"Rob, we both know it wouldn't be that way." She shook her head.

"I hate this finality, Alyssa. I'll never know if you make it or not. All I can do is hope I've done my job well enough that they'll never find you."

"I hate it too. I'll never know what happens to you, either. But there's no other way."

She paused. He would never understand, wouldn't even care whether she used him as Joan had her father. She chose a different angle, still true enough. "It'll never work. In time I'd end up feeling like your prisoner. There are too many choices I'll never have if I go with you. It's too much to ask. I'm so sorry."

Also holding her back was the unrelenting sense of peril she felt every time she even came close to a decision in favor of his request. It restrained her now, and kept her from saying more.

"I wish things were different."

"I know. Me too."

"I wish there was some other way."

"You could go public," she said.

"It would only get us both killed. We've been through this already." A sigh. "I wish you would come. I love you so much."

"I know. I'm *sorry*."

"Is there anything else I can say to change your mind?"

She shook her head.

When he finally rung off she lay on her bed and wept bitterly into her pillow. Only afterward did the heavy sense of danger subside.

Chapter 25

Formal Introductions

Please disregard my earlier memo detailing a predicament involving agent 47. The matter has been quite satisfactorily resolved.

Victor Caldwell,
private memo

The large man sat puffing a fresh Cuban cigar behind the marble kidney-shaped desk, inlaid with gold. He liked the large furniture. It suited him. The shade of the picture window was half-darkened, as usual, so it was never too bright in his office. Too much light hurt his eyes.

He had been awaiting the cigar shipment for weeks, so it pleased him greatly when his secretary Gerome brought it in. He didn't believe his order had really been held back due to short supply. The cigar company was either poorly managed, or they had delayed his order intentionally to annoy him.

But they produced the finest, *finest* tobacco to be had on the planet, so he had waited patiently, ever so patiently, for the order to come, and ordered more long before he ran out. Even then they were unbearably slow. He hadn't had one in months.

These simple pleasures didn't ease his worries much today, however. There was a definite problem. He had to find the girl. Robert had been quite good at keeping his secrets. Too good. He knew that now. They had few leads as to who she was. A blonde, knowing Rob; early twenties at most, college student. Probably Central U, from the location of Rob's research post. Still, not much to go on. No exact matches had shown up yet on the university rosters; the leads hadn't checked out. So far.

He chewed the end of his cigar, thinking. He had other agents checking medical records for recent overdoses, but the ambulance companies, the medics, were never cooperative.

She was the only hope left for finding the proof he sought. The two or three other recent leads . . . Well, perhaps they had put a bad batch of Elation out on the market. It was a shame. What did show up on the news after that had created bad PR. The public was wary now, warned away from the possible dangers. Yes, it was a definite shame. But some negative reports couldn't be helped, in order to preserve the illusion that the government doesn't controlling the media. Otherwise, the public might catch on.

Now even if they found this girl they would have a difficult time covering up her disappearance. It was likely Rob had tipped her off, and she might struggle or tip off others. He mentioned she was related to some public figure as well. That could be awkward to explain politely, if it proved true. Some people disappeared more easily than others. That was a shame too. It was always more difficult when they had to bring them in alive.

He swiveled in his heavy black chair to face the window, turning away from his desk to stretch his legs. His superiors wouldn't be pleased by this turn of events. He had even lost his anticipated scapegoat. He should have killed Robert when he had the chance, quickly and easily. Now he had vanished.

He thought all along that's what Rob would attempt, but he had placed his bets on the man doing something desperate before he disappeared, something careless . . . bringing the girl along with him for his final disappearing act, for example. That would have been foolish, and certainly would have tripped him up. It's what a man in love would have done. And his agent was such a man. He'd read that in his eyes, clearly. No mistake there.

Either Rob would attempt escape with the girl, or bring her in and resume his position with the service. He hadn't considered that Rob would disappear alone.

None of his other agents could find him. He was nowhere. But that meant the girl was still out there, somewhere. With the information. He only had to find her.

"I believe you've been anxious to meet me," said a voice from behind.

The man dropped his cigar and stood up swiftly, drawing his gun as he turned around cautiously. His office was locked. Why hadn't he heard the door open? Hadn't he told Gerome not to allow anyone in?

A shadowy figure sat in the large alligator chair in front of his desk. It was definitely human, but he thought he could see through it. Almost. The figure *almost* appeared solid. He blinked his eyes to make sure he was seeing correctly, blinked again.

"Who are you?" he said gruffly. "How did you get in here?"

The figure laughed. "You can put the gun away, Victor. It won't hurt me. I am what you humans would term *immortal*. I assure you, however, I mean you no harm. On the other hand, if you shoot me you'll only ruin this lovely chair. We wouldn't want that, now would we? Alligators are so hard to come by these days." He seemed to sigh and ran an ethereal finger along the armrest. "It would be difficult to replace."

"I said, who are you?" the large man repeated. He could smell the cigar burning a hole in the carpet. It was too bad. It was excellent carpet, and new. But he would have to leave it there. He shifted the weight on his feet.

"Your particular problem is that you need proof of my people's existence, is it not?"

"Your . . . people?" His jaw dropped.

"You can pick up your cigar, Victor. I won't harm you." The figure smiled.

The large man squatted down to reach the burning object with his left hand, keeping the gun sighted on his target as he moved. He rose and stamped out the smoldering spot on the carpet without taking his eyes off the figure. Cautiously he sat down in his chair and lowered the gun onto the marble desk slowly, keeping his hand on it. He took a long drag on the cigar while he stared at the man—was it a man?—facing him.

"You still haven't told me who or what you are."

The figure smiled pleasantly. Yes, *smiled*. He looked absolutely human, with well-defined, handsome features. He appeared to be wearing an inky black cloak that wafted about him as though there were a breeze in the room.

"We are the beings you have discovered with your quantum sub-phase readings. Congratulations. I have been most impressed by your dedication to this research."

Victor was speechless.

"I am, therefore, the solution to your problem, am I not?"

"Can you help me find the girl?" he asked.

"Perhaps, but I'm certain she'll be inconsequential to our plan . . . though I may have further use for her. She was doing so well." A flicker of anger seemed to cross his face, then vanished.

Victor nodded. "How about my missing agent? Can you find him too? We think he's had his identity altered."

The creature chuckled softly. It was uncanny how *human* he looked and sounded.

"You are overly concerned with petty things," he said, crossing his wraithlike legs. "These individuals you spend so much time on, I can take care of them for you in my own way, in my own time. And so I will. You needn't worry about them any more. Just relax."

"Right. Relax when my position's on the line and I've got the President himself ready to—"

"You need to raise your vision higher than the Presidency," the figure said, straightening and moving toward him. Victor's hand automatically picked up the gun on the desk and aimed. "Much, much higher. I've watched you for some time. You have an amazing, untapped potential. I see marvelous things available to you in your future. With just a little assistance from us, I can help you gain all the power that until now you only dreamed of in your wildest fantasies. Let me tell you a small portion of what I can do for you."

Victor listened.

****

A few days after Rob left, Debra found Alyssa's stash of sleeping pills under some towels in the bathroom.

"Would you like to explain this?" she said, confronting Alyssa with the bottles.

Alyssa looked up at her blankly. "No," she said, and went back to her computer screen.

Deb reached over and flicked the power switch off.

"Hey! Do you know what you just did?" Alyssa said. "I was talking to someone about a job and you disconnected me!"

"Yes, I do. Do you know what you've been doing with all these?"

"Getting to sleep, that's all."

"Do you think I want to come in here someday and have to call an ambulance again? Or a hearse? Forget these! You're going to learn to go to sleep by yourself!" She whirled into the kitchen, bottles in hand, Alyssa following her.

"What are you doing with those? They're mine!"

Deb furiously opened the bottles. "How long have you been taking these things? Was this Rob's idea too?"

She dumped their contents into the drain, ran the water, and turned on the garbage disposal.

"No!" Alyssa screamed. "Don't do that!" She began to weep as she watched, helpless to stop her. "The nightmares will come back!"

She sounded like a whining child, and mentally cursed herself. She used to have so much control over her emotions. Lately it seemed all she did was cry.

"If it was Rob, I swear, I'm sorry I ever tried to like him. He'd have you fawning all over him for drugs like the sorriest dog that ever lived in no time at all. What a *jerk*!"

"No, no, it wasn't him, honest," Alyssa said through her sobs. Her pills were gone. She would never rest now. The nightmares . . . "He didn't know. I've needed those since before anything ever happened between us! I've never been able to get to sleep by myself since . . . since I quit the other."

"Are you sure?" Deb asked, turning off the disposal.

"I'm sure. He didn't even know about them. What's the big deal about them anyway?"

She went over to the sink and looked down, picked up the empty bottle and shook it, then felt the inside to see if there were any traces of powder left in them. Part of her couldn't believe it was empty. Gone.

"Stop that!" Deb said, grabbing the bottle. "Cut it out! You're being ridiculous."

"I am not!" She yanked the bottle back and sobbed, looking inside again, then flopped down on the kitchen floor. "The nightmares will come back now," she moaned.

Deb grew calmer, as she watched Alyssa's obvious grief.

"What nightmares?" she asked.

"The nightmares." Alyssa sobbed, leaning against the cupboard.

"Good grief. You need professional help," Deb said. She found the phone book and slammed it down on the bar. "Why didn't I see this coming? I should've known. I should've done this a long time ago. I'm getting you a psychiatrist."

"*NO!*" Alyssa screamed. "I can't be involved with the government."

"A psychiatrist is not part of the—"

"They keep records and case histories. Please. My life depends on it. I won't talk to a shrink, not about this." She cowered in the corner on the hard kitchen floor.

Deb put the hand-held phone down. "You're not telling me everything, are you?"

Alyssa shook her head, still weeping. "I can't, Deb."

The sobs shook her frame until it hurt. All she could think about were the empty bottles, and the fear that she wouldn't sleep tonight without waking up in a cold sweat, tormented by the creatures of her nightmares.

"Why not? I'm your best friend. And I will be, no matter what you're hiding."

"Rob . . . Rob was actually working for the government. Secret service. The whole time. He got in trouble and had to get away before they traced him," she said, sniffling. "That's why he had to leave so suddenly."

"What?" Deb said, startled. "The government . . . I had no idea."

"They might be looking for me too. I don't know. I have to be extremely careful. If they find me, I don't know what would happen to me. It's the Elation . . . it was a research thing. Oh, the nightmares are going to come back!" She had a look of absolute terror in her eyes. "Deb, please, please don't call a psychiatrist. I'll be good." Finally her tears subsided. "I'll be good. Just don't call anybody, please."

"Not even the medics? What about them?" Deb sat down on the floor next to her.

"No, you could get them in trouble too."

"Why? I don't follow you."

"It's a long story, and I can't tell it all. I don't even understand it all."

"Okay. Look. Why don't you talk to me about these nightmares. Start with that. There must be a way to make them stop without sleeping pills."

"No, there isn't," Alyssa said.

"Have you tried?"

"There just *isn't*," she said, whining again. "I have to have them to go to sleep."

"Tell me about it."

"In the nightmares . . . I relive all the awful parts from when I was getting high," she said. "All the creatures, the pain . . ."

Alyssa continued, explaining the details, the recurring grisly scenes. When she reached the part about meeting the inky black taskmaster, Debra turned pale.

"Whoa, stop for a minute," she said, standing up from her position on the kitchen floor. She leaned on the kitchen counter and rubbed at her forehead. "So these creatures were torturing you, and he showed up and then what?"

"He said I had to want the pain first," she said. "I knew you wouldn't understand. That's why I never told you."

"Oh, no, I understand," she said, looking down at her. "Maybe even better than you do. I'm just . . . just a little freaked. Give me a minute." She rubbed her head.

"You see why I need the sleeping pills then?"

"I understand perfectly why you're terrified. But there has to be a way of controlling your nightmares other than sleeping pills."

"How?"

"I don't know. But I do know you'll have to try it tonight. I'm not letting you out of my sight until you're peacefully asleep, if it takes all night."

She moaned. "It's impossible. I don't want to go back there again. Please don't make me."

"It's for your own good."

"Deb," Alyssa started, then stopped. There was nothing else to say.

"Were you ever able to get rid of them before? Stop them from scaring you or hurting you?"

"The nightmares, no. I can't stop the nightmares."

"Is it every night?"

"Not as long as I take the sleeping pills. Then I don't even remember dreaming when I wake up."

"No, I meant the spiri . . . the things, whatever you called them. Were you ever able to stop them? Make them go away on your own?"

"Oh. Once or twice. I think. They fed on my pain, the fear somehow."

"What did you do? What did you say to them?"

She thought hard. "I said I wanted to go to the sun."

"The Son?"

"The sun of joy I told you about, that's where I meant."

"And what happened?"

"They just kind of . . . recoiled," Alyssa said.

Debra swallowed hard. "Okay, then," she said slowly, "If you start having a nightmare, you tell them that. If it worked once it should happen again, right?"

"But I didn't get to go to the sun. That's when the taskmaster showed up, was after that," Alyssa said.

Deb let out a puff of air. "Well, it seems worth a try, don't you think? Maybe you should be more forceful about it. Don't show them your fear."

"Yeah, right."

"You had to want it, didn't you? Isn't that what they said?"

"I guess so . . ."

"Then make it clear you *don't* want those things anymore. You have to cast . . ." she paused. "You have to be bolder with them. Tell them to get out, tell them no. Above all, remember you're dreaming. Whatever it was, you're not really there anymore. These are only dreams, memories, not actual events. You can change them, if you concentrate. We had a unit on dreams in Psych class last term. Studies prove you can control nightmares by taking a proactive approach when you start to have one. People with recurrent nightmares have been able to change the endings. It really can work."

"Nice pep talk," Alyssa said humorlessly.

Deb kept vigil by her bed all that night, and the night after.

****

"Jon?" Debra whispered into the phone, early on the morning after the second night. Alyssa was still asleep.

He was groggy. "Huh? What is it, Deb?"

"You have to come over ASAP and . . . ah, throw out the spirits at this apartment."

"'Throw out the spirits'? Oh, I get it. Right now? But . . ."

"Maybe it'll wait till this weekend. We'll have to do it while she's not home, I know, but it has to be done. And I mean, soon. I'm going to call Bishop Vernon and see if he can help."

"You sound freaked, hon. What's the matter there? Are you okay?"

"I'm fine. It's Alyssa I'm worried about. Look, I don't want to explain anything further over the phone."

****

Alyssa hated to admit it, but over the next few weeks Deb's suggestions worked better than she thought they would. It sounded too silly to be effective. But when she mentioned the sun, refused to participate, refused to be frightened, it repelled the monsters. It was hard work, especially at first. She had to try hard to remember they were merely dream images. She also realized, with surprise, that the nightmares didn't come every night. And when they did come, she fought to take over the dream and control it. Or wake up.

She didn't sleep well the first two weeks. It was incredibly hard to fall asleep without the chemical aid she'd grown used to. Sometimes she stayed up far into the night, playing computer games to divert her mind, or organizing all the things in her desk for the hundredth time.

Gradually she began to win out. It was a long, slow progress, and she faced each bedtime with trepidation.

In the meantime, her financial and job prospects were few. She sold the Nagel from her father right away. It was small, and turned out to be a print, not an original. Neither was it one of the more famous pieces. Still it went for a decent price. Not as much as she had hoped, but it would pay for groceries and her share of the rent for a little while. She felt much better about that than leaning on Debra's funds to carry them both through, though Deb didn't complain or seem to mind if she did.

She did find a little computer work here and there, but nothing more than temporary; still, it paid her basic expenses a while longer. She had once prided herself on her programming skills. But the technology had advanced while she had been at school, and now without funds to update her software, she was behind. She needed more capital to turn it into a profitable business.

****

In July, Debra went home for a week-long holiday. Jon had returned home earlier, for the summer, and she made no secret about missing him now that she could no longer see him every week. She still went out dressed up on Sundays though; Alyssa attributed it to the fact that everyone needed personal space. It was Deb's time to herself.

She invited Alyssa to come home with her, offering to pay part of the ticket price.

"I'm worried about you. Please come."

"No. Really. I'm fine. Your house is too close to *my* house for me to be comfortable."

"You're sure you'll be okay."

"I don't need a chaperone! Don't worry!" She smiled, a rare occurrence now. "Deb, you go and have fun. I know you're dying to see Jon."

"Did I tell you he's not seeing anyone else anymore?" she asked. "He just wants to be with me. I think being away from me this summer is getting to him." Her flushed excitement was obvious.

"Yes, you told me," Alyssa said, amused.

"Are you sure you don't want to come along? I'd like that so much."

"I'm sure I'd be a third wheel. It's okay. Don't worry. No sleeping pills while you're gone, I promise." She laughed a humorless laugh. "Plus I'd feel guilty for not visiting Mother. And you know how I feel about that." She still hadn't contacted her mother since the funeral, and Joan hadn't called either. It was a part of her life Alyssa sincerely did not miss.

"I know. But I haven't left you for this long since . . . since all that mess happened. I'm afraid to."

"That's over, Deb. I'm all right. Honest. Go on, pack your stuff and get out of here."

Alyssa smiled, but inside she worried that she'd be lonely. She depended on Deb to be there for her, much more than her independent spirit liked to admit. Deb was her only family, in the sense of the word that transcends biology. Her constant presence was one reason she hadn't gone out to buy more sleeping pills. She could have hid them better, maybe, so Deb wouldn't find them again; she knew that. But she also knew she would keep her promise while Deb was gone. As the nightmares subsided, it was becoming easier to do without them. She felt a sense of relief about that. It was finally feeling good to be free of them, even though getting through each night was still difficult.

Besides it was only for a week.

****

During that week Alyssa organized the kitchen cupboards twice, and went through her files, throwing away useless papers and junk. She spent some of the time looking for steady work, again without success. Deb was due back Saturday. By Friday she had watched every movie she ever wanted to see, played through every computer game she owned, and was still restlessly bored.

At two o'clock Friday afternoon, the phone rang, jarring her from an unpleasant silence, an endless reverie of muddled thought. She had been watching a mindless daytime television show. She went to her room to take the call, since it was ringing from there, her personal number, not the apartment number she shared with Debra.

It was scrambled, and a message came up on the screen requesting a string of passwords.

Her heart jumped. *Rob! He's found a way to reach me!* She couldn't help but smile.

She opened her desk drawer and rummaged through the papers. The passwords were written down on a paper somewhere. She had just seen them . . . Ah, yes. There they were.

Quickly she entered the required series of encoded symbols, her heart pounding in her throat. Why was she so excited? She forced herself to calm down, straightening her hair as she entered the last password and the picture cleared. She remembered she hadn't even brushed it yet, or taken her shower, and felt chagrined.

It was a shadowy picture. The room she looked into on the screen wasn't illuminated. She thought she saw a large chair positioned behind a white, kidney-shaped desk, but she couldn't make out the figure sitting in it.

"Why, hello there. You must be the girl we've been looking for," a deep masculine voice said. From his tone he sounded pleased. It was not Rob's voice.

"What girl? Who are you?" She felt uneasy, and wondered if she should terminate the connection. Then she wondered what good that would do. No. She had to know what this call meant.

"You are an acquaintance of Robert Giles, I presume?"

"I don't know anyone named Robert." She made her voice nonchalant.

"I think perhaps you might," the man said. "We found this number and encryption sequence among his effects. Since you were able to unscramble this call on your end, I must assume that you do."

"So what if I did?" she said. "*His effects?*" What did that mean? She didn't dare ask.

"We'd like you to come in and identify him. It would seem that he had no other family. You may be his sole remaining . . . connection."

A voice in her head said, *Don't listen to him. He's lying.* It was kind, unlike the voices from her nightmares, and calmed her surging fears.

"No family, huh. Why does he need identifying then?" She remembered Rob saying his mother lived on the other side of Central, but he never spoke to her. "Can't he tell you who he is?"

"It's his body that needs identifying," the man said.

"You're saying that whoever this guy is, he's dead?"

The man cleared his throat. "That would appear to be the case."

She ignored the flip-flop in her stomach at these words, and said tersely, "*Appear?* You can't even tell if he's dead? Now that takes a special kind of stupid. Who are you? I'm not going anywhere to look at some disgusting corpse. I'm not into dead bodies, creep. I have an automatic call tracing program installed on this machine, and in a few second's I'll know where you're calling from and prosecute you for obscene phone calls. Identify it yourself."

The man sighed. "A feisty one, aren't you. Young lady, I do not wish to make this more difficult for you than it has to be. We need you to come in here for identification purposes. It's a simple thing and should only take a few minutes of your time. If you will verify your location for us we'll send an escort there to pick you up."

"You need my location?" Alyssa said, a knot forming in her belly.

"If you'll please verify your address, we'll send an escort for you."

The knot sank lower in her abdomen. This couldn't be happening. "Escort? You've got to be kidding. I'm a big girl. Why don't you tell me where you are and if I feel like it I'll come in." She felt it best to play tough, not to show any emotion. She had years of practice at that; she could sound convincing.

The voice in the dark room dropped its artificially cordial tone. "I am certain we will eventually find a way to bring you here, whether you wish to come or not." It was a distinct threat.

"You don't know where he is, do you?"

The thought came to her suddenly, a bright flash of understanding. His game became clear in an instant. She wished the room on her screen was not so dark. She adjusted the controls, played with them, trying to get a better resolution, carefully keeping her hands out of the tiny computer camera's view.

"I said we need you for identification," the man said.

She needed to keep him talking. "You can't possibly have him where you are, because I talked to him this morning," she said, lying.

She hoped it was a good lie, one the man would believe. She still might be able to get good visual resolution. Her computer auto-recorded all incoming calls. Her mind whirled. Rob had taught her a few tricks after the day at the library, in preparation for something like this.

"If you're so sure, then you'd know where he was calling from."

"How do you know I didn't see him in person? You think I'm going to give you information like that, free?"

"You are hardly in a position to be bargaining information prices here, miss."

"Oh? I think I am. You don't know where I am, you don't even know *who* I am, and you don't know where he is, either. I know exactly what you want from me, and let me tell you something. You won't get it. Not without making it worth my while."

"What we want is for you to come to our office for identification purposes."

"What a way to put it." She loaded her voice with contempt.

"Miss, erhaps you don't understand your situation here," he said.

"Perhaps *you* don't understand *yours*," she said, as the information she was searching for popped up in a corner of the computer screen. Robert had encoded it and she had then hidden it in embedded files on her drive, and it took a few long, tense moments to access. "I've got a positive visual match on you . . . Victor. Victor Caldwell, head of the Federal Department of Research and Development, isn't that correct?"

There was silence on the other end of the connection.

She continued, reading from a corner of her screen, "Perhaps you'd like to explain your connection to creating the bad polio vaccine that was intentionally sent to Arizona three years ago, crippling thousands of innocent children?"

It was a shot in the dark. Rob had mentioned once that he thought his supervisor was involved, but he was never able to make a positive connection. "Two can play this game. I have files right here that point the finger directly at you."

"I had nothing whatsoever to do with that! It was not my fault!" the man said, clearly angered.

"So you admit there *was* a cover-up? That you *are* Victor Caldwell, and that you are aware of the details of that case?"

She wondered if he was glowering. The screen was still too dark to make out good details, but he didn't have to know that. His name, along with other useful information, was included in the files Rob had uploaded to her before he made his escape. "If these files get into my father's hands he'll do serious damage to your career. You'll certainly never hold any high office. I assure you that *you* are the one who has no idea who you're up against, Caldwell."

"I don't have to tell you anything," he said.

"Fine. And neither do I," she said. "Good day."

She terminated the call.

She was trembling all over. Quickly she checked that the conversation had been recorded, made copies under several filenames, encoded another copy, transferred a coded copy of the video to a disk and stashed it in her desk, unmarked. She was certain she didn't want to lose the information. It might be valuable some day.

Rob had explained how he mentioned her "celebrity relationship" to his boss without being specific, and suggested that she use it as a trump card if needed. At the time she thought Rob was exhibiting excessive paranoia and barely listened. She was glad she had remembered in time. Caldwell would look for the daughter of a powerful *man* who fit her description. He wouldn't know her father was not only an inconsequential figure but dead. With luck her deceit should throw them far enough off the trail to give her time. She took a deep breath and leaned against the back of her desk chair, shaking.

The knot in her gut twisted again, this time demanding attention. She ran into the bathroom and threw up. All along she had entertained the hope that somehow, none of it was true, that Rob was just a little bit nuts, and it was all a desperate (although decidedly bizarre) ploy to win her over. She had begun to believe that. No more.

She could only hope her gut feeling was right, that they didn't have Rob after all. It didn't seem possible. He would have given them the information they wanted if that were the case, even become the "ambassador" to the aliens himself, if need be. She believed he would make that sacrifice. He would do anything to protect her—anything to save her from that fate. He had told her so.

But what if he didn't? she thought. *Then what would happen to me?*

Fear crept back in, a cold spike impaling her spine. She hadn't considered that possibility, not as a reality.

She took a deep breath and tried to relax. The answer to that worry was simple. Rob knew where she lived. If he betrayed her, they wouldn't need to call like this. Agents would have shown up at her door already, if not Rob himself. So the excuse the man gave her had to be a ruse.

That realization came to her as she wiped her mouth on the bathroom towel, still feeling ill. Rob must be alive. They hadn't come for her, not yet. They found her, but only her personal number, not her location in real latitude and longitude. Central City was vast, but obviously not vast enough. Rob had been afraid of that machine he mentioned. If they ever did capture him, and attempted to extract information . . . She couldn't count on his love for her, or his strength to resist them, or on his self-proclaimed genius as an escape artist.

She knew what she had to do. Two things had to be resolved if she was to stay hidden. First, she must eliminate her computer. It wouldn't take long to track its signal. She must do that today, immediately.

She could take a tram downtown . . . No, to the richer neighborhoods, across Central to the New Seattle district, where many politicians lived, and drop it there, perhaps on the lawn of the Presidential Palace itself.

She chuckled at the thought. *That* would be something. It was Friday; the President's big bashes were always on Fridays. She could easily duplicate a ticket to get in.

No, she decided. That idea was too risky. New Seattle would do. The tram ride would take the rest of the day, but it had to be done.

Then she would have to find a new place to live, someplace where she would never be found.

Chapter 26

The Immortals

They call themselves The Immortals. They've been here since before Man first scratched flint to stone and harnessed fire. In fact they claim to have given Neandertal the gift of fire; the wheel as well. It may well be true. This one, who calls himself The Caretaker, is their leader. His store of knowledge is utterly remarkable. There is nothing I cannot ask that he cannot answer or explain. So far the scientific truths he has taught me seem to pan out with the research I am able to conduct on my own, in my limited spare time . . . His knowledge of our genetics is unparalleled by any human researcher to date. And that is merely the beginning.

I am still in the process of learning exactly what it is they want from us. It strikes me that they must need something, for with their superior knowledge and power it seems odd for them to take such a personal interest in our kind . . . If I can find that out I may be able to use it against them as a bargaining chip in the future. Perhaps they have a weakness or desperate need of some kind, that now draws them out in the open.

The Caretaker claims it was simple boredom . . . Our research fascinated them because we humans had never before discovered their existence scientifically and forced contact like we did . . . He said they still could have chosen not to show themselves, but thought it was interesting how far we had gotten with our experiments . . .

He says I have a most promising character . . .

Victor Caldwell,
private research notes

"**N**ow you know I speak the truth."

"You did that? You can cause traffic accidents?" Victor asked, peering through the shade of his window.

Below in the intersection was a bloody scene, the aftermath of several bicyclists and four cars colliding into a semi. The truck had rolled over on top of yet another car and was burning. Police cars had just arrived, sirens blaring, blue and red lights flashing dimly in the bright sunlight. He blinked. He didn't like the glare.

The dark wraithlike figure laughed again as he sat in the alligator chair. "Oh, my dear Victor. You have no idea. We all have learned a little bit about controlling the elements over the eons we've had to play with them. You are such simple corporeal beings. It must be awful for you, going through life chained to those high-maintenance physical bodies of yours. What a chore. The miniscule understanding of science that your limited brains permit you is trivial compared to our combined vast stores of knowledge."

"Get to the point," Victor said.

"Traffic lights are child's play." His voice was chilling.

"Yeah? But how do I know for certain *you* did that?" He puffed his cigar and squinted through the glare.

Two or three survivors were trying to crawl out of their vehicles. The cyclists, who had been pedaling along gracefully in the bicycle lane moments before, were crushed.

"Always the skeptic. That is a good quality, but not when it comes to believing in me. I predicted exactly what would happen while you watched the events play out."

"Yeah, but it doesn't mean you *caused* them. There's a difference."

The figure sighed. "You are beginning to exasperate me," he said tersely. "If you want your proof then you shall have it." He made a gesture with his arm, a flipping motion.

Suddenly Victor felt a *push* and found himself on the outside of his window, on the ledge. He gasped for breath and dropped his cigar. It went spinning down, spraying glowing cinders as it fell. It was bright, far too bright, outside. He squeezed his eyes shut.

Just as suddenly he was back inside. He leaned on the window and gasped heavily.

"What'd you do that for?" he yelled angrily.

"I could as easily have left you out there. Take care that you do not doubt me again or you will not find yourself as fortunate."

"Uh . . . yes, I understand. I see now. My apologies."

The figure leaned forward. "If you complete this contract, when that flimsy heart of yours gives out and your frail mortal body expires, we possess the power to make you one of us. I can grant you immortality. You mortals have no souls, you know. Believe me, we would know by now if you did. Your puny, worthless lives end at death. And we don't miss many of you."

He rose from the chair. "But sometimes, when someone especially talented like yourself comes along, we take compassion on you. Enough compassion to make you one of us. You can belong to our elite group. You will live on forever, with us, free of that confining mortal body and having more power than you can now comprehend." He smiled with disdain. "It's an opportunity I would not pass up, if *I* were mortal."

"How can you do that?" Victor came away from the window and opened a drawer in his desk, taking out a fresh cigar from his special box and peeling the label.

"Simple rearrangement of your molecules from your bulky matter into the far more refined particles that make up our bodies. It's not a complicated process . . . for us. That's why no one ever found Hitler's body, you know. We changed him. He was . . . most useful to us."

He chewed on the end of the cigar. "If that's true, can I meet him, someday? There are things I've always wanted to ask . . . if I ever had the chance."

"Perhaps. If you do well."

"And you're sure you don't want any money for these . . . services?"

"What would I do with money, Victor? I already know where every treasure of the earth is buried. I know where the richest diamond mines are. I have no use for these things. I've watched civilizations come and go for millennia. Don't be foolish. Your glory will be great, Victor. You have the potential to become the first true world leader, to unite the nations as one. The others who aspired before you—from Alexander the Great to Stalin—I'm afraid their technology was far too underdeveloped. The world wasn't ready then. I did the best I could with what they had, but none of them achieved their dreamed-of success. You alone have the potential. And the price we ask is so small. Only your complete and unquestioning trust and acceptance of our demands."

"Trust, huh? Hmm," he said, chewing and puffing on the new cigar in earnest. "But I don't see what you get out of that deal."

"I've already told you our reasons for showing ourselves."

"It doesn't seem to me that boredom justifies all this benevolence. What are you getting out of it?" He narrowed his eyes to slits.

The Caretaker smiled, almost kindly. "We are a benevolent race, Victor. We have been the benefactors of mankind for millennia, giving you gifts of knowledge, power, invention. We have asked for so little in return. So little. But humanity's gross ingratitude toward us and our gifts is not acceptable. You ask what I want, and I see you will not rest until you know. I want you to place your trust in me. I want the recognition that belongs to me, and only to *me*."

"Not to your people? What about them?"

"My people follow me. They are my faithful subjects. They do my bidding and mine alone. *I* am their leader. Anything they do glorifies *me*. Is that not clear?"

"Yes, I think so," Victor said slowly.

"With your help, I can receive the respect that is rightfully mine. You show the world what I have done for them, and I shall reward you with power beyond your comprehension."

"You've sure waited a long time to tell us you want our thanks," he said. "Why is it so important to you now? What do you get out of it?"

The Caretaker smiled, and it seemed his eyes glowed with a strange sort of inner fire. "Before your technological age, it was easier for us to obtain your trust and receive our due respect. When humans foolishly believed in magic it was easy to get them to accept us, to appreciate our gifts and acknowledge our leadership. A few tricks here and there were enough to encourage their fear and appreciation." He paused, eyes flickering. "I especially miss the human sacrifices . . ." he said, laughing softly to himself. "So fascinating to see how far they would go for us . . . But this is a different age. Even though you obtained scientific proof of our reality, you still doubted. Did you not?"

"Well . . ."

"When I first showed myself to you, you didn't believe what you were seeing. You're still stubbornly difficult to convince. Nearly all of you humans now find it equally difficult to . . . accept our reality. We've given you more gifts and shared more knowledge with you as a species in the last two centuries than ever before, and what is the unfortunate result? You don't even acknowledge our existence, let alone yield due regard for our services. This does not please us."

"I think I understand," Victor said. "But you still haven't answered my original question."

"Would you like to spend more time on the ledge?" the creature asked. "I've been more than generous in sharing information with you!"

"No," he said, "That won't be necessary."

"My dear Victor," The Caretaker continued, "If you must *ask* to know what the reward is for having thousands upon thousands of inferior beings place their complete trust in you, and accept, even *worship* you as their leader, then I have misjudged you. If you cannot fathom the deep satisfaction that comes from . . . being worshipped as the very *god* of this earth . . ."

"Ah, yes. It's getting clearer now. Yes, I'd like very much to help you with that." His mouth was dry. "As long as I'm in. One of the . . . leaders."

"Very good. And of course you will be. Oh, and one other thing."

"What's that?"

"You must stop frightening that girl. You upset everything I have in motion when you pull such half-witted stunts. I quite dislike the fact that you tried to call and bully her into coming to this place. That was foolish and interfered with my plans."

"But I almost had her," he said. "And why should you care? She's nothing to you."

"You most certainly did not 'almost' have her. Every time you frighten her she gets farther away from my . . . from *your* grasp. You must move slowly, use stealth, use her curiosity. Gently, gently, draw her in. I watch you make mistakes like this and I wonder if I have made the right choice in selecting you. Let *me* take care of her from now on. I know what I'm doing. I've worked at this for millennia."

"All right, all right," he said.

"If you are to join our elite group we *require* your complete trust. *Complete.* You must follow my counsel explicitly. We are a superior race of beings. You are expendable, Victor. Do not forget that fact or you could find your life rapidly foreshortened. You have received much from us. Much is expected from you in return."

"I understand," he said. "I'll do my part, I swear. Whatever you say."

"Excellent. I'll be back . . . to give you further instructions," the figure said with a twist of a smile. Suddenly he was no longer visible in the chair. He was just *gone*.

It unsettled Victor when he disappeared like that, but he was slowly becoming accustomed to it.

He sat puffing, dreaming of where those diamond mines might be and if he might be allowed to excavate them for himself. He could be richer than his wildest dreams.

****

When he left the building that evening and found his cigar on the sidewalk he was more than slightly shaken. Glancing around, he leaned over, picked it up, and stowed it in his pocket.

Chapter 27

Article 28

ARTICLE **XXVIII**, SECTION **I, 1**. *As it has been proven that professing or holding to a religious belief is a serious psychological disorder, and considering that the exercise of such beliefs has led to the destruction of an inordinate number of innocent lives both historically and in the last two decades on this Continent (as documented in the case of People vs. Alluvius Blankenship), we the People declare that any and all citizens who claim or profess belief in a Supreme Being shall be required to undergo professional and timely psychological therapy for treatment of a pathological condition.* **2**. *This Article shall be enforced by Act of Congress, and shall be punishable by fines, inprisonment, or both, as Congress shall determine, punishment to depend upon severity of resistance offered by any citizen or group of citizens who refuse to comply.* **3**. *Therapy is mandatory without exception, as stated in* ART. *XVII* SEC. *III. 12 (Limitations on Rights of Citizens with Known Psychoses).* **4**. *Therapy may be administered immediately upon imprisonment or arrest.* **5**. *Citizens unsure if they are affected by this psychosis shall submit to a standardized test.*

ART. **XXVIII**, SEC. **II, 1**. *Acceptable forms of therapy for this disorder shall be as follows: A) Psychological reconditioning. This shall be the preferred method of treatment . . .*

The New Constitution

"You can put the gun down, Jeff."

Peter stared calmly at the young man, three years his junior, who held a shotgun aimed at Peter's waist.

They stood inside Hutchinson's Feed & Grain. Peter had come in to pick up the oats for the horses, the winter wheat seed, and some potting soil for his mother. He heard things were getting rougher in town since Article 28 passed, but Jeff had caught him entirely by surprise.

"Ain't no way I'm putting this shotgun down," Jeff said. "You folks are outright religious, and there's a law now says you're nuts. You're comin' with me."

Peter smiled, hoping his nervousness didn't show. "Jeff, we've known each other a long time. Have I ever done anything to hurt you?"

"No," he said.

"Why don't you just let me go about my business? My horses are anxious for their oats."

Jeff grinned a terrible grin. "'Cause the law says if you all don't get yourself some nice good old-fashioned therapy, we can do whatever we want with you. You going to go do it?"

"Now you know the law isn't worded exactly as you put it," Peter said calmly. "I'm not planning on going in for therapy. I'd like to stay who I am."

"You got a nice piece of land out there," Jeff said, the crooked smile still on his face. "Wonder if you'd feel like giving it to me as a donation? For a good cause?"

"Not particularly," he said, as politely as possible. "It was my grandfather's farm, and it's my father's now. I'm fairly attached to it." He cleared his throat. "What might that good cause be anyway?"

"On a *cause* that it's *gooder* for my family to live there since *we* ain't nuts and you *are*. On a cause that you're a menace to all proper society, and the law says so."

"I don't believe that's a good reason to move off my family's land," said Peter. "We've owned it fair and square for generations. Sentimental value, you understand."

"Then that proves you're crazy," Jeff said. "Because I'm the one with the gun, and you're not. And I'm gonna shoot you down right here unless you change your mind 'bout this right quick. You all march yourself down into town for some of that mind-fixin' therapy, and correct yourselves of those infirmities, or else you can give me that farm of yours. What'll it be, Richardson?"

"It'll be neither. This is ridiculous, Jeff. Put the gun down," Peter said firmly but softly.

Jeff didn't answer. He shifted his weight from right to left leg and stared.

"You don't want to kill me, Jeff," he said calmly. "You'd be facing something much worse than therapy. And you don't want my farm. You're going to put the gun down now and walk out of here, and head back home to your wife, and when you get there you'll tell her how much you love her, and how glad you are that you won't be going to prison for killing an innocent man."

The point of the shotgun wavered.

"And on your way home you'll wonder why you ever thought to pull a shotgun on me like that, acting so badly towards a man of God," he added, his voice commanding but gentle. "I know your mama raised you to be a God-fearing man yourself, Jeff. Do you think your own *mama* was crazy? What would she say if she was still here?"

Jeff seemed in a trance. He lowered the shotgun slowly and turned away from Peter, then casually walked to the back entrance of the store. Peter heard him say, "Joe, you got that harness ready yet?" as he passed through the doorway.

Peter breathed a sigh of relief. "Well, what do you know?" he said nervously to Mitch at the checkout, who had watched the whole scene in silence. "What are things coming to these days, huh?"

Mitch stared at him. Peter cleared his throat, paid for his goods, and went out to his truck. It had been loaded with his order while he was inside. He floored the gas pedal. As far as he was concerned, he couldn't get home fast enough. He had to tell his parents it was getting worse.

****

"Did you see that? Did you *see* that?" Jeff said to Mitch, about half an hour later. "They have powers, I tell you. They're all creepy like that, every last one of 'em. The President's right. They oughta be fixed."

"I saw," Mitch said.

"He put some kind of spell on me. Moved that gun right down to the floor all by itself. All by itself. Like I wasn't even holdin' it at all. Just grew a mind of its own and before I knew it I wasn't even in the store. Felt like he transported me out. Did you see that? Did I get transported?"

"You walked out yourself, Jeff. You asked Joe something, and you walked out."

"Well, I don't remember doin' it."

"All said and done, Jeff, next time you pull a stunt like that, do it outside," Mitch said. "If those 'powers' of theirs, or whatever, fail and you do manage to blow a hole in one of 'em, you do it in my store and you'll lick up the mess with your own sorry tongue. I don't need my supplies pumped full of buckshot. You take your arguments elsewhere next time. Is that clear?"

"Aw, you'd be so glad to be rid of him you'd lick it up yourself."

Mitch stared coldly. "He brings in good business, crazy or not. Business is business. Plus I don't need any creepy curses on my store neither. Don't you go thinking I'd be glad for his death. Not for a single minute. I ain't gonna be responsible for none of that."

"Chicken. Are you even with us on this, Mitch? You a sympathizer?"

"Call me whatever you want, but I ain't no sympathizer. All I know is they're paying customers. And they never make up lame excuses for not paying their bills like *other* folks I know." He cleared his throat loudly.

"Come on, Mitch, you know it's hard times. You'll get your money. I'm fixing to settle my account here any day."

"You've been saying that for weeks."

"But the wife, you know she's having a baby. Any day. Have a little pity. I gotta feed my family. She's been eatin' enough for a horse. I can't keep up with her."

"Yeah, and I gotta feed mine. So don't give me any of those 'have mercy' lines. If you'd quit spendin' your whole check on gun polish you'd have enough in no time. You pay up your account right quick or I'll be after you with *my* shotgun."

"Oh, you will not. You're all hot air and you know it."

"Don't tempt me. You've got till next Friday to make a payment or I'm closin' your account."

"Friday? You've gotta be kiddin'!"

Mitch stared hotly.

"Okay, okay. I'll bring in a check," Jeff said, and stomped out.

"No checks!" Mitch called after him. "You bring me cash."

****

"I can't believe Dad lost his job," Debra said. She was walking with Jonathan, arms around each other, after dinner. It was a nice evening, but humid. It had rained earlier in the day.

"I hate to say it, but it was inevitable," Jon said. "We've all seen this coming for months. They were pushing him out gradually."

"I know. It's so hard not being right here. I feel so out of touch with everything."

"It's hard not having you here," he said.

She stopped, and he had to stop also.

"Really?" She looked up at him.

"It's true, Deb. I've missed you."

"I've missed you too."

They started walking again.

"Is everything set up for the move?" she asked. "It's so exciting to be called to this new pilot program, to prepare for the time when we'll build the New Jerusalem. Us, Jon! It can't be that far away now."

"Yes, it's exciting, Deb, but it'll be interesting to see if we really can live the United Order the way it's given in scripture."

"Are you so worried about that?"

He thought a moment. "You know, not really. I'm more worried about establishing the colony and being left alone by the government in Iowa, than sharing everything in common."

"Didn't Dad say the head of the FBI in Iowa is one of us? As well as half the local agents?"

"That's true, but who knows how long he'll stay in charge if he doesn't enforce the law."

"I'm sure God will provide for us, Jon, you have to have faith. This project comes direct from the First Presidency. They wouldn't ask us to do it if it wasn't by revelation and if they didn't have faith we could succeed."

"You're right," he said.

"How many have been called to build the colony? I like the name. 'New Hope.'"

"Many were called, few are going," Jon said. "I don't know total numbers for sure, but I think each colony is supposed to have about five thousand to start with. From our local area, everybody still active in church was called. The Harris's aren't going. He doesn't want to leave his practice yet. We're going, along with your family, of course. Then there's the Jones, Beales, Humphreys, Rafaels, and the Sweets, from what I know so far. We're to head out one or two families at a time so as not to attract attention."

"What about the Georges?"

Jon shook his head.

"I can't believe Melanie at least isn't going."

He sighed. "We've lost a lot of people since this new article passed."

"I hoped so much it never would. Still, I hate to see people fall away like that. You'd think they had more integrity."

"I guess they don't."

"Well, I'm going to miss them."

"Me too."

They came to an elementary school and started around the perimeter. The recent rain made the grass-covered fields look beautiful, fresh and clean. A few children played on the wet playground equipment, splashing in the puddles left on the asphalt courts. The air was thick with humidity, and although it wasn't too warm out it felt sticky. Everything smelled fresh, dirt and oils washed away, leaving only the sweet green scent of growing things. The couple reached a chain link fence on one side of the school's perimeter and stopped. Leaning against it, they watched the children play.

"You know, all this excitement has gotten me thinking," Jon said.

"About what?" she asked.

He put his arm around her shoulder and squeezed her tightly. "I've been thinking about us," he said.

She turned to face him, a mischievous smile on her face. "And why are you suddenly thinking about that?" she teased. "I didn't know you ever thought about us!"

"You know I haven't wanted to see anyone else."

"So you've told me."

"Do you know why?"

"I hope it has something to do with me."

"Well, I love you, Deb," he blurted out. He looked uncomfortable saying it, and afterward looked down at his feet. "I don't know how else to put it."

"What did you say?"

"You know what I said. Um, I don't expect you to say it too," he said, still staring at the ground. "Don't feel you have to . . . it's okay. If you don't feel the same, I'll understand."

"Jon!" She lifted his head up with her hand to make him look at her. "Do you know how long I've waited to hear you say those words? I was beginning to think I never would. Of course I love you. You've got to know I've had it bad for you ever since we started dating." She smiled.

"Well, how come you never said so?" he asked.

"I was waiting for you! I didn't want to scare you by saying it too soon."

"Three years is too soon?"

"Hey, you're the one who suggested dating other people, not me. You think that was easy to take? I couldn't say it, not then."

"Deb, I didn't know. I thought you'd want some freedom, that's all." He sounded exasperated.

"No," she said. "I didn't want 'freedom.' How could you *not* know that?"

"Hey, look. I don't want to fight about it," he said. "Of all the things to fight about, we have to pick this one." There was a long pause between them. "I guess you're right, though. I should've said something sooner. It was so hard. I wasn't completely sure for a while. I hate to admit that but it's true. I didn't want to hurt you in case I didn't mean it one hundred percent. But now I *am* sure. And I *do* mean it."

"Then the waiting was worth it," she said.

"I've had the hardest time lately not having you near me." He looked back down and fidgeted with his fingers.

"Really?"

"Yeah, really." He spoke quietly. She took his hand in hers.

After a moment, he continued, "Well, the other thinking I've been doing, is, well, none of us knows what's going to happen now, except we hope it'll all be okay. And if it weren't for that I might take more time and not rush into what I have to say next, but please, listen to me, okay?" He looked at her. "Promise to hear me out?"

"Okay."

"Debra, I would be honored if you would . . ." He dropped to one knee in the mud and fumbled in his pants pocket for something, but came up empty. "Where'd it go?" he said, checking his other pocket, then patting himself in search of the object. "I'm sorry, hang on a minute," he said, standing up. "Don't go away."

"I'm not going anywhere," she replied, amused.

"No holes in my pockets . . ." he muttered.

Deb watched him with interest, her eyes glittering with a combination of amusement and excitement. Finally he found what he was looking for, a pretty little diamond ring, in his shirt pocket, which he had checked twice already.

"Aha! There it is," he said. "Couldn't feel it in there." He laughed an embarrassed sort of laugh, and looked back up at Debra while he presented it to her. "I'm sorry, I wanted this to be the perfect moment, and I feel like it's turning out lousy. I knew I should've kept it in the box." He sighed. "What I mean is, Deb, it would make me the happiest man alive if you would marry me."

He held out the ring to her. Belatedly he dropped to one knee again and pulled the ring back out of her reach.

"After all that, I forget to kneel. I'm botching this so badly. Let me try again." He paused and gathered his breath. "Will you marry me?"

"Jon," she said. "It *is* perfect. You worry too much. And yes, I will marry you!" She knelt down in the mud next to him. "I thought you'd never ask." She took his hands in hers.

"You will? You did? You mean it?"

"I mean it. Did you think I'd say no?"

He smiled. "I didn't have any idea. It's kind of sudden."

"Three years is hardly sudden," she laughed.

Gently, he slid the ring onto her finger. It was far too big and the diamond slipped down to the palm side of her hand. She laughed again.

"I can't do anything right," Jon moaned.

"You're doing plenty right, Jon. Plenty," Debra said, smiling wide. She slid the diamond up to the correct side of her hand and squeezed her fingers together to hold it in place. "It's beautiful," she said. "*And* perfect."

"Once I got to thinking, I knew there was only one thing I wanted, and that was you. Then it's been all I could think about. I could hardly wait for you to get home, to see you again. I might've waited longer . . . but with all the changes in the air, I had to know right now if you wanted me or not."

"Oh, Jonathan, I do," she said, looking into his eyes.

"Wow, the mud's cold," he said, looking down at his knee. "Sure blows the romance of the moment, doesn't it?" His jeans and shoes were caked with it.

Deb shook her head. "No way! We'll remember this moment the rest of our lives. We'll tell our children about it."

"We will, won't we?" he said softly. "The rest of our lives. And forever after that."

She nodded.

He leaned forward to kiss her, pulling her into his arms. As they embraced, the mud slid out from underneath Jon's knee and toppled them both full into the puddle.

"Whoa!" Deb cried, laughing and righting herself.

She tried to brush herself off, but it only streaked the mud across her clothes.

"Jon, sometimes it scares me that you want to be a surgeon. You know that?"

"Hey, my *hands* are steady," he said, laughing with her. "Even if the rest of me isn't."

"Well, there's one good thing about this," she said, slipping a little as she tried to wipe her hands off on her jeans.

"What's that?"

"At least I'll always be able to say I felt the earth move when you proposed."

He groaned.

••••••••

Debra came home from vacation Saturday evening bursting with the news. She rushed in the door, whisked off her coat and dumped her bags with a thump, then crossed the narrow living room. Alyssa sat at one of the barstools, eating dinner.

"Guess what?"

"What?" Alyssa asked, turning around.

"Look." She held out her left hand to show her the ring, a gold band with a small sparkling diamond. "Jonathan proposed! I'm so excited!" She did a little dance around the living room.

"Wow," Alyssa said. "I thought he'd never get around to it."

"Me either!" Deb sighed.

"So, when are you getting married?" Alyssa asked.

She felt instant apprehension. Even though she knew she would have to move and soon, she didn't know what this change in Deb's situation would mean. She had pegged Jon for one who would go on for years without making a formal commitment.

"Soon," she said. "We haven't set the exact date, it depends on a few things. Oh! It was so romantic! You'd never believe it. We went out for a walk after dinner Wednesday. It had just rained and everything outside was so lovely . . . Alyssa, I didn't have any inkling he was going to ask! I'm still surprised he actually did." She continued excitedly reciting the details of how it had all happened, including their fall in the mud.

Alyssa smiled while Deb told her the story. She was certain Deb would be very happy. But it meant Deb's life would move in a different direction. She still had to tell her about the strange phone call the day before.

"We had to have the ring resized the next day, that was Thursday . . ." Deb stopped suddenly in her narration, looking at Alyssa. "Oh!" She sat down on another stool, leaned on the bar and looked at her. "Are you all right?"

"I'm excited for you, Deb," Alyssa said. "I am."

"Alyssa, we talked about you—my family and I—almost as much as we talked about our engagement. We all want you to come with us."

She laid her hand on her friend's. The thrill of excitement danced in her eyes.

"Come with you? To the wedding, sure. I wouldn't miss it for the world, even if it was next door to my mother's house."

"No, I mean come *with* us. . . .My dad just lost his job at Weaver."

"I don't follow you," Alyssa said.

"Sorry, I'm getting ahead of myself. We're all moving. My family,

Jonathan's family too. We're all going farther north."

"That doesn't make sense, Deb. Moving, maybe, but north? The jobs are in Central City, if he's looking for work. Nobody lives up north. There aren't even good schools up there. It's a virtual wasteland until you hit Sioux Falls, and even that's not . . ."

"It's much more complicated than that."

"You've completely lost me."

"Don't you know by now?" she asked. "Haven't you ever figured it out? No. You *still* haven't."

"Know what? What am I supposed to figure out?"

"Okay, okay. Look. Can I trust you?" Deb said, in a hushed voice, suddenly secretive. It was unlike her easy, carefree manner.

"Sure," Alyssa said. "You know that, Deb."

"I have to tell you something. It's important. But you can't tell anybody else. Ever."

"You're acting very strange," she said. "What is it? If this is what being engaged does to you, boy am I glad I passed."

"It's not being engaged. Listen. You've told me a few things you wouldn't want me to repeat, right? Things it would be bad for the government to find out?"

"Yeah, but what does that have to do with you? Did they connect you to me?"

"No. Alyssa . . . we're *Christians*," she whispered. She waited a moment for it to sink in. "The Church of Jesus Christ of Latter-day Saints to be exact. It's too dangerous for me to live here any more. It's even bad back home. We have to go farther away, set up our own place where the government won't enforce the law. We hope."

"You?" Alyssa asked.

She took a deep breath. *Law?* Someday she would have to pay attention to the news. She had heard something recently, but what? She couldn't quite remember. The news programs and talk shows and movies she'd watched all week blurred together in her head. But she knew it meant something. Perhaps it would come to her.

"Is this a new thing? How long have you been . . .?"

"My whole life. Born and bred." Deb grinned. "I'm surprised you never noticed. You never figured out me and Jon go to church every week?"

"Is that where you go?" she said. "I never thought about where you went. I just figured you wanted some privacy." She was embarrassed to say what she'd always assumed they went off to do.

"Well, we went to church," she said. "You never even guessed?"

Alyssa shrugged. "Does it matter?"

"It does now. I'm taking a risk even telling you this, but I know you won't turn me in. See, that's why my dad lost his job. He was asked to do a favor for some of the other professors in his department. Some fudging in the personnel records in the computer system. It would've gotten him and all the others a nice bonus next term, and no one would have been the wiser. But it would have compromised his integrity, and he wouldn't do it. So they teamed up and found a way to fire him. If he fights it it'll go to court, and if it goes to court, his religion will become a public issue. He'll be in real trouble." She spoke rapidly, her dark round face visibly flushed. "So we're moving up to northern Iowa, where it's safer—at least for a while anyway—to build our own community. Up there the people won't mind us being around as much as here, and if we keep to ourselves we should be left alone." The last sentence came out wistfully.

"What kind of trouble? What can they do to him anyway? What's the big deal whether you're Christian or not?"

"Didn't you hear? They just passed a major amendment to the New Constitution. It's been debated on the news for weeks. They've been deliberating this thing in Congress for the last couple years and it's finally come to a head."

Maybe that was it. "I guess I heard something, but I don't remember what."

"Oh, I forgot. You don't pay attention to the news."

Alyssa shook her head. "I try not to, especially since Rob left. It makes me ill."

"Religious beliefs were officially declared a psychological disorder last year. The amendment they just passed, Article 28, legalizes mandatory therapy. Especially for people who believe in any of the Christian faiths, and Islam or Judaism. Some other religions they're overlooking for now, but they're coming down hardest on Christians."

"Why?"

She shrugged. "They say we're the most dangerous group."

"A psychological disorder? What kind of therapy?"

"I've heard it's some kind of drug therapy. Or neural laser surgery."

Alyssa was horrified. "Neural laser . . . the treatment they give serial killers?! It's just a belief, isn't it? How's that going to hurt anybody?"

Deb sighed. "Oh, they've been trying to get this passed for a long time. Ever since Blankenship nuked L.A. The whole issue is older than we are." She got up for a drink of water. "Frankly, I'm surprised it's taken this long, when I think about it. The government thinks we're all just terrorists waiting to happen."

Alyssa thought a moment. "Oh yeah. We studied a whole unit on that guy in high school, I remember now. You helped me prepare for the test."

Debra leaned back against the kitchen sink, sipping her glass. "It's had serious repercussions for all of us ever since."

"I suppose so," Alyssa said.

"My whole life, it's been a struggle over what I can say and what I can't say, to people. What I could even tell you, and you're my closest friend. In the old days we could share our feelings and beliefs freely, without fear of any punishment. Missionaries went around on bicycles and knocked on doors spreading the gospel. It's hard for me to imagine that kind of freedom. It must have been wonderful. At worst maybe we might've offended someone or injured their feelings, or gotten a few strange looks, teasing. But I'll have plenty of time to tell you about all that later."

"If I come with you, you mean."

Deb nodded, finished her water, and put her glass down.

"I don't know if I can do that." Alyssa sighed.

"Why not? We've got most of the details worked out. There'll be plenty of work where we're going. I'll student teach, Jon will finish up, and I'm sure you could find something better than what you're doing now. Maybe you could finish school too." She walked back around to her seat, carrying her glass.

"Jon will finish med school, in the middle of northern Iowa?" Alyssa raised an eyebrow.

Deb cleared her throat. "Well, he'll have to go with private tutoring, but he'll be taught by some of the best surgeons and physicians in the country."

"Really?"

"Yes, really. And you could have whatever education you wanted, too."

Alyssa sighed heavily.

"So. What did you do while I was gone, watch videos all week and play computer games?" Debra asked.

"I looked for a job," Alyssa said defiantly.

"Yeah, right."

"I did. Is it my fault nobody wants to hire a nonexistent person?"

"All the more reason for you to come with me. What have you got to lose?"

"For one thing, I can't believe in that stuff. You can't expect that from me. I mean, no offense intended, but you can't expect me to buy into any of that religious mumbo-jumbo."

"I don't. And I'm not asking you to. I just want you to come with us. I don't want to leave you here alone. I worry about you. You're my best friend."

"Why can't you just tell them you don't believe it? If they pick you up for therapy, talk your way out of it. Tell them they have the wrong person, or say you have nothing to do with religion. Then you won't have to leave. They leave you alone, you get to go on with your life like nothing ever happened. Simple."

Debra smiled again, amused. "How can you be so naïve, Alyssa? You think they'd take our word for it?"

She thought of Rob and the things he'd told her about the government. Deb was right, of course. They'd want more evidence than just her word.

"Then why don't you just renounce it for a while? Long enough for them to believe you, that you're well now . . . or something."

"You don't know much about what we believe, do you?"

"I was never too interested in finding out. I'm sorry."

"Well, it's like this. Once you have a testimony of Jesus Christ, that He lives and is the Savior of mankind, you don't go around denying Him like that."

"Why not? Wouldn't this Savior of yours want you to save yourself? What's a little lie, compared to losing who you are to therapy?"

"Try to understand. I couldn't live with myself if I did that. I love Him too much. He redeemed my soul. His love means much more to me than saving my own life."

"I suppose bribery is out of the question."

"Of course."

"Well, then maybe you are crazy," Alyssa said, shaking her head. "I mean, Deb, listen. It's nice to believe something hopeful, like when you die you get to go to heaven and live happily ever after, but who knows what's going to happen then? Who *can* know? There's no way for any of us to know what comes next until we're actually dead. Even I don't know that and I was almost dead once." She felt odd when she said it, as though she *should* know something; but the feeling passed. "Don't you see? It can't be real. Or at least it can't be proven. This is just not worth screwing up your life over, is it? What if this *is* your only life? Have you considered that possibility?"

"Alyssa." Deb looked her squarely in the eye. "It is *very* real." She was dead serious.

Alyssa sighed. "Okay. It's real to you. I'll accept that. I'm trying to understand. But is it worth getting into trouble with the government? Look at what happened to Rob. I won't ever see him again, much less know if he's still alive."

She stopped, realizing the same thing was about to happen to her and Deb. Her heart sank.

"It won't be the same as that," Deb said, following her thoughts. "Once we're out of the city it's very likely they'll let us alone, as long as we keep quiet. It won't be the same as the Salem witch trials, I don't think."

"Salem witch trials?" The reference was unfamiliar.

"You never heard of them?"

"No."

"Never mind. What I mean is they're not going to hunt us down for extermination, at least not yet . . . I hope. The FBI's in charge of enforcing this law, and half the force in Iowa is Christian, or at least sympathizers who don't think the law is right. So if you don't come with us, you'll still be able to call and visit if you want. I won't be gone forever."

"This is crazy. Why are they so set on this? I don't see what's wrong with you. You're the most harmless person I know. I mean, even if it is a psychological disorder, it's certainly not a dangerous one."

"Well, we do believe a lot of things the government doesn't like, that they perceive as dangerous. Establishing Zion, preparing for Christ to return and reign over the earth. Not to mention our being politically incorrect on every moral issue. If our views became popular it would ruin their power base, their *revenue*. If they push us all out of the main core of voters and isolate us, they hope to eliminate that risk. But you won't have to worry about any of that if you come with us. I promise. No one will push anything on you that you don't want to hear. I know how you feel about that. I never have, have I? Listen, we'll be close to each other, and you can find decent work up there, I know it. The people I know won't worry about your not having a degree . . . or being a 'nonexistent person.' They'll accept you for who you are. And I'm positive you won't need ID's or anything like that up there."

"But Deb, there's still something *you* don't know."

"What's that?"

She told Debra about the phone call, and her trek across the City, using precious grocery money on transportation to and from, to dump her computer in the New Seattle district.

"They could have traced my terminal from the call. It was only a matter of time until they found me. Now it'll be a little longer. I left it turned on, so they'll be on a wild goose chase for a while. I made sure I went during rush hour and used cash, so it would be hard to trace the ticket sales back to me."

She felt a rush telling the story. It had been exciting, and she felt a sense of impending danger and espionage she had only felt vicariously before, watching spy mystery videos.

Deb was silent a moment. Then she said, "Alyssa, this is the perfect opportunity for you. Don't you see? The timing is *perfect*. You have no reason to stay here anymore. You can't even make one up. And I want you to come with me. We all do. You won't get in the way, if that's what you're worried about. Can't you see that? Maybe this was meant to be." She wore a shining smile.

"It's nothing more than coincidence, Deb," Alyssa said. "Coincidence. Look. As much as I'll miss you, I can't go. I'd only endanger you. What if the government found me? My presence would lead them straight to you. Then you'd all be in trouble. No. I can't be responsible for that. I have to disappear. Someplace where there aren't any central computers or DNA files on anybody, and those stupid palm and retina ID's they scan in order for you to buy anything . . ."

Deb sighed. "Alyssa, there won't be any of that up north. Promise."

"Deb, I can't. I *can't* endanger you."

"You won't. No more than any of us are already in danger because of Article 28."

"Plus, what if they do come and round up your colony, or whatever, and there I am? If they pulled me in for some kind of mental testing or whatever they might figure out who *I* am and send me off to my fate. I can't risk that. Besides, you could get in trouble for harboring a fugitive. No. It won't work. I'm sorry."

"But where will you go, then?"

"Look, I was going to tell you all this anyway as soon as you got back. I've found a place. I spent some time on the monorail after I ditched my computer, and I think there are places in Central where I can slip between the cracks. I've heard rumors. I've seen some neighborhoods from a distance. They look old. I couldn't get close enough on the rail to be sure, so I came home and looked it up on the net. These buildings, they don't show up on the city map like they should. Where they should be, the map says there's some kind of nature reclamation project."

"That sounds dangerous. At least with me your life won't be threatened. The crime rate in those places must be—"

"Phooey. You only hear what the news reports want you to hear. I can take care of myself."

"Why can't you come with us?" Deb's voice pleaded with her.

"I made up my mind." Alyssa set her face in a determined look. "Before you came home. In fact, this thing with you makes my decision easier. I was worried how you were going to take it. How to break it to you. I was afraid of deserting you and leaving you here all alone, especially with Jon home on vacation. I didn't want to abandon you. Now I know you'll be fine. And I'll be all right too. You've got to know that."

Deb sighed heavily. "I guess you will. It was too much to hope that you'd come along. I know how crazy it sounds."

She smiled. "It does. For all I know, you *could* be nuts. But if you are, I don't see anything wrong with it. You're the finest crazy person I've ever known, Deb."

Silence hung between them for a long, long moment. They could hear the clock ticking in the background.

"I'm going to miss you so much," Deb said.

"I'll miss you, too." Alyssa leaned into her friend and hugged her, as emotion flooded uncomfortably into tears. "You're the only real family I've got."

"I'll call," Deb said, sniffing. "You know, I have to leave in two weeks. I was hoping you'd be with me." She wiped tears from her eyes. "I had it all planned in my head. You know how you do? I imagined you with us every step of the way. Jonathan's coming down to get me and all my stuff. Well, everyone is, Mom and Dad too, this time, and then after everything's all settled up north we'll have the wedding. That's the reason we don't have a date set. I figured on your being there, too, somewhere in the background."

"I'll call you . . ." Alyssa started to say, then remembered she no longer had a computer.

She felt completely disconnected from everything important to her, as though all her friendships, familiar activities and habits had been ripped out with the wiring to that terminal. All that was left on her desk was a jumble of wires and cables and a useless docking station.

"Man. Without my computer you won't be able to get hold of me very easily. I'll call you when I can. Whenever I can. When I earn some money, I'll call from somewhere and let you know how I'm doing. Just make sure I have a number where I can reach you."

"I will," Deb said. "You can be sure of that."

"Good luck."

"You too. You'll probably need it more than I will."

****

The next two weeks they spent packing up their things; Deb's in boxes to be moved back home, and Alyssa's in piles, mostly to be tossed or sold. She decided she would be better off taking only a backpack and duffel bag with her; she didn't want much luggage to drag along.

Debra continually tried to change her mind, but Alyssa was even more set on this decision than she had been when she decided not to go with Rob. While she didn't want to hurt Deb's feelings, apart from the danger to both of them, it was not a cause with which she could imagine associating herself.

Once Debra confessed her faith, it seemed it was all she could talk about in the remaining weeks. A floodgate had opened, and Alyssa couldn't help thinking Debra was stranger than she ever knew, though she listened politely.

Once Deb said, "One group that used to be Christian says it's been too long already, it's past the time, that Christ isn't returning, and we're silly for believing any more that He will. They're responsible in large part for getting this thing passed. They're afraid of more man-made Blankenship-type events. But I know the prophecies haven't all been fulfilled yet. I haven't lost my faith. He's coming, and it won't be too long now I think."

Another day, she said, "All his life, Jon grew up wanting to be a missionary, to preach the gospel. Then right when he was old enough, they called all the Elders home, worldwide. He took it pretty hard. Now this. A couple of his close friends volunteered to go in for therapy, guys he grew up with at church. It's hurt him deeply."

Alyssa didn't respond, much. The subject of religion always caused a door to slam inside her mind. She wanted nothing to do with it, though she couldn't rationally explain why.

She remembered that the horrible separation from Peter had to do with religion. Exactly how or why was fuzzy, unclear thoughts at best, something she tried valiantly to keep shut off from her active memory.

There were things she would rather not think about. Religion and the possibility of God were definitely on the list.

She also knew how uncomfortable she would be among a large group of people who actively practiced religion. Never in her life had she set foot in a church. She didn't want to be identified with that. She wondered if there might be a tad of psychosis involved; after all, scientifically conducted studies over a number of years had demonstrated that this was the case. It was difficult for her to refute hard scientific data. *If it was hard and scientific.* The possibility of government involvement in the studies passed through her mind. But Debra did seem a little touched, by *something*, now that she was 'free' to discuss her beliefs.

****

Time passed quickly, but with a feeling of pending sadness on the horizon. The promise of change and uncertainty hung in the air. Jon arrived and Debra's family. With a whirlwind of gathering boxes and loading and embracing and hugging and saying their good-byes and promising to keep in touch, then more hugging, Debra was gone, all too suddenly.

Their apartment felt incredibly empty after she left. It had the feeling a place always does when the familiar and loved things are moved out and it stands waiting to be filled by the next occupants. Alyssa spent several hours after Debra's departure wandering around the small space, looking in all the cupboards for missed items. She scrubbed and cleaned the sinks and bathroom one last time, and went through what little remained of her things.

Her duffel bag was heavier than she liked, but she unpacked and repacked it and finally kept all the things in it. She had done well, taking only items absolutely necessary for her survival anywhere she might go. There was a change of clothes, her warmest winter sweater, some food, a set of utensils, a plastic bowl and plate, a little pan, her old pocketknife and a sharpener, some paper and a pen, a small clock. She tossed in one of the encrypted disks, incriminating Rob's boss, as well, just in case she might need it.

She stuffed all her remaining cash in her wallet, and hoped it would be enough to find a place to live until she got decent work. This was no more than a vague hope. The possibility of not finding a job nagged at her, but she pushed it back away from the corners of her mind. There had to be something she could do. Somewhere.

She kept a hologram of Debra and Jon, and there was a small holo of Rob she had a strange urge to keep. Those two pictures were the sum total of the meaningful personal items she brought with her, and if they had been heavy she might have left even them.

She zipped the bag and hefted it over her shoulder, then headed for the door. At the threshold she paused and looked back one last time at the space, now void of all the personal touches they had added in the years the two of them had lived there, as blank and plain as the day she first arrived in the City.

It was only then that she realized she needed to cry. She let the tears come. It was the middle of the afternoon and no one was around. She knew she would be better off letting the tears out now. The apartment complex was quiet. No one would hear her or stand by to see her go. During the last long months, Debra had taught her to cry. It was a lesson she was glad to have learned, and now she allowed herself to succumb to the need.

Then as suddenly as the feeling came, it passed. With the emotion released, she took a deep breath and stepped off the threshold to leave it all behind.

She did not look back.

PART THREE

Chapter 28

Moving On

We haven't heard from Phil in seven days. I'm completely beside myself. He's just disappeared. No one has seen him. The one lead we have says he saw a man of Phil's description get in a blue truck near the feed store in town with three other men and drive away. Our lead said the men all seemed to know each other, a friendly encounter, no coercion. None that he saw, anyway. Nobody's found a ransom note, or a single clue to explain what happened. If he was arrested for therapy, or anything like that, it would've been public.

The week before this happened, Phil said an old college buddy called him. He seemed glad, but he said nothing about meeting him or getting together. I'm grasping at straws, but my mind jumps at anything that might give us a clue. He's just gone. Gone.

I feel so sorry for Peter. He tries to hold up under the pressure, to be strong for me, the man of the house. He's got to hurt as much as I do. Well, nearly. I don't know. He won't say. And I feel the worst for Kellie and Jordan. It's so confusing, especially to them. We're all in shock. I keep expecting at any minute he'll walk through the front door like nothing has happened. Or I'll wake up.

Even my prayers go unanswered. Maybe I'm not asking the right questions. But I just can't bring myself to hear the worst, if it is the worst. Oh, I couldn't stand to hear that. I can't even stand to think it. He's got to be out there, somewhere. He's got to be. I love him so much. We were always so good together, such a team.

And all I can think about is the last time I saw him, I fussed at him for getting a late start going into town and coming down too hard on Andrew the night before. I was so frustrated with him that morning, I didn't even want to kiss him goodbye. So I wouldn't. I didn't know. I didn't know he wouldn't be home in a few hours like always. I didn't know.

We take too many things for granted, too many. Until we find him I'm afraid all I will have is this terrible guilt.

Beverly Richardson,
personal journal entry

It was the first week of August. The weather was sunny and cooler than normal. Alyssa took a tram north for a distance, but the ticket price had suddenly gone up in the last two weeks, something about an oil shortage. She had been too busy to pay attention to the details.

The first night she stayed in a cheap motel, where the room stank and the bathroom was stained. She ate fast food for dinner. In the morning she counted her money again and realized she would have to walk from there to the poorer sectors. She had used up more cash than she thought on the tram, the room and the food. She'd have to be more careful. She had no knowledge of when or how she would earn more. The reality of her situation, in the dim light of early morning filtering through the motel curtain, slowly sank in. It frightened her.

She missed her computer much more than she thought she would. But she reminded herself that dumping it was absolutely necessary. Even so, she felt disconnected from the world, unplugged from everything familiar. She thought idly of how it would be useful for mapping her progress, researching apartments and prices, other things like that, and with a sigh pushed those thoughts away.

Shouldering her pack and duffel bag, she started walking. It was funny how heavy they seemed. Yesterday the bags hadn't felt like such a burden. She had to keep moving generally north and east to get to the neighborhood she had noticed riding the monorail. She had to find the sectors that didn't require a palm ID for every transaction, the places she saw that didn't register on the official map of Central City. She had heard strange rumors, of places where people could go and live without the usual technology, even disappear from society. She had enough cash left from her last bit of fortuitous computer work for maybe a month's rent there . . . she hoped.

By evening her legs were tired and aching and her belly was yearning for a meal. She stopped once in a wonderful smelling restaurant to use the facilities, but didn't buy. The price was prohibitive. She had to save her money, at least until she knew whether there'd be any left over after finding a place to live.

Hunger she could manage. It bit hard, then faded as she fought down the pain in her stomach. In an odd way it kept her going, giving her something to concentrate on while she traveled. She had brought a little food with her. Twice during the day she allowed herself to eat a few crackers, rationing her supply much better than the day before.

City scenes passed before her in a blur. Her legs ached. She stared down at her feet as she walked, and concentrated on forcing her body to keep moving, resisting the urge to drop the bags and collapse. The buildings stretched out before her, an endless labyrinth.

At length she reached the slums.

She felt a strange sensation come over her, as though she had crossed a threshold of some kind, and when she looked up, she was relieved to see the crippled old buildings before her. This had to be it, the area that, according to the government, didn't exist. It was an embarrassment, a mockery of all the established success of the social systems the President had carefully legislated into place. If his master plan was truly working as well as the press claimed, there should be no more poor, no more poverty, no sign of want in the entire City, or even the country.

But the sector Alyssa stepped into was like nothing she had ever seen before. The buildings were old, outdated, crumbling. It was like walking into a time warp. The streets hadn't seen any federal improvements in many years, judging from the number of potholes in them and their badly cracked pavement. Pedestrians were few, and auto traffic minimal. The cars she did see passing or parked on the streets were neither new nor sleek. Most of them were at least ten years old, she thought, if not more, and in poor condition. Chipped paint and missing hubcaps, shattered windows and rusted-out holes in the bodywork were the fashion here.

A stereo blasted raucous music from somewhere; in another direction came laughter and the sound of doors opening and closing. The buildings loomed above her as the sunlight faded away into dusk.

Her legs cramped and begged to be rested. Her stomach ached for attention. She hadn't eaten more than the crackers all day and the journey had been slow, strenuous work, hauling her bags. She was unused to that much exercise. She felt her body beginning to weaken and grow faint, dizzy.

In the twilight she approached a tall building that looked like it could be apartments, and opened the front door. There was a dusty sign that said "For Rent" in one window. She wandered down a dim hallway, found the door labeled "Manager" and knocked.

A dark fat man with a short bristly beard answered. "What do you want?" He wore an undershirt with holes in it and striped boxer shorts.

"Do you have a room?" she asked, swallowing hard.

"Six hundred a month, and three hundred deposit, don't complain about the rats and I don't fix nothin' for free," he said. It was a gravelly voice that sounded like he had marbles in his mouth when he spoke.

Exhausted, she said, "Is there anything cheaper close by?" The words were out of her mouth before she could think about them. She realized it was rude about the same time she realized how large the man was, and bit her lip.

The man examined her for a minute, then grumbled something unintelligible. "Five hundred . . . plus the deposit," he said after another pause.

"I'll take it," she sighed.

The hallway was dark, with peeling wallpaper. The stairs at the end were wooden and bare, and a few of them showed large splits in the wood. A few old-fashioned incandescent bulbs provided the only light.

The manager disappeared behind the door and returned with a metal key. "You can take 601. You got cash? I only take cash," he said.

"A key?" she asked, dumbfounded.

"Yeah, a key. You got a problem with that?"

"No, no." She shook her head. "It's just been a while since I've seen one like this."

When she thought of it, the last place she had seen such a thing was somewhere in her mother's antique collection. She took out the money and handed him eight one hundred dollar bills. She had less than fifty dollars and some change left over. He gave her the key.

She walked up six creaky flights of stairs to find her room, then struggled to fit the key in the lock. It wasn't easy to figure out how it worked. The house she grew up in, even the old house, had a computerized locking system. It opened with either an electronic key card or by punching her ID code into the keypad. It gave her the distinct feeling that she had been thrown back in time farther than her age.

Teeth up . . . no, down . . . there. It finally went in. The doorknob wobbled in her hands as she turned it, like it was about to fall off. She flipped the light switch and a single uncovered bulb in the middle of the ceiling filled the room with yellow light.

The apartment she had shared with Debra was a dream compared to this. But she couldn't complain. This was her choice. She would rather live like this for a while and take her chances. She couldn't endanger Deb any more than she could have endangered Rob. And once Deb had started rattling off things that sounded more than a little kooky, she was sure she didn't want to live in a whole community of people who shared the same ideas.

It was only one room, and it smelled rank, worse than the motel the night before. The odor nearly overpowered her. She left the door open as she stood in the threshold, hoping it would air out. There was a small bed with a rusted iron headboard in the far left corner, an electric two-burner stove in the near corner on her left, a sink and one cupboard next to it, followed by a small white old-fashioned refrigerator with rusted chips in its enamel. On her right was a small rickety-looking table and two wooden chairs. Behind them was a closet and small bureau. In the far right was a door, barely hanging on its hinges that led into what looked like a bathroom.

She headed there first, overcoming her aversion to the smell out of need to use the facility.

The bathroom was just large enough for the toilet, a wall sink, and a hand-held shower attachment. It screwed into the sink for its water supply. The floor was mildewed gray tile sloped into a drain.

She picked up the shower attachment and looked at it. "I'm supposed to use this?" she wondered out loud, then sighed. Perhaps it would do.

There was a barred window on the wall by the bed. A cracked pull-down shade, the only window dressing, had been pulled halfway down. She went to it and opened the window as far as it would go, then pulled the shade the rest of the way.

The stained, blue striped mattress had no bedding. She didn't want to think what had caused those stains. Between the bed and the refrigerator was a radiator for heat in the winter. There was no air conditioner.

She inspected the tiny closet. Inside were a few wire hangers and a small water heater. The single kitchen cupboard was empty. She opened the refrigerator. There was a gallon jug of soured, curdled milk inside. She made a sound of disgust and closed the door. It would have to stay there until she learned when the trash pickup was.

When she found a job, she could buy sheets, paint, dishes, perhaps even a window air conditioner before next summer. Food she would have to find in the morning, and more importantly, disinfectant. But it wouldn't be too bad. She could survive here until her income grew.

Again she denied her hunger, allowing herself only a small portion of crackers. She was too exhausted to go out and find anything else. Closing the door to the hallway, she lay down on the bare mattress and fell asleep, leaving the light on.

Chapter 29

The Gardens

We are pleased to report that poverty is no longer a problem in our beautiful capital, Central City. Thanks to the success of our Freedom to Eat and Right to Work programs, unemployment is at a record 0.2% among registered citizens, and little children no longer have to go to bed hungry at night . . .

During the next three years, we plan to implement these trial programs nationwide. Their success has been phenomenal . . .

President J. A. Garrison,
Fourteenth State of the Union Address

In the morning Alyssa found a grocery store nearby and bought some oatmeal, pasta, dry beans, flour, rice, a badly needed can of powdered cleanser, and a soup kettle. Fresh vegetables were too expensive. The items she purchased were the least costly things, per pound, to be had.

She was grateful for Debra's careful training in the kitchen. Deb was full of stories about how her family skimped and saved on groceries and learned how to stretch every item. She remembered now some of the things she had learned, though she never figured such trivial knowledge would be useful. She had never planned on having a large family, if she had any family at all, and she certainly had never planned on being poor. It wasn't something she even imagined as a possibility. But now poverty surrounded her, and hunger stared her coldly in the face. This was totally new, and she felt a deep sense of culture shock.

She counted every penny at the checkout line and put some of the pasta back. She had never counted her change like that before. It made her nervous.

The woman at the cash register watched her carefully. When she rang up her purchases Alyssa again felt the strangeness of this place, looking about her in wonder. The stores where she was accustomed to shopping totaled all her purchases by computer; she simply gathered her things into the cart and passed through an exit lane, where she swiped her ID card or placed her palm on the print scanner to pay for it all. If she wanted, she could order ahead on-line, and have everything packaged and delivered, or waiting for her to pick up.

Here, she had to have her cash ready and take everything out of the cart. This woman looked at a price tag sticker attached to the item, and rang each one up individually. It looked as though there used to be an old-fashioned laser scanner there, and the aisle had a belt that moved the items along it. Alyssa had seen this kind of thing in period films before. She watched, fascinated. But the woman didn't seem to be using the scanner at all. She was keying in the prices by hand.

"Is it broken?" Alyssa asked.

"Huh?" the woman said, and Alyssa pointed to the scanner.

"Sure, honey, been broken a long time now," she said. "Don't you worry none. I won't overcharge."

"Oh. No, ma'am, I wasn't worried."

"You new here?" the woman asked.

"Me?"

"Yeah, you. You see anyone else here?"

There were a few other shoppers, elderly people, in the store, but none at the checkout line. The woman's voice was gruff and deep. Alyssa looked up at her, making solid eye contact. The woman was about fifty, graying from dark brown hair, and she had deep lines around her eyes. She smiled, and Alyssa could see the lines were from smiling often, which surprised her. She strained to smile back.

"Yes," she said. "Yes, I'm new. Moved in yesterday, a place down the street a ways."

"There's a lot of places." The smile stayed on her face.

"Manager's this great big guy with a beard. Dark, Indian maybe. Didn't get his name."

"Oh, yeah. Know the place. Make sure he don't overcharge you, now."

"I think I'm all right there." She shuddered at the thought of confronting the man again, demanding to pay even less than she had already bargained for. She cleared her throat. "Actually, I'm looking for work."

"You are?"

"Yes, I . . . would you happen to have any positions available here?"

"You know how many times a week I get asked that question?"

"No, ma'am, I don't." She did her best to be polite.

She didn't ask Alyssa for an ID or fingerprint when she paid. In fact, there was no print scanner in the store that she could see. That in itself was odd. Perhaps the rumors were true and she'd found the right place.

Alyssa accepted the change, and realized the woman was still smiling. She didn't understand. The woman's expression didn't seem to match her words. She wondered if it was just a habit; she knew of people who smiled constantly without meaning it. But no, her eyes seemed sincere.

"I'd be happy to work long hours, as long as I earn enough to pay my rent and eat a little. That's all I need."

"Really?"

"I think so. I have nowhere else to go, or anything else to do but work, if I can find it."

"Well." The woman was silent. She fiddled with the supplies around the register, organizing them. Alyssa wasn't sure if this was a cue to leave, or not, so she cleared her throat again.

"Uh, I'm smart, and I know computers inside and out. I can do all kinds of math in my head, and I'm well organized," she said. "I'm also honest and I know I'd make a good employee. You wouldn't regret it."

The woman hadn't put her things in a grocery sack as she expected, so Alyssa piled everything inside the kettle and hefted it onto one hip.

After a pause she added, "If you don't have a job open, if you could tell me where I might find some work, I'd appreciate it very much." She used her politest voice.

The woman turned back around with a sigh. "You Christian?" she asked.

The question startled Alyssa. Her eyes widened. "Why no, ma'am."

"Hm. You were sounding like it. Too bad."

"Too bad?"

She wondered if there was a reward for turning in Christians here, if the woman had hoped to get one from turning her in to authorities.

"Yes, too bad!" the woman said, smiling again. She pulled a necklace out from underneath her cotton blouse. It was a little cross pendant. "See? I keep Jesus close to my heart." She put the necklace back. "Used to wear it outside, you know, so everybody could see. Too dangerous now, but I won't give it up."

Alyssa was more than startled at the woman's casual revelation.

"My best friend on earth is Christian," she said cautiously, wondering at the purpose for this turn in the conversation.

"Really?"

"Yes. She went north, though, with her family, when the Article passed last month. I came here."

"What brings you?"

"Long story."

"It's religion, government, or family problems brings people here who wasn't here before," the woman said. "So which is it? Nobody else comes for the fun of it. Obviously."

"Oh." Alyssa was quiet a moment, looking down at the tile floor. She shifted the kettle to her other hip and looked back up. "Government, mostly. But I can't go home either."

"Hm. Well, if you was Christian I was going to tell you where to go to meeting on Sunday. Guess I won't. But tell you what. You seem like a nice girl. Even if you're not a believer." She grinned. "I suppose that friend of yours rubbed off on you a bit. But honest, I can't afford to pay much, see, I already got my stockers and checkers filled and another gal who comes in and spells me with the managing from time to time. I can only give you about what you offered to work for and a bit of food from the store. How much he got you paying for rent?"

"Five hundred," Alyssa said.

The woman made a face. "For those rat holes," she muttered.

"I got him down from six," she said.

"Well, good for you then, dearie. What's your name?"

"Alyssa."

"I'm Ash. Short for Ashley. You help improve sales around here and maybe I can raise you a little, if you work out. I usually don't do this. Hope you don't take advantage."

"Oh, I won't. You can trust me."

"I hope so."

"When can I start?"

The woman—Ash—gave her a long, hard look, sizing her up. "Tomorrow," she said. "I'll start training you tomorrow. First thing. Be here before we open. 6:30."

"I'll be here," Alyssa said. She smiled again. "And thank you. This is more than I hoped for."

"Nice to see some gratitude," Ash said. "See you in the morning. Today, you get some rest and eat something."

On the way back, Alyssa wondered how on earth she had "sounded Christian" to the woman. It disturbed her a little, although she knew if she was ever turned in for therapy, she would have no trouble breezing through it. She carried no religious convictions. That would be obvious to anyone testing her. The only problem would be someone in the wrong department discovering her identity. She sighed. It was an unlikely scenario anyway, from the sound of things.

The other strange thing that nagged at her were the woman's laugh lines around her eyes, and how much she had smiled at her. She couldn't figure out how anyone could live in a place like this and smile so much. It didn't make sense to her that anyone living in such a backwards, poverty-stricken place would be that *happy*. She could survive here, after a fashion, but anyone enjoying this kind of life that much was beyond the realm of her comprehension.

She thought of her mother, and the lines that formed on her face. They made her appear as though she was constantly frowning, down-turned lines around the corners of her mouth, deep vertical lines between her brows that caused a scowl even when she was relatively unperturbed. It was a very different set of lines Ash wore on her face.

When she got back to her apartment, she made oatmeal using the small saucepan she had brought with her. Thankfully the stove worked. She never cared much for oatmeal before, especially plain, but this time the aroma was delicious to her while it cooked.

When it was ready she almost burned her tongue in her eagerness. After that, she blew on it, letting it cool just enough, and gulped it down. She was still hungry after the first batch, so she made more, a larger helping this time. It tasted so good.

She continued to eat until she was quite full, planning to take a long nap afterwards to let the food digest. Then a surprising thing happened. Her stomach felt queasy, at first just a little, but the nausea grew quickly until it demanded action. She ran into the bathroom, which she had yet to scrub. It still smelled terrible, and immediately she lost everything she had worked so hard to cook.

She knelt over the toilet, sobbing and shaking. Her stomach felt horrible. She had eaten almost half the oatmeal she bought, and now it was all wasted. Wasted. She cried over the loss of her food supply as much as the pain of her nausea.

She hadn't felt sick at all earlier in the day. Could she have caught a germ somewhere? If so, how could she make it to her new job in the morning? The thought frightened her.

When her system had calmed down again and she realized she didn't have a fever or any other symptoms of illness. It must have been the food. She wondered about food poisoning, but had never heard of that coming from something as benign as fresh oatmeal, or anything that acted so quickly.

She cleaned herself up and sat down on the bed. After sitting there a while she began to feel hungry again, which also surprised her. She got a cracker out of her duffel bag and nibbled it, then waited.

She proceeded slowly this time, eating one cracker every half-hour or so until she felt better. That was all it was. She had simply eaten too fast and too much on a long-empty stomach. It was a lesson she would not soon forget, one she couldn't afford to forget, in fact.

What a stupid way to lose perfectly good food.

****

Her first day on the job went well; she arrived on time and learned fast. There wasn't much to it. Working the cash register was simple, and restocking and organizing shelves, equally so. Ash was pleasant, though brusque and not overly chatty, which Alyssa liked. She was also quick to correct, meticulous about her store, and friendly to her customers. It seemed she knew everyone; no wonder she had known Alyssa was new.

Ash was a widow, she learned. Her husband had passed away five years before of a stroke, leaving her the store and not much else. Her children, three of them, were in their late twenties. They rarely visited her, she said, not that she minded.

"But you'd think they wouldn't be ashamed of where they come from, after all I done to help them improve themselves, especially with me alone now and all."

Alyssa wondered what kind of mother Ash had been. It wasn't an easy thing to judge. She just knew there were plenty of good reasons she'd never go home to visit, even if distance and finances hadn't been a barrier. Better not to offend her new employer, though, by saying anything out of turn. Ash had been kind. So Alyssa kept her thoughts to herself and concentrated instead on learning the details of her new job.

At the end of the day, Ash praised her for her diligence and handed her a carton of eggs and a quart of milk. "You'll need these," she said. "Take 'em."

"I couldn't," Alyssa said.

"Part of your pay. You need more protein in you than what you bought yesterday."

"Thank you," she said, feeling more emotional over the gift than she wanted to show.

"Just don't take advantage," Ash said, patting her chest where the necklace lay. "I can't let a young gal like you go starving while she's working for me. Just can't. But you start manipulating me around, 'cause of that, and you'll be out of a job in no time. Can't afford that."

"I understand," Alyssa said.

"Good. Be back tomorrow, same time."

And so it went. Ash paid Alyssa what she had promised, always making sure she had at least enough for the rent and didn't go hungry.

After her first day of work, Alyssa spent the evening on the front step of her building staring at her surroundings. She had made more oatmeal and scrambled two of the eggs for dinner. She had no butter or oil, so they stuck to the little saucepan, but she ate every bite she could scrape out. Slowly this time.

It was cooler outside than in, and she wanted to get a feel for the place anyway, to know where she was and who lived near her.

The buildings were crusty yellow brick, crowded together, and much of the brick was crumbling to ruin. They were in desperate need of renovation. She overheard people talking about one building a few blocks away that collapsed last month, killing many of the occupants. It didn't make her feel very comfortable.

The sun began to set, turning the yellow stone into a burnished orange, reflecting golden light off the glass panes. The street was quiet. There were others like her who sat outside, having nowhere else to go. Rusted cars lined one side of the street, many of the parts missing, stolen or removed for salvage. From her observations, none of them ran anymore. There was a man who lived in one. He was asleep in it now.

There was a middle-aged woman wearing an odd yellow wig, who hunched over an empty shopping cart and pushed it along the street, calling, "Caps for sale. Caps for sale. Come and buy. Caps for sale. Fifty cents a piece." The cart had a persistently squeaky wheel.

Alyssa noticed the evening before that she had pushed it around and around the block until she finally fell asleep next to it in front of the building, endlessly repeating the same words. Today was no different. It gave her an eerie feeling.

A woman named Margret, in her early twenties, lived across the hall from her with two young children. Tonight, she came out and sat on the step next to Alyssa. She had long curly brown hair, dark skin and mahogany eyes. The children bounded over her and ran off to play in the street.

She had first met Margret when she arrived home a little earlier, exchanging a brief hello.

Pointing to the woman with the cart, Alyssa asked, "Does she always do that?"

"Who, Mary?" Margret asked.

"Is that her name?"

"Yeah. Mary. Poor thing. She should be in an asylum on meds, but the family couldn't afford it. So they dumped her here."

"Where are they now?"

"Gone." She shrugged her shoulders.

"How does she live?"

"Well, we all try to feed her, if we have anything left over." Margret smiled faintly. Her dark eyes were distant. "It's the most any of us can do."

She had a faint Hispanic accent, though she didn't quite look the part. Alyssa couldn't place the difference exactly. She wore a short, low-cut tank top that showed off her middle, with cutoff jeans. Alyssa noticed that she had a small ring in her navel, and raised her eyebrow. She also wore several pairs of large pierced gold hoop earrings, dancing halfway up her ear. They jingled together when she shook her head. She wore a different ring on nearly every finger.

Margret leaned back, shook her hair, and rested her elbows on the stair behind her. "Turds," she said, angry now. "Don't even care what happens to her. We get a lot of that around here. 'Specially lately. Like this is some kind of dumping ground, you know? Like we put up a sign, eh? I *hate* those people."

She spat, casting it out a few feet to land ungraciously on the sidewalk below. Alyssa wrinkled her nose, and the eyebrow unconsciously went up again. But Margret's words weighed heavily on her mind.

"A week ago I didn't know anybody lived like this," she said. "I mean, I know the media won't report anything, but *this* . . . this is something I never even imagined." She blew out a puff of air.

"So. What happened to you?"

"I'd rather not discuss it. It's kind of . . . complicated."

"You got family?"

"None I want to see."

Margret nodded. "Know what you mean. I can't go home neither. Papa disowned me. Told me he'd shoot me if I ever set foot near his door again." She cocked her head and smiled. "You know, I believe him."

The comment reminded Alyssa of her own family troubles. Again they seemed petty in comparison, as they had when Rob talked about his life.

"Why?" she asked, then thought it might not be polite. "I'm sorry. You don't have to tell me."

"Aaah." Margret waved her arm, a gesture that said she didn't mind. "These kids," she said, pointing. Then she sat up straight. "Marcus! You *loco!* I told you a hundred times, stay away from that grate!" The boy complied, running off in a different direction, waving at his mother.

"Oh." Alyssa said, not understanding.

"Papa said I should marry Pablo, or get rid of the baby. Marcus, there," she said. "That one. I don't get 'rid of' no babies, not me. Just look at him. I can't believe he's six already. He is *muy* good-looking, don't you think? Just like his father." She grunted in satisfaction. "But Pablo wasn't looking for a wife. You know the type. No way was he going for that."

"Mm-hmm," Alyssa nodded.

"Slam, bam, thank-you-very-much ma'am, now I'll be on my way!" she said, laughing out loud. "Ay! Well, some things are worth it. Know what I mean? Man, I thought he loved me though . . ." She sighed.

"Later there was Ralph. I did marry Ralph. *Stupido*," she cursed, and spat again, this time hitting the stair below her. A long string of expletives followed, in Spanish. "Papa didn't like that move either. That was the last straw. But I was pregnant already with Natalie, I had to do *some*thing. I thought that's what he wanted, since I didn't marry Pablo. But no, see, he didn't *like* Ralph. He *hated* Ralph." She waved her hand upward in the air for emphasis.

"Oh," Alyssa said, thinking maybe she shouldn't have asked after all.

"Papa was right. Oh, Papa. He was always right." She shook her head and looked down between her knees. "See. Ralph gave me this as a wedding present." Her voice bristled with sarcasm.

She raised her leg up with her hand and showed Alyssa a ragged white scar on the underside of her calf. Alyssa gasped.

"And this, and this, and this," she said, pointing to small round burn scars on her arms, thigh and one on the back of her neck. She lifted up her hair to show that one. "And plenty in here," she said, a hand on her heart, "but those don't show. Oh yes. Living with Ralph was a nightmare. He was *loco*, *muy loco*. We ran away from him when Natty was a baby, two years ago. Saved all our lives, I know it. Poor Marcus. I may never know what he remembers."

Alyssa knit her brows together. "So whatever happened to Pablo?" she asked, looking down at a tiny crooked white scar on own her hand, between her thumb and forefinger. Joan had given her that, throwing something . . . she couldn't remember. Oh yes. That china plate, the day after she last saw Peter.

"*Ay caramba*, girl. I don't know now," Margret said. "He's long gone. I thought we had such a great love, a strong love. That kind of love you only find once in your lifetime. Oh, yes. That's what it felt like." She was quiet a moment and closed her eyes, a faint smile on her lips. Then she opened them and looked at Alyssa. "First time for everything, eh? I'm older now, not so naïve. I was just one in a long line of young girls."

"I'm sorry," Alyssa said.

"Don't be. I don't regret it. Even if, you know, he didn't care about me, he was *very* good, you know?" She winked, her voice suddenly sultry, and nudged Alyssa with her elbow. "Like I said, some things are worth it, eh?"

"Ah," Alyssa said, nodding as if she understood. It didn't appear "worth it" to her.

Margret sighed. "Well, it's my life. I chose my way; I can live with it. And I do love my babies. If I have nothing else, I have my two beautiful babies. I wish I could give them a better life, though, or a good Papa even. My Papa, he was a good Papa. He tried to teach me, but I was a lousy excuse for a daughter. Oh, well . . . at least I can give them love. They've got that from me, and plenty of it."

"Mm-hmm," Alyssa agreed.

They both were quiet, watching the colors of the sunset. Marcus and Natalie played tag along the opposite side of the street, laughing. Their voices echoed off the walls of the buildings.

"What about that one over there, counting his fingers?" Alyssa asked after a while.

"Oh. Bert."

Bert was a young black man, with beautiful features. He sat across the street from them next to a basement windowsill, and did nothing but count out loud—fingers, toes, bricks, the cracks in the pavement.

"What about him?" She wondered if he also belonged in an asylum, like Mary. "Was he dropped here too?"

Margret shook her head, tossing her long brown curls. She looked very sad. She had looked merely wistful a moment before, but there was no trace of her jovial smile now.

"No. He was here when I moved in. Such a nice man. So kind. You never met a sweeter soul in all your life."

"Until when? What happened?"

Margret sighed heavily. "They found him. He was a Christian. I'm sure you've heard what's going on."

Alyssa sat up straighter and felt a catch in her throat. Deb could have ended up here, like that? *Is this what happens to them? The government's idea of "therapy?"* It both turned her stomach and angered her at the same time. She felt a chill go up her spine.

"He said he wanted to die for Jesus. He hoped they would kill him. He was singing when they dragged him away. Singing, 'I'll Tell the World That I'm a Christian.' I can still hear it echoing in my mind."

Margret looked away, blinking rapidly a few times. "Now he can't even remember his name, much less who he used to be or what he believed in. His beliefs got him a long way, *si?*" Her voice broke, and she wiped her eye as though there was something caught in it.

"Is he—was he—your friend?"

Margret nodded. There was a long pause before she continued. She swallowed hard. "I told him to be quiet. He never listened to me. The goonies dropped him back here afterwards, an example to anyone who might think about speaking up."

Alyssa thought of Ash, and her carefree, easy admission of her faith. Surely she must know about Bert. This didn't frighten her? "Just don't take advantage," Ash kept saying. Her phrase took on a new meaning. Alyssa resolved not to take advantage of her beliefs, ever, or of the knowledge that Ash held those beliefs.

The sunset faded into dusk, golden orange fading rapidly to dun yellow-gray. Alyssa felt more hopeless and helpless than she had all week, or in her entire life. Here were people with problems she never imagined. She had spent much of her life feeling sorry for herself, completely self-centered, without ever thinking that somewhere people lived in far worse conditions, their lives a nightmare compared to her own. She felt small and ungrateful.

She was used to having money. She had always had it, taken it for granted. Even the brief scare after her father died, before she found out about the inheritance, hadn't frightened her that much. She always assumed money would come from somewhere, like it always had; that she would finish school and pursue a professional, high-paying career.

Living like this wouldn't be an easy adjustment, even with a job that had come to her so easily. The job would give her enough to live on, to feed herself and keep a roof over her head, but not much more. It was survival, not a career path, not a ticket to financial security.

This was the dumping ground for society's outcasts. Now she was one of them. It wasn't an easy label to affix to herself. She had frequently tagged others with it, with some disdain, always assuming they had brought their misery on themselves.

Silently she realized she had done exactly that.

She considered her options. It seemed she was not destined to enjoy a normal life after all. She wondered about calling Deb, maybe tell her she'd changed her mind. But she had no money left for travel, and Deb wouldn't have any extra to send her.

Calling home would only result in Joan gloating over her plight. She was sure of that, if Joan would even accept a collect call to begin with. She wasn't ready to try that avenue. She doubted it would help her, anyway. No, going back was simply not an option. She would stay here and take her chances.

She shuddered. A cool breeze drifted through them as they sat on the stoop. Fall was coming early.

****

"I have been displeased with the state of world affairs ever since the fall of the Soviets," the shadowy figure said, his inky cloak shifting around him.

It was mesmerizing to watch. Hypnotic. Victor leaned back in his chair and crossed his legs, listening intently to the speech. He enjoyed the Caretaker's impromptu visits, now that he was used to them. He had learned so much.

"It was quite an unsettling time for all of us. We had great hopes." He seemed to sigh, although from what Victor could tell, the man (if he was a man; Victor thought of him as male) did not breathe.

"You have no Mao? Hmm. No matter. Marx. Yes, good," he continued, floating in front of the teak bookshelf, and laughed to himself. "Karl was so malleable. He had a good ear. Better than you, Victor. Don't forget you still have much to learn."

"I won't."

"Nevertheless, I must compliment you on your work lobbying for Article 28. I find it most satisfying to have you doing things on your own initiative."

"Thank you," Victor replied. "Been a personal vendetta of mine for years."

"Since your mother died in Los Angeles. Yes. Such a tragedy."

Victor nodded his head. "Hey," he said, excited. "Is there any way you can do that thing for her? Make her immortal too?"

"Impossible. It must be done at the point of death. Remember, Victor, you humans have no souls or essence or what-have-you beyond the lives of your loathsome corporeal tissue. She is gone forever. But I must add I'm not impressed with your peevish devotion to her. If you want to succeed, you must transcend your attachments to others. That includes anyone!"

He punctuated his sentence by suddenly appearing, twice as large, inches away from Victor's face.

"I am grooming you very carefully. If you prove untrustworthy, I can find another to put in your place. You are expendable. Is that clear?"

Victor's face paled. "Yes, yes. Quite clear, but entirely unnecessary. I will earn your trust. You'll see, and I . . . apologize for my weakness."

He kept feeling like he should call him *Sir*. Cursed military training. He wouldn't succumb to it.

"Good." The Caretaker resumed normal size. "The next item on our agenda is this. There are several Senators partial to meeting the Saudi's new demands."

"Yes, I was aware of that. What of it?"

"You must use all your influence to prevent such a move. You will be aided much in your personal gain by encouraging an oil embargo. It won't be difficult. Have you not read the works of Stalin you so proudly display on this shelf? You disappoint me yet again."

"It's been a while. I remember the basics."

"You must prove to the remnants of this country and the world that free trade is not the pathway to a utopian society. The longer an embargo continues, the more frustrated the people will become with the system. When their frustration peaks, you can lead them to freedom from this moronic capitalism. The world's resources must be re-appropriated *fairly*. For example, it isn't good for you to be kept from your Havana cigars indefinitely, is it?"

"Of course not! The idiots!" Victor said.

"Then you understand, and the public can be encouraged to see it as well. When their cars no longer run because gasoline prices are too high to afford the luxury, they will also become angry. Much good will come from that anger. And it will separate the wolves from the dogs quite nicely, like a fine sieve; only the rich will be able to maintain their vehicles. You see?"

"Ah, yes. Quite right."

"It will be easy to tell who belongs with you in the ruling class if the situation is allowed to continue long enough. And equally easy to establish who is unworthy of your appropriations and favors."

"Right. But my cigars, in the meantime? Can't you do anything about those shipments? Hurry them up a little?"

"You fuss about a cigar when I offer you the world? Perhaps I have chosen the wrong man for the task!"

Victor felt a pain in his chest, radiating down his left arm.

"No! No, never mind," he gasped out. "I can live with a little inconvenience."

The pain dissipated. Victor took a deep breath and shook his arm with relief. He would have to figure out how the Caretaker managed that little trick. It could come in handy.

"Good, then. You know what you need to do. Annoy the Saudis every chance you have and they will not be partial to negotiation. I do not need to teach you any more than you already know about sabotage."

Victor grinned.

"One more thing," the Caretaker said.

"What's that?"

"It would be best if you continued to keep my—my *people's*—existence a secret a little while longer. The world isn't ready to know about us yet. It could ruin the entire plan. You must wait until your power is secured to introduce us to the public."

The large man sighed, tearing the band from a new cigar. "All right. I'll keep it quiet. You're the boss."

"Yes. Never forget that. Trust in me, Victor."

He nodded his assent and lit up.

Chapter 30

Confinement

And ye shall know the truth, and the truth shall make you free.

John 8:32,
Holy Bible (KJV)

Margret was only a few years older than Alyssa, but the dark circles under her eyes were permanent, and she already showed fine lines from worry on her face. She sewed blouses in a factory, and worked the graveyard shift. She walked three miles to the factory in the dark and carried a gun. The children were instructed to open the door to no one while she was away. Her dearest hope was that they slept the duration of her shift and had no nightmares.

Alyssa learned of this during her first week.

"What else am I supposed to do?" Margret asked her, hotly. "I can't afford day care and feed them too. I gotta work while they're sleeping. There *is* no other choice. Not for me. I do what I have to do. You got a better idea? You think I got me some fairy godmother or something, gonna grant me my every wish? Huh? Don't you *dare* tell me how I gotta live my life, you stuck-up little . . ." She launched into a string of Spanish expletives, none of which sounded nice.

Standing outside her door as Margret left for work that evening, Alyssa said, "I'll watch them," before she knew the words were out of her mouth. That interrupted Margret's blue streak.

"Oh, *you* will. What do you know about kids?" She blew her bangs upward with a puff of air and crossed her arms in front of her.

"Not much, but enough to help if they need anything. It's better than nothing, isn't it?"

"You sure?" she asked dropping her arms to her side.

"Yeah."

"Why?" she asked, her jaw still set.

"I . . . I don't know," Alyssa said. "It's just . . ."

"What are you going to charge me? Huh?"

"Nothing," Alyssa said, exasperated.

366

"You think you can make a buck off me? Is that it?"

"No! You just said you can't afford . . ."

The look on her face changed to gratitude. "Are you serious? You have no idea how much it would mean to have somebody who cared, who could be here for them when I can't." She smiled, then looked hard at Alyssa. "But I don't know you. You seem like a good kid. I bet I can trust you. But let me tell you, you mess with my kids and I'll shoot you myself."

Her eyes told Alyssa she meant it. She had learned enough about Margret to know her comments were often made in jest, but she was sure anyone caught "messing" with Margret's children would regret it. The handgun she wore in a holster around her waist was hardly an empty threat.

"Understood," Alyssa said. "Tell them if they need anything they can come to me. Deal?"

"Okay. Okay, I'll try it," Margret said, still sounding hesitant. She looked down at the floor for a minute, then looked up. "Hey . . . thank you. I'm sorry. I'm sorry I called you a—"

"That's all right," Alyssa said, interrupting her.

Margret grinned wickedly. "Yeah, only 'cause you don't know what I called you."

"Let's leave it that way, huh?"

"Deal." She grasped Alyssa's hand and shook it firmly. "I'll be back in the morning."

Afterwards Alyssa wondered what she had been thinking. She never babysat in her life. She didn't even *like* children. At least they would be asleep, most of the time. She needed to rest for her own job, and was unaccustomed to volunteering, especially to help someone without the possibility of improving her own situation as a result. She had offered to do this for free.

As it was, she had to leave for work before Margret got home in the morning. Still it was something. Something better than leaving them unprotected all night long. That, at least, made her feel better.

When Alyssa got home from work the next day, Margret brought her a key. "This is to my apartment," she explained. "I had it made this morning, a place by the factory does it."

"Thank you," she said, taking the key.

"I told Marcus he can come get you if he needs you, anytime. Natty too. If anything sounds fishy in there, with this key you can get in and see what's up, but you don't let anybody else use it, ever, or you're toast.

Especially no strange men, you got it? I think sometimes, Ralph, he might still be looking for me. You never know. He swore he'd get me back if I ever left him. He forced me to promise I never would."

"Understood," Alyssa said.

"He did this," she said, showing her a long white line along her wrist and palm, "so I promised."

Alyssa didn't want to see any more of Margret's scars, but she seemed strangely proud of them, so she took a quick look.

"Mm-hmm," she said.

"Come up to the roof with me," Margret said, as soon as Alyssa put the key in her pocket.

"Why?"

"I got something to show you. You'll like it," she said. "Come on!"

Alyssa went. It was a ten-story building. Together they climbed the remaining flights to the roof exit and stepped out. Marcus and Natalie came too, running ahead of them and bursting through the heavy steel door to let the sunlight spill into the stairwell. It was hot up there, in spite of the fading sunlight. Alyssa stepped out of the doorway and gasped in surprise at what she saw.

There was a garden on the roof. All was green around her, vibrant with life.

"How did this get here?" she asked. "This is amazing!"

"Manager lets us keep it," Margret said. "Even lets us have the water for it. Long as we give him some of the stuff. It's about the only nice thing he does for us, but he likes fresh tomatoes."

Alyssa walked over to the nearest planter. All the vegetables were planted in raised boxes filled with soil. Some of the plants were staked. Some she didn't even recognize. It had been many years since she'd been in a garden.

"This is absolutely amazing," she repeated. "How do you do it?"

"I take care of it, mostly. A few of the others do, too."

"How was it built?"

"Hauled up dirt from a couple old vacant lots, I think."

"Must've taken forever," Alyssa said.

"That was before I got here," Margret shrugged.

"How do you keep the rest from taking it all?" she said.

"Not everybody knows about it. Most don't care. The people that do, help."

"Why?"

Margret looked confused. "It's just the way we are. We're all tight on money. We help each other out."

"That's amazing, too," Alyssa mumbled.

"What do you mean?" Margret asked.

"It's hard to imagine nobody comes up here and steals everything," Alyssa said.

Margret laughed. "Steal a garden?" she said. "If somebody wants to come all the way up here to eat, nobody minds. There's plenty. Besides, we'd all know if somebody came off the roof carrying boxes of stuff. Those stairs are so loud."

Alyssa laughed. "Yes, they are."

"Besides, it keeps growing more," Margret said. "If the weather holds out we should keep it going until November, maybe. Some of the plants, the ones that like cool weather. Others will die sooner." She paused and walked over to a tall plant winding itself around a long pole, and started looking through the leaves. "Green beans," she said nonchalantly. "See over in that other corner? That's a greenhouse. Some of the panes are cracked, see? We can't replace them, but it still manages to keep a few things going even in the winter. Cool weather crops. Broccoli, celery, beets."

She handed Alyssa a green bean. She took it eagerly and crunched into it. It was delicious.

"This is unbelievable," she said, mumbling as she chewed. Her stomach began to rumble.

"Look around you."

She looked, but saw nothing else. "What?"

"Not here. Look around. Look at the other rooftops."

She looked again, expanding her focus to a wider view and gasped.

The rooftops she could see were all green. Every roof had a garden. It was surprisingly beautiful, more like a rainforest than a cityscape. Their building was slightly taller than most of the others in the neighborhood, so she could see some distance. Everything glowed with the brilliance of the sunset.

Margret laughed at her. "How else would we survive? You've seen the prices at old Ash's store."

"Yeah, I noticed. I just thought vegetables were scarce."

"They are if you don't have your own garden. Tell you a secret, I think she grows the stuff for her store up on her roof."

"No, she doesn't. I saw the shipment come in on a truck," Alyssa said. "She takes what doesn't sell for herself, after it's gone too bad to sell. I've seen her do it."

"Hmm," Margret said. "Maybe so."

"She doesn't order much produce either. Doesn't sell well. I figured it was the prices. Maybe not."

"Some of the old people would rather buy it anyway. Pride, I think. But you shouldn't have to go hurting, except maybe in the winter."

"Why didn't you tell me sooner?"

It would be difficult to make her food supply last to the end of the week, when she got paid. She feared it wouldn't hold out, even with Ash's occasional gifts at the end of the day, and today Ash had offered nothing.

"I had to trust you," Margret said. She picked up a basket from somewhere and rummaged through the green beans.

Alyssa nodded, even though Margret wasn't facing her.

"See, once in a while the goonies will come up and trash one of the gardens, just for kicks. Have to be careful. Watch your back. So I had to trust you first. Make sure you aren't with them."

"Goonies?" Margret had used that term before.

"Government goons. They have some fancy official title. I forget. We all say goonies. Black uniforms, red trim. You'll see them every so often. Best to stay clear if they're in sight."

This information made Alyssa's skin crawl as she stared at a bean plant, her eyes aimlessly following the pattern of the vine on the pole.

"You going to help or not?" Margret asked.

"You'll have to show me how," Alyssa said.

"Easy."

Margret taught her about each different plant, showing her the proper way to pick their fruit as Marcus and Natalie played tag around them, full of energy. Alyssa noticed that they occasionally stopped and grabbed something from a vine and ate it quickly, then continued in their play. Watching them would make her dizzy if she paid too much attention. She glanced quickly toward the roof's edge and was glad to see it was bordered by a wall at least one meter high. *Good*, she thought. That way they couldn't accidentally fall off in their exuberance. The wall was topped with barbed wire.

"The rules are," Margret said, "only take as much as you yourself can eat. Don't take any more. Don't pick everything in sight. Only pick the ripest things. Only what you need."

There did seem to be plenty. The roof was large, bigger than she expected. The planter boxes seemed unending. Mentally she calculated the building's architecture, remembering there were eight units on each floor, and realized that the roof was indeed the right size, if some of the units were bigger than her own. Her own place felt so small, she had assumed the entire building was.

There was a lot to learn. Margret spoke rapidly and showed her so many things at once it was hard to grasp. Twice she asked her to slow down. Several times she picked a vegetable the wrong way and was chided for it. But she cooked a delicious dinner for herself that night, green beans, tomatoes, carrots, and a little of her rice. She slept well, feeling a sense of peacefulness for the first time since she had moved in.

****

Margret met her at the door the next day just as Alyssa got back from work. She seemed upbeat, even excited.

"It's Friday," she said. "You know what that means?"

"No. What's the big deal about Friday?" Alyssa asked.

"You gotta work tomorrow? Same time?"

"A little later, actually. Ash says she wants me to learn to close up on Saturdays. The girl who managed for her part-time quit yesterday. I think she wants to train me to replace her. So I won't go in tomorrow until ten."

"Wonderful! She must really like you, huh?"

"I guess so," Alyssa said. It was good news, but she still had a hard time reading Ash. It was hard to tell what she really thought. "Then I'll have Sundays off because she's closed. Isn't that strange?"

"That's Ash's way," Margret said. "For her, Sundays are the Lord's day, for keeping holy and worshipping God."

"You'd think she would need the money," Alyssa said.

"It's her way. Be glad you know when your day off will be. I never know. Sometimes I go fourteen days without a break if they're trying to make a quota."

"Slave labor," Alyssa said.

Margret made a rude noise, and spat right in the hallway. "You don't gotta tell *me* that," she said.

"So what's Friday all about?"

"I got the night off," she said, excitedly. "I'm going down to the Hall like everybody else. Wanna come?"

"The Hall?" Alyssa asked.

"It's a few blocks down. Call it a block party if you want. Place used to be a soup kitchen until a few months ago. When that Article looked like it was gonna pass, the church that ran the place cleared out. But we all gather there Fridays and hang around. C'mon, it's fun."

"What about the kids?"

"They come too. You coming?"

"I guess so. I don't see why not."

"I only get to go when I got Friday off. But those days, I never miss."

"What time?"

"Anytime. Usually not much of a crowd till about eight though. Only the old farts come early."

"Aren't you afraid of taking the kids out that late, after dark?"

"Why?"

She hadn't thought of Margret as naïve before. Now she gave her a look with her eyebrows raised.

Margret laughed. "Alyssa. You *are* new here. I told you, we look out for each other. We stick together."

"If you say so."

****

Margret knocked on her door at eight, sharp. "Ready?" she asked.

"Guess so." Alyssa said, but she felt nervous.

Outside the building, Natalie ran on ahead. Marcus called to her to stop, but she ignored him.

Margret called to Bert. "It's Friday. Are you coming?"

"I thought he didn't know anything anymore," Alyssa said, in a whisper.

"He doesn't," Margret said, not bothering to whisper. "But still he likes to come. Bert?"

"Twenty-eight," Bert said, his head turned upwards and his eyes darting about.

"Marcus, go get your sister," Margret said, then knelt down to face Bert at eye level where he sat on the pavement.

Marcus ran down the sidewalk after Natalie.

"Bert, you know you don't have to sleep out here. You got a room inside. You remember? Mrs. Gomez keeps it for you. If you're not going in, come with us to the meeting, eh?" She spoke kindly.

"Four," Bert said. "Four, five." He stood up. "Five."

"What does he mean?" Alyssa asked. She hadn't planned on this. He made her uncomfortable.

"Four, five," Margret repeated, musing, counting on her own fingers. "It means he's coming. There were four of us, now there's five. Come on, we don't want to be late!"

The three of them walked quickly to catch up to Marcus, who came toward them holding his little sister by the arm. "I told you all the time not to run off like that, Natty," Margret scolded, scooping her up when they reached the children. "Thank you, baby, for getting her. You're a sweet boy." She leaned over to kiss Marcus on the forehead. The boy beamed with pride.

"I'm fast, Mama," he said.

"I know you are," she replied.

They continued on their way, Margret carrying Natty in one arm and leading Bert with her other hand much like another child. He dwarfed her in height, but meekly followed along.

"Lori told me last week she'd make biscuits and gravy tonight for you, special. She told me she hoped you'd come."

"Eighteen," Bert said happily. "Eighteen, nineteen, twenty." He smiled. He had perfectly straight teeth. His smile was attractive and endearing, but more like a child's than that of a grown man.

Alyssa watched the little procession as though she wasn't actually with them. She felt apart, lost, completely out of her frame of reference. Margret and Bert continued to talk to each other during the walk. From their cadence and tone, it would have sounded like a normal conversation between two old friends if Bert's language hadn't consisted entirely of numbers. It gave Alyssa a weird feeling in the pit of her stomach. It was as though the two actually *understood* each other, though she couldn't fathom how.

It wasn't far, as Margret had promised. Alyssa was grateful. She wasn't sure how much longer she could manage listening to the two of them, and she couldn't bring herself to join in the conversation.

The Hall was on the ground floor of a downtown building. It looked as though, once upon a time, it had been a department store, with large glass display windows to either side of the entrance. The displays were empty of all but a handwritten sign saying "Hall Meeting Tonight!"

They entered through the glass double doors. Alyssa was the last of their little group to come inside. She moved cautiously, unsure of what she would find.

Loud greetings were called to them on all sides as they entered. Alyssa saw that the wide open space of the "Hall" was already quite crowded. It was set up with long metal tables around the walls and a jumble of folding chairs scattered in no particular pattern. There was a group of seven to nine children playing in the center with a pile of toys. Marcus and Natalie were already there with the other children by the time Alyssa came in the door. Food had been placed on a table near the back of the room, and some of the people crowded around it with plates or trays.

"I thought you said it wasn't a soup kitchen anymore," she said.

"It isn't," Margret said. "But if anybody's got anything to share, they bring it. Helps feed those like Bert, Mary, and some of the others who don't do so well for themselves. I didn't have anything leftover this week," she added, "and I figured you didn't either, so I didn't tell you. But feel free to eat if you're hungry. Nobody minds."

Several people Alyssa recognized were there, customers she had checked out of the grocery line at work. Ash's rule was that she had to be friendly if she was going to cashier, and she tried hard to live up to that expectation, though it was difficult. It would have been much easier for her to keep her eyes down, merely looking at the prices of the food items, than to look up and greet the customers. But Ash prided herself on her store's customer service, so Alyssa worked at it. Maybe here some of that friendliness would pay off.

Some others she recognized from her building. She recalled passing them in the hall or stairway, and they waved when they saw her.

Margret had many friends there. She pulled Bert gently toward the back table with the food as she greeted them. It was noisy with the chatter of many different conversations going on at once. Alyssa felt overwhelmed, and when Margret disappeared into the crowd, she felt lost.

She thought about heading back home where it was quiet, but something held her there. Her apartment would be too quiet tonight, with everyone here. There would be little to do there besides dwell on her situation, and she didn't feel like doing that tonight. Though unnerving to her, the mood here was buoyant and cheerful, and the bright fluorescent lights dispelled the gloom she had felt all week.

It was a mystery to her why Ash and some of the others she'd met were so cheerful. Didn't they know their lifestyle was technologically backward, disconnected from the rest of the world? No one here had any sort of computer at all. To her, that was primitive. She had found Ash balancing her books the old-fashioned way, with a calculator. It amazed her completely. Ash had smiled and laughed at her. Maybe here, at the Hall, she could learn what it was that kept the morale of these people so high.

"So you must be the new kid on the block." A voice startled her. She turned to find its source.

"Excuse me?" she asked, looking around.

"Hi," said an older man, about sixty. He grabbed her hand and shook it vigorously. "I'm Walter. Heard of me?"

"Uh, no," she said, wondering if she should have.

Walter laughed. He was quite short, and his face was ruddy and kind. "Well, of course not. I was just checking. Have to go catch that doll Margret and set her straight on telling newcomers who's who on this block. What's your name, miss?"

She realized she had been too flustered by his approach to introduce herself properly. "Alyssa," she said. "So what do you do?"

"I'm the plumber," he said, grinning. "You won't forget to be nice to me!"

She smiled back, and gently disengaged her hand from his grip. "I'll have to remember that," she said.

"You bet you will," he said, and grabbed her other hand. "Come meet my wife, Beth."

He pulled her along much as Margret had led Bert. It made her tense. She was unused to physical contact, especially from complete strangers. It was quite uncomfortable, but she allowed him to lead her through the crowd.

Beth looked much like her husband. Alyssa might have thought they were brother and sister from their appearance. Beth also patted her and welcomed her, then took her by the hand and led her around the room to meet everyone. She saw so many faces they all became a blur before much time had passed. Names and faces and occupations jumbled into a log jam inside her head. A lot of the women hugged her.

This is certainly a convivial group, she thought with some surprise despite her increasing discomfort.

Eventually she bumped into Margret again, who had settled Bert at a table with a plate of the promised biscuits and gravy. Margret took her all around the room again meeting and talking to even more people. Alyssa tried to remember who she had met and who she hadn't, but it was difficult.

After a while, many of the people trailed out the door. Most of these were older folk who must have felt the need for rest. The room became quieter and someone turned out a few of the lights. One of the mothers came out of a closet, her arms filled to overflowing with blankets. The other mothers helped to lay them out in a corner of the room for their children, if they were tired. Most of them were not worn out yet, though it was approaching ten o'clock. Alyssa felt tired herself and sat down in an empty chair with her elbow on the table.

"One, or two?" The voice was familiar. She looked up to see Bert, who sat down in a chair opposite her and smiled.

Alyssa wrinkled her brow.

"One, or two?" he repeated, and pointed to her.

"Oh. One," she said, remembering how he had counted their little group earlier. "I'm single. I live by myself."

"One," he said. He reached a long, lanky arm out toward her. She was careful not to flinch. He was harmless, but she didn't know what might happen should she hurt his feelings. She watched as he reached toward her. Softly he touched her hair, pulled a lock between his fingers and stroked it. The admiration in his eyes was obvious.

"Thousands," he said, with a tone of awe in his voice. "Thousands and thousands."

"Thank you," Alyssa said. It was some kind of compliment, she was sure.

He dropped the lock of hair and looked at her a long moment.

"What is it?" she asked.

"Only one is One," he said, apparently meaning something deeper than she understood. His words came out with great effort, slowly. "Only one is One. We . . . aren't one. You . . ." here he waved his arm, encircling the room, "Two hundred forty-three. Five. And two. Yes, always two. Prob'ly three." The last he mused nearly to himself. "Yes, three . . ."

"You've lost me, Bert," she said with a sigh.

"Two hundred forty-three." He waved his arm again and looked at her like she was supposed to understand.

"Okay," she said.

She wished Margret would come and translate.

"Okay," Bert said, satisfied. He got up again and went off, heading toward the kitchen area.

She sighed.

"You made a friend," Margret said. She plopped herself down in the chair Bert had just left, turning it around backwards before she sat down. Her earrings jingled.

"There you are," Alyssa said.

"Having a good time?"

"Yeah. Wish you'd been here a minute ago though."

"Why? You two were doing great."

"I have no idea what he said. How do you understand him?"

"I don't." She shrugged.

"Come on."

"Sometimes I can guess. I knew him pretty well, you know, before they . . . So I know what he's like. What he talks about."

"What does 'one is only one' mean?"

"He told you that, eh?"

"Yeah. He asked me if I was one or two and I said one, and then he said no, only one is one."

"Only one is One. Yeah."

"Huh?"

"I know that one. He means you're never alone."

"Oh," Alyssa said, as though that explained everything.

"It all makes sense if you pay attention," Margret said. "All Bert's numbers. You'll figure it out."

She didn't want to figure it out. It made her uneasy. She didn't want to think of Deb reduced to this kind of existence, and every time she considered the possibility it sent a chill through her.

"He's also talking about Jesus," Margret offered. "Only Jesus was ever truly left alone, when he hung on the cross. We aren't ever alone, because he's always there for us. Something like that, I think."

"Oh," Alyssa said, and was quiet for a moment. "What about you, Margret? Do you believe in that stuff?"

"You're a spy now, eh?" she asked, teasing.

"No way," Alyssa said, hurt she could think such a thing.

"*Kidding*," Margret said, with a mock punch to her arm. Then her lighthearted demeanor became more serious. She sighed. "I can't afford to believe it. It's not worth it. I see this thing happen to Bert, and I'm afraid. I have my kids to think about, my family to protect." She gave Alyssa a searching look.

Alyssa could see from Margret's eyes that she was deeply troubled about this.

"But you said when we met, some things are worth it," Alyssa said, raising her eyebrow.

"You are one wicked woman, you know that?" Margret said. "Yeah, I said that, but I was talking about *fun* things, girl, not things that make you wind up brain dead, or worse." She laughed, but without humor. "I just hope, if there is a God, he understands," she continued, looking away. "I hope he forgives me for my weakness. My family . . . I was raised counting on a rosary, but I can't bring myself to believe in any of it now. Not anymore. I've seen too many things happen. Too many scary things." She crossed herself, an involuntary motion.

They were both silent, listening to the lull of conversations buzzing around them. Suddenly, shifting moods, Margret jumped up.

"Come on. Let's go see what Eleanor and Jennie are gabbing about over there, huh?"

It turned out they were gabbing about childbirth, a subject on which Alyssa could only be silent. Margret joined in with gusto, telling the tales of birthing Marcus and Natalie. Alyssa tried not to let it show that the conversation horrified her. The details they described included things she had never heard of before, procedures that sounded excruciatingly painful. When the topic didn't change after more than an hour, she politely excused herself from the group claiming she was tired.

As she got up she saw that Natty had fallen asleep on the blankets curled up next to her brother. How peaceful and serene they looked in sleep. She stood there, watching their gentle breathing, and wondered why it was that one had to go through such a terrifying process to bring children into the world. She wondered, if it was so dangerous and life-changing, why anyone ever did it.

How amazingly innocent and pure they looked, asleep like that. Maybe, she thought, for some parents, like Margret and the others in this group, it was worth it. But she couldn't comprehend that, and doubted she ever would.

"Going already?" Margret asked.

It broke Alyssa out of her reverie. She set herself for the door. "Yes, I have work in the morning."

The group of late stragglers waved her goodbye as she left for home, and called out their enthusiasm at having met her, encouraging her to come again. She smiled and returned their thanks and goodbyes.

In the weeks that followed, she came to enjoy the Friday Hall meetings. She got used to the social group and the relaxation of being around them. When Margret had to work on Fridays, which was often, she brought Marcus and Natty with her. She felt responsible for them, and found to her surprise that she didn't loathe that feeling.

At first the others at the meetings teased her about being a "spoiled little rich kid." After her initial shock at being labeled that way, she understood both that it was meant in fun and that it was painfully true. She had never thought of herself as spoiled. She had focused instead on the things she didn't have, experiences she had missed, chances she had lost. Now that she had nothing left at all, she felt more comfort here, with these people, than she ever enjoyed before.

Her neighbors were friendly, frank and down-to-earth, and gradually, they pulled more personal information out of her than she ever thought she would reveal. Many of their weekend evenings were spent in storytelling. The group took turns telling their own stories, how they came to be there, tales of their families, their histories, tales of bygone days from the older folk, how things used to be, how it all changed before their eyes in a matter of years.

At first Alyssa sat and listened to everyone else, remaining silent. But as the months passed, and the days turned from the crisp cool of early autumn to the bitter wind-chill of Midwestern winter nights, she started to speak up.

It was frightfully cold and snowing the first night she said anything. She might have stayed home that night if Margret hadn't gone, but they bundled the little ones up and crunched through the snow. Ash managed to get in a shipment of hot cocoa mix that week, and donated a portion of it for the Hall meeting, which Alyssa had to bring along. Ash came only rarely, saying she was too old for that kind of thing, even though quite a few of the group were much older than she.

It was after the cocoa had been passed around and all had drunk their fill of it, after the evening had worn down and become still, that Alyssa started to speak. For some reason, people were quieter than usual this night. Alyssa wasn't certain what came over her, but she felt a need to tell them where she had come from.

Once she started talking she had the floor. All the rest were obviously curious about this newcomer, this quiet girl who smiled at them at the grocery store because she had to and not because she was truly happy inside. When she realized the room had gotten quiet it made her nervous, and she stopped.

But she received such positive encouragement, everyone urging her to continue, that she went on. Once she started telling her story, feeling comfortable about it, it was hard to stop. She told them about her family, her father's death, and everything that happened to her after that. Even about the drugs and the government involvement, and how she had been removed from the federal computers, which erased her citizenship and official identity; all the things that obliged her to seek out this place.

She was met with understanding, no judgment, only acceptance. Most of the group knew of such things from personal experience; she knew this from months of hearing their stories. There was one man everyone called Ed (though no one knew his real name), who was a former scientist. He had worked for the government, for a cloning project that went awry. That was five years ago. Alyssa felt relieved when she heard of Ed's story. He didn't tell it himself. He came to the meetings infrequently, and when he showed up, he was quieter than Alyssa. But the others filled her in on what details they knew, or had heard, or guessed. Knowing he had hidden there successfully for so long helped her to relax and adjust, without worry that some day unknown agents would come knocking at her door.

So she told her story with a degree of confidence, without fear of the details becoming known. These people didn't believe in turning anyone over to the government. Most of the population in this sector were wanted themselves, for one thing or another. Generally it was for things the government now labeled "treasonous acts," threatening to take information to the public, exposing a public official's corruption, refusing to participate in activities they found distasteful or unethical. One woman was there because she refused to fix an election so her candidate would win. Someone else had fixed it anyway, the man still won, so she truly felt she had lost everything for nothing. She was still quite bitter.

A significant percentage were deeply religious, hiding there to escape "therapy." Alyssa slowly grasped that Bert's misfortune was a reminder to them to keep quiet, that he had been left alive as an example to the rest that the government was in control, even here. It had the ability to swoop down on any of them, like a circling hawk, if they called attention to themselves. And occasionally, some people did disappear.

There were also a fair number of the mentally ill and disabled, like Mary. Many were elderly. Their natural families had found they could no longer care for them. Others had lived there in poverty for as long as they could remember, as long as their families before them could remember. For them, life had always been this way.

The population of the place came from all walks of life, all nationalities and races. No one ethnic group was more predominant than another. Harry, the janitor in the next building over, sometimes teased Margret about her ancestry. She was bilingual in Spanish and English, but it was hard to determine from her appearance what her nationality was.

Alyssa was shocked when she first heard this teasing. She had been raised with her mother's careful political correctness about such things. But Margret just laughed in her usual good-natured way. It was obvious she was used to this, and didn't mind it.

Seeing Alyssa's wide eyes, she laughed again and explained, "If I was born a dog, I'd be nothing but a mutt."

Alyssa choked at this explanation.

"My mother was mostly Mexican, *si*," Margret explained, over-emphasizing the Spanish word. "*No habla Ingles* . . . not without spitting first anyway. But Papa was mostly black, and *never* spoke Spanish. One of my grandmothers was Korean. My other grandmother, if she even *knew* who my grandfather was, she never told."

It was clear Margret enjoyed telling the story, and was proud of her unusual heritage. "It gives me *culture*," she would say, "and plenty of 'em!" They would all laugh, and Alyssa would shake her head in disbelief.

****

As Alyssa finished telling her story that night, she saw many thoughtful and caring faces around her. She had never felt so understood in her life, except perhaps with Rob, though that was different. That was one to one, and emotions ran high and strong when she was with him. This was a community, a family, in a strange way, and she felt accepted into it. It was a good feeling.

"This place is a prison without walls," Emma said, the next one to speak. She was a large black woman with a deep throaty voice, who kept her hair pulled back into a severe bun, tight against her scalp. Her husband George was the pastor of a small church that several in the group attended. Their services were held in the basement of one of the apartment buildings.

"How do you mean?" Alyssa asked, even as all the others around her murmured their agreement.

"It's a prison without walls," Emma repeated.

"Amen," George said, sitting beside her.

"Look at you, Lyss," she said. "You aren't happy here. Don't you see? They've taken all your dreams away, they've taken your true love, they've taken your friends, everything important to you. It's not your fault. But you're stuck here, like the lot of us, and can't leave, now. Can you?"

Alyssa shook her head. "No, I guess I can't," she replied. "But I'm not entirely without blame in that."

She avoided correcting the shortened version of her name. At first she tried. She had never used a nickname before, and was unused to it, but it seemed to be a form of endearment here, and eventually she gave up trying to get these people to use her whole name. It also bothered her that Emma called Rob her *true love*, though she didn't want to argue that point either.

"See? A prison with no bars," Emma said again. "Ain't no bars, ain't no magic forcefields, ain't no fancy technology, ain't no walls, but we're all stuck here just the same, for our own reasons, and the sad thing is most of us came here all on our own. Locked ourselves up."

"Amen," said several more people in the little group.

"They do have a forcefield," someone said. It was Ed. Everyone turned to look. "Doesn't keep anyone in or out though. It's a holographic projection, so satellites and planes flying over this sector see a park. Didn't you feel anything weird when you arrived here? A kind of vibration?"

"Yes," Alyssa said suddenly, remembering. "I did feel something, but I didn't think anything of it at the time."

"It's not a difficult illusion to maintain, with all the gardens up there on the rooftops. You hear about that big wildlife reclamation project they wanted to put in the middle of the city that got big in the news several years back? Ever wonder where they built it?"

"I never thought about it," she answered.

"It's right here," Ed said, speaking from the shadows in a corner of the room. "We're the reclamation project."

It was dark, but Alyssa thought she could see him smile.

"I used to get a kick out of watching people try to find this great big green park. Shows up on all the satellites but nobody can ever *drive* there. Rich guys make all kinds of donations to its cause, and the Feds pocket the money. Pretty great fundraising trick. Anybody who figures it out, of course, doesn't get the luxury of ending up *here*."

"Oh, Ed. That's as wild a tale as your lame old asteroid-headed-for-Earth story," someone said.

"Believe what you want," Ed said.

They all waited to see if he would add anything else. But he was silent, fading into the background.

"Anyway, what is it that keeps us here?" George said after a pause, straightening up in his seat. "What is it? Do you know? They've got us all tied down by fear."

"Fear," repeated the same several people who said "Amen" before.

This repeating thing, Alyssa noticed, was something of a habit with these few. It had something to do with their being religious, she thought.

"Come on, George, save your preaching for the Sabbath," Emma said, pulling on his sleeve with a smile.

"Oh, hush, Emma, I got something to say," he said. He leaned over and kissed her on the cheek, then stood up. "It's fear! They got us imprisoned here by fear and fear alone. That's their jail key. And what does the Lord say about fear?"

"What?" said the ones paying attention.

"He does not give us the spirit of fear! Where does fear come from?"

"Where?" The group was getting lively. Alyssa sat back and halfway listened. Margret rolled her eyes, and Alyssa suppressed a chuckle.

"From the devil! The devil gives us fear. It's his fault we're here. He's the one controlling the politicians! They've sold their souls!"

"Amen!"

"He's the one who's imprisoned us here. He wants us to be downtrodden, downhearted. He wants us to give up, to be afraid, not to show our faces for what we believe. And do we believe?"

"We believe!"

"We believe!" George repeated, after his group. He spoke even louder, using his resonant, deep-throated preaching voice. Something about it reminded Alyssa of an audiotape she heard in school of Martin Luther King. "And people, let me tell you something. They can close us in. They can make us stay here. They can deny our existence in the media. Maybe they can even put up that fancy hologram Ed talks about. They can try all they want to scare us into submission. They could build walls around this whole quarter, but it wouldn't make any difference!"

"Amen!"

"And do you know why? Because we shall know the truth, and the truth shall make us free!"

"Amen!" they said, with exuberance.

"We are all made free in the Lord! They can knock us down, they can take all we own, they can even take our families, our loved ones . . ." Here he paused and looked pointedly at Bert, who was also there. "But they can't take our *souls*!"

"Amen!"

"As long as we do not succumb to fear, that fiery dart of fear, then that old menace, the devil, can't win the battle! We still triumph by the grace of Jesus! The devil has not won! Isn't that right, Bert?"

"One," Bert said, who up to this point didn't appear to have been listening.

"We shall triumph at the end!" George said emphatically. "You feel like singing tonight, Bert? Tell us all about it! Tell us all how to overcome our fear! Give us the answer!"

"George," Emma said.

"Hush," George said to her, in a whisper. "Maybe he will. Wait and see."

"Come on, let's go," Margret said to Alyssa. "Time to get out of here."

Alyssa agreed. She put on her coat and helped Margret gather the sleeping children, each of them carrying one. While they were occupied with that, the rest of the room became deathly silent. Alyssa looked to see what would happen, but Margret rushed her.

"Come on," she said. "I hate it when George does this."

As she opened the door to the frozen wind, Alyssa heard Bert begin to sing. It was a beautiful baritone, a true Gospel singing voice, and he sang words, not numbers. His voice was exquisite. She had to stop and look back.

"The Lord has not given us the spirit of fear," Bert sang out. "But a spirit of power, and of love, pure love, and of a sound mind, of a so-o-ound mind."

"Come on," Margret said, pulling her out the door into the snow. "We're letting the cold air in."

"I'll bless the Lord who counsels me . . . I've set the Lord always before me; And I shall not be moved . . . My heart is glad, my soul shall also rest in hope, in sweetest hope; And I shall not be moved . . . Shall not be moved. Because . . ." As the door swung shut behind her, Alyssa heard the rest of the group join in on the repeating chorus. "Has not given us the spirit of fear, but a spirit of power. . ."

"What's the matter?" Alyssa asked, carrying Nat as best she could while trying to keep up. "That was beautiful. I've never heard anything like that."

She fell behind, listening until the door was fully closed and she couldn't hear them anymore. Margret continued to walk quickly.

"It's nothing, just a song he made up himself from verses in the Bible," Margret said. "I think that one's Psalms and Timothy or something. He used to do that a lot. Man, would he quiz me on his Bible verses. Look. Once he gets singing he won't stop until he falls asleep. It's not fair to Bert. He's tired. But once George gets started on one of his sermons, he doesn't know when to quit."

"How do you know he's tired? Like he does anything all day."

"I can just tell, okay?"

She said nothing else, and Alyssa didn't press her for more details. As talkative and open as Margret usually was, Alyssa could tell she didn't want to talk about this. She regretted not being able to listen longer; his singing took her breath away. They made the rest of their way home in silence. The only noise was the sound of their footsteps crunching through the snow and the wind whistling through the tall brick buildings. Alyssa thought it was one of the more lonesome sounds she had ever heard. She hugged Nat close to her chest for warmth.

•••••••

The residents called their sector The Gardens, for lack of an officially designated name. Whether Ed's story about the large-scale holograph was true or not, they couldn't know. But it was clear the government did everything it could to deny the existence of the place. It was a thorn in their side, an embarrassment. The suffering and deprivation was never reported in any media Alyssa had ever seen. According to the general public, poverty had been wiped out in Central City. A large part of the President's power and control stemmed directly from this false image of prosperity. It had to be maintained . . . at any cost. Lives were dispensable, the image was not.

One Saturday in February, Margret pounded on Alyssa's door with her usual loudness. It was still dark out and Alyssa was bleary-eyed opening the door.

"Don't you ever get tired?" she asked.

"Sure, but I deal with it," Margret said cheerfully. "It's clinic day. You been here six months, you gotta go now or the goonies are gonna start nosing around."

"Clinic day?" She struggled to wake up, and ruffled her hand through her hair. "What's that?"

"They have clinic day every month. Everybody has to go get a shot every three months. You're late going."

"I had all my vaccinations when I was a kid. This is stupid. You sure it's not some kind of research?"

"It's required. We gotta get there early, or we wait all day in line. Come on."

"How come you didn't say something three months ago if it's so important?"

"I forgot then. But it's my month and I realized you didn't know about it yet," Margret said.

"I have to work later this morning. Thanks, but no thanks. I'll pass."

"You can't. If you don't go they'll come find you, then you're in trouble. I already called and told Ash, she says she'll see you when you get back. She understands, trust me."

"How the heck will they know? Who're *they* anyway?"

"They know. Believe me. They don't know *who* we are, but they know how many there are and which ones live where and how many move in and out and when and all that kind of stuff. They keep stats."

"The government?"

"Yep."

"No way. Not going," Alyssa said.

"You have to."

"What kind of shot is it anyway? I had all my shots."

"Believe me, you don't want to catch this one, eh?" Margret said, grinning. "And I'm sure you're not immune."

"Come on, enough already. What's the vaccine for?"

"Babies!" Margret said, and laughed. "Birth control. Ever notice the only infants in this place belong to newcomers? You see many pregnant ladies walking around?"

"No," Alyssa said, considering. "I never paid much attention. But why?"

"They don't want us *reproducing*," Margret said. "We're threatening enough as it is."

"No, I meant why on earth would I need to bother?"

"You could have sterilization surgery instead. It's free."

"Margret."

Margret shrugged. "It's required," she said. "Part of getting to live in this *lovely* atmosphere."

"Let's not and say I did. I'll tell them I've already had surgery and skip it."

"They'll check you for a scar. Probably scan you too. Won't work. They catch you lying, then you're in *deep* crap. You don't want that. There was this lady, Dolores, she tried that trick and disappeared the next week. Besides, you don't want no kids anyway."

"I never said that."

"It's true," Margret said. "I can tell. You're great with Nat and Marcus. In fact, you surprise me, girl. But you don't have that longing in your eyes. You're happy to play with them a while and then give them back. Girls who want to grow up and be mommies, they look at kids different than you do."

"You can tell all that from my 'look'?" Alyssa asked. She didn't like how Margret could read her personality; she also didn't like being called a "girl" by her when she wasn't all that much younger.

"Of course I can," Margret said. "I'm a *mother*."

"Well, whatever," Alyssa conceded. "But I won't be putting myself in any situation where I'd risk getting pregnant. I'm smarter than that."

Margret laughed openly. "Girl," she said, "You never *have* been in love, have you? I thought so."

"Yes I have," Alyssa said, defensively.

"Well, then you didn't love him long enough or close enough to know anything about anything," she said. "It happens too fast. And then, well, look. I got Marcus to show for it, and some incredible memories."

It happens too fast. She remembered the night with Rob and the marijuana. If things had been only slightly different . . . This thought made her uneasy. "So? Who am I gonna go for around here anyway? Harry the janitor?" she said with disgust.

Margret laughed again. "I see your point," she said. "But there's always rape. You never know."

"I carry a knife." But the thought was unsettling. She hadn't considered it a real risk, but maybe it was.

"And you thought I was naïve," Margret said, folding her arms across her chest. "Look. I should've taken you to the clinic when you first got here, but I forgot last time. Now you gotta go, since they're gonna know you been here six months already and haven't got the shot yet. They'll come looking for you. You call more attention to yourself if you don't go than if you do. You don't even want kids anyway, so big deal!"

"My *problem*," Alyssa said, "is the mandatory part. It's wrong to force that on anybody."

"It's a free service," Margret said.

"Oh, great."

"No side effects except stopping your period. Ever wonder why Ash is so short on feminine products all the time? We don't need them. Think of the money you'll save."

Alyssa considered this too. It was as though a few puzzle pieces suddenly fit into place. Ash was always in short supply and could only get one inferior brand in stock. Alyssa figured it was because Ash was an older woman herself and much of the female population was older too, past needing them. But this explanation made more sense.

"Why didn't you tell me about this before?"

"No rush. You don't have a guy. Why bother? Besides, I forgot."

"That was *my* point, I believe." She smiled.

"If you'd got a guy, I would've told you right away," Margret said. "I'd have remembered. So you'll come?"

"I don't see that I have much choice."

"Good," Margret said. "I'll get my coat."

"I have to get dressed," Alyssa reminded her.

"I'll wait. Come knock when you're ready."

She did.

After the second shot, and the third, it became routine, something she hardly thought about, except to circle the calendar for when it was time to go.

•••••••

Thoughts of Debra also faded away as time passed. Alyssa tried to call soon after she arrived, but found the number busy. Another time she tried and got no answer, and the next few times her call wouldn't go through at all. At first it bothered her very much that she couldn't connect with her friend, just to talk to her, let her know things were all right. But when she started going to the Hall meetings, and fitting in to her new life, her past became less important. Eventually, it seemed a universe away. While there were occasional days when she missed Deb, Margret's friendship was bubbly and bright and satisfying. It filled the emptiness she had felt at first. Deb had a new life too, surely long married to Jon by now. She probably didn't have time to spend wondering how her old friend was doing.

Life here was about survival, and helping those to survive who couldn't do so on their own. She had little time that wasn't devoted to finding ways to stretch her budget, ration her supplies and pull together enough to make up her next meal. Ash was as generous about raising her pay as she could afford to be, but money was always tight. In time Alyssa dressed up her apartment with sheets, curtains, and a comforter for the bed from a second-hand store. A few other decorations made it feel cheery and homey inside, her own little place.

She learned to appreciate it. In fact, she found a greater sense of enjoyment and satisfaction with these people than she'd ever known before. She hadn't believed it possible, but she enjoyed a sense of well being and peace in this place she had never known . . . without material possessions. The friendships she created here were deep; she came to know the people well. To her they were the family she never had.

And they noticed changes in her, or so they said. She smiled more often. She was more relaxed and easygoing, laughed more when she was teased. Her life here was unexpectedly comfortable, and as time passed, she discovered that this meant she was happy.

Chapter 31

Recruiting

I still haven't found any way to contact Alyssa, especially since the phone lines were rerouted through a new server. Jon tells me I'm worrying far too much, but I can't help it. I don't know what else I could've said. She just wouldn't come. I thought she would have called long before the rerouting happened. Maybe she's forgotten about me. I try not to dwell on it, but . . .

Jon worries about me. He dotes on me, actually, so much sometimes it's annoying. I chalk it up to his anxiety over becoming a new dad. Only two weeks to go. He's seen a lot of things go wrong with this whole maternity process during his internship. He doesn't talk much about that, for my sake. But I'm not worried. I have great peace inside. Pregnancy is nothing like I imagined, so uncomfortable, but so thrilling every time I feel this tiny life move inside me. It's a joy like no other I've ever had. I wish Alyssa was near me to share it. I miss her so much. Not knowing, that's the hardest thing. The hardest part of all.

Debra Gray Pike,
personal journal entry

Eventually George and Emma took their little congregation and marched out of the slums, chanting glorious Gospel songs about finding freedom. Bert stayed behind.

They were never heard from again.

It didn't help the ever-growing perception, even among the poor, that religious fervor must be, at its root, no more than a psychological abnormality. It was said of George, and not nicely, that he led his lambs straight into the lion's waiting jaws. When people can be so easily led to an unpleasant fate it seems nothing short of psychotic. None of those who said such things knew what actually happened to the little group. But it didn't matter much. The perception stuck.

Alyssa, however, didn't agree with that mindset. She had been too close to Debra, knew her too well to believe she was mentally ill. She felt a person should be allowed their own beliefs, whatever those beliefs happened to be, and she saw nothing wrong with the way Deb, or Ash, or many of the others she lived with, behaved. George and his followers were the exception. But the way she saw it, one could become a fanatic about any cause, religious or otherwise. Most of the others she knew who professed a religion were not so eccentric.

The oil shortage, which began about the same time as Alyssa's arrival in the slums, had steadily worsened. Relations with the Middle Eastern oil cartels simply could not be worked out diplomatically. They flatly refused to sell, placing a full-fledged oil embargo on the United States before a year was out. By the end of its second year, the media reported tales of terrorist groups sabotaging forbidden shipments.

Numerous other injustices against the United States were reported that worked the general public into a riotous frenzy. They wanted to drive their cars, fly away on vacations. But prices were so high that only the wealthy could afford those things. The real damage was felt in the trucking and air traffic industries. Price increases there dramatically inflated the cost of all goods, not just petroleum products. Foreign products of any type were a challenge to find, even if one could afford the outrageous prices.

Many corporations were able to compensate with virtual commuting and networking with their employees' home computer systems, but even this was little help against the enormity of the problems the shortage caused. The stock market plummeted.

As time wore on, selections on grocery shelves became meager. There was serious talk of rationing, but that too resulted in controversy. Those with wealth didn't wish to be rationed if they could pay the prices.

The cry came increasingly for war. It appeared there would be no other way to regain what the people had lost. The States alone could not produce enough crude oil for the needs of the entire country, prices notwithstanding. Public unrest peaked as the frustration became too great to bear. War propaganda filled the airwaves, all the media cried for redress of the injustices suffered by the American people.

In The Gardens, however, prices would always be high, food shipments to their sector always shorted. It was just more meager than usual. They pulled together, pooled resources, shared as best they could. Few owned cars or could afford to keep them running it they did, so that aspect of the crisis mattered little to them. Alyssa, along with nearly everyone else in her neighborhood, ignored it. They ignored it, that is, until the President became serious enough about pursuing war to reinstate the draft.

Then it became personal.

•••••••

Near the beginning of Alyssa's third summer in the Gardens, they began to hear the march of army troops echoing through the streets. Their synchronized footsteps rang up to the skies from the pavement below, reverberating off the glass and brick of the tall buildings. They set up recruiting stations, some quite nearby.

Many of The Gardens' inhabitants hailed the armed services as an easy way to make quick money. The military rewarded voluntary enlistment with the complete dismissal of any charges one might have, automatic reinstatement of citizenship, and a sizable paycheck. The offer was attractive.

What was not attractive was their method of drafting those unwilling to serve voluntarily. Unpleasant stories began to circulate. Soon riots and street fighting broke out as soldiers coerced selected individuals to join, at gunpoint. The soldiers sought out those whose bodies and minds were able, looking for anyone healthy or young enough. Any who refused their "invitation" were shot for treason. No arrests, no trials. Judgment was swift and the sentence immediate. Bodies were left on the streets as examples.

Fear permeated the entire sector. As the stories became more widespread, the echo of marching patrols, even a considerable distance away, caused everyone to hide quietly in their apartments. The streets were unusually quiet. All here were guilty of some crime or other, real or imagined, and it appeared the government would no longer leave them alone. It picked them off, one by one, coercing them to swear new allegiance to their country or pay the price with their lives.

Alyssa's own neighborhood was lucky. Such incidents hadn't happened there yet. To them, the reports were more like rumor than truth, though none doubted they were real.

In mid-June of that summer, as Alyssa stocked some shelves near the registers, she heard Ash collapse with a gasp. It was closing time, and Ash had been counting out the drawer. Alyssa ran to her.

She had knocked her head against the corner of the drawer when she fell, and blood ran down her face from the cut.

"Are you all right?" Alyssa asked.

"My heart," Ash gasped. "My chest hurts. And my arm."

"Can you stand up? I don't know what to do!"

"Call Larry," Ash wheezed.

"Oh . . . right!" She remembered that Larry was once a surgeon, and picked up the phone behind the register. Larry was at his apartment. He said he'd be right over, and not to move her until he got there.

"Call my kids," Ash said, when Alyssa hung up.

"I'll take care of this scratch first," Alyssa said. She ran to find the bandages. First aid she knew from years before returned to her mind. Stop the bleeding first. That was the rule.

By the time she had the wound cleaned and stanched, Larry walked up to the register. He said Ash had had a mild heart attack, from the look of things.

"You got insurance, Ash?" he asked.

"You kidding?"

"Can't call the hospital then, they'll eat you alive. What about your kids?"

"I think Jewel has coverage," Ash said, wincing with the pain. "But I'm not on the policy."

"Call Jewel," Larry told Alyssa.

"I don't know the number," Alyssa said.

Ash gave her the number from memory, and she punched it in. While Larry got Ash as comfortable as possible, she talked to Jewel on the public videophone, practically ordering her to come right away and pick her up.

Jewel whined, "It'll take me a good half-hour to get there, if I can even find a place to get gas for the car," she said. "I'm not rich, you know, Mom. No matter what you think."

"She'll pay you back for the gas!" Larry said, angrily. "Shoot, I'll pay you extra! Just come as soon as you can!"

"This better not be some cute little trick of yours, Mom," Jewel said, and rung off.

"Wonderful child," Alyssa remarked.

"She's my angel," Ash said sourly.

"And you *want* them to visit?" Alyssa asked.

Ash started to laugh, but coughed instead.

Larry had brought along a stethoscope. "How bad is the pain?" he asked, taking her pulse as he listened to her heart.

When people were sick in The Gardens they went to Larry. He made crude penicillin the old-fashioned way, distilling it from mold, and he provided what small services he could for a low charge. Alyssa had rarely been sick in her two winters there, outside the occasional cough or flu. She maintained good personal hygiene, and kept her apartment as clean and sanitary as possible.

"It's getting better now," Ash said.

"Good. Very good," Larry said, listening through his stethoscope. He started to smile. "I think you're gonna make it through this one. Have you been taking your aspirin?" he asked.

"Too expensive lately," she said.

"Ashley," Larry said, chiding her.

"I've been fine," she said. "Figured I could do without."

"Don't do that again," he said. "You might not live through the next one. You think I've got a heart-lung bypass machine stowed in my apartment? Never mind anesthesiology, there's no way I can operate on you in this place."

"Okay, okay," Ash said.

Alyssa stood watching, a helpless bystander. When she could see Ash would be all right, she finished the closing procedures by herself while Larry attended to his patient. The three of them stayed there until Jewel arrived nearly an hour later, in a fluster.

The next day, when Alyssa arrived at work, Jewel was there with Ash. She had decided she could no longer *bear* to see her mother suffer in this forsaken place, and insisted that Ash come back and live with her and her children.

Ash protested. "I'd have to close your Daddy's store. Can't do that."

"Mom, you'll have to. I can't come running down here like this every time your heart troubles you. Ricky's got good insurance now, didn't I tell you? We'll have to get you on it, and figure out what this is all about, take care of you right from here on out. I couldn't *stand* it if something worse happened."

"You care?" Ash asked in wonder.

"You're my *mother*," Jewel said.

Within two weeks the store was closed. Ash sold off her inventory at a discount, and gave a generous portion of the leftover groceries to Alyssa as a going-away present.

"You were my favorite employee," she said, smiling, when she gave her the boxes of groceries. "Ever."

"Thanks." She blushed. "Are you sure about this? I mean, I could run the store," Alyssa said.

Ash laughed. "Now dearie, I just can't do that," she said.

"Why not?"

"Simple. You can't buy the store, honey. You haven't got money. And besides, I've sold it."

"To who? Can I work for them?"

"Highest bidder," she said. "And the highest bidder wants it closed."

"Who'd want to do that?" Alyssa asked.

"Government," she said.

"How could you do that to us, Ash?"

She patted her blouse where she wore the cross underneath. "They been taking advantage of me long enough now, what with their taxes and regulations and all. Figured it's about time I took advantage of them a little. I got retirement to think about, honey, and my heart. Can't be fixed for free. I need that money, and frankly, nobody else is buying. They've been wanting me to sell for years."

"I can't believe you'd do this," Alyssa said.

"Have to. No other way. Look, hon, it won't be that bad for you. You've got Delbert's place in walking distance."

"Why do they want to close the store?"

"Oh, you know. They let us all live here, all right, but they don't like it and they don't like us getting comfortable. Anything they can own, or do, to make us uncomfortable, well, they like that. See?"

"And you're just going to let them."

"I have no other choice, Honey. You got to understand this. There's nothing else I can do."

"I see," Alyssa said, but she wasn't sure she did.

Borrowing a shopping cart, she pushed her boxes of groceries home. The situation frightened her. It was hard enough to take in the fact that the store was closing, Ash was moving, and she was now out of a job, one she had held for nearly two years. Knowing *why* made it that much harder.

At her apartment, she shared the food with Margret, who was grateful and explained why Ash was selling out.

"Can you believe it?" Alyssa said.

"Sure," Margret said. "I'd sell too. Nothing wrong with Delbert's."

"He charges too much and puts additives in his produce to make it look bigger."

"Ash told you that. Don't mean nothing," Margret said. "They hated each other."

"But what will I do?" she asked.

"Find another place," Margret said, shrugging. "Big deal."

"Any openings at the factory?"

"*Nada*. Besides, I got the *skill*. I can sew anything. And these industrial machines are touchy. You got to know what you're doing. Spoiled rich girls like you never had to sew your own clothes like I did, now did you?"

"Hey. I'm neither spoiled nor rich . . . anymore." She laughed easily at Margret's teasing.

"I know. Still, did you?"

"No."

"You'd sew through all ten of your fingers before you got through a single shift," Margret said, smiling. "Find something you can do. Look around. Something will turn up."

But something did not turn up, and the manager nagged her when the rent came due. She was able to pay him half, which bought her a little more time. She applied at Delbert's and got on a waiting list, but all the other employees from Ash's store were also on the list. It would be a long wait.

Businesses were closing everywhere. Little shops that barely turned a profit were found empty, abandoned as fear of the draft and the mandatory "enlistment" procedures grew stronger.

There were few places to go from here. Alyssa assumed she had hit absolute bottom when she landed in The Gardens. But every day it seemed someone else vanished inexplicably, gone into further hiding, moving on before they could be discovered or drafted or worse.

She had plenty of food for the time being. Ash had seen to that. As long as she could hold off the apartment manager, she could bide her time for a little while. As long as she had food to eat and a place to stay, she had all she required.

But it was strange to be at home during the day. So she spent her days walking, talking to people she knew, trying to find a business that would hire her, that offered a job for which she had any skill.

Being summer, there was the garden on the roof to tend as well, and she spent time up there in the evenings tending it, thinking, trying to plan what she would do. Competition for even the smallest jobs was tight.

Hall meetings on Friday nights became noticeably smaller. Conversation turned to talk of the impending war: what it all meant, political views, what they would do if the troops marched down *their* street. If there were rumors to fear before, they were reality now, creeping like unwelcome insects into their lives, nibbling at their thoughts, nagging at their hearts.

More than once Alyssa thought about enlisting. She brought it up one Friday, postulating, "Why not?" She was twenty-two and still had her life in front of her. After all, what she needed was work, and this would mean a regular paycheck.

Her query was met with many objections.

"You honestly think they're gonna overlook what you came here for? Anything you might have done?"

"Did you ever think they might be trying to get us to turn ourselves in? Whole war's probably a hoax."

"Now that's farfetched," Alyssa said. "That's even more out on the fringe than some of Ed's old stories."

Ed had disappeared a year ago, on his own.

"Not really," came the reply.

"And what makes you think they won't throw us all to the front lines when the shooting starts?" someone else asked. "Convenient way to get rid of us without attracting attention. Likely it's part of their plan. You know The Gardens are the biggest government embarrassment since Area 51. They pretend we don't exist. What? You think you'll get some desk job filing papers for a general? Yeah, right."

Alyssa sighed. "Okay, okay. I see. Bad idea."

The more she thought about it and what everyone had said, the worse the idea sounded. They could all be right, as the buy-out of Ash's grocery proved. She cringed to think that the voluntary enlisting of Ash's former employees might be exactly what the government planned as a result of closing down the store.

The fear existing among the inhabitants was an energy that crackled through the streets, nearly tangible, something that hid just around the next corner, waiting, stalking every resident mercilessly. She could feel it. It made her skin feel prickly all over whenever she was out in the open air. It was a queer feeling, paranoia, looking over her shoulder whenever she left her apartment or walked down the street.

Some residents did enlist, planning to ditch the army as soon as they got their first paycheck and had their citizenship restored. She thought of them and wondered how simple it would be to get away with that trick. She doubted it would be as easy as they thought it would.

What would she do if the troops came and "requested" her service to her country? She wondered if she would object, make an issue out of it, dying in the process, or if she would meekly go along. She guessed she would probably go along and endure it. It couldn't be all that bad, she thought, better than death.

But then, from the deepest corners of her mind, came a nagging worry. If that happened, and they discovered her actual identity, and that disgusting man in the Department of Research was still looking for her, they would send her off to her fate as a human guinea pig before she could blink.

The thought frightened her anew. She had survived there for two years in peace, but the political unrest, and the general fear that characterized the expressions on the faces she passed on the street every day, had changed all that.

That night she tossed on her bed in the July humidity. She never had quite enough money for a window air conditioner, and had to settle for a fan. The heat and humidity were miserable at this time of year. Rest didn't come easily under the best of circumstances. Her room was always stuffy, even with the window open and the fan running on high.

Tonight, however, her sleep was even more disturbed. The old buried fear had become fresh again.

Chapter 32

Silent Prayer

It's a boy! Zachary Jonathan Pike, 8 lbs., 3 oz., and 21" long. I am so in love with him I can hardly stand it. I feel like my heart will burst. He's absolutely beautiful. Jon is so proud. He's going to be a great dad . . . What an incredible, amazing thing this gift of life is.

Debra Pike,
personal journal entry

Four weeks after Ash left with Jewel, the manager again pestered Alyssa about the rent. It was the beginning of August. She still had no source of new income, living cautiously on the groceries Ash had given her. She had to remind him he had rooms standing empty and that people were not exactly moving in here in droves, so there was no good reason to evict her whether she paid rent or not. She explained he would get her whole paycheck as soon as she found work, and promised to make him some fresh *gazpacho*, from Margret's mother's recipe, as soon as she could. With a grunt, he conceded to wait a little longer. She hated having to deal with him this way. Always, always before she had been exactly on time. Never a day late, no matter what.

Later that evening, in Margret's apartment, she helped her friend feed the children their dinner. Marcus was nine now, and Nat, five. Margret's place was somewhat larger than her own, with a bedroom off to the left of the entrance that all three of them slept in. Other than that it was a mirror image of Alyssa's, only messier.

"Still no openings at the factory, even if you were qualified," Margret said. "Hiring freeze is on. Profits are down again, or something. It's bull, but there's nothing I can do."

"It just seems there should be something else I could do," Alyssa said. "But everywhere I look, someplace else is going out of business."

The phone rang. It was that old-fashioned, audio only variety, and Margret only carried the service so that the factory could reach her if they needed her for an extra shift.

"Hello?" Margret said, and went silent.

Alyssa looked up.

Margret slammed the phone down violently and cursed, in English for once. "He *found* me, " she said, her eyes wide in horror.

"Ralph?" Alyssa asked.

She nodded. "Come on, kids, put your most special things in your backpacks and don't forget a change of clothes. We have to leave *now*."

"Where are we going?" asked Marcus.

"Mama, I don't wanna go anywhere. I wanna go play with Frances," Nat said, her voice a tired whine. "You said I could play with Frances."

"Just come with me, kids. I'll explain later. Come on! We have to hurry!" She rushed to a ceramic cookie jar on the tiny counter and turned it upside down. Cookie crumbs and a small sum of cash spilled out. "He's too close," she said to Alyssa, and swore again, a long sentence of muttered Spanish phrases. "How did he get this number? Somebody at work must've . . ."

She left off her sentence, picking through the crumbs and counting the cash, then picked through the remains for any change. She began to cry.

"I don't know where to run," she said, sobbing. "I thought I was safe here. It's been so long. I figured he forgot about me, or gave up. But no. He'll track me down eventually no matter where I go. That's the way he is. Damn, I should've moved a long time ago."

"Do you have enough for a ticket out? How far can you get?" Alyssa asked.

Margret counted. "Maybe a little ways. I might make it out of the city limits. I try to save, but their milk costs so much now. It slips through my fingers soon as I cash my check." She fumbled with the green bills, trying to sort them out and straighten them into a neat pile, dropping the stack more than once.

"I don't have to drink milk, Mama," Marcus offered, putting a small car and a T-shirt in a ragged pack.

"I have a good friend north of Central City, somewhere in northern Iowa. I'm pretty sure she'd take you in. Can you get that far?"

"I don't have that much cash. Why would she want someone like me around anyway?"

"She's Christian. She'd take you in. She went up that way for safety herself." Alyssa found a pencil and a small piece of paper and jotted down the name and general location of the colony as well as she could remember it. It had been quite a while. "Her name's Debra Gray. Well, probably Debra Pike, by now. She was getting married. We roomed together in college. I don't have enough money to go myself. I was never sure before that I'd want to, but I'd do it now if I could, the way things are."

Margret sighed. "Well, can't be more trouble than I'm already in. Long as I don't end up like Bert, I'll be all right. I guess." She wiped away tears. "I'll see how far we can get and head that direction, then. Better than staying here and waiting . . ." She shuddered.

"Stay here. I'll be right back," Alyssa said, and ran across the hall to her apartment.

Not knowing why, but only knowing that she had to, Alyssa reached her arm deep between her mattress and box spring for a little wallet she kept there. She had saved every dollar that she could in the last two years, hoping to have enough someday for a ticket out, perhaps to see Debra. But ticket prices kept going higher and higher; it was a vain hope, but she had felt driven to save every coin she found that she didn't absolutely need.

She pulled it out and counted it quickly. She had a little over four hundred dollars saved. She looked at it in her hands in surprise. She had never counted it before. It never occurred to her that she could have saved that much. Briefly she thought about replacing it in the wallet and stuffing it back under her bed; after all, with this much she might be able to bargain with the manager for a little more time. And the food Ash gave her wouldn't last forever.

Shaking away that thought, she grasped the bills in her hand and ran back to Margret's.

"Here," she said, holding it out. "I want you to have this."

"Girl . . ." Margret said. Her tears came again. "I can't take your money. It's all you got." Then, seeing the amount, she added in a whisper, "How'd you get all this?"

"I've been saving, a little every week, ever since I came here," she said. "Don't worry about me. I'll manage. Please, take it. Maybe this time you'll get far enough away and he won't ever be able to find you again."

Alyssa stepped toward her and pushed the money into her hand.

There had been nights, not a few, when one or the other of the children had come knocking on Alyssa's door after a bad dream, and she had comforted and held them until they fell back asleep, finally feeling safe again. Sometimes they fell asleep in her arms, whimpering if she so much as moved to let them go. Those times she would lean back against her iron headboard and try to sleep that way, holding on tightly until morning came peeking its pale light through her window.

Their nightmares were disjointed and strange, and to the children perhaps made no sense; but there were sufficient details here and there and the occasional clue from Margret, that she had been able to piece together much of their story. Her heart had ached as she discovered each new fragment of truth. She knew more in this way, of what they had endured, than their mother ever suspected. And she knew she couldn't live with herself if she failed to help them get as far away from that awful man as possible. Margret needed that money. There was no real choice to be made. It was just what had to be done.

Margret looked at her through grateful tears, clutching the bills.

"I've looked out for myself long enough, my whole life. Look where it's gotten me. Nowhere. This'll do you more good than me," Alyssa said with a flip of her hand. "I won't need it."

She turned to see Marcus zip his pack then help Nat fix hers. He talked to his sister in hushed tones, offering words of comfort. She looked back at Margret.

"Now go," Alyssa said. "Get out of here while you still can. The train station's at least a twenty-minute walk away."

****

She watched them leave as she stood on the front steps, Margret carrying Nat, Marcus hurrying along beside her into the enveloping darkness of the city streets. Margret didn't look back.

Alyssa had never prayed before in her life, but she prayed now, not knowing to whom or to what, that they would make it to somewhere safe. She didn't know whether there was any god that could hear her silent longing, or had the power to answer her earnest request. But she wished for their safety. She wished it desperately.

Chapter 33

Purification

Larry: What are we rerouting all these pipelines for, anyway?

Hank: I don't know. Some lame-brained government project. Personally I think they're wasting our tax money again. Is that joint secure?

Larry: Secure enough. Leaks a little, but I'm tired of working on it. I've sealed it five times already.

Hank: Let's get to the next one. Fool project anyway.

Larry: Yeah. But hey, whatever brings in the paycheck, right?

Hank: Right. They're never gonna come all the way down here and check every single pipe fitting.

Central City Water Utility,
Transcript of surveillance video

"Are we ready to initiate Operation Purify?" Victor asked Gerome.

"Almost. The east reservoir is ready to be pumped when needed. Tactical is still working out some details. We do have several major potential problems though, sir," the secretary said, clearing his throat.

The large man sighed and swiveled in his chair to face the window. It was raining today and he had the curtain open wider than usual. "What are they sniveling about this time?"

"It's possible all the water pipelines may not be totally separated by the time the reservoir is pumped. You haven't given them enough time. Tactical is quite concerned that the contagion could spread to the upper-class sectors. They recommend waiting—"

"That's why we developed the vaccine!" he said angrily, turning back to face Gerome. "In case of any accidental exposure!"

"Yes, but how quickly can it be distributed? Can we ship it out ahead of time without raising alarm? Doctors up there aren't going to take well to that," he said. "There's also a concern among the scientists about the techniques used to create the initial virus. They don't like the gene sequences you ordered. They say that the virus is too unstable. The specimens they've cultured in the reservoir could have mutated by now."

402

"Send a team out to check on that."

"Yes sir. But they're worried. They can't tell what it will do once it gets inside a human host. It could mutate again and negate any effect the vaccine might have. Besides, the vaccine is only effective on the virus, it doesn't kill the—"

"*Is* there anything else in that report?"

He stopped and glanced at the paper he held in his hand. "Yes. At the last evaluation the infected bacterium appeared to be emitting large amounts of hydrogen."

"Is that pertinent, Gerome?"

"They're still working to determine the significance. I'll have the full report in about a week."

"Then why are you bothering me with it now?"

"Well sir, hydrogen is highly flammable, explosive. Remember the stories of the Hindenburg? It's a safety hazard."

"Hazardous to burn those fetid slums out of existence? I think not! That would be more than we could hope for! The President would be elated. In fact, this could be useful. Yes . . . quite useful indeed." He felt almost giddy as he considered this new side effect.

"Uh . . . yes sir. As you say, sir."

"Dismissed."

Gerome stood in front of the marble desk silently.

"I said, dismissed."

"Sir, if I could venture an opinion," he said.

Victor sighed. He needed no one else's opinions. The Caretaker was in charge of this operation. Everything would proceed as planned, no glitches. He was certain of that. The Caretaker himself had given him the instructions and technological information necessary to create the new virus. *Unstable?* Nonsense. That was part of its brilliance. It was designed that way. They would see.

It was a lovely thing, really . . . quick enough, but certainly not painless. The virus itself appeared innocuous. But it was engineered using some radical DNA sequences taken from another experiment he directed. That experiment had to do with germ warfare, a federal weapons development. He considered it his life's work, a field in which he could use his expertise to its fullest extent. But this new project was so much more appealing, the plan so much more subtle than simply exploding a bomb loaded with biological toxins.

When they took the virus to the second stage of the procedure and exposed it to the common Streptococci Epidermis bacterium, the results were truly fascinating. Alone, the virus produced symptoms resembling a nasty form of lingering stomach flu in human subjects, not enough to serve his purposes. But it could also infect certain bacterium with new nucleic acid sequences. Coupling it with the streptococcus was like a marital union. The two were made for each other . . . literally, at least in part.

He was still surprised that it actually worked; the scientists had had their doubts about his instructions, and for good reason. He would have doubted the formulae himself, had the knowledge come from any other source. It was genetic engineering taken to a new level, using techniques never conceived of before.

From what he could determine, introducing the virus to the bacterium resulted in a synthesis remarkably similar to the introduction of a viable sperm into an ovum. The two sets of DNA recombined, intertwined, and rearranged themselves into sequences unlike those known in any other lifeform. It became an entirely new organism, virulent and toxic to every living creature it infected, and its various mutations made it unpredictable.

They had lost three good scientists to it already. It made developing any kind of antibody-based cure or vaccine difficult, and the resulting hybrid bacterium was extremely resistant to all known antibiotics. But its composition also made it nearly impossible to trace or identify . . . as long as one didn't know what to look for or how to look for it. And his laboratory employed the only individuals on earth with that information.

The most fascinating aspect of the experiment was the creation of what seemed to be a completely new genus. The latest reports showed that it had developed some poorly understood virulence factors, reacting differently as it came into contact with various human tissues. The last scientist they lost—just last week—reported the sensation that he was being consumed from the inside. And, if he hadn't known better, he would have thought that was exactly what it did. Of course there had to be a more scientific explanation than that. That didn't make any sense. But it systematically destroyed every system in the man's body. It was absolutely fascinating to observe. He had watched it personally, seen with his own eyes how the man begged for mercy, for anything to relieve the pain.

Victor shook his head with a sigh. Such things had to be studied to their final end without interference from other chemical compounds. There could be no variables. In the end, they did sedate the man, after all, to prevent him from committing suicide. It was a shame to lose him, of course. He had been instrumental in developing the virus and deserved far more than the honor of acting as a test subject.

But Victor enjoyed the thought, the hope that glimmered deep inside his dark soul, growing brighter daily as the reports came in, that he had engineered something *new*, something the world had never seen before. More than that, this was something *alive*, capable of not only eating and reproducing, but of changing, developing. It evolved faster than he ever imagined a lifeform could. When they performed the autopsy on the scientist (on what was left of his body anyway), they found the new bacterium mostly in clusters of sixteen cells, not single-celled any longer.

They hadn't determined yet whether it was merely a strange anomaly, or if the organism actually consisted of *sixteen cells* now. He awaited the results, but it was entirely possible. He would have to discuss the development with the Caretaker to find out if this was part of his plan.

In the meantime he reveled in his power, his brilliance, the genius of what he had created. What the organism was, or might possibly become, he didn't know for certain. He didn't care that the concept was not originally his. He would take all the credit. It was his due. He thrilled at the thought, feeling godlike, nearly omnipotent.

He looked up from his reverie to realize his secretary still stood there expectantly.

"What is it, Gerome? I'm tiring of this." He was irritable now. He had expected the man to leave.

"I personally don't believe this is a good idea, sir. I would recommend waiting much longer before implementation. There are so many loose ends, so many avenues that can, and probably will backfire, knowing human error. It will be impossible to cover up the operation should anything go wrong. The contagion could become widespread. You might even be in danger yourself, sir."

Victor laughed. "Nonsense, Gerome. Trust me. I know exactly what I'm doing."

Chapter 34

Searching

Just as we were finally settling into a routine without Phil, this happens. Now I'm anxious all over again. Not that I quit worrying, but I don't know what to make of this.

We have a note. We were out in the pasture all day yesterday, all of us, exercising the horses. Having such fun we could almost forget Phil wasn't with us. Though lately I've begun to think of him as with us in spirit. It might be morbid of me, to assume his death like that, but in many ways it's easier for me. Helps me get on with things, keep moving when everything else feels like it's falling apart around me.

Now this note. It came in Phil's own handwriting, addressed to me. Taped to the back door where we all saw it on our way back into the house. Jordan and Kellie got especially excited. It took a while to calm them down. It means he must still be alive, or at the very least, he was recently. We left it there untouched until Peter could scan it for fingerprints. There were none.

Such an enigmatic message though. All about how he can't return to us yet but he's safe and he wants us know that. Nothing to give a clue as to his whereabouts. Nothing even about what he's doing or who he's with. We even tried that trick of reading every other line, to see if there was a hidden message in it. Nothing. He wrote that he loves me and pleaded with me to stay true and faithful and not give up hope. Very like Phil. It was his handwriting and his "voice;" I don't see how it could be a fake. It sounded so much like him.

The police are no help, of course. They're so wary of us. I hate that.

I've put it under my mattress right by my pillow. Nights are the hardest to get through, even when it's been so long since he left. The bed is so empty. I even miss that awful snoring.

And nothing shakes that creepy feeling I get when I think someone came right to our door to deliver it, and not one of us had a clue. I've asked the family to please not leave the house empty or unguarded from now on. The dogs didn't even put up a racket, which is strange. Even if Phil himself had brought it (oh! what a *thought) they would have been so excited. I guess to be fair, three of them were out in the pasture with us, leaving only old Bobbsey close by, and he was probably sleeping in the barn. Still Mimi's ears are keen. I'd have thought she at least would have heard something strange. Oh well. I know. I worry about every little thing, too much. But how can I help that . . . considering?*

All we have now are clues that leave even more questions. No answers, just questions.

Beverly Richardson,
personal journal entry

Alyssa felt absolutely vile about it, but the next evening she walked the three miles to Margret's factory to see if she could replace her. It would be a job, at least, a chance at earning some income. She spent the morning making the promised cold tomato soup for the manager, and took it to him on her way out. He was not pleasant and made reference to the possibility of her trading sexual favors rather than currency. It made her wish even more fervently for some real money, some cash, just enough to get her by.

The place smelled of machinery, oil and human sweat. The foreman pointed to a large sign above Alyssa's head when she stated her request. It said, "NO POSITIONS AVAILABLE."

"I'm here to take Margret's place," she said. "She's left town. Won't be back. She didn't have time to tell you she'd be quitting."

"Margret who?"

She hesitated. "Probably went by DeVray," she said.

She remembered seeing that surname on Margret's pay stubs. It was not the children's surname, she was sure; Margret called herself by several different names. She hoped she had picked the correct one.

The foreman looked it up on a computer terminal and grunted. "You sure she left?"

"I'm sure."

"How do I know you know?" His eyebrows were bushy. He lowered them to indicate his disbelief.

"I'm her best friend," she said, faltering, wondering what she would say next. She had no proof. "Has she ever missed work before? Check your records. She even came in when she was sick, just to keep her job. She wouldn't pull a no-show, not unless she was gone. Her ex-husband found her and she had to get out of town fast to save herself and her kids. He was going to kidnap them, or worse."

The foreman raised one of the bushy eyebrows and typed some commands into the computer.

"You're right," he said after a minute. "Perfect record. Hate to lose those. Not many of 'em." He sighed. "But that don't tell me *you're* qualified. Says here she got six awards for turning out the highest quotas while she was here. Those ain't easy to come by either. Looks to me like she was fast and good. What you got? You know how to work an industrial sewing machine?"

"No," she said, biting her lip. "But I'm here. Who else have you got?"

He laughed out loud. "Lady," he said after he calmed down, "That's the best joke I heard in a long time. We post a notice saying we got even one opening, and we'll have a line three blocks long in less than a hour."

"Will any of those people be any more qualified than me?" she asked. "Are they here to fill the empty slot? Nobody else'll come till morning. I'm ready to work now."

"You're a stubborn one, ain't you," he said.

She just looked at him.

"Shoot, lady, I ain't got nobody who can train you tonight anyways."

"My *name* is Alyssa," she said firmly. "Can't I at least watch and learn?"

"No. I can't be liable for any accidents. You get hurt back there and tomorrow you turn around and sue me blind. Forget it."

"I'll sign a release."

"What part of "no" don't you understand?" he said, grumpily. "I ain't got nobody free to train you tonight. Job'll be posted tomorrow morning. You be here at 7:30 in line like everybody else, to fill out your application. *If* it's posted. We might just see if we can get along without her. Might decide not to fill it at all, see? Now go on."

"That's all?"

"Yep. Go on. Come back in the morning and check the board for any postings."

"I'll be here," she said, and left.

She considered staying there and sleeping against the building. It would be three miles again home and then three back. But it wasn't safe. The area near the factory was much more dangerous than her own neighborhood. There were good reasons Margret carried a handgun. So she walked all the way back and set her alarm clock, already tired, wondering how Margret had walked that route nearly every day.

****

She slept through the alarm, waking up at 8:00, and cursed when she saw what time it was. She was supposed to *be* there half an hour ago. Well, she would have to get there as soon as she could.

When she arrived she found no long line to stand in. She went inside and found someone who looked like a secretary.

"Is the night foreman here?" she asked.

"Jim? No, he leaves at six," the woman said. "What do you need? I'm the day shift supervisor."

"I talked to him last night about a possible opening."

"We have a hiring freeze going on, were you aware of that?"

"Yes, but my friend, Margret DeVray, she worked here and had to leave town suddenly, and he said if I came back in the morning I might—"

"Hiring freeze means *freeze*, Miss," she said. "I don't know what Jim thought he was telling you, but he knows as well as I do that when we lose somebody we have the others work harder to pick up the slack. It's tough, but that's the way it is. We get our profits back up in a few months and maybe we can talk to you." Her demeanor was crisp and businesslike.

"I don't have a few months," she said. "Are you sure? I mean, Jim said—"

"Jim's an idiot," the woman said, interrupting again.

"So I came all the way back here for nothing."

"Guess so."

Alyssa sighed.

"Have a nice day," the woman said. "Better luck somewhere else."

"Yeah, right."

****

Her legs were already tired, having walked nine miles in less than twelve hours. She didn't want walk all the way back home right then only to twiddle her thumbs and do nothing, so she sat outside the building and rested, feeling frustrated and irritable. Just in case she had to wait in line all day, she had thrown together a backpack with some lunch in it. She opened it now, pulled out a package of cookies and munched on them. Ash had been generous, but hadn't given Alyssa any choice in the matter. The food she got consisted mostly of whatever Ash had left over after the clearance sale. The cookies weren't exactly tasty, or fresh, but they sated her hunger for the moment.

After the snack settled in her stomach like a small, hard rock, she remembered it was August. She was due for her next shot, and it was the second Tuesday, Clinic day. The clinic was not too far from here, she guessed. She still thought it silly to bother, but as there was always the risk of being discovered, and since she had nothing else to do, she headed in the direction of the Clinic.

Paula was the nurse on duty. Margret liked Paula very much, and in times past, she and Alyssa would sit and chat with her afterwards, purposely arriving when it would be near her lunch break so they could visit longer. Margret had known her first, but Alyssa was glad to see her there. Her presence made her pointless morning venture a little brighter. She hadn't thought about Paula in a while, and during the walk from the factory to the Clinic she wondered if she would even be working today.

She told Paula all about how Margret had gone so abruptly, and filled her in on all the other events of the last few months since they had seen each other.

"It's so sad she's gone, just like that," Paula said, as she withdrew the needle from Alyssa's arm, carefully placing a bandage on it.

"I know," Alyssa said, watching. The stuff was cold going in and she never could get used to it. She rubbed her arm to warm it up. "I didn't think he'd ever be able to find her. She thought it must've been someone at work."

"Could be," Paula said. "Anything for money, eh?"

"Really," Alyssa said. "Glad I'm not like that anymore."

"Used to be?"

"Well, I wouldn't do anything, no, but money was important to me. Now I'll just be happy if I can find a job. Any openings here?"

Paula smiled. "This is a Federal job, remember," she said. "Gotta have full citizenship."

"Oh, yeah, I forgot," Alyssa said, feeling sheepish.

"Her kids were so cute," Paula said. "Remember last time, when Natty got herself all tangled up in that blood pressure cuff?"

"Yeah." Alyssa grinned. "I'd have left her there, myself, if it weren't for the racket she put up."

Paula laughed. "Yeah, she had quite a set of lungs on her, didn't she?"

She sat down next to Alyssa, her expression turning serious. "Hey, you ever thought about having children of your own, you know, someday?"

"I've thought about it, sure, but I haven't thought highly of it. I don't

think I'd do a great job of it. Margret . . . she was a natural. Not me."
She shook her head.

"So you'd be fine, maybe, if you never had any?"

"Probably. I don't know. I could change my mind, I guess." Alyssa
tried a small smile. "I doubt it . . . But I do miss those kids. More than I
thought I would. Why?"

"It eases my conscience," she said. "A little."

"Hey, these are *voluntary* shots, remember?" Alyssa laughed, trying
to lighten Paula's mood.

She looked so sad all of a sudden. They both knew the shots were
hardly "voluntary," though it was made to appear that way.

"Yeah," Paula said, her look unchanged, and sighed. "I shouldn't tell
you this, and you've got to promise not to tell anybody else . . ."

"I hate sentences that start that way," Alyssa said, trying to be
lighthearted.

"But the thing is, these shots? After your fourth one, you're sterile."

"Excuse me?"

"Yeah. It's illegal to tell you though, so I've just, like, committed a
crime here. But I thought you ought to know."

"So why are you telling me now?"

"I like you," Paula said. She shrugged her shoulders. "Thought you
ought to know."

"So what you're saying is these shots have made me sterile for life?"
Alyssa rubbed at her arm again.

She felt heavy and dark inside, a foreboding feeling.

"Yeah, see, what we give you here is more than the standard
hormonal treatment normal citizens take. They add a toxin to this stuff
that kills your eggs. Takes three or four doses, but it always works."

"Why?" she asked in disbelief.

Paula shrugged again. "They're serious about not wanting you guys
to reproduce, I guess."

"Why do we have to keep coming then?" Alyysa asked. This was her
seventh shot, she thought, trying to add the visits together in her head.
Or was it eight? Nine? She had lost track. At any rate, the damage was
done.

"Gotta keep up the appearance, you know."

"Well, why is it only women? That's unfair."

"Most men are snipped," she said, making a scissors-like motion with
her fingers. "It's still not foolproof, though, and a lot of them won't go for
it. Those who don't are supposed to take the pills every week, but we

don't always know whether they do or not. So it's harder to regulate. No guy's gonna come all the way here every single week so we can watch them take a pill they could just as well take at home. Plus if they stop taking them they go back to their normal counts again. They still haven't developed a reliable male shot."

"I guess I didn't know that," Alyssa said, her mood increasingly glum.

"So, with the men, we try our best, but it's a sure shot with the women." Paula lowered her voice even further. "And I heard about these tests they tried, doing the same kind of sneaky sterilization thing on a guy, but there were these *really* noticeable side effects. Like some guys' *huevos* shriveled right up to nothing. Can you imagine keeping that a secret?"

Paula grinned mischievously, closing up her hand while she spoke, as though holding a shrinking object.

With a half smile, Alyssa said, "I see your point."

"Talk about rioting in the streets!" Paula laughed. "So they haven't figured out a convenient way to get away with it, that's all. I'll bet they're still working on it." She took a deep breath. "Anyway. You still gotta come back in November. Keep up appearances. Else they'll start getting suspicious . . . either of me, or you."

"Did Margret know?" Alyssa asked.

"No," Paula said. "But then, she's got kids. I don't feel so bad about it when a gal's had a chance to have babies already. Mostly, I don't think about it much. I just do what I'm paid to do. But I hate my job when it's gals like you coming in. Your whole life's in front of you and all. Never married, never had babies yet." She sighed. "That's when I feel bad. So I feel better knowing you weren't planning on having a dozen someday. Know what I mean?"

"Yeah, I guess I see your point."

"In fact, you're the only one I ever told in seven years working here. Don't ruin my career for me, huh? I got kids to feed too."

"I won't," Alyssa said. "Don't worry."

"Figured I could trust you. You seem the quiet type."

Alyssa nodded her head.

She went straight back home after that, feeling worn out, tired, and heavy. It was as though she had lost something she never quite wanted, but it struck her as a painful loss nonetheless. Two years ago she might have been ecstatic. But after caring for Marcus and Natalie, becoming like an aunt or a second mother to them, this news struck her far more deeply than she would ever have expected.

All the rest of the day she sat on her bed, replaying the conversation with Paula over and over in her mind. She tried mentally replaying the events of the morning differently than they had actually played themselves out. Imagining what might've happened if she had come directly home. If she had forgotten about the clinic altogether. If she just hadn't gone in today, had forgotten, done something else. But she knew that if Paula had never said anything, the situation would still be the same. Even if she hadn't gone today, the damage was done, long ago. Today's shot was literally unnecessary. She just wouldn't have known.

She wondered which scenario she preferred. Neither way changed the facts. Not knowing the truth didn't change the truth. That much was absolute. She kept coming back to that thought.

Her thoughts and her sense of loss circled around each other until she finally fell asleep, fatigued but restless. Her dreams were fitful, resonant with shadowy images of shriveled eggs and nests without young.

When morning came, Alyssa awoke in her clothes on top of her covers. She felt uneasy, with a sudden acute distaste for the place. There were no jobs here. She remembered the manager's allusions to letting her stay for sex instead of cash. The thought revolted her. She couldn't live that kind of life. Not ever, especially not with *him*. Her stomach turned as she pictured it. She shuddered, shaking the awful images away.

Slowly she got to her feet, all the while wondering why she even wanted to get out of bed. Part of her wanted to curl up and stay there all day. Doing anything seemed utterly pointless. But she was too restless. It was like having an itch without knowing where to scratch it.

Before she realized what she was doing, she began packing things into her tattered duffel bag. She crammed in as much of her remaining food as she could carry, a few utensils, a change of clothes. Vaguely she realized she intended to leave, and that she was going away with even less than she had when she arrived. It was too lonely without Margret. There were other friends, acquaintances. But it was as though a light had burned out. Life here felt gray and dull now, as though all the color had been washed out of her life.

She went outside, lugging her duffel bag without even a backward glance at her apartment. She even left the door open and the key on the kitchen table so the manager could find it, whenever he bothered to check. Anyone who needed her other things could have them. She had no way of carrying more.

She slumped down on the sidewalk and leaned against the brick of the building, suddenly feeling too heavy to do anything else. She had no idea what she was doing. She only knew she wanted to get away, somewhere. Where, she didn't know, but it was time to move on.

Mary made her way to Alyssa's side of the block with her empty shopping cart, calling her incessant cry of "*Caps! Caps for sale. Fifty cents a cap.*" Her short blond wig was askew. Alyssa thought maybe she had put it on backwards today. She caught sight of Alyssa looking her way and stopped.

"Excuse me, miss," Mary said. "Have you seen my baby? Surely you have . . ."

Alyssa furrowed her brows and shook her head. "No, Mary, I haven't seen any baby." She didn't know what else to say. They had been through this before, more than once, and just now talking about babies made Alyssa even more irritable. *Lost babies.* She felt angry. She wanted Mary to go away.

"Are you sure?"

"Yes, Mary, I'm sure."

"You know, it was my baby's favorite book. *Caps for Sale.* I can't find that book anymore. Have you seen it?"

Again Alyssa shook her head.

"You haven't seen my little baby either? Do you think he took the book with him?"

"I'm sorry, I don't know."

Mary took up the call again and continued around the block without another word to Alyssa.

In the background Bert suddenly began to sing in his powerful baritone, "*Mary had a baby, Yes, Lord. Mary had a baby, Yes, my Lord. The people keep a'comin' and the train done gone . . .*"

It was too much.

Alyssa wandered that morning, leaving the familiar neighborhood of Mary and Bert and their eerie behavior. She knew that once Bert got to singing he wouldn't stop until he fell asleep, which would be quite some time. He seemed wide awake. It saddened her and made her even more anxious to go. She wished she could help them, but there was nothing, nothing she could do. She was certain of that now.

She shouldered her duffel bag and walked, relieved when she had gone far enough she could no longer hear Bert's voice. She wondered why she had felt so uneasy. Part of her couldn't stand living around that street anymore. On the practical side, she thought, no one there threw away much food. She had to find a neighborhood with restaurants, or more income, anything that would mean more to eat. More food discarded. Her supplies would not hold out forever. And there had to be a job somewhere, if she could just find it.

She wandered for days in an easterly direction, purposeless, dirty, having nowhere to shower or clean herself and few places to take care of her other physical needs. Her food was gone within a week. After two, she could no longer keep track of what day it was. She was weak, frequently dizzy and rapidly became gaunt where she had merely been thin before.

Forced to focus only on finding her next meal, her hope of finding employment soon faded. Her sense of purpose and direction clouded with malnutrition. She thought of little but survival. If she thought of more, of all the things she might have been or done, it made her too sad, too heavy to move. Dreams she once had were lost forever. Memories of friends and companions she once enjoyed were like vague dreams, unfounded in reality.

Many made their homes on the street. She wasn't the only one living there, though she rarely spoke to anyone. They were mostly the mentally ill, the handicapped and genetic testing subjects who had been released. Some had been physically maimed by hospitals extracting their cruel form of payment from those who couldn't afford to pay with cash. They were missing hands, a foot, eyes. Some had strange scars. The rich never had to wait long for donors any more.

All these things were done *legally*, in the name of freedom. Freedom to buy anything with money. Freedom to do anything to those who had none or little. Freedom for the rich, perhaps. It made her ill. Soon the word *legal*, the very idea, made her cringe.

In several quarters she passed, she heard the marching of soldiers in the street, gathering recruits. At such times, she hid until she could hear their marching no longer.

There would be war soon. The crackle of it was in the air. She could feel it all around her, a tense kind of excitement. Hatred for the Arabs and their allies for holding back their precious petroleum had grown strong and thick, massaged by the government into a call for vengeance, a cry of wrongs that required redress. The current fiscal depression would end only if they would sell at a fair price. And if they couldn't be persuaded to sell, then oil could be taken by force. Only then would life get back to normal, back to the good old days when driving a car was neither a luxury nor a privilege, available to the poorest of citizens.

The American military was certain to win. It was stronger and more technologically advanced. A swift conquest awaited, the proud eagle swooping down on its prey to claim the easy victory. So all the news programs said. They announced it with confidence, as casually as if they were stating the odds on an upcoming sporting event.

She read the signs on all the public notice boards, advertisements that made the armed services look so attractive. Enticing, almost. She would stare at the posters for long periods and wonder. It would be a job. It was money, reinstated citizenship, which meant food, shelter, a home, possibly even new friends. She could create a false identity for herself, start over fresh. And if she survived the experience, she might come out of it far better off than she was now.

Sometimes it sorely tempted her. She would stand there, staring at a poster, imagining herself in uniform, having a bed to sleep in, a blanket to cover her, and plenty of food just given to her three times a day.

It was an alluring thought to her starving body and soul, until she remembered how the same government had stripped her of her dearest friends. Then she thought of the others who shared the homeless life with her, strangers she passed every day. Most of them had been injured in some way by a society that utterly failed to help them or harmed by a ruthless government in some experiment to advance the cause of medicine, a medicine now entirely devoted to diseases of the rich.

These were things the media would never unveil. The rich, and even the pleasantly comfortable, never asked how it was that medical science had progressed so rapidly in recent years. They didn't know of the rampant testing on human subjects. It was a terrible, well-kept secret.

But Alyssa knew. She saw the results of it firsthand, and overheard the stories people told one another on the street. Stories of being enticed by offers of large sums of money for participating in a simple study, participation that sounded no more difficult than answering questions for a survey. But the money never came. Instead they received strange illnesses, lost capabilities, sometimes even death.

At these times, she remembered how they had deprived her of her own body's precious gift, the repeated doses of toxin injected inside her body to kill her ova. She felt consumed by an irrational surge of rage. She would stand in front of the posters, rubbing her arm where the shots had pierced her, until she spat on the ground and told herself again, *Some things aren't worth it for any amount of money.*

Spitting like that was a strange habit she had picked up from

Margret. Sometimes she remembered that her mother would be mortified if she saw it. The thought usually made her spit twice.

She calmed herself by remembering that motherhood was never something she desired in the first place. She was probably better off this way. But that choice should have been hers to make, and hers alone. When she thought of that she became angry all over again.

She cycled through this torrent of thoughts, until she came back to what she told herself the last night she had spent in her apartment: *Not knowing the truth doesn't change the truth.*

But knowing the truth was better.

She carried the thought a step further, looking beyond herself. If the public knew the truth, the real truth, about what the government was doing to the poor, maybe things could be changed. Maybe some of the needless suffering could be stopped.

Of course, the public would have to *care* first.

And would they? she wondered. There was no way for her to know whether anything would be done to alter the situation if it became public knowledge. Outside these slums, in spite of the current rationing talk and shortages, would the people living in relative comfort be willing to give up their medical advancements, their rapid organ transplants; would they want to share their health care, their food, their clothing? Would they share such things freely with her and the other homeless with whom she shared the streets, those who had no citizenship and no rights, nothing to give in return, no way to pay? Could they be made to understand who the poor were, that they were good people, her friends, her only real family?

She doubted a positive outcome, remembering well the person she used to be. She knew how easy it had been to ignore those in less fortunate circumstances; knew how much store she had once put in material possessions. She knew she'd been exactly like the majority, concerned only with self and personal gain.

And with the government's behind-the-scenes control of the press, even releasing the truth was impossible. She had no power to change even the smallest thing.

She knew she could never sell herself to serve this country, this government that was so far debased from its original design, a dark shadow of what America had once been.

It wasn't always so. She remembered things Debra taught her, in the days before they parted. In the past, atrocities like those she saw on the streets today would never have been permitted. There had once been soup kitchens and "missions" to the homeless where food, a bed and a shower could be had on occasion. She knew that from stories she heard at Hall Meetings. But these had all been run by religions, religions now declared enemies of the state.

All too frequently, her thoughts cycled back to Debra. Her soul cried out for her companionship, to see her face again, to cry on her shoulder as she had once done. At these times, she was more lonesome than she could bear.

Chapter 35

New Hope

And the multitude of them that believed were of one heart and of one soul: neither said any of them that aught of the things which he possessed was his own; but they had all things common.

And with great power gave the apostles witness of the resurrection of the Lord Jesus: and great grace was upon them all.

Neither was there any among them that lacked: for as many as were possessors of lands or houses sold them, and brought the prices of the things that were sold,

And laid them down at the apostles' feet: and distribution was made unto every man according as he had need.

Acts of the Apostles 4:32-35,
Holy Bible (KJV)

"Can I bring you a pillow?" Jon asked.

"I already have six." Debra laughed.

"Footstool?"

"Got it," she said.

She sat comfortably on their couch nursing their new son. Sunlight streamed through a large picture window in their living room that looked out on a pleasant neighborhood of townhouses. It was a small place, but cheery with plenty of light, on the end of a building of four units.

"Is he eating all right?" he asked from the kitchen, where he worked to finish up the breakfast dishes.

"Jon, come sit down," Deb said. "You're too nervous."

"I know," he said, drying his hands on a towel. "He's gaining fast enough. But I worry, Deb, I mean, the lab hasn't been able to come up with a good baby formula yet. If he wasn't nursing well . . ."

"You worry too much," she said, laughing again. "This system's been working since the dawn of time." She patted the cushion next to her. "Come on, sit down. Besides, Jane Parker's baby is doing fine on goat's milk. If anything goes wrong, we can go that way."

"I know, but it seems so unsanitary."

"Oh, please. It's pasteurized. It's not like they let her drink it straight out of the udder."

Jon laughed. "I guess you're right." He came over to her and sat down, putting his arm around her. "You thirsty?" he said. "Let me get you a drink of water." He popped back up.

"Jon."

He sat down again. "Okay. I'm here."

"You've got the day off and you're not on call. Just relax. *Be* with me."

He sighed. "I'm sorry, honey. I feel so lost. I mean, I'm used to being the one giving other people advice, and now I feel like I don't know anything at all."

"Feeling's mutual," Deb said. "But just look at him."

They were silent as they watched the baby. His skin was newborn-soft, and he had dark black hair. His eyes were open and intent on his business, his tiny fists clenched up with the effort of eating as he made small suckling noises with loud swallows in between.

"He'll be all right, Jon," she said.

"Yeah," he agreed. "Little Zack. I can't believe he's ours. And finally here." He reached over and stroked Zack's tiny fingers. The baby moved his hand away with a grunt. Jon laughed. "Look at that, it's like he's saying 'Don't bug me, Dad, can't you see I'm busy?'"

"Mm-hmm," Deb said, and leaned her head back against the couch, closing her eyes.

"Sleepy, hon?" Jon asked.

She nodded.

"You know I worried so much about you in those last weeks before delivery."

Deb made a little laugh, keeping her eyes shut. "You worried enough for both of us. I hardly got a chance to do my own worrying." She looked over at him and smiled, then leaned into his strong shoulder. "I can't believe it's been six weeks. But then every day seems to go by so slowly, as though these few weeks have lasted a year. It's weird."

"That's probably because we're awake nearly twice as long. Makes the day feel longer."

"You mean, *I'm* awake nearly twice as long," she said.

"I get up with him too."

"I know, I'm just teasing. But you don't spend the entire night trying to satisfy his monster appetite," she said.

"I know. Debra." He paused. "I'm sorry for worrying so much. I know I bugged you. I was so afraid of something going wrong."

"You need to work on your faith," Deb said, nudging him with her elbow. "I always felt everything would be all right. From the beginning."

Jon sighed. "True, but the hospital's so new. We're still trying to figure out where to get all the medicine we need, not to mention equipment, and—"

"Hey. I couldn't imagine a better place to deliver. They've done a great job pulling together that birthing room. Think about all the places our ancestors had to have babies. 'Course I can't imagine going through that process in the back of an ox-drawn wagon, like Jane Manning James."

"I can't imagine it either."

"So I count my blessings. We have it pretty good," she said. "All the nurses told me it was a great delivery."

"It was," Jon said. "Nothing unexpected. By the book."

Deb laughed. "Maybe for you! As for me, I don't think I'm ready to go through it again for a long while, even if this little guy's worth every bit of it." She looked down at him. His eyes fluttered closed. His suckling noises were slowing. "But it's been a hard year."

"It has," Jon said.

"A hard two years," she added, and sighed.

"But good ones."

"Now that's true."

Zack dropped away from his mother and lay fast asleep on her lap. Debra lifted his tiny body up carefully, with one hand holding up his head, rested him across her shoulder and chest, and pulled her shirt down with the other hand. Then she leaned back into Jon. He wrapped his muscular arm tightly around her shoulder.

"Who'd have thought it would be so hard?" Deb said. "Two years, and we're still having trouble figuring out the basics, from design and construction, to how to route the electricity, to the Storehouse and division of labor and how all the property sharing is supposed to work. I don't think even Nauvoo took this long to build and organize, and they had to drain a swamp."

"We've got our own place now," Jon said.

"Sure, after twelve months with your folks. Or mine. I thought that bouncing back and forth would never end. And I still feel lucky just to have electricity and running water."

Gently, she patted the baby's back. He responded with a burp and a little grunt as he snuggled his dark head into his mother's shoulder.

"There," she said to him. Then to Jon, "I still miss having a microwave. Isn't that petty of me?"

"I know you do," he said. "It's hard going without the basics. We've all gotten soft, too used to technology doing our work for us. When they built Nauvoo they weren't trying to wire the town for electricity and phone lines, let alone digital cable."

Deb smiled. "I know. It's just so frustrating to know that anywhere in any other city there are microwaves for sale everywhere and we can't just go get one."

"Deb," he said.

"I know, I know. Remember the Dalton's. Well, Don was pretty stupid about it."

"You're not saying they got what they deserved . . ."

"Of course not! The whole thing was horribly unfair. But they were still pretty stupid to go trotting off after a new television just because Nadine couldn't *stand* to live without one of her own. I mean there's a big difference between a TV and a microwave, don't you think?"

"Not really," Jon said. "They're both conveniences."

"TV is for entertainment," Deb said. "A microwave helps me cook. *Your* dinners, I might add."

He laughed. "All right, all right."

"And stealing money out of the treasury vault for it was just plain wrong. No means no, you don't get one, and that's that."

"We all know that," he said. "I wonder how they thought they were going to hide it from everybody once they got back with the thing."

Deb laughed. "Really." After a pause she said, "And the biggest shame is that we never got the money back, either."

"Debra!" Jon scolded.

"Well?"

"It wasn't their fault their bus was stopped and inspected on the way home."

"Well, I wonder why," Deb said. "From the stories we heard it sounded like they practically announced where they were headed. Even the driver could've tipped off the authorities, for all we know. We're all lucky they didn't have someone follow them all the way here."

"You're right there," Jon said. "But what's done is done."

"Yeah." She sighed.

"You know as soon as there's enough in the treasury for everyone to have a microwave, they'll order them," Jon said. "It's just a matter of time. We have to be patient. They have a priority list. First things first."

"What if no one wants to sell them to us? What if they think an order for hundreds of microwaves is some kind of subversive Mormon plot? You know? Like, we're going to take them all apart and make a weapon to blow up the world."

"Then we'll deal with that when the time comes. Worst comes to worst, honey, you may never see a microwave again the rest of your life. You should plan on that and move on. You know, I'm more surprised you've been all right so far without air conditioning."

"Oh, come on. I don't know what we were thinking when we planned to have this baby in August. That was so miserable. Thank goodness it's cooling off."

"I never heard you complain," Jon said.

Deb smiled and looked up at him. "The Lord did." Her smile turned into a broad grin, then she sighed. "You were worried enough. You didn't need more to fuss over."

She patted the baby's back some more, and he gurgled in his sleep.

Jon smiled back. "You got me again."

"At least this wasn't the first summer without it," she said. "You do get used to going without it, after a while."

"Same goes for a microwave."

"You know what I miss most?"

"What?"

"Alyssa."

"I had a feeling you were going to say that."

She sighed. "I keep torturing myself wondering if there was something I could have said . . ."

"Deb, honey, this life wouldn't have been her style."

"I know. I've resigned myself to that. She'd have a rough time without the creature comforts she's used to. But I can wish, and I wish there was some way to know if she's all right. That she's safe, or happy, or even if something terrible has happened . . . I just wish I knew."

"I know," Jon said.

"And then I have days where I'm not sure I want to know after all. Maybe it's easier believing she found a great place and got a great job and everything's fine. But if that were the case, I have to think she'd have found a way to call, or something. Don't you think we'd have heard, at least by now, if she was all right?"

"Deb . . ."

She sighed. "I mean, I pray for her still. I ask for her to be kept safe if she's still out there, but I can't bring myself to ask whether she is or not. I just can't. Because if she isn't . . ."

"Deb." He spoke more tenderly this time. "Sometimes, some things, you just have to let go."

"I know, Jon. But it's so hard."

"I've had to leave things behind, too. I know it's not easy."

"Missing your remote control again?" She nudged him, trying to lighten the mood. "How many men have you treated for 'twitching thumb syndrome,' huh?"

"Plenty." He smiled. "But no, I don't miss it. I meant not having the chance to finish school at New Hopkins and get that official seal of approval. Sure I'm practicing medicine here, sooner than I expected I would, and there are excellent doctors and researchers here to continue my training—hailing from some of the best schools—but it's just not the same."

"I know how much Jerry means to you," she said.

"Yeah, he's been the best mentor I could ask for. But no other hospital in the world will ever recognize me as a qualified physician, not to mention surgeon. Ever."

"Honey, you'll never live anywhere else. Nowhere else in the world will recognize you as being sane." She smiled.

"You're right. So I know it doesn't matter, but I do miss that sometimes." He paused. "Overall? The big picture? I'm so happy to be with you, and to have Zack with us, our own little family. You mean everything to me, Deb. I'd be lost without you. I mean that."

"Jon, you're getting misty."

"No I'm not," he said, wiping his eyes under his glasses.

"Yes, you are." She laughed. "That's okay. Me too." She looked down at the baby and wiped her own eyes, then looked back up. "I love you, Jon."

"I love you too."

She kissed him, and they fell asleep on the couch for a late morning nap.

Chapter 36

Riot

> Victor: *Have we reached our quota of infantry yet, Gerome?*
>
> Gerome: *Almost, sir. We're stepping up the draft procedures even as we speak.*
>
> Victor: *Good. Very good. Are the tactical armies all moved out to the southeast? Only enlisted men should be in those troops.*
>
> Gerome: *Yes, sir, enlisted voluntary according to Presidential specs. The General reports all tactical troops are settling in, camps are in place.*
>
> Victor: *Good. We start tonight. Tell the technicians to initiate Operation Purify, Underground Sequence, Phase One.*

Office of Victor Caldwell,
transcript of security camera tape

The day came, in the chill of an early fall morning, when Alyssa awoke after sleeping uncomfortably on the sidewalk, and realized she would die if something didn't change soon.

Her survival instincts were strong. There had to be some way to change her circumstances, something, somewhere. It was always just around the next corner. Giving up was not in her mind. She would keep looking, searching, until she found it.

But she was short of breath. The night before she vomited the tidbits of molded food she found in a dumpster, after trying desperately to keep them down. In the light of morning she returned to the same trash heap to see what else it might hold. The stench didn't bother her now; she no longer noticed it. There must be something edible in there, she was sure of it. If there wasn't . . . She had exhausted the other bins in the vicinity.

She hoped for a stroke of luck, that someone might have thrown out something fresh this morning. Every passing day made her weaker, less able to travel, to search for new sources of food. She was driven solely by her hunger now, a fierce need that begged to be satiated.

Intent on her rummaging, she ignored the sounds in the main street around the corner from her. It was dim in the alleyway.

"You look strong enough," a gruff voice said behind her.

Alyssa jumped and turned around, then fell into a sitting position on the cement. Her hips hurt. She scooted back into the steel of the dumpster with another thud when she saw who, or rather what, addressed her.

A soldier in full uniform and holding a rifle pointed directly at her chest stood facing her in the alley.

"I . . . I'm not very strong," she said in a tiny voice, wiping a stray wisp of hair out of her eyes.

Her own voice sounded strange to her, but it was all she could muster in her shock. She felt paralyzed, looking from one side to the other. There was nowhere she could run, even if she had her full strength. She couldn't escape the barrel of that rifle. She swallowed hard.

"No sense arguing. Evaluations come later. You're coming with me."

She didn't need to ask why. Slowly she stood up. Hunger gnawed in her belly.

"Do they feed you well, in the army?" she asked as she walked in the direction the rifle indicated.

He didn't answer. They walked, she in front, out of the alley into the main square. Once there had been a beautiful fountain there. It hadn't seen water in years, and the bronze statuary in the center was crusted over with bird droppings and mineral deposits.

There were soldiers everywhere. Alyssa couldn't believe she hadn't heard their approach. They must have moved quietly. That would be necessary, she realized, as the "drafting" continued. The rumors she had overheard were increasingly bizarre.

An old woman peeked out from behind a curtain in one building they passed. The face vanished so quickly from the window she wasn't sure she had seen it.

The soldiers were rounding up a large group of potential recruits in the middle of the square, north of the fountain. Some came out of apartment buildings with their charges. Some of these were handcuffed.

Alyssa was surprised. For some reason she thought only people like her, caught out on the street, were at risk. She hadn't heard of people being pulled from their homes.

Not all the charges were as compliant about going with their captors as she was. A shot rang out from somewhere and a man went down on the other side of the square. She barely caught the movement before it was over. It made her extremely nervous.

"How can you do this?" she asked the soldier behind her. "It doesn't bother you to round up other human beings like, like cattle?"

"Hardly human," the soldier said with contempt. "Look at you. Eating trash. Disgusting."

"Like I have a—"

"It's not hard at all." There was menace in his tone, and she imagined him grinning behind her.

"How do you expect me to go out and be like that? That hard? Or any of us? I won't be able to—"

"Training. Sims. Virtuals. Good stuff . . . it's a rush. Look, I ain't supposed to talk to you. Shut up or I'll shoot you right here. Nobody'll check me out. I just say you resisted."

She didn't ask any more questions.

They arrived at the gathering point where she was shoved roughly into the midst of a growing group of civilians. The infantry took their places surrounding them, rifles held ready to fire. The crowd was unruly, not silent or cooperative. Alyssa wished they would shut their mouths and hold still.

She smiled at the irony. They resisted, while all her daydreams of courageously resisting the draft, her high ideals, her imagined haughty refusal to be coerced into service, had vanished as soon as the reality presented itself. Bravery was out of the question. Couldn't they see that?

Some of the men around her started whispering to one another, something about an escape plan.

"Frank, we're going t'all push east. Got that? On my mark."

This frightened her more than walking with the soldier. "You're going to get us all killed," she hissed.

She was surprised it came out of her mouth. She felt too weak, too mousy and small, to do anything. The dizziness she had come to expect lately had returned, and it was hard to stand up. But the group was too crowded and close for her to sit down. If she couldn't stay standing she would certainly be trampled.

"It's die now or die later, babe," someone said from behind her, kicking her in the back of the knees. "I'd rather go now, fighting for a cause I believe in."

Regaining her balance only by the press of the crowd, she didn't do the man the courtesy of turning to see who had kicked her. She refused to look over her shoulder.

She never thought her childhood training on how to avoid her mother's blows would come in handy in her adult life. Reflex taught her now. Hold still. Be quiet. Avoid attracting attention. Above all, listen carefully. Her ears twitched, trying to gather in all the information possible about her situation, her location in the crowd.

She was dizzy. Her mind struggled to come up with a plan, what to do if the crowd bolted, visualizing different outcomes. All the outcomes she saw ended with spilled blood. She desperately hoped she could come up with some plan that would avoid it being *her* blood.

A man with medals on his uniform stood before a podium and adjusted a microphone. Alyssa assumed he must be in charge of this recruiting endeavor. He began to speak.

"We've graciously gathered you here this morning . . ."

His voice was drowned out by shouts from the crowd, but he continued to make his speech. Alyssa could only catch parts of it. It was standard. The same paragraphs written on all the propaganda posters, nearly word-for-word. "Benefits are greater than any you enjoy here . . . Resistance is an open manifestation of treason . . . in these desperate times we have Presidential authority . . ."

The crowd was getting worse. She tried to shift herself toward an outer edge, then changed her mind and worked her way back into the center. There seemed to be no way out, no way to avoid worse peril if the mob didn't settle itself. And that didn't seem likely. She heard more whispers, saw hand signals. The general plan was to bolt eastward *en masse*.

"Wait," she said aloud, hoping someone would pay attention. "If we all run the same direction we'll be mowed down in minutes!"

"Shut up," someone said.

"You have to run *toward them*," she said, "in all directions. The outer ring will fall, but you'll scatter them. Then overtake them one by one, and take their weapons."

"Those are machine guns, idiot," someone else said.

"Oh," she said. She knew nothing about weaponry. She had thought they were rifles. But she continued. "Well, it's a better shot at coming out of this alive than if we run in a herd. Don't be stupid!"

"She's right," one of the others said, one who had spoken before. "We have to scatter their forces."

She heard more words tossed around between them, but she kept quiet after that as confusion entered into their plans. The military leader droned on above the crowd, reciting the speech by rote, as though he had repeated it so many times the words had lost their meaning.

"As we have now fully explained the consequences of non-compliance to you, we would ask you all to come along quietly. The vans are waiting at Checkpoint 63 where you will be escorted . . ."

At this phrase the people began to chant, *"Ne-ver! Ne-ver! Ne-ver!"* The boom of their collective voices deafened her and she covered her ears. Then the mob bolted.

The majority ran eastward, as first planned. Others ran in every direction. Machine-gun fire echoed through the square, followed by shrieks and screams as people tried to escape the bullets.

Men and women fell before her eyes as she stood paralyzed. All her brain could process was the sight of red everywhere. Red blood splattered onto the sidewalk all around her, red flowing everywhere she looked.

Finally she ran. She didn't know or care which direction. Fear completely overwhelmed her and she ran without thinking, with more energy and adrenaline than she ever imagined she had left. The wind whistled in her ears.

She heard a whining noise behind her. A split second later *something* slammed into her right thigh and carried her through the air at least two meters, forward and a little sideways. Her leg felt ripped out from under her.

She had time to recognize that it felt very strange to move in that manner, and that her right leg was in agonizing, crushing pain. Then her head hit the pavement with a resounding crack, and everything went black.

Chapter 37

The Stranger

A funny thing happened today. I was changing Zack on the bed, and when I straightened up a sharp pain shot through my right leg. It was awful. I almost dropped him! It was a lot worse than that sciatic nerve problem I had while I was pregnant. It went away about as quickly as it came, but my leg's been aching all day. I didn't tell Jon. And I'm not going to, either, unless it comes back. He was doing rounds when it happened. Thank goodness he wasn't home. He'll just worry, and it's probably nothing.

Debra Pike,
personal journal entry

When Alyssa regained consciousness it was chilly and looked like dusk. She was somewhat surprised to find she was still alive.

Pain returned with consciousness, and with it the wish that the shot had killed her. Never had anything hurt like that. It radiated streams of agony through her entire body, little knives running up from her leg to scream into her brain that something was wrong, terribly, terribly wrong.

She was face down on the pavement. Her face felt sticky and moving made her gasp. Trying again, she raised her head, struggling through the intense pain. Slowly she made her arms lift her torso off the ground and righted herself, hissing in agony. After a long moment she managed to roll over and prop herself up. The fabric of her pants stuck to the sidewalk when she turned causing her nearly to pass out. Her vision was blurry, but it cleared after the pain subsided. She felt terribly faint and dizzy.

Alyssa looked down. The puddle of blood frightened her, and it frightened her more when she realized it was *hers*. The pain emanated from her right leg. Dried blood crusted around a large tear in her pants, revealing a sizable wound. That was why the fabric had stuck.

She felt sick, and coughed. If there had been anything in her stomach to bring up, she would have vomited. Realizing it would be too

430

painful, she used great effort to suppress the reaction.

Using her arms, she scooted herself to the wall of the building nearest her. It was a distance the width of the sidewalk, but it felt like miles. As she slid she noticed the square was littered with dead bodies. More than one wore a military uniform. The sight of the carnage didn't help her queasiness. She closed her eyes and concentrated. It was too quiet. The small swishing noise made by the fabric of her pants sliding across the sidewalk seemed to echo around the square.

Finally, she felt the brick wall against her back and rested herself on it, opening her eyes. She leaned over to inspect her wound and feel the back of her leg. The bullet had entered there and gone all the way through. It felt like a very large hole for a bullet. She didn't know much about guns, but Margret had told her about a type of ammunition the troops had begun using which detonated on contact with the target in a miniature explosion. It could penetrate almost anything. It must have been that type of bullet to create this much damage with one shot.

She remembered the flying sensation as she moved through the air. Dimly she realized she had been nowhere near this close to the building before she was hit. From what she could tell, it went straight through her thigh bone, splintering it. Feeling around it she began to weep. Her leg would never work again. That was certain. But it was her least concern. She would die in this spot, whether from loss of blood, infection, or starvation.

Why didn't they just finish me off? she thought idly.

Sobbing was nearly as painful as coughing, but her thoughts tormented her, and hot tears burned her cheeks in spite of her efforts to stop.

Why was I ever alive in the first place? Why didn't I just go home? Was it really worse than this? I could have gone with Debra. Or Rob. Rob would have taken care of me. He loved me. He wouldn't have let this happen to me.

Her vision blurred around the edges and she faded into unconsciousness.

Each time she awoke during the cold night it was with surprise that she was still alive. She lost a lot of blood before the bleeding finally stopped. In a way she wished she didn't have to die now, like this, without dignity or hope. But she was anxious for death to come. At least then the pain would stop. No matter what lay beyond the great mystery of death, she was sure the current pain would end. It must. It had to.

****

Morning came with a fever. She was amazed she had survived the night. She awoke hot, sweaty, panting. The next minute she felt so cold she thought she might freeze to death before starvation took her. Infection must have set in. She shivered violently. The movement irritated the angry gash in her leg and caused her to moan. Then she was hot again.

A few hours later a goonie wearing a sealed yellow rubber environmental suit came by and poked her. It was the type of suit she had seen on television, the kind scientists wore to protect them from radiation, or biohazards.

"I'm here, I'm here," she said. "I'm alive."

"You're injured," he mumbled through the speaker on his face mask. "Do you wish transportation to a hospital?" The standard phrase.

"No," she said, shaking her head.

That would be far worse than death. She would certainly be relieved of her leg, and a variety of other organs, then returned to the street to die an even slower death, if she survived the process at all. It would be better to get it over with here.

He walked on.

She noticed then that there was a whole crew in the square, engaged in the unpleasant task of cleaning up the bodies. She wondered that she hadn't heard them before. They were making quite a commotion, lifting and hauling the corpses, zippered in plastic, into a large military truck. They all wore the sealed environmental suits with face masks. The suits puzzled her, but she couldn't spare the energy to consider why. A soft breeze wafted muffled voices toward her, but she couldn't make out the conversation.

Then she knew why she hadn't heard them. That was it. She had been dreaming, a strange fevered dream in which she was talking to someone. She didn't want to wake up. Was it her father? She had to think. Yes, maybe it was. She missed him suddenly. The emotion overwhelmed her, and she wept again. This time it seemed she would never stop.

She watched through tears as the crew finished loading the truck and sprayed down the square with high-pressure hoses. After a long time, they were ready to go.

" . . . *good enough* . . ." she thought she heard.

One of them pointed in her direction and seemed to ask a question of another one.

" . . . *that one?*"

It was hard to make anything out. Their heavy suits, and the distance, made reading expressions impossible. But she fancied the two were arguing over what to do with her. Would they put her in a zippered bag and take her away as well? Her mind raced with panic.

But they didn't. They stopped pointing, and seemed to resolve the matter without coming toward her. All of them got into the cab of a truck or hung onto the canvas sides. With a roar, the truck shifted into gear and drove away.

After it was gone the street regained its pall of silence.

She wondered if they would come back, if they were waiting for her to die so they could be about their business. Then her body would be a pile of ash to be thrown into the wind. That is, if they came back to collect her at all.

It wasn't a heartening thought. She continued to cry, shaking with new chills, until she faded back into a dream.

****

"Alyssa."

Startled, she raised her head, with great effort, to see who had addressed her. Was it the same day or a new one? What time was it? It must be near evening. The sun was low in the west.

Her dried tears left her skin feeling tight. Had she looked in a mirror, she would have seen where tears left clean crooked streaks down her face, washing away the dried blood, dirt, and filth.

A man knelt on one knee in front of her, looking at her intently. He didn't wear the standard black uniform of a goonie, or a yellow environmental suit. Instead he had on a long pale linen robe, apparently seamless. It had a loose hood woven into it, which covered most of his longish hair but not his face. It was an unusual style of dress. She rubbed at one cheek with the back of her knuckles and stopped, remembering how pointless it was to rub away the grime.

She thought she should be afraid, but instead she felt a strange calm. His face looked vaguely familiar, as though she should know this person, but she couldn't recall having seen him before.

"Alyssa."

She realized she hadn't answered. She opened her mouth, but only a grunt came out. She cleared her throat.

"How do you know my name?"

"I have come to heal you, Alyssa.

She made a noise in her throat that would have been laughter if she had more strength left. She spoke slowly, carefully, each word coming with strenuous exertion.

"This leg will never work again. I'm dying. It's much too late for any cure." She waited for his response.

He continued to watch her. His eyes were unusual, so filled with compassion that she wanted to weep.

"Please," she said, "Please, sir, whatever you do, don't take me to a hospital."

She tried to scoot away, her natural suspicion overcoming the peculiar calm she felt.

"Alyssa," he said. "Arise and walk."

His voice was soft but commanding. His eyes pierced hers with an intensity that couldn't be ignored, as though he could see inside her heart. She couldn't turn away. Something buried deep inside her began to stir.

"What did you say?"

He stretched out his hands to her, and said, "I have watched over you always. I have much yet for you to do, and many have petitioned for my help in your behalf. Now, if you will but believe enough to act on my words, rise up and be whole."

His touch was kind, gentle, entreating. No one had been kind to her for so long.

She thought about his words. Any attempt to get up, much less walk, would not only cause excruciating pain, but could possibly open clotted blood vessels, causing her to bleed to death in minutes. It was foolhardy even to think about it.

But she couldn't resist his request. His eyes, his voice, his presence gave her the most comforting reassurance, a feeling of inner warmth that surpassed anything she had experienced before. She would do it.

What does it matter if it fails?

She put her hands in his and he pulled her carefully to a standing position. With all her weight on her left leg, she stopped and rested against the building.

"Put your weight on both legs," he said.

She felt a persistent throbbing from the infection in her thigh, the shudder of chills from the high fever, and the streaking, radiating blackness of pain from the crushed bone.

"It hurts too much," she gasped.

"Put your weight on it. Go ahead."

She took a breath and quickly shoved half her weight onto her injured leg in one daring effort. It buckled beneath the pressure, and she gasped in pain. His arms pulled her close and held her firmly upright.

"Why are you making me do this?" she wailed, shifting her weight back to her left leg. "What kind of man are you? You want to torture me!"

"I would never do that, Alyssa. Just believe me enough to do what I say."

Again she felt overwhelmed by the love that flooded her in his presence. It was so compelling she shifted her weight again. Waves of pain radiated throughout her body. She shook as the sensations intensified, and her head spun.

I can't do this, please let me die, she meant to say. But she looked down at her leg and stopped, watching in horror as purulent fluid, streaked with blood and filth, flowed from the wound. She thought she might vomit, but she couldn't close her eyes.

The agony increased, and at the same time she felt an excruciating pain in her chest. It was a pain she had denied expression, a pain built up over a lifetime, layer upon layer of emotional damage; but once released, it filled her entire being with a torrent of overwhelming grief.

She let out a strangled cry that was half gasp, half wail. Then she felt an extraordinary calming peace that resonated through her whole soul, helping her ride out the throes of exquisite agony that wracked her body.

Just as she felt she would succumb to death, the remnants of her frail existence caught up, removed from her body to meet death with grace, her vision fading into a colorless gray, the bleeding stopped. Momentarily, she felt an intense itch where the bullet had penetrated, then all discomfort dissipated completely, disappearing into oblivion. She shivered violently as he held her gently in his arms.

"Now, you can walk."

His voice was kind but compelling. She put all her weight on her right leg and balanced on it, expecting pain again from even the smallest movement. Instead she felt nothing. No, not nothing; a sensation that had been lost with the injury. Her hazel-gray eyes went wide.

"I can feel my toes again," she whispered, then smiled. "I can feel my toes!"

She wiggled them inside her tattered shoe and suppressed a giggle, then took a timid step with her right foot as she balanced, holding on to the man's arms for support. Rapidly she placed her left foot in front. She watched her leg move in disbelief. It tingled with a new-found aliveness, a vitality, a freedom from pain that was exhilarating.

She dropped his hands and reached down to feel for the wound in her thigh, putting her hands through the bloody tear in her clothes. She had felt crusted scabs forming in it already, and knew that even with time and proper medical treatment it would leave a devastating scar. But she felt only smooth, unbroken skin. She looked back up.

"How did you do this? Is it some kind of regenerative treatment you're testing? You're a genetic scientist, is that it?"

"No, not at all," he said kindly.

"Then why did you come down here? Why did you bother with me?"

"I have descended far below this place to rescue my own."

"Your own?" she asked, confused. "Who are you? What does that have to do with me?"

"You will know me in due time, Alyssa. Yet you needed to believe in me to be healed. When you obeyed my words, you exercised faith in me. Do you understand?"

He smiled, and she felt the sincere pleasure in his voice. It warmed her all over.

But she didn't understand. "Faith? In you?"

"Yes," he said. "Your faith was manifest in your obedience. And you must continue to nurture this faith so it may grow. Your kindness and compassion toward others, your willingness to sacrifice for your friends, have given place for this seed of faith to be planted in your heart."

"How do you . . .?" she was bewildered by his words, though they wrapped her soul like a warm blanket in the lifeless chill of winter. She couldn't continue for a moment.

Then she shook her head, unable to sort out what he had said, shocked that he seemed to know things about her.

"How do you know . . . how did you know my name? . . . Are you with the government?" she asked, as sudden, old suspicions rose.

"Do you see anything of their corruption in me?"

She didn't, and shook her head. His eyes were not only kind, they radiated purity. She didn't believe him capable of the slightest evil. He smiled. It was a look she had seen once or twice in her father's eyes when they worked together on his train sets. She recalled the warmth of his love lost now, so long ago.

Puzzled, she asked, "You remind me a little of my father. But he's dead. Are you dead too? Is this death? Am I dead?"

"No," he said, still smiling. "We are both very much alive." He paused, looking into her eyes until he had her complete, rapt attention.

"Tell me, Alyssa," he said. "Look at me. Am I real?"

"Real? I don't know."

"Touch my hand. Feel me and see. Am I real to you?"

She did as she was asked, feeling his hand. When she looked closely at it, though, she gasped.

"You can heal my leg without a scar, but you can't heal yourself of this? This is awful, how did you get this?"

There was a sizable mark in his palm. She turned his hand over and saw that it went clear through to the back, as though something large had pierced his palm completely and torn the flesh a little. Then she noticed a similar scar on his wrist.

"I have no need to be rid of these," he said. "I must keep them, in fact, to be recognized in the house of my friends." He seemed patiently amused by her questions. "But you haven't answered my question."

"Oh. I don't know how, but yes, you have to be real. My leg is better. Unless I'm dreaming again."

"Good." He smiled again, still looking pleased. "Can you tell this is not a dream?"

She looked around, touched the building, felt her leg again and closed her eyes. Then she looked back at him.

"Yes," she said with relief. "I don't believe it, but it doesn't feel like a dream. Besides, this is about when you usually wake up, right after the dream starts getting good."

She let go of him and took a step or two on her own, grinning with delight at her ability to do so. She looked up, her mind on a new thought.

"You saved my life. How can I ever thank you? I have nothing, no way to repay you for this." The look on her face was pained. Surely he would want something in return. Money? What?

"All I ask is that you believe and follow me. Follow my words, from now on, faithfully," he said. "It is crucial that you leave the city now. You will not be safe any longer if you stay."

"Is that all?" she asked, realizing he hadn't asked for more. "I can work for you. I don't have any money, but I can work hard, and I've been looking for a job."

He smiled the same amused smile, a twinkle deep in his eyes. "You will, someday, when you're ready. For now, I ask only that you always remember me, and all I have done for you."

"How could I forget this? But follow you where? Out of the city?"

She looked down and rubbed her new leg as she spoke, inspecting it as best she could in the fading daylight. It seemed odd to her, but there was no question how she felt. She didn't follow Rob or Debra when they begged her, but she would go with this man, a total stranger, anywhere he led her. He had saved her from certain death. If he wanted her to come with him, she was more than willing. In fact, there was no place she wanted to go more than with him.

When she heard no answer she looked up. He had walked away, and was almost at the corner of the block now. She blinked. His feet didn't seem to touch the sidewalk as he strode along. It must be her imagination, a trick of the fading daylight. She blinked again.

"Hey, wait!" she called as he turned the corner and smiled back at her.

She tried to follow, to catch up to him, but though her leg was whole again, she had barely moved in two days, and she stumbled twice on the way.

"Wait!" she called.

Something deep inside her wanted desperately for him to stay. This was longing of a nature she had never experienced before, a fierce, irrationally attachment to him. Her voice was frantic as she called out.

"Who are you? Wait! How can I follow you if you don't *wait* for me?"

When she reached the corner, she looked around, wide-eyed, panting. "Where did he go?" she gasped, out of breath.

The street was empty. She was alone.

She leaned against the building, and sighed, exasperated, trying to remember what he had said.

Follow me.

But he had vanished before she could. It confused her.

Well, he had said she must leave the city. *No longer safe?* That much was obvious. If the goonies came back, it would be dangerous for her to be found alive and well. Yes. Very dangerous. That much of what he said made sense, at least.

She picked a direction, east she thought, and started walking. The edge of the city had to be somewhere. In her weeks of wandering on foot she had come a long way east already, but she still hadn't found the outskirts.

****

It was much later that night, after she had finally cleared the city limits and stars shone brightly above her, after she had made a bed of fallen leaves under a grove of birch trees, that she realized something else was missing.

It was an old ache. As long as she could remember it had been there, a dull pain, the half-forgotten, half-remembered experiences of a fractured, broken life. It was so familiar to her that she couldn't quite place what it was that also felt somehow well. It was as though an engine running in the distance, in the background of her life, had suddenly been shut off.

The peaceful silence of a healed soul settled sweetly inside her, a thousand clamoring voices finally put to rest.

Chapter 38

Heading Home

*And I was led by the Spirit, not knowing beforehand the things
which I should do.*

1 Nephi 4:6,
Book of Mormon

When morning came Alyssa awoke refreshed, though she had slept on bare ground. She was surprised how little her muscles ached. Earth was softer than cement, even if it was more lumpy. She rolled over and stretched into the sunlight.

Her stomach grumbled.

After her weeks of near starvation, her renewed health felt wonderful. But there was still the basic task of finding food before she could ensure her health would continue.

She stood and surveyed her surroundings.

To her left was the tree under which she had slept. In front of her the hills stretched as far as she could see, rolling up and down gently. To her right the trees became thicker and gradually turned into a forest. Behind her lay the suburban outskirts of the city.

She thought about her experience of the day before and wondered again where the strange miracle worker had come from, where he might have gone. Why did he come to her? How did he know who she was? He called her by name. That alone defied logic. She had not used her name since she left her familiar neighborhood in The Gardens. It was not asked for on the streets.

If there was an experimental tissue-regeneration technique, or some stranger circuiting the slums practicing new healing arts, she would have heard of it. She asked about all the rumors. But even if she missed something, there was no way such a man would know her personally.

She reached down and ran her hands over her leg again, massaging the perfect pink skin and muscles, feeling the solid bone beneath. There was no trace of scar tissue. Twisting around, she looked at where the bullet had entered her leg at the back of her thigh. There was nothing there either, except the bloodied hole in her pants, now the only proof of what was once there.

In the distance she recognized the sound of a running brook. Water. Clean water. She walked rapidly toward the sound and soon discovered a bubbling stream winding its way through the forest. She threw herself down and drank. Afterward she rolled into the rocky stream, and laughed as the coldness of the water chilled her body. It felt good to be covered with something so fresh.

It could be polluted, so close to the city, she thought. But weeks ago she had ceased worrying about the possibility of poisoning or illness from the things she ate or drank. So what if she vomited later. It filled her now, and that was what mattered. After all, she was still alive, and today she felt more full of life than she had ever felt before. Exultant in the feeling of the current against her body, she drank more, then sat on the bottom of the brook until she felt cleaned off and quite cold.

She walked around briskly to dry off and found a wild raspberry bush, but the berries were gone. It was too late in the year. There was a tree growing not far from the water with lots of odd looking things on the ground underneath it, black and leathery. Sitting down, she gathered a few, curious, and tore the skin-like coverings open. It stained her fingers brown as she worked it off. Although she was aware many plants were poisonous, she didn't care at this point whether these were. She'd eaten worse.

"Walnuts!" she said aloud, surprised. She hadn't realized the nuts began life with an odd leathery coating.

Crushing the shells with a rock, she picked out the insides. They tasted good. She gathered more, and crushed and ate them until she felt reasonably satisfied. It took a long time to pick the nutmeats out of their shells.

Then she checked her pockets to see if she still had her old pocketknife. It was there, but it was dulled from the uses she had put it to on the street, prying open half-empty cans, scraping mold off discarded food, scraping her initials into dumpsters for lack of any other useful activity. She walked back to the riverbank and found a flat stone. Wetting it, she attempted to sharpen the blade. It took some time before she felt the knife was sharp enough.

Finding a long dry stick, she whittled the end to a sharp point. By then it was getting to be afternoon. Alyssa knew she would have to have more than walnuts if she was to last for long.

She went back to the brook for another drink, and followed it upstream about a kilometer, she guessed, to where the water ran a little deeper. She was in luck. The water was clear. There were minnows, and a few catfish swam near the bottom. She spotted a medium-sized one and watched it carefully. When it stopped moving, she thrust her spear into the water with one quick, fluid stroke. Her aim was slightly off, but the startled fish swam into the point of the spear before it hit the bottom, piercing it neatly near the tail. She scraped the point along the muddy bottom as the catfish wriggled to get away, finally dragging it out of the water.

Sighing with relief, she grabbed the fish by the gills and pulled it carefully off the stick. It struggled to get away, but she held it tightly, in spite of getting stuck by the dorsal spines more than once as it thrashed in her hands. She looked back into the water. She had stirred up a good deal of mud. There were no more fish.

"Well," she said to it, "Looks like you're dinner."

Back at the spot where she spent the night, she struggled for over an hour trying to start a fire. She had never been much of a camper, but she knew how to make sparks using her knife and a stone. Twice she had a small flame that was blown out by the wind. For a while, she considered eating the fish raw. She had eaten worse things than catfish sushi. But the cool feel of the afternoon sun and a brisk wind told her she would need heat during the night. That was a better argument for persistence than cooking.

Finally the flame took, catching on some dry pine needles she collected. She nursed it carefully, adding tiny sticks at first, then larger ones, until she had a strong fire going.

She roasted her fish on the stick. Cleaning it was a mess. She didn't know where to begin, but left it mostly in one piece, minus the head. Still, it was the most delicious food she had eaten in a long time. Some walnuts, roasted in the coals, were tasty as well. It was more food, and better, than she had eaten in several days. She felt rejuvenated.

A peaceful feeling filled her, though she knew there wasn't enough food around her to last very long. She didn't have the skill or the tools needed to survive in the wilderness. City survival tactics wouldn't work out here.

After much thought she decided to head for home, as unpleasant as that still sounded. She would start walking in the morning, after a good night's rest.

Go now, a small, penetrating voice whispered.

It startled her. She looked around, to see if anyone was near. Not that it would matter. She hadn't spoken her intentions aloud.

Again she heard it, adding some strange words this time. *Go now. Go ye out from Babylon, for the hour of her destruction is at hand!*

The sense of urgency the words carried with them sent a chill through her body. It could not be ignored. It was a warning of danger that made her feel a sudden, powerful urge to bolt.

She fought it away with an effort, then stood up involuntarily. Turning herself around, she had a rush of adrenaline that made her legs feel bouncy. She saw no one.

"Who's there?" she asked, drawing her knife in a defensive stance.

She heard nothing.

"I need rest before I go," she said to the unseen voice. "Sleep. And I need daylight. I won't know where I'm going. I need water, and food. Let's be practical here."

There was no answer, only dead air.

She had heard voices in her head before, years ago. Frightening ones. This voice was different. It was reassuring and calm, peaceful in spite of the urgent warning. She was inclined to trust it, but . . .

She sat on the ground with a thump. *More things that make no sense*, she thought. Then she remembered the words of the man who had healed her leg: *Believe in me. Follow me.* Could this strange voice be how he meant for her to follow him?

She felt her chest glow with warmth and joy at the thought, and *knew* that it was. She didn't know how, only that she *knew*. It was certain this was her guide. Then she remembered there was one other time she had heard a voice that helped her. It was when that boss of Rob's tracked her down. The voice told her he was lying, and helped her. It gave her peace then too. It was the same voice now.

"Okay," she said aloud. "I'm going."

She scattered the fire and the ashes, and stomped out the embers using her stick to cover the rest with as much dirt as she could scrape up. She buried the remains of her fish and double-checked that the fire was out. Then she went back to the stream and drank all the water she could.

After breaking camp, she headed north, out of the forest.

The moon was full and bright. The clouds billowed and danced across its surface like paint meandering without a brush on the canvas of the sky, coloring and erasing at will, as though freed from the hand of the artist and allowed to roam joyfully. Occasionally a star winked out from between the patterns in the clouds.

The moon provided light to see well enough, but she had no real sense of which direction she was going. She followed the dance of the clouds, moving to a rhythm she felt in the very marrow of her bones, the melodic rhythm of nature itself. Her blood pulsed in time to it. She had heard of the harmony of nature long ago, maybe in grade school, but thought it was a fairy tale, a myth of days long gone when the natives tracked the beasts of the earth in their nomadic search for food.

Her heart surged within her breast as she felt the exhilaration of oneness with this strange new landscape around her. The earth was alive here. It was not the dead cement paving of Central City. She was too used to square walls and skyscrapers, smoggy skies and the acrid smell of plastic, pollution and overcrowding. The scent of the dry leaves she crushed under her feet exhilarated her. She broke into a run, thrilling at the feel of soft earth giving beneath her feet, springing back to push her forward. The cold air came in deep, rhythmic breaths, chilling her hot lungs as it filled them.

She pressed her renewed legs on harder, sprinting faster, surprised that she didn't tire or cramp. The ground itself seemed to guide her feet, pressing her forward, urging her on.

After crossing several gently sloping hills, and winding around the outskirts of a grove of trees, Alyssa slowed as she approached a wooden fence. In the distance to her right she could see a house, outbuildings, lights. Farther off there were more lights. She stopped and leaned on the fence, breathing deeply but easily. She didn't know how far she had come. She stretched out her legs, which tingled at the cessation of movement, and looked around.

Walk alongside the fence, or cross it? she wondered. The other side was wet plowed land. Puddles of water reflected the moonlight above. Before her mind knew it, her foot found the first rung of the fence and pushed her body upward. She felt a glowing, warm feeling in her chest. The feeling urged her onward, over the fence.

She stepped into the mud. Slowly she crossed the field, and the next one, following the warm glow that, she realized now, had been with her since she left her campsite.

She continued the rest of the night, walking, running, or skipping, filled with joy and delight as she leaped over boulders that loomed in her way. Always when the path in front of her divided, her inner sense knew the way to go. She didn't even consider looking the other way. There wasn't a shred of confusion in her mind. She possessed a clearness of direction that seemed natural to her, though as a small girl she could get lost in her own neighborhood.

Late in the night, she reached a pond of dark water and an overwhelming thirst welled up inside her. She knelt down to drink, but as she reached out her hands to cup the cool water, she was repulsed by a terrible, ominous feeling of blackness that seemed to exude from the water itself. The warm feeling fled, replaced suddenly by fear.

Shocked, she staggered back, away from the water, then ran along the length of it. It was more a small lake than a pond.

The black feeling stabbed at her. Her dry thirst pounded mockingly in her throat. It called her to come closer, taunting her to drink. But she had an irrational fear that the oily black taskmaster of her former nightmares would rise up out of the water and pursue her.

She ran faster. Her legs ached. Her blood pounded in her chest, and her lungs gasped for oxygen. The clouds obscured the moon, which refused to shine through them. The inky water reflected nothing. It was as still as a sheet of ebony on the landscape beside her. She felt she would never be free of the menacing sensation that pulled at her, dragging her toward the murky depths like an undertow in the atmosphere. She ran harder, forcing her body past its natural limits as fear drove her on.

At last when she felt she could run no farther and would have to submit to whatever evil the water held for her, the clouds separated. The full moon burst out of the blackness, and at the moment she looked up at its light, the awful dark pull she felt vanished into nothingness. She slowed to a walk, panting.

A few yards more and she leaned on the trunk of a large tree. Slowly, slowly, as she gained her breath, she felt the warm light returning. Her soul embraced it gladly.

She took a look behind her. The land there was much darker, more shadowed than the area ahead. She had run through no forest of trees, nothing that would cast natural shadows. The moon shone liberally on the terrain, yet she couldn't make out any ridge or other natural cause for the pervasive darkness that surrounded the pond.

She was now out of visual range of the water itself. She breathed her relief. Feeling safe again she sat down with her back against the tree, pulled her knees to her chest, and hung her head low over them.

The younger, more scientific Alyssa would have teased the murky water, tempting it back, perhaps drinking as it beckoned, even bathing in it. There was no objective reason for her fear. She recalled the days when she had toyed with danger, risking the frailty of her life and body at will. She shuddered. It was terrible to think she had been so stupid and careless. Now she had no curiosity for the danger that the lake held. She was certain it was real. That was enough. Every nerve in her body had flooded with adrenaline, forcing her to flee it. She would not look back.

When she looked up again after her brief rest, the night seemed brighter. Daylight must be approaching. She didn't know where she was or how far she had traveled, or even if she was heading in the direction of her home, her mother and sister. They were the only people she could call home, but she doubted they would welcome her, even if she made it there.

Still, she continued on. There was no more sense of danger, but no other water either. Her throat burned with thirst. Gradually, she became aware as she ran that she was growing tired and weak. Her muscles complained of the strain of the arduous exercise, but she didn't grant them the luxury of rest. She slowed to a stroll when she absolutely had to, but she felt a sense of urgency, a need to reach her destination by morning.

Gradually daylight appeared to her right. *East must be that way somewhere*, she thought idly as she ran. *I must be heading north.*

When full dawn came to the landscape, she saw that all her surroundings were different. The landscape was flatter, not quite so rolling, with wider valleys and lower, sloping hills. She slowed to a brisk walk, breathing deeply, feeling the sensation inside that had led her, feeling it tell her she was almost there.

Before her stretched a road, oddly the first she had noticed all night, although she must have crossed others as she ran. Vaguely she remembered crossing a large bridge, some time after she passed the black lake. She wasn't sure though.

Climbing a barbed-wire fence, she surveyed the road. It ran east-west. Heading north she would soon intersect it, though she was unsure if she had come in a straight line north or not. She searched for a glimpse of something, anything, she recognized. Why should she expect to find something familiar? She only felt there should be.

There was a line of tall, old trees stretching as far as she could see in either direction on the other side of the road. It was a two-lane paved road. She crossed it and stood under the trees. From this angle, looking east, a memory flickered.

"The Richardson's!" she exclaimed aloud. "They can't be far!"

She remembered driving eastward along this very road, years ago, when her family and the Richardson's went camping together. There was a campsite many miles east of here where she had been several times.

Two cars went by, heading that direction, and Alyssa ducked behind a tree trunk. Instinct had taught her to be cautious of anyone rich enough to own or drive a car. She sat down in the brush and her intense fatigue overcame her. Crawling under a bush, she got as comfortable as possible, and fell asleep.

When she awoke she guessed it was mid-afternoon. It was difficult to ignore her complaining stomach. All around her were open fields except for the road and the single line of trees and brush. The fields had been emptied of their crops long before she arrived.

When she stood, her legs ached with the strain of so much use, and every muscle complained at the harsh treatment they had received. But the Richardson's farm couldn't be more than three miles west of here.

She stretched, wincing, her mind oddly rested even as her body complained. She looked at the road. There was no more traffic at the moment.

Walking as quickly as she could force her legs to move, she soon was able to maintain a good pace. After another half hour, she came to a familiar intersection. Traveling so close to the road, she was thankful for the lack of traffic. She made a right turn to head north again and felt increasing hope. She had been on this road before. Her pace quickened when she made out a familiar white farmhouse off to the left, in the distance.

Then she began to worry. Her inner feeling was that it would be all right, or she wouldn't have come. But it had been so long. She was a child the last time she traveled this road.

What if they moved by now?

She struggled to remember. There was Peter, Julia, an older brother, a little boy . . . or was it a girl? Were there four, or five? *A huge family, anyway,* Alyssa thought, *about as big as Debra's.* She only had Lauren. Her thoughts kept her occupied as she came to the drive that led to their home and crossed the street, then started down the long gravel driveway.

Their acreage wasn't yet plowed under. The brittle yellow cornstalks looked odd and eerie in the fading sunlight. She kept her pace steady, fixing her gaze on the house as she came up to it. Did they still live here, after so many years? Would Peter be here, or elsewhere?

She was uncertain, not knowing how much she cared to meet his wife in person, and any children he may have by now. Anxiety and anticipation filled her. It would be better if he wasn't here. She hoped that whoever did live here was friendly, but it was a faint hope.

Alyssa stepped onto the long wooden porch and the boards creaked. It was filled with potted ivies, ferns and flowers of all kinds. A dog barked from somewhere behind the house. She smiled as she recognized the wrought iron music stand and the nameplate next to the doorbell. It still read "Richardson."

A light was on in the front room. She rang the bell and waited nervously. Suddenly she realized that her appearance must be less presentable than the most miserable of strays who appear on people's doorsteps. In spite of her bath in the river, she was sure that she would not be appealing to anyone's senses. *Too late to worry about that*, she thought, as footsteps approached from inside.

She started to feel dizzy when the door opened, and a tall, handsome man with dazzling blue eyes looked at her from behind the screen. She remembered those eyes. Or did she?

"Hello?" the man said, puzzlement in his voice.

"Peter? Is that you?" she said as the dizziness overpowered her.

Her vision blurred around the edges, and she collapsed into the enveloping, comfortable blackness of unconsciousness, falling limply onto the worn wooden slats of the porch.

Chapter 39

Immortalized

> *My people (wait for applause) my dear people, I greet you with a depth of sorrow for the losses we have recently endured . . .*
>
> *As we all know, no man or woman could hope to replace our late President . . . his passing and untimely death saddens us all . . .*
>
> *It is with great honor, not to mention trepidation, that I now assume his position with your ~~overwhelming~~ enheartening approval. I am overwhelmed by your support . . . I only hope I can continue to bless your lives as he did, as we move forward to ~~repairing~~ the damage . . .*
>
> Victor Caldwell,
> Inauguration speech(rough draft)

In the core of Central City, Victor smiled. "You see, Gerome? Everything is proceeding perfectly. As planned." He reclined comfortably in his chair.

When this project was wrapped up he would be the highest-ranking official remaining in the nation. The social problem of the poor would be neatly taken care of, and he could easily assume control over the rest of the population. They were sure to be devastated after what they would perceive to be a great loss.

Fools. For him it was a bargain, gaining two victories for the price of one, wrapped neatly in a single package. In the people's distraught state he could easily claim the Presidency. Success was inevitable. He had only to wait and watch, patiently ready to claim the prize.

Earlier in the day he toyed with his acceptance speech. He savored the feeling as a wine connoisseur would approach an exceptionally fine vintage, inhaling the luscious bouquet of victory, his mouth alive with the flavor of it. It was intoxicating to him, arousing even, to be so close to his objective.

This was his favorite part of the game. The planning stages were so tedious. After the plan was set in motion, that was when the true excitement began. He felt it deeply. The tingling nervousness resonated through his body in sweet anticipation.

"The infected bacteria do appear to be taking hold well and spreading rapidly," the secretary answered. "However there are reports of disease in some of the upper-class sectors." He coughed, covering his mouth nervously.

"It could hardly be the same infection," Victor responded. He waved his hand as though swatting a fly. It was an insignificant anomaly.

"The symptoms are remarkably similar, sir, and they are not exactly common."

"We double- and triple-checked every single pipe coupling, Gerome. We've been over this already. There are *no leaks*."

"No leaks *reported*, sir." He coughed again. "In fact, whatever it is, it's spreading quite rapidly in the New Seattle district. Some of the Congressmen who sympathize with you are—"

Victor stood up and pushed his leather chair backwards. "Send out the vaccine then." Gerome backed up toward the door. "That's what we made it for!"

"Yes, sir," Gerome said meekly. "It's being sent by helicopter as we speak. But there are doubts as to whether it will be effective. It appears to have mutated again at the last testing. The vaccine may not target the current strain. One other thing. The fires are increasing exponentially. The southeast slums have been hardest hit, as expected, but we received reports in the last hour that there have been unexplained explosions near main water lines in the Dakota, Vegas, and New Angeles sectors. If it isn't on fire, it's flooding. I again apologize for disturbing you, sir, but everything is *not* proceeding as planned. There are serious issues here that need to be addressed immediat—"

"Send out rescue teams. Mobilize one of the western military units if you have to. Fix it!"

He launched into a stream of expletives that caused Gerome to flee from the room, slamming the door behind him, before Victor could decide to throw heavy objects in his direction.

Victor leaned heavily on the marble-topped desk, muttering curses under his breath.

"Where are you when I need you?" he called to the air. But the Caretaker did not appear. "You promised everything would go perfectly. Your people were supposed to take care of any leaks we humans might've missed. What's going on?"

He wished he could summon the wraithlike figure on command, like the mortals he had under his control. But it never happened that way. The Caretaker came and went as he pleased, and only as he pleased.

Victor's needs didn't seem to matter. He wondered how he could change that situation. He had yet to find a weakness, a need the being had that he could exploit to his advantage. It would come, eventually, he thought. He just hadn't found it yet. Exploiting a being's need to be worshipped . . . his only confessed need . . . Well, that presented a challenge.

No shadowy figure appeared in the room. It was deadly silent. He needed a cigar. He definitely needed a cigar. He unlocked his special drawer, the drawer where he kept his last reserve of the fine Havana stock. Only three left, and no more coming for a long while, with the embargo still on.

Now would be the perfect time to have one. It would help him relax, think straight, come up with a way to cure the rich who became sick, who would then proclaim him a savior and elect him their new leader without hesitation. How much could he reasonably charge for the vaccine? he wondered.

He had made certain to contaminate the President's personal drinking water, the Capitol building, and the homes of officials above himself in rank. He rolled his cigar in his fingertips, contemplating.

First he would own the country, an easy victory. Then he would claim the world. For that, he would have to make war. He sliced off the end of the cigar with a tiny mother-of-pearl handled blade.

Millions would fear his armies. Germ warfare against which no merely human force could protect itself. With the help of the Caretaker and using his own personal brilliance, he had developed new weapons that made atom bombs look like firecrackers when it came to body counts. Together they would achieve what no mortal had in the history of the earth, total world domination. It was within his grasp. These reports today were only minor glitches. Minor. The solutions would be found. And soon, if the Caretaker would only show up and explain; that was all he needed.

He took a deep breath, comforting himself with these thoughts, and flicked his solid platinum lighter.

With a deafening boom, the room exploded.

It was an instant fireball. Victor didn't even have time to feel it. He found himself watching, a casual observer, as his body blackened and then vanished before his eyes in the brightness of the flames.

He was in shock. *Am I dead?* he thought. *It can't be. I am the next world leader. The Caretaker said so. It was in the contract.*

There must have been a hydrogen leak from the bacterial emissions *inside* the building. That was definitely not supposed to happen. The labs were cleared of all specimens last week. This was the most secure place in the City. He had checked the pipe couplings personally.

But he was obviously standing in the middle of a growing inferno. That much he could not deny. It quickly consumed the building. The floor of what had been his office moments ago crumbled. He could hear the screams of the workers below him who were just this second finding out what that loud noise meant. Screams of people running desperately for a fire escape, who could never reach it in time, filled the air.

In an odd way he enjoyed that noise, knowing he had caused it, knowing that in moments they would all cease their puny existence forever. He smiled to himself. He had not ceased to exist. He was special. The Caretaker had taken notice of him and saved him from their fate. The knowledge burst upon him in a rush of glory that he was now one of the *Immortals*.

Perhaps he wouldn't be the next world leader after all. Well, not the next *mortal* one. Surely his friend would be along soon to tell him what to do with his new form, his new plane of existence. He didn't miss his charred body. He felt free, released from a heavy weight. He enjoyed the floating sensation, no longer subject to gravity. He had seen the tricks the Caretaker could do, and looked forward to learning them.

He was one of them now.

"Ah, there's my little Victor-y," a familiar voice said.

He looked around until he could make out the familiar black-caped form walking easily through the flames.

He smiled and moved toward the figure. "There you are," he said. "What took you so long? I was trying to call for you. Everything is backfiring! There are leaks everywhere! Even this building. What's going on? What about our plans?"

"Oh, Victor," the Caretaker said condescendingly. "I told you those cigars would kill you someday." He wore a menacing grin.

Victor hadn't seen that particular expression on his face before. Something about it unsettled him.

"But what about my lab? We checked everything out. Why'd it blow?"

"I didn't need it anymore," he said, seeming to shrug. "In fact it was important to destroy all evidence that the virus was genetically engineered."

"Well, you could've warned me," Victor said. "This is kind of extreme."

"Oh. Yes, I suppose I could have." He still wore the malevolent expression.

"At least . . . I am immortal now, right? You changed me. I'm one of you, aren't I?"

The Caretaker let out a chuckle and nodded. "Oh, yes. You're mine. Be certain of that."

Someone else came through the flames, moving rapidly, obviously frightened.

"Where am I? What happened?" the person said. "Help! Help!"

The being came closer until Victor made out who it was. Gerome.

Instantly, Victor was hot with anger. He couldn't feel the flame of the fire, but this rage burned him fiercely. It was intensely painful, and enraged him further.

"What's Gerome doing here?!" Victor screamed. "You said I was special! Did you make a deal with him too?"

"Why, no," the Caretaker said, and laughed again.

Gerome screamed when he recognized Victor standing in the flames. "Get away from me!" he shrieked. "Murderer! You killed my Pietro! My darling Pietro! Do you think I didn't know? Do you? You killed him too! I hate you! I've always hated you!"

He rambled on, wailing as he tried to run, moving like a person thrown into water without knowing how to swim. With a rapid floating motion, he finally disappeared beyond the wall of fire.

Then Victor became aware of others around him, rising up from the depths of the inferno below, more than a few looking utterly bewildered.

"Are these your people?" he asked.

"Not all of them, unfortunately," the Caretaker said, "but most." He inspected an imaginary fingernail. "Some," he sighed, "just don't know it yet." He grinned again.

Victor decided he didn't like that grin. He looked around again and was aghast to find he recognized many of the faces. The secretary from the third floor, the pretty woman on the eighth, he counted three . . . no, four of his agents. He was aware of *hundreds* of others.

"What is the meaning of this?" he demanded. "*I* am the chosen one! Why did you change all these nobodies? Why are they all here? They're dead!"

"Yes, Victor, you are all *dead*," the Caretaker said, taking great delight in his predicament.

"But I am the chosen one! I'm the only one of these humans you selected to join you in your world of immortality!"

"Oh," he said casually. "Is *that* what your fussing about?"

"As if you didn't . . ." Victor left off as his anger seared him again with pain. He seethed in agony.

The Caretaker chuckled again. "Simply put, I had no further use for you, Victor. I told you more than once you were expendable. It shouldn't surprise you so. I only needed you to create the virus and set it free. Your work is done here."

Victor gaped at him. "But . . . but what about my end of the contract?" he stammered.

"*Your* end? Oh, Victor." It was the same condescending tone. "I'm afraid you should have read the fine print."

"Fine print?"

"Oh, now will you look at that," the Caretaker continued, disregarding him. "All your pathetic little souls *are* immortal after all. Isn't that something? Amazing, don't you think?"

"You . . . you lied to me! You *lied!*"

"Did I? Oops. You'll forgive me, won't you? Nasty habit I have. I come by it so . . . naturally."

The chuckle burst into a booming, evil laugh that rung in Victor's mind louder than the rupturing flames and crashing steel girders that surrounded him. He put his hands up as if to cover his ears but it had no effect. He wished there were some way to avoid it, to make it cease.

"Stop it! Stop it!" he screamed. "It's too loud, too loud! Somebody make it stop!"

The Caretaker moved very close to him, forcing him to look up at his suddenly terrifying face and that horrible menacing grin. He had never been more afraid of anything in his entire existence.

"You're mine now, Victor, and you'll hear what I want you to hear. Do you think I intend *Hell* to be a pleasant experience?"

The ringing laughter echoed in his mind until he was deaf to any other sound.

Chapter 40

A Dubious Welcome

I feel more rested today than I have in quite some time. Zack slept for six hours straight last night, and that was wonderful. But more than that, I feel somehow different, as though a burden has been lifted off my shoulders.

Debra Pike,
personal journal entry

"**I** don't know who she is," a man's voice said.

Alyssa groaned and blinked. A bright light shone in her eyes, and she decided to keep them shut. The light was turned off.

Where am I? she thought. *Oh yes. I found the Richardson's house.*

"Or how she knew my name when I answered the door," the same voice continued. Alyssa struggled to focus in the dimmer light of a lamp beside the bed.

"She's coming to," an older female voice said.

"Alyssa," she said with an effort, at last comprehending the conversation around her. "I'm Alyssa Stark."

She moved to sit up and realized she was in a comfortable, clean bed. Her clothes were filthy from her weeks of homelessness, and she pulled the covers up to her chest to hide them.

"Alyssa?" Mrs. Richardson asked, startled. "Joan's daughter?"

"Yes, but I doubt she'd claim me anymore."

"Alyssa?" said Peter. His voice was a hushed whisper. He swallowed hard. "I didn't recognize you." He leaned over and looked into her hazel-gray eyes, searching. She held his gaze steadily. "Yes. I'd know those eyes anywhere," he said. "It's her all right."

"It's me," Alyssa said. "But don't feel bad. I doubt anybody I know would recognize me right now."

Peter turned away from her to face his mother, and sat down heavily in an antique wicker chair in the corner of the room. He had grown into a fine-looking young man. His blond hair, wavy now, didn't fall into his eyes anymore. He reminded her a little of his father, only a younger copy; handsome and strong, carrying himself well. He had a strong chin and high cheekbones. Except for his eyes, that same bright starry blue, he didn't look at all like the gangly, awkward young boy Alyssa remembered.

She felt self-conscious, and wondered for the first time in weeks just how she looked right now. She shifted the covers nervously.

"Well," Mrs. Richardson said, "Since you're awake, I have some dinner here. You look starved to death. Are you hungry? It's not anorexia, is it, I hope?"

"Yes. No, not anorexia, hardly," she said. "Yes, I'm hungry."

She placed a tray in front of Alyssa with beef stew, rolls, and fresh steamed garden vegetables on it. There was both milk and ice water to drink. "Wait, please, I don't have any money . . . Are you giving this to me?" she asked.

She picked up the glass of water before it could be pulled away and drank it down. The water was delightful on her raw, dry throat.

"Certainly it's free," Beverly said with a small laugh. "This isn't a restaurant. In fact, there's plenty more where that came from."

"More?"

Alyssa ate hungrily before Mrs. Richardson could change her mind and snatch the tray away. She thought she must be dreaming, but the reality of the food filling her stomach assured her she was not. She could barely use the spoon fast enough, and she wished she could pick up the bowl and drink the stew. But stray thoughts of etiquette returned and she constrained herself to be content with the spoon.

A memory passed through her mind, of the time when she first arrived at The Gardens too hungry, and had gotten sick from eating too fast. She forced herself to slow down, imagining the scene that might take place if she didn't exercise some control.

Beverly sat down on the double bed and straightened the corner of the handmade quilt, watching her.

"How did you get here? What's happened to you?" Peter asked.

"Peter, wait for her to finish. Can't you see she's famished?"

Waving with the spoon, Alyssa said, "It's okay. I was trying to find my way home, but I seem to have ended up here. For the moment," she added. She would have to get home as soon as she could, though staying anywhere that gave out free food was mightily appealing. "I left Central U. two years ago, I never finished." She picked up the fork for the vegetables. Her tray was almost empty. Looking at Beverly she asked, "Is there more or would it be too much to ask?"

"Of course. Eat as much as you like. One thing about farming these days, you grow enough food to eat, share, and still leave half to rot in the field." Beverly left the room for the kitchen.

"I can't believe that," she said to Peter. "In the City you'd think an abundance of food anywhere was a myth. I can't remember the last time I ate a meal like this."

"Really? We hear rumors of shortages, but we have a hard time finding buyers for our crops, City or not."

"Oh, there's plenty of food if you have the money to buy it. It's just expensive. For people in my situation, anyway."

Peter wrinkled his brow. He leaned over toward her from his chair. "What situation is that, exactly?"

"Oh, well, I . . . I left my apartment several weeks ago, after I lost my job." Where to begin? To explain? She didn't know.

"You've been homeless?"

"You could call it that." She looked around the room, not meeting his eyes. "It was by choice, though. In a way."

"Why would you choose . . ."

"Well, without me paying rent the manager didn't like me staying there very much," she said. "Even though plenty of units were standing empty."

"Couldn't you find another job?"

"Not where I lived. Unemployment rate there soared. I probably could've hung on, had I wanted to . . ." She stopped and frowned.

"But?"

"Let's just say I didn't like his terms for keeping my apartment." She shrugged her shoulders and scraped the last bite of vegetables from her plate as Beverly returned to the room. "This is the most delicious stew," Alyssa said, looking up at her.

"Thank you," Beverly said. She handed her another bowl of stew and more homemade rolls.

Peter made a face. "What kind of offer?"

Alyssa smirked. "Not the kind of job I wanted. Not worth it."

She didn't volunteer anything further. No sense in either offending Peter's sensibilities or turning her stomach thinking about all that, especially when good food was in front of her. Fresh hot bread. It smelled more than divine.

"Thank you so much," she said. "I never thought I'd see food this good again." She spread butter on a roll and slowed down. Beginning to feel full, she savored the taste in her mouth. "This is delicious."

"You're welcome," Beverly said.

"So you moved, but there were still no jobs?" Peter asked.

"Not for me," she said, uncertain how much of her story to tell. Much of it was so embarrassing . . . especially *why* things happened the way they did. She had been so self-destructive, so foolish. "Two years ago my citizenship was erased from the central government mainframe. Technically, I don't exist. Hard to apply for work or get credit when you can't prove who you are."

"Really?" Peter said. "We had to do that . . ." He stopped short and his face lit up. "Did you . . . are you . . . do you mean?" Turning to his mother, he said "Article 28, Mom!"

"Article 28 . . ." Alyssa said, comprehension forming. "No, that's not it . . . wait a minute, Peter. Please."

Peter's face fell.

"No religion for me, sorry," she said, and shrugged. "No. It's a long story. I'd rather not go into the details." She didn't feel like telling about her drug involvement, her suicide attempt, Rob . . . that whole nightmare was long behind her. "But after it happened I moved to the lower income sectors, the places that don't require ID for everything, and found a job there," she said, choosing her words carefully.

"Then the rumors *are* true," Peter said.

She nodded. "Yes. I managed fine. Week-to-week, though. It didn't pay much but it was work. The people were great, so wonderful to me, like a huge family. I loved them so much. Anyway, in July the grocery was sold, the owner moved away, and after that there weren't any jobs to be found."

"And since then you've lived on the street?" Peter asked.

"I've survived," she said, looking away again, pretending to study the wallpaper.

"So you came to be here by . . .?" Beverly asked.

Alyssa looked down at her empty bowl, noticing the floral pattern on it. "Well, I wandered aimlessly most of the time, looking for food, shelter. . . After a while I figured I may as well try to go home, since there was nowhere else. I started walking, and just kept going."

"You came here on foot?" Beverly asked.

"I couldn't exactly afford airfare," she said, with a little laugh. "Or the tram."

"You walked here, all the way from Central?" Peter asked.

"I reached the city limits yesterday—or was it the day before? Anyway, I headed north after that. Like I said, I figured I'd try to get home if I could. I never had a good sense of direction though. I just kept going until something looked familiar. This was familiar. And that's about it."

"So you weren't coming to me," Peter mumbled to himself.

"Hmm?" Alyssa said, not sure she heard what he said.

"You weren't looking for us?" he said, louder.

"It's lucky I remembered this place at all. I don't mean to impose on anyone. The road looked familiar this morning when the light hit it, that's all. I'll find my way home as soon as I can, don't worry. I'm not sure why I knocked, except that it was familiar, and it's been a long time since I've seen a friendly face. I guess I thought . . ."

All of a sudden she was completely unsure of what she was doing there, uncertain how welcome she might be, showing up on their doorstep in this condition. She pulled the covers tighter around herself, feeling small and out of place.

"Wait a minute. You started *last night*? From the outskirts of Central City?" Beverly asked.

Alyssa nodded. "I think so. I cleared the city limits the night before, and spent the day in the countryside, but I think that's right."

"On an empty stomach?"

"I managed to catch a fish and find some walnuts before I started. I walked all night, and part of the day today."

"You caught a fish?" Peter's voice was incredulous. "Right, with what? You're not carrying any rod or tackle."

"I got lucky. I sharpened a stick with my pocketknife." She unconsciously reached to feel it in her pocket. It wasn't there. "It was cool. I didn't think I could do it but . . . Hey, where's my . . .?"

Peter cleared his throat. "Mom put it over there, on the dresser," he said cautiously.

A weird feeling came over her when she realized this meant they had searched her pockets. How long had she been unconscious? She hated passing out. Well, she was obviously unhurt.

"Oh," she said finally, taking her hand out of her pocket and returning to the task of finishing her roll.

"It could be done in one night, I suppose," Beverly said with an exhausted sigh. "If you were in excellent condition. But forgive me, you don't look it."

"Her fingertips are stained brown," Peter said. "Like she's been peeling walnuts, as she said."

"I haven't been in shape," Alyssa said. "But I did run most of the way," she said. "Honestly. It felt good."

Beverly's voice was suddenly anxious, "Look, this is hard to believe. Getting here in one night all the way from the City is very farfetched. Only a trained marathon runner could make that distance in that little time. Something's not right here. You're not telling us everything. Who are you, really, and what do you want? Why don't you tell us the whole truth and get it over with?"

"I am who I said."

Alyssa was flustered at Beverly's unexpected outburst. She felt caught. No, she hadn't told them everything. But who would believe her? Nobody. They didn't even believe this much.

"Mom," Peter said. "Who else could she be? She said herself she wasn't trying to find us."

"We have to be careful. She could've been told to say that," Beverly said.

"I know," Peter said.

"It's too uncanny, Peter," Beverly said.

"I did do it. And I am Alyssa Stark," she put in.

Both of them ignored her. "Who would remember Alyssa?" Peter asked. "That was too long ago."

"No it wasn't. People remember things. Anybody who vaguely resembles her could've been sent here."

"I recognize her eyes, Mom. Nobody else has that exact color."

"She could be wearing special contact lenses for all we know."

"I'm not wearing contact lenses!" Alyssa said.

"You're getting paranoid again. It's hardly the same thing, Mom."

"Why are you defending *her* all of a sudden?" Beverly asked, upset.

"I'm not. You'd get like this no matter who she was and you know it. Who she is or isn't makes no difference. Plus, if she had some agenda she'd have come with a more believable story, and not looking like something the cat dragged in." His tone was angry also.

Alyssa watched in confusion as the odd conversation unfolded.

"I know, I know," Beverly said to him, shaking. "It hasn't been the same since Phil . . ." she broke off her sentence and sat on the bed again without looking at Alyssa.

"Well, I *can* leave," she said. "I didn't ask to stay, and I didn't ask for food or shelter, or anything from you or anybody else!"

She got out of the bed abruptly.

"I've been taking care of myself for quite a long time and I intend to keep on doing it. *You* must have carried me in here when I passed out. *You* gave me food, and thank you. But *I* didn't ask for anything. I wasn't planning on inviting myself in. I know I'm filthy. I know I must look awful. I can't help that right now. I was only trying to get home. And I think I can find my way from here, unless they've moved without telling me. I shouldn't have knocked on your door. I'm sorry. I'll be more than happy to get on my way."

She stood stiffly, feeling far weaker than she hoped she looked, and waited for a response.

"Mom, now look what you've done," Peter chided. "It's not *her* fault Dad's gone."

His mother began to cry quietly.

"I'm sorry, Alyssa," he said. "I'm sorry I said you looked like . . . Please, sit back down."

He ran his hand back through his hair, even though it was perfectly in place, and if he had done it in a less intense moment she might have laughed. It really was Peter. It was the same adolescent gesture she remembered.

But she didn't budge.

"You have to understand something," he continued. "A few months after Article 28 passed, Dad went up to town on errands, and he never came back. Witnesses say he got into a truck with three men and it didn't look like it was by force, but no one has seen him since. We don't know who they were, where he is or what happened to him."

She sat down on the bed, wrinkling her brow. "I'm sorry."

"Mom suspects they may have posed as old friends of his. So of course with anyone new coming around, Mom gets this way. She's afraid someone else will disappear next." Beverly was crying softly. "It's been terrible for all of us. A year or so later we got a note in his handwriting. It appeared on the back doorstep. It said not to worry, that he'd be all right but he couldn't come back yet, and sent his love, things like that."

Beverly said, "Seventeen months later. And no, it said things were *going* to work out for the best and he wouldn't be returning for some time. It did not say anywhere that he either *was* or would be *all right*."

Peter winced at his mother's correction.

"We've heard nothing since. In some ways it would be easier if we found his body somewhere, or something, *anything*. Not knowing what happened to him . . ." his voice broke off and he cleared his throat, blinking away a tear.

"I think I understand," Alyssa said quietly. She imagined the note tucked away somewhere in Mrs. Richardson's most private things, that she must have memorized every word.

After a pause, she said, "I can prove it's me. I think. I can try anyway."

"It doesn't matter," he said. "Mom would wonder about you anyway. You remember she and your mother didn't part on the kindest of terms."

Again the memories flashed, of crashing china, bandages, Joan screaming threats. She only nodded. The religious issues . . . Article 28. It struck her suddenly that this family must be in a similar situation as Debra's had been, only not so lucky.

"I hate to say anything negative about your mother, but . . ."

"Why not?" Alyssa said with a laugh. "I don't hate to."

Peter returned the smile briefly. "She is the *type* of person who might want to cause us trouble, just to be vindictive. We just want to live our lives in peace."

"She is vindictive. But look, you can bet if she wanted me to do anything for her I wouldn't do it. Just because she wanted me to would be reason enough. It wouldn't matter if all she wanted me to do was floss." She would vastly appreciate dental floss at the moment, but that was beside the point. "We haven't spoken in years."

"Then why are you going back?" Peter asked.

"There is such a thing as having no options left," she said. There was an uncomfortable pause. "I swore I'd never return, no matter what. Yet here I am. I doubt she'll even take me back, and I seriously doubt I'll like being there. But I've been trying not to think about all that." She sighed. "Thanks for the reality check."

"Sorry," he said.

Beverly wiped her eyes and looked up. "It *would* be easier if you weren't claiming to be anyone we know. I'm sorry. I didn't mean to make you feel unwelcome. Peter's right. I do get this way. I try not to, but . . . Some things are hard to handle even when it's been . . . a while."

"I understand," Alyssa said. "But there's no need to worry. I won't be here long."

Beverly said, "There's no rush. Feel free to stay and rest as long as you need. Please."

Alyssa hesitated. "Are you sure you mean that?" she asked.

Beverly nodded, then said, "Just promise me you won't take anyone else with you when you go." She attempted a smile, but looked up at Peter.

"I promise," Alyssa said.

It was the silliest thing she had ever promised to anyone, but she felt she must, if only to reassure Mrs. Richardson. What did she think, that she was there to kidnap Peter? Maybe it was an attempt at humor, but she couldn't tell. She had no intention of bringing harm to anyone, much less these people. They had given her food. Right now that meant more to her than anything else. If she could be allowed to stay a few days and eat, freely, where food was plentiful, it would be more than bliss.

Beverly nodded. "Thanks."

"What in the world happened to your pants?" Peter asked with surprise, noticing their condition.

She looked down. The dried bloodstains hadn't washed away completely in the cool of the river. The shredded fabric was obvious. She swallowed.

"It's a long story," she said.

"That's okay," Peter said. "We have time."

She hesitated. "Well, they were Margret's pants," she said, trying to think quickly. "But she gave them to me when she left. She couldn't take much with her."

What else could she say? She couldn't explain what really happened. It was impossible. They would be even more afraid of her.

"Who's Margret?"

"A friend. She's gone now," she said, more softly. "Her trouble caught up with her too."

"Is her trouble what's on the pants?" Peter asked, repulsed. "How could you even *wear* those?"

"No," Alyssa said, distressed. "No, she's not dead. Well she could be. I don't know. She was headed for safety last time I saw her."

She stopped before her voice could betray her emotion, and pushed it back. She hadn't allowed herself to think about Margret or what might have happened to her since she left.

"That's my blood."

"Your blood," Beverly said with a heavy sigh of *here-we-go-again*. "I noticed the tear earlier. I didn't see any trace of injury there."

The truth would have to come out. She didn't want to talk about it. It was *her* secret. It was private; and besides, they wouldn't believe her if she told them. Or would they? No, they'd send her away immediately, accusing her of lying again. But she couldn't think of a good lie fast enough that would plausibly answer all their questions.

She felt uneasy at the thought of telling a lie about him. No, she couldn't tell anything but the truth . . . Somehow it would be wrong any other way. She had a full stomach, but she still felt weak. She wasn't sure she would get far if they did ask her to leave. In spite of that she had to say something, fast, and it had to be the truth.

"I was caught in the crossfire of a military drafting riot," she said. "It was very serious. I'm lucky I survived." Maybe that would do.

"You seem to have a rather high degree of luck," Beverly said. "How long ago was that?"

"Military riot?" said Peter at the same time. From his tone, it was clear he didn't believe her either. "Drafting?"

"I'm not certain," she said. She wasn't. That part was not exactly a fib. Days and nights were fuzzy.

"Couldn't have been too long," Peter said. "That's a fresh bloodstain."

"Can you show us the scar?" Beverly asked, sourly. "The injury?"

"I . . . don't have a scar," Alyssa said, dropping her eyes. She rubbed her forehead with her hand.

"Yes, I noticed that too," Beverly said.

Peter dropped his head into his hands and shook it.

"I'll ask," he muttered, finally. "You can't claim a fairly recent bullet wound without any sign of it. You couldn't possibly pay for reconstruction surgery, unless you're lying about your finances. And even the best recent surgery would still show some kind of incision. I might believe you're Alyssa, but there's something wrong here." He looked up at her. "You never used to lie to me. As far as I know. You lied to your parents all the time, but not to me. Listen. You can tell us. What's going on?"

"I think she shot somebody, stole their clothes, and now she's on the run. What else could explain it, Peter? She's been living in *Central City*, after all." Beverly said it with obvious contempt. "You know how things are there."

"No, no, no, I couldn't hurt anybody," she responded with a small moan. "If I could I'd have easily found a high-paying job, ID or no ID. Honest. Look, I can see I'll have to tell you everything. This is the whole truth, okay? But you won't believe me," she said mournfully. "You already don't believe how I got here." She took a deep breath. "Look. It was only a few days ago. It was a terrible injury. I was dying. They have this new explosive kind of ammunition . . ."

"I've heard of it," Peter said, twisting in the chair. "Nasty stuff."

"Fever set in fast, so I was unconscious a lot of the time, thankfully."

"Which hospital were you in?" Peter asked, looking up.

She paled. "Are you kidding?! Don't you know what they do to uninsured people in hospitals?"

He shook his head.

"Well, that's another long grisly story I'd rather not go into. Let's just say, there are good reasons privileged people never have to wait long for donors. Organ cloning never did work as well as scientists hoped, no matter what the media says."

"Oh," they both said. Beverly wrinkled her nose.

"The goonies came out and cleaned up the bodies and the mess but they left me, I guess because I wasn't dead yet. I don't know if they meant to come back or not . . ."

"Goonies?" Beverly asked.

Alyssa sighed. She'd forgotten the term was unique to The Gardens. "Government employees. They do the clean-up duty in the slums, take care of . . . well, waste material. The news never tells you anything about our district."

"They say there aren't any slums," Peter said. "All we hear is how well-organized Central City is, how well taken care of the usual social problems are, and so on."

Alyssa grimaced. "They 'take care of the usual social problem' with these living garbage disposals. They have a more professional name, but I've forgotten it. Street name is 'goonies.' Part of their job is to pick up corpses and dispose of them. Joke on the street was that some of them worked on commission." She laughed.

After waiting for them to absorb the information, she continued, swallowing hard.

"Anyway, about three nights ago I was very weak . . . I heard a man call my name. He had the most wonderful voice. It was so beautiful to listen to. I remember that." She paused again, a far-away look coming into her eyes. She remembered how sweet it had sounded in her ears. "He talked to me and told me to stand up and walk, and I stood and he held me in his arms. This is the only explanation I have, but I swear it's the truth. I felt this . . . this awesome power flow through me. The infection, the fever, the bullet wound. . . they were gone instantly. When he let go I could walk again, and there was no scar, nothing left but new pink skin." She sighed.

"I don't know who he was. He didn't tell me his name. He didn't want any money either, and that was very strange. The only thing he asked for in return was for me to remember what he'd done for me. Like, sure, I could forget? Well, he also asked me to follow him, and I tried but he vanished. He went around the corner and then he was gone . . . there was no one there.

"But look, the bullet went all the way through, see?" She turned her leg over to show the hole on the other side of her jeans. Her skin was soft and pink, dusty but without any trace of injury. "I know it crushed the bone completely. I could feel it. It had to be some kind of, I don't know, unexplained phenomenon I guess? He might have been some kind of genetic doctor. I've heard about these regenerative experiments . . . I didn't think they worked. But look. I don't know how else to explain this. I'd be dead if it weren't for his help. I don't expect you to believe me, but it's the truth, and it's all I have. He told me I had to leave the city, or I wouldn't be safe anymore. So I did. I started walking and kept going, and here I am."

Beverly said, "You said earlier you claim no religion."

"That's right."

"But you insist your leg was healed by a miracle."

"I guess you could call it that, yes." She nodded emphatically. She hadn't said the word aloud, but hearing it, she knew it fit. "Unless I'm dead already, or delirious, and I'm just going to wake up back in the city." She shuddered involuntarily. "But the man said I wasn't. No. He said so." The last part she said more to reassure herself than anyone else. "He had me check to be sure it wasn't a dream."

"And you have no other explanation," Beverly said.

"No. My best guess is he was some kind of doctor with a new technique he wanted to test quietly. That could explain why he didn't ask for money. It would hardly be the first time the poor were used for medical experiments, willing or not." She grimaced, haunted by memories of the maimed people she had seen in her wandering. "I've seen more failures . . . more results of failures than successes. But I've never heard of a medical procedure like this. No pills, no machines . . . He made me stand up, then all he did was touch me. I can't tell you how or why it worked. All I know is that it did, or I wouldn't be alive to tell about it. So maybe that does make it a miracle."

"Yet you have no idea who he was?" Beverly asked.

"No, I don't know." She shrugged. "And I doubt I'll ever bump into him again to ask." That thought left her with an insatiable longing.

Beverly nodded her head. "Well." She was quiet a few moments. "I still have things to take care of tonight and it's getting late. Please, stay as long as you need to. I do mean that. We'll put you to work if you're strong enough. We could use an extra pair of hands lately." She got up and headed out the door. "Do you need more to eat?" she asked.

"No, I'm full, thank you," Alyssa replied. It was good to feel full. Once it was a feeling she took for granted. She doubted she ever would again.

She paused. "You believe me, then?" she asked.

"I'll have to," Beverly said, a wan smile on her face.

Alyssa could hear her slow footsteps as she went downstairs.

Peter stayed in the room. He sat quietly in the wicker chair, chin in his hands, not looking at her. Alyssa was acutely aware of her own despicable condition, the odors she had been apathetically used to that now insulted her nose, informing her of her own filth. He must be aware of them too, but he said nothing and didn't seem in a hurry to leave her. She sat wishing for a bar of soap or at least an open window to ease her embarrassment. But opening the window would only call more attention to the problem.

She couldn't imagine what Peter must be thinking, except for his unintentional insult. And it could hardly be considered an insult as much as the truth. She probably did resemble something the cat killed and dragged home.

"So, it's been how many years? Eight, isn't it?" Peter asked, after a long and scarcely comfortable pause. "Mom mentioned once you'd gone to CU, but . . ." his voice trailed off. "What happened before that?" he asked. "While you were still at home?"

"Well," she said, "Mom did go out of control after we were separated. Dad started drinking, a lot . . . I didn't know how much. Well, I mean, I didn't know that what he had was a lot. We got closer, though, for a while . . ." She sighed. "We moved, did you know that?"

"Yeah, uh, I knew," Peter said, shifting his legs in the chair and looking down.

"Really?" she asked. "How?"

"Well," he said, and made a cough, "Well, I tried looking you up once. Couldn't find you, though."

"You did?"

"Yeah." He looked up at her.

"You really did? You looked me up?" She looked at him, considering it, a smile beginning on her face. It was nice to hear. She had imagined he never did . . . that he forgot her completely as soon as her letter reached him.

"Well. It was a long time ago." He looked away again.

"Yeah," she said, at first disappointed, but forcing herself to remember: this was a married man, and she had absolutely no intention of interfering, especially not with Beverly's desperate paranoia firmly in place. "Well, anyway we moved to this huge house, like old Joan always wanted. I found out later Dad made a deal with her not to hurt me anymore if he let her get her dream house. Isn't that nuts?"

"Did it work?"

Alyssa shrugged. "Mostly. Not always."

There was a silence, then Alyssa said, "Man, I haven't thought about any of that for so long. Not since Dad died. I went to Central U after graduation, with Debra, and I've never gone back." She paused. "Well, I did go back for the funeral but that's all. I didn't stay. Just up and back."

"Funeral? Your dad died? When?"

"Oh. I've lost track of the time. Let's see . . . I was nineteen when he died. My sophomore year of school, January . . ." She counted on her fingers. "Was that only two years ago? I guess so . . . no, it's closer to three. Seems like a lifetime." She shrugged.

"I'm sorry."

"He did it to himself. Drank too much. His heart gave out. His liver would've gotten him sooner or later. He started losing jobs the year he died, because of the drinking."

"That's still so sad."

"Would you believe Mom tried to blame me for it? I even kind of believed her, for a while there."

"Really?"

"That was a bad year," she said.

Peter nodded. "Sure was." He looked away.

"What's that?"

"Oh, nothing. Uh, sounds like it was, I meant." He cleared his throat again.

She stopped for a minute. There were plenty of things she didn't need to tell him about. The drug addiction after Chuck's death. Rob, and his part in all of it. "So, do you still live here or are you just visiting?" she asked, deciding to turn the conversation. "How's your wife? Do you have any kids yet?"

"My . . . wife?" he asked, with a gulp. "Excuse me? How did you . . .?"

"Yeah, I talked to your mom once, she said you were in China and I met this girl on the phone, she was there when I called—Topaz, wasn't it? They told me you were getting married as soon as you got back."

"Oh. *Topaz*," he said, seeming relieved. "Oh."

"Yeah . . ." she said, trailing off. His tone of voice made her curious. "Is something wrong?" She noticed, only then, that he wasn't wearing a wedding ring.

He cleared his throat. "I just . . . I didn't know that you called."

"I told your mother to say hello for me. She wouldn't give me your number in China."

"I didn't have a number," he said absently. He seemed very far away.

"So how is she?"

"Who?"

"Topaz."

"Oh, she and John have a little girl now," he said.

Alyssa registered surprise, raising an eyebrow.

"She didn't wait for me to come home, like we planned. She married this other guy before I got back. John Bryant. He was a couple years ahead of me in high school. I hear they're very happy together."

His tone was dry, void of emotion. He shrugged.

"Oh."

She was having difficulty taking in this news. Maybe she *should* have called again, later on, just to see if things actually went through. At the time, she assumed it would be a serious social blunder to do so, and avoided the possibility of further embarrassment. The one call had been hard enough.

"Well, it's all right," Peter said. "She was too flighty for me, anyway. I doubt I'd have made her happy, or vice versa."

She decided to change the subject. "So . . . China was good?"

"Yeah," he said, but his voice was flat. "China was good."

"And . . ." she paused, unsure whether to proceed. But she had to ask. "There's nobody else? That's hard to believe . . ."

"I never married." His demeanor stiff. He paused. "I live here still. I took over the farm after Dad . . . well, since he's been gone."

"I see."

"What about you?" he asked.

"Me?"

"I would guess you're single, showing up like this, but . . . you never know, these days."

"Oh. Right. No, I haven't married, either. Never felt like it. It's a lot of commitment."

He nodded his head. "Yes, it is."

He still seemed stiff, uncomfortable with the subject. There was a long, difficult pause.

"Well," she said. "So how's everyone else doing, then?"

He perked up a little at this. "Isaac got married about five years ago, married a nice girl named Anna. They have two kids, a girl age two and a baby boy. They live in another town, oh, twenty miles from here or so. Julia got married last summer and lives in town. I'm still here, and so's Andrew."

"That's the one I couldn't remember," she said. "I was trying to think who there was. Andrew. How old is he now?"

"Nineteen."

She nodded. "And this is Julia's old room."

"Right. Good memory. And Jordan and Kellie will be seven in the spring," he added.

This was news. "Who?"

"The twins . . . you didn't know about the twins?"

"I thought there were four of you."

"Mom had twins. Oh, that's right. That was the year after we fell out of contact, I guess, so you wouldn't know. Those two are inseparable. It's unusual," he said, "for a boy and girl their age to be good friends—especially siblings—but these two must have been cast from the same mold."

"Which one's which?" Alyssa asked.

"Jordan's the boy."

"Oh, of course. Wait, *six* children!" She was aghast. "Isn't that illegal?"

Peter laughed. "Illegal? Who has rules about how many kids you can have?"

"Central City. You didn't know?"

He shook his head. "That's awful. Sounds like holdovers from twentieth-century communist China. It wasn't like that at all when I lived there, but the older people still remember the horrors."

"It wasn't that bad," she said, and shrugged. "Higher tax penalties, that sort of thing. But whatever compelled your parents to have more? Wasn't four enough?"

Peter just smiled. "Our family never felt complete until the last two came along."

"Did they have anything to do with why my mother broke up with yours?"

"What did your mother tell you?"

"She wouldn't tell me anything. Ever."

"That would be like her, wouldn't it?" Peter grinned. "Mom having twins at 42 had a little to do with it, but it's more complex than that. We can talk about it more tomorrow. You look like you still need some rest."

"It had to do with a religious choice, didn't it? I remember that much, from what you told me back then."

He nodded but said no more.

Remembering Debra, and her family, Alyssa thought she could tell him she understood, that there were some things people had to do, even if she didn't relate to it personally.

"Debra was religious too," she said. "She was a Christian."

"You mentioned her earlier. Who is she?" Peter asked.

"She was wonderful. A great friend. My best friend. We met in high school after we moved to the big house. We roomed together through college."

"But you said earlier you didn't finish school?"

"No, not quite. After Dad died the money dried up." She felt bad blaming the loss of money on her parents, but couldn't bring herself to explain how she had wasted her inheritance.

"So where is she now?"

"Oh, she wanted me to come with her, but I couldn't. It was too much to ask."

"Where'd she go?"

"Well, the summer after Dad died was also the year Article 28 passed . . ."

"I remember," Peter said. "That would be the year."

"So, all of a sudden she tells me she's a Christian and she has to leave Central City or else. Funny I never saw it coming, I never thought about where she went every Sunday. I always figured she needed time alone with her boyfriend, is all, and she kept quiet about her beliefs."

"She'd have had to. They passed laws years ago against sharing religious beliefs or information with non-believers. It's against the law to encourage anything that leads to a 'dangerous mental illness.'"

"Oh. Well, that makes sense. Anyway, she said they were going up north somewhere to build this experimental new colony or something, where it was safe and they wouldn't be bothered by the government. Her dad lost his tenure over some ethical thing he defended, and the college was going to prosecute for the mandatory therapy, so they were all moving to this new place to live. She was going to marry her boyfriend there, he was one of them too. He was a nice guy. I'm sure it must have worked out for them."

"A colony?" Peter asked, showing a little excitement. "North, hmm, yes . . . but which one, eastern or western Iowa?" he muttered.

"All I know is north. I never did look it up on a map. Why?"

"Just curious."

"She wanted me to come with them, but I wouldn't. It all sounded too strange; forgive me, but I've never been into religion. I didn't think I could deal with it, and there is that Article . . . I thought it would be dangerous. Plus I had my own problems . . . Well, we ended up going our separate ways. But what I meant to say is, I supported her. I understand there are things you just have to do, when you feel something's right, in your heart, like she did. You should know, I would never dream of turning anyone in to the authorities. I swear. You don't have to worry about saying things in front of me."

"That's interesting," Peter said, smiling. "I'll keep it in mind."

"I still miss her sometimes," Alyssa said. "I moved to The Gardens after she left."

"Do they really have a secret forcefield around the place?"

She laughed. "No." Then she added, thoughtfully, "Well, I don't know. There could be."

"What was it like?"

"It was hard. Hard work. Good company though. Good people. They were like family to me, more than family, in a way. We were all very close. Look, it's not easy for me to talk about them right now." Suddenly she felt a surge of emotion, and had to pause. "Living there changed the entire way I see life, but I've seen a lot of things happen there I'd rather forget, too."

She looked up at the ceiling, and studied the pattern. Margret's lively friendship . . . George and Emma and their little congregation marching out of The Gardens, never to be seen again . . . Crazy Mary, Bert and his beautiful baritone singing, Marcus and Natty with their sweet little faces looking up at her. She thought of them all and had to stop talking completely. It seemed they lived in a different universe than this one.

Peter said, "Maybe another time."

"Sure." She looked at him.

After a pause he said, "It's strange to think your father's dead," Peter said. "I liked Chuck."

"I did too. But I mostly felt sorry for him. When I wasn't mad at him for being such a loser."

She tried a laugh, but was too tired. She felt terribly sleepy, and struggled vainly to keep her eyes open.

"Hang on," he said. "I don't think Mom knows he passed away. That was three years ago? No, two?" He stood up and went to the doorway, calling loudly to be heard downstairs. "Mom, get up here, you need to hear this."

Footsteps were heard on the wooden stairs. "What is it?"

"Did you know Chuck died?"

"He did? How long ago?"

"Alyssa says about three years ago."

"What from?"

"Heart attack. Brought on by alcohol abuse."

"I'm sorry to hear that, Alyssa," she said, reaching the doorway.

She looked in, but Alyssa was barely conscious, beginning to doze off. It was far into the night. She was just aware of Peter passing Beverly in the doorway, and Beverly coming close to switch off the lamp.

Chapter 41

Revelation

I believe she was as startled as we were.

Beverly Richardson,
personal journal entry

Alyssa was so exhausted she slept until afternoon the next day. Even then it was hard to wake up. When she finally did, she found a breakfast tray by her bedside and ate eagerly.

She had found the way to the restroom in the middle of the night and now went back and took a long, much needed shower. She scrubbed her skin hard with a washcloth until it was red and raw. Soap was a rare luxury, and it felt magnificent to get completely clean again, but it took some time.

She recalled her first look at herself in the mirror last night. Her face was so gaunt it frightened her. She could hardly tell it was her own reflection. She took a long look now. Her blond hair hung wet and limp, and although she tried to brush the matted tangles out before her shower, it still looked frizzy and unkempt. It hadn't been cut in months, and she had only Margret to cut it for her before that. She remembered, in college, slapping down over a hundred dollars at a time to keep her hair in perfect shape by the perfect stylist. That was back when it was long and healthy. Well, that was a lifetime ago.

Someone else's life, she thought. *That's not me anymore.*

She thought her eyes looked different. They were the same hazel-gray, though. She couldn't place what it was. Her shoulder and hip bones protruded obviously from her bare frame, and each rib was pronounced under her skin. She was much thinner than even she had guessed, like a walking skeleton. Sighing, she looked away, much saddened by the reflection she saw.

She put on the clothing Beverly had left out for her. The pink blouse and denim jeans fit quite loosely. She would need to ask for a belt to keep them from falling off. She wondered whose they were. They couldn't be Beverly's. She was a stout woman. These clothes were not her size. Oh, yes, Julia. These must be hers. She brushed her hair one more time. Well, she had looked worse yesterday and they accepted her, if barely. But she doubted that what she saw in the mirror could be considered pretty any more.

Then she wondered why that mattered at all, and sighed again. She had never cared about being attractive anyway. Her beauty always attracted the wrong sort of attention from men. Even the expensive haircuts and the designer clothing she once owned had been justified as necessary, not to be attractive, but to appear professional, smart.

But . . . *Peter had never married . . . maybe it* could *matter. Stop*, she thought. *Stop now*. It was hardly a good time to think of such things.

Beverly had also left out a new toothbrush, which she used gratefully. It felt wonderful. Her gums bled from the scrubbing. Only now did she begin to wonder if her teeth might have suffered permanent damage from the neglect, the intermittent vomiting of poor food choices. Two of her teeth had hurt badly, she knew that. As she brushed she realized they were no longer giving her trouble. Odd, she thought.

She found cleanser under the sink and scrubbed the bathroom clean of the dirt she had left in it. She was embarrassed, now that she was in a normal house among normal people, to see the mess she made simply cleaning herself. The sheer volume of filth that scrubbed off her body and lay like silt at the bottom of the bathtub was alarming.

She wondered who would be home at this time of day, what their schedules were like. She had heard voices in the house earlier in the morning, but had fallen back asleep. She had no idea when she had fallen asleep the night before, and had the odd feeling she dozed off in the middle of a conversation. She couldn't recall either saying goodnight to Peter or turning out the light.

They were certainly kind to take her in, considering the circumstances. As she scrubbed the shower, she wondered what reasoning her mother used all those years ago to justify slicing these wonderful people out of their lives. She wondered what "unforgivable" religious thing Beverly had "done" that Joan would never talk about.

Her mother had never mentioned Beverly's pregnancy, either, but from what Peter said, Joan must have known about it. Joan had always been a staunch environmentalist, strongly opposed to what she called "irresponsible overpopulation of an overtaxed earth." It was not a subject to which Alyssa had given much thought or any opinion. Maybe that was the clincher, the last straw. Too many children? Or was it merely the religious issues, whatever they were?

This morning she found herself intensely curious to know the reasons behind her mother's wrath. She was well aware Joan's rage could be set off with little provocation. While she was here, she might as well discover what lay behind the mystery. Get the answers to the questions that had always puzzled her, that had never been answered because neither her mother nor her father were ever willing to explain them.

She finished rinsing out the sink and shower and thought about going downstairs, but she was overcome by drowsiness. The heat of the long shower and the energy she used cleaning the bath out taxed her strength more than she realized.

Oh, well, she thought. *One more nap won't hurt.*

She went back into her room. Beverly had left out a clean set of sheets. Alyssa stripped the bed down and put the fresh ones on. She had made a grimy mess out of the ones she slept in during the night, a fact that caused her further embarrassment. She climbed in. It was heavenly. Quickly, she fell asleep.

Late that evening she awoke again. It was dark. She felt foolish for sleeping so long. The clock said ten-fifteen PM. She turned on the lamp by the bed. The cotton sheets were soft, clean, and comfortable, the pillow made of soft down. It was absolute luxury. She hadn't slept in a bed for so long. She yawned.

The light revealed a new tray of food by the bed. It felt weird to have trays of food appearing out of nowhere. She knew someone must have brought it, but it seemed magical. She had slept so deeply she didn't hear anyone coming in or out.

Dinner tonight was a roast beef sandwich on a roll with assorted condiments arranged on the plate, and a cold salad with dressing. It was chilled, so it couldn't have been left out for long. She ate with gusto.

She was almost finished and wondering what she should do next when Peter appeared in the doorway.

"You're up," he said quietly, startling her.

"Finally, huh?" she said with a grin. "It's about time I woke up."

He smiled back and came into the room. "I just came up to see if I needed to put that dinner away or not. I guess not." He sat down in the wicker chair.

"Thanks. It was delicious."

"I hope you have everything you need. Can I get you anything?"

"I'm fine. I feel strange, sleeping so long. I did get up earlier. I was going to come downstairs and say hello, but I was too tired after my shower. I hope I haven't imposed on you too much already."

"Not at all."

"I haven't eaten too much?"

He laughed. "Of course not. Mom meant it when she said you could stay as long as you like."

"Are you sure?"

"Sure."

"I suppose I should try calling home and make sure they haven't moved before I leave?"

"I suppose."

There was a pause.

"So what did you do today?" she asked, putting her tray back on the night stand. She wasn't sure what else to say. Still it sounded odd.

"Oh, the usual stuff."

"What's that?"

"Milking, grooming the horses, feeding all the little critters. We'll be plowing the fields under soon, before the first hard frost comes."

"Hmm."

"Do you feel strong enough to come down to the living room? Mom's there, and Andrew's been rather curious to meet you." He smiled.

"He always was a curious little kid, wasn't he?" She struggled to picture the brown-haired ten-year-old. "He could never keep his mouth shut."

Peter laughed. "Some things never change."

"I feel all right. I feel stronger now than I have in a long time. It's amazing how much better a real shower and sleep in a real bed can make you feel."

She stood up, and noticed her own clothes, the rags she had worn when she arrived, had disappeared. She thought she didn't mind, at first. Then she remembered they were Margret's, and they were all she had left to remember her by.

"Where are my clothes?" she asked, clearing her throat.

"They were pretty torn up," Peter said. "Did you still want them?" He looked at her quizzically.

"Oh, um, no, I guess not." She took a deep breath, telling herself it was silly to hold on to them.

"I'll pull them out of the incinerator pile, and we'll wash them for you instead," he offered.

"Would you? I know it must sound odd, but I'd appreciate that."

They went out of the small bedroom. To the right of it the hallway opened up into the staircase landing. The stairs curved fully around to the left going down into a large, open living room.

When Alyssa reached the bottom, she stopped suddenly and gasped. On the far wall hung a beautiful framed portrait of a man.

"Where did you find that picture?" she whispered.

She could barely speak. She felt struck by lightning . . . a fire, an intense thrill, coursed through her chest the moment she saw it.

Beverly was sitting on the sofa, doing some kind of stitching. Peter had come down first and was already in the middle of the room when Alyssa stopped. Beverly exchanged a glance with her son.

"The one on the far wall?" Beverly asked.

Andrew lounged in a large recliner facing his mother and sat up straight when they entered the room. His hair was the deep black his mother's used to be and he had soft hazel eyes.

"Who is it? Do you know him?" Excited, Alyssa moved a few steps into the room.

Peter asked, "Do you?"

"I would know those eyes anywhere."

She took a small step toward the portrait and stopped. She felt a shuddering thrill of joy run through her seeing that face again. What was it doing *here*?

Beverly looked at her. "You've seen this man?" she asked slowly.

Alyssa nodded. "That's the man who healed my leg." Automatically, she felt for the nonexistent wound. "You must know him. Is he a relative? A family friend?"

Her thoughts raced. If the Richardson's knew him personally, perhaps they could arrange for her to see him. Her heart leaped, imagining it. They would certainly believe her now, if there was still any doubt in their minds. Here was something unexpected they had in common.

Peter said, "I think you should sit down, Alyssa."

He led her to the sofa and sat her down between himself and his mother. Peter looked straight into her eyes for a long moment, until he had her complete attention. She was brimming with excitement and anticipation.

Then he said, "Alyssa, that is a portrait of Jesus Christ."

Her eyes widened. "No. That's impossible." She turned quickly to Beverly. "Isn't it?"

"Peter is telling you the truth," Beverly said.

A river of electric shock coursed through Alyssa, burning in her soul, confirming the truth of his words. She turned back toward Peter and looked up at the painting again. Her excitement transformed itself into shock, in spite of the strange burning, glowing sensation that filled her being. She turned again to sit straight forward and stared out the front window. She felt faint.

"It's also impossible for you to walk nearly 180 kilometers over rough terrain in one night, days after being shot in the leg. By your own account," Beverly said.

"I walked that far?"

Beverly nodded. "At least."

"Not to mention crossing the Missouri River," Andrew said. "She didn't say anything about crossing the river."

Alyssa felt flustered. "I don't remember." It was possible she had crossed a riverbed, she thought, but it had only been muddy. She had splashed through a stream or two . . . it was unclear. "Yes, I think there was a large bridge, somewhere." She was uncertain. Her memory of crossing the terrain was fuzzier than she expected.

"You can understand why we thought your story was farfetched, until you told us all if it. Then we started to piece the possibilities together," Beverly said.

Peter watched her closely. "We weren't sure who it was you saw, but we do believe in miracles." The expression on her face must have shown she was having a difficult time taking in the meaning of what happened to her. "What happened to you, and how you got here, must have been a miracle."

"Don't you see, it can't be," she said. "Jesus is a myth. Maybe he was a real person once, with some nice ideas, but . . ." She sighed and was silent a long moment. "You have to realize this shatters my whole concept of the world, of the entire universe, even." She continued, fumbling for words. "Debra left Central City because she believed in him. She said it was real and I'm sure it was real to *her* but believing in something doesn't make it true no matter how hard you believe it. Don't you see? I think it's a harmless belief, but . . ."

Her voice rose slowly. "I mean, it's not right to punish somebody for thinking it, or believing in it, but don't you see? It just can't be. Jesus Christ is *dead*. He's been dead a couple thousand years if I remember right. He's not walking around anymore healing people. He's just . . . just an *idea*."

She paused, took a deep breath, her mind running in circles, trying to piece together a logical train of thought. "Maybe a good idea, for some people, but just an *idea*." She rubbed her hands back and forth on her pants, wiping off the cold clammy sweat that broke out on her palms. "The man I met was *real*."

"No, he's not dead," Peter said quietly. "He lives."

"Look. Debra couldn't convince me to go with her a couple years ago and this won't work on me now. I know I'm not crazy. What if . . . what if that's just a picture of some guy you know, who happens to be the same person I saw, and now you're using this opportunity to get me to believe in your 'cause'? How do I know that?"

Inwardly a part of her realized how ridiculous her line of thought was. There was no way they could have known in advance who she'd seen or what that person looked like. Neither could they have known she would show up on their doorstep, any more than she knew it in advance. But the alternative was too difficult to accept, impossible for her. She felt hot and rubbed at the collar of her shirt.

This isn't real, she thought. *It's not real, it's not real, he can't be real. No.* She rejected it.

Andrew spoke up. "I don't know why you'd think we were lying. That picture's been right there on that wall since I was thirteen. Uncle Nick, Mom's brother, sent it to us for Christmas that year. It was commissioned by the leaders of our church a long time ago. We've had some trouble lately over it being there, but we're not taking it down. We're not afraid to admit who we believe in."

"That was my next question," she said. "You could be sent away for therapy for displaying that picture in the city, if it's supposed to be Jesus. How *do* you get away with it? Don't you understand what it means?"

Abruptly she remembered Bert. A heavy weight sank into her chest thinking about him, his counting of everything from his fingers to the bricks in the crumbling yellow wall, his booming incessant singing. Margret said he wanted to die for Jesus. She had wondered why anyone would want to go through that kind of torture rather than give up on a silly belief. She continued to fidget with her collar and scratch her neck, which was also sweating.

"Tell me," he said. "Look at me. Am I real?"

"Real? I don't know."

"Touch my hand. Feel me and see. Am I real to you?"

Her memory brought the words back. She remembered the scene clearly, the feel of his hand in hers, the strange scars on his hand and forearm that didn't seem to bother him. Her mind reeled.

He made certain I knew he was real. She thought the line of questioning was odd at the time, but was in no position to question his reasoning. He was determined that she answer him.

Yes . . . you have to be real, she had said. How could she have said no? He was standing right in front of her. She felt a familiar queasy feeling, her stomach churning its contents, upset with them. She fought it. Her dinner wasn't spoiled food that caused the feeling this time.

"This can't be happening to me," she whispered. In a quiet voice, she continued, "This man . . . this man had a body. I felt him. He held me up in his arms so I could stand. He was as tangible as you or me. God is . . ." she paused.

She had never been to any church, never sought any religious experience. The only theology she knew consisted of a few things she had overheard by accident, during George and Emma's emphatic preaching at Hall meetings, Friday nights in The Gardens.

"God is something people feel . . . love or something like that. He's not a, a *person*, if there even is a God at all."

"Why not?" Peter asked, gently.

"I don't know why not," she said, frustrated. "None of this makes any sense."

"That depends on what you've been taught. What does your heart tell you?" Peter asked. "What are you feeling right now?"

When he asked this question, she recognized the bright, warm burning inside her that she had felt earlier. It was the same feeling that led her here to find this forgotten family, *and* this painting, when her intention was only to return to whatever fragments were left of her home. It burned like a fire in her bosom, and refused to be ignored or put aside.

It was the same warmth she had felt in that man's presence, the feeling that caused her desperate longing to be with him, to be near him. She felt it vibrate through every fiber of her soul, telling her that what she was hearing was the truth.

But she didn't want to believe it. Something else inside her desperately did *not* want it to be true. That something rebelled against the warm feeling, refusing to trust anything so ethereal, so immeasurable and intangible. It was an internal war that threatened to tear her apart.

"I do feel something," she said. "I can't deny that. But I don't understand how this can be."

Peter said, "Believing in something doesn't make it true, but just because you *don't* believe in something doesn't mean it's *not* true. No one believed the world was round a thousand years ago, but that didn't make it flat. The truth is that Jesus lives. He is a tangible being. And you have experienced something most of us only long for, our entire lives."

She stood up and walked over to the picture. "His expressions were different, but very detail is perfect," she said in awe. "How can it be so perfect? It could have been taken from a photograph."

"The leaders of our church are called Apostles," Peter said. "They're called as special witnesses of Jesus Christ. They had the artist do it over several times until . . ." His voice trailed off.

The burning sensation intensified as she studied the painting, saturating, it seemed, every cell in her body. The negative feelings began to fade, the warmth she longed for winning the battle that raged inside her. She felt so good, so right, so at home.

"I would have died if he hadn't come to me," she whispered. She couldn't pull her eyes away from the eyes in the painting. "Right after it happened, I kept wondering who he was and why he found me and how he knew who I was. He knew my *name*. I completely forgot to ask him how he knew that. Nobody for miles around me knew that." She was quiet a long moment. "How did he know?" she whispered to herself. The others in the room were silent.

"I kept wondering why someone would bother to help me instead of just letting me die. But if he truly was," she swallowed hard, "Jesus Christ, or God, that only makes me more confused. Why would God care enough about me to save *my* miserable life? Why? I had no good reason to keep living. My life was worthless no matter what he said about me."

"What did he say about you?" Peter asked.

She flushed. "Oh, nothing, really . . . He said I exercised faith in him, and talked about my compassion. He knew I'd sacrificed some things for my friends. I . . . I didn't understand how he could know anything like that about me."

As she said this, she remembered the incredible love she had felt from the man when he said those things to her. In his eyes her life was *not* worthless. For the first time she felt a true sense of personal worth, a sense of being valuable to someone else, someone great and wonderful, of being loved for who she was, for everything she was, no matter what, of being completely understood and highly valued, like a rare and precious gem.

The wave of emotion that struck her then was too much for her weakened body to bear. She crumpled to the floor, overcome by a feeling of love that permeated her entire being and completely overpowered her.

Beverly and Peter rushed to her side. "Are you all right?" Beverly asked, kneeling and placing a hand on her shoulder.

"I think so," Alyssa whispered, looking up from the floor. "I've never felt this way before. I don't know what to do about it. I honestly never believed there was a God," she said, close to tears. "Especially not a God who took any notice of anybody personally, anybody like me. The world is so messed up. My whole life has been so messed up. It doesn't seem like any higher power could possibly have been watching over me."

She was silent for a very long time.

"But I can't deny what happened to me," she said finally, her voice a still whisper. "I *can't*."

Peter helped her up and she stood again facing the portrait.

"Can you help me understand all this?" she asked, pleading in her voice, reaching up gently to touch its frame. "Everything I ever thought about life has changed. I don't know what to think now. I don't have any idea why I'm here, why I'm still alive, who I am anymore. I thought I knew, you know . . . I thought I had a pretty good sense of myself for a while there . . . until the day I lost my job and all my friends were gone and I had nowhere to turn, nowhere to go. Now I feel like I never knew anything about *anything* and I still don't."

She paused, remembering something. "The marks in his hands . . . in his wrists . . . He had these ghastly scars. I asked him how he could heal my leg yet not himself . . ."

"His hands?" Peter asked, an expression of wonder on his face. His tone was one of awe, filled with emotion. "You . . . you felt the prints of the nails in his hands?"

"His wrists, too," she added.

Understanding formed in her mind. Yes, she had heard of this before. *The prints of the nails in his hands and his feet* . . . Something George the preacher had referred to, on occasion. "Those were from his crucifixion," she said softly. "From when he gave his life, on the cross."

"Yes," Peter said.

The realization weighed on her mind . . . the reality that he was once dead, and rose again, seeped into her soul.

Always remember me, and all I have done for you . . . His phrase took on a far deeper meaning.

She didn't say it out loud, but as she stood there she recognized finally what the feeling was that made her want to follow him anywhere, immediately, as soon as he healed her. From the moment he came to her, she had loved him, thoroughly and completely. She hadn't recognized it for what it was until this moment.

It was a different kind of love, more wonderful than anything else she had ever known. Different from the love she had felt with Rob, or even Peter, so many years ago; different from the love and sense of companionship she had with Debra or Margret. It was deeper, a love she felt resonating in every cell of her body.

Her soul and mind now understood that this feeling meant she loved *Jesus*. That was something she would never have imagined herself feeling before this day. But she did, and she knew she always would. What was more, it was certain beyond doubt that he also loved her.

It was an amazing thing. It was a thought and a feeling she never asked for or cared to have, but now that it was *hers* and she knew it completely, she could not imagine that she had lived so long without it.

The battle was won. The earlier dark feelings of unbelief had vanished, and in their place came a sense of total relief.

Is this what other Christians feel? she wondered. *Is this why Deb left her future behind?*

She thought she had understood her friend before; now she realized her understanding was merely tolerance. Only now did she truly comprehend.

Oh, Deb, she thought, *I finally understand you.*

Again she heard his voice in her mind. *"All I ask is that you believe in me and follow me."* It was a soft and gentle voice, but it pierced her soul to the very center.

Deep in her heart, she answered quietly, *I will.*

Chapter 42

Outbreak

Today we heard of a bizarre new disease taking Central City by storm, a terrible plague. Thousands are reported to have its symptoms and no one is sure yet how it spreads. Jon is absolutely fascinated by it. He can't get enough information. I, for one, have avoided hearing the details as much as possible. It's too gruesome. No ordinary "flu," this thing. But Jon is inquisitive as always. Keeps wondering what kind of germs could spread so fast, and how. So far the reports say scientists are at a loss. It doesn't follow any of the usual patterns.

I know I should be even more concerned about Alyssa than I have been in the past. Naturally I would assume her to be at risk, hearing all this. But somehow I feel calm. I'm not sure what that means . . . but I hope it's something good.

Besides, how can I have a worry in the world when my little Zachary smiles up at me? He laughed today for the first time . . .

Debra Pike,
personal journal entry

"I don't get it," Andrew said when Alyssa was gone.

"What?" Peter asked.

He sat in the brown recliner with a scowl on his face. "Well, that's a cool story, don't get me wrong, but I don't get it."

"What don't you get?" Beverly asked.

She and Peter turned to face him. They were standing by the stair landing.

"I saw her when you carried her in here, Peter, she was filthy. Why would *he* go to *her*? We're out here struggling, trying to do all the right things all our lives and nothing remotely like that ever happens to any of us. It's not fair. We need help all the time to protect ourselves and where is he then? Where was he when Dad disappeared?"

"Watch your tongue, Andrew," Beverly said sharply.

"Mom, let him talk," Peter said, going to the couch to sit near his brother.

She sighed.

Andrew continued. "How could he go into such a filthy place? How could he even *touch* her when she was that dirty? I can tell from her reaction she wasn't making it up, but I just don't get how it can be true." He pulled at the hole in the arm of the chair.

"Don't pick the stuffing," his mother said.

"Well, you could put duct tape over it if you care that much, Mom," he answered, and continued to pick.

"Andrew," she said with a stern look.

He patted the armrest firmly and stood up.

Peter said, "Andy, none of us has been shot and left to die."

"That's beside the point," he replied.

Beverly said, "May I remind you that God *is* all-powerful and if he has to go to the darkest corner of the darkest city to rescue one soul he can do it, and will do it, if necessary."

"I think the key word here is *'necessary,'*" Peter said quietly, looking up from his seat at his brother. "He doesn't need to visit us personally to teach us. You know that. We've got the scriptures, his words. We've got each other. She had nothing."

"Why not leave her with nothing? She was just a street rat."

"You forget the worth of a soul," Beverly said. "And to judge not. You see why I asked him to hold his tongue, Peter. Some things are better left as thoughts and not words until one can work them all the way through." She folded her arms across her chest. "Andy, you should know I have my doubts about her. But I invited her to stay, and she will be welcome to stay as long as she wants. I won't have you or anyone else interfering with that. And more than that, I spent a long time on my knees last night, until I felt a witness from the Spirit that she was telling the truth."

"How can you possibly know everything she's done and everywhere she's been?" Andrew asked with disgust obvious on his face. "She was filthy. A homeless . . . bum."

"We can't know," Peter said.

He wasn't sure he wanted to find out, either. There were those rumors he heard long ago, when he looked for her on her sixteenth birthday . . . everything pointed to her turning down an undesirable path. "But the Lord looks on the heart, right? Outward appearances don't mean much to him."

"She lived in *Central City* of all places," Andrew continued, unwilling to drop the argument. "Her soul can't possibly be less filthy than what we saw on the outside. You know what people are like there. You know the kind of sordid lifestyles they all live. It's a modern day Sodom and Gomorrah."

"I don't know what kind of lifestyle she lived," Peter said, standing to face him. He was taller than Andrew and had always been glad his younger brother hadn't passed him up, especially when they disagreed. "And I don't much care to guess, either. But I do know one thing. I'd be very careful about passing a verdict on her that differs from God's."

"You know the Lord answers your prayers as well as mine," Beverly said quietly but firmly.

"I know that, Mom," Andrew said with a sigh. His shoulders slumped a little. "I'll go try."

"Promise me," she said.

"Yeah."

He left the room, walking past the portrait without a glance, and turned left into the hall opposite the stairs, where his room, Peter's, his parents' and another bathroom were located.

"I hope she's not a burden for you, Mom, or doesn't become one," Peter said.

Beverly came over and sat down on the couch. Peter sat again, facing her, wrinkling his brow.

"I hope so too," she said. "We'll have to wait and find out." She looked at him and paused. "What is it?" she asked. "You look worried."

"I'm afraid I might've prayed her here," he said in a whisper.

"How so?" she asked, furrowing her brow.

He fidgeted, twisting on the couch. "Every so often I ask for her to be kept safe. You know. We never knew what happened to her . . . Did we?"

Beverly shook her head slightly.

He looked at her. "And I wanted to make sure she was okay."

"Peter, I don't think that constitutes praying her here," she said with a warm smile. She reached over and touched his shoulder. "Unless you've specifically asked for her to come back, I don't think it's anything to worry about."

"Yeah, I guess you're right," he said, still looking uncomfortable.

"Goodnight, son." She hugged him. "Don't worry about that, okay?"

"Okay."

But later that night, Peter couldn't sleep. He hadn't slept well since Alyssa arrived. He had brought the food, removed the empty trays, disposed of the filthy clothes. Did she actually want them? Strange. He'd have to go pull them out of the incinerator pile, as he promised, and put them in the wash instead.

I will come to you, Peter, the whispered voice of his dreams had said.

Two years ago he assumed it was simply a warning about Jackie, a warning he hadn't heeded. Especially when Alyssa didn't present herself to his arms immediately afterwards. For over a year after he sent Jackie away, he had bruised himself daily for ignoring that warning. But that didn't matter now. It didn't matter that he hadn't been able to date anyone seriously since, or be interested in or trust another woman.

Now she was here, in his house, no longer a shadowy dream. But she was hardly the glamorous image of Alyssa he had conjured up for himself, a dashing blonde bombshell who would waltz into his life and sweep him breathlessly off his feet.

Oh, Peter, he imagined her words. *I've waited for you for so long and finally found you. Did you wait for me?*

He would whisk her away and they would be married instantly, flinging headlong into eternal wedded splendor. She would be wearing white when they met. She would be pure and clean and her hair would sparkle like diamonds in the sunshine. She would . . . She would *not* come to his doorstep starving, smelly, homeless, straight out of the heart of the most depraved and wicked city on earth.

His mind was in turmoil. Andrew's questions only fueled his own, as much as he had put up his outward defense of her. Where had she been? What kind of life had she lived? What could he believe about her? His imagination wandered, picturing scenarios that tormented himself with images of things she may have done.

Realizing the path his mind was taking, he forced himself to stop. He knew the Lord could forgive, would forgive "whom he would forgive . . ." Yet he had tried forgiveness with Jackie, and she had only used it against him. He could not, could *not*, get close to anyone remotely like that again.

He couldn't ignore the fact that a miracle had brought Alyssa here. It couldn't have been an accident that she found her way. Or could it? Maybe he prayed her here after all. He felt ill. Absolutely ill, torturing himself over and over with the old saying: *Be careful what you ask for, you just might get it.*

Whatever she was, she was certainly not the woman of his dreams. Not the one he had foolishly been waiting for in the vanity of his hopes. She was not the soft echo of a dream. The reality was a stark contrast to his fantasy. Indeed, the very fact that the reality existed was a burr in his side.

He tossed and turned, shaking his pillow, unable to find a

comfortable position on the mattress.

Well, it was not as though she was making advances, or as though he was under any obligation to make any of his own. No, she would be on her way soon. Then he could forget she ever came.

•••••••

The next morning Alyssa woke at a normal hour. There was no breakfast tray waiting for her.

It must not be magic after all, she thought, smiling to herself.

She looked out the window to get a feel for her surroundings. She felt disoriented. It was night during the only times she had been awake long enough to think about it. Her room faced the front of the house, east, and the window looked out on the old live oak tree. It was a bright morning and the tree looked odd with the sun shining brightly on its dead brown leaves, which had yet refused to fall.

She showered again. It was wonderfully refreshing to have hot water and as much soap as she needed. She put on the jeans and pink blouse from the day before.

The bathroom was on the far end and opposite side of the hall from her room. Leaving it, she passed the door to her room and went downstairs.

She looked around to get a feel for the house. Her memories of the place were fuzzy. As she stood on the staircase, the kitchen was to her right, the living room to the left, and the portrait on the wall directly faced her. Just to the right of the portrait, a hallway led to another wing of the house. She remembered there was a bathroom that way, bedrooms, and stairs to the basement.

The living room and kitchen were open, separated only by a short wall concealing the far portion of the dining area. The curtains were pulled wide in the living room to let the morning sun pour through the large picture window, brightening the house. She moved to the kitchen.

The rear of the kitchen was not wall, but all windows. Old-fashioned French doors in the center led out to a sizable wooden deck. The room was bathed in the sunlight from the front, the deck outside still in shadow. The cooking area was to her right as she faced the kitchen, divided from the dining area by a counter. A long rectangular table filled much of the space in front of her.

Peter sat at the table looking out toward the deck when she walked in. "You're up," he said, standing. He smiled as she sat down at the table.

"Do I still look like the cat dragged me in?" she asked with a twist of a smile.

His smile disappeared. "I already apologized for that. It just slipped out."

"Hey, no offense. I scared *myself* when I looked in the mirror." She grinned.

"Well, um, you do look . . . better," he said.

"I'm not fishing for compliments. I think I'll need a belt to keep these pants up though. I'm happy just to have something clean to wear. It feels nice."

"I'll ask Mom about a belt when she comes in. Can I get you something to eat?" he asked, moving into the kitchen.

"I'm pretty hungry."

Peter turned on the stove and placed a skillet on it. "How do you like your eggs?"

She laughed softly. "*My* eggs," she mused. It was difficult, even though they had been bringing her food, to understand that it was given to her for free.

Peter dropped some butter into the pan and it began to sizzle. He cleared his throat. "Like we told you, we don't have any shortages here. The chickens lay plenty of eggs every day. Too many." He tried to smile at her, then looked back into the pan, intent on watching the butter melt.

She made a mental note to stop saying things like that. It was hard not to, though. She had been deprived for so long of so many basic things, things most people took for granted.

"I think I like them scrambled," she said, suppressing the urge to add "used to" to her sentence. "Not gooey and not dry and brown. With pepper." Freshly ground, black. The way her father did it. Add a touch of fresh chives and grated parmesan cheese sprinkled on top . . . *Whoa*, she thought.

Memory came back too quickly. Chuck had been an excellent chef in his days in the old house, before he quit altogether to devote his time to trains. Her mouth watered, remembering.

It was strange to think she had been so spoiled once. In college, she would send her restaurant orders back if the food wasn't prepared correctly, if she detected a trace herb or seasoning missing. No wonder Rob had noticed it. She couldn't imagine ever being so picky again.

Peter nodded that he understood her directions and cracked six eggs into a bowl. "Did you sleep well?" he asked.

"Wonderfully. I forgot how divinely comfortable it is to sleep in a bed."
She had done it again, without thinking. There was a break in his
whisking rhythm. "I'm sorry," she added. "I'm trying not to do that."

"Do what?" he asked, looking over while he stirred.

"You know."

He looked back at the eggs and continued whisking.

"I'm trying not to talk about it. I'm sorry if it bothers you where I've
lived lately. Circumstances were beyond my control."

"It's okay. I know that."

"Do you think it doesn't bother *me*? What else could I do after I lost
my job? Living on the street was the only option I had left."

"I know, you said there wasn't work anywhere." He whisked faster.
The egg sloshed out of the bowl and he slowed down.

"I didn't have any friends left, I was afraid to go back home, besides I
didn't have enough cash for a ticket out of the city if I wanted one. There
was no other choice."

He looked up to stare out the kitchen window while he stirred.

"Why are you judging me? I can't help what I've been through."

"I'm not," he said, and looked over at her. "I said, I know that."

"Then what is it? Do I still smell funny or something? I know I was—"

"No," he said, exasperated. He stopped stirring. "You're fine. It's just .
. ." He broke off and stared out the window again, leaning his hands on
the counter.

"Just what?"

"I don't know." He picked up the whisk again to stir. The eggs were
already frothy.

"You do know. You don't believe the story about my leg."

"That's not it. No. I believe that."

"Then it's where I've been. What I am. What I represent?"

Silence. He stopped stirring.

"Ah. That's it then. I will *try* not to refer to it if it makes you
uncomfortable, but it's hard not to. I learned more about myself living in
poverty than I did in all my life before that. I learned more about what's
important in life and what isn't than I ever thought I needed to before."

Silence except for the soft sizzle of the butter in the pan.

She felt she would never fit in anywhere normal again, and exhaled a
sigh. The street was a place where she didn't need to explain herself.
She could stay or go as she pleased, and didn't need to conform to any
standards of expected behavior. Perhaps it had been a short time. Yet
that part of her life had changed her. The daily burden of finding a meal,

the chore of struggling not to vomit bad food and losing the battle, the need to defend choice morsels from would-be thieves; and sharing her findings, when she could, with those nearby who were physically unable to search for food. All these things were permanently etched into the core of her being. None of that lifestyle was considered socially acceptable. Not here, not anywhere else but there.

"I barely survived . . . I'm sorry . . . I've forgotten how to be socially correct about things, but I'm trying. I don't know how to be normal anymore."

"It's not just that," he said. "It's everything. It's how you've lived, before that happened. Ever since we parted ways."

"What's that supposed to mean?"

He took a deep breath. "Our values are different. You're not the same as us. We follow a certain moral code . . ."

"Why should you care what my values are, or aren't?" she asked. "And what makes you so sure mine are different?"

"Listen. I know there's a lot you're not telling me. You're holding back, I can tell. I can feel it. And there's a real concern you may have brought those values along with you. Andrew's having a hard time right now. Well, we all are, and . . ."

Alyssa felt a twinge of irritation at this turn of the conversation. She felt accused of something, but didn't know what. Was eating out of garbage cans a 'value' she would 'bring along with her?' Hardly. What were they—was Peter—afraid of?

"Excuse me?" she said, finally.

"It's just . . . Look. I told you I looked you up, once."

"I wondered about that, since you told me. When exactly was it?"

"You would've been sixteen . . . that day."

She tried to remember her sixteenth birthday.

"It was a little while after I got your letter . . . Well, I met the lady who bought your old house."

"You came all the way to the house?" She was taken aback.

"Yeah. One of those rash teenage ideas." He shrugged it off. "Well, the lady told me something your mother said during the mortgage closing, about moving to get away from the reputation you seemed to have earned. And after they moved in, the neighbors told her about the revolving door of boyfriends you seemed to have—in and out, all the time, all hours of the day as long as your folks weren't home. That's what I mean. Can you explain that? I mean, what got into you, Alyssa?"

She looked at him in shock. It was impossible. He'd heard . . . what?

Her mother told people *what. . .?* Again the blame had fallen on *her?* It was she who had the "reputation." She bent her head to the table, struggling for emotional control.

"Oh, *Lauren . . .*," she whispered.

"What? What did you say?"

"There were boys all right. Dozens. Just like they said. But they had the story all wrong. All wrong. They were there to see Lauren. Only Lauren. She started that not too long after we were separated."

"Lauren?" he asked, puzzled. "She never seemed the type . . ."

"And I *do?*" she asked, devastated by the pain of his suspicions.

"No! I didn't mean it that way. I'm sorry. Sorry."

"After high school she turned her little hobby into a full-fledged occupation. She had quite a career in adult film last I knew. She forced me to swear never to tell Mother the truth, and I never did. She wouldn't have believed me anyway. You remember how she doted on Lauren. Lauren was *perfect.*" She paused to gain control of her emotions. "Are you going to cook those eggs, or just burn the butter?" she added, feeling hunger in the pit of her stomach, and badly needing a diversion, however small.

He was silent. He put the whisk in the sink and poured the eggs into the pan with a loud sizzle.

"None of it—absolutely none of that—was me," she said. "Honest. It's the absolute truth."

Peter's eyes widened, then narrowed. He cleared his throat.

"That still doesn't clear up one thing," he said. "Why would Joan say your reputation was a reason for moving?"

Why did his suspicions hurt her so much? They seared through her heart like hot coals. She struggled to hold on, to stay in control of her feelings.

"That's another matter entirely," she said at last. "As usual, she had that all wrong too, entirely wrong . . . but I'm sorry. I'm far too upset right now to go into *that.*"

"Oh," Peter said. She couldn't tell what he thought of her explanation.

"Mother never believed anything I said, even when it was true. She got it into her head that I had a rotten reputation. How was I supposed to change her mind? I told her the truth. I told her. But she never believed me. I could never please her, Peter. Don't you remember? I could never get anything right, no matter how much she tried to beat her idea of sense into my head."

She trembled. Vivid memories of the literal truth of that statement came crashing back into her mind. It was too much. Losing the shreds of control she'd been clinging to, she began to cry, surprising them both.

She was terrified of going back home, but she knew she had to, and soon. Her predicament made the tears flow harder. She couldn't burden the Richardson's, whether food was plentiful or not. It was painfully obvious she didn't fit in. But the thought of facing her mother in person filled her with unspeakable dread. She could almost feel the bruises she expected to come her way when she arrived home. She ached inside, her tears spilling freely.

"Alyssa Stark does not cry," Peter said firmly, waving his spatula at her.

"Alyssa Stark did not cry," she said back, "until a few years ago, when she learned how . . . but it wasn't easy."

She wiped her tears on her shirtsleeve, embarrassed by her outburst. Especially in the last week, she had allowed her tears to come freely, whenever she felt the faintest need. Now, here, they were out of place again. Another thing she would have to relearn.

"How do I know that?" Peter asked. "How do I know any of this is true, anyway? Who are you, really? Now that Mom's not around, why don't you prove it, to me. The Alyssa I knew would never cry in front of anybody about anything no matter how much it hurt, not even me."

"Except for *once*," she said, no longer hiding her pain at his accusations. "That's how you know that. Because I cried when I broke my stupid leg in that field and I made you promise not to tell, when I was ten years old. That was our first secret. After that we shared a lot of secrets. Is that enough or do I have to list them all?" She struggled on, crushed that he would demand this of her. "There was the time you locked Julia in the back shed. There was the powdered laxative in the—what was it?—the bottle of peach jam. And last of all . . ."

"Hey," he said, raising the spatula as if to defend himself from her words. "I didn't mean it that way!"

"Then what did you mean? How often must I prove myself here? Every day? What do I have to do, before you believe me?"

"That's not what I meant," he said. "It's enough."

"Because I can leave now, I really can!" Tears flowed as she thought about it, even though she fought to hold them in. "Right now. As much as I'm absolutely terrified of going home, I'd rather be on my way than stay where I'm not wanted!"

"No, please," he said, more calmly, lowering the spatula.

They looked at each other, her eyes red and hot, his piercing through her in a way she didn't like. She had stood up somewhere during her outburst, and only now realized it. She sat down hard in her chair and looked out the window.

"What are you going to do if they don't want you?" he asked, softly.

"I don't know," she said. The thought had just barely begun to creep into the corners of her mind, before he asked. "I don't want to think that far ahead. If I can't find work, I guess I'll just go back to living on the street again." She spoke firmly. "Which would suit me fine, since that seems to be the only place I belong anymore."

"No, that's not true, don't say that," he said. "Please. Alyssa . . . I needed to know it was you. It threw me when you started to cry, that's all. That's not the Alyssa I knew."

"What, was I supposed to stay exactly the same? I suppose you're exactly the same as when you were sixteen? You haven't changed at all I suppose, in what, eight years? You expect me to pick up where we left off, like nothing ever happened? Like no time has passed? What?"

She turned back to him. She was instantly sorry she said it. The conversation had brought back a powerful memory of just *where* they left off, and she didn't want to think about that. His lips soft against hers, in the field just outside this very house. It made her extremely uncomfortable.

"No, of course not," he said, "I just thought . . ."

"The eggs are burning," she said.

He scooped them out of the pan and onto two plates. "Sorry," he said.

"Oh, I don't care if they're burned. I'll eat anything."

She was distracted, not wanting to think about the fact she once kissed the man in front of her. Or that he might possibly remember it too. She felt a strange, weak sensation in her knees, and shoved the memory away.

"No, I mean, I'm *sorry*. I'm sorry I asked you to prove it. It wasn't nice."

"You told your mother it didn't matter who I was," she said, glad of the fresh tangent.

"*I* needed to be sure."

"Why? If it doesn't matter it doesn't matter."

"Do you think losing my father hasn't affected me? Do you think it's only my mom who worries? I'm the oldest son home. I have to be strong for everyone else to lean on. But I have to know it's *you* so nothing else happens to threaten my family. I had to know for me. For my sake."

"And if I'm really Alyssa Stark I'm not a threat?"

"I don't know that, but if you're not pretending, there might be less risk, more chance we can trust you."

"You people are the most paranoid I've ever met."

"No, you have to understand. See, we had a lead that Dad was abducted by old friends. But one of the men we first thought was with him was out of the country then, and we have sources that prove it. He was shocked to find out Dad was missing. It really is possible somebody impersonated him."

"Are you sure this man was telling the truth?"

"Absolutely. But none of us were there. We'll never know exactly how it happened. That's just our best guess."

"So you'll trust me if you know I'm really me. Is that it?"

"I trust in Christ. And I believe your story. So I don't believe you've come here to harm our family. Not intentionally, anyway."

"I see," she said, but wasn't sure she did, or that she hadn't just been insulted, again. Learning everything he had imagined about her was insult enough.

"I forgot about that. I flipped when you started crying, it made me think you might be an impostor, though I can't fathom why. I'm sorry I upset you. I'm sorry that it bothers me where you've been and I'm even sorrier that it shows. I don't want you to be uncomfortable. It's just that we get a lot of unpleasant surprises these days . . ."

"And I'm one of them," she sighed.

"That's not true."

"Yes it is. My being here is troubling all of you. I can feel it. It's not a matter of you making me uncomfortable. It's more that I'm bothering all of you by being here. I see that now. I think I'll just give up, find my way back to the slums and sleep on the cement until I starve. Safe or not. At least there I didn't have to be sociable. All of us belonged there and we all knew it."

"You can't do that," Peter said quietly, bringing the plates out around the counter and setting them on the table. He went back for forks.

"Who are you to tell me what I can do? I'll do what I want."

"I didn't say you *may* not do that. I said you *can't* do it."

"And the difference is?"

"Do you want juice or milk?" he asked.

"Juice, please." She sighed. "So?"

He brought the drinks over with the forks and sat down next to her. "You can't go back because the slums aren't there to go back to."

"What?" She had picked up her fork but set it down now, uncertain she had heard right.

"We were going to tell you last night. That's why I asked you to come downstairs in the first place. Then all the excitement happened with you seeing the picture and all. We didn't expect that," he said, clearing his throat. "And overnight it's gotten worse. There's been an outbreak of some kind of disease no one's ever heard of before. An epidemic. There are huge casualties. They think the symptoms started about four days ago, but they didn't call it an emergency until people started dying, last night.

"There seems to be no cure. They think it's a new virus. They can't figure out what spreads it either. It doesn't have to be direct contact, but they're not sure if it's airborne, or something else, since they're having a hard time isolating it. No theories yet about where it came from."

Alyssa just looked at him.

"This disease is spreading so fast it's taking everything they've got just to quarantine it. They're reporting its heaviest concentration is in what they call the 'lower income sectors.'"

Alyssa coughed. "So that's what they're calling them."

"People are so sick there's not even any looting going on."

"Nothing to loot, where I've been. Wait, they're actually reporting The Gardens sector on the *news*?"

"Yes . . . yes, I think that's the name they used. The upper class sectors have been hit too, but not as heavily. There are reports of random explosions all over as well, especially along water mains, which doesn't make any sense. That investigation is going more slowly. The strange thing is the explosions are concentrated where the disease is most rampant. They think there must be a connection. The explosions have broken so many water mains there's no way to fight the fires. No water pressure. The flooding from the broken mains is mostly underground, so that doesn't help either. Most of the slums have burned to the ground."

She was silent for a time. "I can't believe it," she said eventually.

She picked up her fork. In spite of the shock, her stomach called anxiously for the food in front of her.

They were both quiet while they ate. When her plate was empty, she looked up.

"That means Mary and Bert might be dead," she said with a blank look, the realization finally settling in. "And all the people living outside that horrible hospital . . ."

All the people she left behind, all those she had met in her wanderings; all now more helpless than herself. At the time, apathy had hardened her to their separate plights, her own desperate need preventing emotion for others. She had no way to help them then. Now their possible deaths, even those of strangers she had seen but never knew, struck her like the loss of close family members.

"I should have been with them," she said, tears coming again as she remembered the faces she had seen. So many more pitiful than her own. So many in greater need of mercy. "I shouldn't be here at all. Some of their faces . . . Why did he rescue me and not them?" She looked at Peter, hoping he would have an answer.

"Hey," he said. "You're not the captain of a ship, you're not expected to stay on while it sinks or anything like that."

"But why?" she asked. "Why *me*?"

"I can't answer that," he said, and looked out the window again, then sighed. "Maybe it's better for them this way. You said yourself you would have starved to death even if you hadn't been shot. They won't be suffering anymore, not for long anyway."

"But how could he leave them all there to die? Why rescue only me? I don't know much about God, but that doesn't seem fair, does it? Isn't he supposed to be fair?"

"Death isn't so awful."

"Oh, right. Like you've been there."

"It'll be an end to their mortal suffering. They won't be hungry anymore. They'll be with their loved ones who've passed on. They can be at peace."

"How can you be so sure? What if it's worse?"

"I suppose it's faith."

"Faith?" She sighed heavily. There was so much of which she had no concept.

"Well, it's like you said last night. You felt something, right? You just knew, didn't you? In your heart, you felt the truth. That's how it is with me, it's a spiritual witness."

"Well if death is so much better, why can't I be with them? I could've died three or four different ways by now."

A bleak memory caught her by surprise: her near-fatal overdose, reminding her of yet another time her life was spared. Why did she go on living, always escaping the odds?

"It must mean you have more to do with your life. Your work isn't finished yet. Otherwise he might've allowed you to die."

"My 'work'?" she asked skeptically. "What work? I haven't done anything, and I have no skills he could use."

"You may not think so, but apparently he does."

"I guess. I told him I'd work for him. He said . . ." He said, *You will, someday, when you're ready* She left the thought unsaid. "Well, I would do anything for him. I know that much."

The sun streamed into the room from the front of the house, behind her, warming her back. It seemed out of place. It should be cloudy on a day like this. She got up and rinsed her plate in the sink.

"Thanks for breakfast," she said.

"Still hungry?" he asked.

"I'm all right." Her tone was sullen.

"I'm sorry to be the one to break the news. None of us knew how you'd take it. Mom thought she might do it better, but . . ."

"It's okay. I would've found out sometime anyway."

"There are live reports on all the stations if you want to see for yourself. The TV's in the alcove wall under the stairs. The remote's on the little table."

"No, thanks. I have a hard time watching the news." She moved into the living room.

"Too negative? Graphic?" Peter asked.

Putting his plate on the counter, he followed after her.

She shook her head. "Too hard to know what to believe. The simple fact that they've admitted the 'lower income sectors' exist says it must be serious though." A new thought came to her. "Are there any government officials dead? That they've reported?"

"Several," he nodded. "The President himself is sick. He's been quarantined inside the Presidential Palace with his staff for the last two days."

She raised her eyebrow. "They said *that*?"

"Yeah. So? That's news."

"They still have the usual news anchors?"

"A few are sick. Most of the usual ones are still on."

"If very bad news about the President himself made it to the public, it could mean the entire agency that monitors the media is *gone*."

She thought hard, trying to remember all the things Rob said the day before he left, teaching her about the way the system worked.

"The government has a strict policy not to release negative reports about the President himself. They exercise extreme control over any news like that. If those reports are coming out, it must mean . . ." she paused, piecing it together. "You might actually be able to believe what you're hearing." The last sentence she said thoughtfully, considering the meaning herself. "He may truly be sick."

"How do you know so much?"

She smiled faintly. "I had a friend once who knew all the ins and outs of the system."

"And I have to take your word for that?" he asked, smiling back.

"No. You don't have to." Her smile broadened. "I don't care if you do or not. But it sure doesn't help me feel any better knowing it's probably ten times worse than they're letting on." The smile vanished as abruptly as it began and she was sullen again. "If you don't mind, I think I might like to go up to my room and think this over for a while."

"That's fine."

"I mean Julia's room," she said, correcting herself. "These must be her clothes." She pulled at the loose shirt.

"Right. She left a lot of junk behind when she got married. Keeps coming back for visits and picking through it, but won't let Mom toss it out. Drives Mom nuts. Don't worry, she won't mind loaning a few clothes. Oh, and I was supposed to tell you, Mom said feel free to wear whatever's hanging in that closet."

"Thanks. By the way, where is she?"

"Out shopping. Oh, and the twins are in school, and Andrew left for work an hour ago. Mom figured I could take care of you if you happened to wake up. Didn't know if you'd sleep like you did yesterday or not. I was getting ready to bring up some breakfast when I heard the water running for the shower."

"Oh." That explained why there was no tray when she woke up.

"She'll be back soon. I have to get started plowing the corn under, so I'll be out there." He motioned toward the back door. "I'm getting a late start as it is. You'll be all right?"

She nodded and turned toward the portrait again, leaning her hands on the end of the couch for support. Those eyes drew her, beckoning her to look, to see. She stared into their depths, searching for some kind of understanding, answers to her multitude of questions. There were so many mysteries. She had to search, deeper than she ever had in her life, to find out who she really was. There were so many things missing, so many empty places, so many aches, and then new losses today. She had to find meaning in it all.

Something deep inside whispered to her that somewhere, there was meaning to be found.

****

Peter stood a few feet away from her, closer to the kitchen. As he watched her, with the room drenched in sunlight from the front window, it seemed to him she began to radiate the light, reflecting it, shining with an internal glow. He became as absorbed looking at her as she was looking at the painting.

She shone pure white in the morning sun, and in that moment he no longer saw the gaunt, malnourished skeleton of her frame. He saw a beautiful face shining through her pale skin. Her still-wet hair sparkled, the drops of water catching the rays like dew and reflecting the light with their tiny prisms, breaking into thousands of rainbows around her head. It was like . . . like *diamonds*. An aura of diamonds. He stood transfixed, and caught his breath in a silent gasp. The diamonds he always imagined . . .

This is what I see, Peter, said a voice in his mind. It was a penetrating, soft voice, so quiet he wasn't sure he actually heard it. *Remember, I look on the heart*, it said.

Suddenly she radiated purity with a glow of whiteness that nearly blinded him. He was unable to fully apprehend the beauty of what he saw, nor did he understand it. But the sense of her perfect loveliness distilled through his soul, and stunned him frozen in place.

After an impossible time, one of those rare moments that are both an eternity long and an infinity too short, she turned to him. He blinked. He felt blinded by her radiance.

"What are you looking at?" she asked, wrinkling her brow. "Do I look all that bad?"

"No! No . . . not at all!" He squinted and gave his head a shake. "Sorry, I think the light got in my eyes, I didn't mean to stare. I . . ."

His voice trailed off as he squeezed his eyes shut in a prolonged blink. He felt embarrassed and ran his hand through his hair. The brilliant light faded back to normal and she again appeared as she had looked earlier that morning. It was just Alyssa, a young, gaunt, slightly disheveled woman who stood before him now. He took a deep breath.

"It's bright out there this morning," he said.

"Yeah, I guess it is." She looked out the front window. "It doesn't seem right, with everything happening today. Should be gloomy."

Peter nodded. "Weather doesn't always match the mood of the day, that's for sure." He tried adapting to the turn of the conversation. "It'll be good for plowing, though. Not too cold yet, but the hard frost will be here soon."

"I guess so . . . I'll just go upstairs now," she said sadly, taking one last glance at the portrait before turning to the stairs.

"Oh," Peter said. "Please, don't feel you have to stay up there."

"I don't. I need some time to think," she said. "I think I said that already."

"Oh. Yes, you did. I understand."

After a moment he heard the latch click on the door. He stared after her in wonder with a vague sense of longing, wishing he could regain the vision of beauty he had just seen. He shook his head to clear it, and remembered there was work to be done. It was a very late start. He put on his hat and pulled on his old leather work gloves, then slowly walked out the back door in a daze.

****

Alyssa spent much of the morning thinking, remembering her time in The Gardens. She realized she had been happy there. She had changed so much, cast off her old self-centered materialism and learned to function as part of a community, to see the whole picture, to truly care for the others around her.

Now all those others were gone.

It was too horrible to consider . . . yet she must. Gradually she realized she was weeping, unashamed hot tears of grief. She fixed her mind upon the man, her healer—he whom she now knew as Jesus Christ—and the eyes in the portrait. In her heart she knew that if anyone could help her understand, he could. Only he could. If he could hear her now . . . if he was watching over her still . . . She begged that he would help her understand why . . . *why?*

After her lengthy weeping had spent itself, worn her tired, weakened her body out, she fell into a deep sleep. And in her sleep she dreamed.

There were many images in the dream, but it seemed she was among her friends again, in a beautiful place, a garden place, and there were smiles on the friendly faces.

She looked for Margret, to say hello, to see Marcus and Natalie and hug their little bodies tightly to her chest, but she couldn't find them, no matter where she looked.

Mary came up to her. It was a much younger Mary, her hair a natural, pretty blonde with a soft curl to it, but it was still Mary. She cradled a toddler on her hip, a blonde boy, two or three years old. She smiled at Alyssa and the boy waved.

"Oh, Alyssa!" she said brightly. "Look, just look. I've found my little boy! Smile Danny, say hello. This is Alyssa. She's my friend. She used to help Mommy all the time." The boy beamed a bright smile and said a shy hello, then snuggled tightly into his mother. Tears of joy streamed down Mary's radiant face. "I'm so happy. I've found my little Danny. Shall we go find your book, sweetheart?"

The boy nodded his head, and they moved on.

The scene shifted, and she saw Bert singing in a large choir. She could pick out his baritone above the rest of the voices. He sang a song she had never heard before, yet it resonated through her soul with a deep sense of familiarity. She knew this song . . . from somewhere . . . yet the words were strange to her.

". . . The veil o'er the earth is beginning to burst. We'll sing and we'll shout, with the armies of heaven, Hosanna, Hosanna, to God and the Lamb! Let glory to them in the highest be given, Henceforth and forever, Amen, and Amen."

As the song ended, Bert turned and saw her watching. He came to her, his smile wider and brighter than she had ever seen it, his long, lanky form full of bounce and energy.

"Did you like it?" he asked. "We're rehearsing."

"I loved it," she said.

"I'm singing for Jesus now, Lyss," he said. "I'm so full of joy I could burst."

He looked at her with warmth and enveloped her in a huge bear hug. She began to cry, and couldn't respond. Bert was speaking . . . in language she could understand, for once, and she could think of no words to say.

"Lyss, don't you cry," he said. "Don't you worry about me none. I'm home now, safe in the arms of Jesus."

He drew back from the hug and regarded her, the wide smile never leaving his face. He seemed satisfied with what he saw and gave his head a slight nod.

"And so are you," he added, after another moment. "Oh, that is wonderful."

He beamed and hugged her again, and she wept on his shoulder.

"Yes," she said, "I suppose I am."

Chapter 43

Home

Peter and I had a huge fight today. He was waiting for me outside when I got back, when I went to stable the horses. It was awful. It was my fault. I was wrong. Apparently Alyssa mentioned calling here while he was on his mission. I know I should have told him, but at the time, Topaz didn't want him to know. She was very firm about it. I did mention—well, I had to be honest, didn't I?—how Peter had pined for her, off and on, for over a year after their forced separation. Topaz was adamant that Peter not know Alyssa had been "found," so to speak. It made perfect sense at the time . . . and well, I put it out of my mind after she broke it off.

After all, there were those rumors Peter brought back. I did some checking myself, and it seemed there was some truth to them. Enough to substantiate the claims, anyway . . . and Central University is such a party school, a den of iniquity where morality is concerned. Am I all that much to blame? I hardly wanted him chasing off there, fresh off his mission and vulnerable . . . Since then, quite honestly, I forgot all about it.

Oh, but Peter was livid, absolutely livid. I suppose I should have told him. He had a right to know. Still he was far more upset than I ever suspected he would be, after this much time. As it turns out, he spoke to Alyssa, and it appears the rumors were about Lauren, not herself. As far as she says. There's still the matter of her years at CU, though . . . and afterwards.

I really shouldn't have reminded him of the torture Jackie put him through. I just wanted him to think straight before even considering . . . I was very reassured to hear him say it was the farthest thing from his mind, and he doesn't still think of her like he used to. He's hoping she'll get on her way as soon as possible, in fact. Apparently Jackie was on his mind before I brought it up . . . he was uninterested in reliving something like that again, and I trust he'll maintain a solid sense of caution and reserve.

Beverly Richardson,
personal journal entry

"Have you been asleep all day?" Beverly asked with a smile when Alyssa came into the kitchen late that afternoon. She was fixing something that smelled divinely Italian. Alyssa's stomach rumbled.

"No," she answered. "Not all day." The memories of her dream clung to her, warming her inside, as though Bert still had his arms around her. It helped her through the intense grief she felt, easing it with a remarkable sense of peace. "I've been thinking . . . sorting things out." She walked up to the stove to see what Beverly was doing. "Can I help?"

"Are you much of a cook?"

"I'm used to cooking for one," she said, amazed by the size of the pot and the quantity of sauce inside. "Debra and Margret taught me most of my cooking skills. I tried, but my cooking never quite tasted like theirs."

Beverly put her to work chopping vegetables for a tossed green salad. Alyssa was appalled by the vast amount of food required in order to make dinner for six people. She hadn't seen so much food in one place in ages, not since tending the garden on her roof. But that was a community garden, not a single family's harvest.

"You grow all this?" she asked.

"Oh yes, we have quite a large garden out there." Beverly laughed. "You poor thing. It must've been so hard for you."

Alyssa only nodded, remembering how rapidly the argument had developed between her and Peter that morning, his extreme discomfort over the subject of her past. She wondered what suspicions Beverly might hold. It was best not to discuss it.

"Go ahead, taste as you go," Beverly said. "I do. Just wash your hands after."

She did so, biting into a wedge of succulent, ripe tomato. It was delicious.

"Where's Peter?" she asked when she finished fixing the salad, noticing no one else was around.

"Still plowing. Andrew went out to help when he came home from work. They'll be in by six-thirty."

For the first time Alyssa realized she hadn't heard any engines running in the distance. Something occurred to her.

"Don't those things run on gasoline?" she asked. "Where do you come up with money for the fuel, if you can't sell all the crops?" Her mathematical brain automatically tried to calculate the figures. "Oh, I'm sorry," she said after a minute. "That's not polite, is it?"

"It's all right," Beverly said. "You don't have to worry about politeness nearly as much here as you had to with Joan, if I remember correctly. In fact, they used to run on gasoline, right." She looked over at Alyssa while she stirred the sauce. "Isaac is something of a mechanical whiz. When the prices started to inflate a few years ago—you remember that, don't you? I'm sure it was the same everywhere."

Alyssa nodded. "It didn't matter much, since I didn't have a car. Everybody in The Gardens walked."

"Well, back then he started working on an electrical system for the farm equipment. It's quite ingenious what he was able to come up with. It took him over a year. That was in addition to working full time at his engineering job, Anna having another baby, and living twenty miles away from us besides. It was quite a sacrifice."

It was easy to see she was beaming with pride for her son, but all Alyssa could think about was *electrical system*.

"What kind of system?" she asked. "I heard the major car corporations tried to invent electrical and solar powered cars, and all they could come up with were models that were so expensive it was cheaper to buy the gasoline. Or things that wouldn't work for much longer than thirty minutes, and couldn't drive faster than about twenty miles an hour. Has Peter been out there all day?"

Beverly grinned. "Yep." A timer buzzed, and she poured a pot of pasta into a large colander in the sink.

"How does it work?" Her long-dormant scientific mind shifted into gear, fascinated by the possibilities.

Beverly rinsed the pasta and poured it out into a large serving bowl. "Solar generators. We garage the tractors at night to recharge and plug them into the generators. The tractors have a booster panel on top that allows them to use the sun's energy during the day instead of depleting the battery. Like I said, it's quite ingenious."

"That's why I haven't heard an engine," Alyssa said.

"That's right. They're very quiet."

"If it works so well why couldn't he sell it to an auto company?"

"He tried," Beverly said with a sigh. "One said there were problems with the system that would make it impractical for personal auto use. Another said it wouldn't be marketable. Everybody had a different excuse. At the last company, he frustrated the consultant he talked to so badly she finally told him they were getting a substantial government subsidy *not* to produce any new type of motor, and nobody was ever going to buy his idea no matter where he went."

"I didn't know that," she said.

"He was told to keep quiet. In no uncertain terms."

"So he couldn't make any money on it. That's rough."

"Actually, he's sold and installed the system at several farms since then. He's done fairly well for himself. And in all fairness, it works wonderfully for tractors, but he didn't think it would work well on cars. Like you said, it's difficult to come up with something that runs faster than twenty miles an hour. A tractor doesn't have to go fast. But he never did try to adapt our cars. They're rusting in the garage like everyone else's."

"Twenty miles an hour is still better than walking," she said.

"True. But we get along fine without them. Besides, such a thing would call attention to itself, and that's not 'keeping quiet.' Doing that wouldn't be practical, either."

"But Peter said you went shopping this morning," Alyssa said.

"I did." Beverly pulled a loaf of homemade French bread out of the oven.

"Did you walk, or take a tractor?" she asked. The mental image created in her mind made her smile.

"Oh, no," she said. "We use the horses."

"Horses." In an instant, she felt as though she had been pulled centuries into the past.

"We have plenty of fuel for horses," Beverly laughed. "We can grow all the hay we need. And they're wonderful animals. Worked for man for millennia before the old 'horseless carriage' was invented." She shrugged her shoulders, seeing Alyssa's look of disbelief. "We already had the stables. It made perfect sense."

"I suppose," Alyssa said slowly. This place was becoming more strange by the moment.

"And if it ever happens that the oil embargo lifts and gasoline goes down to an affordable price, I suppose we'll put them out to pasture and repair the cars. I'd rather they were pastured, anyway, they'd be happier than they are in the stables. But until that happens, we're getting around just fine. One of our neighbors welds, and has a thing for antiques—he made us a nice little carriage for things like grocery shopping."

Alyssa shook her head. "I never thought of horses."

"Large animals in a place as vast and crowded as Central City wouldn't be practical," Beverly said. "I'm not surprised it never occurred to you."

"True."

Alyssa began setting the table as the twins bounded up from downstairs where they had been watching television.

"Ew, Mom, it was so gross," Kellie said. She had brown hair pulled back into a short ponytail, brown eyes, and freckles.

"Nah. It was *cool*," Jordan said. "This one guy threw up his whole *stomach*."

"Jordan," Beverly said. "Please, not before dinner."

"What's for dinner?" he asked. "Spaghetti? Are you the new girl?" He directed the last comment to Alyssa.

She looked up and nodded. "I'm Alyssa," she said.

"Okay. Then these other people, their *eyes* fell out," he said, continuing his narration with hardly a breath.

"Jordan, Mom said to cool it. I don't feel like eating, Mom."

"I'm not surprised, Kellie," Beverly said. "Why were you watching that? I thought you had a nice movie on."

"We were going to. But Jordan wanted to watch the news."

"The news?" Alyssa blurted.

"Did Peter get to talk to you this morning?" Beverly asked, quickly. "Did he tell you anything?"

"Yes, he told me about the epidemic. Or so I thought," she said, looking at Jordan.

"Jordan, please be considerate," Beverly said. "Alyssa used to live there. She knows a lot of people there. It's much more personal to her than it is to you."

"Oh. Sorry," he said glibly, and grabbed a piece of bread from the table. He had light brown hair and blue eyes similar to Peter's, but was not freckled like his sister. He was deeply tanned.

"Not right before dinner," Beverly said.

"Aw, Mom, it *is* dinner." He put the bread, minus a large bite, down on one of the plates Alyssa had placed around the table. "C'mon, Kellie, they don't need us. Let's go watch some more." He pulled at his sister's arm.

"No!" she said, resisting. "You're disgusting."

"No you don't," Beverly said. "You two can help finish getting dinner ready."

"But it's done already," Jordan said. "She's doing it all."

Alyssa had finished setting the table. She went to the stove to stir the sauce. It was odd being referred to in the third person while she was in the room. Well, he was only seven. She looked back at Beverly.

"You can go get your brothers and tell them it's time to eat, then," Beverly said.

"They know it's time to eat," Jordan said.

"Do it anyway," said Beverly.

With a grunt he opened the French door and stomped out onto the deck.

"What can I do, Mom?" Kellie asked.

"For starters you can remind your brother to shut the door."

She did so, yelling out after him, then shut the door herself. "Now what?"

"Why don't you go wash up. Your face is dirty."

"It is?" she asked, putting a hand to her face, and heading for the bathroom.

"She hates it when her face is dirty," Beverly whispered, smiling. Then, becoming serious, she said, "I'm sorry you had to hear that, Alyssa. We weren't going to tell you all the details."

"They were talking about the disease, weren't they?" she said, an ominous feeling in her gut.

"Unfortunately, yes. It's a nasty thing. I doubt Peter mentioned the details. I apologize. Jordan doesn't find that kind of thing as troubling as some people do. I have no doubt he's a perfect fit for some field of medicine when he grows up. But until then, he still hasn't learned when to keep his mouth shut."

"Wasn't Andrew like that at his age?"

"Still is," Beverly smiled wanly. "But about different things."

••••••••

Andrew said they stopped working for over an hour just to listen to the radio broadcast. He worked as a vet tech for a large-animal veterinarian a few miles away.

"Nobody could believe what they were hearing," he said. "Eddie even came up to me and said *we* were responsible for the whole thing. If that rumor takes off," he took a bite of food, "we're sunk."

"Mouth full," Beverly said.

"Sorry." He swallowed.

"What'd you tell him?" Peter asked.

"I said, of course we weren't."

"Where did they get that idea?" Alyssa asked.

"Some of our people have said Central's wicked, and needs a good dose of repentance," Peter said.

"Oh." She thought a moment. "Why do you have to go around getting people mad at you? Don't you have enough to worry about without stirring things up like that? I mean, from Blankenship to Article 28, you'd think—"

"We try not to," Andrew said, interrupting. "It wasn't all of us saying things, and not any of our leaders. Just the wing nuts."

"The wing nuts?"

"Yeah, the ones on the fringe, chasing every wind of doctrine. The ones who *are* maybe a little unstable."

"Oh," she said. "Still. Is there that much to worry about? How can they blame so much destruction on one little group?"

"Remember Alluvius Blankenship?" Andrew asked in an ominous tone. "What happens once can happen again, or so they think."

"We're not that small of a group, either," Peter added. "Counting worldwide membership."

"But it's a *disease*," Alyssa said. "You can't have that much to worry about. Nobody *causes* epidemic illness. It just happens."

"Tonight they were saying something about this virus being released on purpose," Jordan said.

"Oh, great," Andrew said. "That's all we need. I'll have to buy a gun to protect myself at work."

"No, you won't," Peter said. "All you need is faith. You'll be fine at work. Dr. Hilbert isn't going to give you a hard time. He's a good man. He won't let the others bother you, either."

"What else did you hear, Jordan?" Beverly asked.

"It's in the water supply," Kellie said. "That's how it spreads."

"She asked *me*," Jordan said, elbowing his twin. "It's in the water supply," he repeated. "It looks man-made because some of the pipes that haven't blown up look like they were rigged. They found this reservoir east of the city that was totally contaminated with the virus, and the pipelines were connected to it. Everybody who went out to investigate it got sick." He took another bite of spaghetti. "Nobody else wants to go out there to collect more water samples."

"Why didn't you say something about that earlier?" Beverly asked.

"You sent me *outside* first," he said, whining.

"Even if someone was depraved enough to do that, it certainly couldn't be you or anyone like you," Alyssa said. "You're the nicest people I've ever known."

"When something like this happens, it's common to lay blame on someone quickly," Beverly said. "Preferably someone unpopular."

"Like the nutty Christians?" Alyssa asked, with a half smile.

Beverly nodded.

****

After the dishes were done, Peter walked over to his mother and whispered in her ear.

She nodded. "Yes, I think it's for the best," she said.

He came over to Alyssa, who was wiping the table clean.

"It's a nice evening," he said, and cleared his throat. "Would you like to go for a walk?"

"I could manage a walk," she said, putting the cloth back in the sink.

Peter opened the back door to the patio.

"Since you haven't been out back yet, let me show you around."

"I've been here before. It's just been a long time."

She walked slowly to the door and stepped over the threshold.

"Are you sore?" he asked.

"Not anymore. I was very sore the first day, though. I guess that's why I spent so much time asleep."

She turned back toward the house. The lights were warm and inviting. Andrew and the twins were laughing and wrestling in the living room.

"Is something the matter?" he asked.

Alyssa took a deep breath and stepped out into the evening breeze. It was a little chillier than he expected.

"No."

"Am I making *you* uncomfortable now?"

She smiled. "No. Not right now, anyway." Her smile broadened.

Peter ran his hand through his blond hair. He looked back in through the window panes as he closed the door behind her, taking a deep breath. Crossing the deck to the two wooden stairs that led to the pathway, he put his hand on the railing. From inside, someone turned on floodlights, illuminating the stable, barns and pens. A horse whinnied in the distance. He turned and gestured to Alyssa, who was still standing by the door.

"We don't have to walk, if you're tired. We can just talk."

She crossed the deck and stood near him.

"I mostly wanted to say I'm sorry about this morning," he continued.

"Oh, that. It's okay." She sighed.

"I thought you might want to talk. After everything that's happened today, in Central."

"I'm fine." She crossed her arms, folding them tightly to herself to shield against the breeze, and leaned against the railing. "I did a lot of thinking today."

"What about, exactly?"

"All those people." She sighed again. "I just can't comprehend it. But somehow . . . after I took a nap this afternoon . . ." Her voice trailed off. "Since I woke up, I've had the strangest feeling of peace about the whole thing, like it's all going to be okay. I do feel sad, but it seems like I can bear it. But I can't figure out why I'm still here, alive, out of all of them." She paused. "I know I can't stay and burden you much longer. It's been nice, but I think I ought to be on my way. I don't fit in here. You have your own problems, and it looks like they're only going to get worse, with what Andrew was saying."

"Andrew likes to hype things up," Peter said. "It won't be as terrible as he makes it out to be."

Peter came back up the two stairs and leaned on the opposite side of the stair railing from Alyssa, facing her.

"I did some thinking today too," he said.

"What about?"

"Well, Mom brought it up first yesterday, and I thought about it today, and we agreed . . . Well, maybe it would work out best if you . . ."

He had to pause. His mother suggested the plan for asking her to stay, after their intense fight this afternoon had been resolved. He preferred to have her ask Alyssa, rather than himself, but she insisted he should. He thought about their argument, and wondered, briefly, if he should tell Alyssa about it. No. That wouldn't be wise, or nice. And afterward they had talked about Jackie, something they had not done in ages. It brought back the pain and more fears.

"You want me to leave," she said. "I understand. I'll be off in the morning before I can be any more trouble. Don't worry."

"No. You keep jumping to that. No. I talked to Mom today about how afraid you still are to go back home. We both wondered, how much worse did Joan get after . . . after our families broke apart?"

"Oh, that," she said, and shook her head. "It got worse. A good deal worse. I don't really want to talk about it." She made a strange face, frowning. "After we moved to the big house, she did ease up a bit."

"I always figured it was worse."

There was silence for a moment.

"I did try," Peter said. "I wanted to know. I sent that letter . . ."

She looked over at him. She had been staring out toward the barn.

"I know, you said so before." She paused. "That letter! Do you realize what would've happened to me if she had gotten the mail that day, instead of me? I could've killed you for that. I wouldn't have lived through it!"

"I'm sorry."

"It's the truth. I wish I was exaggerating."

"I'm very sorry," he repeated. After a pause he said, "Well, what I was getting to was . . . we'd all like very much if you would stay with us."

"I am staying with you."

"No, I mean, *stay*. Don't leave. Don't . . . don't go anywhere. Don't go back there."

He hoped his nerves didn't show. All day he had vacillated on the question while he plowed the fields and was still uncertain which choice he preferred. It would be *easier* to have this strange episode over, have her sent peacefully on her way, in spite of the strong feelings her nearness brought to the surface of his heart. If only she wasn't here, the feelings would subside.

Or would they? He had thought about her all day. He tried not to, but the memories kept surfacing. He loved her long before he kissed her. But today, the memory of that kiss was like a video on continuous replay, with his mind trapped there, spellbound, unable to press the stop button. How often he'd thought of that moment in the years since. How often he had wished for one more opportunity, just to touch her, to feel her lips again, her soul close to his heart.

He looked at her standing opposite him, a puzzled look on her face. Right now, in her presence, he felt as intensely as if she had never been gone, as if he were sixteen all over again.

But Jackie had scarred him, terribly. He didn't want any romantic feelings to return, not now, not even for Alyssa . . . especially not Alyssa. Too well he remembered Jackie's assurances that past was past, her lies twisting him into believing whatever she wanted. The pain ate at him, held him back. He didn't want to find out things, unpleasant things, he would then have to forgive. He didn't want to have to forgive anything, even if Alyssa were pure now, as the vision seemed to tell him.

Was it truly a vision, a voice from God, or had the light played tricks on him this morning? She looked so beautiful in the sunlight . . . like the girl she used to be. So *pure*, so radiant. The memory filled him with awe, but he still wanted to shake the emotions away. Yes, it would be easier on him if she chose to go. Far less complicated, at the very least.

And if she chose to stay . . . Well, he couldn't see into that future.

The thought filled him simultaneously with illogical, delighted anticipation and a deep, painful dread. He only knew he needed to ask. That he *must* ask. That it was right for his family to make the offer. It would be wrong, somehow, not to give her the choice. His personal preference was secondary, something that shouldn't factor into her decision at all. He tried to remember that.

He watched her as the impact of his offer sank in.

"Stay?" she repeated. "Not go back to my family? Live here?"

Peter nodded. "We'd be happy to have you around."

"For how long?"

The question took him off guard. *Forever*, his heart whispered, but he pushed the word, the thought, out of his mind. "Um . . . as long as you want. We'll be, you know, your family."

She took a deep breath and let it out. "But you're uncomfortable around me, Peter."

"I'm not right now, am I?" He tried a smile. It didn't come as easily as he hoped it would. He felt confused, but she mustn't know that. His heart pounded. He was, indeed, deeply uncomfortable, but for none of the reasons he thought she might imagine.

"I guess not." She shifted the weight on her feet. "Are you sure you know what you're asking? Why would you want to?"

"You need a home, don't you?" he asked in return.

"Well, I was going home," she said, and paused. "Oh, no . . . Look, I can't stay. Peter, I know I need to go home. When I made the decision to go home it felt right. I know it did. You said yourself I must still have a purpose in life, right?" She paused. "Maybe it means I *have* to go back there. For some perverse reason."

She became agitated, twisting a lock of her hair, shifting her position against the railing. Peter moved nearer to her, watching her closely. Seeing her agitation made him long to hold her close, to comfort her, yet he feared to touch her, afraid of her reaction and his own.

"Peter, why would *he* make me go back there?" she whispered, looking up at him. "Rescue me from death only to toss me back to that horrible place . . . *that* I seriously do not understand." Her anguish was clear in her eyes.

"It's been years since you talked to them. Maybe things have changed."

"My mother? Change?" she scoffed.

The silence hung thickly between them for a moment.

There was something else he needed to say. The sentence was nearly pushed out of his mouth by an unseen force, almost before he realized he had formed the thought.

"What do you mean by *home*?" he asked softly. "What does that word mean to you?"

"Huh?"

"What is *home*? Is it the place where your biological parents and siblings live or is it a place where you're welcomed and cared for?" He didn't add *loved*. His tongue tripped over the word and it wouldn't come out. It was too frightening. "For me it's one and the same place, but for you maybe it isn't. Think about it. What does *home* mean to you?"

"I hadn't thought of it that way." Her fidgeting motions settled down. She seemed more calm, more composed. "I was trying to get home, and I wound up here. I assumed this was a stopping point on the way."

After a moment she continued in a whisper. "It feels good just to imagine calling this place home. Looking out at this yard. It brings back nice memories, memories that as a teenager I thought were the only happy ones I was ever destined to have." She took a deep breath. "Teenage angst," she said, and laughed. "But being here, sleeping in Julia's old room . . . I remember all the good times, the fun, how much I enjoyed coming here when I was a kid. I would've jumped at the chance to live here then." She paused. "Are you sure you really mean it?"

"Yes," Peter said quietly. "We mean it. Maybe . . . maybe you already *are* home."

The thought amazed him even as he said it.

A brilliant smile lit up her face, bursting through the anguish he had seen in her eyes moments before.

"Home," she said slowly, softly.

Her eyes lit up with a flash of recognition, as though she suddenly understood something she had been puzzling over.

"What is it?" he asked.

"Maybe," she said, "Maybe . . . I *am* home." Her voice trailed off again. She looked at him. "Thank you," she continued, her eyes brimming. "This is the kindest thing."

He smiled. "I'm glad you want to stay."

In spite of his reservations and fears, a deep sense of relief washed over him. It was odd. He had assumed he would feel that relief only if she chose to leave, making his life easier. Yet there was no denying the reality of the feeling.

She turned away and cleared her throat. There was another long silence.

"You are?" she asked, finally.

"Yes. I am."

Alyssa looked back at him. Their eyes met. The cool fall breeze blew through her hair, and time slowed its hands for a moment, wrapping him with her in the embrace of eternity, a blanket of soothing peace.

He found he couldn't turn from her gaze. For Peter it was one of those rare moments that incise themselves unforgettably into the mind, etching each detail into the memory with flawless artistry. Her eyes compelled him. He longed to pull her close, to kiss her again as he had dreamed for so long, as he imagined in his daydreams today, but he was frozen to his position on the porch, motionless.

In the same instant he also desperately wished she would vanish. Her very presence brought emotions bubbling powerfully up from the injured wellspring of his soul, emotions he had long denied and kept buried. Part of him wanted very much for them to stay that way. He felt so confused, unsettled. What pain might he be forced to endure because of her past?

A vision of Jackie the last day he saw her flashed through his mind. It would hurt far worse than anything Jackie ever threw at him. He knew that in the core of his being. His feelings for Alyssa were more deeply ingrained in his soul, since childhood, some of his earliest memories. He wasn't sure he could handle that. If she were gone, no longer standing before him, vanished as though she had never come . . .

The thought struck his heart like a dark, unseen knife, more painful than anything he had felt before. *She can't vanish again, not now.* He held back a gasp as the awful reality of what it would be like to live without her swept through him. This was Alyssa. *Alyssa.* The girl of his childhood, his best friend, his first love, the echoing voice in his dreams. If she left, the emptiness would leave a gaping wound in his soul, a scar more painful than anything her secrets could inflict, more than anything he might ever need to forgive.

He wanted to say something, anything. But no words came. There were no words, none appropriate to speak aloud at least, none that would capture all that he felt.

He hoped that the possibility of her disappearing out of his life again was as unlikely as rain on a cloudless day, as unlikely, even, as the sun rising in the west. He couldn't know what the future would bring, and his nerves trembled to think what it would, for either good or ill. Worry over secrets she might hold in her past still nagged at him. Yet, as he gazed into her eyes, he felt strangely calm.

Her life had been inexorably intertwined with his for as long as he could remember. She was part of him and always had been, always there, a part he could neither forget nor let go. He was certain he could never manage to live without her again, not now; and he was willing to use all within his power to convince her of that.

"Alyssa."

She held his gaze, expectant, with a look of uncertainty in her eyes, raising that eyebrow in just the way he remembered.

"I've missed you so much."

"It's been the same for me." She nodded and turned away to look at the ground. "It's just that I . . ."

It was an impulse, but he reached his hand toward hers, then drew it back and grasped the railing, as though he had meant to put it there in the first place. He hoped she hadn't noticed.

"I've been through so much lately," she said.

Perhaps she was afraid also, he thought. As afraid and confused and upside-down about him, about being here, as he was about her.

"There are so many things," she continued quietly. "It's been such a long time. We need to get to know each other again . . ."

"I know," he said. "I want to."

She looked up once more, the smile back on her face. Though still gaunt, she was beautiful, impish, the Alyssa he once knew. Rolling her eyes, she let out half a giggle, and looked away again.

He could tell she wasn't ready to hear more, not tonight. His hand suddenly felt empty without hers. But she was right; it was too soon. Perhaps, in his mind, at least, he knew that better than she did.

Someday, he hoped, at the right time, he would confess the feelings of his heart aloud, and sweep her into his arms again, never to leave his side. Was that a dream, an unrealistic fantasy? Perhaps, but he could be patient. For the love they once had, he could wait nearly forever. In a sense, hadn't he already been waiting?

Yes, he reminded himself, he had, and one dream had already come true. Alyssa had come home.

And she had said she would stay.